Beads on a String

Beads on a String

A Novel of Southern Siam

Paul Wedel
Yuangrat Wedel

RIVER
BOOKS

First published and distributed in 2021 by
River Books Co., Ltd.
396 Maharaj Road, Tatien, Bangkok 10200
Tel. 66 2 622-1900, 224-6686
E-mail: order@riverbooksbk.com
www.riverbooksbk.com

Editor: Nicholas Grossman
Production: Narisa Chakrabongse
Production supervision: Paisarn Piemmettawat
Design: Ruetairat Nanta

ISBN 978 616 451 048 7

Printed and bound in Thailand by Bangkok Printing Co., Ltd.

 Contents

Southern Siam in 1900

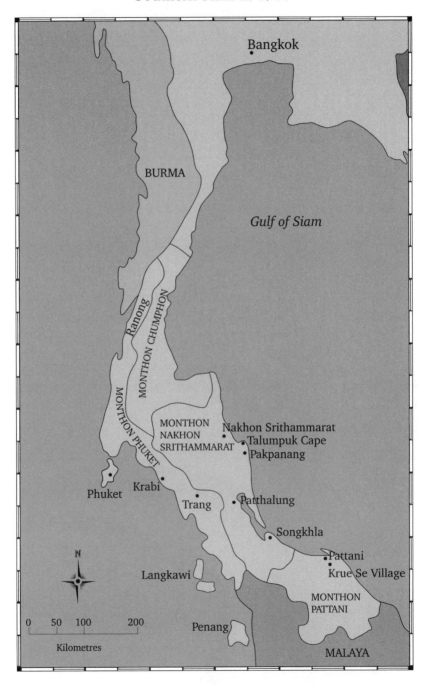

Part One : Loss

1

ABDULKARIM
Waiting for the Light

PAKPANANG, APRIL 14, 1896

The slim young man looked again at the dark windows of the two-story shophouse across the red dirt street, searching for the promised lantern —the light that would surely change his life. Like other shophouses along the street, it was built of weathered wood with a sliding iron grill that stretched the width of the building. Through the narrow alley between the shophouse and the next building Abdul could see the sunset glinting off the ripples on the river beyond. The uneven glass of the second-story windows reflected a shimmering image of the rosy evening sky.

The coffee shop owner put a small oil lamp on Abdul's table alongside a heavy glass tumbler of weak tea. He looked up at the shophouse again, but there was still no light in the window. He smiled at his own impatience. She shouldn't be making him wait so long to complete something she had started. He savored the bitter taste of the coffee softened by a dollop of sweetened condensed milk. Bitter and sweet, dark and light. Enough of the bitter, now he would get a chance for the sweet.

He thought back to her smile at the *Songkran* water festival earlier in the day and the thrill it sent through him. Her large brown eyes gazed into his. Then she dropped her eyelids and looked away, giggling and covering her face with her hands. What did that mean?

Songkran was the biggest holiday of the year. It brought thousands of merrymakers into the district town of Pakpanang where he had lived his whole boring life. During *Songkran*, the normal population would double or triple. Hundreds of farmers, workers and orchardists paddled down the river from the hills and rice-fields of the interior to join the celebration in the port town.

It would be strange to leave Pakpanang, but there would be other places and better. Leaving his younger brother would be hard. That afternoon he had coaxed Saifan to go with him to celebrations outside the big Buddhist temple, Wat Nantharam, on the bank of the river. His brother should enjoy himself for a change. Still a teenager, he acted like a glum old cleric, quoting the Koran as an excuse to avoid life.

He chuckled as he recalled Saifan's frown at the sight of monks paddling in the boat races that were popular attractions of the *Songkran* celebration in Pakpanang. He had laughed when a team of young women sped ahead of the monks' boat to win the first race. But Saifan shook his head in disapproval.

"Muslims would never act this way, much less religious teachers," he said.

"They may be monks, but they are not teachers," he had said. "Most of them are just young men in the monkhood for a short time. In a month or two they will be back in the town courting and maybe marrying those same girls."

High-pitched wailing music had pulled their attention back to the temple and a colorful stage set up just inside the gate. A young woman in yellow and green satin raised and lowered her arms like wings to the music of drums, tiny cymbals and a two-stringed violin. Perched on one leg, she swiveled around to the cheering crowd.

She portrayed the *Manora* bird in slow, graceful flight. She twirled on one foot, searching for a safe landing place. A male dancer, the hunter, came stalking her in time to the *ching chap ching, ching chap ching* sound of the tiny cymbals. A painted backdrop depicted an azure pool of water in a forest. The performance was graceful; the stage was colorful, and the girl was pretty.

As they watched the dance, a trio of teenaged girls came up behind Saifan and poured water on his back. He started from the sudden cool and jumped back against his brother. The girls ran away giggling. Abdul had laughed, but Saifan shook his head.

"We don't belong here," he said.

"Why not?" Abdul had answered. "We belong here just as much as anyone."

"But we are Muslim. This is a Buddhist festival," Saifan said.

"Really it's not even Buddhist. It's something older from India," he said. "My teacher at the temple says the heart of Buddhism is in the teachings of the Buddha. The rest is leftovers from old superstition. Anyway, *Songkran* is just for fun. Don't be so serious. You're becoming worse than Father, unable to see the bright side of anything. The world awaits us. So much to see and do."

"I would love to make the pilgrimage to Mecca. That is the way to see the world, Abdul, in the company of believers at the holy sites, the places where Mohammed lived and preached."

"Well, that doesn't sound like much fun to me," he had told his brother, "but it's better than spending your life selling goat meat or praying in that dark old prayer hut."

He had pulled Saifan through the crowd along the waterfront road through the temple gate. They paused at the bottom of the stone stairway leading up to the prayer hall. He admired the intricate gold designs on the façade and the gold-painted wooden extensions that soared heavenwards from the orange tiled roof. He smiled at the large limestone phallic symbol in the temple courtyard. Thais could be so shy about sex, at least in public, yet still put a carving of a male sex organ in a compound devoted to abstinence from worldly desires.

Around the temple yard, venders sold a variety of sweets wrapped in banana leaves or displayed in large glass-covered trays. An old woman roasted shrimp over a small charcoal broiler. A plump girl flipped over a line of pandanus leaves wrapped around sticky rice sweetened with palm sugar and coconut bits. A crowd of people pushed towards a long row of bamboo huts along the temple walls.

"Saifan, look there—that is the business that could make us wealthy," he had said. "Look at all the people lining up for a chance to throw their money away."

Each of the thatched huts had a sign proclaiming the game of chance offered within. Some advertised *Fantan* or mahjong—favorites among the Chinese women. Others proclaimed the best odds for *Po Kam* where gamblers crowded around a bowl of cowrie shells to guess, from a brief look, how many shells were in the bowl. There was no minimum bet for *Po Kam*, so the poorest gamblers, some dressed in only tattered cotton sarongs, crowded into the *Po Kam* hut.

"Over there, that's Kamnan Paen's stall. That's where the high-stakes gamblers go," he had explained, pointing to the largest hut.

A pair of portly matrons with big gold necklaces squatted on a mat. Next to them were three officials wearing high-necked white jackets above heavy cotton *phajonggraben* secured with ornate silver belts. They stared at a pile of cowrie shells in the center of the mat. Dominating the other side of the circle was a large man, his forehead glistening with sweat despite the efforts of a scrawny girl fanning him. The man leaned forward as another man started pulling shells from the pile with a small bamboo rake.

"That is Jate, the big merchant and money lender," he told Saifan. "Look how much the bastard is betting."

They watched as Jate slammed his bets down on one of the four betting possibilities. A slim, teenaged girl dressed in pale blue silk *phajonggraben* and a frilly white top knelt on a mat behind a pile of casino markers. A gambler put a sack of coins down and she exchanged them for markers. Her long, glossy hair shimmered in the dim light of the hut. Her large eyes darted between the operator and the bettors. With quick movements, she marked down the wins and losses of each game in a small notebook without ever looking away from the game. She was skinny, but someday she would be beautiful.

"The way to get rich, is not to play, but to own the gambling den," he told his brother. "Kamnan Paen not only runs the big casino on the other side of the river, but has one of the sub-concessions for *Songkran* gambling at the temple. I suppose that is one of the privileges that come with being part of the old ruling family."

Working in the market was hot and smelly, but chatting with customers gave him inside knowledge. Saifan should see the benefits of knowing what was going on in the town. He should learn which people were important and how to make friends with them.

"That's Paen's daughter, Ploi, handling the exchange."

Too bad she is so young and so wealthy, he remembered thinking. He could never have a chance with her. What would it be like to be part of the aristocracy, to have money, privilege and protection? Why was it that a few people had so much and the rest had so little? He envied Paen his wives and his sprawling teak house on the north side of the river. But most of all, it would be good to have the confidence that came with status and power. He had watched Ploi as she counted the casino's take from the latest bet, calculated the odds and then paid the winners. She gave the losers a sympathetic smile and encouraged them to try their luck again. So young, but so sure of herself.

"Look at the money the casino is making. Much better than selling goat meat, eh brother," he remembered saying. But Saifan had been unimpressed.

"Religious commerce, business Buddhism," he had sniffed. "Religion should encourage enlightenment and abstinence from physical pleasures, but the monks have to offer gambling, *Likay* shows and worship of a sex organ to attract people. And they only want to attract people to make money. Our mosques are above such crass money grubbing."

Saifan was negative, but this just reflected the views of their father. Father Hussein was always complaining about the Buddhist dominance of life in Nakhon. He didn't seem to understand that insulting Buddhism was not the best way to get ahead in a town where most of the people were Buddhist. Besides, he and his brother both had learned to read and write Thai at a Buddhist temple. Their teacher, Phra Sirithammuni, had taught them well. Father should think of the good side. How many times had Father told the story of the Nakhon king invading the sultanate of Pattani? His voice would deepen with emotion as he told yet again how the family suffered from being taken prisoner and sent to Nakhon as war slaves. That had caused all their problems. Unlike most of the Muslims in Nakhon who had long ago become accustomed to Thai ways, Father could not give up his grievances.

"Our people never wanted to come here," he would often say. "We were prisoners then and we are prisoners now. The Thais call it 'putting slaves into towns like putting vegetables into baskets.' To them we are little more than vegetables."

Whenever Abdul did something Father disliked, he would get the same lecture.

"Abdulkarim, your name means 'servant of god' but all you serve is your own whims. Never forget I named you for the heir to the throne of Pattani. You owe your allegiance to the throne to the south, not the one in Bangkok. Your people are the Malays of Pattani."

When he asked why the family didn't move back to Pattani, Father mumbled about better business in Pakpanang and instability in Pattani. Father talked a lot about religion, but he cared more about making money, no different from the venders at the temple.

He had pulled Saifan back to watch the *Likay* performance when he felt another cool stream of water on his shoulder.

"Welcome to the new year!"

He turned and there she was, with a smile that lighted up her face. Her long dark hair spilled onto her bare shoulders.

"Welcome to the new year, Malee," he responded with a smile.

He had chatted with Malee almost every day for the past three

14

weeks. His father would glower at them as they chatted, but wouldn't say anything until later. Malee was a regular customer, though she didn't buy much each time. Unlike his father, he enjoyed talking with his customers, especially the women. When Father told him to stop his flirting, he would reply: "It's good for business. That's why we sell more than Mohan."

This argument always quieted his father who disliked the boastful Mohan who claimed to be the biggest goat meat vender in the market.

He often explained to father that pleasing the women shoppers was the key to better sales. His friendly chatter had made him a favorite with them. His flirting and promises to provide only the tenderest cuts of meat attracted female customers to his stall. Malee was his favorite.

She had dark eyebrows that highlighted the smooth skin of her face. Her large brown eyes sparkled with mischief. She wore the same batik sarong that many of the housewives wore, but it revealed a flash of leg when she walked. Malee wore a thin cotton top with a square cut that showed the top of her breasts. The delightful movement under the top showed she had not adopted the new practice of wrapping the upper body in an undergarment.

"The old man is busy gambling now, but then he is going to Nakhon to visit his suppliers. He'll spend the night with his first wife and his sons. I get left behind while he celebrates *Songkran* with them," she had told Abdul. "So, I am free to enjoy *Songkran* with any handsome man who might be interested."

Abdul took his water bucket and moved closer to Malee.

"May you have happiness and health in the new year," he said as he poured water onto her shoulders. He could not help noticing how the cool water affected her nipples, now outlined under her sodden blouse.

She smiled and looked away.

"Health perhaps, but happiness with the old goat is impossible. You slaughter goats, so maybe you can help me," she said with a laugh. Then she frowned. "No, really, you must help me. I can't stand living with that man anymore."

Malee was the second wife of Jate, the man they had just watched gambling. He was the town's biggest purveyor of fishing nets, floats and other fishing equipment. He made more money as a middle man buying up rubber and coconuts for shipment to Bangkok. Jate's businesses included making loans to fishermen and farmers desperate for capital. Abdul had heard the loan business gave him leverage to buy latex sheets and fresh fish at low prices.

It was fun to flirt with the wife of such a man. He might be rich and powerful, but he couldn't make his wife happy. Jate was in his late forties. Malee was not yet twenty. Abdul had seen the burly Chinese with a receding hairline at his shophouse and watched him oversee shipments of rubber on the riverfront. Two or three tough-looking men often trailed behind him. Malee had told him that Jate's first wife lived with their children in the provincial capital while the merchant shuttled between that house and the rooms over the shop on the riverside where Malee lived. Jate had everything that he wanted—power, wealth and Malee. But maybe he could have Malee.

"Happiness? You deserve to be happy and perhaps I can help," Abdul said. "May I start by buying you some sweets?"

"First we have to wash away the smell of old goat from both of us," Malee said, pouring the rest of her water over them.

He had seen Saifan's scowl, but said nothing. Why spoil the mood? Sometimes the only thing to do was to ignore his little brother, just like he ignored Father.

"I'm going home, brother," Saifan said. "Not that you would notice."

"You should stay and have fun for a change," he had urged. "Go back to watch the *Likay*. They brought in a famous troupe from the capital. The costumes are amazing."

He wanted his brother to enjoy life more, but he wasn't sorry he was leaving him alone with Malee. He had watched Saifan hurry away from the temple without a backward glance. His brother was already a little imam. Not much fun, but if that was what he wanted, fine. Maybe Father would focus his religious fervor on his second son and let his first son go his own way. Well, soon it wouldn't matter.

He remembered the soft, smooth feel of Malee's arm as the pair struggled through the jostling crowd around the temple. It was nice to be with her, nice to walk so close. They made their way through the main part of town. Dark splotches speckled the dirt street, the signs of earlier *Songkran* blessings.

In front of one shophouse a plump woman dropped small dabs of dough onto a hot iron pan. She flattened them with a wooden spoon and topped them with shredded coconut and palm sugar. The sweet smell of the toasted treats mingled with the earthier aroma of Malee's body, sweating despite her dampened garments. He bought a dozen in a box made of banana leaves. They strolled down a side street, nibbling the sweet snacks. He edged closer to Malee, bumping gently against her as they walked further from the crowd. She looked up at him and smiled. She pushed him away, but her fingers lingered on his arm. Her touch felt warm, and her smile made him feel hot.

Away from the temple and the river, there were fewer people. Shophouses gave way to patches of fruit trees and small, thatched-roof houses. The sound of music from the *Manora* performance faded as they wandered down a narrow path. They found a spot under a large tamarind tree shielded from the path by a thick line of banana trees. They sat down and leaned back against the tree, their shoulders touching and their legs stretched out before them. The damp cloth of Malee's sarong clung to her slim legs.

He remembered reaching for another coconut sweet and finding her hand instead. He admired the delicate tracery of bones, veins and tendons under the skin. He brought her hand to his face and sniffed. This was the "Thai kiss" he had learned from other liaisons.

He had sighed. Malee had laughed. "What do you think you are doing?"

"I am showing my deep appreciation of your beauty."

"Is it only the beauty of hands that win your appreciation?"

"No, there is much else to admire."

He released her hand, leaned over and sniffed her neck. He enjoyed the view of the swelling of her breasts. She waited a moment, then pushed him back.

"You are just playing with me," she said. "You don't really care."

"No, no, I have never felt like this about anyone," he had protested. "I must be in love."

The words had slipped out, but they might be true. He had never felt like this before.

"That is what you tell all the women," Malee said. "I hear the gossip. I know about the others."

"Not since I met you. If only you were free."

"I could be free if there was someone to help me get away from him. We would need to go somewhere he could never find me. Surat? No, still too close. Maybe Phuket. Better would be Bangkok or even Penang."

Going to the royal capital. That would be an adventure. If they could live there, his life would be transformed.

"I too would like to get away. See other places. Become someone important," he had told Malee as he leaned back and nuzzled her neck. Malee's hand dropped to his upper thigh.

"Don't forget that I am a married woman," she had laughed, with a tinkling sound like the little cymbals in the *Likay* orchestra.

"Then you have the experience to teach me."

"Like this," she said, stroking his thigh, and leaning over to sniff at his chest.

"That is a good start."

"One I see you appreciate," she giggled at the movement under Abdul's long *phatung* garment.

"What else would you teach?"

"A good student must help the teacher," she said. "All that water has made me cold. Can you warm me up?" Malee guided his left hand underneath the silk blouse to the cool damp skin of her breast. The memory of that touch still thrilled.

"That is a big task," he had mumbled as his hand explored her breast, grazing the nipple with his thumb.

"Not the only big thing," she said as her hand closed around the swelling under his *phatung*. "But we can't do such big work here where anyone might pass by."

"We could try to find a place nearby," he had said. His voice sounded strange, husky with desire.

"No, no," she had said. "We can't. Not now."

His spirits had fallen only to revive a moment later.

"Jate is still around somewhere, but tonight I will be alone at the shop. Perhaps you could come then. We can talk about Bangkok and other things. But you must be serious about taking me far away."

"Do you mean it? I have some money saved. Tonight can be the beginning of new lives for us."

Malee's smile had collapsed into a grim look. "Only if you are serious."

He nodded and pulled her closer. She felt so soft. Malee exhaled and pulled back. She gave a parting squeeze and stood up.

"I'll light a lamp on the second floor to show you Jate has not returned and it is safe to come upstairs."

Abdul nodded and smiled.

"Come ready to do some real homework," she giggled. "But better stay here until you have calmed down. You don't want to attract too much attention."

He had looked down and realized he was in no condition to follow her. He watched her as she hurried down the lane. Tonight would be his chance, if he had the courage to seize it.

Malee excited him like no one else. The rest of the *Songkran* celebration had lost its attraction. He had scarcely noticed the other revelers as he walked home to get dressed in his best clothes.

Now he waited as shadows lengthened on the street. He finished the last of the strong coffee and looked up at the window for what must be the tenth time. Still dark. He examined his reflection in the coffee shop window. Not too bad. He wore a long white tunic and a sarong with a bold blue and red pattern that reached down to his ankles. His black hair, combed straight back, glistened with pomade. His skin contrasted nicely with his hair. He smoothed his mustache, still a little thin. He practiced a friendly smile and then a confident look of command. The image in the glass didn't look like a goat meat vender; it looked like an official at the district office, a person of culture and importance, a man who could impress a woman like Malee. A man who could rise, would rise. A man with a future.

He had enjoyed such assignations before, but they had been with older women bored with their fat and lazy husbands. Malee was different—younger, more beautiful and more playful. She was a worthy prize herself, but it would also feel good to take something belonging to Jate, who was known for taking advantage of others. The man deserved to lose her.

They would have to plan carefully. Malee had told him that Jate was sometimes as rough with her as with his non-paying borrowers, slapping her if she was late with dinner or unready for his advances. Jate insisted the man had to dominate in a Chinese home.

Yes, it would be enjoyable to pleasure Malee behind her husband's back and even more thrilling to take her away from him forever. They would have to make sure he never found out where they went.

But maybe it would be best to avoid the risk. He had to think of her welfare, too. Living with Jate was already bad enough, but if he found out she had cheated on him and couldn't escape, it would be hell.

Stay away from Malee or leave Jate and his thugs far behind. Staying away was the smart thing to do. Why take the risk? But maybe it was time to leave Pakpanang behind. Go someplace new. Selling his father's goat meat in the hot market was not what he wanted. He was tired of the constant conflicts with Father who resisted all his efforts to improve himself. There was so much more of the world to see beyond the market. He would do something more exciting—start his own business or even join the civil service. He was a quick learner and already had more education than most. He could emulate the polite manners of the royal officials in town. He enjoyed making the elaborate gestures demanded by social etiquette—the deep *wais* and bows, the special pronouns and elaborate words. He would become respected and wealthy, not just a despised Muslim boy. He would have Malee to himself. They would have long hours to enjoy each other, not just moments of furtive fumbling.

He looked up at the shophouse once again. A yellow light flickered against the weathered wood of the shop wall. His heart raced as he rose. He smiled, dropped a coin on the table and hurried out of the shop.

2

CHAO
Father and Son

Hai Sae-tang stomped into the middle room of the shophouse.

"Son of a whore, did you tell your mother you don't want to go to sea anymore? That you want to leave the business?"

Chao-xiang looked up from the book he was reading. His father's sun-darkened face was red and his hands were clenching and unclenching as he stood before his son. He was a wiry man over 60, with a small belly that protruded over his loose sailor's trousers. Chao saw he would have to mollify the old man.

"Honored Father, don't be upset," he said, using his father's preferred Teochew dialect. "I was just thinking it might be better for the family if I continued my education. The teachers in the temple think I could go to one of the new schools starting up in Bangkok. Mother wasn't supposed to tell you because I haven't decided anything yet."

"You decided? You decide nothing. You are not the father in this house. I decide. And who are you to tell your mother to keep secrets from me? I make the decisions for this family, but your mother doesn't seem to understand that."

"But, going to school in Bangkok I could make connections valuable for the business. It could mean higher profits," Chao said. "I could learn more about the new commercial laws my teacher says are coming. I could find new customers and handle the Bangkok end of the business. We could work with the *farangs* coming into the economy—the British, the French, even the Americans. We can get the stuff in the south those *farangs* want to buy: tin, rice, fruit, wood. The days when Nakhon was an independent kingdom are long past. We are connected now."

"I don't need a history lecture from you," his father said.

"Of course not, Father, but I know you want to be well-informed and you are already thinking of ways we need to adjust to changing times," Chao said in his most soothing tones. He was only seventeen, but he could usually handle Father's tempers.

"King Chulalongkorn has visited the south several times; he is changing the old ways. There will be more movement of people back and forth to the capital. The big merchants in Bangkok will buy more. All this is good for the family shipping business, if we modernize to keep pace."

Father looked interested. He sat down at the table, his scrawny legs straddling the stool, his belly pushing against the heavy wooden table. This might be the time to press ahead with the plans he had been thinking about for weeks.

"I have taught both younger sisters to read and write," he said. "They can do the accounting, correspondence and record-keeping I do now. Huat is big for his age and he can take my place on the ship or in the warehouse. Mother can help with the customers, making this a real family business. Some of your friends have already taken their Thai wives into their businesses or given them a business of their own to run. It pulls the family together."

Hai scratched his balding head and frowned.

"Being in Bangkok, I could not only boost the business," Chao rushed ahead, as he bent his head and shoulders to be lower than his father's head. "I could study medicine. I want to learn more about science too. I could..." he stopped. He had said too much.

Father scowled and pulled at the long hair sprouting from a mole on his chin. Chao watched the expression on a face lined and leathery from long hours in the sun and wind.

"With science I could learn how to run steam engines," Chao said. "One day they will put all the sailing junks out of business. We could be the first steamship owners in Pakpanang. We could compete with the *farangs* for the big shipping contracts."

Father scowled, so he hurried on.

"Sailing ships take too long and transport times are too unpredictable. Trade has boomed, linking the producers in the south to the capital in Bangkok and the British colonies in Malaya. We are still profitable thanks to your careful management, but sailing junks can no longer meet the demands of the customers. Already steamers are taking all the long hauls and most of the passenger traffic along the coast. Look how much money that Scottish-Oriental Steamship Company is making. Father, you know all this. But knowing is not enough. We have to take advantage of these trends."

Father rubbed his chin. He had often complained about losing business to the coastal steamers. Chao had suggested buying at least a share in one of the big steel steamships before, but Father had always hesitated because of the expense.

"How am I going to pay for one of these fancy ships? And keep it supplied with coal? Those ships just burn money."

"Maybe we could borrow—an investment that would pay off in the long run."

"No, I have already borrowed from the clan association. I can't ask for another loan. Anyway, we already have a ship and without the cost of coal we make a good profit on every trip, even though we can't charge top rates," Hai said. "*The Wind Uncle* is still a profit-maker, why should we change?"

"Father, *The Wind Uncle* is old and leaky. Just yesterday I found dry rot around the rudder slot and the lime putty is crumbling in the seams. The crew spend half their time operating the pumps."

"You are too easy on those lazy bastards. We've hired too many Thais, and Wei Fan doesn't know how to crack the whip to get work out of them. He's too soft to be a good captain. Things have gone to hell ever since I started to stay ashore to run the warehouse business here."

"Well, we don't pay them much."

"You have to keep the expenses low to survive. That's what you have to learn. That's why we can't run a coal-gobbling steamer and that's why you can't go to school any more. You need to toughen up. You have to sacrifice to get ahead, like I did."

He looked past his father to the unpainted wooden walls, the floor of cheap red tile and the cobwebs drooping from the ceiling. Keeping costs down – whether on the boat or in the home – was Father's obsession.

He had heard his father's story many times. How he had come to Siam as a crewman on one of the big junks that sailed between Bangkok and Kwangjo at the end of the fourth reign. How he had jumped ship to work as a coolie loading ships in Klong Toey harbor. How he had eaten only salted rice gruel and saved his meager salary to buy a share in a ship trading along the coast between Bangkok and the provinces of the south. How, by living on the junk and parlaying his share of cargo space into profitable trade, he was finally able to buy out the elderly owner of *The Wind Uncle*. How he could marry at age 44, making arrangements to take the daughter of one of his Thai customers as his wife. The bride price had been steep, but he always declared she was worth it— giving him two clever sons and two daughters who would care for him when he was old. The two babies who had died were unfortunate, but acceptable losses.

"But there is so much more I have to learn. It could be a benefit to the family," he offered.

"You already know how to calculate, keep records, bargain for better prices. You speak Thai better than most Thais and you can write both Thai and Chinese. What else do you need to know?"

"There is so much – science, chemistry, biology – how to cure disease, medicine, technical knowledge, how things work. I would like to…"

"Useless," Father interrupted. "That's all useless. No more school giving you crazy ideas. The family business is shipping rice, dried fish and rubber from Pakpanang to Bangkok on *The Wind Uncle* and bringing stuff back for sale here. That's it," he said, slapping the table.

"From now on you work on the ship full time. No more school. And you'll take your brother along to teach him the business. If you don't mess up, I'll make you *chuan zhu* and we can stop paying Wei Fan so much."

Father looked up at him.

"Chao, my son," he said more softly. "You are a man now. You have a duty to your family and to the family business. I won't be here forever. We need to build the family fortune to protect your mother and your sisters. The world honors you only if you have money and power. You must concentrate on those. If you have money and power, you get respect. I am coming to the end of my time. The family will soon depend on you to build the business into something great, something everyone will respect."

"I understand my duty to the family, but I don't want to spend my life chasing money."

"Money is just the means. You need money to gain respect and to provide for your family, especially the women. Like your mother says, men are paddy and women are hulled rice. As a man, you can be planted anywhere and sprout. Women need to be protected."

Chao knew his father calculated that his mother's words and his duty to his sisters would be telling arguments. He said nothing.

"You are the only one I can depend on," his father continued. "Your uncles are all back in China. I need you. The family needs you."

He looked out through the open front of the shophouse across the Pakpanang River. The tide was receding, pulling the dark water of the river out to sea, taking old crates, dead fish and a few sticks of bamboo with it. Like these bits of flotsam, he felt himself being pulled along, helpless to struggle against the current of father and family.

3

DAM
Obeying the Boss

Dam sat on a crate sagging beneath his weight on the dock behind the boss's house. The sun had disappeared behind the trees on the other side of the river. The last colors were seeping from the sky. He watched a fishing boat ablaze with kerosene lanterns as it headed out to sea. Going for squid. Must be spooky, being at sea in the dark. Worse than the blackness of the rubber groves at night. He had hated waking up at night in that hut in the hills where the trees blocked the light from the moon and the stars.

It was there he first had the nightmare that troubled him even now. He could still see the monster with white fangs lurking in the rubber grove. It followed him as he moved from tree to tree collecting the latex from half shells of coconuts fixed to the trunks. The white latex dripping down into the shells was the same color as the teeth of the monster. A monster that reared up to sink its fangs into him like the python he had once watched kill and swallow a rat. He had learned to lessen his fear by conjuring up other memories. The warmth of his mother who slept beside him. Her sleepy smile in the morning. The sugary smell of roasted bananas on the charcoal stove contrasting with the sharper, spicy scent of reheated curry. The sounds of birds singing in the mango trees behind the hut. Good memories battled the bad.

One time, when he clutched at the body beside him, it was not his mother. She must have gotten up in the night. It was his father's arm he grabbed. There was a rumble of sleepy anger and then the shock of a smack across the face. It sent him sliding across the sleeping mat. The monster had struck. He huddled against the bamboo wall in fear, trying to see through the darkness. A light appeared. He saw he was not in the forest, but in his house. His mother hurried across the hut with a lit candle. He could see his father glaring at him before he turned over and went back to sleep.

It was not the first or the last time he had felt his father's hard hand. Any small misdeed – spilling latex, letting the fire go out, asking for food – all these earned him the bony back of his father's hand or a sharp kick to his rear that left him aching for hours.

He thought of the last time he saw his father. He must have been about seven or eight years old that evening when he heard his mother's screech. He stumbled into the hut. Father was holding his mother's arms as she tried to slap and claw him.

"You can't do this to us, you bastard!" his mother screamed. She tried to kick his father in the ribs, but he punched her in the face, threw her to the floor and kicked her twice in the stomach. She doubled over, moaning on the floor.

A hot surge of anger sped through him. He rushed to his mother's side. Blood trickled down her face. She was weeping.

"How can you make us slaves? What kind of man would do that?"

"It is done," Father said as he towered above them. "I sold the house. The plantation manager will come for you and the brat tomorrow. They will find someplace fit for slaves."

He remembered Father's face glaring down at them. It was a face dark with anger. His mother moaned again. Without thinking, he had grabbed his father's leg and sunk his teeth into the flesh of his calf. He remembered the rich, metallic taste of the blood as the skin broke under his teeth. Then came the pain ringing through his head as Father swatted him away, sending him skittering across the wooden floor. His father followed up with a kick to his backside that slammed him up against the wall of the hut.

"You filthy lizard. You dare to bite your father. Nothing but a stupid animal."

He looked up to see his father, a large cloth bag over his shoulder, pause for an instant at the door. He could still see the broad silhouette of his father in the doorway before he disappeared forever.

After that night, life changed. The next morning, a pair of men in a rough, open-sided horse cart pulled up at the house. Without a word they pushed Dam and his mother into the cart. Mother pulled Dam to her as the cart lurched over the rough road towards the mountains behind the town. He remembered watching as their house, with its pleasant garden and spreading mango trees, grew smaller in the distance. The rocking of the cart lulled him to sleep on Mother's lap. When he awoke, they were in front of a tiny thatched hut in the shadows of rows of trees that leaned towards the hut from all sides. It was the rubber plantation where Dam's father had often hired them out for a daily wage.

Life became a familiar pattern of rising late at night and stumbling into the long rows of rubber trees. Once they finished the tapping and collecting, Mother had to mix the sticky white latex with chemicals from a large tin and watch it expand into a thick sponge. She then fed the spongy rubber into a press. It was Dam's job to crank the wheel that squeezed out the water and turned the latex sponge into a hard, flat sheet. They hung the sheets on racks behind their hovel. The sheets turned a dirty brown as they dried, filling the air with an acrid smell, a smell he had grown to hate. It was good he didn't have to do that anymore. But at least the rubber had led him to the boss. He remembered how it started.

"Mother, what do they do with the rubber?" he had asked her when the plantation owner's horse-drawn wagon made its weekly visit to pick up rubber.

"They sell it."

"And get money?"

"Yes, they get money."

"Why don't we get money?"

"We get food and this hut to live in."

"But if they get money, we should get money, right?"

"It doesn't work that way. It's complicated. We are slaves. We have to work for the master."

"Why?"

His mother looked at him and sighed.

"Your father couldn't pay his debts. He gambled and lost. He borrowed money from the plantation owner and gambled again. Lost again. He sold us to the master in exchange for the debt. We are debt slaves."

"Because father didn't have enough money?"

"Yes, not enough money, but enough questions."

"If we had enough money, could we buy ourselves back?"

"Just turn the handle so we can finish."

"Why don't they give us some of the money from selling the rubber?"

His mother turned and smacked him on the side of the head.

"Enough. We are what we are."

He still remembered the surprise and sting of that smack. But once he thought about it, the realization he was a slave because he didn't have enough money hurt him far more. He had only been eight years old, but from that time, he had started to think about ways to get money. He started picking up scraps of rubber that had sloshed over from the trays. He scraped dried latex from the trees when the other tappers had finished. He formed the rubber into balls he hid behind the hut. The first time he took the balls into town, he walked until he saw a warehouse full of rubber sheets. A big Chinese man was directing the coolies bent under bundles of rubber.

"I have rubber for sale," he said holding up his sack of scraps.

The big Chinaman had laughed at him, but gave him a coin.

"You can call me Boss Jate," the man said. "There will be more coins if you can bring me more rubber, but better quality next time."

That was the start. Soon he became more adept at stealing whole sheets of rubber. Boss Jate welcomed the extra rubber on the cheap. He not only paid Dam but gave him food, including the fatty pork they could never afford to eat on the mountain. Sometimes he ran errands for the merchant for an extra coin or two.

At the temple where he learned to read and write, the monks taught him stealing was wrong, but they also taught him to honor and respect his mother and father. How could he respect a father who beat him and made him a slave? And how could stealing be wrong if it was the only way to get the money to free his mother and himself? The monks taught that desire for money was an attachment that would cause suffering, but he and his mother were already suffering, not because they were attached to money, but because they didn't have any. He was not stealing because of love of money; he was stealing because of love of his mother. That must make it right.

The money from Dam's extra work made life better. Each month the plantation manager gave them a sack of rice from his fields along the river. They had banana plants, papaya trees and morning glory growing around the hut. In the forest, Mother showed him how to collect plants and wild fruits. Bamboo shoots and mushrooms were plentiful in the rainy season. He found frogs, crayfish and land crabs along the streams running through the plantation. At the end of each dry season, he would scoop the water out of the tiny pond behind the hut and then root in the mud to pull out the catfish that burrowed into it. He looked at his hands. They still had the pale marks left by the catfish spines.

They had used some of his money from Boss Jate to buy some chickens. After that, they had an egg or two every week. They had never gone really hungry. But sometimes, especially as his appetite grew with his size, they ran out of rice before the end of the month. They had little cash to buy clothes, so they wore rags that his mother kept clean and mended, but still rags. Once in a while they spent his extra money for palm sugar or spices, but saved as much as possible in a box he buried next to the hut. Someday, he promised himself, there would be enough to pay back the debt and buy their freedom.

As he grew tall and powerful from his work on the plantation, Boss Jate began taking him along on visits to collect money from debtors. A scowl from the hulking Dam helped persuade some debtors to pay up. Jate would call him "my mountain buffalo" and tell anyone with payments overdue to beware of the hooves of the buffalo.

The first time he had gone on a debt collection call he was 16 or 17 years old. They called at the hut of an elderly man. With only a *phakaoma* around his scrawny waist, the man looked small and frightened. He made a deep *wai* to Jate and promised payment soon. Jate smacked him across the face.

"Not soon. Now," he said. "I hear you have been to the opium den. How can you have money for opium and none to pay your debts?"

"But I have no money right now. I will work to get some soon."

"You have a gold chain hidden somewhere. Give it to me."

"No, there is no gold. I am a poor man."

"Dam, my big buffalo, help him remember where he has hidden his gold," he said.

Dam could still see the cold look in Jate's eyes. He could still feel his confusion at what was expected.

"I don't want to dirty my hands with this piece of garbage. Show him what happens when you don't pay your debts to Jate."

When he grabbed the man and lifted him up, he could feel each of his ribs. The man looked at him, his eyes wide with fear. They looked like his mother's eyes when his father drew back his hand to hit her.

"Give him a friendly little hug—until his ribs crack," Jate ordered.

The man's eyes rolled back.

He couldn't do it. He let the man drop.

Jate erupted. "You worthless lizard. Do as I say. Beat him up."

But all Dam could do was stare into the man's eyes.

"Stupid buffalo." Jate lashed out with a kick to the old man's stomach, doubling him over.

Dam watched as Jate stomped on the man's hand. What he couldn't forget was the look of disgust that Jate gave him when the man gave up a thin chain of gold. After that he feared more kicks, but the greater fear was disappointing his boss. That fear was mixed with anger like that against his father. But he had learned it was best to keep it hidden.

He obeyed Boss Jate's orders to beat up debtors, but he always feared something would go wrong. What if they fought back? What if they had weapons or friends? Hitting the helpless ones was a different problem. They made him think of his father smacking his mother.

One day he went back to the forest temple where he had learned to read. The abbot was known as a man of knowledge — occult knowledge. He had always been curious about the burly, tattooed men who came to the temple and sat with the abbot. The abbot offered them magical protection against harm. Since Jate was forcing him into violence, he needed protection. He still remembered the abbot's frown when he explained what he wanted.

"I am sorry, but not surprised to hear of your need," the old man said. "The dharma and the discipline of self-control are the real source of protection from evil, but you have a restless spirit and little discipline."

The abbot pulled a thin sheet of tin from a drawer behind him and he used a stylus to press strange symbols into the surface. He chanted something Dam didn't understand.

"This is your *takrut*, with powerful words written in the ancient Khmer language and a set of symbols I have devised especially for you." The monk's gnarled fingers took a thick white cord and bent the tin sheet around it into a small cylinder. "This will protect you from ghosts, wild animals and human enemies. Wear it at all times, except when lying with a woman—if worn during sex, it will lose its power," the old monk said.

He still felt a flash of fear when Jate insisted he carry out a beating, but he could touch the *takrut* around his neck and feel better. Once a slim young fisherman had fought back with a stunning kick to his head before dashing away with Jate screaming at him. The next day Jate gave him a wooden staff topped with an iron knob.

"Don't let anyone get away again, ever."

Whenever Dam whacked a debtor with the staff or smashed the

knob into someone's stomach, he was rewarded with a grin from his boss. He came to like the feel of the wood as it smacked into flesh or bone. The fear in the eyes of the debtors felt even better. He was no longer the target of Jate's kicks. He was no longer a despised slave. He could intimidate. It felt good to see grown men cower before him.

Even the plantation overseer, respecting Dam's size and growing reputation as a young *nakleng*, or tough guy, spoke more politely to him. As Boss Jate branched out into other businesses, especially fishing supplies and boat equipment in the nearby port of Pakpanang, Dam became one of his regular collectors. He was still subject to Jate's ridicule for reasons he only half understood, but over the next two years, he learned to anticipate Jate's demands. He spent less and less time working on the plantation. The plantation overseer, who heard the stories of his slave's work for Jate, chose not to object.

By the time he was 18, he thought proudly, he had saved quite a few coins. He took them to the plantation overseer and asked to repay the family debt. The overseer promised to help and a few days later told him that under the King's proclamation on debt slavery, there was enough money to pay for his freedom, but not for his mother's. He grew angry again at the memory of the foreman's patronizing tones because he learned a few months later that the King had already freed all children of slaves once they reached 18. So, he had been tricked into paying for freedom he already had and Mother was still a slave.

He never worked on the plantation again. He went to Jate and told him he could now work for him full time.

"I have a better idea," Jate had told him. "You can read and write. You are strong and in good health. If you can get a bit more book learning into your thick skull, I think I can get you an appointment to the police force. You will be my man in the police station. If you do what I tell you, you will soon have enough money for your mother."

It had been two months since he joined the police force. Now the message from Jate said he was needed. He was supposed to wear his police uniform. Where was Jate? Why did he have to wait in the dark behind the house? He had already been sitting for an hour.

Finally, the door opened, the boss silhouetted by the light within. The boss waved to him impatiently and he hurried up the stairs.

"I have an important job for you," Jate said. "Don't fuck it up."

4

ABDULKARIM
Into the Dark

Abdul headed down the darkening street. Most of the shophouses were shuttered. A few slivers of light spilled out of the windows onto the reddish-brown dirt of the street. Behind the row of wooden buildings, sagging docks and tall wooden pilings lined the river bank. He walked around Jate's shophouse to the river bank. He eased his way past a stack of wire fish traps and buoys. A pair of huge rusty anchors leaned against each other next to the wooden stairway leading to the second floor. Jate must have built this stairway to bring in goods from the dock without being seen from the street.

He hesitated at the first step and looked out over the river. A full moon slid from behind the clouds. The moonlight sparkled off the ripples of the ebbing tide. He felt a surge of excitement. Malee was special. None of his other conquests had been as young or as pretty. More than that, she offered the promise of a different future. If they left Pakpanang together, they could build a life better than selling goat meat or suffering from a cruel husband. A Thai wife in a new place would open possibilities for him beyond the constrictions of Malay society in Pakpanang. Would she go through with it? If not, at least he would have the pleasure of tonight.

The dark beauty of the river and the bright moon above it grabbed at his heart for a moment. The moonlight was an auspicious omen, a promise of a brighter, more beautiful life ahead. He drew a deep breath and climbed the stairs.

He knocked on the wooden door at the top of the stairway. No response. He knocked again, louder this time, and listened. Nothing. He should just leave. But she had placed the lantern in the window. She must be waiting for him. He took a deep breath and pushed on the door. It squeaked open onto a narrow hallway with two doors. A soft orange light seeped out from under the one to his right. He knocked on that door. There was a murmur from within.

"Malee, can I come in?"

From behind the door he heard her voice. What did she say?

"It's me."

"Come in," he thought she replied. There was something strange about her voice. Must be as nervous as he was. He smoothed his hair, straightened his shirt, opened the door and strode into the room with a smile on his face.

A small oil lamp glowed beside a wooden bed. Malee was sitting on the bed. As his eyes adjusted to the light, something looked wrong. Tears glistened on her cheeks. A dark bruise curved under her left eye.

"I'm so sorry," she said.

Something hard slammed into his left side and he stumbled to his knees. A kick to the stomach doubled him over. Two pairs of hands grabbed his arms. He tried to breathe. Someone in front of him. It was Jate, his face twisted in a sneer. A wave of pain washed over him. All he saw was the glow of the lamp in a field of black.

"Dam, get this *khaek* trash out of here," he heard Jate order. "Everything is arranged at the police station."

Jate pulled Malee by one arm and pushed her head down towards him. There was pain and fear in her eyes.

"Look at your pitiful little boyfriend now. No one cheats on Jate."

He saw Jate through the fog of pain raise something in both hands. It looked like a table leg. Why?

Pain exploded in his head and the hazy light in his vision went dark.

5

PLOI
Family Business

Ploi counted the proceeds from the *Songkran* gambling, forming the coins into neat stacks. The gambling hut was dark, with only a single oil lamp. The staff rolled up the mats and placed the cowrie shells in a leather bag. In only two more days the celebration would be over and they would take the hut down. All that would remain, she smiled to herself, would be the biggest profits they had ever made from the holiday gambling. She checked the ledger with the day's accounts and made a quick calculation. If the last days were as good as this, the family would make 50 percent more than last year. Father would see how well she had handled the collections and the accounts.

She looked around the darkened hut for Elder Brother Chit. Although entrusted by their father to oversee the gambling den, her brother had taken off with a group of friends in the late afternoon, promising to return "soon". She didn't want to wait much longer to make the long walk back home in the dark and she didn't want to make the trip alone with all that money. Where was Chit?

"Uncle Daeng, I know you want to go home, but I need you to come with me to deliver the money," she said. "I can't wait any longer for Elder Brother Chit. If you don't come with me, I'll go alone and you will have to answer to Father if anything happens."

The burly croupier frowned at her. She smiled up at the man, one of her father's former slaves. Daeng had been with the family ever since she was a baby. She knew he would never let his boss's daughter go out into the night alone with a sack of money. Pakpanang could be dangerous at night. Daeng sighed and slung a sash holding a long, curved sword over his shoulder.

"Let's get going then," he said.

Without speaking, the pair trudged together down the dusty path from the temple to the road. They walked along the raised road of hard red laterite with the rising moon lighting their way. The moonlight picked out the stubble in the dry paddy fields on both sides of the road. The small earthen walls between the paddies were dark strips dividing the fields into irregular squares.

When the pair reached the house, Daeng grunted good night and disappeared into the darkness. She took off her sandals and washed her feet in the water jar by the side of the wooden stairs up to the house. She pushed open the heavy door to the central platform. It was bordered by rooms on three sides, each a small step up from the platform. A walkway of weathered teak led to the room of wife number two—her mother.

The rooms around the platform had linked roofs of heavy orange tiles. Carved leaves and flowers decorated the doors. She felt relieved to be home in the big house where she had spent her entire life. Normally it bustled with slaves and servants who lived in huts around the main house, but it was quiet this late at night. There was no light in the main room. Mother must be asleep. She had seemed tired and dispirited for the past two months. Father must still be at the main casino along the river. Maybe he stopped off to visit his new girlfriend, the one she wasn't supposed to know about.

Sleeping mats and mosquito nets were rolled up against one wall. Family photographs lined one side. Father looked stiff and uncomfortable in a formal jacket and *phajonggraben* in a group photograph with the Nakhon Srithammarat governor and other members of the family that had ruled the area for centuries. Father stood in the back row of the group, but at least he was part of it. If that photograph were taken again, Father might be moved closer to the governor. He had been appointed *kamnan*—the head of the sub-district of nearly 20 villages between Nakhon town and Pakpanang. He was important, and therefore, so was she.

A sepia photograph showed Father seated with his first and second wives on one side and baby Chit on the other. The dim light flickered over other pictures of elderly monks seated in the lotus position. Why were there none of Ploi? She should ask Father to take them to the new photography shop in town. She could wear the new *phasin* her father had promised her if the *Songkran* takings were good. Mother might let her wear some of her jewelry.

Muffled voices came from the next room. She peered around the corner. Her mother and an older woman were kneeling in front of the family altar. Nine Buddha images sat on small tables arranged on both sides of the main image. The two women bent over a small object. She shouldn't interrupt.

"...an ancient Khmer amulet. Its power has been renewed and strengthened by Phra Plaek, the most revered monk in Nakhon. When you wear this, no rival can win away your husband. It will make Kamnan Paen think only of you and bring him back to you, like a hungry bee to honey."

Who was this old woman?

"If you put it under your sleeping mat, it will revive your romance, enhance your erotic power and deepen your intimacy, infuse your love-making with the fire of youth," she heard the woman say.

Ploi pulled back and listened. They were talking about sex—something her mother had always refused to discuss with her.

"What do I do with this?" Mother said holding up a small glass vial of dark brown liquid, its seal wrapped in red thread.

"That is the other part of my service," the old woman said. "This is Necromantic Oil—rare and powerful. It is diffused from the bodily fluids of a woman who died in childbirth. The oil was extracted from the chin of the deceased—the only way to ensure potency."

Mother held up the tiny bottle to the lamp light.

"*Mae* Chaem, listen carefully," the woman said. "Use your right hand to apply the oil above your eyebrows, smearing it on your skin with the middle finger."

"And that will make him love me, desire me again?"

"To be absolutely sure, put three drops of the oil on your middle finger. When he lies with you stroke his *lingam* with that finger, from the base to the tip and nothing can stop him from loving you."

"You know I do this not for myself, but to save my family. Paen is drifting away to some other woman. He doesn't even bring her here to be part of the family. I am the second wife. The major wife is honored even though she left long ago to live in Bangkok. I have no money of my own. I have not given him a son. If I lose him, I will have nothing. My daughters will have nothing."

"Do everything as I have explained and you will get him back," the woman said.

"Please take this," Chaem said and pressed a handful of coins into the hands of the old woman, who rose to her feet and shouldered a woven bag. Ploi pulled back and walked back to the outer door, opening and shutting it with a bang.

"Mother, I'm home," she called out as the old woman entered the front room followed by Chaem.

"Ploi," her mother said. "Where are your father and your brother?"

"Elder Brother Chit has gone off somewhere with his gang. I wouldn't depend on him getting home anytime soon."

"And your father?"

He probably had gone off to see his new girlfriend, but she hesitated.

"As for Father, he must still be at the casino."

Mother frowned. Ploi looked back at her with what she hoped Mother would see as a smile of innocence. But she too felt angry at the loss of Father's attention. Until a year ago, he had taken her everywhere with him—to the casino, to inspect the rice fields, to oversee the rambutan harvest. She had taken notes for him and recorded income and payments in a ledger. He called her 'my little minister of finance'. He would joke and tell stories in funny voices. They would sing songs together as they drove the little horse carriage along the rutted trails on the west side of the river.

But for the past several months she hardly saw him. Maybe, as Mother suspected, it was the new woman he was seeing. Maybe she just wasn't doing as much for the family business as he expected.

Father was drifting away from them, but Mother was a fool to think magic would bring him back. Father cared about the business. He was just too busy with his work as *kamnan* and distracted by that new girl. She would impress him by showing she could manage the family businesses—certainly better than her worthless brother.

6

SAIFAN
Family Shame

Saifan wrapped three slabs of flat bread in a clean white cloth. He had risen early to cook them on the charcoal stove behind the house. He placed them on top of a pot of curry in a shoulder bag and went into the house. The sound of footsteps from the second floor made him look at the stairway. He swung the bag into a corner of the room. When no one came down, he picked up the bag and walked out the door.

The hard dirt of the street was still damp from a late-night shower. He walked around a large puddle and looked back at the ramshackle house. He could see nothing through the windows of his father's bedroom. It was almost time for morning prayers. His father and mother were unlikely to come down for another hour.

Ever since the news of Abdul's arrest, their prayers had taken more time. Mother was praying for Abdul's release. She was sure the arrest had been a mistake. Father refused to talk about his elder son. He wanted to lose himself in the sounds of the prayer and forget the shouts and whispers in the market.

"Hussein, the rapist's father, is this what you teach your son?"

"*Khaek* rapist, spawn of Hussein,"

"Head of the Hussein crime family."

These were only a few of the comments he and his father had endured in the market. Two Chinese venders did more than mutter. They swaggered up to his stand, knocked over the goat meat table and spit on the meat.

"*Khaek* rapists go away," one shouted.

In the month since the news of Abdul's arrest, daily income had dropped by more than half, Father had grumbled. Why was he more upset by his business problems than by Abdul's arrest?

Mother had been worried when Abdul had not returned from the *Songkran* festival, but Father had declared he was probably off chasing some girl. Two days later, however, they were all frantic with worry.

Then three of the district policemen had come to the house and asked questions about Abdul. Was he married? Did he have a girlfriend? Had he ever been arrested? Were there complaints against him?

Hussein, always uncomfortable dealing with Thai authorities, at first said little. Then he tried to defend his son.

"He is mischievous, but he is a good boy," he said. "Yes, there were complaints but only from men jealous of their wives' interest in Abdul."

Father demanded to know why they were asking questions.

"What did you do with my son?"

One policeman pushed Father down hard onto his chair.

"We ask. You answer."

The policemen then turned to Saifan. They wanted to know whether he had helped his brother break into a house. Before he could say anything, the policemen asked another question and another. The big dark one just glared at him and tapped a wood staff with a big knob. He felt like he had done something wrong, but there was little he could tell them. He tried to explain he didn't know where Abdul had gone that night or what he had done. They nodded and wrote down notes like everything he said betrayed his brother.

Finally, they said Abdul was in jail on charges of rape and there were eyewitnesses against him.

"He beat her and then raped her in her husband's bed," he said. "Your son chose the wrong woman to rape, the wife of Mr. Jate."

"Malee? That is stupid," he blurted out. "They were friendly. She liked him." The big policeman smacked his face with the back of his hand.

"Better shut up or you'll be in jail with him."

He was stunned by the blow and confused. Mother rushed to him, weeping, but his father sat unmoving.

"Jate, the money lender? No."

"Jate. Yes," one of the policemen said. "He wants this over quickly. Don't interfere."

The next day they learned Abdul would come before a judge. He had assumed the family would go to the court to support his brother, but Father had forbidden them to leave the house.

"Abdul has disgraced us. He has put us all in danger and he has ruined the family business," he yelled when Mother said she wanted to go.

Father stood in front of the door and pushed his weeping wife back into the house. "We cannot help him now. We can only hurt the rest of the family."

Saifan thought of all the passages in the Koran calling for justice, honor and honesty. But he knew Father would not listen, so he just sat with Mother, ashamed of his silence.

A friend later told him the trial had ended in minutes and Abdul had said nothing in his own defense. Sentenced to ten years in prison. How could this happen so fast? His fun-loving brother could never beat and rape a woman. He loved women. And Malee more than any. Why would he rape her when she seemed so eager to be with him? They had witnesses, his friend said, and the judge had believed them.

The family could have helped him, could have explained to the judge that Abdul was a good and kind person. He could have, he should have, told the court Malee had often met with Abdul and she clearly liked him. He could have told the judge they had been together at the *Songkran* fair earlier that day, laughing and smiling. But Father had forbidden him to get involved. And he had just stayed home. He was a coward, a coward who failed his brother.

In the days after the trial, Father closed the stall, unwilling to face more abuse in the market.

"We are disgraced. The business is finished. We are moving away from Pakpanang to some place where Muslims are treated justly," he announced.

They were set to move the next day, but he couldn't leave without seeing his brother. He had already gone to the jail twice, trying to catch a glimpse of Abdul when the prisoners were taken out for exercise. Once he thought he had seen him in a line of prisoners shackled together as they cleaned the yard in front of the police station. Was it Abdul? He had looked smaller and older, his head bent over and his shoulders stooped as he lugged the heavy chains linking his ankles and wrists.

The prisoners had disappeared back into the jail before he could decide what to do. When he tried to enter, a guard stopped him at the door. Official permission was needed. But the official responsible for approving visitors was not there. He must write a letter, the man sitting at the desk said with a yawn.

As he trudged away, a younger policeman put a hand on his shoulder.

"You want to see a prisoner—this guy Abdul. I can arrange that," he said. "But I have to give some money to the jailers."

The policeman surveyed the teenager dressed in a frayed sarong. "Forty baht—not for me, for the jailers," he said.

How could he ever get forty baht? Father kept a careful watch on the family's money. But he had ten baht from selling some of their knives earlier in the day. "I can only give you ten," he told the policeman. "That's all I have."

"Well, I don't know. Try to find more and come tomorrow before eight when the station opens," he said.

"Then you'll allow me to go to Abdul?"

"Of course, if you pay, I'll show you right to Abdul's cell."

At least he could see his brother, give him some food and money. Saifan headed towards the river and then turned to walk along the bank. The misty morning sun glinted silver off the river dotted with fishing boats sailing out towards the bay. He looked ahead towards the town jail behind the new district police station.

The small bag of coins felt light in his hand as he entered the courtyard in front of the police station. Would it be enough? He had gotten another eight baht from one of his friends saying he needed it for their trip. He had three more coins to slip to Abdul.

The police station, with large white pillars and a peaked roof was one of the biggest new buildings in town. It fronted onto the river where there were three boats tied up at the police pier. The sun slanted down the river from the expanse of Pakpanang Bay. He was glad to see there was no one else waiting for the station to open.

He walked around behind the station to the old jail. It looked deserted, but the thick wooden door was slightly ajar. He pulled it open and entered a dark room. It took a moment for his eyes to adjust from the morning sunlight to the gloom of the jail. The young policeman looked up at him.

"Did you bring the money?"

"I have fifteen baht."

"That's not enough, but let me see the money and maybe I'll take pity on you," he said with a grin.

He took out the bag of coins and placed it on the desk.

"And all you want to do is to go to Abdul's cell?" the policeman smiled as he swept the coins into a drawer.

"I have food for him too," Saifan said.

"Well, I guess even rapists need to eat," he said. "Leave the food here and come with me."

The policeman picked up an iron ring of keys, unlocked a door and beckoned to him. They entered an even darker corridor with a ceiling only inches above the policeman's head. Barred cells lined both sides of the corridor. In one cell, two prisoners in grimy loin cloths were lying asleep, their mouths agape. A crude opium pipe lay between them. In another cell, four inmates squatted together in the gloom, looking up at the policeman. Their bare backs glistened with sweat. Saifan wrinkled his nose at the stench. At the end of the corridor, the policeman selected a key and opened the lock. He tried to see past him.

"Here you go. This is Abdul's cell. Just like you wanted," he said with a laugh as he swung the door open and pushed him forward.

Saifan grabbed the bars of the door and stared, trying to make out the figures inside. There were two men lying on mats in the cell. They stared up at him. One had a rough beard and dark hair as stiff as rice straw. The other glared out of a pale narrow face, the dome of his shaven head making his face look stretched out like a sheet of rubber.

"This isn't my brother. This isn't Abdul," he cried.

The policeman was now laughing out loud. "You wanted to see Abdul's cell. Well this is it. If you want to see the honorable Abdul himself, you will have to go to his luxurious new abode at the provincial prison. We moved him last night. Should be arriving there about now."

Saifan stumbled back down the corridor, the laughter of the policeman echoing behind him. He was a fool. Once again, he had failed his brother. He rushed out of the door, blinded by tears and the glare of sunlight off the river.

7

DAM
Services Rendered

Dam looked out over the wind-swept beach curving into the hazy distance. Four fishermen rolled a boat on coconut logs down the damp sand. They pushed it into the small waves. The fishermen leaned their weight onto the stern until the bow lifted with a wave. They pushed hard, scrambled aboard and set the sail. The steersman swung the tiller and the boat beat to windward against the strong sea breeze.

Dam felt the damp wind on his face as he watched the boat head up the coast. *I've faced a headwind all my life, but now I see there are ways to tack forward against it. From now on, I will sail more smoothly. I am a policeman now. I'll soon have money. Mother will be free.*

A horse snorted behind him and he turned back to look down the long, straight dirt road from town. He watched as a horse-drawn buggy moved up the road. Two men stepped down from the buggy, tied the horse to a post and walked toward the small restaurant where he waited. He recognized the silhouettes of the two men against the afternoon sun and smiled, but where was Jate?

"Uncle Nit, you're getting fat," he called. "Not enough exercise since you helped me work over that *khaek* kid? We did a good job, eh, hurt him where it doesn't show."

"You're proud of that?" Nit asked.

What a strange question. It was just work—the Boss's work. Nit was a tough guy, a true *nakleng*. He wanted Nit to think he was tough too.

"We were just following the boss's orders, right? Anyway, that *khaek* is young. He'll recover." Was that a look of disappointment in Nit's eyes? What the hell? Nit was the only one of Jate's men who did not look down on him. How was doing what the boss wanted a bad thing? Maybe he didn't have to be so rough on the boy.

"Dam, you need to be more careful. You're a policeman now, so it's better if no one connects you to the boss. When he wants you to work for him, he'll send you detailed instructions. You'll be told exactly what to do, just like before, but without meeting the boss. The way you work will change. You should protect your position in the police. Sometimes the boss may not remember that."

He nodded. Nit was right. Jate treated him like he was a simpleton. When he was younger it hadn't bothered him. It had been reassuring to know exactly what to do. But he was grown up now and he could think for himself. Nit, at least, understood he had to look after himself.

"Now, about the *khaek*. Is it all done the way the boss wanted it?" Nit asked.

"Yes, everything has gone as planned. I testified, and the judge believed everything. I made sure the kid wouldn't dare to speak up. He just sat there terrified. My talk, my testimony, went fine. I used all the fancy words. Boss Jate was in court. He knows this already. The *khaek* kid got ten years and there has been no appeal. The fool doesn't understand how badly he was screwed. He's already on his way to the provincial prison."

"Can he appeal later?"

"The poor guy is too ignorant and too scared. I made sure of that. Now, the money."

"Here is everything the Boss promised," Nit said. "Use it well, but don't forget you made someone else suffer for it."

"It's for Mother."

"Ah, of course. Understandable."

He hefted the small leather bag. It was pleasantly heavy. He opened it and saw the glint of silver. He counted the pieces, and when he looked up, the two men were already in the buggy and heading to town.

He looked around, but there was no one else in the shabby, open-sided restaurant. A clatter of metal came from the kitchen area at the back. Must be the old lady who ran the place preparing vegetables for the evening customers. The shoes he had to wear now as a policeman were pinching his feet. He slipped them off and leaned back. He sipped the rice wine in front of him and looked down the beach at the thatch-roofed huts scattered along the shore. They were simple sheds of woven bamboo slats lashed to poles of weathered rubber wood. Two small boys stood on the sand watching the fishing boat sail into the distance. One was naked, and the other wore a tattered *phakaoma*. Both were skinny with extended bellies, their hair tinged with yellow. Not enough food.

Once, I was as poor as them. Never again.

He looked at the bag of coins in his hands. This would do it. He hadn't minded roughing up the Muslim kid. Slapping him around before the trial had shown the other policemen he did not shy away from dirty work. Athough the youngest in the station, he now got more respect. Then he had made sure of the *khaek's* silence by giving him another working over the day he left for prison.

The boy deserved it for raping Jate's wife. The court appearance, though, had made him nervous. He had spent hours memorizing Jate's instructions on what to say in court. The boss made him repeat it over and over again, even after he said everything correctly.

He strode down the path towards town, eager to show his mother the money and tell her she would soon be free. Behind him, a rising wind whipped the waves into froth-topped peaks. Things were working out. The gusts at his back seemed to lift him up and push him forward.

8

ABDULKARIM
A Gate Closes

Nakhon Srithammarat, May 20, 1896

The horse cart jolted along the laterite road, knocking the six manacled prisoners against the sides of the cart. Abdul was still nauseous from the rough boat trip from Pakpanang. His head ached. Had ever since Jate hit him. Now there were new pains. His blackened eyes were nearly swollen shut from that policeman's final punches. Every breath sent searing pain through his right side where the ribs felt like they were cracked. He forced himself to swallow the sour acid taste rising in his throat. The iron manacles on his hands and feet made it difficult to adjust to the sharp rocking of the cart after a full day of the rolling at sea. The neck ring chained to the manacles chafed with each bump in the road.

At least this was change. After weeks in the Pakpanang district jail, anything was better. There was no air in the small, dank cages of the jail. His stomach ached. Some prisoners had family or friends who paid for extra food, but all he had was the watery rice gruel provided by the police. Where was Father? Why didn't Mother come to see him? Not even Saifan. His own brother couldn't be bothered. Nobody came at all. Where were all the friends he had laughed and joked with? Where was the teacher from the mosque? Or the monks from the temple? How could they have forgotten him? What had happened to Malee? He could still see her bruised face, wet with tears. What more did Jate do to her?

Even on the day of his trial, no one from his family had shown up. The proceedings were over so fast. The main witness was the police officer who arrested him. Abdul tried to remember what the policeman said. It made no sense. The pain in his ribs had made it difficult to breathe. He felt dizzy and confused. The guy came to his cell. Took a club wrapped in cloth. Hit him on both sides of his head.

The policeman had jerked his head up and hissed into his ear: "Don't say anything or you'll get more of this tonight."

The same policeman had sat stiffly on the tall wooden chair in front of the judge. He had looked nervous.

"I heard screams coming from the shophouse," the policeman told the court, "so I, uh, ran up the stairs and found this fellow raping the wife of Mr. Jate."

Rape? Rape? What rape? The words were confusing. There was a pounding in his head. He heard "written statement from the victim… too distraught to come to court." The policeman told the court that he had confessed to the crime during interrogation. Confess? No.

"Was he tortured?" the judge asked.

"He resisted arrest, so we had to take measures to control him, as usual in such cases, your honor," the young policeman said. "We did knock him around a bit, but it didn't take much to get him to confess. As you can see, there are no marks on him."

He had wanted to cry out he was still in pain from the beating, but no one would believe him. The policeman was right. The beating had left no obvious marks. Better to say nothing. He had tried to focus on the judge who was saying something. The words were long and unfamiliar. Two men seized him by the arms, his ribs screamed with pain as they pushed him into the seat the policeman had occupied. He struggled for breath. Would they hit him again?

"If you confess, your sentence can be reduced," he heard the judge say from what seemed a long distance away. He tried to recall what he had said. There was no rape. But reducing the sentence sounded good. He looked around the almost empty courtroom. None of his family had come. He was alone. Jate and his men sneered at him from the other side of the room. He didn't want to go to prison. He didn't want the big policeman to hit him again. What did he agree to?

"In view of his youth, his confession and his lack of any prior criminal record… ten years imprisonment," he heard the judge say.

Ten years! He would be over 30. Ten years was forever. He felt the manacles biting into the flesh of his legs. He looked at the prisoner sitting across from him staring into the distance. Did he look like that? Hopeless, indifferent to his own fate? Abandoned? Without even family to help? The cart came to a halt.

He looked through the bars of the cart. A white wall loomed above them. A big black gate flanked by two towers. The gate opened. The cart lurched forward. Abdul looked back in despair as the gate swung shut behind him.

9

SU SAH
A New Beginning

The horse-drawn carriage slid to a dusty stop in front of a long, two-story wooden building. Su Sah leaned out and read the sign in English and Burmese over the entrance: "Pegu Provincial Hospital."

She adjusted her pale green cotton *longyi*, picked up the woven bag stuffed with her clothes, took a deep breath and stepped down. She looked around. No one was there to meet her. She shrugged and climbed up the stairs to the wooden veranda running along the entire front of the building. At one end, a line of people waited outside a door. The double doors in the center swung open and a tall Englishman in a white coat strode past her with a quick sideways glance.

"Excuse me, sir. Where is the nurses' room?" Su Sah asked in English. The Englishman looked startled, then looked at her more closely. She was glad she had worn her new Western-styled jacket. She touched her hair; the bun was still tight. She stood straight and looked him in the face.

"I am Nurse Su Sah and I am supposed to report to the hospital superintendent."

"You must be the new girl from Dufferin?" he said.

"I am a graduate nurse from Dufferin Hospital, sir," she said emphasizing the word graduate. "I am here to report to the superintendent and the head nurse."

"Uh, that would be Dr. Myers," the Englishman replied as he inspected the young nurse. He smiled and thrust his chest towards her. She didn't know why he was getting so close. She looked like most women—light brown skin, a long neck and black hair. She knew the other girls at school said she was pretty, but she was not here to be stared at.

"The nurses' room?"

"Of course," he said. "Come with me. I'll take you to Dr. Myers. By the way, my name is Malcolm Richardson—Dr. Richardson, Malcolm."

"Thank you, but I would like to go first to see the head nurse," she said. "Tell me the way and I shall find it on my own."

He took another step towards her, looming above her.

She took a step back and looked down to adjust her *longyi*.

"Well then, go through this door and up to the second floor," he said, pulling a large watch from his pocket and examining it.

"I am busy anyway, but welcome to Pegu Hospital."

She nodded, turned and climbed up the stairs. She looked forward to seeing Ma H'La Yin, who had been two years ahead of her in the training program at Dufferin Hospital in Rangoon. They were among the first Burmese women to undertake the course set up by Lady Dufferin, the wife of the British viceroy. The advanced program had been adapted from the Women's Medical College of Pennsylvania. She felt confident her training in modern methods at Dufferin meant she was more capable than most of the Burmese doctors. She had graduated at the top of her class and had practiced with Nurse A.M. Barkley in her home town of Zigon. She was ready to start this new job where she would be on her own, a long way from her teachers and her family.

Going through the door from the sunny veranda, it took a moment for her eyes to adjust to the nurses' room darkened by shades pulled down over the two windows. A heavy-set figure in white bent over a ledger.

"*Mingalaba*, Nurse Ma, I am here to report," she said as she pressed her palms together and bowed to the head nurse. The woman looked with a questioning glance and then a broad smile.

"*Mingalaba*, Su Sah. We have been waiting for you. It is so good to see you after—what is it? Nearly two years," Ma said. She stood and walked over to the new nurse and embraced her. Su Sah looked into her friend's broad face creased by lines at the corners of her eyes. She didn't remember those lines from their time together at school. Ma had always been full of fun and energy. Now she looked weary.

"You will be a big help—a fellow Dufferin nurse. There is so much work to do. I am glad you are here."

Their embrace told Su Sah that Ma, already chubby at Dufferin, had gained more weight since leaving school. But it seemed to suit her—made her seem more substantial, more dependable.

"I am glad to be here. It wasn't easy. My father wanted me to stay in Zigon. He even made an appeal to the health advisor."

Father wanted her to work in the local hospital and live at home. But after three years of nursing school in Rangoon and a relatively independent life, she didn't want to return to the confines of the family household and her traditionally-minded mother. She had been allowed to study nursing because she had won over her father. Getting approval to work in Bago meant another long struggle against Mother's angry tears and her father's reasonable arguments about helping the local people.

"It was you who gave me this opportunity," she had told him. "You taught me to read and write. Taught me to think logically – like the Buddha – accepting as true only what can be proved. You taught me I have a duty to help people," she said. "As a nurse I can do that."

"You can do that here where everyone knows you," he said.

"That is the problem. Everywhere I go people know me. They'll gossip with Mother about this and that. I'll be like one of those Siamese fish in a bowl. Worse, with Mother watching me all the time, we'll be nipping at each other like those fighting fish."

Father groaned at the thought. "You are too much alike. Both determined to get your way."

"Besides, the hospital in Bago is larger and more advanced. There are foreign doctors. I would learn much more there."

"You are the first educated woman in our family," Father conceded. "Your mother knows literature and music, but nothing of science or foreign languages. I suppose it would be a shame to waste it."

Father had always been able to see her side. It saddened her to refuse his request to return to their home town. But within the family, she had no clear role anymore. Her oldest sister took care of the house. And her second sister, two years older, had already provided her parents with grandchildren.

"I want to make my own way," she told him. "I have friends in Bago and I promise to come home every vacation."

"You always were the independent one," Father smiled, a little sadly, she thought. "You must write often."

She to must do that as soon as she got her belongings settled. Ma led the way through the hospital corridors and out through a rear door. They walked along a stone path lined with papaya trees to one of a half-dozen small houses with thatched roofs.

"Put your things here," Ma said. "Then we must go see the superintendent."

The wooden door opened with a screech. Inside were two rooms. In one, three sleeping mats were rolled up against the wooden walls and a rack held white nurse uniforms. In the second room there was a small table and four chairs. Pots and pans hung on one wall. An open door to the back revealed two charcoal stoves and a water pump.

"Do you live here?" she asked her friend.

"No, they have me next door where I have a room of my own, a privilege for the head nurse," Ma said.

"We heard back at Dufferin. Only two years out of school and already the head."

"Sounds good, does it? Well, not really. The other nurses have little formal training and not much English, so I got the promotion when the old head retired. There was no one else."

"So, how is it here?" Su asked.

"Well, Bago is quieter than Rangoon. Not much industry other than a few rice mills and a pottery factory. Not much commerce, so it's a quiet life."

"And the hospital."

"It's not Dufferin."

"What do you mean?"

"It's not a teaching hospital. Some of the doctors do a bit of training, but not much. Most of them want to be somewhere else – Mandalay, Rangoon, Prome – or back in Britain. So, we have some doctors who are still green, and some older doctors who haven't done well elsewhere. Many of the old ones don't keep up with the latest medical information. There are still some old inflamationists who swear by their jars of leeches. Some of the Burman doctors prefer traditional medicines to British medicines. Those, at least, seem to do less harm."

"That's not so different from Zigon. I thought it would be better. Is it a problem for the nurses?"

Ma sighed. "It means we get caught in the middle between the British and the Burmans, between the Burmans and the Mons, and between the old and the young. From one shift to another, the diagnosis can change and so the treatment changes. Then the original doctor complains the nurses are not following orders. To avoid a clash, we sometimes end up giving double treatments."

"Difficult."

"I feel more like a diplomat or a translator than a medical practitioner," Ma said with a short laugh. "But now I have an ally. Let's go see the superintendent."

10

CHAO
Brothers at Sea

GULF OF SIAM, MARCH 2, 1899

Chao had been reading in his cabin since the noon meal, studying a new book on biology. The system of arteries and veins described in the book was so complex! He looked at his arm, tracing the veins on the back of his hands, seeing how they twisted over and under the bones and tendons. He counted the beats of the artery in his wrist. If he slowed his breathing, could he slow his heart beat? He imagined he could feel the different parts of the heart contract as the heart muscle pushed blood from one chamber to another. His eyes closed, he focused on his breathing. In and out; in and out. He felt the warm, salty air enter his nostrils and slide down to his lungs. In and...

He started and looked up to the smiling face of his younger brother leaning against the cabin door.

"Lost in your own world again, huh, Chao?" Huat said, pushing into the cabin. "How do you do that?"

"Just concentrating and being quiet. You should try being quiet for a change," he said.

"Then you wouldn't know how to find me to order me around. Then nothing would get done on board," Huat said with another smile. "And then you would be the one in trouble with Father."

"So, your loud chattering is all for my benefit?" Chao asked.

"Exactly."

"How can I ever thank you enough?"

"Well, you could stop an extra day in Pakpanang and give me and the crew some time off."

"Time to gamble and chase women, you mean."

"Well, there are some good-looking girls there—Thai, *khaek* and Chinese. Why don't you look around a bit? It's time you were married anyway."

"You just want to get me married off so Father will let you take a wife yourself."

"A wife would be nice, but I want to have some fun first; then find a wife who is fun, so we can have even more fun together."

"Fun, drinking, gambling and women—is that all you think of?"

"Well, shit, I have you to think of everything else."

He felt his smile fading.

"You have to start thinking for yourself. I don't know how much longer I want to do this." He gestured to the row of account books and the frayed charts on the table next to his bunk.

"You need to know how to do everything I do—the buying, selling, accounting. Next voyage, I think I'll sit back and let you be the *chuan zhu*."

"Me as ship lord. You are crazy. Father would never agree to that," Huat said.

"Well, we don't have to tell him, do we?"

"Then I am not sure I would agree to that," he said.

Chao thought back over the six months since the old man had made him *chuan zhu* in charge of the sailing junk, *The Wind Uncle*. He had soon learned how to select the best merchandise to sell at their ports of call and how to negotiate shipping contracts with merchants along the way. *The Wind Uncle* plied the east coast of the peninsula from the mouth of the Chao Phraya River, to Songkhla or even to Pattani in the far south. Along the way, the ship stopped at the tin-mining port of Kanom, and on to Ban Dorn, Chumporn and Prachuap. Sometimes they would venture further north to the big city of Bangkok. Or head all the way south carrying cargoes of rice from the mills in Pakpanang to the sultanates along the east coast—Kelantan, Trengganu and Pahang. At first the sailing and the ports had been interesting, but now it was getting boring.

As ship lord he had to decide what cargoes to take and where to land. He was in overall charge of the ship, but sailing the big junk was left to the sailing master, Wei Fan, a wiry old Chinese who had worked for Father for decades. The old man, who had always sided with Father against the crew, now cast himself as the crew's advocate. Just the other day he called for another pay rise for everyone. He whispered that Chao's inexperience was making the crew spend too much time at sea. The crew should not have to make repairs during voyages, he grumbled. But whenever there was real work to be done, Wei Fan was hard to find.

Chao knew he did not inspire the fear his quick-tempered father did, and he did not inspire the affection his brother did. Often, when he needed something difficult done, he would ask Huat to lead the work because the crew would pitch in to help without too much grumbling. He wanted to win them over with higher wages, but Father refused. The old man was quick to anger if he saw any increases in expenses, so he tried to help the crew with better food and small consignments of cargo, but that only led to more squabbles. It would be good if Huat could take over from him.

"You have to be ready," he said. "There is so much I am missing out on."

"But *The Wind Uncle* is a big part of the family business. It fits with the warehouse operation and our import and sales business," Huat said. "Besides, father will never let you quit. He sees *The Wind Uncle* as a member of the family. You have less chance of getting his approval than a bleeding fish escaping shark alley."

"I know, I know."

"I think he loves *The Wind Uncle* more than Mother," Huat said. "They've been together longer."

"I am not saying we should give up shipping," Chao said. "But we should have a more modern ship. Mother would like to be more involved in the business and the girls are smart. Toh is fourteen and already has a head for business. Wan is only twelve but already she can do all the arithmetic needed for keeping the books and calculating the best use of our cargo space. They could do all of the pricing and bookkeeping better than I do it."

"I'm convinced, but good luck convincing Father," Huat said. "He sees our sisters as pretty ornaments. I suppose he loves them, but he doesn't see them as carrying on the family business. That is your job."

"Maybe I don't have to convince him. Just leave. It's my life."

"But, it's the family business. You would screw things up if you left."

"Just be ready; that's all."

11

ABDULKARIM
A Change of Fortune

Abdul thought for a moment and then added the final sentences.
"I am no longer getting drunk, but as the poet Suntorn Phu has written, I am still drunk with love for you. I think of you every night. Come visit me soon and don't forget to bring the dried fish and shrimp paste."

The poetic reference sounded good even though he knew the woman would have to ask someone to read the letter to her. The clear black letters looked good, even on the cheap paper. Getting a metal nib made such a difference, and the squid ink was nice and dense. The graceful swirls of the letters, the precise placement of the tone markers and the occasional alliteration all added beauty to the letter.

"Is it finished, Pak?" asked Bear, the heavily muscled man who had squatted beside him as Abdul worked on the letter.

"Yeah, it's done and it's a beauty," he said, pleased that more inmates were calling him by the nickname he had adopted. Pak could mean uncle in *Jawi*, but it could also be short for Pakdee in Thai. The name Abdulkarim was so Muslim, not the best thing in a Thai prison.

Like everywhere else, people in the prison were better known by their nicknames than their real names. Many of those nicknames, given in childhood, seem ridiculous when applied to the full-grown men now serving prison time for decidedly un-childlike crimes. His friend Tiny had become a hulking brute. Chubs had been pared down to a near skeleton by prison and opium. Red was burned black by the working in the sun on the prison road crews. Bear was one of the few whose nickname fit.

Pak was different from the old carefree Abdul. Pak spoke carefully and politely. He considered the feelings and intentions of others. Pak spoke only in Thai. He was no longer the headstrong Muslim boy in love with fun, food, music, gossip and women. The boy who had been beaten and thrown into prison had nearly given up. Huddled in a cell with ten years to serve, he had wanted to die. When Bear had loomed over him that first night in the provincial prison, he had cringed in fear, but the big man reached down and pulled him to his feet.

"Hey, it's not so bad here. We prisoners have to help each other or we're screwed." Other inmates gathered round and gave their names and their sentences. Several had even more time to serve than he did, but they seemed proud of their punishments.

"Chai—twenty years for sticking a knife in the ribs of a money-lender," one said. "It was worth it to see the look on his fat face. Anyway, it's better to be in prison here than to be struggling every day to pay the interest."

Over the following months, as his injuries healed and his health recovered, he had begun to see possibilities. There were amnesties each year on the king's birthday, so ten-year sentences never lasted ten years. There were chances to work outside the prison and see the provincial capital with its busy flows of people and animals. Good behavior in the first year made him a first-class prisoner, one freed of the hated neck ring and manacles. Careful attention to prison rules put him in charge of ten other prisoners. The ability to write gave him something many of the inmates and even some of the guards needed, a way to communicate with those outside the prison walls. He didn't have money or connections, but his skill with a pen gave him something to trade.

He always delivered more than he promised. The gratitude of his fellow prisoners would somehow, someday be useful. Now after more than three years in the prison, he was popular with both the guards and the prisoners. Some prisoners shared their food when a relative brought them something special. They had noticed he never received anything and never had a visitor. Helping guards with their letters earned him protection. The change of wardens a year earlier had meant kinder treatment from the guards, better food and less violence. Life was better, but he was still in prison. He turned back to his latest client.

"This should get you not only a wifely visit, but food too," he told Bear. "I wrote that you dictated the letter yourself, so you get credit for the romantic thoughts. I'll submit it to the prison office this afternoon for clearance and she should get it in a couple of days."

"Thank you, thank you," Bear said with a broad smile. He must be thinking of his wife's visit and the conjugal shed, against the back wall of the prison.

"No need. Happy to help. Someday, maybe I'll need your help," Pak said. He enjoyed helping others, but it was also helping him. The plan was to do as many favors as he could for guards as well as inmates, to earn return favors.

He felt another headache coming on as he began to put his pens, paper and a block of dried ink in a shoulder bag. He leaned back and closed his eyes. The headaches had been much worse when he first arrived. They had made the occasional beating from the guards or a fight with a fellow prisoner seem like minor annoyances. An offer of opium had tempted him, but he knew if he gave in, he would never leave the prison. He would end up like that old Chinese prisoner who one night drifted away in his sleep.

Fortunately, the headaches had become less severe in the past two years. If he could just close his eyes, keep still and relax, this one should pass. He tried to think of something pleasant, a memory of his mother playing with little Saifan. The chubby baby gurgled with delight each time his mother hid her face behind her hands and then opened them—and sniffed at his forehead. She gestured to her oldest son. He joined the game, drawing laughter from his little brother.

The pain was already easing when he heard a murmur from the inmates lounging around the prison courtyard. He opened his eyes to see the prisoners step back to let through an imposing figure in a white jacket. It was Warden Krit. The big man lumbered straight towards him.

Why would the warden want to talk to him? He hadn't done anything wrong, had he? There had been a delay in the road-building his group was working on, but that wasn't his fault. Someone had forgotten to order stones for the roadway.

He and Warden Krit got along. The man was from the far south, with a broad, dark face. He was loud and officious, but seemed to care for the welfare of his prisoners. Life in the Nakhon prison had been far better than the cramped torture of the Pakpanang jail where he had spent a month hoping the ruler of Nakhon would review his sentence and reverse the judge's decision. The governor should have noted the lack of physical evidence, the failure of the supposed victim to appear in court, the collusion between Jate and that policeman and the harshness of the sentence for a first-time offender. Asking about this had only earned him kicks from the Pakpanang guards.

In his first year in Nakhon he clung to hope his sentence might be reduced. He had written seven letters to the governor asking for a review of his sentence without a single reply. Not even a rejection. He had gone to the warden to confirm the letters had been delivered. Warden Krit had assured him that all the letters had been taken to the provincial administrative office and showed him the signatures of the officials who had received the letters.

"Don't you have family or friends working on your behalf? Anyone with the ear of the governor? An aristocrat? A wealthy merchant?" he asked.

Pak shook his head. Even his own family had deserted him and his friendships with local officials in Pakpanang had proved worthless. Only one had replied to his notes from the Pakpanang jail. "Don't try to contact me anymore," wrote a municipal clerk who had been a classmate at the temple school. "You are a convicted criminal and you have a powerful enemy. I can't know you anymore."

"If you can scrape together some money for the officials working at the governor's office," Krit said, "that might help."

"I have nothing and I have lost contact with my family."

"Then you must make the best of it. You have to understand the way things work. People are not convicted and imprisoned just for committing a crime. They are convicted for a lack of status and influence. Look around at your fellow prisoners. Are any of them wealthy? Are any of them aristocrats? Are any of them well-educated?"

The warden was right, but he couldn't give up. There had to be something he could do. He devoured the few tattered books available in the prison and cajoled the warden into providing him with old government announcements and copies of the laws and regulations. He saved every coin he earned from his writing services and he dreamed of ways to win his freedom.

Earlier in the month, the other prisoners had asked him to approach the warden with their complaints. They all agreed better food was the most urgent need. He drafted and presented a petition from the prisoners to increase the amount of fruit and fish in their daily rations. To everyone's surprise, the warden added pomelos and bananas twice a week to the rations. The warden said there was no budget for more fish.

"No fish, but more fruit is better than nothing, isn't it?" the warden said.

Pak then suggested digging a fish pond and diverting water from the city moat running beside the prison. The warden promised to think about it. Maybe that was what he was coming to discuss. He had already made drawings and a budget with estimates of fish production. He began shuffling through the papers in his bag to find them.

"Prisoner Abdul, what are you doing?" Krit asked gruffly.

"Just helping a fellow prisoner with a letter, honored warden sir," he said with a deep *wai*.

"I have heard about your letter writing. Do you have a sample?"

He hesitated, then took out the latest letter and gave it to the warden, who sat down on a patch of grass in the shade. He squatted down beside the big man, careful to keep his head lower than the warden's. Krit straightened his uniform jacket and leaned back against the whitewashed prison wall. His forehead wrinkled in concentration as he read, mouthing the words.

"Suntorn Phu, eh? I have heard of him; he was a randy one."

"Well, a romantic one, appropriate for an appeal to a lover."

"Your writing style looks good—very clear, even the complex letters. No ink smudges," Krit said. "Not like my reports," he added under his breath. "Can you do numbers? Accounts?"

"I used to keep the accounts for my family's food business," he said.

"Look Abdul, your writing for the other prisoners is all well and good, but I have more important work for you. I want you to help me with reports to the ministry," Krit said. "You'll work in the office; no more ditch digging; no more road repairs."

This is what he needed. Without family to help him, he needed to have the protection of someone powerful. Someone who would help him in exchange for service and loyalty. He looked up into the broad face of the warden.

"If that is your wish, I would be honored by such work," he said. "I have only one small request: I don't want to be Abdul anymore; I want the name Pakdee, not just Pak, to be official."

12

CHAO
Off Course

A shaft of light stabbing through the cabin window broke Chao's concentration. With a sigh, he put his book aside and walked out of the cabin. The setting sun sent orange light raking across the waves, casting long shadows on the deck of *The Wind Uncle*. He squinted against the sun, but couldn't see the dark outline of the shore. Why hadn't he noticed sooner? They were supposed to sail no more than 15 miles off shore. Navigation was Wei Fan's job, but something was wrong.

Night was coming. Without the lights on shore, the only instrument they had to stay on course was an old compass. Monsoon clouds would hide the stars. If they sailed far enough offshore, out into the middle of the gulf they would be safe, but they would have to dodge seven or eight islands scattered in the way.

He leaped down from the forecastle and headed towards the stern. A group of sailors squatting on the fore deck looked up from their game of *Fantan*. Flat copper coins and a few old bullet-shaped silver baht coins were scattered on the gambling mat. Huat looked up and smiled.

"Chao, come join us. My luck is running strong. Maybe it will spill over and your messed-up luck will change for the better."

He didn't like gambling on board, but there was little he could do. Gambling was a necessary diversion on the junk's long, uncertain voyages. At least it was better than getting drunk or smoking opium— other activities he tried to stop. He just wished his brother was not such an avid participant. Huat was popular with the crew for his bright spirits and generosity. When he won at *Fantan* or mahjong or dice, he often gave all his winnings back in loans or rounds of rice wine. Huat liked entertaining the crew with songs he had learned on trips to Bangkok or picked up from temple fairs around Pakpanang. He had a great number of lewd jokes in both Thai and Teochew and told them with a mischievous smile. His selection of songs included wistful ballads, ribald ditties that got the crew erupting in laughter and rhythmic chants for hauling up the sails. His smooth voice sounded good with Thai folk tunes, Chinese songs and the new "international style" music that was becoming popular.

When in Bangkok, Huat would lead the group to the nightclubs near the Klong Toey docks to enjoy the female singers in *cheongsams* slit to the waist. Now 18, his bubbly nature and generosity allowed the crew to forget he was a son of the owner—an owner they cursed for his stinginess.

The sailors, intent on their game, didn't even notice him. Maybe the crew had no affection for him, but they should have some respect. Since taking over management of the ship, he had made improvements in the lives of the crew—better food and less abuse. But the crew thought he still demanded too much work. He couldn't hide his disdain for those who drank or smoked opium. He did the best he could as *chuan zhu*, but he never felt part of the crew and never in full control.

The only sure way to dominate them was with fists and club. That was what his father had done and wanted Chao to do. He wasn't ready for that. He was taller and better fleshed than any in the scrawny crew, but they were more experienced in the brutal brawling that often erupted in port. It wasn't just that. How could he hurt the people he spent most of his time with? Their lives were already tough enough.

"Huat, take a break," he said. "I need to talk to you."

He put his arm on Huat's shoulder and steered him away from the game. His brother was now as tall as he was, and much broader. They had both been toughened by work on the ship, but he had been pared down to lean muscle while Huat had thickened, with a broad chest and powerful arms. Since beginning work fulltime on the ship, they no longer engaged in the wrestling matches of their early teens. Now he would probably lose to his younger brother. Huat had always had a greater appetite for food, drink and fun. He quickly picked up reading and writing both Thai and Chinese, but he was content to do no more than their teacher demanded.

"The sky seems strange," he told Huat. "I think the weather is turning bad."

"No worry, we performed all of the rituals," Huat said. "We burned paper money to appease the sky gods. We sacrificed a chicken to the *Jao Mae*. The soothsayer predicted a successful voyage. You worry too much."

"You think the smoke of some fake money will deflect the winds of a storm?"

"Well," Huat grinned. "It makes the men feel better and it can't screw things up any more than they already are."

"Feeling better won't keep us afloat with all those leaky seams," Chao said. "Better take a couple of men and go below to check on the patches we made in port."

"*Ayah*, if there is a storm, there is nothing you can do about it now," Huat shrugged. "We have gotten through storms before. Screw it, we can do it again. Just head for Pakpanang Bay. We can shelter behind the cape."

"That's part of the problem, we have swung well to the east of our usual route," he said. "We are a long way from shore."

"Maybe Wei Fan was trying to find us some better winds. There is not much. At least a storm would get us moving faster."

Chao looked up at the patched brown sails that hung slack on the masts. The square sails of woven matting were divided into sections by long battens of split bamboo that stretched parallel to the deck. Now the sails were raised to their fullest, trying to catch the fitful breeze. The battens smacked lazily against the mast. At least they were not heading away from the coast very quickly. There were dozens of ropes tied to the ship's railing. Each raised or lowered a different portion of the sails.

The old junk was flat-bottomed with a shallow draft. Its big advantage over the steamships was that it could enter the silted-up river ports along their route with little problem. The downside was it was hard to control in big seas.

"Better get below and see about those seams," he said. "That's more important that your card game."

"Yes sir, Exalted *Chuan Zhu*, sir," Huat laughed. "Just let me finish this round. I'm on a winning streak. And that doesn't happen too often."

Shaking his head, Chao turned and headed toward the rear cabin, which looked like boxes stacked on the deck. Peering into the twilight shadows as he climbed up to the steering platform, he saw Wei Fan, seated on a stool, but slumped over the heavy wooden beam that served as a tiller. What the hell? The helmsman reeked of sour rice wine and snored softly.

"Wake up!" he shouted and slapped the worn wood of the tiller. Wei

Fan woke with a start and fell off the stool.

"What? What?" he asked as his eyes tried to focus. "I wasn't asleep."

"Worse, you are drunk. Get below," Chao said.

"But I am the steersman. I am the navigator."

"And you have steered us off course. You don't even know where we are."

"We are on our route. Uh, you can see the Surat mountains right there," Wei Fan said, pointing unsteadily to the west where only a sliver of the sun could be seen between the clouds and the horizon.

Wei Fan peered again into the slanting light. "Where are they?"

"No, the question is where are we. I think you have steered toward Samui Island."

"We are west of Samui. It should be right there," Wei Fan said and pivoted to point to the east. "See there. That's it. Isn't it?"

Chao looked to the east and saw a mass of clouds tinted dark red by the setting sun.

"That is not an island. Get below and send someone to take your place while I try to get us back on course."

Wei Fan started to object, then thought better of it. He trudged forward, shaking his head and grabbing the rail for balance.

Chao took hold of the thick tiller and pulled it towards him. Sluggishly, *The Wind Uncle* turned towards the sun. It was good having the tiller in his hands. The stout wood, grayed by exposure to salt and sun gave him a feeling of control, something he lacked in his life.

All he wanted was to continue his studies, but Father had loaded him with more responsibilities: drafting contracts, dealing with royal officials, keeping the accounts, maintaining the list of stuff in the warehouse, and finding new customers. Father was a lot harder to steer than *The Wind Uncle*. He was the leader of a group of older Chinese men, most of whom, like Father, had moved to Siam in their youth.

The men agreed the problem was that their children had abandoned the traditional ways. They all spoke Thai more than Chinese. Although despised by Thai society as "Chink children," they strove for a place in that society. The old men preferred their Teochew dialect and longed to return to their home villages on the southeastern coast of China. Unfortunately, they agreed, the time was not yet right.

China was in turmoil, Father had often explained, reading from the Chinese newspapers reaching Pakpanang. He had been excited by the

100 days of reform, but then the emperor was overthrown and the Empress Dowager Cixi took over. Foreign troops occupied Beijing. It was a disgrace, he often said. According to Father, the Siamese king's approach to the aggression of foreign devils was far more clever.

"The white ghosts just want to make money. If you stop them from making money, they want to take over the whole country. Look at Burma, Laos and Annam," he lectured. "So, the Siamese king lets them make some money, gives them a few bits and pieces of outlying territory, but never gives them a chance to take over."

The day after a drinking session was always difficult for Chao, as Father, battling an aching head, complained angrily about dropping profits or rising expenses. He found fault with the accounts he no longer understood. Anything but the most patient explanation would only lead to a bigger storm of cursing. He no longer feared his father's fists. But he he had to make sure Father would not take out his anger on Mother.

Out at sea, at least, he didn't have to deal with Father. Despite the frustrations of running the old ship, there were times of peace when a moderate wind pushed *The Wind Uncle* on its course. Even now with this fitful breeze he could lean on the tiller and enjoy the night sky. But those seams were a problem. Where was Wei Fan's replacement?

If the wind didn't pick up it would take a long time to get back on course, but at least he would have time to finish reading that biology book. It showed all the parts of the human body and how they fit together. But he had a lot of questions and there was no one to ask.

When next in Bangkok he would visit that herbal medicine shop near the docks. The shop was small, but its walls were lined with hundreds of glass jars. Some contained exotic medicines: rhino horn, bear's gall bladder, tiny dried sea horses and strangely shaped fungi. Different odors spread through the tiny shop as the shop-owner dumped a variety of herbs out of their bottles, ground them to powder and measured the powder into paper packets for a customer. Ginseng, wolfberry, wood ear mushrooms, cinnamon bark, ginger, licorice and *Ephedra sinica* were the most popular. The wizened shop-owner told him the names of each and how they had to be mixed in just the right proportions to treat different conditions. He explained how herbs classified as hot treated cold diseases, while cold herbs, like menthol, were used to treat diseases caused by overheating.

"But how do you know they really work?" he had asked the old man.

"Thousands of years of treating illness," the shop owner said. "You have to have faith, faith in the Chinese tradition of medicine."

The old man's explanations, however, didn't fit with what he had been reading in the biology text. The causes of disease, it said, were tiny animals seen only with something called a microscope. Cures came from killing those animals. The book cited experiments by doctors named Pasteur, Lister and Koch. There was nothing about overheating or imbalance of forces or the twelve meridians in the body. Which was right? Why were there no Chinese experiments like those of the *farang* doctors, to prove the Chinese herbs really worked?

He heard soft footsteps on the ladder to the steering deck. He looked up, expecting to see one of the crewmen trained to steer the ship. But the slight figure moving hesitantly towards him was Tum, the young Thai who helped with the cooking.

"*Chuan Zhu* Sir," Tum said with a shy smile. "My apologies, but Wei Fan said I should come back to help you steer. The others didn't want to leave their gambling."

Why didn't Wei Fan force a more experienced crewman to come? He was just too damn lazy. But that wasn't Tum's fault.

"Do you know how to steer?" he asked with a sigh.

"It's not so hard. I've helped Wei Fan before, when he was... sleepy."

"How do you keep a straight course at night?"

"Wei Fan told me to watch the wake to see if it is straight and to align the first mast with something on the horizon."

"But it will soon be dark. What will you do then?"

"Stars—see there are stars," the boy said, pointing to a patch of clear sky to the west. "Don't worry, sir," his gaze lingering on Chao's face.

He felt something flip in his stomach and looked away from the boy.

Tum was a good boy, with a sweet disposition, always eager to help. He had worked in the godown for more than a year, carrying goods, sweeping the floor and fetching tea. He had begged for a chance to work on the ship. After only two weeks at sea he had proved his worth. Tum kept Chao's cabin clean and made great improvements in the food served on board. He and Huat would often work together over the charcoal stoves in the galley, debating recipes and spices. When Father captained the ship, the usual fare had been little more than dried fish and boiled rice. Now Tum livened it up with the spices he brought on board along with the fresh morning glory leaves and water cress he grew in pots alongside the cabin. He also put out fishing lines that brought in fresh tuna, squid and bass.

Tum's work on the food made him popular with the crew, but it was his sweet smile and large eyes that made a few of the seaman look at him with special warmth. He worried Tum would be forced into relieving the desires of those crewmen unwilling to wait for a woman in the next port. But Tum didn't seem to mind the calloused hands that stroked his slim arms or patted his behind when he passed on the narrow passageways of *The Wind Uncle*.

This threatened to become the cause of more brawls among the crew, so he had put out the word Tum was not to be bothered in that way. He knew the crew wondered about his protection of Tum. They must think his interest was due to something more. Tum enjoyed curling up at Chao's feet as he read from one of his Thai books. He tried to ignore the knowing looks of the crew when they saw them together.

"Alright Tum, you keep the bow pointed just to port of the brightest star, that one there," Chao said. "Double check the heading with the compass. Head southwest."

Tum would have to do until he could get a more experienced man to take the tiller. Now he had to get Huat to inspect the hold. Looking back, Tum seemed tiny next to the massive tiller, but he smiled confidently.

When Chao got back to the game, he saw that the pile of coins in front of his brother had disappeared. He stared at Huat until he threw down his cards.

"Time to call it quits," his brother said. "We have work to do. Who will come with me to check the seams?" he asked. Two of the gamblers raised their heads in mute appeal as another round of cards was dealt.

"Just one more hand, then come see me in the hold," Huat muttered as he headed towards the supply box to get a lantern.

"I can't let my baby brother go into that deep, dark hold all by himself," Chao teased and put his arm on Huat's shoulders. Huat grabbed him by the arm and spun him into a headlock.

"*Ayah*, the mighty *chuan zhu* is trouble," he said. Chao struggled to get free, but his brother was too strong and he gave up after a minute of thrashing.

"Fortunately, his baby brother has taken mercy on him," Huat said as he let him go.

"Enough foolery," Chao said with a frown. But it had felt good to play with his brother the way they had growing up.

Huat dusted off an oil lamp and lit the wick. The orange glow of the lamp lit the hold as he slid down the ladder. Great bundles of cloth, wooden crates of mining equipment, coils of telegraph wire, boxes of medicine and bundles of fishing nets lined the narrow passageway in the hold. Huat handed him the lamp and lifted one of the walkway planks. A foot of water sloshed below. That was nothing new. Some of the lime and coconut husk caulking was old and small leaks dribbled water down the sides of the hull. The crew had patched some of the leaks in Kanom, but new ones were weeping water into the hold.

He helped Huat muscle some of the heavy boxes away from the sides of the ship for a better look. The Wind Uncle was overdue to be beached and given a thorough overhaul, but Father insisted they make one more voyage first. He saw several small leaks, but nothing big. If a storm hit, they could run before it without putting too much strain on the hull. The wind would likely come from the east. That should blow them into port without much tacking.

On all the voyages he had made since he was twelve, he had never seen *The Wind Uncle* get into serious difficulty, not even in the late monsoon storms. His first storm, on only his second voyage, had scared him, but after that he had come to enjoy the fierce weather. Huat, he knew, also liked seeing the storm clouds gather. Easily bored, his younger brother loved riding the winds of a storm.

"It doesn't look too bad. Nothing more we can do until we can beach her," Huat said.

"I guess not, but I hope the weather won't get much worse."

"What? And miss a fast, fun cruise into Pakpanang?"

Chao chuckled, but as they shoved the hatch cover back into place, he looked to the east where the clouds reflected the last red tint of the sunset. A dark mass was growing in the center of the horizon, sucking the last light from the world.

13

SU SAH
Vocation

Carrying a tray of supplies, Su Sah used her knee to nudge open the door to the main operating room. She always felt excited coming into this room. It was here doctors and nurses dealt with the most difficult cases. It was here the surgeons worked, here the doctors examined the most seriously ill. It was here lives were saved or lost.

In the nearly two years since coming to work at the hospital, there had been days of great fulfillment. She delighted when a treatment worked and a patient recovered. She had contributed to that recovery, not only with medicines and treatments, but with kind words and personal attention. So many patients were fearful and in pain. The words she spoke to them and the way she touched them, could lessen that fear and ease that pain. On a few occasions she had seen something the doctors missed. Once she saw an error in the medicine prescribed and quietly corrected it. She was truly useful.

Her happiness, however, was sometimes clouded by frustration and anger. The ignorance and carelessness of the patients themselves often led to needless suffering. When the patients were children, it was worse. The parents, who were supposed to protect their children, were often to blame for the illness. Some children came in on the brink of death from diarrhea caused by drinking dirty water. Babies suffered disease and malnutrition because their mothers stopped breastfeeding too soon. Too many children shivered with malaria because they slept without mosquito nets. Others came to the hospital too late because they had been treated by useless home remedies or magical talismans. Some women suffered difficult pregnancies because they had too little to eat or worked too long in the fields. Her job was more than easing suffering, it was fighting the ignorance that led to suffering.

It was frustrating, but at least she could understand why the simple villagers, mostly illiterate, didn't understand the harm they were doing. Much worse was the attitude of some of the doctors who were supposed to know better. Some criticized her for spending too much time with patients. Few accepted her medical suggestions. Most refused to explain their treatments. She was just a nurse. She didn't know who was worse, the older Burman doctors with their refusal to change their treatments in the light of new research, or the younger British doctors with their airs of superiority trying to cover up a lack of experience or understanding of the medical problems in Bago. One or two of the young doctors, at least, seemed to listen to her. The saving grace was her dependable friendship with head nurse Ma H'La Yin. Ma had been through it all before and urged patience.

"The doctors will eventually come to accept you," Ma consoled her. "They will still be arrogant and still pretend to be all-knowing, but most will see your devotion and expertise. Give it time."

"I'll try, but I can't help speaking up when it affects the patients. Dr. Richardson is the only one who listens to me. Often, he agrees. He too feels shut out by the older doctors and says they are behind the times."

Ma looked at her and sighed. "Su, be careful of that one. It may not be your medical knowledge that interests him."

"What do you mean? We only talk about our patients. He has medical journals that come straight from England and he lets me read them."

"Su Sah, dear, we must accept that we are not doctors. We are junior members of a team and doctors are the leaders. If you have to speak up, do so in a way that does not threaten them. Now that takes different skills than we learned at Dufferin."

Su Sah laughed quietly. "I'll try, but it's not easy. There are days when I have to check the mirror to see if there are wounds from biting my tongue so often."

The older nurse took both Su's hands in hers and looked into her eyes.

"It is what it is. If you let the hospital take over every bit of your life, you will suffer. You will grow bitter. That would not be good for you or the people who come here for help. You need to find something else in your life, something you can turn to for happiness and solace when things go badly here."

"Well, the hospital is important, but I have joined a Mon music group. One of the Mon landowners, Nai Tun Way, invited me."

"Well, that is progress. I have heard good things about him. He is a leader in this community. You should understand more about Bago, not just its medical problems. Besides you are over 20 now. You should think about marriage and a family."

"What about you? You are older than me, but all you think about is the hospital and the nurses."

"The nurses are all the family I need," she said with a smile. "Besides, what man is interested in me? I am not beautiful and have no land or wealthy relatives."

"You have an inner beauty everyone can see. I would like to be like you. The hospital can be my family too. I love being a nurse and helping people. We can think of the old doctors as senile grandparents and the young doctors as naughty, annoying cousins."

Ma laughed and then composed herself.

"No, you are pretty and smart," she said in a serious tone. "Men like you. You don't notice how they look at you. I think you are destined to be married and have a big happy family."

"Maybe someday," Su Sah said with a laugh, "but I won't give up the hospital. I want both kinds of family."

14

PLOI
Rising Waters

Ploi looked up from the accounts ledger as a clap of thunder shook the zinc sheets that formed the roof of the gambling den. She looked into the main room where two dozen gamblers were intent on their games, barely noticing the growing storm. Four games were in progress. In one corner the *Fantan* players were hunched over their cards, eying each other warily. The biggest group of gamblers was around the *Po Kam* mat. Most were men, bare-chested, calling out loudly for their preferred number as the bowl of cowries was uncovered. Ploi looked at the *Thua* mat—that was the high-stakes game that generated most of their profits. The *Thua* dealer was counting out the cowries as the gamblers watched. As usual, the Thais chatted merrily while the Chinese placed their bets with ferocious intensity. Most of the *Thua* players were well-dressed. Women with a dozen bracelets, men with chains of gold, even a top-knotted little boy holding his mother's hand. The district officer, his white official coat tossed to one side, had made a series of bets on the numbers two and three. A *saw-oo* player provided a piercing tune that lent a rhythm to the betting around the gambling mats, but failed to drown out the sounds of the gamblers. Smoke from a dozen cheroots chased around the room as the wind blew through the barred windows.

Located well off the main road to the provincial capital and with its own pier jutting out into the Pakpanang River, the Jaikla Casino – or Daring Casino – was one of the best-known buildings in the district, she thought with pride. It had one main gambling room, one private room and a room for records and accounts. The walls were rectangular wooden planks held together in a frame of dark teak wood. It was the only licensed gambling den in the district. She was proud that her casino now generated a good portion of the income that Sia Leng, the *monthon* gambling tax concessionaire, sent on to the *monthon* office in

Songkhla. It was her job to ensure there were credible records to show the Chinese concessionaire while ensuring that the tax paid was as low as possible. Still only 16, she had become expert at shaving a few baht here and there from the income and adding a few baht here and there to the list of expenses. She had taken over from Elder Brother Chit when the concessionaire had sent his thugs to threaten her father with broken thumbs if the casino continued to insult him with meager payments. When Father grudgingly admitted that Chit had caused the problems, she eagerly volunteered to replace him.

She had increased the payment and the concessionaire now seemed happy. He probably knew she was still cheating him, but she did it carefully, respectfully. She made sure she paid enough to keep him from getting angry. She controlled all the casino finances: token exchange, payouts, accounts, employee salaries and tax payments. Elder Brother Chit was left with the job of keeping order on the gambling floor, handling disputes and making sure the big bettors were enjoying themselves. He seemed to like chatting up the customers and offering free rice wine to the best ones. Whenever there was a fight, he was enjoying themselves to wade in, swinging the ornate walking stick he liked to carry. But now he was nowhere to be seen.

"Where is Elder Brother Chit?" Ploi mouthed to the head dealer. He shook his head and looked away. It didn't matter. The casino ran just as well without him, though her father would never admit it.

"Do the best you can whenever Chit is away," Father would say. "Leave any serious problems for him to handle."

Unlike many of her girlfriends, Ploi no longer idolized her brother. When she was little, he just ignored her. Lately, however, he seemed to take delight in tormenting her. His tricks and insults were intended to let her know that, however much their father might love her, there was only one eldest son. He had mocked her quick facility with numbers and her beautiful handwriting.

"Why does a girl need to write and calculate? You only need to warm some man's bed and tend to his babies, that is, if anyone will have you."

She knew Chit was behind the scorpions left in her bedding and the smelly stains that appeared on her best clothes. He would always give her a smirk to make sure she knew. She had complained to Father, but he said she was imagining things. After that she never complained again, but made sure Father could see that she, not her brother, was the one devoted to the family business.

It was not just his treatment of her that led Ploi to despise her brother. As she grew older, she saw he was the slave of his own whims and urges, whether for liquor, for excitement or for women. He was shallow, weak, undisciplined and lazy. Why did mother and father make excuses for his failings? That only made him worse. He thought he could get away with anything.

His absence during the evening peak gambling time would also be excused. Now, with the storm growing in intensity, they better close down so customers could get home safely. It might already be too late for those who had come by boat. She glanced out the door and saw wind-whipped waves surging over the dock. The river was rising and high tide was still two hours away. It must be raining in the mountains to the west, swelling the streams feeding the river. Storms like this sometimes sent a surge of water from the gulf into Pakpanang Bay. If the runoff, the storm surge and high tide all came together, it would be bad.

A crash reverberated through the room and stopped all the gambling. It must have been a dried palm frond smashing into the zinc roof. There were a few nervous laughs from the bettors. She straightened her *phasin* and strode into the main room. The roofing rattled like a giant bowl of cowries. The wind whistled through the widening cracks.

"Honored customers, we are going to have to close early because of the storm," she announced.

Immediate cries of protest arose from the gamblers.

"But I am on a winning streak."

"I need to recoup my losses."

"You can't do that. Where is your father? Where is Kamnan Paen?"

Another branch hit the roof. The wind lifted one of the metal roofing sheets. Rain whipped into the front corner of the casino. Gamblers around the *Po Kam* mats grabbed their wagers and moved to the middle of the room.

"Who came by boat?" she asked. "It is already too rough for you to go home that way."

Groans and protests went up from the group now huddling in the dripping room.

"Make sure your boats are well-secured. You will have to spend the night on this side of the river. We will all have to move to higher ground," she said. "Finish the current games and then pick up your betting counters."

She issued orders to the dealers who quickly wound up the remaining games. They picked up cowrie shells, collected mah jong tiles and rolled up the mats. She was busy exchanging the bright-colored ceramic betting counters for dull coins when a cry arose as the wind tore off one of the roofing sheets, letting pellets of rain slant into the betting room. She glanced through the door at the bettors scrambling to avoid the rain. She grabbed the account book and strapped it around her waist. She raised the lantern. Its light picked out the frightened faces of the gamblers. She could feel the fear radiating from them, but she felt calm. She knew what she had to do.

"Uncle Daeng, lock the cash box and bring it with you."

The *Fantan* dealer closed the lid on the wooden box when a gust of wind blew open the door. A wave of warm river water sloshed through the door and across the floor of the casino, sweeping gambling mats and betting counters with it. Several bettors screamed and rushed towards the door. The dark water was already ankle-deep and rising.

15

CHAO
Dark Storm

The first sharp gust of wind hit the sails as Chao walked forward. The wind came from a quarter off due east.

Good. That will get us back on course even sooner.

The Wind Uncle surged forward as the wind filled all three of the giant sails. He rechecked the heading against the last glimmers of light in the west, knowing once that was gone, Tum would have only the ship's compass for navigation. Heavy clouds swallowed up the darkening sky.

He climbed down to the main deck and frowned when he spotted Huat squatting behind the gamblers on the fore deck, not even noticing his brother's approach.

"Huat, what are you doing? You saw the hull. The caulking is working loose. You better organize the pumping crews," he said. "Once we get moving faster more water will leak in."

"Shit, there is plenty of time for that, Chao," Huat grinned. "A few more little leaks, but basically okay."

"Those little leaks could get bigger fast. Get two-man crews for each of the pumps with back-up crews to take over when they tire," he said loud enough to get the gamblers to look up. "Now."

The gamblers looked back to their game and accelerated play. "Let us finish the hand," the dealer said. "It will only be a minute."

"Where is Heng Wing?" Chao asked. "I need him to take over as helmsman."

One of the men shrugged and the others resumed a quarrel over their bets. Heng Wing was nowhere to be seen. He would have to get Huat to track him down. Tum would have to handle the helm for a few more minutes.

The wind roared through the rigging, adding a low-pitched hum to the sound of the waves smashing into the blunt bows. He looked astern.

The waves had swelled quickly, white foam topping each. The spray and the darkness made it difficult to see into the storm. He couldn't recall ever seeing the wind rise so quickly. Now the wind was whipping the foam off the waves and sending it skipping across the dark sea to pelt the ship with salty spray. The wind was suddenly cold and drove the spray so hard it felt like grains of sand hitting his face. He watched as a rain squall scudded across the angry water. The first large drops were followed by a downpour driven almost horizontal by the wind. The rain sent the men scrambling to pick up the cards and coins. They crammed together in the cabin. They could feel the ship rise as a large wave lifted the stern and sent the ungainly junk careening down the face of the wave.

What if the ship simply nosed into the wave ahead? But the bow lifted up. The ship slowed as it crested the wave. Lifted high above the sea around them, Chao looked down on the angry waters pounding the sides of *The Wind Uncle*. The hull shuddered with the impact.

"Get the pumps going," he shouted.

The command sounded like a whisper in the wind, but Huat didn't need to be told.

"Two of you lazy motherfuckers on each pump—get all four going! And two standing by to relieve each crew," he shouted to the men.

Good. Huat was following orders. He looked at the faces of the men. They looked surprised and afraid. Through other storms he had never seen that look on the older crewmen. Where was Wei Fan? He should be doing this.

The crewmen clambered down into the hold carrying lengths of rubber hose for the heavy pumps. He peered through the hatch as Huat led the men into the cluttered hold, holding up a lamp to guide their way. He was pleased to see how quickly Huat positioned the pumps and thrust the hoses through the pump holes. Huat called out a rhythm; the men grunted to his cadence and the pumps began a rhythmic rasp.

Good, this will all work out okay. His brother was proving useful. Just a bit of heavy labor for a few hours. He looked up at the matting sails, now bulging with the wind despite their stiff battens. It would be good to make up time with such a strong wind, but this might be too much.

"Get aloft, take the fore and main sails down three battens," he shouted at a half-dozen crewmen crouched against the front of the cabin sheltering them from stinging wind. The men didn't even look up. Wei Fan should be dealing with the crew on this. They were used to following his orders.

"Get aloft," he yelled into the wind. "Sails down."

He plunged into the wind and grabbed one of the crew by the arm.

"Trim sails," he shouted into the man's ear and pulled on the arms of the man next to him. He pointed up at the sails now vibrating with the strain of holding the wind.

Two of the crewmen crawled to the fore mast and started to climb, but a lurch forward down the face of a wave and a gust of wind sent them tumbling across the deck and into the railing. He grabbed two more crewmen and pulled them with him as they stumbled towards the mast. He would have to lead the way. He put his arms around the mast and started to climb, his bare feet finding purchase on the hemp wrappings every three feet up the mast. Lek, one of the strongest crewmen, started climbing on the other side. They climbed cautiously, stopping each time the ship came to the peak of a wave and slewed down the other side, then scrambling up as *The Wind Uncle* climbed the next wave. Finally, they reached the massive spar holding the top of the sail. Far below, two crewmen, wet and glistening in the light of the ship's lanterns, struggled to loosen the lines.

The heavy top spar under his feet gave a sharp lurch as the line came free, but the wind pulled the iron sail ring tight around the mast. A second lurch and the other side came free, but the sail was not going down like it should.

"Bounce," Lek shouted and flexed his knees, pushing down on the spar. Chao did the same, clinging to the mast. The wind plucked at his fingers, threatening to send him plunging to the deck 30 feet below. The beam inched down. They bounced again. He felt one foot slipping on the wet spar as a wave smashed into the ship from the side. He hugged the mast and regained his balance. Lek grinned at him from behind the mast. They pushed again. The spar lurched lower, then stuck again. He looked ahead and saw only the massive slope of a wave looming. The wind drove the bow into the froth and a surge of water swept down the deck as the bow lifted. The water threw the crewmen working the lines off their feet, sending them sliding sternward until they could cling to the rail. The crewmen looked like little wet mice huddling together. Astern an even larger wave gathered behind them.

Excitement swelled in his chest. The crew, the ship, he himself— all were nothing more than toys for the waves. They just kept rising and streaming past, ignoring the fears of those on the ship. The vast darkness of the sea and the indifference of the wind overwhelmed him.

I am nothing. This is all so much larger than I am. It doesn't care. Why should I?

If he fell into the sea, it would welcome him like a warm bed. There was nothing he could do. Men were helpless. All the supposed gods were impotent. Nothing could challenge or change the blast of the wind or the power of the waves. He felt hollow. The wind seemed to blow through him as if his body was nothing more than a thin netting of flesh. He was nothing in this vast world. It was liberating, exhilarating. It didn't matter what Father wanted. It didn't matter if the voyage lost money or even if the ship was lost. Nothing really mattered because the storm, nature, the world, didn't care about any of that.

Far out on the horizon a strange light curved around the edge of the world, crushed under the weight of dark clouds. He shivered with a kind of exultation. The wind whistled like an insane flute. The ship shook under his feet. He drew a deep breath and looked around at the darkness that vibrated with the power of the storm. In the dim light of the ship's lamps he watched as wave after wave rushed out of the blackness and hurled the ship forward. He had never felt more alive.

He looked at Lek and grinned.

"Bounce some more," he shouted. "Get this sail down."

He bent his knees and straightened up. Lek joined him and the beam dropped a notch. The sail bellied towards the bow. He could see the crew below trying to tie down the slats as the sail lowered, but the wind was too strong. The sail writhed like a big shark furious at being hauled on deck. The waves that surged across the deck kept throwing the men off their feet. He laughed at the sight of them slipping, sliding and scrambling. What a joke to think we can control our fate.

The beam lurched downward. With less sail area catching the wind, the beam began to move more freely. Like village boys riding their water buffaloes, Chao and Lek rode the beam all the way down to the bottom boom. They dropped to the deck, and the crew scrambled to tie down the sail.

"Good work," he shouted, clapping Lek on the shoulder. But he knew it didn't matter. The wind and the waves would do what they wanted no matter what he and the crew did.

"Next one?" Lek asked and gestured to the big main sail that was stretched to the full. Chao nodded and they crawled on hands and knees to the main mast. He felt the motion of the ship had changed. It was more sluggish now, riding lower in the water. The ship was slower to rise up on the waves. More of each wave broke across the deck, torrents of water grasping at them as they struggled forward.

A blast of wind hit the sail from a new angle as a wave swung the stern around. The crew were thrown against the railing as *The Wind Uncle* began to skid broadside down the wave. The wind hit the back side of the main sail. With a crack, the sail twisted around the mast with the bottom boom and the lower battens going one way and the upper battens the other way. He ducked as the boom swung over his head, snapping one of the stays. He looked up at the tangle of matting, battens, ropes and spars.

Ah, this must be what the old sailors called a "fan-up", the most serious problem for the junk rig. Now there is no way to lower the mainsail. The wind will drive us wherever it wants. The wind strengthened as he marveled at the mess it had created in the once neat rigging. The mast strained in the struggle between the power of the wind and the mass of the hull. The main mast was curved like a bow from the power of the wind, but with part of the sail twisted by the fan-up, it might hold. The loss of power from the fouled mainsail put more pressure on the aft mast. It too bowed under the strain.

The darkness deepened. The shifting squalls blasted the ship like a boxer battering an opponent against the ropes. Left then right, the wind swung the ship as the waves rolled from behind, speeding it up, then slowing it down, lifting it up, then pushing it down the face of a wave. He watched as the largest waves swept the deck again and again.

After each attack *The Wind Uncle* rode a bit lower in the water. Huat and the pump crews must be losing their battle against the leaks. The water pouring through the hatches was making it worse. Except for Lek, the crew on deck had given up trying to manage the sails and lay scattered along the forecastle, hugging the railing. He couldn't blame them. He clung to the mast straddling the main boom. Staying on deck risked getting washed overboard. But each lurch of the ship threatened to tear his arms from the mast and throw him to the deck below. He gestured to Lek and they climbed down towards the deck. Timing the waves, he leaped to the deck and slid to the main hatch. He pulled it halfway open and peered below.

In the hold, dimly lit by a lamp swinging from a hook, he could see the pump crews were working hard, but water had risen above the floor boards and sloshed around their feet. Each pounding of the waves sent small spurts of water through the seams.

"How are you doing?" he shouted at the figure of his brother, glinting wetly in the yellow light. The scraping sound of the pumps competed with Huat's chants and the heavy breathing of the men. As the deck pitched forward, one of the men slipped in the water and hit his head. Huat jumped in to take his place on the pump. Water surged down the hold as the ship pitched forward on the face of a wave. Now knee-deep, the water threw two more crewmen off their feet and the rhythm of the pumping faltered. One man clutched the Buddha amulet around his neck.

"Come on, you black-faced bastards," Huat shouted. "We have to keep going. If we work together, we can keep afloat."

Chao felt a surge of pride in his brother, taking charge and getting the men to work together, but he knew it wouldn't matter. He heard a strange groaning from the aft mast. He looked up from the half-open hatch. With a sound like a big New Year's firecracker, the mast split and pitched forward. It ripped into the bottom part of the main sail and smashed to the deck in a tangle of matting, ropes and splintered spars. He climbed quickly up to the deck. The aft sail slumped over the side and trailed in the froth streaming past the rail.

He looked back below. Water was now knee-high and the men struggled to pump. One by one they gave up in exhaustion. Only Huat and his partner worked on.

"Enough," Chao shouted. "Everyone up on deck."

One by one the men struggled up the ladder, staring in amazement at the mess on deck. The main sail was bulging on either side of the mast with splintered battens and a half dozen ropes swinging around the mast with every lurch of the ship. The aft mast was a splintered stump with half its sail on the deck and half trailing in the angry water surging no more than an arm's length from the deck. Several men clung to the rail; others had clambered into the cabin where a lantern cast quivering shadows on the deck. Dark seas rose astern and the ship slid sluggishly forward.

Chao grabbed his brother's arm as he slid on the wet deck.

"Come with me," he shouted into Huat's ear.

The brothers scrambled over some ropes towards the fore deck.

"I'm sorry," Huat yelled between deep breaths. "We just couldn't pump any more. Too much water."

"There was nothing you could do—nothing any of us could do."

He seized his brother's arm as another wave lifted the stern. He looked down at the trough of the wave below them. The ship lurched down the wave and the stern rose again. The largest wave yet curled far above the boxy stern cabins. It surged under the ship, lifting first the stern, then the bow.

He felt weightless, rising from the deck high into the air. He was far above the main mast. The ship was a toy cradled in white froth. He could see himself far below, holding onto his brother's shoulders. Higher still and the ship was little more than a brown smudge in the darkness. The wet wind roared through him from the dim line of the horizon. Flashes of lightning lit up the clouds that looked like huge hands cupping the sea and the tiny ship.

Then he was back on the deck again. He felt his brother's powerful grip on his arm.

"*Ayah*, this can't be the end, can it?" Huat yelled.

He leaned over Huat sweaty neck, "No, not the end. There is no end."

He smiled into Huat's eyes, eyes wide with fear and excitement. The stern lifted under the next wave and the bow dipped. He looked at the sea ahead. A line of white froth glimmered through the black just beyond the bow. This time the wave did not slip beneath the hull, but broke over it, surging over the deck and smashing into the main cabin. The bow tilted down and hit something hard and then broke free. A harsh scraping sound reverberated from the hull. Huat clung to his arm as the wave rushed towards them and the cabin lanterns went dark.

16

PLOI
Swept Away

A gust of wind slammed the casino door shut. Two customers screamed. Another gust whipped it open and left it quivering on its hinges. Ploi waded into the water rushing past the doorway. She held up her lantern and waved to the group in the doorway to follow her. A quick glance toward the dock showed nothing in the dim light from her lantern. No boats, nothing but white-capped waves.

She turned to head up the slope from the river. The rain had churned the bank into a thick porridge of wet clay that grasped at her feet. She slipped back. They would have to walk along the path halfway up the bank until they could find firmer footing. She searched for the path with her feet.

"Hold hands. Help each other," she shouted. "Follow me."

The water was now up to her knees. She leaned against the rush of water to angle up the riverbank, bent over by the gale blasting in from the bay. She pulled her sodden *phasin* up to her thighs with one hand and dragged the district officer forward with the other.

Behind her, Daeng and Tim carried the casino counters, the *Thua* mats and the cash box. They struggled to stay upright. The river was rising fast. A heavyset Chinese lady fell back into the mud and shrieked for help. Brown water swirled over her. Ploi dropped her lantern and slid back down the bank to grab her hand.

"Get her arm," she shouted. Tim hesitated, then pushed the cash box to Daeng who struggled to hold it out of the water that pulled at the mats in his arms. Tim lurched forward and took the woman's arm. They heaved her upright. The water was now up to their waists.

"Don't leave me. I'll drown," she screamed.

"No one will leave you. We are all together. Just lift your foot straight up and then forward. Now the other one," Ploi urged.

A market lady got behind the woman and pushed. Ploi and the district officer each took a hand and pulled her up the bank. Each step took an effort. She could feel her heart pounding and she was breathing hard, but the bank was firmer now. The ungainly group moved a few steps forward and a half step up the bank.

She stopped for a moment. Was everyone still with them? She could see Daeng far behind everyone, struggling to hold the cash box and stay upright in the current. Ploi gave the market lady a final push and slid down the bank towards Daeng.

"Drop that stuff," she yelled into the wind.

Daeng fell and the dark water surged over his head.

She reached into the water and felt his shirt, holding on with one hand as she leaned into the bank, straining against his weight. Daeng regained his feet and took a step up the bank, reaching his hand out. Ploi hauled on his shirt. Tim grabbed his hand. Another step up the bank and the water was below their waists.

They would make it.

"I am so sorry," Daeng wailed. "The money, the counters, they are gone. All I have is this," he said holding out the mat slung over his shoulder.

"Don't worry about it," she said. "We have all the people, don't we?"

They were standing exhausted in water now only knee deep. She counted quickly. Yes, everyone made it. What about the casino?

The glimmer of light from the casino lanterns flickered out. The muddy torrent in front of her disappeared into the darkness and then lit up in a series of lightning flashes. The river water tore off one of the casino walls and then another. The glistening planks of one wall were seized by the water and pulled into the darkness. One by one the wind lifted up metal roofing panels and sent them spinning off into the night. Her casino was being torn apart. She turned back to the people struggling through the mud and water.

"Everyone—follow me. Keep moving this way," she yelled as she trudged forward. She couldn't see more than a few feet ahead. All she knew was that they had to get higher, angling across the slope, fighting the water trying to pull them into the river. She paused and waited for the group to catch up. Several of the men struggled past her, but the older women kept slipping. The dark water was surging higher. She felt like running away from them. She just wanted to get up the bank and out of the grasp of the fast-flowing water. If only Father was here. But he wasn't. She couldn't leave anyone behind. The fat lady was stuck again, wailing in fear.

There had to be a way to get her moving. She slid back down the slick mud of the bank and unslung the *Thua* mat from Daeng's shoulder. The wind straightened it out like the flying carpet in one of her story books. She pulled it down onto the fast-flowing water.

"Lie back on the mat," she shouted. "We'll pull you up."

The woman stood frozen in fear.

Ploi put both hands on her shoulders and pushed her back on the mat.

"Everyone take hold. Keep her above the water," she yelled against the howling wind. "Uncle Tim, get the other side. Hold on. Pull."

At first the grip of the water seemed too strong. Then the district officer slid down the bank and grabbed one edge of the mat.

"Again," she shouted. "We are making progress." She wasn't sure they were, but she dug her toes into the soft mud and threw her weight forward.

"Heave. This is working."

Daeng and Tim strained against the weight of the mat and the women clinging to it. The district officer yelled something into the wind and one of his men pulled at his shoulders. Then, a half-step at a time, the whole group began moving—one, two, three steps forward and a half a step up the bank.

She could feel the strain on her legs and shoulders, but she didn't feel tired. The wind and the rain gave her strength as the group slipped and trudged up the river bank.

Finally, the ground leveled off and the mud was not so deep. More hands reached down from the top of the bank and helped pull. She stopped the group on the higher ground that formed the road along the river. She counted again, touching each person as they bent over in exhaustion or squatted in the mud. All 32 of the people at the casino had made it. Wet and cold, the survivors were exhausted, but they couldn't stop here.

"Follow me," she shouted. "Uncle Daeng, you go last and make sure no one is left behind."

She felt her way through the darkness to the main road to Nakhon. The heavy rain had flooded both sides of the road. Flashes of lightening showed the road had become a long thin island. Two small houses near the road were dark and partly flooded. A buffalo, its eyes large with panic, swam past, unable to climb onto the road.

"We'll go to my house. It is the nearest," she shouted. The road of hard-baked laterite made easier going, but the wind and the rain continued to assault them. Finally, she saw the multiple roofs of her home emerge from the darkness. The water streaming off the road helped push them into the family compound. Once they left the road the water came nearly to her waist. She struggled to open the gate that swung back and forth in the water flowing through the compound. Yellow light leaked around the window shutters. She turned and helped the others through the gate. She pulled herself up the steep stairway into the house and pounded on the door. She pounded again, but there was no response.

"Open the door," she screamed. "It's me."

She was rewarded with the sound of the iron bolts being withdrawn from the door. It swung open and she staggered onto the central platform of the house and into the arms of Awn, one of her father's assistants.

"Where is Father?" she asked. Awn nodded to the reception hall on one side of the platform. She opened the door and stepped over the raised door frame. She welcomed the warmth and light of the room. A dozen men sat around a long mat with bottles and glasses beside them. Several trays of prawn crackers lay between them. At the far end of the room, Father looked up with a scowl.

"What are you doing back here so early? Where is your brother?"

"The storm. The river rose. The casino washed away," she said. The other survivors pushed their way into the room and stood dripping.

"That is ridiculous," Paen snorted. "Why are you all in my house?"

"I almost died," the Chinese woman wailed.

"The wind felt like a whipping with palm fronds."

"Give me something to drink."

"The river was wild. It just kept rising and rising with big waves."

"Alright, alright, come on in," Kamnan Paen roared. "Ploi, where is the money and where is your brother?"

She looked back at Daeng and the other casino workers and they looked down at their empty hands. Daeng started to say something with a plea in his eyes.

"We had it when we left the casino," Ploi said, turning to face her father, "but we had to pull people up the bank to escape the flood. The river was up to our waists and trying to pull us into the current. We had to leave things behind."

"But not the cash!" Father said.

"The cash box is big and heavy," she said, looking at Daeng, who hung his head. "The weight was pulling him down, so I told him to drop it. The important thing is we managed to save everyone. Other than a few cuts and bruises, no one is seriously hurt."

"But the money? What about the casino counters?"

"It was just one night's take," she said. "And I did save the accounts." She pulled out the sodden account book she had strapped around her waist.

"You lost our money? How could you be so careless?" he screamed at his daughter.

"We saved everyone's lives when they could have drowned. You were not there to help. Chit was not there to help."

Paen took a step back. He looked surprised she had yelled at him.

"Well, where is your brother? He was in charge of the casino. If you had only waited for him—he wouldn't have lost the money," he said.

"Isn't he here? He said he was not feeling well and was going home," she said.

"Would I ask if he was here? How could you forget your brother and save everyone else?" he demanded.

"But he wasn't there. I don't know where he is," she said. "If we had waited for him, we all would have drowned."

Daeng stood up. "Kamnan, sir, Miss Ploi did everything possible to save everyone at the casino. Chit left the casino long before the storm and we never saw him again."

"We need to go back to the casino and find him," Paen said.

"There is no one there. There is nothing left but the building posts," Ploi said. "Chit has probably gone to one of his friends' houses. You can't see anything in the dark and rain."

"He is my son. We need to find him," Paen said. "Ong and Art, get some lanterns. We've got to go out to search."

Kamnan Paen and his men surged out the door, letting another blast of rain and wind into the room. She tried to tell him it was futile, but Father wouldn't listen. She busied herself getting food and drink for the casino group. Her mother brought out sleeping mats and blankets for the people lying exhausted on the floor. Many were soon asleep.

Ploi couldn't sleep. She just lay listening to the storm. Father hadn't said a word about her own survival or her efforts to save the casino customers. He cared only about his money and his son. What did she have to do to mean something?

After what seemed like hours of fury, the whistle of the wind softened. Its high-pitched sounds lowered into a moan. The sound of the rain lashing the tile roof faded. Finally, she slipped into an exhausted sleep.

It seemed only a moment before she heard shouting at the doorway. Father threw open the door with a bang and trudged into the main room. Three of his men followed, looking cold and exhausted. She brought some cloths for them to dry off as Mother came in with a pot of tea. Paen collapsed to the floor in front of them.

"We went to all his friends' houses, but nothing." He sat slumped in a corner and grabbed for one of the liquor bottles still on the floor.

"Father, I…"

"Don't talk to me now," he grunted and grabbed a bottle.

For the first time that night, tears welled in her eyes as she watched her father take another drink, staring at the darkness beyond the door.

The thin grey light of a morose dawn filtered into the room, glinting off the bottle as it was raised and lowered, raised and lowered.

17

CHAO
Sea Loss

Chao woke with a start, puzzled at the wet sand scraping his neck as he twisted around. The dense green of a wet jungle came into focus. Where was he? He sat up on the sloping beach and looked into the gray dawn. Spread out before him was a curved sweep of sand with small waves breaking through yellow-brown foam.

The storm. The struggle through the water in the dark. Swallowing salt water. Somehow, he was alive. Where was the crew? Scattered along the beach were bodies. Dead? No, there was movement. Three men were walking slowly along the water line. Beyond them seawater swirled around what must be the hulk of *The Wind Uncle*. Its stern was hung up on a reef. Waves foamed against the hull. They swept a tangle of torn sails, ropes and broken spars back and forth. The once straight line of the hull now formed a slight angle between bow and stern. The reef has broken her back. He quickly surveyed the beach on either side, counting the sleeping lumps that were his crew. How many men did they have? He couldn't remember. He leaned over and shook the body beside him. Huat looked up and groaned.

"Wake up brother," he said and shook him again.

"Are we dead? I thought for sure we were dead," Huat said with an amazed smile. "We made it. But where are we?"

Chao looked down the beach, curving away from them at each end.

"We must be on an island. We were too far off the coast for this to be the mainland. It must be an island, but I don't know which one."

He looked at his brother who shrugged.

"Who cares? As long as it is dry land and we're safe."

"We need to make sure everyone is here," Chao said. "Rouse the crew and make a head count."

Huat rose to his feet, shaking sand from his shirt and his hair. He walked along the beach, nudging each of the sleeping lumps with his bare feet. Chao looked back at *The Wind Uncle*. How did we get over the reef? He remembered the crash and shudder of the ship as the waves pounded it on the rocks. He thought they would die if they stayed aboard while the junk was broken to pieces. He shouted to the crew to grab the cork fishing trap floats from the cargo and leap overboard.

Looking around him, he saw the beach was littered with the white-painted floats, bits of wood and a variety of crates and sacks. The cargo. He had to save the cargo. Huat led a group of sailors up to him.

"It looks like we are missing only two—Wei Fan and Tum," Huat said. "No one has seen them."

"Okay, Lek, you search along the beach to the south. Xi-yang, you look to the north. Don't forget to check the bushes along the beach."

"We're thirsty," Xi-yang said. "We tried drinking rainwater from the leaves, but it is not enough."

"There are kegs of water on the ship. You go search and we'll bring back drinking water. The rest of you come with me. We must find the others and save everything we can from *The Wind Uncle*."

He waded into the frothy sea and stroked towards the broken ship. Behind him the crew reluctantly followed, some swimming, some clinging to a float and kicking through the troubled water. The hulk of *The Wind Uncle* waggled morosely in the waves. Torn sails and tangled lines drooped into the water. Chao used them to clamber up the steep sides of the junk. Soon the crew stood around him on the tilted deck. The foremast had been swept away and the main mast had splintered and crashed to one side. The rear cabins were still intact, but one corner of the fore cabin had been crushed by the main mast.

"You two search for Wei Fan and Tum, one forward and one aft. Pu, see if you can find the drinking water. The rest of you start bringing the cargo up out of the hold. We need to save as much as we can."

The men followed his directions, working in weary concert. They halted only to broach a water keg and pass it around. He sent two of the men to search the ship for food. The men in the hold handed up crates of roofing tiles, plowshares, mining equipment and soaked bags of spices. Another group lashed together spars and battens to make a rough raft. A shout arose from one of the stern cabins. He ran back and found his crewmen pointing at the form of Wei Fan snoring in a hammock. He smiled grimly and punched the sleeping man in the shoulder.

"Wei Fan—wake up you idiot."

"What?" he mumbled in Teochew. "Have we arrived already?"

The three laughed, glad to see the old navigator still alive.

"Yes, we have arrived, no thanks to you, you drunken old fool," Chao said. "Come see what is left of our ship."

They emerged from the cabin. Wei Fan's eyes widened as he surveyed the tangled wreckage on the deck and the jungled hills beyond the beach. Already crewmen were lowering the first load of cargo onto the raft. Soon they were poling it into the quieter waters inside the reef. The slate gray of the dawn was brightening to the east, tinging the dark clouds to the west with streaks of pink. Looking back to the shore, Chao saw a group of villagers coming down the beach.

We need to save the most valuable cargo before they start picking her clean, he thought. We can wipe the steel and iron stuff down with oil from one of the barrels. We'll have to rent a boat to take us to the mainland. *The Wind Uncle*, though, will never sail again. Maybe that is a good thing.

"Doesn't look too good does it?" Huat said.

"I think it is time we got out of the shipping business," Chao said. "Father can focus on his trading and warehouse business and we won't have to make any more voyages."

"But what will we do?"

"Whatever we want," he said with a smile.

The possibilities seemed to rise within him like those paper balloons that rose into the air on the heat of a candle. Study, Bangkok, medicine, whatever we want. No more facing the indifference of the sea. No more storms. No more tedious accounting and scraping to show a profit. A chance to break free of Father's control. A smile spread across his face as he looked out to a sea horizon that was no longer confining.

His thoughts were interrupted by a shout from the stern of the ship.

"Come quick—it's Tum."

He climbed up the ladder to the steering platform, feeling sorry for the old *Wind Uncle*, but happy about the future. There pressed into the one wall was the slight, silent form of the boy, the massive tiller pinning him down. The slim body was bent at an unnatural angle and his skin was pale and damp. Chao bent down, grabbed his wrist and felt for signs of a heartbeat.

There was nothing.

18

DAM
Sea Gain

Dam followed Jate as they picked their way over the wreckage along the bank of the Pakpanang River. They headed towards a fisherman squatting on the dock. Bent over a damaged fishing net, the skinny old man didn't notice their arrival until they loomed over him. He squinted up at them, the dark skin of his face crinkling into sharp creases.

"Boss Jate, good morning sir. I didn't know it was you," he said raising his hands in a deep *wai*.

"Have you got my money?" Jate asked.

"I will get it. Somehow. But I need more time. My nets were damaged in the storm. All the fish traps were blown away. We haven't been able to fish since the storm."

"That is too bad, but it looks like your fishing boat survived," Jate said. He pointed to the new fishing sloop tied up at the dock. "You are fortunate. Many were lost."

"Yes, I moved it into the creek when the storm loomed. Some of the spars were cracked, but those can be replaced."

"That is good to hear." Jate smiled. "Since you cannot make your loan repayment, I am taking the boat you pledged as security."

"No. You can't do that. The loan was only for half the cost of the boat, the rest of the money was from my savings," the fisherman cried. Dam watched as Jate loomed over the man.

"Don't tell me what I can't do. You signed an agreement. If you can't pay, you forfeit the boat. That is the law and this policeman is here to make sure the law is followed."

"If you do this, all the fishermen will protest. We will boycott your store. We won't buy again." The fisherman stood and took a step forward. "We are not slaves to be pushed around this way."

Jate nodded to Dam and stood back. He knew what he was supposed to do, but he hesitated. He was a policeman now, even though he wasn't wearing his uniform. He shouldn't be doing his old job. What would the captain say?

"Dam, what are you waiting for? Show this fool what happens when you don't pay your debts to Jate."

The old fisherman scrambled backward and picked up a boat hook.

Dam lurched forward, grabbed the fisherman's wrist and slammed a big fist into his face and another to the side of his head, sending him crashing into a wooden fish trap. Blood trickled from his ear.

For an instant he saw his mother lying on the floor of their hut, blood dripping from the corner of her mouth as his father stood over her. He cringed at the memory, confused by Jate's look of approval. He watched as Jate gestured to two of his men, who boarded the boat and untied it from the dock.

"A boycott?" Jate laughed. "You fishermen need my equipment more than ever. You'll have to replace what was lost to the storm. You'll need my loans, so from now on I am raising the interest rate. The storm may have been a disaster for many, but for me, it was a gift from heaven."

"How will I feed my family?" the fisherman pleaded. "If you let me keep the boat, I will pay next month. Have mercy. I'll be grateful."

"There is nothing about mercy in our agreement, but I am a merciful man. I will let you work on the boat as a crewman and pay you a wage. When you have saved enough, you can buy the boat back."

"Even with a good wage, that will take a long time," the fisherman moaned, one eye already starting to blacken.

"My calculation is that you should be able to pay for the boat in say—the afternoon of your next life," Jate said. His harsh laugh sounded more like a cough. He turned and headed towards the next dock. He clapped Dam on the back.

"Good work, Dam. My investment in you is paying off again."

Dam nodded and pulled his gaze away from the bent figure of the fisherman and the blood dripping onto the rough wood of the dock. Once more the image of his mother rose in his mind, her face marked by the bruises and blood from his father's fists.

19

PAKDEE
Appeal

Pakdee sat cross-legged on the floor next to Warden Krit. The big man was bent over the packet of documents that had arrived earlier that morning. He watched the sweat trickle down the warden's thick neck as he squinted at the cover sheet. The packet looked fatter than usual. On top was the schedule of reports expected by the ministry. Then there were two letters with heavy wax seals. He leaned over and saw the first was from the High Commissioner of *Monthon* Nakhon Srithammarat, Phraya Sukhumnaiwinit. He watched as Krit slowly read through the elaborate wording, making a tick mark at some of the words. He gave up with a sigh and turned to the second letter. After looking at it for a few minutes he handed it to Pakdee.

This one was even more elaborately worded. At the bottom was the distinctive signature of the Minister of Justice. He read it aloud to Krit. The letter explained that His Majesty King Chulalongkorn had authorized work on a new criminal code based on Japanese and European law. A first draft was enclosed. All organizations in the ministry, including police, prisons and courts, were requested to provide comment on the draft. They should also speed up implementation of earlier legal reforms, especially the Law on Evidence. Krit groaned.

"More complications."

"Don't worry, the Law on Evidence won't be an issue for us in the prison," Pakdee said as he read through the document. "That is a problem for the courts and the police."

"Are you sure?"

"Yes, but there are also some new rules for prisons. It appears His Majesty the King has visited prisons in Europe and the British colonies. According to the minister, the new rules forbid beating prisoners, withholding food, and all forms of torture. See, he writes there are strict requirements for food, exercise and pay for prisoner labor."

"I've already made improvements," Krit said. "Do you think they will be enough?"

"You have gotten the warders to treat prisoners better. They still sell food and opium to the prisoners, but you have worked hard to cut out the kick-backs for sales to the prison. That has meant more of the budget for food and clothing. Life in prison is better than before, but you will have to improve the food. And we need to make sure senior officials are aware of all you have done and how it helps them."

The warden unbuttoned his uniform jacket down to his bulging stomach and squinted at the document.

"Pakdee, can you help me?"

"Yes, sir, of course. Perhaps we should also demonstrate your understanding of the proposed laws by offering comments."

"We should? Won't they think I am criticizing their draft?"

"The comments must, of course, include praise, but they will show you are thoughtful and helpful. It will be good for your reputation, especially if you have ideas that make your bosses in the ministry look good. Let me work on it."

Hours later Pakdee lit a lamp to look over the documents as daylight faded. He had copied the draft Criminal Code and the Law on Evidence onto fresh pages and begun making notes. In the four months since coming to work in the warden's office he had re-organized the filing system and set up new budget procedures that lowered costs. He had persuaded the warden to adopt policies that were better for the prisoners and the warders. He expanded the reports to the ministry with additional details. The objective was simple. He had to make Krit look good and he had to make Krit dependent on his help in looking good. If Krit had power and protection then so did he. Already he had used access to prison records to make a name change, replacing Abdul with Pakdee, though there was little he could do about the conviction and sentence recorded in the district court and reported to the ministry. Father would be upset if he ever learned he had exchanged his Islamic name for a Thai name. But Father had failed him. Family and friends had failed him. He had to create new links above and below. He had to use the system the way the Thais did.

As he pored over the new criminal code, he saw how he could find grounds for an appeal. The problem was the new code had not yet been promulgated at the time of his trial. As he studied the document and the accompanying letter, he saw that the Law on Evidence had been enacted five years earlier, nearly a year before his arrest. Torture during interrogation had been banned just a month before he had been beaten in the Pakpanang jail. A beating was torture, wasn't it? The stupid policeman had admitted beating him to the judge. Perhaps it was in the court records. As he searched through the painful memories of his own arrest, imprisonment and trial, he saw there had been violations of both the spirit and the letter of the king's reforms.

He had been kicked and slapped every day by the jailors in Pakpanang. Without money for food, he had eaten only thin rice gruel. When he couldn't pay them, his jailors had torn up his letter to his parents. He had no one to help him at the trial and the judge had not let him explain what had happened. No physical evidence of rape had been given. Malee had not been called even though the laws of evidence required her testimony. Malee's husband had given evidence when he should have been disqualified as an interested party under the new law. He would appeal! With rising excitement, he wrote late into the night.

The dawn light slanting through the window of the prison office and the cries of a rice congee vendor outside roused Pakdee from his sleep, slumped over the appeal letter on his writing table. He rose and went to a red clay pot of drinking water. He threw water on his face and smiled. The injustice of his conviction would soon be erased.

He went back to his table and started to read. What a mess. The hastily scribbled letters were hard to read. Several pages were smudged, including a large stain where his forehead had rested on the final page. The tone and language were all wrong. He sounded angry, ignorant and petty. There was no evidence to support much of what he claimed.

He would need to find records of his trial. He would have to change the tone and use more elevated vocabulary. He would quote from the draft criminal code and the Law on Evidence. Most important, he must praise the king's reforms as wise and say that such wisdom should extend beyond the capital to reach the majority of the king's subjects in the provinces. Taking a fresh sheet of paper, he began with the traditional address to "the dust under the feet" of the king. He worked carefully and slowly, with hope.

20
DAM
Protection

Dam felt the itch of the wound on his neck and the deeper ache in his shoulder as he sat cross-legged on the polished wooden floor of the prayer hall. The wounds were healing, but still painful. The bite wound on his neck was red and swollen, but the shoulder was worse. If he moved the wrong way, a sharp pain would rip down his arm and across his chest. He would see again the glint of the knife in the semi-darkness and feel again the burn as it sliced into him. He was glad to have removed his heavy blue police jacket and feel the cool, damp air coming out of the forest. His old teacher, *Ajahn* Klai, and two younger monks approached. The monks placed a wooden box next to him. The abbot looked at Dam.

"You have been wounded and you doubt the effectiveness of your *takrut*," he said. "What you may not understand is that the blows that injured you would have been fatal without the protection of the *takrut*."

Dam fingered the slim tin tubes that held the magical words and symbols strung around his neck.

"*Luang Paw*, I don't dare doubt the power of the *takrut*, but I wonder whether it is enough. I am a policeman now. I battle criminals and pirates. They are armed with pistols or rifles. They have swords. They lie in wait in the dark. We never know when we might face death."

"You are wise to return to me," the old monk said as he touched the bandage around Dam's shoulder. Dam couldn't help wincing.

"Yes, you need stronger protection. It is several years since I gave you the *takrut* and its power may be fading. The threat of bullets requires a higher level of occult knowledge and a higher level of discipline from you. The *takrut* you wear could be torn from you. We must give you something that can never be taken away. Even then you must come back to me every year to renew its power."

"Another *takrut*?"

"More than that. The power of the *takrut* does not come only from the symbols and its maker, it comes from inside of you. First, you must never fail to protect your mother. Second, you must perform good works. Third, you must live a moral life. You can have women, but you must not lust after another man's wife. You must live by the Five Rules for lay people, but that is not enough. There are other rules I'll teach you to preserve the power of the *takrut*. Most important, to become a real man, you must ordain and spend time as a monk. You must learn meditation and explore the deeper internal power possessed by all men."

He was still on inactive duty while recovering from his wound. The rainy season retreat had several more weeks left. This would be the ideal time to enter the monkhood for a short time. Ordination would impress the captain and draw attention to his wounds and his bravery.

"*Luang Paw*, I will ask permission to ordain and I will place myself in your hands. But is there nothing that can be done today?"

The old abbot laughed.

"I expected you would be impatient, so I have prepared. First an additional *takrut*, learned from the most powerful of the Khmer monks and used successfully in battle against the Anamese. This will protect against bullets from guns."

He pressed his forehead to the floor and *waied* three times to the old man. He took the slim tube of tin, added it to the cord that held the earlier one and retied it around his neck.

"Now we must ensure you can never be separated from your protection," the abbot said and gestured to his assistant. The young man opened the wooden box and took out a blue-black slab of dried ink and a set of long needles. He began to grind the ink, adding drops of water as he worked.

"I will tattoo a magical design, a *yantra*, on your skin. This *yantra* can never be taken away from you and will be visible to your enemies. This is the best way to protect you against both blade and bullet. I have selected some ancient Khmer designs specifically for your needs—both to protect you and to inspire fear in your enemies," Klai said.

He felt the first jabs on his back as the old man tapped rapidly on the needle starting just below his neck.

"Pay attention. This round one on your back is the eight-point protector—providing escape from dangers in the eight directions of the universe. Once you have ordained, we can do more. I will place the

Five Deva Faces on your chest to ward off danger or perhaps the tiger *yantra*. Yes, the tiger is best for you. Just as important will be the *Yot Mongkut* on the top of your head for good fortune and success in battle. Once your head is shaved for the monkhood, we can do that one."

His mind drifted as the old man described the different *yantra* tattoos, their histories, powers and variations. The rapid pricking of the needle was painfully ticklish, but it was a welcome distraction from the ache in his shoulder and the thick residue of fear from the struggle that had left him wounded.

Before that day he had always felt invulnerable. Police operations often had seemed like his collection work for Jate. The victims might run or put up token resistance, but they were not a real threat. He was bigger, stronger and fiercer than any of them. They might argue or cringe or beg, but always they would submit.

This time had been different. The bandits, cornered and caught with a large amount of loot, refused to surrender. They attacked with a desperation that surprised him. When the leader's pistol misfired, they pulled out swords, clubs and gaff hooks. They charged, screaming curses. The fighting was hand-to-hand. He remembered the sour smell of rice whisky on the breath of one bandit who had pinned him down. He twisted the wiry bandit's knife hand backward until it broke and the knife fell free. The man screamed, but then sank his teeth into Dam's neck, rooting for the artery. He clawed at the man's eyes, but nothing stopped him until one of the policemen clubbed him from behind with a rifle butt. He had only a moment to shout his thanks and pick up his rifle when another man leaped at him with a long knife in his left hand. All he could do was raise his right arm and twist to the side to protect his face from the blow. The blade cut into his shoulder. Furious, he pushed his bayonet into man's stomach with both hands and pulled upwards against the burning in his shoulder.

He shook his head at the memory. The small pain from the tattoo needles was assurance he would never face such a threat again. As the pin pricks completed a circle, he felt a calmness returning to him. He had not slept well since the fight. Now the tension was flowing out of him. The cicadas in the forest began their high-pitched drone as the afternoon stretched towards dusk, providing a monotonous backdrop to the clink-clink of the tattoo needles. He felt calm and protected again.

21

CHAO
Facing Father

Chao and Huat stood, heads bent, in front of their father seated at the table. Chao could feel his younger brother shifting his weight from one foot to the other. He touched his brother's arm trying to calm him as Father glared at them.

"You really lost *The Wind Uncle*?" Father finally asked. "Can't it be refloated or salvaged?"

"*The Wind Uncle* is caught on a reef and cannot be repaired. It is gone," Chao said. "The fittings, parts of the rigging and some of the wood can be recovered, but the keel is broken and many of the planks are cracked. Two of the masts are gone and all of the sails."

"How did you stupid buffaloes let this happen?"

"We were off course and the storm drove us onto the reef."

"Who was steering?"

"It was the boy, Tum. He was crushed in the storm, the only death."

"Why wasn't Wei Fan at the helm? He has a lot of experience in storms. We always got through them before."

"He was drunk, so I told him to sleep it off."

"So, with a storm approaching, you replaced our most experienced helmsman with a boy who had never steered the ship before."

"Yes, sir, I did—and the boy died because of my decision."

"Did you check on him during the storm? Did you wake up Wei Fan? Did you send anyone to help steer?"

"No—the storm came quickly. There was so much happening. The sails wouldn't come down. The foremast broke. The main sail got caught in a fan-up. The ship was leaking and we had to pump."

"So, you ran her smack into an island. Chao, you are responsible for all of this. You have ruined our family."

Father was exaggerating. They still had the warehouse, tons of goods and a large amount of rice bought for shipment to Pattani.

"The family business will recover, but I have caused the death of a young boy. There is no recovery from that. I need to apologize to his parents. I would like to offer some money as compensation."

"*Ayah!* You lose my ship, you wreck the family business, you send me into bankruptcy and you want money for compensation," Father shouted. He stood up knocking over his stool. His face was contorted with rage. "You have a duty to the family. If you do not accept that duty, you are not my son."

"I understand the duty of family members to help each other, but there must also be love and understanding."

"What kind of love do you show by wrecking my ship, a ship I bought with my own sweat and sailed for 30 years? Understanding? All I understand is that you have ruined our family business and you worry about some little faggot cabin boy who is no relation to us."

"I will work to repay you," he pleaded. "I will find a job in Bangkok and send all I can back to you."

"Bangkok! That's what you wanted all along. You lost the ship because you didn't want to work at sea anymore. You did this deliberately," he screamed. "You might as well just kill me now."

How could Father say this? But, maybe in some way, somehow, his failure to save the ship was due to his desire to get away from the shipping business. Maybe he had wanted this.

"Honored Father, I don't think that is really fair," Huat spoke up mildly. "Chao did everything possible to save the ship. Even with all the leaks, it might have survived the storm if we had not strayed east of the islands—that was Wei Fan's fault."

"You defend him? I had such hopes for the two of you and now both of you turn against me. My life is over. My own sons have killed me. Get out and never come back."

Father glared at them, breathing heavily.

"Get out. Get out. I never want to see such ungrateful sons again."

Chao bowed and stepped back. Fine, if Father didn't want to listen to them, didn't even want them in the house, then there was no reason to stay and take his abuse.

Pulling Huat with him, he turned his back, threw open the door with a bang and stomped out of the house.

22

SU SAH
Invitations

The afternoon sunlight slanted through the window of the nurses' room and glinted off the pages Su Sah was studying. She shifted to the other side of the little table to avoid the sunlight that made the dry season heat even more stifling. She bent again over the article by Professor Angelo Celli.

His methods of malaria prevention would probably work in Bago, but would the older doctors accept the connection between mosquitoes and malaria? Too many people in Bago still believed that malaria was caused by an imbalance in the blood or by vapors from the swamps. Many monks and villagers blamed angry local deities. The Italian professor had run experiments showing it was the bites of mosquitoes that spread the diease. He advocated individual protection with clothes and mosquito nets in addition to efforts to destroy mosquito habitat.

Someday, perhaps, she could further her studies—go to England or Italy to meet the authors of the articles she read in the medical journals Dr. Richardson had given her. She appreciated his help, but she wished he would be quicker in getting the journals to her. He said they had to be placed in the doctors' library so all the doctors could read them first. The edition she was reading was already a year out of date and medical knowledge was advancing so quickly she felt like she wasn't keeping up. If she could get to England, she would be at the center of those advances. She had been excited to hear of the establishment of the London School of Medicine for Women where the first woman doctor in Britain was the dean. Another possibility was the medical school at London University where women had gotten medical training for almost 20 years. Dr. Richardson, who had graduated from the school, often had talked of his friends and mentors on the faculty there. Would it be possible someday for a woman from Burma to study there?

Heavy footsteps echoed from the hall. It was Dr. Richardson. Doctors rarely came to the nurses' room. Usually, they sent one of the sweepers to notify a nurse she was needed. The tall British doctor smiled at her, his thinning blond hair plastered against his sweaty forehead.

"Ah, Nurse Su, I am glad I found you," he said and leaned against the doorway. "I see you are reading *The Lancet*."

"Yes, there are two excellent articles on malaria in this edition. Professor Celli has some good recommendations on malaria prevention."

"The Italian? Well, if it is in *The Lancet*, then it is probably quite alright, but I recommend the articles by British experts like Dr. Ross, or what is his name? That colonel who works for the Viceroy."

"Of course, those are good too, but there has been great progress in reducing malaria in Italy. The Italian methods could be applied here."

"Yes, but you need not be so serious. You work all the time. You should have a little enjoyment. I understand there will be a concert at the town hall this evening. I was thinking of going and would like to invite you to join me."

"The Mon music concert? I was already planning to attend," Su Sah said.

Nai Tun Way had invited her. She had first met him at the hospital when he brought in the daughter of one of his tenants. He had been truly concerned for the girl and his visits to the hospital led to long conversations about malaria, worker health, Bago's history and Mon culture. Once the girl recovered and left the hospital, they began going to Mon music events. Tun Way had invited her to the evening concert, and she had agreed to go.

"I am going with a friend. Perhaps another time."

Richardson frowned.

"A friend... one of the nurses, I suppose. Well, that's alright. We can go somewhere after the concert. It would be good to talk about something other than medical work."

"Well, my friend is..."

The British doctor surprised her by suddenly reaching out and touching her on the arm. The pale skin of his hand contrasted with the honey color of her arm.

"It's settled then. I would really like to see you away from the hospital. We'll go to the concert and we'll have a pleasant evening."

She opened her mouth to speak, but Richardson abruptly nodded, wheeled around and left the room.

23

PLOI
Business on the Brink

SONGKHLA, FEBRUARY 4, 1900

Ploi sat behind her father, straining to hear his unusually quiet voice. He leaned forward, carefully keeping his head well below the level of the broad-faced man across the rosewood desk. The man was dressed in a dark blue, embroidered silk jacket with a high collar. A dozen sepia photographs of old Chinese men and women hung on the paneled wall behind him. They seemed to be providing support to the man glaring at them. She felt like she and her father were outnumbered.

"Honored Sia Leng, sir, you will appreciate our difficulties since the storm," Father said softly. "As I have explained, we lost not only a full day of proceeds, but had to close the casino for five weeks of repairs. Then there is the cost of the repairs. Even more important, the flooding and the loss of ships at sea left everyone short of cash for gambling. Betting has been way down.

Ploi had never heard this whining tone in Father's voice before. She turned to watch the tax concessionaire. His face was soft with fat and his jowls bulged out over the tight collar like the fat on pork legs in the market. His small eyes were hard.

"Enough. I am not stupid. I know all this. You have had some losses. But you run a gambling house. Losses are part of gambling," Leng said. "What I am waiting to hear is how you will limit my losses. My casinos in other parts of the *monthon* are bringing in more money and did not suffer from the storm because they were built on higher ground. I didn't gamble with the river and the weather. Why should I suffer losses because of your carelessness?"

"Honored sir, I will try to increase revenues by getting more customers and changing the games to improve the odds for us. We have a detailed plan," Father said.

She could see little sympathy in Leng's eyes.

"What are the details of this plan?"

"Well, we will get more small bettors to come in at better odds and more big bettors, too."

"How?"

"We have a plan."

She waited for Father to explain the plan she had detailed to him the previous day. He seemed to be shrinking as she watched, like the big *chedi* growing smaller in the distance as their boat left Pakpanang.

Father had seemed to listen to her then. He must have understood what they had to do. If only he had not gone out drinking. Didn't come back until nearly noon the following day. He had hardly had time to bathe and dress before they left for the sail down the coast to Songkhla. She had tried to go over the plan again on the voyage, but Father, looking bilious, had lain down in the cabin and fallen asleep.

She remembered leaning on the ship's rail and watching the long sweep of beach slip by. Beyond the deep green of the trees behind the beach were pale blue mountains, hazy in the distance. It had been six years since the last time they had made this same trip together. How different it had been. Father was lively and fun back then. They stayed on deck together, playing a rhyming game for things they saw along the way, and singing duets that challenged the sound of the wind sighing through the rigging.

Father told her the name of each of the villages they passed, what they produced and what problems they faced. He explained how each of the lines on the ship was used to control the sails and he took her to the tiller, persuading the helmsmen to give her a chance to feel the pull of the wind and the punches of the waves. Like many of their trips together, it had been exciting to learn more. It had been comforting to have her powerful father teach her.

This trip she was left on deck by herself, watching the shoreline, like time, move steadily on, indifferent to her feelings. At intervals the boat glided past clusters of brightly painted fishing boats pulled up onto the soft white sand. There were more boats and more thatched houses along the beach than on their last trip down the coast. The area was prospering. Tin, coconuts, rice, fruit and wood were all bringing in money from markets in Bangkok and British Malaya. It was an opportunity Father should be seizing with his old enthusiasm.

Now he seemed weak, struggling to reply to the big Chinese. The gambling concession was the key to the family income and the heavyset man in front of them controlled the concession. He frowned at Father's hesitation and spoke with a harsh tone, anger deepening his Chinese accent and odd grammar.

"Paen, we've done business together for a long time, but I don't like the way things are going. Your payments—no increase for two years," he said in staccato cadence like the lefts, rights and knee thrusts of a boxer.

"More people—more potential customers, yet you pay me no more for the concession. Worse, you tried to cheat on your payments last year. I gave you another chance, but now I hear disturbing things, very disturbing. You rarely go to the den. You ignore your duties as *kamnan*. The *monthon* commissioner is replacing the governor's relatives one by one. I hear you will be next. You always drank too much, but now worse. You've lost interest. I know you have a new young wife, but you can't let that interfere with business. Your son, what's his name? Chit? He is supposed to be in charge, but he leaves early and takes money from the till. On the night of the flood, where was he? Nowhere to be found. It turns out he was with a girl all night and never bothered to think about the casino. Hundreds of your tokens went missing. You have no idea when they will be exchanged for cash. Your most popular dealer quit last month after a brawl with your son. Your staff loses the night's receipts and you were lucky no one died. The people of district say their *kamnan* did nothing to help them during the flood, but spent two days searching for a son who was never in any danger."

Father seemed to reel before the blows like a beaten boxer.

"Am I wrong about these things?" Leng demanded.

Father looked down, unable to meet Leng's eyes. Ploi thought back to his assurances that he and Leng were old friends. They went out drinking together. They had worked together for more than a decade. He told her he had paid thousands of baht to the man, so he would be understanding of their current problems.

"I can fix these things," Father finally said. "I will be at the den every night. Income will increase under our new operating plan. My second great uncle is still the governor. I have connections. My family is the most important in Nakhon. You need my connections."

"Your connections get weaker and less useful every day. The governor no longer has much power. The royal court in Bangkok is running things through the *monthon* commissioner," Leng said coldly. "Your days are over."

Explain the plan. Explain the plan, she urged silently as she looked at her father. He seemed to be sinking into the heavy chair under the baleful gaze of the Chinese. Their family needed the concession. Father's rented lands and other businesses brought in money, but not like the gambling den. The den was the key. She leaned forward. Father looked around the room helplessly.

"We have a good plan. It is written down. There are charts and numbers."

"You have become incompetent and unlucky," Leng said with a sigh. "I ask you again. What are the details of your plan?"

She had worked on the plan for more than two months, talking to customers and discussing options with employees to come up with ways to increase revenues. She had explained it all to her father who now seemed punch drunk.

"Honored Boss," she said softly, "Permit me to go over the details of the plan Father worked out and asked me to write down."

She felt his eyes focus on her. She knew she shouldn't be speaking, but Father was going to lose the concession. She had heard that Leng had welcomed the improvements to the casino financial reporting since she had begun work. She felt his eyes travel down her body. She knew she looked older than her 17 years and she had become accustomed to the appreciative stares of the casino customers. Despite her mother's objections, she wore a fashionable Western-style dress like the upper-class women in Bangkok. It was tight in the front and the skirt had ridden up on her legs as she turned in the chair. She didn't bother to push it down. She looked directly into Leng's broad face.

"Go on, explain," he said.

"Of course, you understand this business much better than we do," she smiled, "so we look forward to your suggestions to improve the plan. Here, I have made a copy for you."

She leaned over the big desk as she extended a sheaf of papers to Leng. She felt his eyes linger on the tops of her breasts showing through the lace of her dress. She moved a bit closer and pointed to the chart on the final page.

"This shows our projections for boosting revenues and increasing payments to you over the next five years," she said.

"But how do you do that?"

"Look back to the first page. When we rebuilt the casino, we added another room covering the whole second floor. It is well-decorated and paneled with wood. That will be exclusively for the big bettors. It will make them feel special. We will have pretty women to serve them drinks – *farang* liquor brought in from Singapore – for free. We will have a singer and music. It will be like the nightclubs in Shanghai. The liquor and the women will distract the customers and encourage them to bet. We have made a list of our biggest bettors. They will be allowed to use a special boat to bring them across the river. Only those who have bet more than 200 baht a night will be eligible. In addition to *Thua* and *Fantan*, we are bringing in a roulette wheel, second-hand from a casino in Macau. That will appeal to those who want to play like the rich in Europe and China. The percentage of house take can't be changed much, but we will have greater volume. The wealthy bettors are crafty people who can work out the odds and play the games with the best chances to win. So, we have to make them feel special, privileged to lose money at high stakes games with the elite. We already have explained the idea to our key customers and they are eager to join."

"Hmm, that might work," Leng said. "But what about all the missing gambling tokens? In my casinos all tokens must be returned each evening according to government rules."

"Actually, sir, the more missing tokens the better," she said. The fact that some bettors don't cash in their tokens right away is not a problem—it is a benefit. Since we hold their cash until they exchange the tokens, it is like we are getting an interest-free loan. We can use that money to lend to customers at a high interest rate. We make the tokens shiny and beautiful to encourage the gamblers to keep them as mementoes. By the time we have to return the money for the tokens we will have earned a nice little profit on it. If bettors lose some tokens, and we know many were lost in the flood, then that is free money for us."

A smile split Sia Leng's face, "So missing tokens, free money?"

"Another way of thinking about this is that the casino is a bank. We can use our surplus cash to make short-term loans. You know how those who are losing want to keep gambling, desperate to turn their luck around. We give them an advance and charge interest. This way the gamblers who don't redeem their tokens are depositors and those who want credit are borrowers—except unlike a bank, we don't have to pay interest on the deposits and have no limits on the interest rates."

"So, we can make more money?"

"Exactly. We just have to be careful to have enough government currency to exchange for the tokens," she said. "So far, however, we find only a small portion of the outstanding tokens are likely to be redeemed on any one night. That gives us the money for our loan business. Already we provide a good portion of the cash circulating in Pakpanang. Jaikla Casino, in practice, is the central bank for the district. You could do the same in your other casinos."

Sia Leng sat silent for a moment. Then his face twisted into a frown.

"Your father said you were going to earn more from the small bettors. I don't see how that is going to happen. Why not focus on the high rollers?"

"The big bettors have more money, but they cling to it more tightly. The small bettors have less, but their grip on it isn't so strong," she said. "With the big bettors moved up to the new second floor room, we can expand downstairs to five mats for *Po*. We will also offer small bets outside the casino under canopies on three sides of the casino. In the outside areas we will go for the mass market while keeping our expenses low. These are small bets, fast and easy to make, but the odds will be heavily in our favor. Each week we will put up posters with sketches, or maybe even photographs, of the biggest winners. People like to show off."

"That should help, but I don't think it will get you to the numbers in your chart."

"Perhaps not," she said, feeling more confident. "But we won't depend on the gambling alone. We will have food available at prices a little higher than the market. Up to now all of the food profits have been going to outside venders. Now, we have a fence to keep them out. Those venders we let in will pay a fee. Or we can provide food ourselves. The small bettors will have to pay for their drinks. More important, we will use the area behind the den for a pawnshop. We know many of our customers pawn their valuables when they lose, so we should get some of that business. When people are desperate for cash, they don't worry about the interest rate. Some losers go to soothe their pain at the opium den in town. We will provide the opium operator with a building near the casino—for a percentage of the income. That is shown on line four in the chart. The opium will not only provide income, but will attract more customers, especially the

Chinese mine laborers who come down from the mountains with a month of wages. They can either seek the sweet dreams of the opium pipe or the dreams of wealth at the *Po* mats—both available at the Jaikla Casino. Either way, we profit."

"This all sounds good for you, but how is it good for me?" Leng said.

"We will take what we owe you now and convert it into a share of the business, so you will not only get the regular tax payments, but also a percentage of our profits, from the food, the pawn shop and the opium as well as the gambling," she said.

"And that income won't be gambling tax, so I won't have to report it to the government," he said with a smile.

"Correct. We will keep the gambling tax payments steady, and move as much income as possible into the business account."

"How will I know that you are not cheating me on that account?"

"I keep detailed accounts, as you know, and I will share them with you. Each month I will sail down to meet you, answer all your questions and meet all your demands," she said and looked into his eyes.

"Yes, that should work."

"Sia Leng, sir, rest assured," Father suddenly spoke up, "my son and I will oversee everything in our plan. We have the experience needed to make it work. You have nothing to worry about."

Why had Father finally found the courage to speak up? Chit oversee everything? Never! She was about to speak when Leng stood up and smiled at her father.

"I am no longer worried. Paen, you and your son do not need to trouble yourselves with such mundane matters. You have the rest of your businesses to care for and you should do something to save your position as *kamnan* before the commissioner finds someone else to do the job."

Father looked crestfallen.

"About the casino, your lovely daughter and I appear to understand one another quite nicely."

24

CHAO
Irreparable

Pakpanang, March 20, 1900

A boyish figure gripped the tiller of the ship. In the darkness, it was hard to make out who it was. Then the bare-chested steersman stepped out of the shadow and looked straight at him. It was Tum, with a mischievous grin on his face. The boy waved as if to say that steering the ship was no problem. He felt himself smiling back at him. Then he saw a huge black wave gathering behind the grinning boy. It rose higher and higher. He tried to shout a warning, but his tongue felt trapped in a mouth that would not open. He watched in horror as the wave smashed down on Tum and surged towards him.

Chao awoke with a start, wet with sweat and tangled in the thin satin sheet on his sleeping mat. It was the third time this week he had dreamed of Tum. He had gone to the boy's parents and offered them his meager savings as compensation, but they had refused to talk to him. He left the money on their table. He heard the sounds of weeping from the back of the tiny house. What more could he do? Father had refused his repeated requests to contribute to the payment.

"What? Me pay to cleanse your conscience? No, you wrecked the ship, you must be responsible for all the losses."

Father was intent on blaming him. He had refused to listen to his explanation that the storm was indifferent to human efforts, that there was nothing that could have been done. Each time they talked they both ended up angry. Huat and Mother had tried to soothe tempers to little avail. Wei Fan had also faced Hai's wrath, but had meekly submitted to his boss's curses.

"I am at fault," he said softly. "I never should have obeyed the order to give up the helm."

"You were drunk. You could hardly stand," Chao had protested. "You fell asleep while we drifted off course."

Wei Fan ignored him and moved closer to Hai.

"Remember that storm off Songkhla—when we had to sail into the lake for shelter. That storm was worse, but you got the sails down and I steered before the wind. *The Wind Uncle* surfed down the face of the waves like a dolphin and we glided safely through the inlet."

"That was a bad one," Father agreed.

"But we got through it without the loss of a single piece of cargo," Wei Fan said. "We didn't fuck it up like this time."

"Father, he was so drunk he slept through the storm. How could he know anything about how we dealt with it?"

"Go to your room. You have made me suffer enough for one night," Father said. He stomped to the cabinet where he kept his rice liquor and pulled out a bottle.

There was no point in saying anything more. He bowed and left.

His head on his wooden pillow, he listened to the indistinct murmur of the two old sailors talking over their cups. He couldn't sleep and he couldn't concentrate enough to read.

Father was right. It was his fault Tum was dead. He should have insisted the ship be overhauled before the voyage. He should have noticed sooner they were off course. He should have plotted a new course to avoid the islands before turning back to the west. He should have forced Wei Fan to sober up and steer the ship. He should have sent someone to relieve Tum once the storm hit. He should have lowered the sails sooner. If he had gotten the mainsail down first, there would have been no fan-up.

The next morning, bleary-eyed from lack of sleep, he left the house before any of the family awakened. He stuffed some clothes and his books into a cloth bag that he slung over his shoulder. He wrote a short note and left it on the table. "I am an unworthy son. I am sorry for all the losses I have caused, but there is nothing I can do to make amends. I am going away for a while to avoid causing you any more pain."

He paused at the door and looked back at the room in the gray light of morning. This was where the family ate, where he had learned to read, where he had played with his brother and sisters, where Father had conducted business, where Mother had served them spicy curries and Chinese soups. It was plain and spare, the walls dark with the smoke of family meals and family memories. He turned and walked through the door, closing it quietly behind him.

25

SU SAH
Suitors

Su Sah bent over the infant in the wooden crib. The tiny girl's pulse was fast and weak. Diarrhea had drained the child of fluids and it was necessary to restore them as quickly as possible.

The child was only six months old, but the mother had stopped breastfeeding her to return to work in the fields. The woman had said all she had to feed the baby were mashed bananas and rice gruel. Su Sah had to choke back her impulse to scold the mother for stopping the breast milk too soon. The woman had little choice. Now the child was suffering. She would probably recover, but might never develop properly. She would always be under-sized and susceptible to illness.

When she became a mother, she would take advantage of all the latest medical information to ensure her own children got the best start in life. In the meantime, she had to do everything she could to teach the mothers of Bago how to care for themselves and their babies.

Her mothers' training program was a beginning. The next session was only two days away and she wasn't prepared. She needed to draw some charts with pictures the women could understand. She had to buy samples of the right foods to give children.

She looked up to see Dr. Richardson watching her with an odd expression on his face.

"Dr. Richardson, I didn't see you there."

"Su, you seemed lost in thought, but beautifully lost in thought," he said with a smile. "Please call me Malcolm when it's just the two of us."

"Of course." She tried to smile. "Malcolm."

Her heart raced, as it often did when speaking with the British doctor. His attention was flattering, but confusing. None of the other British doctors spoke to her unless it was a hospital matter. He is courting you, the other nurses teased. If he had been Mon or Burman, there would have been intermediaries contacting her family to see if a match was appropriate. In the village there would have been games or dances to make intentions clear. With Malcolm, nothing was clear. He seemed interested, but she never quite knew what he wanted or how she should respond.

What would life be like as the wife of a British doctor? A new world would open up. She could travel to Europe, further her studies, perhaps one day become a doctor herself. Meet leading researchers. Go to medical conferences. She could be the first from Burma.

There were a few British-Burmese marriages, but usually the women were uneducated and the men were clerks or soldiers—never a doctor. Those marriages seemed slightly shameful. Neither British nor Burmese society fully accepted them. Women from families like hers did not marry foreigners. Mother would be furious. She was already unhappy she had shown no interest in the young men she had introduced to her. If she were to move away from Burma, her parents would be devastated. Silly to worry about it, Malcolm wasn't really interested in her that way, was he? Probably he wanted to be just a friend and colleague.

Nai Tun Way was a more appropriate match. He too had been paying her a great deal of attention. Their attendance at Mon cultural events had become a regular outing. He seemed happy whenever she was with him, but she had yet to meet anyone from his family and there was no formal indication of his intentions. It was all a bit confusing. Better to just focus on her work at the hospital.

Richardson interrupted her thoughts, taking her hands in his.

"I hope you can join me for dinner tonight. My houseboy makes a very acceptable curry and I have just received a tin of fruit cake from London that I would like you to try."

"That is very kind of you, but I have a second half shift tonight, so I have to work."

"I saw that on the chart and made a change. I moved your extra shift to tomorrow, so you are free."

Why did he think he could move her shifts around to please himself?

Still holding her hands, Malcolm drew her closer to him and she looked up at his face. His eyes were deep-set and that strange, pale blue——like the sky in the cool season. This close, his nose appeared even larger and she could see a tracery of blue veins beneath the translucent skin of his temple.

"Su, I would like it if you come tonight. We have much to talk about."

His eyebrows rose for an instant and then dropped. He showed his teeth in a half smile.

"Who else is coming to this dinner?" she asked, looking away.

"Who else is coming? Well, a couple of the doctors should be there—with their wives, of course."

It was good to be invited to a social occasion for the doctors. Did Malcolm see her as the equal of the doctors? Or, if not exactly equal, then at least worthy of inclusion?

"Thank you. That is most kind. I shall look forward to it," she said, a little uneasy that he was still holding her hands. "Right now, there are patients waiting for me."

As she turned and walked back to the children's ward, she thought about Malcolm's invitation. It was exciting to be meeting doctors socially. Perhaps they would accept her suggestions after this. She looked forward to discussing the different options for dealing with the outbreak of dysentery now filling the hospital. She wanted to recommend the hospital conduct tests of the wells serving the townspeople.

But why had Malcolm invited her? Usually, Malcolm's invitations were to see a play or watch the sunset over the river or listen to music. He had become more persistent in his attentions over the past month. He seemed to know when she would be alone in the nurses' room and often dropped by for a chat. He had been generous with advice and with useful medical publications. His support had been helpful when her treatments or her approach to patients were questioned or criticized by the senior Burmese doctor, an old man uninterested in keeping up with medical research. Too bad the other nurses were making something romantic out of this.

"Isn't he handsome—so tall and with hair the color of rice straw," that new girl recruited from town had teased. "Your babies will be pale and beautiful, no?"

"You know what they say about the nose. If the nose is big then so is the appendage we cannot see," one of the married nurse aides teased.

She ignored the giggles of the others in the nurses' room, but that didn't stop them. They teased her about going out with Tun Way even though she usually invited Ma to go with them. Their chats had always been rather impersonal—about health problems, work at the hospital, issues with Tun Way's lands or Mon culture and customs. He felt so strongly about the need to preserve Mon language and literature. He had told her he would like someday to create a Mon cultural institute to teach Mon language and music. The other nurses scoffed at her accounts and refused to believe that was all they talked about. They insisted that Su Sah was dallying with two lovers.

"It's unfair," one nurse pouted. "Su Sah takes all the handsome ones and leaves the old, fat ones for us. Every night one or the other. Sometimes both. I don't know why she isn't too sore in the morning to walk," she said to peals of laughter in the nurses' room.

"That's enough. Leave Su alone," Ma scolded. "But that Mon fellow would be a catch. All that land and no siblings to share it," she said to Su Sah. "He is educated and mature, but not too old. If you don't show an interest, he might move on. I'm surprised he has been unmarried this long."

Why were they all so interested in her supposed love life? They were too easily bored with the routine of the hospital. She was never bored. There was always an interesting case, or a problem of public health to research. She could sense which patients were lonely or fearful and tried to spend time with them. She'd better stop in to see that boy who had lost fingers in a rice mill accident.

Dinner at Malcolm's bungalow. It was a chance to show the doctors she had some social graces. They should already know she was a serious medical practitioner who kept up with the latest developments. If she could charm their wives a bit, that might help.

26

KRIT
High Commissioner

Warden Krit stared at the note in front of him. He tried to force down the dread rising in his throat. He spun to look at the corner desk usually occupied by Pakdee. It was piled high with papers, but no Pakdee. That's right, he left an hour ago. What should he do? He could feel the sweat sliding down from his forehead, stinging his eyes. He wiped them with his sleeve, trying to re-read the note.

Monthon High Commissioner Phraya Sukhumnaiwinit was coming to inspect the prison and its accounts. The note said he had questions about recent prison reports. What questions? Was something wrong? He had not even read the reports for the past four months. He trusted Pakdee. He simply signed the reports Pakdee prepared. Now the high commissioner was coming and Pakdee was out somewhere buying supplies. Pakdee was a prisoner, so if the commissioner saw that he was out of the prison on his own, he might demand an explanation.

He looked again at the note. It didn't say when the commissioner would come, but it took most of a day to sail up from the *monthon* office in Songkhla, so there should be time for Pakdee to get back and brief him on the reports. Maybe even two days. Yes, there was time. No need to panic.

He had been the assistant warden the last time the commissioner visited the prison. He had watched while the commissioner questioned his boss. Politely, but relentlessly, the commissioner had asked about discrepancies in the prison accounts, falsehoods in the monthly reports, mistreatment of prisoners and violations of regulations. The commissioner already had detailed notes for each problem. Even Krit himself had not known everything the warden was doing wrong. How had this scholarly aristocrat from Bangkok learned all of that dirt? It had been a relief to see the prison's many problems brought to light. Within a week the warden was transferred back to the ministry with no position. To his surprise, Krit was named as his replacement. Now, however, he feared the commissioner's sharp eyes would focus on him. Where were the copies of those reports?

Like other officials in Nakhon Srithammarat, he had tried to learn as much as possible about their new boss. Pakdee had been a big help in getting information. He had reported that the commissioner had first won royal favor as a scholar teaching the king's children. When the king sent four of his sons to study in England, he assigned Sukhum to look after them and tutor them in Thai. Before long the young teacher was also serving as secretary to the Siamese embassy in London. Within a few years, he rose to head the mission. Then he came back to Siam with the new name given by the king, Phraya Sukhumnaiwinit. Now, as commissioner of *Monthon* Nakhon Srithammarat, he was the most powerful man in the south.

It was dangerous to draw the attention of such people, especially when they seemed bent on shaking things up. He had always gotten ahead by staying in the background, doing his job without fuss. The commissioner had already fired one prison warden. Was he next?

With all of his work on the king's reforms, why did the commissioner care what went on in his prison? Maybe it was part of the effort to wrest control over Nakhon away from the local elite. Surely, the commissioner knew he wasn't one of them, didn't even come from Nakhon. Maybe the man doubted his competence. That was it. He would be fired for incompetence.

There were shouts outside the window. He watched as the prison gates swung open and an elegant carriage drawn by two black horses wheeled into the prison compound. Sitting erect in the open carriage was a stiff figure in a white uniform with a plumed hat. It was the commissioner—here already. Shit! How had he arrived so soon?

He cleared papers from his desk and stuffed them into a cabinet. He struggled to put on his uniform. It took him three tries before he could button the white coat over his stomach. The top button was even harder to close. The stiff collar felt like a noose tightening around his throat. He rushed into the hallway, crashing into a young man. It was the commissioner's secretary, carrying a sheaf of papers he barely kept from spilling to the ground. Right behind him was the high commissioner looking straight at him. Flustered, it took him a moment to make a deep *wai* and bow. He opened the door, bowed again and followed the slight figure of Phraya Sukhumnaiwinit into his office.

"Honored High Commissioner Phraya, I am humbled by your visit. What can I get you to drink? Some tea? We have Chinese and Sri Lankan. We also have four types of coffee brewed from beans grown in the mountains of Nakhon. I have sent out for some Chinese pastries. Just tell me what you want and I will get it for you."

It was too early in the day to offer his guest anything alcoholic. Did he even drink? Where was damned Pakdee?

He waved to the office boy.

"Cool water. And tea. The best. And coffee. Quickly, quickly now."

"Warden Krit, your hospitality is most appreciated," the commissioner said in the measured tones of central Thai. "Normally, I would enjoy a leisurely chat with you about the different Nakhon coffees. I am sure they are most delicious. Today, however, there are a few matters I would like to go over with you."

The commissioner's secretary crawled on his knees to the low table and placed that sheaf of papers before the commissioner. Phraya Sukhumnaiwinit opened the stiff marbled paper cover and glanced down.

Gotta keep my head lower. The man is too small. Oh, shit, is that the prison report from March?

"Honored sir, our meager refreshments will be here shortly. Please do not feel in a hurry. May I suggest a tour of the prison. You can see for yourself it is in good repair and the prisoners are in good health. We have been able to overcome some of the problems of order and discipline that once troubled the prison, sir."

"I have no doubt. I have no doubt. All that is reflected in your monthly reports. I see the use of corporal punishments has been reduced in each of the past four months, with no punishment administered at all last month. Unlike the prisons in the capital or Songkhla you don't seem to have prisoner uprisings or escape attempts—none at all in the past two years. How do you maintain order without punishment? Moreover, how have you been able to afford an increase in the allotment of fresh fruit and fish shown in this chart? You have some additional income. Where did that come from? Are these reports accurate, or just intended to make you look good?"

"Honored sir, I am… I am sure the reporting is accurate, but I am uncertain of the details. May I look at it to refresh my memory?"

The commissioner swiveled the report around and pushed it towards the warden, now on his knees in front of the low table. He looked at the report a long time. It didn't look familiar, but he forced himself to smile and nod to the commissioner.

"Hmm, ah yes, this number is quite correct. In general, sir, we try to treat the prisoners well. That means they stay healthy and work better. My assistant handles the budget and expense reports. I find it is wise to delegate the small details, but unfortunately, he is not here right now. Please forgive me."

"You don't understand the details of your own reports? Here, is this not your signature attesting to the correctness of the report?" The commissioner pointed a slim finger at the final page of the report.

What could he say? His knees ached. His head spun.

There was a soft knock on the door. It opened and a familiar face peered in and bowed.

"Here is your tea, sir. Do you like it in the British fashion? We have some fresh milk."

Krit felt a bubble of relief rising in his throat.

"Honored High Commissioner, sir. This is my assistant, Pakdee, who would be pleased to provide more details on the reports."

"Your assistant? I don't recall any such position? Where is the budget for that?"

Pakdee, seated on the floor between the two men, clasped his hands in a graceful *wai* and bowed again to the commissioner.

"Honored sir, I am pleased to serve without pay. It is one of the economies that have enabled the prison to become more efficient. One of several initiated by the honorable warden."

"Is that so?"

"For example, sir, we have used part of the prison compound as a fish pond with water from the moat circulating in and out of the pond, so we can raise more fish in a smaller area. I see you have marked the chart with our income from skilled labor. Once the prison earned only meager fees from heavy road work. But under the honorable warden we have identified prisoners with valuable skills and we charge market rates for those with skills—blacksmiths, wood carvers, even mechanics."

He felt relieved. It all sounded so good when Pakdee described it. How could he sound so confident when speaking to someone so important? Somehow his accent sounded refined. What happened to the swinging tones of the southern dialect?

"Go on," the commissioner said, leaning forward. "How can the prison afford to provide so much fruit to the prisoners' diet?"

"Honored sir, 27 percent of the increase is from the prison's own orchards of fast-growing fruit—bananas, papayas and pineapple. Another 13 percent comes from fruit gathered in the forest west of the city—mostly wild jackfruit and durian. The prisoners enjoy getting out into the forest and some of them are skilled at climbing trees to harvest durian. The rest of the fruit is purchased in the market with the proceeds from the skilled labor of the inmates. We divide that income into three parts: 30 percent for food, 30 percent for general expenses, shown on the next line, and 40 percent, by agreement with the prisoners, is paid to those who do skilled work."

"That means that the prison only gets 30 percent of the labor income. Other prisons retain a greater proportion."

"Yes, that is true, sir, but by putting some of that income towards better food, we improve the health of the prisoners and therefore have more available labor, whether skilled or unskilled. The prisoners see they get something out of it, so they work harder. The honored warden requires the skilled prisoners take on younger prisoners as apprentices. Therefore, when they are released, they can support themselves without resorting to crimes. So, please don't consider the percentage, but the overall total income. By taking a longer-term view we, the warden, that is, has increased income while providing needed services and reducing the tendency of prisoners to return to crime. The prison therefore makes a greater contribution to the development of the province."

The commissioner looked at Pakdee.

"How old are you?"

"Twenty-four, sir."

"How did you come up with these ideas?"

"The warden has a strong desire to improve the prison. I have merely implemented his intentions."

"Yes, yes, but training prisoners to have new skills. That has never been done before."

"Not in Siam, sir, but I read a report on foreign prisons after His Majesty the King visited prisons in England where such programs have shown good results."

"His Majesty would be interested to learn about this. Can all this be sustained? Are there hidden problems somehow omitted from the reports?"

"No, sir."

"You are the one who has been writing the prison reports, are you not?"

Krit winced. He would be blamed for failing to write his own reports.

"Under the wise guidance of the warden."

"Of course. And those reports are written in your hand?"

"Yes sir."

"Where did you learn to read and write?"

"At Wat Sao Thong in Pakpanang, honored sir. I was fortunate to have Phra Sirithammuni as my teacher."

"Ah yes, Phra Sirithammuni is a good teacher and speaks proper Thai. Just last year His Majesty provided a grant to establish the first government school in Pakpanang. I appointed Phra Sirithammuni as the school supervisor. He is also helping me establish schools throughout *Monthon* Nakhon Srithammarat."

The commissioner shuffled through the report again, marking several pages with a pen. Was there a problem?

"Hmm. Since His Majesty is interested in prison reform, I plan to send your reports on to the palace as a good example of what can be done to improve our prisons. However, I need to know if there is anything in the administration of the prison that would cause me embarrassment."

Krit saw Pakdee turn to him with a questioning look. It was all going so well, Pakdee shouldn't say anything.

"There is one thing, sir," his young assistant said. "It might be better if you do not mention my role. It is really the inspiration and leadership of the warden that has led to our successes so far."

That sounded good. Now just stop talking and let the commissioner leave.

"Why shouldn't I mention you? It is clear to me your role is important."

"Sir, the benevolence of the warden has enabled me to be of use, but I am not an employee of the corrections department."

Sukhumnaiwinit raised an eyebrow and looked at the warden.

Here it was. He would have to explain. How would the commissioner take it? He had exceeded his authority to trust a prisoner with such important tasks. He would get the sack. What would he do? All he knew was the prison. He had to explain.

"Honored sir, Pakdee is in my care. He is a prisoner and, like other prisoners with skills, his talents have been put to use for the overall benefit of the prison," he said in a rush of words.

"And how, exactly, did this young man come to be a prisoner?" The commissioner looked at Pakdee. "He doesn't look like the usual prisoner."

"Honored High Commissioner, sir. It is possible he did not quite deserve the sentence he received."

"All prisoners say that," Sukhumnaiwinit said.

What could he say? It would be dangerous to criticize the courts or the police, all under the commissioner.

After a long pause, Pakdee spoke up. "Honored commissioner, sir. It is complicated. I have prepared a document to explain how I came to be here. I would beg your indulgence to read this at your leisure." Pakdee bowed and *waied*. He placed a set of papers on the table.

It must be the appeal Pakdee had been working on.

The commissioner looked at the handsome young assistant for a moment, then picked up the papers and began to read.

27
SU SAH
Proposals

The soft lights of the Lake Temple reflected off the dark water of the pond. Nai Tun Way slowly paddled the slim boat along the shore. Su Sah sat back, enjoying the cool, moist air of the early evening. She held an oiled paper umbrella against the chance of rain, but the clouds had thinned and a sliver of moon was peeking through them. Nai Tun's invitation for a boat ride had been puzzling. Usually, they would go to a traditional dance drama or a music recital, sometimes for dinner. Only last week he had taken her to a *sabaa* courting game in a village outside of town. They didn't play the game, but maybe he was trying to show he was courting her. Since neither had family in Bago, the normal steps of a Mon courtship were missing. No relative to speak to her father. It was more like what she was experiencing with Dr. Richardson. He too had taken her to dinner, to music recitals and the occasional traditional dance-drama at the fairs, festivals and weddings that filled the Bago social calendar.

It was all flattering, but there were days when she resented the way this was distracting her from her work at the hospital. She had not gone through all that training just to get married. She wanted to care for her patients, learn more about disease and improve her abilities as a healer. But it would be nice to have her own family.

She was becoming a specialist in birthing. The hospital doctors recognized her empathy with young mothers and assigned her to all the difficult cases. She loved helping to bring tiny new lives into the world. There was much she could contribute to the health of mothers and newborns. Too often they suffered from traditional post-partum beliefs, such as "roasting" the new mother in front of a fire for weeks after the birth. Nutrition was another problem. Far too soon mothers gave up breastfeeding so they could return to the fields.

Whoever she married, she would never give up her work. If it was Dr. Richardson, they would be a team working together. Someday they might go to Britain where she could further her studies. London was the medical research capital of the world!

But that would mean living far from her family and the culture she loved. That was a love she shared with Nai Tun Way. He knew all the old stories and had memorized much of the classical poetry. Often, he would recite for her at dinner or provide amusing critiques of the dance-dramas. Life with him would be familiar, comfortable. In many ways he reminded her of her father—quiet, studious, but sometimes showing flashes of deep emotion.

Tun Way guided the boat to a rickety bamboo dock on the far side of the lake, threw a loop of rope around one of the posts and turned to face her with an intense look. His smile seemed forced.

"There was a reason I asked you to come with me for a boat ride tonight," he said. "I didn't want you to run away."

"Why would I run away?" she laughed.

"You might, when you hear what I say," he said. He paused, looking at the temple across the water.

"It is beautiful here, but for me, it is you who gives it meaning. I think we could have a beautiful life here—if we were together," he said in a rush. "I know I haven't yet spoken to your father, but I want to ask you first. You would want me to ask you first, wouldn't you?

"Ask me what?"

"Would you be willing? Would you be happy? Would it be possible for you to become my wife? Before I met you, my life was lonely, but you have changed all that. You know I have lands and social status. I promise to care for you, support you and love you."

She was stunned. She had thought this might come, but now that it had, she was unprepared. Life with Tun Way would be pleasant, secure, maybe a bit boring. She would have to give up her dream of studying medicine in London. She looked up at him. His normally calm face seemed charged with emotion as he leaned towards her and took her hand. She knew she should say yes, but she hesitated. If she married Tun Way, would she become like her mother—frustrated with the limitations of running a traditional household? Would she be tempted to dominate her husband and her children? But she had her work at the hospital. That would save her, save them. But London and the chance to see the world—that would be gone.

"Tun Way, I am honored by your proposal. I enjoy being with you.

You are kind and respectful. I care for you a great deal, but I am not ready to make a decision. I must ask for some time to think and to be sure in my heart."

A look of disappointment flashed across Tun Way's face. He seemed to shrink and dropped her hands to grip the sides of the boat.

"I understand. I am unworthy. I am too old and not a professional man."

"Tun Way, I am not saying no."

"Then I have hope. I do love you. More than you can imagine. I will wait for your decision."

An hour later, Su Sah was back at the hospital. They had walked back from the lake without talking. She smiled and said good night.

What should she do? She felt comfortable with him. She usually knew what he would say and what he meant when he said it. With Dr. Richardson, she was often excited and confused. What would he say next? What did he mean by it?

That dinner at his bungalow. Only two other doctors had attended, only one with his wife, who seemed offended by her presence. The dinner had been quiet with most of the conversation about London— the politics, the theater and events in the medical world. She could feel the longing of all of them for home. She tried to steer the conversation to medical matters. As the house boy cleared away the dishes, the two doctors abruptly rose and said they had to get back to the hospital. Suddenly she was alone with Richardson.

"Would you like a brandy?" he asked.

Already a little dizzy from the wine with dinner, she declined. Richardson took her hand and walked her to the sofa. He sat uncomfortably close and did not let go of her hand. The air was warm and moist in the bungalow and the candles on the table cast a warm glow on Richardson's face.

"Malcolm, I really should be going back now. Thank you for inviting me."

"In a moment. I just want to tell you how much I appreciate your coming tonight and the time we have spent together. You know that a foreign posting like this can be quite lonely for a single man. But you have changed that for me," Richardson said, putting his brandy glass down on a side table.

He had taken both her hands and brought his face close to her. She was thinking how to respond, when he pressed his lips to hers. She felt a quick thrill at the touch of his lips. A kiss. Her first romantic kiss. His hand reached behind her back and pressed her against him.

She tried to move back, but she was pinned against the sofa. She felt trapped. She pushed back against his chest and pulled her face to one side.

"Malcolm, please, we shouldn't do that."

She remembered the sudden flush on his pale face.

"It is just that I care so much for you. Please stay with me."

What did that mean? Her head whirling, she had stood up, thanked him and walked quickly down the steps of the bungalow.

They hadn't talked about the kiss in the days that followed, but she couldn't help thinking about it. Why had it excited her so much? What did he mean by it? Was this what British men and women did? She wondered what it would be like to do it again, when she was not so surprised. Was that what she wanted? Was it love? She had avoided being alone with Richardson again even though he had pressed her to go to a concert and a walk on the following evenings. Their conversations at the hospital became constrained. She kept them focused on medical matters.

Now Tun Way had proposed. Her thoughts swirled back and forth between the two men as she walked through the quiet hallways of the hospital. She walked out the back door of the hospital and headed to the nurses' quarters. She was surprised to see Dr. Richardson sitting on the steps. He rose as she approached.

"Ah, there you are," Richardson said, clearing his throat. "I have been waiting. There is something important I need to discuss with you and we never seem to have the time during the day. Earlier today I received notice that I am being transferred to the hospital in Rangoon. I will head the communicable disease section. This is a promotion for me. I will have a large private bungalow and will be on track for a transfer back to London in two years."

"That is good news," she said. "But I will miss our discussions and our work together."

"You don't have to. I want you to come with me. If you want to continue to work, I can arrange a transfer for you. This is not just for Rangoon. I don't want to go anywhere without you. In two more years, I can return home and you could come with me. My family has money and estates. You would enjoy London. We would have a wonderful life together."

Richardson must have felt her confusion.

"I don't need an answer right now," he said, "but I have to start the paperwork in the next few days."

The tall doctor abruptly turned and walked away from the lamplight. Su Sah sat down on the wooden stairs and watched him disappear into the gloom. He hadn't even said he loved her.

28

HUAT
Salvage Mission

Huat leaned against the rail near the bow of the sloop. He could see the dark green shape of the island rising out of the sea as the boat sliced through the water. Maybe this would restore the family to something close to normal. Chao had been gone for four months. Father was drinking even more than before, starting with a bottle during work hours and then joining his friends in the evening for a few more. Mother and Father argued more than ever—about his drinking, about household expenses, but mostly about Chao. Mother wanted to beg him to come home. Father refused to even consider it.

Meanwhile, nothing had been done to salvage *The Wind Uncle*. Then, last week Father had called him in. He dropped a small leather sack on the table.

"Here is some money. It's most of the cash I have left. Take it and hire a boat to go out to the island. Take everything of value from *The Wind Uncle* and sell it in the market. We will need the money for a deposit on a new ship. Your brother has abandoned his father."

"He just needs some time to get over the wreck."

"He should be trying to help the family recover from the losses he caused instead of deserting us. You haven't had any word from him?"

"Nothing really. I got a note that he is safe and he is staying with the monks in a monastery."

"A monastery? Which one?"

"Well, I am not sure. I think it must be outside of town," he said. He had to lie to save his brother from more grief. He had visited Chao several times on quick trips to the old temple on the west side of town. Chao was sleeping on the floor of the prayer hall and helping the monks make repairs to the ordination hall. Chao had begged him not to tell Father where he was.

"About the salvage. I will need a half dozen men to help. We need to go as soon as possible."

"Ah, Huat. Chao is gone. You are my only son now. You need to help me save the family business."

"Father, the storm was months ago. I don't know how much will be left. Maybe it would be better to save the cash and forget about *The Wind Uncle*."

"You too abandon me? Why can't my sons just obey me?" Father turned away and stared out the window before continuing.

"Listen to your father. There should be more cargo left in the hold. You didn't bring everything. I want every bit of that cargo, all the brass fittings from the ship, wood planks, anything of value. For once, do as I say. Recover everything you can, sell it in the port, and bring the money back. We need to find the cash to buy a new ship."

He had gathered six of the old crew, hired a sloop and set sail for Phangan Island. As they rounded the rocky point near where he remembered the wreck lay, he searched for *The Wind Uncle*. It should have been right there on the reef, but there was nothing. As they sailed closer, he peered into the clear blue water of the bay. He could see the thick keel jammed into the reef. The ribs of the ship reached upward like the fingers of a beggar. There was little else.

"The waves must have washed it away," he told the crew.

"Not water waves," said one sailor. "Waves of villagers, picking the carcass clean like crabs picking at the bones of a fish. The people here know what to do with a wreck. The old man sent you on a fool's mission. He should have known."

Father did not want to know. He hadn't shown much interest in anything after Chao's disappearance. He brooded most of the day, shouting at Huat for little reason, cursing his wife for food he claimed was tasteless. Now, he would have to go back to face his father and explain they had wasted the money on hiring the boat and had salvaged nothing.

The men pried a few brass cleats from the wreckage, found two boxes of rusted tools in the sand, and pulled some heavy coils of telegraph wire from the reef. Luckily, they found one of the anchors buried in the sand, but could find little more.

The long sail back to Pakpanang had been a quiet one. They sold the bits of salvage in the market and the men headed home.

Waiting on the pier to cross the Pakpanang River, he tried to think of what he would say to Father. He felt the leather bag of coins—all that was left of *The Wind Uncle*, like ashes after a cremation.

The first time he had seen the junk it had seemed impossibly grand, plowing through the river water under a steady breeze. It swerved to come alongside the dock where the family waited, the sails luffing. He had looked up to the tall stern of the ship where Father was waving to the family waiting on the dock. He felt proud of his father and proud of the tall ship that was theirs. Now there was nothing left of it but a bag of coins.

He looked across the dark water flowing out to sea and wished he could drift with the tide far away from the family problems. But he had to report to Father that the salvage effort had yielded little. Who would he blame? Me.

He let one boat go by, then two. He could hear music from the *Songkran* festival at Wat Tai. *Songkran* celebrations were fun, but not this year. There was nothing to celebrate and little chance of good fortune in the new year. It was hard to look at the happy crowds along the river. Maybe he should wait until the next morning to talk to his father. It was late afternoon, so Father had probably started drinking already. That would make him even more unreasonable. But he was grouchy and unreasonable in the mornings too. Maybe seeing him just after the midday meal tomorrow would be best.

Another boat crowded with revelers rowed up to the dock, the oarsman standing on the stern, pushing the oars forward against the tide. Passengers waiting on the pier jostled him towards the boat. He stepped down onto one of the seats. He caught his balance and sat.

Father would say he got too little for the wire. If only there had been more to salvage. To make a payment on a ship, even one smaller than *The Wind Uncle*, they would have to sell most of the merchandise they had stored in their warehouse. His mother had already offered to sell the gold jewelry Father had given her on their wedding day. It would be humiliating. Father would blame him for the loss of face. Why had Chao abandoned him to face Father by himself? Maybe he should just disappear like his brother. He looked up with a start as the boat pulled into another pier, decorated with flowers and a big sign saying "Jaikla Casino."

Ayah, he had gotten on the wrong boat—one taking him upriver rather than across. Now, he would have to wait for another boat. Fellow passengers climbed up onto the new pier, pushing him ahead of them.

At the bottom of a stairway up the bank stood a beautiful woman. She glowed like a candle against the muddy bank. She wore a yellow silk *phasin* and thin red top that left one shoulder bare. A large red hibiscus flower glowed in her dark hair. She bowed and *waied* to each of the passengers, pouring a few drops of scented water on their clasped hands before they headed up the bank to the casino. He felt drawn towards the young woman like a piece of driftwood pulled by the current.

"Happy New Year! May you have health, friendship, and most importantly, good luck, in the new year," the young woman said as she smiled up at him. His hands were at his sides, so she poured some water on his shoulder. He shivered as the cool liquid seeped down over his chest. She looked younger than he had thought at first. She must be younger than him, but she seemed so self-assured. She did not pretend to be shy like so many girls.

"Welcome to the Jaikla Casino," she said, looking into his eyes. "You must be a new customer. My name is Ploi and I am here to help you have a good time. You look like a big bettor. Shall I put you in the elite room? You need at least 500 baht. Do you have that much?"

He felt for the leather money bag under his shirt and nodded.

The girl smiled even more broadly. She just wanted to attract more customers. Why was she still looking at him? His clothes were rough and his skin was darkened by the sun. He didn't belong here. What did she think of him? He had never had a problem attracting girls. They seemed to like his sense of fun as much as his broad chest and thick arms. He knew he looked a bit Chinese, but had the large eyes of the Thai and a long straight nose. This girl must think he was lower class, entirely unsuitable. Why embarrass himself? He should just go home. But he could not stop looking at her. What was her name? Ploi—jewel, a fitting name. She sparkled like a ruby.

"Come with me," she said and climbed the wooden steps up the bank.

I have time to kill. No point seeing Father tonight. Maybe I can win some money. That would make him happy. It would also be nice to learn more about this girl. She is waving to me. It would be rude not to go.

He climbed the steps behind her, watching her long legs move smoothly under the thin silk of the *phasin*. His face felt hot. There was a strange feeling in his chest that made it hard to breathe as he ascended towards the casino. Maybe his luck would finally change.

29

SU SAH
Choices

"Ooh, two proposals," Ma said. "Lucky girl."

"But what should I do?" Su Sah asked.

"How should I know? I have never had even one proposal, or even any suitors," Ma laughed. "Could I borrow one of yours? Don't be greedy. You can have the tall pale one and I'll take the rich brown one."

"You are no help," Su Sah whined. "You are supposed to be my friend, my wise mentor whose sage advice saves me from a terrible mistake and all you do is make fun of me."

"Well, if you ask me how to disinfect a head wound, or treat a sore throat, I can give you good advice, but this is a problem with a different part of the anatomy. I am not a heart specialist. There is only one person who can work out the diagnosis you need."

"I know, I know. I'll have to figure this out myself."

She slumped back against the wall of Ma's room. Malcolm had invited her to dinner at the British Club, making it clear he expected to celebrate her answer. He was so sure of himself. She should have declined, but she got flustered and hadn't been able to think of an excuse. He expected her to agree to go with him to Rangoon. She had to decide.

Malcolm offered an exciting future of travel and study. He would be a professional partner who would understand her work, who could advance her career, perhaps helping her become a doctor. What would life be like in London? At the center of the British Empire, where so much medical research was taking place. With big hospitals and women doctors.

What would his family be like? Malcolm didn't talk of them much, but she knew his father was the director of a large London hospital and his mother attended many social events. What would they think of a Mon daughter-in-law? What would it be like living with a man who knew so little of her culture, who spoke only a few words of Mon and with an ear-grating accent? A man who would be happy never to return to Bago again?

Marrying Tun Way would be much simpler. Her father would like him. Her mother would see him as a suitable match. It was only a short trip home from Bago, but when Malcolm returned to London, she would be away for years at a time. A pang of fear shot through her. Never seeing her parents or her family. Could she endure that?

With Tun Way, she could continue her work at the hospital in Bago. She could care for her patients, and work with Ma and the other nurses who had become such good friends. She had two young mothers with pregnancy problems she would have to leave behind if she went with Malcolm next month. Maybe she could delay her transfer. Would Tun Way support her career as a nurse? Staying in Burma meant she would always be just a nurse. It was too conservative, too backward here. Britain already had female doctors. What if she said no to both of them and continued on as before? Her life was good. How had it become so complicated?

A patch of sunlight crept across the worn wooden floor as evening approached. She would have to face Malcolm soon. She thought of his kiss and the press of his body against hers. Her breasts tingled when his arm brushed them. It made her feel strange and excited. Was that love? If he kissed her again, should she kiss him back? Unlike Tun Way, he had never said he loved her, but she had felt the emotion in his lips. If he didn't love her, why would he ask her to marry him? There was much about the doctor that left her confused. She knew her English was good, and she rarely had a problem talking about patients or medical treatments, but somehow with Malcolm nothing was clear. There seemed to be meaning in the pauses between words, in the talk about life in Britain, in the looks he gave her. His words often seemed to say something she didn't quite understand. Life with him would be an exciting challenge.

With Tun Way, she never felt puzzled. They could chat in Mon, Burmese or English and understand each other almost before the words were finished. His small, neat features, his smile and his gentle laugh, all seemed dear to her in a calm, sweet way unlike the heated confusion she felt with Malcolm.

With Tun Way, there was little uncertainty. He would be a loving father. There seemed to be a hidden depth to him. Did his polite words hide real passion? She could see his feelings about family. She could feel his care for the children of his tenants, his description of his parents and his sisters, now all gone. A new family would fill a void in his life. That could be a problem. He would love her more than she could love him. It was unequal, unfair. She could see his emotions and hopes rise and fall with every gesture she made. She had already seen that even an unintended slight could wound him deeply. He never said anything about Malcolm, but she could see he suffered every time he learned that she had been with him.

Malcolm never mentioned children, while Tun Way always asked about the children of friends and her work with babies at the hospital. He often talked about his sisters and the family life they had before death took them. He would care about family the way her father cared, as a protector, a mentor, but not a controller. But did she love him? Would she get tired of him? He did not rouse the emotions she felt with Malcolm. Just the touch of his hand sent the blood rushing. She could not forget the hammering of her heart when he kissed her.

Sometimes he seemed so eager and passionate, other times cold and aloof. He told her a lot about his achievements, but little about his feelings. Even talking about his mother and father, he was correct and formal. There was something held back. Malcolm was exciting but disturbing.

As the room darkened, she could feel the time for a decision slipping past. She stood up and straightened her embroidered *longyi*. Ma looked up at her from her desk with a lifted eyebrow.

"Thank you so much. I know now what I want."

"Well, what?"

"I'll tell you later," she said. "There is something I have to do first."

30
HUAT
Luck and Love

Huat awoke with a start. Where was he? He lay on a mat in a large, wood-paneled room. His heart lurched. He was alone. Where was she? His head felt sluggish, but patches of memory drifted back to him like the morning mist creeping up the river. He remembered the feel of her soft, smooth skin under his hands, the way she had touched his face, his chest. The warm whisper of her breath as she sniffed at his neck. His astonishment as she slipped the red blouse over her head, the warmth of her breasts as she pulled him towards her. Her smile saying all was permitted. Her little cry as he entered her. The explosive joy as they made love.

Ploi. Like her name, she sparkled with light and color. They had spoken like they had known each other forever. What had happened? Where was Ploi?

He lay back to enjoy the memories of the evening. Her smile. The flick of her dark eyelashes. The toss of her hair. The touch of her warm fingers as she led him into the gambling den.

She had introduced him to the dealers and the other bettors. Another young woman had served him a glass of something she called gin tonic. It looked like rice wine, but tasted much different. Peculiar, but, after a few sips, good. The games in the casino differed from those he played with his crew members, but Ploi explained how each of them worked. The spinning of the roulette wheel, with all its numbers, was fascinating. It was like the indifferent luck of life—one number wealth, another number poverty. Like a shipwreck—some lived, some died. No reason why. Unlike *Po, Mahjong* or *Thua*, there was no skill to winning. It was pure luck. He had always been lucky—until the storm, the wreck of *The Wind Uncle* and Father's anger. Last night, with Ploi beside him, he once again felt lucky.

He had bet cautiously at first. He placed the colorful ceramic tokens on red, inspired by Ploi's red blouse and the red flower behind her ear. It was a lucky color and won three times in a row, leaving him with a pile of tokens. A fourth red in a row would be too much. If I am lucky, he remembered thinking, then I should go for the big odds. He asked Ploi her age. Seventeen, she said. So, he bet on seventeen. It lost. He smiled at her and tried again. This time the wheel spun round and slowed as it neared his winning number, landing on 17 on the last click.

Ploi gave a little yelp and grabbed his arm.

"You won!"

Her large eyes sparkled as she looked up at him. She had seemed even more excited than he was. The smile on her face was as much a prize as the money.

The people around the table cheered for him as the croupier pushed a large pile of counters to him. He took a deep drink of the strange-tasting *farang* liquor. Another win like that, he had calculated, and he would be able to return much more money than his father had given him. It might even be enough to put down a first payment on a new ship. Thirty-five to one, he remembered her telling him. He put half his counters on seventeen again. Others around the table also bet on the number. The wheel whirled around and again slowed as it approached 17, but stopped two agonizing numbers short.

He still had more money than he had come with, but maybe this foreign game was not for him. He had turned to the *Thua* mats and placed his bets. He bet carefully, but couldn't help watching the beautiful girl who swirled through the crowd, chatting with the customers and exclaiming over their wins. She directed the serving girls to give more drinks to the big winners and consoled the losers. In his mind he saw again her graceful form moving like a dancer through the crowd. His heart had raced each time she returned to his side and touched his arm or looked up into his face. He focused on her when she spoke to the musicians who played in a corner of the room. She then turned to the customers.

"Our regular singer was unable to come tonight, but it would be a shame to deprive you of a song," she announced in a strong, sweet voice that hushed the murmur of conversation at the betting mats.

"So, I would like to make my own unworthy effort to entertain you."

The bettors applauded.

"We are honored," said one of the elderly officials at the *Thua* mat.

"You have pleased us before."

Ploi smiled, bowed and *waied*. "This is a composition by His Majesty King Chulalongkorn. It's called 'Khmer with a Glass Flute'," she said.

The ensemble behind her began with a gentle ripple from the wood xylophone followed by the melody from the three-string violin and a silk-stringed lute. Her clear, low voice began the song of a country girl longing for the return of her lover. The high notes of a tiny bamboo flute flitted between the verses. The sounds of gambling faded, then stopped.

Everything else in the room had faded away for him as he listened. He could see Ploi once more as she gestured in time with the music, her hands as supple as strands of seaweed in the tide. The emotions of the song became his emotions. Her longing was his. Her sadness was his. Her desire for love was his.

Ploi's voice was deeper than the shrill tones of so many singers. It touched something inside him—mixed feelings of sadness and hope. The words of the song spoke of love and loss. He had never actually experienced that before. But now he felt again the deep mingling of need, pain and joy that Ploi stirred in him.

The impact of the song and the girl was still vivid as he tried to recall everything about the evening. When her song ended, Ploi bowed and thanked the crowd for listening. There was a moment of silence. Then she smiled and waved to the musicians who started into a lively folk tune Huat had often sung when out drinking with his shipmates.

"The next song is male-female repartee," she announced. "Can any of you gentlemen help with the male part?" Ploi looked around the room. After a moment's hesitation he found himself stepping forward as Ploi launched into the song with a teasing question. He responded with the male reply and the audience cheered. The song, filled with word play and sly insults, drew laughter and applause from the gamblers. When they finished, to a chorus of hoots and claps, he felt flushed and pleased he had stepped in to help her. They bowed and *waied* each other and the audience. Ploi looked into his eyes and mouthed the words 'thank you' before turning back to the gamblers.

"Enough singing for tonight," she said. "Our real business is getting rich. So, place your bets. Who will be the next lucky winner?"

The croupier spun the wheel and the *Thua* man dumped a bowl full of cowrie shells onto the mat. Somehow the songs had raised the energy of the gamblers. They pleaded for luck. They called on the roulette wheel to stop at different numbers. The clack of the Mahjong tiles was overcome by laughter at a foolish play and then cheers for a big *Thua* win.

He had watched Ploi as she walked through the room. She walked up to him and stood so close he had trouble breathing.

"That was fun. You are not such a bad singer. Are you feeling lucky tonight?" she asked.

"Yes, I have already been lucky just to be here, to be here with you."

"Well, let's see if we can convert that luck into some money. How are you doing so far?"

He told her he was losing a bit, and the sympathy she expressed led him to tell her the story of the wreck of the family ship, the departure of his brother, the pressure from his father and the failure to salvage much from the wreck. She had looked at him like she cared about his problems. She said she understood his need to win some money. The rest of the night, she stayed by his side, guiding him on his bets. She celebrated his wins and sympathized with his losses.

Games and gambling had always been fun, but this was special. He needed to bring back some money to Father, but all he could think of was the girl beside him—the way she touched his arm, her delight in his good fortune, the slight coconut scent of her hair. The hours passed in a swirl of sounds, colors, sensations and emotions. The pile of ceramic markers rose higher and higher in front of him. The girl and the winnings made him feel like he was living on a higher plane. Energy and life surged through him. His luck and his joy came from the girl beside him.

"It's time. Play your last bets now," the croupier announced.

He couldn't help smiling at Ploi. He took two handfuls of heavy porcelain markers and pushed them onto number seventeen once again.

"That is nearly everything you have won. Better not to risk so much," Ploi said. "Here take back enough so you still have a sizeable profit for your father."

The wheel spun. The silver ball whirled around it and settled far from 17.

There was a moment of disappointment and then a surge of gratitude to Ploi.

"It's good to take chances, but never risk everything," she said. "Hold something back so you can survive to play another time."

His eyes could look nowhere else but at Ploi as she busied herself exchanging the casino markers for cash, smiling sympathetically at the losers, jesting with the winners and inviting them all to come back the next night to try their luck again. He sat in a dark corner, content just to watch her.

As the bettors trouped out of the room, some boasted about their wins while others bemoaned their losses. The casino attendants rolled up the mats, put away the cards and stored the roulette wheel. Ploi bent over a notebook and thanked the staff as they headed for the door.

"Uncle Daeng, take the cash box back to the house," she called. "I'll close up myself."

Then, like the moon emerging from the clouds over the sea, she sought him out.

"You haven't exchanged all your markers. Bring them over here. I must lock up."

"I want to keep a few to remind me of this night."

"Don't be foolish. You need the money for your family," she said as she counted out three more silver coins from her bag.

"You did well tonight, but there is not enough for a new ship. Without a ship, you have no job. What will you do now?"

"I haven't thought of it. Well, I guess I could help my father with the trade and the warehouse, but I don't want to."

"You don't want to work in the family business?"

"Not anymore. I loved sailing with my brother. There was a good feeling being part of the crew—all working together. Mostly I just followed my brother. Whatever he decided was good enough for me, but now he has gone to a place I don't think I can follow."

"Stand up. Let me look at you."

Huat recalled smiling in bewilderment as he rose before her. Ploi looked at his shoulders and arms, then walked around behind him.

"Hmm, you look strong."

He felt her hands move down his back and he turned around, his lips brushing her forehead. He felt himself trying to look bigger. She looked up at him, her eyes large in the semi-darkness. She smiled and bent her head to bring her nose to his chest and took a long breath. She pulled him into a side room lined with account books and shut the door.

His excitement rose like a dolphin leaping from the sea. He had been with girls before—tea house girls at ports of call, but never had they made him feel like this. Never had they shown they desired him. Always they had been limp, waiting for the act to be over.

The thought that Ploi wanted him exploded in his brain and sent tremors through his body. Her fingers reached beneath his shirt and stroked the muscles of his chest. His body responded with a still higher pitch of excitement and he felt his manhood push against her stomach. Without thinking his arms encircled her. He bent to kiss her neck. His tongue relished her warm saltiness. He heard her take a sharp breath, and she pulled him towards her as she lay down on the mat.

The blood rushed to his face as he relived the warm feel of her breasts, the smooth skin of her thighs and the soft smile on her face as they made love. He grew hard again. He looked around the empty room.

Where was she now? Why did she leave him? He rose from the mat, found his clothes and dressed. A leather bag beside the mat bulged with coins. Enough, maybe, to placate Father. The slant of sun through the shutters showed it was already late morning.

He heard a soft murmur of voices in the next room. He straightened his clothes and cautiously opened the door.

31

SU SAH
Rejection

Su Sah looked up at the dark teak building of the British Club. The two-story club loomed over a British-style garden surrounded by trimmed hedges. Jacaranda trees lined the driveway up the hill from town. A veranda stretched around three sides of the building. The yellow light of oil lamps reached out from the line of windows around the upper story. A part of the building extended over the entrance to provide protection from the rain for guests stepping down from their buggies or rickshaws.

She had decided to walk up the hill from the hospital. She wanted time to plan what to say. As she drew closer, her steps slowed. She could hear the clink of silverware and the murmur of conversation. She had been to the club once before as Malcolm's guest. They had arrived as a group with doctors from the hospital, but still she had drawn stares from the turbaned Indian doorman. He relaxed only when Malcolm had assured him she was with the hospital group. Inside, she saw that she was the only local woman there. There were several Burmese men—officials in the British administration, merchants and a wealthy landowner, and two of the senior doctors. The buzz of talk was all in English. The white-clad waiters were Indian. An elderly British man with a military-style mustache and an erect posture greeted them at the top of the broad, curving wooden staircase.

"Welcome to the British club, Dr. Richardson," said the man, who Malcolm introduced as the club manager. "Your reserved table is this way."

This time she would be entering alone. Would she receive the same welcome? With relief, she saw Malcolm emerge from the double doors of the entrance and wave to her. He looked pleased to see her.

"Su Sah, thank you for coming," he said. He inspected her new silk dress, and the top embroidered with butterflies. "You look smashing."

This was a compliment, but she had never understood why. She smiled uncertainly as Malcolm extended his hand and drew her to him. She felt uneasy to be so close to him with the burly, bearded doorman watching impassively. Malcolm led her up to the dining room and then into a small private room overlooking a small pond at the rear of the club. A stiff white cloth covered the table. It was set with an array of cutlery and four tall glasses. Bottles of wine and water stood on a side table. She could hear the click of billiard balls from the next room. Malcolm gestured to the waiter who nodded and slipped out of the room, closing the door behind him.

"Before we start dinner, I just want to tell you I've cleared everything with the hospital administration both here and in Rangoon. They have given you leave to transfer in record time. It helps to have a father high up in the profession. So, we will be able to travel together."

Su Sah felt a mixture of anger and sadness rise in her throat. He had not even waited to hear her decision.

"Malcolm, I…"

"Yes, I know you will need to pack very quickly, but I will send transport for your things the day after tomorrow. I don't suppose you have that much."

Anger got the best of her.

"Malcolm, I do not want to live my life with a puzzle. I cannot marry you."

"Of course not, my dear. And I cannot marry you. But we can still love each other and enjoy each other. We have a custom in the landed classes in Britain not so different from the Burmese tradition of minor wives. Those with the means can always have someone they love, even if the official marriage has to be for duty or family obligations."

"You mean I would not go with you to London?"

"Of course you would," he said in a soothing tone. "I want you with me wherever I go. There is someone back there my family expects me to marry, but she is a pale, bony thing with buck teeth. I want only you."

She stared at him, mouth open.

"You will have your own apartment close to the hospital run by my father. You can have an appointment there, if you want. That way we can continue to work together and we can be alone together every day after work before I have to return home."

"What? I didn't know…" The blood rushed to Su Sah's face.

"That I had worked out all the details? Of course. You will find I am very thorough when something is important to me and you are important. Another year here in Burma and then back to civilization."

"You don't understand," she said. "I thought you were proposing marriage. I thought about that proposal and I decided against it."

Malcolm sighed, looking peeved.

"I expected you to understand. I told you about my father. Our family has a certain position in society that creates some constraints."

Su Sah stood up and looked down on him.

"I came here thinking I would have to explain my reasons for declining your proposal, but I see now that will not be necessary. I reject your wonderful offer. I will not be your mistress, your minor wife or even your major wife. I would not marry you even if that is what you intended. And I can no longer be your friend."

Su Sah stared down at him, her chin thrust forward, as Malcolm gaped at her.

"But, but it's all arranged," he spluttered, reaching a hand for her arm.

"Go un-arrange it. I would be grateful if I never have to see you again." She brushed away his hand and turned her back on him, striding to the door.

She had reached the stairway before she heard Malcolm shouting behind her.

"You little tease, you will regret this. You will rot here in this stinking backwater forever. You have lost your chance with Dr. Malcolm Richardson."

Su Sah marched through the door, surprised to see the big doorman smiling at her through his beard. She was halfway down the driveway to the main road before tears of anger began streaming down her cheeks.

32

PLOI
Another Kind of Gamble

Ploi looked up from the box of gambling tokens she had been counting when the door opened and the young Chinese sailor walked out of the inner room clad in the rough garb of the previous night.

"Ah, our sleepy gambler has awakened," she said, suppressing a smile.

"I let him stay the night to make sure he came back to gamble again," she explained to Tim, the roulette operator who was helping her with the count.

"It's Huat, right? Well, Huat, you can wait here while we finish this up," she said. "I have ordered some rice congee for the morning meal."

She stopped herself from staring at him and turned back to the tokens as the roulette operator restarted the counting. Her mind was no longer on the task. She thought about the previous night.

It had not been the first time she had taken a lover, but it was the first time she had felt like she had lost herself in someone. Somehow this half-Chinese sailor had ignited feelings within her so suddenly, like a lightning strike. Their talk had flowed. He had been so attentive. Even when she had to chat with other customers, she had felt his eyes follow her around the room. As the heat of the hot season ebbed from the room at dusk, she felt the growing heat of his interest.

As the evening wore on, she had spent more and more of her time at his side. She told him things she had never told anyone—about her father, the conflict with her brother, her mother's weakness and her hopes to be something more. They both felt they were losing their fathers to drink. Fathers who had once seemed large and powerful, now seemed small and helpless. He had understood when she told him of Father's bursts of anger amid long periods of fuzzy inattention. They both feared for the impact on their families and couldn't understand why their mothers couldn't do more to stop their fathers' downward slides. Their similar sadness had sealed a bond strengthened by the thrill of betting and winning.

At first, she told herself, she was just encouraging him to bet more, but she soon felt a desire to help him, not just to bet, but to win. Each time he hit on the right color at the roulette wheel or guessed the right number at *Thua*, she felt a thrill. There was a special satisfaction in his success because she knew it would help him with his father.

"850—correct?" Tim asked her.

"Yes, that seems right," she said, startled out of her reverie.

She took a quick look at Huat. His hair was still rumpled and his eyes still clouded with sleepiness, his face fixed in a smile as he watched her.

She blushed again and turned back to her account ledger, trying to hide her own smile. The sight of him brought back the feel of him. His hands were rough, but his touch was gentle. A thrill surged through her as she remembered those hands touching her in places no one had ever touched before—not just on her body, but in her heart. She felt again the warm weight of his body against her. She had enjoyed running her fingers over his body, from a narrow waist to hard chest muscles. His body was so unlike the soft, slim bodies of both the boys she had lain with before. Her tongue felt again the feel of his nipples hardening at her kiss and his firm length pulsing against her lips as she took him in her mouth.

She had intended to stop there. Surely it was too soon. But she couldn't stop. Didn't want to stop. She felt again the heat of her own sex at the image in her mind. The color rose still higher in her cheeks as she bent over the account ledger. She looked back at Huat, still staring at her and then back to the accounts.

"I think that is enough for my report," she said. "What other business do we have?"

Tim frowned. "You told me you wanted to discuss hiring a floor manager now that your brother has gone to Phuket. Are you sure he won't be coming back?"

"Not any time soon," Ploi said. "There is a girl there from a wealthy family. Elder Brother Chit wants to get into the shipping business and her family owns several ships. Anyway, Sia Leng doesn't want him involved with the casino, so it is a good option for him."

Good for her too. No big brother to cause problems in the accounts or start arguments with the dealers. No big brother to make her feel small. Now she could do what she wanted and now she wanted the handsome sailor.

"Ploi—the floor manager?" Tim reminded her.

"Yes, of course, a floor manager," she said as she took another quick glance at Huat, still smiling, still staring from the other side of the room.

"Ploi, you said you wanted someone who was tough enough to deal with unruly customers, keep an eye on the staff, deal with the outside venders and make sure we get our cut from the opium den," Tim said. "You said you wanted to be free to entertain the big bettors."

"Yes, yes, all that," she responded, as an idea grew in the back of her mind. "Uncle Tim, let me introduce Huat, our big winner from last night. His family owns a shipping and warehouse business."

Tim looked at the young Chinese as Huat *waied* him, a smile still pasted on his face. The door opened and one of the dealers brought in a basket filled with bowls of rice congee, a pot of tea and a plate of light Chinese doughnuts.

"Huat, if I may ask, what are your plans for the day, sir?" Ploi asked.

"Miss Ploi, I have to go home and report to my father about the ship and give him the money from last night."

"And after that?"

"I don't know. It depends on my father."

"Perhaps you could return tonight. Since you were so lucky last night," she smiled, "you should give the casino a chance to win its money back."

"I would love to do that, but I don't think I will have any money to gamble. It all goes to Father."

"That's a shame. You seemed to enjoy the gambling and you know all the games now. Perhaps your good luck will continue," she smiled.

"I would like to try, but it seems unlikely."

"I see," she said and made a decision.

"Let me offer a proposal then. As you have heard, we are seeking to employ a floor manager. Would you like the job?"

"But we don't know…" Tim said, halted by her glare.

She saw Huat lean forward. His smile widened. It was a good smile. He wanted her. He would accept. She would get what she wanted. But then he shook his head sadly.

"That is very kind. I would like very much to work for you, but I cannot."

"Not work for me so much as work with me," she said, pleading with her eyes.

"I can't. I, I just can't. It's my father. You understand."

"I understand, but I don't accept," she said as she touched his arm softly. "You think about it and come back after you talk to your father."

"Thank you. Thank you for everything," Huat said as he rose. He looked confused and knocked over his stool. He set it back up and hurried to the door, leaving his unfinished breakfast behind. Then he came back for the bag of coins.

"Talk to your father," she said. "It would be regular income and it would be fun working together."

He *waied* awkwardly with the bag in his hands before hurrying out the door.

She watched him walk reluctantly down the path from the casino. He looked back. Maybe he was changing his mind. Yes, he had to come back. She wanted him. Then he turned his broad back to her. He was walking away again, faster now.

33

SU SAH
Wife and Mother To Be

BAGO, DECEMBER 4, 1900

Su Sah jotted down the weight of her patient—only 94 pounds. The woman was thin and burned dark by the sun. Her cotton *longyi* was crusted with mud at the hem and her feet were bare. She had gained too little weight going into the seventh month of pregnancy.

"It is time to take more rest. If you work in the morning, you should rest in the afternoon. Drink only boiled water," she said, noting the look of alarm in the eyes of the woman who looked younger than her seventeen years.

"You are doing fine, but you need to eat more, especially foods like fish and eggs. Lentils and beans are good too."

Saliva rose in Su's throat at the thought of food. She had vomited that morning before coming to the hospital, but it didn't bother her. It was another sign her pregnancy was progressing normally. She reassured herself the way she had reassured so many pregnant women. Morning sickness was nothing to worry about.

But being pregnant yourself was different. It was intense and intimate. Her body was creating a baby, a new person, week by week, pulling her into a new role—mother. She could feel the changes in her body, not just hear about them from a patient or read about them in a journal. She must already be at least three months pregnant, maybe four. That meant the baby would be born at about the time of the traditional water festival. So, the baby would enter the world in a celebration. Maybe that would help Tun Way get over his fears.

The day she told Tun Way she was pregnant had been puzzling. She expected joy; instead, he looked stricken. Then she recalled that his mother had died in childbirth. He had told her he never forgave his father for submitting her to yet another pregnancy after four children and two still births. His eyes widened with fear as she explained her missing periods and the morning sickness.

"I am so sorry for doing this to you. I should have been more careful," he said. "What if something happens?"

"There is no need to worry about me," she told him. "I know what problems to look for and I will always get the best care at the hospital."

Tun Way's worries didn't seem to abate. After a few weeks of her making light of them, he just spoke of his fears less often. She knew he had consulted with Nurse Ma and Dr. Tun Yi and they had both told him the same thing—she was young and healthy, so there was nothing to fear. He had insisted they go to see a well-known monk. The monk assured them they would have a healthy boy. Still, her bouts of morning sickness only made him feel more worried and more guilty.

But his fears appeared mixed with the longing to have a family. She knew he had felt an emptiness ever since the death of his father and of his elder sisters before that. They had been like mothers to him until all three had died of a fever that swept through the delta towns ten years earlier. He had been away at school. He reached home only in time to see them laid out on the funeral pyres. His father had passed away from a cerebral hemorrhage less than a year after. Once more he had been away at school. He told her he felt like he had deserted his family when they needed him most.

She knew she had changed his life. Their marriage had changed his life. Not on the outside. He was still a landlord and avid promoter of Mon culture, but on the inside. There was a joy in him that thrilled her. She had done that. He was still busy with his tenants and his properties in town, but now these were distractions. She was the center of his life. It was wonderful and frightening at the same time.

Every day he waited for her outside the hospital in the little horse buggy—even if her shift was late at night or early in the morning. He would leap down and help her up into the buggy. With a light touch on his arm she could release the tension within him that had built through the hours of her absence.

On the way home she would discuss her patients and he would ask thoughtful questions. He would react with anger if she reported any slight from the doctors, so she had to be careful to make light of the usual work frictions and frustrations. Sometimes she worried his love was too much. The Buddha taught that excessive attachment led to suffering. He was too dependent on her. She would have to keep things steady, tempering his emotions with a gentle joke or a smile. Sometimes his love seemed like a burden. But it was exciting to be that important to someone else. And often it was pleasant.

Before dinner they would sit on the broad veranda of the big house and look out over the Bago River. The slow brown flow of water usually generated an evening breeze. Often, they would sip small glasses of green tea cooled by evaporation from a porous clay jug. She would tell him of her patients or the latest advances in medicine. She knew he didn't always understand, but he never seemed bored, gazing at her like he was looking at the moon on a beautiful night.

When she prodded him, he would tell her of his dreams for the Mon Language and Culture Society. These were dreams his father had passed down to him. Unlike Su Sah's father with his many Burmese and Chinese friends, Tun Way's father had stayed aloof from the cultural flux of Burmans, British, Chinese and Indians. He had clung to the past as a minor member of the old Mon royal family, filling Tun Way with tales of the mighty Mon empires. Wise Mon kings ruled much of what was now Burma and most of the country all the way to the Khmer empire in the east. He told of Queen Camadevi who ruled the Chao Phraya River valley, the mighty Bago kingdoms of King Wareru and King Rajathiraj and their long struggles against the Burmans.

More often than kingdoms and battles, however, Tun Way spoke of Mon music, literature and religion. The Mon poetry and stories he recited touched on the great concerns of human existence. What should we strive for? How can one find meaning in life? The Mon had been the first receivers of the Buddhist missionaries from Lanka. Those monks brought a true understanding of Buddhism to the region. Today, he told her, the struggle was to return to those original teachings, to sweep aside the cobwebs of animism and Brahmanism.

It was nice to sit back in the slatted teak reclining chairs of the veranda after a long day with patients and listen to the soft precision of Tun Way's voice. The cool of the evening would bring out the music of crickets from the mango trees in the garden behind the house. She loved the house, so different from the crowded hospital and her noisy family home near the bustling market in Zigon. By evening, traffic on the road along the river would slow to the occasional ox cart hauling rice from the golden paddy fields that stretched to the horizon. Tiny swiftlets would soar and twist in the reddening sky over the river.

Their lives had settled into an intimate routine that continued on the sleeping mat. Their first time had been awkward. Tun Way was afraid he would hurt her. She was afraid she would disappoint him. Those fears had dissolved in their first weeks together. They explored each other's body, learning what pleased and what excited. She blushed as she thought of what she had come to like and how she had learned to please him. And now that pleasure would give them a child. How would that change things? Would it be like her own family? She would create a new family. She could do it the way she wanted. Life would be different, but surely it would be even better.

34

DAM
Mother

Dam placed a damp cloth on his mother's forehead. She looked up at him, her eyes wide with pain and fear. He felt the heat of her fever through the cloth. She had been ill for more than a week. Herbal medicines from the market had lowered the fever for a day, but now it was worse than before. That fast-talking herbal doctor's promise of a rapid recovery turned out to be a lie. He wanted to go back and shove those herbs down his throat, but now Mother needed him.

He spent what time he could with her, but he had to leave her alone when it was time for his duties at the police station. There were no relatives, no friends to help. He had brought her down from the rubber plantation only a month earlier.

"Mother, you are no longer a slave," he had told her. "I have paid off Father's debts with interest and I have a small house for you in town. You are free."

The move to Pakpanang, however, had gone badly. Mother knew no one. She blamed him for leaving her alone. But what could he do? Nothing pleased her. The noise of traffic along the river road annoyed her. She complained there was nothing for her to do. Unlike the rubber plantation, she said, Pakpanang was hot and smelly.

"I miss chatting with the other tappers as we work among the trees," she said. "The rubber grove is cool and quiet. Here there is the noise of carts, rickshaws and merchants shouting all the time. I can't sleep here." It was a slap in the face after all his efforts.

"You want to go back to being a slave—a nobody who has nothing?" he had tried to reason with her. "Don't you remember when we didn't have enough to eat? When we had to drag ourselves out to feed the chickens after working all night?"

"But I don't like it here," she said with a sigh.

"Why did I sacrifice for you?" he had yelled. "Do you know what kind of shit I had to do to get the money for you?"

The hurt in her eyes sucked the wind out of him.

"I know, I know," she said. "You are a good son, but you're never here."

"I have to work," he said. "You know that. Police hours are uncertain and I still have to do things for Boss Jate,"

"He is a bad man. Do you have to work for him?" Mother asked.

"It's money, money for you, so you can live better, have some nice things."

"I don't need anything. I just miss the sounds of the birds and the crickets," she said, reaching out to touch his arm. "It's alright. I will learn to live here. Don't worry about your old mother."

Only a few days later she became listless and then feverish. He knew Mother had suffered from malaria before. There were usually a few days of shivering fever and then a gradual return to normal. This time, though, was different. Her forehead got really hot. Her complaints drifted into incoherent rambling. The stupid doctor said something about a brain infection, a more serious kind of malaria. He said there was nothing he could do but give her some medicine for the pain. What good were the fucking doctors? You paid them money and nothing changed.

He rinsed the cloth in a bowl of water beside her sleeping mat. There was a knock on the door and another. Then it was pulled open. Sergeant Lat stuck his head around the door.

"Dam, we need you at the station. There are prisoners to transfer to Nakhon and everyone else is out," he said.

"My mother needs me."

"I'm sorry, but if we don't get the prisoners to the boat, the court will complain and the chief will be angry. I'll have to explain that you wouldn't help and that will not be good for you."

"I can't go right now."

"Another ten minutes, then you have to go."

"Can't you do it alone?"

"No, there are six of the bastards. I need you. Look, she is asleep anyway. You'll be back soon."

He looked down at his mother. Her eyes were closed and her breathing was shallow. The dark skin of her face sagged back and made her high cheekbones more prominent. Her eyes twitched beneath her eyelids. He wiped her forehead again, but she didn't respond. He pulled the thin cotton sheet over her stick-thin arms and rose from the mat. He looked back at her sleeping form as he closed the door. The light from the doorway highlighted her face. Something inside him broke.

He would make an offering at the temple near the market. That would give his mother merit. He would ask for a special prayer—better than any fucking doctor.

It was four hours before he could return. The prisoner transfer turned out to be a total screwup. Two of them refused to move from their cells and then the others started shouting that they wouldn't move either. Furious, he pulled open the door and grabbed one by the throat. He had to make him an example so the others would cooperate. He smashed him up against the bars. The prisoner tried to shake free, but he drove a fist into the man's stomach and followed with an elbow to his face and continued to rain blows down on him as he slumped to the floor of the cell. Maybe it was too much, but the slimy lizard shouldn't have made him angry. The sergeant hurried into the cell and pulled him off the man. The other prisoners were yelling and jeering.

"You lizards want some of this," he yelled at them and raised his fist. The prisoners went silent, but they refused to leave their cells until he waited outside while the sergeant put shackles on each of the prisoners. They then had to wait until the unconscious prisoner revived. The sergeant wiped the blood from the man's face and found him a new shirt.

By then they had missed the first boat to Nakhon and had to wait for another. The damn boatmen couldn't wait even ten minutes. Finally, the prisoners were aboard and the sergeant told him he could go. As he ran back to his house behind the police station, a sense of foreboding rose within him. He had forgotten about the prayers at the temple.

When he opened the door, the room was still. There was no sound of breathing. His mother lay still on the mat. Her mouth sagged open and her open eyes stared upwards.

He slumped beside her. How could it be? He came back as fast as he could. It wasn't his fault. Those fucking prisoners.

He touched her softly. His heart felt as cold as her forehead. She was the only person who had ever loved him. He had done everything for her. Why did she abandon him? The strength left him. His head sank to the mat. His body shook with sobs.

35

SAIFAN
Brother

A moist, salt-scented breeze blew through the Krue Se village market as Saifan helped his father pack away the last pieces of goat meat left unsold. The market – an open field along a dusty road – was nearly deserted as the time of evening prayers approached. A few crooked poles held up some old sail cloth that offered patches of shade. Father shook the leather pouch with the day's income.

"Another bad day. There just aren't enough people around here and they are all so stingy. Business was better in Pakpanang," he grumbled. "I don't know why we left."

"Father, you said we had no choice. You were the one who wanted us to move away from our problems," Saifan said, cautious not to upset his father by saying his brother's name. "But you made the right decision. I like it here. As the Holy Koran says, 'Let there be among you a community called to virtue, advocating righteousness, and avoiding evil. That is a successful community.' That is the community we have in Krue Se."

"But we used to make three times this much money in Pakpanang."

"Here we are among our own people. We have our own raja, our own religion. The mosque is a short walk away. Imam Wae Muso is teaching me to understand the Koran. We have our own Islamic courts. We speak *Jawi*, not Thai."

"That may be true, but it would be good to make more money," Father sighed.

Saifan nodded, but he was just as happy they didn't sell more. That would mean killing more of the soft-eyed, long-eared goats they raised behind the house. His job was to catch and hold the goats as his father slashed their throats with a razor-sharp knife in the halal procedure. He hated holding the warm young animals, and tried to avoid the splatter of blood as it spurted from their quivering bodies. There must be some other way to make a living.

He finished wrapping the last of the meat in broad green banana leaves and placed it in a cloth bag he slung over his shoulder. Without a backward glance he headed down the road.

Father was strange. After all his complaints about the Thais in Nakhon, he should be happy in Pattani where Thais were only a small minority and the Chinese kept to the big towns. Both Thais and Chinese pretended at least to respect the raja. It had taken some time to adjust to the local dialect of *Jawi*, but it had been easier for him than Father. He enjoyed using the flowing Arabic script instead of the boxy Thai letters while Father struggled to read *Jawi*. He looked forward to classes at the mosque where he had won praise for his recitations from the Koran.

The peace of Krue Se was a welcome change from the noisy bustle of Pakpanang. It was pleasant to get the breezes from the broad waters of Pattani Bay. If the family needed something from town, it was only a two-hour walk away. Fortunately, there was little need to go into town with its crowds of Chinese merchants, Thai officials and even big-nosed British, stinking with sweat.

He dumped off the meat in the storage cellar below their wooden house and took off across the fields to the mosque. The big square brick building was the center of village life, the center, truly, of his own life. He resented wasting so much of his time in the market, feeding the goats or butchering their carcasses. The Krue Se Mosque was more than three hundred years old—the oldest in the Pattani sultanate. Yet it had never been finished. The bare brown bricks were still exposed. Someday, he thought, those bricks would be plastered over and painted white like the big mosques of Mecca. Krue Se would become the center of Islam in the region. Already, it was a required stop for the roving preachers and imams of the south. He enjoyed following their sermons and their complex debates about the Koran.

Buttoning his clean white shirt as he walked, he hurried across the broad brick platform in front of the mosque. He paused to listen to the soaring tones of the evening call to prayer. The setting sun gave a warm red tone to the bricks of the mosque and the three gracefully pointed arches that opened the way into the building.

He left his sandals in a long row of footwear before entering the first portal. He moved quickly to the tank filled with water from nearby Di Chae stream that ran past the village and filled the little moat around the mosque. Concentrating on washing away the stains of worldly life, he scraped dried goat blood from under his fingernails.

It was time to focus on the divine. He washed his right hand three times, then his left before splashing water on his face and sluicing the dry season dust from his feet. He walked along the arch-covered hallway to the prayer hall. Already a dozen villagers had gathered, chatting quietly. He ignored them. Prayer should be a personal communication with Allah, not an occasion for gossip. He nodded respectfully to the imam who taught Friday classes. He oriented himself to Mecca and unrolled his prayer mat on the red tiles of the floor. As sonorous prayers began echoing through the building, he prostrated himself on his mat, careful to look neither left nor right.

When the regular *salat* prayers concluded, it was time for his evening supplication prayer asking Allah's mercy in returning Abdul to the family. He murmured the verse: "Who delivereth you from the darkness of the land and the sea? Ye call upon Him humbly and in secret: If we are delivered from this evil we truly will be of the thankful."

During the day, he performed the *salat* prayers at home or in a shady prayer area near the market, but the evening prayers were special. They were more powerful because they were performed at the mosque. He dedicated these prayers to his brother.

Where was he? Was he suffering in a cell somewhere? Abdul had often been irritating and arrogant. His teasing was infuriating, but now that he was no longer around, his absence felt like a hollowness in the stomach. He recalled his distant view of Abdul in a prison work-gang, thin, bowed and shackled. How had his vibrant brother been brought so low, so quickly? He felt guilty. The family had done nothing to help. Even his efforts to send him some food had been inept failures.

It was in his supplication prayer he felt closest to Allah. God must be listening with wisdom and mercy. If he subjected himself sufficiently to Allah's will, if he concentrated hard enough, if he prayed with enough intensity of spirit, surely Allah would answer his prayers. Someday, somehow, Abdul would survive to return to the family.

Long after the other worshippers had risen from their mats and left the now darkened prayer hall, he finally headed home. He pushed through the goat pen behind the house and climbed up the wooden steps. He heard the muffled sounds of weeping and pushed open the door. His mother sat on the floor, her hands covering her face, with his father sitting stunned beside her.

"Mother, what is it?"

She shook her head from side to side and pointed to two sheets of paper on the mat in front of her. He crouched down and began to read. The first was a letter from their old friend Hamidy in Pakpanang. It said that a formal government notice had been delivered to their old house. He grabbed the second paper. At the top was the Garuda crest of the royal government. The letter said Abdul had died of a fever in Nakhon Srithammarat prison two weeks earlier. His body had been properly buried in the Nakhon's Muslim cemetery within 24 hours in accordance with Islamic practice. The notice was signed by the warden of the prison.

There must be some mistake. How could someone so full of life and laughter be dead? Guilt rose in his throat like vomit. What had he done wrong? He had prayed every evening for Abdul's return. He had led a virtuous life. He must have done something wrong. Perhaps it was the will of Allah to release his brother from suffering in prison. No, it was the Thai government that killed him. Abdul had rarely been ill. How could he have succumbed to a simple fever? The prison must have mistreated and starved him; must have refused him medicine and a doctor. That was murder.

He tried to recall the verse on murder in the Koran—"O you who believe! Retaliation for the murdered is ordained upon you: the free for the free, the slave for the slave, the female for the female." How could he retaliate for the murder of a brother? Somehow he would make them suffer as his mother was suffering now, as he was suffering now.

He was startled by a strange sound that began low and rose to a high-pitched wail. It was coming from his own throat. It rose above the cries of his mother, carrying with it the anger, guilt and pain of a terrible loss.

36

TUN WAY
Difficult Birth

Nai Tun Way sat stiff and upright on a woven mat, only half-listening to the men sitting in a half-circle before him. He wore a high-collared shirt and a hand-woven *longyi* that covered down to his ankles. An overhead fan lazily beat the humid air just starting to cool as the light faded. A scrawny boy in the corner sleepily pulled the cord that spun the fan. Tun Way's old friend, U Htun Htin, was making his usual complaint about British complicity in the oppression of the Mon people.

"We are now doubly colonized," U Htun Htin said. "The Burmans crushed our king almost a century and a half ago. They banned the use of the Mon language. Even today, the Burmans undermine our language and customs while the British monopolize political power and control the economy. We have to contend not only with our old Burman enemies, but also with the Indian and Chinese bloodsuckers getting favorable treatment."

Tun Way was nodding in agreement when he saw one of his servant girls waving from the doorway of U Htun Htin's house. The ignorant girl should know better than to come into a meeting like this. It would not be polite to interrupt his friend's speech even though he had heard it many times before. He frowned at the girl and shifted his gaze back to Htun Htin.

"Our young people are becoming more and more Burman. They learn Burmese and English at school. To get ahead they have to kowtow to bosses who are British, if not Burman or Indian," U Htun Htin said. "Our farmers are trapped in debt to Indian money-lenders. We Mon, who once ruled all of Burma and most of Siam, are fading away like shadows on a moonless evening."

Shwe Hongsa stood up and recited a poem that concluded:

We were the first people to write.
The Thais and Burmans studied our lessons.
How do they treat their teachers now?

The group was quiet for a moment as Shwe Hongsa reached into the silver betel box for a chew of betel leaves, lime and areca nut.

"Yes, yes, as teachers, as cultural leaders, the Mon should be respected, but we are not," Tun Way said and looked up in annoyance at the girl who was still waving at him with a distraught expression on her face. He glared at her until she shrank away from the doorway. "The question is, what can we do?"

The group mumbled amongst themselves for a moment until he continued. "The essential elements are language and culture. How can we be Mon if we fail to speak Mon? We must establish a Mon language and culture society to teach Mon literature and culture. We must set up a school with Mon as the language of instruction," he said. "This school will be the path to return future generations to the Mon nation."

His friends nodded.

Shwe Hongsa said he would volunteer to teach at the school. U Htun Htin said he would contribute his library of Mon texts and palm leaf books to the school. Aung Mon promised to donate the land, a plot only ten minutes' walk upriver from Tun Way's property. Others in the group promised to raise funds.

"Nai Tun Way, we want you to be the leader of the society," U Htun Htin said. This had all been discussed before the meeting, but he tried to look as though he was still considering the request.

"I am not sure I can take on this heavy responsibility. My fields need much attention and I am finally starting a family," he said. "Before I decide, please review the draft of the charter."

He lay a sheaf of papers in front of them and leaned back as they read. Already more than thirty-two, he had married late. He had put off marriage to pursue his education in Calcutta. Those studies were interrupted by the sudden death of his father. As the only surviving son, he had to return home to clear debts, negotiate land rental agreements and deal with a two-year drought that left much of his crop withered in the field.

All this had delayed finding a wife until well after the age that most Mon men were married with children. But the truth was he had never really liked any of the local girls proposed by eager matchmakers. Sweet, complaisant and dull, they were interested in him because he was a landowner and the only heir of one of the oldest families in the city.

Su Sah had been so different. She had impressed him when he

brought in the child of one of his tenant farmers for treatment. She had given the girl such gentle care and directed the other nurses with brisk confidence. With a white medical coat, a stethoscope around her neck and her long shiny hair pulled into a tight bun she looked so professional. Her large brown eyes showed concern for the little girl as she delivered her diagnosis of malaria.

"The next few days will be critical," she had said, holding the hands of the girl's mother, "but there is every hope that once she survives this crisis, she will recover without permanent damage."

In contrast to the doctors' lack of concern for a peasant girl, Su Sah checked on the little girl at least three times a day over the next five days, ensuring that she drank only boiled water, ate a broth with minced egg and took the prescribed doses of quinine.

He had found himself eager to escort the girl's mother to the hospital and to consult with the pretty nurse instead of the arrogant doctors. He had hoped she would be impressed by his devotion to the health of a tenant's child. Sometimes they discussed her case over tea. He learned Nurse Su was passionate about finding ways to combine the latest medical research with the most effective traditional Mon remedies. She also talked of prevention.

"Malaria is borne by mosquitoes and mosquitoes need stagnant water to breed," she explained. "You should drain the ditches near the workers' houses and give them mosquito nets."

Two days later, he proudly reported he had bought a wagon-load of mosquito nets.

"My workers are filling in every place water collects and we are raising fish in the ponds that remain—you know, so the fish eat the mosquito larvae," he had reported.

"Well done. I say the same things to everyone, but little happens," she had said with a rueful smile.

Even after the girl was released from the hospital, he had found it necessary to consult with Su about her follow-up care and the general health of his tenant farmers. Despite her heavy workload, the young nurse always found a little time to talk with him.

It had taken three weeks, but he finally got up the courage to invite her to join the Mon music society. They had sat side-by-side at several concerts. He had to endure some teasing from his friends, but somehow, even that made him happy.

It had not all gone smoothly. There was that awful time when she seemed to be drifting away from him to that big-nosed foreigner. She had frightened him with talk about furthering her studies in London and someday becoming a doctor. He had feared she would be dazzled by the doctor and the chance to see the world, so he had pressed his case.

Her initial refusal to accept his proposal had devastated him. He thought she would reject him for the British doctor. Days of agony followed. Then there was the marvelous relief when he heard the doctor had been transferred to Rangoon.

More days of uncertainty had followed with Su refusing to meet him. Then she had invited him to dinner at the new restaurant behind the town hall. She had looked so beautiful in the light of the stubby candles on the table. She has decided to say no, he had thought. His face went pale, and he suffered a moment of dizziness. He finally looked up and saw she was smiling at him.

"I wanted to be sure of my own feelings. Now I have had enough time to think," she said as he looked at her in alarm.

"Yes, I would love to be your wife and share your life here in Bago. I want to continue to work at the hospital and to raise a family with you."

The wedding had been a traditional Mon ceremony. Over her protests at the expense, he had bought Su an elaborate sky-blue silk dress for the wedding. He warmed at the thought of how she had looked up at him, her hair freed for once from its bun. It spilled out from under a tiara of pearls and flowed down her bare shoulders. The ceremony included eight white-clad Brahmins who filled a golden bowl with water filtered through a sieve of one thousand holes. The head Brahmin blessed a white cord and draped it between them, connecting their heads and their hands. A long line of relatives and town notables, even some doctors and all the nurses from the hospital, gave their blessings and poured water over their hands. The house was decorated with flowers and candles, but all he saw was Su's smile.

The next months had been wonderful. They found they had an easy understanding of one another. When they had a rare disagreement, he would think: what does it matter as long as Su is happy? The old saying was true: man is the flowing water that must be contained and ordered by the ridges of the rice fields to become productive. His wife provided those ridges, gave an order, a calm to his life, and now she would produce a son.

She worked hard at the hospital, but almost always made it home for dinner. Whether visiting the farmers, inspecting irrigation works or haggling with the rice millers, he found himself smiling to himself as dinner time approached. His management tasks were as annoying as ever, but now they meant something. He was working for Su; he was working for his family. Dinner was usually followed by a stroll through the orchard around the house. Occasionally they would attend a dance-drama in town or listen in on music rehearsals by Tun Way's friends in the Mon music group. He enjoyed reading Mon poetry to her even though she usually fell asleep soon after he began.

When Su told him she was pregnant, a flash of fear swept through him. She was tall, but so slim and small-boned. There were so many dangers. Mother had died in childbirth. And so many others. He couldn't help thinking of all the problems she told him about at the hospital. The fevers that came with childbirth, the babies born dead. Shouldn't she stop working?

But she was stubborn. She made light of his fears and ignored the more recent frowns he had seen on the faces of the older doctors. With only two more weeks to go, she was still attending her patients. As pregnancy filled out her slight frame, the prospect of a child became his new world. The head monk, known for his powers of prophecy, had promised a boy.

"It will be a difficult birth, but your wife will soon recover and you will have a strong and healthy boy," the monk had assured the couple.

A son to carry on the family, manage of the property—but only after a good Mon education. He would teach the boy to read and write, to appreciate the Mon heritage. He would go to the Mon language school. That's what all this struggle was for. The three of them would be a family. It struck him then how lonely he had felt when Mother died. Father had never really recovered and he realized he had done little to help him, leaving for studies far away. Father had daughters to care for him, he had thought then, but they too passed away. When Father died, there was nothing left. A Mon household should be full of sons and daughters, cousins and aunts all living together. Home had been that way when he was a boy, but all the deaths had left him alone in the big house. There was nothing but loss, until Su.

All his work, whether on his lands or Mon culture, was to provide a better future for her and for the child on the way. His son would have a family. Maybe there would be more than one son. And at least a daughter or two to look after Su and him as they grew old together. There would be grandchildren. They would enlarge the house so they could all live together by the river. They would have family meals with many dishes. He would recite poetry. He and Su would sing together. The children would take the parts in their own dance-drama. The grandchildren would chase each other around the house. They would…

"Tun Way, Tun Way, do you accept?" The sound of Shwe Hongsa's cheroot-roughened voice broke his reverie. "The draft is fine, but we need to add your name as founder and president."

"What was that? Oh, the Mon society. Are you sure it must be me?"

"Yes, of all of us, you are the most educated. You know the tales and the customs," Shwe Hongsa said. "You even have your own library of Mon literature. It can only be you."

"As director and headmaster?" he asked, even though this had been proposed and agreed three days ago.

"We will all support you and, anyway, this was your idea," Shwe Hongsa said.

"Yes, but I have some conditions you need to consider," he said. He thought of his wife and her struggles to get an education.

"We must open the school to both boys and girls. We must not let the past history of Mon culture be forgotten, of course, but we must not become mired in the past. We must prepare both male and female for a future in which they play leading roles."

Shwe Hongsa looked startled. "But girls are not accepted into temple schools. It is against the Mon tradition."

"That is why we must allow them a place in the schools of the Mon Language and Culture Society. We are not training monks, but citizens of what could one day be an independent Mon state," he said. "Su Sah had to struggle for an advanced education. Now that education allows her to play an important role in preserving the lives of Mon people. How can we have capable, educated Mon youth unless we have capable, educated Mon mothers?"

There was a murmur among the group as they considered Tun Way's arguments.

"Our women are already much advanced beyond the women of India," Aung Mon said. "The British allow girls in the new secular schools, but otherwise, we are more advanced than the foreigners.

Mon women keep their own names, unlike the British. Women can divorce, they can remarry, and…" he said with a grimace, "they control our money."

Htun Htin laughed. "You are just miffed because your wife won't raise your allowance."

"Our women are advanced," Tun Way agreed, "but isn't this precisely due to the Mon tradition of honoring our women? This must be shown in all the activities of the Mon Language and Culture Society—especially the schools."

"I support Tun Way's condition. Who agrees?" Htun Htin asked.

"I guess I have to agree," Aung Mon said. "If I tell my wife I supported women's education, maybe she'll give me enough to go drinking more than once a month."

The group laughed.

"With your support, then, I accept," Tun Way said. "The Mon Language and Culture Society will be born from this day. But we must accept that it will be a difficult birth and there will be opposition and problems. Let's think about a budget."

He brought out a notebook and opened it. Three kerosene lamps lighted the room as the moon rose outside. The men discussed the money needed for more than an hour, when there was a movement at the doorway.

It was that servant girl bothering them again. But next to her was the midwife who was supposed to be helping Su with her pregnancy. Her head cloth askew, the mid-wife leaned against the doorway, panting. What was she doing here? The baby was more than a week away. Fear stabbed through him.

"Sir, please come now," she gasped. "It's Su Sah. She is not well. Something is wrong."

37
HUAT
Return

Dark clouds threatened rare hot season rain as Huat emerged from the cramped alleys on the western side of town and crossed the dusty main road to the triple-gated temple entrance. The orange tiles of the prayer hall stood out against the dark green of the mountains to the west. Huat hurried past the large teak-wood residence of the abbot. The walls were decorated with elaborate carvings of warriors, animals and flowers. It was beautiful, but odd. Usually monk's quarters were tiny huts, like those beyond the prayer hall. Little in the temple had changed from the month before, yet so much had changed.

At the little hut assigned to Chao he stepped out of his sandals and climbed the steps to the doorway. Elder Brother Chao sat cross-legged on a mat in the center of the tiny room, his eyes closed. Huat tapped on the door frame. His brother opened his eyes and smiled.

"Huat. It is good to see you. You are so kind to come."

"I am sorry to interrupt your meditation, but there is urgent news."

"No bother. My meditation is full of interruptions anyway, mostly from my own mind," Chao said with a smile.

"It is Father. Two nights ago, he came home from drinking and couldn't open the door. It seems he thought Mother had locked him out, but it was only that the door was stuck. He got angry and started pounding on the door and yelling. When mother came down, she found him lying at the foot of the steps. He tried to get up and fell down again. She couldn't understand his words. She couldn't get him up."

"Where were you?"

"I was still on my way home. When I got there, Father was on the ground. At first, I thought he was just drunk, but I saw the left side of his faced drooped like the melted tar we used on the boat."

"What do the doctors say?"

"Mother sent word to the doctor at the clinic on the other side of the river, but he was away. So, she told me to bring you," Huat said. "You will know what to do."

"Is he conscious?"

"Partly. He makes noises and waves his hands, but we don't know what he means. Then he falls back like he is asleep, but he twitches."

"How much did he have to drink?"

"I don't know, but he has been drinking a lot since you left. Almost every night. And he gets so angry over even the smallest thing."

He exhaled as his brother dug through packets of herbs, tossing them into a shoulder bag. Chao would help. He always knew what to do when men on the ship got sick and he had been studying with the temple healer.

Their boat set off on a reluctant breeze. It would take them hours to get home, but he felt better just having his brother with him. Chao had always been the one to cool things down when Father was yelling. He was the one who could get Mother to be less stubborn. He had never seen his brother lose his temper until the fight with Father over *The Wind Uncle*. Maybe everything would work out fine. Chao would stay home to treat Father. The sickness would bring father and son back together. They would forgive each other for their harsh words. Chao would stay at home and the family would be whole again.

38

TUN WAY
To Love Is To Suffer

BAGO, APRIL 3, 1901

Tun Way leaned back against the hospital room wall. His head pounded with pain and his back ached. The heat was oppressive. He had not slept for a long time. But it didn't matter. Everything that mattered was on the hospital bed in front of him.

Her eyes closed, Su looked like she was sleeping. No, not sleeping. Something else, much less peaceful. Her hair spread out like a dark fan around her face, which was as white as the sheets. Her breath was ragged, her body trembling with each slow, shallow breath. She had gotten weaker and weaker over the past eight days. He reached to touch her forehead. Still burning with fever.

He had taken too long to reach her. The horse carriage had been terribly slow despite his shouts to hurry. He had gotten home as fast as he could. But he had been too slow. Why hadn't he gone with the servant girl when she first appeared?

When he rushed into the house, he could hear nothing. The oil lamp shed a warm glow over Su's face. She was so beautiful. Then he saw the darkness puddling below her waist. Blood. So much blood soaking the sheet. Su was pale and weak as she looked up at him.

"There is something wrong with the baby. I think it is a breech birth," she said and then slumped back on the sleeping mat.

"I'll get you to the hospital," he said. But Su shook her head. "Too late, only a few minutes between pains. The baby is coming… now." She gasped and groaned. The midwife took him by the arm and pulled him out of the room.

He sat for hours just outside the doorway listening to Su's cries of effort, pain and frustration. He was useless. The monk had foreseen a difficult birth, but he had promised a healthy boy and Su's recovery. Finally, the midwife came out with a small bundle. He saw a tiny dark face with a smear of blood on one cheek. She extended the child to him, but he rushed past her to see Su. She lay exhausted, only semiconscious. A pile of bloodied cloths was crumpled on the mat.

He sat beside her for most of the next two days, waiting for her to recover, as the midwife promised she would. He recalled her smile when she woke.

"We have a daughter," she said and asked for the baby in a raspy voice. She took the infant to her breast, bending her head to look into the baby's eyes and then lay back in weariness. A daughter? It was supposed to be a son. The little thing was like a leech, sucking the life out of her.

The next morning, he found her hot and flushed. There was a foul smell in the room. Su moaned in pain.

"Water, please, some water."

After a few sips she looked better. She brushed at damp strands of hair that clung to her cheek, then her eyes closed in pain.

"Headache, thirst, fever, rapid heartbeat," she said. "I think it is puerperal sepsis—childbed fever," Su whispered to him. "Now you can take me to the hospital."

Mother had died of childbed fever when his brother was stillborn. He gathered Su in his arms and walked out of the house shouting for his carriage. Every rut in the dirt road pushed a groan from her lips. Each jolt was a stab in his heart. When he carried her into the hospital, he expected a flurry of action, but everyone seemed to move as if they were wading through water. First the nurses wanted to know what had happened, then more people came into the room when they realized she was one of their own.

Finally, a doctor came, then several more—mumbling among themselves. They placed cold cloths on her forehead and tried to get her to drink some broth. He heard a discussion among the doctors, with the Burman doctor recommending she be bled. He heard the words "great derangement of the vascular system...inflammatory... bloodletting." The younger doctor accused the older one of being an "inflammationist," using treatments from the last century that would "worsen her debility."

If the doctors were fighting amongst themselves, who would save Su? The Burman doctors might not treat her properly because she was Mon. That British doctor seemed to want to try experimental treatments. The hospital director seemed more concerned the fever would spread to others in the hospital. He felt angry and helpless.

When the doctor asked whether the midwife had washed her hands and used sterile instruments, he didn't know what to say. How could he know? He hadn't been there. When she needed him most, he hadn't been there. He was at fault for the delay in reaching her, for entrusting her to the mid-wife and for failing to bring her to the hospital immediately.

He put his head in his hands and rubbed his temples, reviewing all of his failings. Getting her pregnant too soon. Allowing her to work until the end of her pregnancy. Attending a meeting when she needed him. His thoughts spun round and round with all the things he had done wrong. Why had he ignored the servant girl? It was his fault. It all came back to that. It was his fault.

"Be careful, you idiot," he snapped at a nurse who washed Su's face. He seized the cloth from her, dipped it into the water bowl beside the bed, and gently stroked her forehead. He thought he heard a change in her breathing. It was raspier, slower. He felt her forehead. It was cold. That was good wasn't it? Maybe the fever was breaking. The skin above her eyes was white, almost translucent. He could see the faint tracery of bluish veins through her skin. Her breathing slowed still more. She didn't seem to have the strength to pull the air into her lungs. Her body trembled and then sank back into the bed. Something was very wrong.

"Doctor, nurse, somebody come," he croaked. "Help her. Do something."

Her eyelids fluttered open and stared unseeing through him. She took a long, unsteady breath. He waited for the next breath, but it never came. Disbelieving, he stroked her face.

"No, no, no," he moaned and collapsed by the side of the bed.

39

CHAO
Natural and Normal

Chao stood on the bow of the boat as it struggled against the tide. The dark water rushed past, but the boat made slow progress. They had sailed slowly down the coast, but soon after entering the mouth of the river the tide had turned against them. When he looked at the river bank, it seemed like they were hardly moving. Slowly the large shape of the warehouse and the two-story house beside it came into view, gleaming faintly in the light of the nearly full moon.

He leaped onto the dock and hurried to the door, his brother close behind. When he burst through the door of his parents' room, he could see a line of candles beside the sleeping platform. His mother and his sisters sat around a still form.

The candlelight flickered over the deep lines in his mother's face. Toh and Wan sat beside him, looking with dread and fascination at their father. His head was on a small wooden pillow and his mouth hung half open. Chao knelt, bent in a deep bow and pressed his head to the floor at his mother's feet. Mother pulled him toward her.

"Son, your father has been this way for hours. The medicine shop gave me something for him, but I can't get him to swallow it."

He sniffed at the cup of medicine next to the mat.

"This smells like *Huang Qi*, good in reducing an excess of blood." He tried to speak with the calm assurance he had used with patients at the temple.

"The monks gave me another medicine that has helped some people recover—*Buchang Nao Xin Tong*. They say it can help remove blockages in the blood."

He found it hard to recognize Father in the drooping face before him. Where was the man who dominated the family? Where was the proud ship captain? His breath came slowly as if it was reluctant to leave his chest. This man, who had always seemed so powerful, the cause of so much frustration and anger, now seemed small and helpless. He staved off a feeling of panic and tried to focus on what he could do to help.

"Huat, stir this packet of herbs into two cups of boiling water. Mother, soak some soft cloth in hot water," he said.

He pulled Father up to a sitting position in front of him. He carefully massaged the back of his neck. When his Mother came back with the hot cloths, he applied them to the base of Father's skull and then massaged again. He took a cup of herbal broth and tried to get Father to swallow a sip, but the thin brown liquid dribbled down the side of his face. He massaged his father's neck again and then laid him down. His mouth sagged open, his breath barely raising and lowering his chest. Father is dying. How is that possible?

An hour later, there were footsteps at the door and a young man came in with Huat.

"This is Dr. Prasert, the new government doctor in Nakhon who was visiting the Pakpanang clinic," Huat said. "He graduated from the Pattayakorn Medical School at the Back-Palace Hospital in Bangkok."

The young doctor was dressed in black, Western-style coat and trousers. He carried a leather bag. He gestured Chou to one side and took out an instrument with rubber hoses that he applied to Father's chest, then his neck. He peeled back his eyelids and examined Father's eyes. He grasped his wrist and pulled out a large watch from a pocket inside his jacket.

"It appears this man has had a brain hemorrhage. A blood vessel in the brain has burst," he said.

"What medicine do you recommend?" Huat asked.

"There is no medicine for this. If there had been merely a blockage, we could provide medicines to thin the blood, but a large vessel has broken," Dr. Prasert said brusquely. "He will die very soon."

The doctor put away his instruments as the family watched in silence. What a cold-hearted man. Chou could feel anger rising at the unfeeling words of the doctor, but he knew they were true. Then he felt angry at Father for dying, dying before he could forgive his son, before he could welcome him home, before they could be father and son again.

Mother broke into strangled sobs. His sisters uttered high pitched cries. Huat was shaking silently as he tried to comfort his mother. How could he think only of himself?

He struggled to calm himself. Birth, illness and death, he recited to himself. These things are all natural and normal. Birth, illness and death, these are inevitable parts of life. Birth, illness and death, natural and normal.

He looked at the family gathered around the still form of his father. His mother's face was tight as she struggled for control. His sisters wept freely. His brother looked to him with a question.

"We'll stay here together," he said. "Doctors can be wrong. There is always hope."

But he knew there wasn't.

40

TUN WAY
The Punishment of Memory

His hands clasped before him, Tun Way stared dully at the monks chanting from a raised platform at one end of the temple. In front of them was the carved white and gold coffin holding Su's body. Beside him, her mother wept quietly.

His mind kept going back to Su's final breaths. He had wanted to tell her how much he loved her, but he had waited too long. By the time he held her to him, she was unhearing, already gone from the world.

That heavyset nurse, Su's friend, fighting her own tears, had pried him away from her body as her father and mother rushed into the room. The old Burman doctor formally pronounced her dead in a sorrowful tone and waved to the weeping nurses and orderlies, telling them to make the arrangements. The doctor asked Tun Way where they should bring the body, but he found himself unable to answer. It was left to Su's father to tell them the funeral would be held at the ancient Shwemawdaw temple.

He looked up at the three large Buddha images looming in front of them. The images with their golden robes and their serene smiles seemed wrong. He watched as the coffin was carried behind a white cloth screen where Su's father and mother carefully bathed the corpse. He couldn't force himself to take part. He did not want to remember her as a cold, dead body. He wanted to remember her alive and lively: dancing with graceful hand movements, carefully examining a patient, tasting delicacies in the market, clapping at a music performance, holding him. He watched as seven members of Su's extended family, each born, they told him, on a different day of the week, carried earthen pots of water behind the screen for the bathing. Su's father took a length of white cotton thread and tied her thumbs together, then her big toes. Why did any of this matter?

The family members then carried the coffin from behind the screen and placed it under a canopy decorated with flowers. He knelt before the coffin, clasped his palms together and then pressed his head to the cold tile floor three times. His mind whirled as he tried to imagine life without Su. All the plans and hopes for a life of love and family were gone. Nothing was left. He couldn't move for a long time. Then someone took his arm and pulled him to his feet. He walked backward to the polished marble floor where Su's parents sat.

Family members came forward to kneel before the casket. They were followed by a long line of Bago notables—doctors and nurses from the hospital, Mon aristocrats, even the British advisor to the governor. Old ladies chatted in the back of the hall and two little boys chased each other out the doorway, oblivious to the chanting monks and the frowns of their parents.

The wail of an infant in the distance turned his thoughts to his new daughter, somewhere in the temple with one of the house maids. Su's sister had already found a wet nurse—something he had forgotten completely. How could he raise a daughter? That was a mother's responsibility. He would hire someone, maybe one of the tenant wives. Maybe Su's family would take the child. How could an old farmer like himself teach her all she needed to know? He felt a surge of anger. Why did Su leave me like this?

The chanting ended and the head monk gave a brief sermon that made no sense. It was the duty of all those present, he said, to observe the corpse and to reflect on the brevity and fragility of life. Death was the inevitable end. Birth, sickness and death were normal elements of existence, the monk said.

But death should come only after a long and loving life together. Death should not come so quickly, so unfairly. Not even two full years together.

Four of Su's male relatives lifted the casket and began a slow procession out of the main prayer hall to the cremation grounds outside. Someone thrust a coconut into his hands as they followed the coffin. A pyre of wood loomed, a dark door into what? Another life? Nothing?

The bearers carried the coffin up the steps, turned it around three times and placed it atop the pyre. Su's father sprinkled water from a silver bowl onto the corpse and nodded to him. He cracked the coconut on a corner of the casket and slowly let the coconut water drip onto Su's feet. He couldn't look at her face. A temple attendant took a silver knife and cut the cords tying her toes and thumbs, murmuring that he was cutting away the desires and sins that had bound her in life. She was now free to move forward to nirvana. There must be something more. It should not end like this. But it had.

He bowed and climbed down the steps as the other mourners climbed up. They placed small candles and flowers made from slivers of sandalwood beside the casket before a light wooden cover was placed over it. Two temple officials thrust torches into the pyre.

He stared into the fire until his eyes ached. The heat of the flames dried his face into a stiff mask. He clamped his mouth shut, fearful any expression would lead to tears. The pyre collapsed in a shower of sparks and smoke. The flames had consumed his own life. Nothing would be left now but the ashes of regret. As the flames subsided into coals, he felt the burning continued inside of him. His chest filled with anger. At what? He couldn't say, but it felt like it would last forever.

As the crowd of mourners began to say farewells and drift away, talking quietly, he stood alone. Su's parents walked away with their daughters, arms wrapped around each other. He had no family to comfort him. No matter. Comfort was not possible. He tried to think of the light on her hair, the smile on her face, the serious voice she used when discussing a medical problem, the laughter when she teased him about his growing pot belly, the touch of her skin when they made love. All this was gone.

His thoughts were interrupted by a thin, needy cry.

"The baby is hungry, sir," said the servant girl. "We need to go."

Anger and hurt surged through Tun Way.

"Well, go ahead then and take it home to the wet nurse," he said.

He looked at the wailing infant, its eyes screwed shut. This was all he had left of Su. All his dreams had burned away in the funeral pyre. This scrawny thing was all he had left. He would have to care for it, raise it, teach it. How could this little life make up for his loss?

Part Two : Gain

1

PAKDEE
Royal Opportunity

Pakdee stood three steps behind the line of prison guards. Ahead of them stood Warden Krit, sweat already staining the back of his tight white jacket. The mid-morning sun blasted through a gap in towering white clouds. In front of Krit were two young women, wives of prison guards, dressed in green and yellow silk. They held silver salvers, each with a thick garland of white jasmine flowers. Behind him, prisoners stood in five long rows stretching across the prison compound. The normally bare-chested prisoners were dressed in new white cotton shirts and blue-print *phakhaoma*. They stood barefoot on the clean sand spread in the compound the day before to sop up the moisture from the nightly monsoon showers. The black iron gates of the prison stood open.

Warden Krit had spent two days drilling the prisoners on how they were to receive the king. He explained that the king felt the old-style kowtows were no longer acceptable in modern Siam. He read out a royal proclamation Pakdee had found in the prison files: "The practice of prostration in Siam is severely oppressive. The subordinates have been forced to prostrate in order to elevate the dignity of the senior officials. This kind of practice is the source of oppression. Therefore, I want to abolish it," the warden read slowly and loudly. "From now on, Siamese are permitted to stand up before dignitaries. To display an act of respect, the Siamese may take a bow instead. Taking a bow will be regarded as the new form of paying respect."

The warden then demonstrated how the prisoners should bow from the waist. "All together. All at the same angle on my signal. I will move my hand like this," he said, demonstrating a slight wave of his right hand. It had been difficult for the prisoners to bow together, but nearly an hour of practice had finally won Krit's approval. Now to see how they would perform.

Crowds of townspeople lined both sides of the dark red laterite road through the main gate of the crumbling brick city wall surrounding the heart of Nakhon town. Some carried flowers. Others held banners welcoming King Chulalongkorn. There was a stir in the crowd and three men on horseback cantered through the city gate. They slowed to a walk at the prison entrance. The figure in the lead wore a simple white jacket, Western-style riding trousers and a broad-brimmed hat. As he dismounted at the gate, Pakdee could see the face he had seen so often in the Bangkok newspapers. The high forehead was partly blocked by the hat, but he could see the king's broad face with its distinctive mustache curling over the sides of his mouth. The two women bowed deeply and knelt, offering the garlands. The king touched each. An aide hurried up to take the flowers away.

Phraya Sukhumnaiwinit appeared at the king's side and introduced Warden Krit, who bowed and saluted the king. The king said a few words in a soft voice Pakdee strained to hear. A man struggled up to them with a heavy box camera on a tripod. The king turned and posed with the prison staff in front of the gates. Sukhumnaiwinit led the king through the gate, gesturing to the lines of prisoners. The warden waved his hands, and they all bowed, all together except for one gangly teenager to his left who stared open-mouthed at the king. The king paused and turned to walk in Pakdee's direction.

"Your Majesty, I believe this prison provides a useful model of how we can implement Your Majesty's desire to improve our corrections system," Pakdee heard Sukhumnaiwinit say in the royal language. Pakdee had rehearsed the key phrases of that language in which one did not address the king, but spoke only to the dust beneath his feet. Sukhumnaiwinit led the king to him. This was his chance.

"We have modeled our new prisons on those in Singapore, but there may also be useful models in your own realm," Sukhumnaiwinit said to the king. "The Nakhon prison may be one. This young man, Your Majesty, has played a particularly useful role in improving this prison, even though he himself is a prisoner. I believe you have seen some of his reports on prison activities."

The king turned his gaze to Pakdee and spoke in soft tones.

"I am glad to meet one who has justified my belief in the possibility of rehabilitation. I have seen prisons abroad that do more than punish. Those modern, civilized prisons return convicts to society as useful citizens. We hope that will happen with you and the other prisoners here. We have seen reports that prisoners here enjoy good health and the prison earns enough income to improve the food it can offer inmates. The high commissioner tells me the prison has a program to enable prisoners to learn new skills and earn money. He says this is partly due to your efforts. How did you go about doing that and what have been the results so far?"

Pakdee looked up at the king. This was his opportunity to make an impression, to win royal favor. He searched for the royal language to explain his ideas that healthier prisoners were the key to better prisons. What was the royal word for health? Was there a royal word for prison? He searched for the words, but they seemed to have disappeared from his head. Oh, he had to use that long pronoun for himself—*kha praputthajao*—then what?"

"I..., yes, honored sir, uh, dust under the feet of Your Majesty... I..." Pakdee panicked. No more words came to him.

The king smiled and turned to Sukhumnaiwinit. "This is the one you told me was such an eloquent talker? No matter. I am tired of people who are good at talking. I want to find those who are good at taking action. We cannot reform our country; we cannot stave off the foreign powers unless we have competent people. Perhaps this fellow is one. Now, let me see that fish pond he manages."

The king walked away, his gleaming riding boots disappearing from Pakdee's gaze. His heart sank as he watched the king and the commissioner turn away from the main prison yard. They disappeared into the mangosteen orchard. There had been so much he had wanted to say, about the court system, about the prisoners, about the prison, about his own case. He could have made the high commissioner and the warden look good to the king. He could have strengthened those crucial relationships. The king had graciously given him an opportunity to speak—and he had said nothing.

2

PLOI
Mother's Advice

Heavy clouds drifted across a full moon as Ploi reached the house. She had asked Mother to tell Father to spend the night at home because she had something important to discuss.

It had only been two months and the new *Po Kham* operator was already trying to cheat the house to help a big gambler from Bangkok. Just because they were far away from the capital didn't mean they were blind or stupid. She would need a couple of Father's tougher men to persuade the operator to start cheating the other way. Once they had cleaned the man out, they would bar him from ever coming back. That was better than beating him up. He probably has some connections. I just need a little help from Father.

The house seemed quiet as she washed her feet with water from the porcelain jar at the foot of the steps. Father should still be in the main room with his buddies finishing the last of their rice wine. But there was no sound. She pulled back the iron bolt and stepped onto the central platform. No one.

She sighed and opened the door to her room, the room she rarely used any more. An oil lamp glowed in the dark, glinting off Mother's eyes.

"So, tonight you come home for once?"

"Mother, what are you doing in my room? What's the problem? I told you I had something to discuss with Father. Wouldn't he come?"

"You and your father are just the same. Do whatever you want with whoever you want."

"Mother, I…"

"Just shut your mouth and listen to your mother for once. Do you think I don't know what you're doing at the casino late at night? Too much work to come home to your family? No, you are sleeping with a Chink sailor like some tea shop girl in the port. There is already gossip."

She felt her face flush. How could Mother speak to her like that?

She should just pretend she didn't know.

"Good. You're embarrassed. You should be. You are the granddaughter of a noble. Your father is a *kamnan* and my family are honest, moral people. You are disgracing us all."

This was too much from a woman who could not hold onto her own husband.

"Mother, I am the one working for the family. If your family are so moral, why aren't they supporting you? If Father is so noble, why won't he give you any money? You have pushed him away with your coldness. That's why he prefers Rung. You can't force him to love you with magic potions."

Mother's face flushed. Was she embarrassed or just angry?

"Who earns the money that buys your food and clothes?" Ploi plunged on. "Father never comes around anymore because of you. So, don't tell me who I can be with."

"But he is a Chink, spits everywhere, barely bathes more than once a day, eats like a pig. Can't speak ploperly. No manners."

"You know nothing about him," Ploi protested, but her mother wasn't listening.

"Soon, he will be fat with a big hairy mole on his chin. You won't like him so much then. What will you do then? Move on to another one, like your father?"

She could feel the pressure rising in her chest.

"If I feel like it. Why not? I can have ten Chinks in my bed if I want."

Mother glared at her for a moment, then burst into tears and sank to her knees on the sleeping mat.

"Please, please daughter give this man up. He is not one of us."

"Why do you care?"

Mother reached up and pulled her down beside her.

"My beautiful daughter. You are my hope. You must make a good marriage. We will find you a suitable husband, one who has land, has breeding, even education, if that is what you want. How can we have a Chink in our family? You are so lovely. Your hair glistens—just have to arrange it a bit better. Your skin is a little dark, but I know how to lighten it. It will be easy to find someone for you better than this ill-mannered sailor."

"He is not ill-mannered. He is smart. He is not a Chink—he is half Thai. He works well with the customers. He speaks Thai perfectly and sings nicely. I like the way he looks and the way he looks at me. So, there is no need to change my looks."

Her mother stroked her hair.

"But we can find you a Thai gentleman."

"Why? So, I can be a second or third wife. I don't need you or Father to find someone for me."

"Father will be furious when he finds out."

"So, don't tell him. You don't talk with him anyway and he never comes to the casino anymore."

Her mother grasped her hands and pulled her close.

"You will get tired of this man. Or he will get tired of you," she said. "You think things will never change, but they do."

She could feel her mother trembling with emotion. She had to control her own. She just had to persist and Mother would eventually give in.

"I know things can change. Just be quiet. Don't say anything to Father and maybe this too will change. Maybe you are right and my feelings will change."

Mother smiled through her tears.

"Yes, this will change. Everything changes. But at least be discreet. Don't let anyone know. Then you can move on to someone better. Yes, this will change."

"Yes, Mother," she muttered as she *waied* to her mother. "This could change."

If and when I want it to.

3

PAKDEE
Rebirth

The sea breeze ruffled the papers on his table. Pakdee crossed the room to lower the shutters to block the wind and sun. He looked out over the sea below. A steam ship was turning into the harbor, a plume of smoke pulled to one side by the wind blowing from the shore. A scattering of fishing boats dotted the silver sea that lay flat as a mirror under the sullen sky. He gazed along the narrow white strip of sand that faded into the distance. He imagined he could see all the way north to Pakpanang Bay. Pakpanang—that place of suffering he never wanted to see again. That was Abdul's home, not his. He had killed the person named Abdulkarim with his pen. High Commissioner Phraya Sukhumnaiwinit had given new life to the man now officially named Pakdee.

After his failure with the king, he had been sure he was destined to remain in the Nakhon prison for the remaining five years of his sentence. Only five days after the royal visit, however, the prison had received a letter signed by Phraya Sukhumnaiwinit, ordering the prisoner known as Pakdee transferred to his personal custody and assigned to work as a clerk at the *monthon* office in Songkhla. With that letter, everything had changed. Warden Krit had given him a new set of clothes and wished him well.

"When you are in the *monthon* office, don't forget your old friend, the prison warden," Krit said.

He had spent his final day in the prison saying farewell to prisoners and guards. He thought they would resent his good fortune, but they seemed to feel his luck offered hope for them all. A pair of guards drove him in the warden's carriage to the port. The guards escorted him aboard the coastal steamer heading south and then left. For the first time in more than five years, he was on his own: no chains, no bars, no guards, no walls. Free.

As the boat passed the sandy shore of Cape Talumpuk at the mouth of the Pakpanang River, he had thought that few in his old home town would remember the skinny Malay boy selling goat meat in the market. He was heavier and stronger from the work in the prison. Even his face had changed. There were lines making him look older than his age. On leaving the Nakhon prison he had shaved off his mustache and had his hair trimmed in the style of Thai officials—cut short on the sides and allowed to grow long and swept back on the top. He checked his reflection in one of the office windows. Few would recognize him as the frivolous boy in the Pakpanang market or the convict sent to the Nakhon prison.

Now he worked for the royal, government, for the high commissioner. His home was now Songkhla. The town was like Pakpanang with its seaside, its coastal trade and its green interior. It was the administrative capital of the *monthon* that included Nakhon, but stretched far to the south. It was here he would take the next steps to ensure he would never be helpless and abused again. Looking around the large room he saw the five other clerks lounging around a pot of tea, nibbling at treats of sticky rice and bananas roasted in *toey* leaves. He would outwork them all. He had already mastered the big black typing machine on his desk after less than two weeks of practice. Only last week he had won the monthly typing competition.

Looking out the window on the landward side, he could see the broad, green-rimmed expanse of Songkhla Lake. The lake was busier than the sea. Bare-chested paddlers, both male and female, propelled slim boats along the shore, weaving through the lines of fish traps reaching out like long fingers into the lake. The sun glinted from the sweaty backs of the paddlers. The women would throw a cloth over their shoulders to cover their breasts when they went into the market, but out on the lake they preferred the older style of bare upper bodies. Four paddlers propelled a larger, blunt-prowed boat piled with pineapples towards the distant shore to the west. Thatched huts on wooden posts rose from the lake water along the curve of the north shore. A handful of boats with steaming pots of rice congee and fish maw soup stopped at the waterfront market just below him. He could see the broad straw hats of the market ladies as they ladled out their food or haggled over fresh fish and vegetables.

In Songkhla, only High Commissioner Phraya Sukhumnaiwinit knew he was still technically a prisoner. The commissioner treated him with polite respect. Others knew only that he was a clerk the commissioner brought in from Nakhon.

"You will be under Somsak, the head clerk," the commissioner told him. "Obey him, but more than that, watch him. He comes from a family of officials. He knows how an official should act. Try to speak like he does, dress like he does, work like he does."

That should not be hard. Somsak didn't seem especially clever or energetic. He was careful with the paperwork. He was deferential to the higher officials and arrived at his desk on time every day. How hard could any of that be? Since he slept in a small shed behind the office, getting to work on time was easy. After a few days, the other clerks teased him for being too industrious. One asked him to type more slowly because he was making the rest of them look bad. He smiled but worked as hard as ever. He declined invitations to go out eating or drinking. Somsak usually paid, but with no money to return the favor, he didn't want to feel indebted. Soon the invitations stopped. None of the clerks were friends. None of them knew anything about him. None of them had shared his suffering like his friends in the Nakhon prison. He didn't mind. The important thing was that he was out of prison and improving his position. Everything depended on his relationship with the commissioner who seemed to take a real interest in him.

Sukhumnaiwinit told him he too had been abandoned by his family.

"They gave me up for adoption to a senior monk. I was only six years old. I cried when the monks took me from my mother and my brothers and sisters, but it was becoming a temple boy and later a monk that allowed me to learn. Learning allowed me to rise. Without wealth or connections, it will have to be the same for you. You must study, work hard, and think carefully."

"I am determined to do that, honored sir."

The commissioner looked at him and nodded.

"There is a verse with some useful advice:

> *Obey your bosses.*
> *Defend them against losses.*
> *Give your family honor.*
> *Provide them succor.*

"In practice, of course, it is not so easy," the commissioner said as he looked up at the portrait of the king behind his desk.

"You must be clever to see when and how to provide for your family. You must have the knowledge and skill needed to serve your superiors. Our whole way of life is under threat and only men of knowledge can deal with it. You can be one of those men."

He told Pakdee he was now a junior member of the team working to transform southern Thailand according to the policies of Prince Damrong Rajanubhab, the minister of the interior and brother of the king. "His Majesty and the Prince are engaged in nothing less than the transformation of Siam into a modern, civilized nation," he said. "Local administration, the courts, the police, business, trade, foreign relations, the military—everything must change."

"That will not be easy," Pakdee said. "People like the way things are, especially the people with power."

"It will take time and great effort," Sukhumnaiwinit said, "but we must eliminate everything that makes us look primitive in the eyes of the Europeans. Prince Damrong says the worst two are opium and gambling."

"From what I have seen of the tax receipts, that would cost us our two biggest sources of state income," Pakdee said.

"Yes, but as you realized in administering the prison, there is short term income that is actually costly in the long term. Opium robs the people of the energy to work. Gambling leads to poverty and family problems, to theft and violence—all those are damaging to state income in the long run. Prince Damrong is already drafting a new law on gambling like the one the British have in Hong Kong. He wants me to implement it in the south before anywhere else."

"But elsewhere, like in Borneo, the British still allow gambling. Maybe we should go slowly so we don't lose so much in taxes."

"Pakdee, these decisions are made at a higher level. They are not for you to question."

Sukhumnaiwinit explained that other changes were coming as well. It was only five years ago, he said, that the Nakhon Srithammarat kingdom had been formally abolished and made an integral part of Siam. The network of old officials and royal relatives was quietly resisting the new centralized administration. So, one by one, he was moving the old elite aside or absorbing them into royal service.

Songkhla felt different from Nakhon. Nakhon, with its old *wats* and ancient carvings, its revered meditation teachers, its quiet groves and jungled mountains, was a place of the spirit. Songkhla, like Pakpanang, was a place of commerce, trade and the sea. There was a merchant spirit here that placed profit ahead of tradition or religion.

Songkhla's central role in the coastal trade and the commerce with the Malay states to the south meant the port bustled with activity. The big steamers that bypassed Nakhon, all stopped at Songkhla. Nakhon had turned inward to its temples and traditions. Songkhla had turned outward to a world of commerce and politics. It was one of the few Siamese provinces ruled for years by an ethnic Chinese governor. The crowds in the streets of Songkhla included Chinese, Indians, Malays and even Europeans mingling with the Siamese.

The last of the traditional Songkhla rulers had been honorably retired and replaced only a few months earlier with a central Thai appointee selected by Phraya Sukhumnaiwinit. The commissioner's office and Pakdee's small room were in the former ruler's family mansion, purchased for use as the *monthon* administrative building. Dozens of officials from Bangkok worked there and more were coming. Unlike in Nakhon, where everyone knew everyone, officials in Songkhla came from all over Siam.

In Nakhon, talk was usually in the rapid sing-song of the southern dialect of Thai. In Songkhla, a slightly different dialect competed with the more somber sounds of *Jawi*, the harsh clang of Teochew and Cantonese, the precise tones of the official central dialect and even the breathy sounds of English.

Three weeks earlier the commissioner had given him a standing assignment.

"I need you to help me with our reform of the courts," Sukhumnaiwinit said. "Somsak was helping me, but he was working too slowly. I want you to take over and devise ways to improve the system. Right now, there are several different courts but no clarity on which ones take which cases. Both Siamese law and Islamic law – *khaek* law – are used."

Pakdee had bristled at the word *khaek*, but he kept his face impassive as the commissioner explained that if there was a dispute between Thais and Chinese, Siamese law applied, but if the dispute was among Malays, sometimes it was Siamese law, sometimes Islamic law. The commissioner lamented that Islamic law was largely unwritten and there were few trained judges, so judges made decisions based on impulse, connections or bribery.

"The raja sits on top of this system and can overrule any decision," he said. "He can order death sentences—a power and responsibility that should belong only to His Majesty the King. Recently, the raja of Saiburi killed his minor wife and her lover, but got away without punishment. This sort of thing cannot continue. We must make the system coherent, just and modern."

"But people are accustomed to the way things are. They will resist," Pakdee said.

He knew from Father that changing the minds of the Malays would not be easy. Even his own name had been a sign of his father's allegiance. Naming him after the eldest son of the Pattani raja – now on the throne himself – was a sign of Father's allegiance to Malay culture, religion and traditions. Change could not be rushed. His first advice to Phraya Sukhumnaiwinit had been to allow exemption from some of the new national laws for the Malays south of Songkhla. Trying to replace local Muslim courts with new courts manned by central officials would only create bitter feelings, he had argued.

"Anyway, the central government courts are not working that well. I know that from personal experience," he told the commissioner. "The things dearest to the Malays are family, village, tradition and religion. Let the local traditional Islamic courts deal with marriage and inheritance along with village level disputes. They can exist side by side with central courts dealing with major crimes and commercial disputes."

"That would make the Malay areas different from the rest of the country," Phraya Sukhumnaiwinit said, "when everything we are trying to do is meant to unify the country, to treat everyone in Siam the same."

"We have different courts for the British and the French," Pakdee said. "Why not for Malays?"

"The *farang* powers forced that on us," the commissioner explained. "We will soon have new laws just as good as any in Europe. Once those laws are operating well, we will press all the *farang*, even the arrogant British and French, to come under Siamese law."

"Then you should wait until that time comes," he argued, "before you extend all the legal reforms to the Malay areas. You have brought the Malay areas into the *monthon* system. If you take away their courts, there could be an explosion. You should not forget how many times the people of Pattani have revolted. My own great grandfather fought against the Thai king."

"Perhaps, but we changed the raja's status without much protest," the commissioner said. "Don't forget each of those rebellions was put down with great cost. We Siamese have invested many lives and much gold in Pattani. We cannot let it slip away."

"I hear the raja is unhappy and wants to restore his former status," Pakdee said.

"It is his income he wants to restore. I hear rumors of secret meetings at his *Istana* after I took away his opium and alcohol concessions," the commissioner said. "We can't let him keep his judicial powers."

"Perhaps we could leave family and Islamic matters to local courts and appoint local people to lead them. That way we are giving power back to the people," he said.

"That makes sense," the commissioner said slowly. "If we can show the British that we are just as capable as they are in administering semi-barbaric peoples, then they have less reason to push us out of those areas. I will write to Prince Damrong. Better yet, Pakdee, you draft a letter with your analysis for me to review."

He felt pleased the commissioner had listened to his views. He had helped put together the committee making unofficial *Jawi* translations of the new laws and regulations issued from Bangkok. Saifan would have been good at this work. He had such beautiful *Jawi* penmanship. Where had the family gone? The death notice sent to their house in Pakpanang had gone undelivered. He might never see his mother again. But it was the family who had abandoned him. His old life was gone. No one could ever learn of his past as a convict.

Sukhumnaiwinit seemed to enjoy their secret. He helped his young protégé perfect his language. He brought him to state functions and meetings with officials from Bangkok. After each event, he would question Pakdee: "Why did I use that pronoun?" "Who *waied* first?" "Why did that woman carry a betel nut box with her?"

At first, the language, rankings and actions in the *monthon* headquarters had been confusing, with so many subtle signs of rank.

"Our society is like that sweet made with layers of coconut cream and fruit gelatin," Sukhumnaiwinit explained. "Each layer has a different color and the order of the colors must be preserved even though all the layers are made of the same coconut cream, sugar and rice flour. But our society is far more complex because it is not static. A common man who serves his lord well can become a *khun*. A *phraya* who serves the king well can become a *chao phraya*. But you must never forget. No matter how far you may rise, you must subordinate yourself to the next higher layer. Always at the top is His Majesty the King."

For centuries, Sukhumnaiwinit told him, the relative status of everyone in society had been precisely ranked with a number. This system, called *sakdina*, had provided a sense of stability despite dynastic fights, succession struggles and frequent wars among the various kings and lords. From slave to king, he explained, each person in the realm had a *sakdina* ranking denoting privileges, powers and responsibilities.

"When my assistants crawl on their knees to offer me a cup of tea, they do not feel abased or abused," he said. "They are acknowledging their place in this system. It makes them feel secure. It is the same for me. When I make a deep *wai* to the prince, even though he is an old friend, I do not feel demeaned. I feel honored to show my loyalty."

"But now," he said, "that system is in flux. We have to adapt to the changes in the world. Officially, the *sakdina* system is gone, though it remains in our hearts. There are no more *sakdina* rankings, but even people meeting for the first time quickly figure out who is the superior and who is the inferior. For the two of us it is simple—you serve me, I serve Prince Damrong, and the prince serves his brother, the king."

The commissioner seemed to see him as a personal educational experiment. Could a low-born Muslim from a town in the hinterlands, someone who had been a convict, who had never even seen a palace, be turned into a Thai royal official? It was his boss's private joke against the system, though it must be more than that. The commissioner needed someone he could trust. Who could be more trustworthy than a non-Thai convict who was completely dependent on him?

Life in prison had taught Pakdee to make do with little and stifle all desires, but he could not help looking at the pretty girls who sold snacks in front of the building. He was tempted to chat with them—just to tease them into smiling at him like his female customers used to do in the Pakpanang market.

There was one particular girl. She must come from one of the coconut groves along the beach. Her skin was dark, but her smile was bright. She wore a red and yellow cotton *phasin* tied at the waist. A simple cloth thrown over her broad shoulders left her arms bare. When the sea breeze played with the cloth, he got tantalizing glimpses of her firm breasts, the dark nipples winking at him. Each morning she carried her coconuts to the market on two trays slung from a heavy split bamboo pole across her shoulder. Despite the weight of her goods, she walked with an easy grace that emphasized the curve of her hips and the length of her legs under the thin cotton. When he watched her walk down the road he would tighten with desire. Then he would recall how he felt as he opened the door to Malee's room. He had to stay out of trouble now, but someday...

4

CHAO
Renamed

Chao sat in his hut with the door open to let in the breeze from the morning shower. He should be meditating, but he couldn't seem to get started. His eyes drifted to the novice monks lazily sweeping up soggy leaves in the temple compound. The rain had washed the dust from the air. The clouds filtered a somber light into the temple. The new day was struggling to break through. Raindrops hung like tears from the edge of the thatched roof.

No, the time for weeping was over. Father had died before they could reconcile, but there was nothing he could do. He had to move on. That was what Huat kept telling him, and he was right. The brief note he had received from his brother offered a first step. He should have been here by now. Huat had always been a little careless about time. At last he spotted his brother striding through the gate.

"Hey Chao," he shouted. "It's time to go."

His brother stepped through the narrow doorway of the hut.

"Quiet. This is a place of meditation, not the deck of a ship," he said with a grin. "I'm ready."

Huat *waied* him and grabbed his arm. "This is an important day. We will change our fates today."

"Your fate is what you make it," he said.

"Well, we will make it different today."

"How is mother?" he asked as he thought of the last time he had seen her, pale and still dressed in white mourning clothes. She had seemed calm and composed as she greeted the relatives and arranged food for the guests. The family's choice of a Thai temple for the ceremony had annoyed some of his father's relatives and friends, but Mother had insisted and he had supported her. Funerals were for the living and Mother was still alive. The sonorous chanting of Thai monks was more soothing than the clanging noises of the Chinese temple. Later he had gone to Father's Chinese temple to make amends with a separate ceremony and a donation. Mother had asked to be excused. She had never been a favorite of his father's friends. She seemed confused about her own feelings. Father had not been easy to live with. She had struggled against him, sometimes in loud arguments and threats to leave him. But once he was gone, she had been stunned. He had tried to comfort her, but she pushed him away.

"He never got over you leaving," she said.

Does she blame me? But when he asked her, she just shook her head and held him. For a week she ate little and said nothing. The girls were taking care of her, so Chao went back to the temple to think. Maybe to gather his things and come home. Maybe not. Then he got Huat's note. He knew immediately it was a good thing to do.

"Mother is good," Huat said. "Eating much better now. She got up four days ago, called me and the girls to come with her to the warehouse. She said we would now have to look after the business ourselves. She's been working there every day since then."

"Does she want me to come back and manage the business?"

"No, not at all," Huat grinned. "She wants to do it herself, but she would be happy to have you and me work with her if we want."

"Do you think she can handle it?"

"Sure. More than that—she needs it. She and the girls have done a complete inventory of the warehouse. There is more stuff there than we thought and all the money that came in from the funeral has been a big help. Father knew a lot of people and they were generous."

"But the customers were mostly Father's friends."

"Yeah, but Father wasn't a very good manager. He thought every complaint about bad service or damaged goods could be dealt with by taking the guy out drinking. Mother says she had to listen to father talk about the business all those years so she feels like she has been trained to take over for him."

"What about the girls?"

"They love it. They were bored at home with little to do. They charm the customers. They handle the accounts as well as you did, but with better penmanship."

"So, they don't really need me?"

"No. They don't need me either. I told them to let me know if they needed any help. The casino is only a short boat ride across the river, but they haven't called on me yet."

Huat took his hand as they walked through the streets of the old town. They had to wait for a trio of elephants with high-domed howdahs to pass through the city's western gate. They turned into the long avenue that was Nakhon's main thoroughfare. They talked as they weaved their way through the traffic of venders with shoulder poles, heavily laden rickshaws, horse carts and riders on scrawny ponies.

"*The Wind Uncle* was always on the verge of losing money," Chao said. "It was old and slow. In a few years the steamships would have put it out of business anyway, so maybe it is good that it is gone."

"Without the ship, there really is nothing for you and me to do," Huat said, "but Mother would still like you to come home. She would make a place for you at the warehouse. The work wouldn't be hard. The warehouse crew has agreed to stay on. Mother wants to make the decisions and do the deals. Already she talked to all the old customers and got them to promise to continue using the warehouse and consign their cargoes through her."

"She managed the house and father and you and me all those years," Chao said. "Compared to that, the business shouldn't be too hard. I want to come home, but if I came back, I would just be an expensive laborer. This is our chance. We are free then to take control of our lives, to go where we want and do what we want."

"What do you want? To go to school in Bangkok?"

"That was an old dream, mostly to get away from Father. I find it peaceful in the temple and I am learning a lot about medicine right here. The abbot has old palm leaf books about herbs that I am studying. I am helping the monks treat the sick who come to us. It makes me feel good, but what are you going to do? You always loved the ship and the crew a lot more than I did. You like having lots of people around."

"I am doing fine," Huat said with a faraway look. "The casino is doing well. I like it."

"That girl—Ploi. Are you still seeing her?"

"Yes, every day," he said with a smile. "I am helping her at the casino. Her father and brother are useless."

"But you must be bored. All that gambling night after night," he said with a grin. "All those different games and the fancy food and the singing. Worse, you have to work long hours with a pretty girl. It must be exhausting."

"It is a real burden, but one I am willing to bear," Huat laughed.

"I always enjoyed the games, but now I get to watch and sometimes explain the rules to new customers. I help Ploi entertain. We sing. She has a wonderful voice, and she always looks so, so... beautiful."

"I've never heard you talk like this about a girl before."

"She is different. We fit so well together. We are a team and we are making a lot of money."

"So, it is just for money?"

Huat ignored his teasing.

"Sometimes we bring in a *Likay* group to attract customers. Ploi and I even take parts in the play if they need us. It's fun. On Chinese holidays we have a Chinese opera group. We have one performance in the afternoon and then another just before midnight and the final gambling session. Because we work so late, Ploi lets me stay in the back room of the casino."

"Don't you get lonely?" he asked with another grin.

"Oh no. Ploi always works late and sometimes the other staff stay pretty late too. We have to put away all the equipment, count the gambling markers, record losses and gains in the ledgers."

"The other staff stay late only sometimes. What about the other times?"

Huat's face flushed. "Don't say anything to mother yet, but we enjoy being together."

"Is a marriage coming?"

"Someday, I hope. But her father and her family want her to marry someone Thai, or at least someone rich. They suspect we are together, but they don't know for sure."

"Working in a casino. That's a big change from working on *The Wind Uncle*," he said as they walked past the massive *chedi* of Wat Mahathat.

"Yeah. I have to help keep books, deal with customers, sometimes break up fights, but worst of all," he said with a grimace, "I don't get to do any gambling of my own."

"When on board I could hardly pull you away from *Mahjong* or *Po* to do a little work on the ship."

"Your life has worked out well too then. As *chuan zhu*, you had to struggle to find time for your books and your herbs. Now you have all the time you want. Once you have finished your studies, though, you will have to come out and rejoin the real world."

"Maybe. Anyway, let's just worry about today. Father never would have agreed. But mother is happy with the idea, right?"

"I don't think she was ever happy with our Chinese names," Huat said. "She always had Thai nicknames for us. But father would not let her use them when he was around and would not register them with the district office. He wanted us to be as Chinese as possible. He even talked about sending us back to his home village to learn how to be a proper Chinese man and to find a Chinese wife."

"I was never sure what to call myself—Chinese name or Thai nickname."

"Nicknames are one thing—everyone has them," Huat said, "but with Chinese names, the Thais see us as foreigners, as Chinks."

"Then we need official Thai names, registered properly with the government," Chao said. "We are half Thai. We don't even look very Chinese. If we use Thai names, we will be Thai. Have you decided on a name?"

"Well, Ploi has suggested Prem," Huat said, "because she wants me to be content."

"Yes, Prem means content or happy, but it also means love in Pali. Maybe that's why she suggested it. So, is it really love?"

"I love being with her and I think about her all the time..." Huat said. "Anyway, if it makes her happy, that's enough for me. I'll be Prem from now on. What about you?"

"I have been thinking since the wreck—how I failed to be conscious of all that was going on. I need to change. So, what about Somneuk?"

"Consciousness?"

"Maybe 'presence of mind'."

"It fits. No one I know has more presence of mind. So, we will be Prem and Somneuk from now on. We will have new names and new lives. You will be free from Father's path."

"And you will be Ploi's Prem."

The brothers turned through a pair of heavy white pillars and walked, hand-in-hand, up the steps into the government offices of Nakhon Srithammarat.

5
PAKDEE
Politics

"Pakdee, His Excellency the High Commissioner, wants you in his office—now," the office boy said, poking his head through the door.

Pakdee looked up from the document he was drafting. His anger flared for a moment at the disrespectful tone of the office boy—like they were equals. He pushed that emotion aside, straightened his high-collared jacket and headed for the door. Only two more sentences to finish, but Phraya Sukhumnaiwinit expected an immediate response to his requests. Those requests had been coming more and more often as the political problems mounted in the far south.

Although several of the sultans were conspiring to get British support against the Siamese government, the most serious threat was Raja Abdul Kadir Kamaruddin Syah, the eldest son of the family that had ruled Pattani and Kelantan for centuries. Abdul Kadir paid elaborate courtesies to High Commissioner Phraya Sukhumnaiwinit when they met. According to a palace cook, however, the raja often railed against Sukhumnaiwinit to his courtiers when no Thais were around.

As the best Malay speaker on the *monthon* staff, he had traveled to Pattani at the high commissioner's request to learn what was happening in the town and in the raja's palace, the *Istana*. As a good Muslim, Raja Abdul Kadir proclaimed he wanted nothing to do with opium or alcohol, but the taxes on those vices had provided much of his income. The commissioner had now farmed out those taxes to the highest bidder, a Chinese merchant. Then he took most of the raja's remaining sources of funds—port fees, poll taxes and salt taxes. To lose that income was a serious blow, both personally and politically. The raja now depended on a budget from the government. Was there now some new measure the high commissioner wanted to discuss?

He bowed and *waied* as he entered the large, elaborately decorated office of the commissioner. A bronze Buddha image presided over an altar against one wall flanked by two rows of candles and smoldering joss sticks. A large, gold-framed oil painting of King Chulalongkorn dominated another wall. A slightly smaller portrait of Prince Damrong hung next to it. The slim, graying commissioner sat dwarfed behind a large teak desk. A thin sheen of perspiration glistened from his high, balding forehead. A trim mustache bristled on his upper lip.

"No need to kneel. Take a chair," the commissioner said in weary, but precise tones. "I have a document for you," he said with a brief smile, "but first I need your counsel."

He sat on a low chair in front of the desk and looked up at the man he had come to admire. Not only had the commissioner helped him out of prison and given him interesting work, but he had a quick intelligence and a deep knowledge of the world that helped him understand much that had confused him. Although careful to maintain a certain distance between them, the commissioner had treated him with courtesy.

"I have learned that Abdul Kadir has written a letter to Swettenham," the commissioner said. "He has complained officially to Sir Frank about the loss of the tax concessions. Look, here is a copy of the letter we got in London." He handed a much-creased paper to Pakdee. He bent over the letter, hand-written in English. He had been working hard to learn this strange language. The key paragraph was: "I trust that the trouble and grievance which are being imposed on my people will be seen by Your Excellency to be so harassing and unendurable that the peace and well-being of the state are endangered...and also that it will be seen that my application for the intervention and good offices of Great British has good ground on which it is founded, and on which such application can be made to Great British or some other of the Great power either Europeans or other."

He looked up at the commissioner, thinking how best to frame his response.

"Abdul Kadir can complain, but if it is just about his loss of income, there is not much the governor of the Straits Settlements can do. He has no authority in Siam," he said. "Does the governor have enough influence in London to get the British government to intervene?"

Sukhumnaiwinit stood up and began pacing back and forth.

"Unfortunately, there is a lot Swettenham can do. Britain's support is critical to how we deal with the aggressive French. With British backing we can stand up to the French. Without it, we are vulnerable."

"You told me the British did not want to share a border with the

French colonial administrators who are often much more aggressive than their home government. So, they have to support us, don't they?"

"Maybe, but the British also want to maintain good relations with the Malay rulers and woo them away from us. The Pattani raja has complained I am undermining the Muslim religion. He claims I allow Thais to molest Muslim women and even charges I brought a dog into a mosque," he said. "What nonsense."

"High Commissioner, sir, we know that these stories are untrue," he said, "but we must accept there are reasons local people believe them. Malays are accustomed to Muslim traditions and concerns—including the Koran's injunction against worshipping idols. They still remember the public procession bringing the new Buddha image to the big temple on Wisakha Day."

"That was in the early days, when I did not understand the Muslim concerns," Sukhumnaiwinit said. "In any case, I cannot deny Buddhists the right to worship in their own way just because it upsets the Muslims. Buddhism is the religion of most of our people. I am a Buddhist and I cannot put unfair restrictions on Buddhism. Still, at my request, the monks have now toned down the processions."

"But people don't forget. They believe whatever agrees with what they already believe. As you know, there have been problems with the way some policemen from Bangkok have treated local women."

"I know there was disrespect and lewd talk, but nothing that amounted to a crime. These are young men far from home. Even so, I had those men transferred once I could get replacements."

"I am afraid, honored sir, that was not good enough. The disrespect was in public and the transfers were made too quietly, too slowly."

A flash of annoyance crossed the commissioner's face.

"Pakdee, I appreciate your directness, but for your own good, you must learn not to criticize your superiors. It doesn't matter whether you are right or wrong. Sometimes being right is even more dangerous. If you are ever to get anywhere in our government you have to understand you never openly criticize your superior, or say anything that he might not like."

"Please forgive me, honored sir," he said, making a deep *wai*.

"This is for your own good. From now on, you will praise everyone in this office, especially me, when there are others around. When they say something stupid, you will agree, or at least keep silent. You are at the bottom of the hierarchy here, so you must treat everyone as if they are wise and wonderful. Speaking to me in private, however, I expect to hear your real opinion, even if it clashes with mine. Do you understand?"

"Doesn't publicly agreeing with stupidity lead to error?"

"Of course it does, but failing to agree leads to dissension. If you are not careful you could lose your position and the ability to serve the country. Find other ways of dealing with stupidity. Work behind the scenes. Agree loudly with stupid orders, but drag your feet in carrying them out. Misplace documents ordering a foolish action. Or make your most incompetent officer responsible for carrying it out. If you have to, quietly find a more senior officer you can convince, subtly, very subtly, to speak against the error. Make friends and allies. Become part of a group you can influence to do what you want without having to step forward yourself."

This was a strange way to operate, but it explained many of the puzzling things he had seen since coming to work in Songkhla.

"Thank you, sir, I am trying to understand."

"Now, how should we be dealing with the Muslim complaints about the court sessions?"

"High Commissioner, sir, many of the complaints are due to judges scheduling court appearance for Malays on the Muslim Sabbath. When they don't show up, they are fined. They see it as a deliberate attack on their religion, one that hurts them financially."

"Yes, but the courts are busy and, according to national rules, they are closed on the weekend. They have to be open on Fridays. We don't allow Buddhists to miss their court dates when they fall on a holy day. We can't have one set of rules for Pattani and another set for the rest of the country."

Even a man as intelligent as the commissioner didn't understand.

"Honored sir, praying at the mosque on the Sabbath is important to Muslims—more important, pardon me, than going to the temple on holy days to Buddhists," he said. "It is, of course, up to you, but you could change the court days, just for Pattani and the border towns, until people get used to the new court system."

"I don't think we can do that. There must be some other way."

"Then I humbly suggest you advise Prince Damrong to set up Muslim family courts to deal with the issues of inheritance and family matters that the Malays care so much about. The details are in my report. We could appoint respected local people as judges. That would undercut the power of the sultans. Other, more important cases would still go to government courts, but you could advise the court officials to avoid scheduling hearings involving Muslims on Fridays whenever possible."

"That all makes sense, but I am not sure it will help. What about the British? I fear they may encourage Malay unrest, ignoring our agreement the *khaek* states must remain under our influence."

"The British fear rebellion and religious emotions as much as we do. Like our own officials, the British are thinly spread. They still remember the costs in lives and money of the uprisings in India. A private note to Swettenham would be useful."

"It would be good to have some of the British businessmen explain to Sir Frank how unrest would hurt British business interests. Maybe one of them, like that fellow Duff, could deliver my note and explain the dangers of letting this get out of hand. He has influence with Sir Frank and a close partnership with the sultan of Kelantan. He is seeking business in Siam so he could benefit from helping us."

"An excellent idea, sir," Pakdee said. "We need to move quickly before the Malay rulers get up the courage to act."

The commissioner paused a moment in thought.

"We need better information on what is going on inside the *istanas*," he said. "You got good information from that cook. Do you think you could find more informants like that? For Pattani and perhaps some other provinces."

"Sir, I would be happy to try, but I will need some funds to encourage cooperation," he said.

"It will be money well spent," Sukhumnaiwinit said. "Focus first on Pattani. If we can bring Raja Abdul Kadir under our control, the others will be more pliable. The raja's call for foreign intervention amounts to treason against His Majesty. That gives us grounds to arrest him."

"But we must wait for the right moment and we must have clear evidence that the British can accept," Pakdee cautioned. "I can travel back to Pattani tomorrow."

Phraya Sukhumnaiwinit turned back to the documents in front of them, signing them with a flourish. "There, I have signed off on your report and approved funds for your assignment in Pattani, but there is something else we need to discuss," he said. He reached into the big desk and withdrew a stiff sheet of parchment.

"Pakdee, I have a document for you, but before I show it to you, I want to express my personal thanks for your service. You have always responded to my requests, whether for advice or action, with intelligence and honesty. It is not often one finds both those qualities in government. My little experiment of bringing you into royal service has been quite successful, I think."

"Sir, it is I who must thank you for giving your trust to a convict, however unjustly sentenced."

"That has now changed. I no longer give my trust to a convict," the commissioner said, his face looking suddenly stern.

"What? I don't understand, sir. I have always tried to be worthy of your trust."

Sukhumnaiwinit broke into a broad smile and extended a sheet of heavy paper with the royal seal at the top. "This is His Majesty's official order reversing your conviction. You are no longer a convict. So, I no longer have to trust a convict. I trust you."

He stared at the document, struggling to see the letters through the tears filling his eyes. He found the signature of the king at the bottom and looked up at the commissioner. "His Majesty was most impressed with the arguments in your appeal, your understanding of the legal issues, and your turn of phrase in explaining the injustice committed. He was most unhappy with the conduct of your case by the police, the prosecutor and the court. This document means you are free. However, I reported on your valuable role here to both Prince Damrong and His Majesty. They have graciously allowed me to offer you a formal appointment to the royal service and a position as secretary to the *monthon* commissioner. Of course, if there is something else you would prefer to do, it is entirely up to you."

He looked down at the document again, but he could not make sense of the words. He looked at the man who had pulled him out of prison. It was a long moment before he could speak. "I want nothing more than to stay here and to serve you and His Majesty's government," he finally managed. "This is what I want to do with my life."

"In that case, I have some advice and a small gift for you," Sukhumnaiwinit said. "I have been impressed by how quickly you have learned. At the same time, I also must warn you that if you continue to rise, you will make enemies. Jealousy is a dangerous emotion. Unfortunately, some people see another's success as their failure."

Sukhumnaiwinit held out a small velvet bag. "I don't know whether you believe in such things, but this crystal is said to have magical, protective powers. Wear it always."

Pakdee opened the bag and found a brilliant white crystal with a silver mounting and a thin chain.

"Put it on. You can tuck it underneath your shirt. You may not understand how this can help you, but believe me it can. If nothing else, wear it as a token of my esteem."

The crystal was brilliant, but the chain and the ornate silver mounting looked very old. He carefully put his head through the chain and felt the stone cool against his chest. He clasped his hands together in a *wai* and bowed to the commissioner.

"Now you will take the office next to mine. I will move Somsak back into the clerk's room and you will take over his responsibilities for controlling the flow of documents in the office. So, move your things in. We'll find better living arrangements for you too."

With that, the commissioner nodded and turned back to the documents on his desk. Pakdee backed away, gratitude, confusion and determination swirling within him. Over the next few weeks he thought of the commissioner's remarks every time he put the crystal around his neck. Although he no longer saw himself as a Muslim, he had never felt comfortable wearing Buddha amulets like many officials. He suspected those who noticed the silver chain thought it held a Buddha image. He could never figure out why his boss thought the crystal had special powers.

6

PLOI
A Proposal

"Prem dear, is all the equipment stored?" Ploi asked as she shut the account ledger. They had closed the restaurant and gambling floor early because of the holy day. The casino room was already empty and lit by only two of the oil lamps scattered around the room. The silence seemed even deeper after the raucous noise only an hour earlier—the clack of the betting tokens, the sound of the cowries shaken in their bowl, the soaring tones of the horns, the thump of the drums, the shouts of the winners and the moans of the losers. Now the silence and the darkness made the casino a different place. After managing the emotions of dozens of customers, her tasks now were quiet and mundane—rolling up the mats, counting the tokens, completing the account for the night and checking the gambling equipment. It was a time for restoring order, not just to the casino, but to her life.

"Yes, everything is taken care of," Prem responded. "I put some coconut oil on the roulette wheel. I am just getting the lamps now."

The casino darkened as Prem snuffed out the last oil lamps with a small copper cone. The full moon sent a column of pale light through the open window. She looked back at Prem. He was staring at her with a half-smile. He looked happy, but anxious.

"The casino looks kind of romantic," he said softly. "The moonlight makes you look even more beautiful than usual. Are you sure you can't stay here with me tonight?"

"No, I can't and you can't either," she said.

Now is the time to take the next step. How will he react?

Prem's face fell. He started to speak, but she held up her hand.

"We can't stay here tonight because we are going to see my parents," she said. "We have something important to tell them."

"We do?"

She took Prem's hand and pulled him to her. She rested her cheek against his chest and inhaled with a sigh.

"First I have something to tell you," she said, looking up at him. "You are going to be a father."

Prem sat down abruptly on the rolled up gambling mat. "You are pregnant? Are you sure?"

She examined Prem's face. Was that alarm? What was he thinking?

"Don't you want to be a father? Don't you want to be my husband?"

"Yes, of course I do. That, that is wonderful. A father. I will be a father and you will be a mother and we will be a family. We will be our own family," he said, a broad grin splitting his face.

"Then you better propose marriage right now," she said with a smile, "because you can't ask my parents' permission unless I say yes first."

She watched the happiness spread across Prem's rugged face. She had made the right decision. The man loved her. Would he be faithful? He was a bit crude, but that was from his shipmates and his Chinese father. Living with her, he would learn more polite manners. He would not be like her father, would he? Moving from one woman to another with little thought of the one left behind. She would never be like her mother—taking her man for granted until it was too late. Men would stay loyal if properly motivated.

Prem was motivated. He had given up his family business to work for her. He had little money of his own. He enjoyed the games of the casino as well as the social interactions around the mats. Most important, he was delighted with their love-making. He loved it when she was the aggressor. Unlike the other men she had been with, he wanted to stay with her when their love-making was finished. He seemed to like stroking her skin. Often, he offered to massage her feet—something she couldn't imagine any other man enjoying. She had only to look at him in a certain way or touch his nipples and he would grow hard. No matter how tired he might be or how recently they had made love, he would become excited when she took him in her mouth. Sometimes the taste was sour or salty, but she enjoyed their oral sex almost as much as Prem. It gave her a feeling of both closeness and power to be able to affect him so strongly. She liked it because it excited him and he was always so grateful afterward. It was good to have that power.

Yes, she had made the right choice. In any case, she needed a man to protect the family business. Father and Elder Brother Chit were useless. Now that she was pregnant, she needed a father for her child. There was no other option. She looked again at Prem's face beaming in the half-light. She took him by the hand and pulled him to the door.

An hour later, they stood in front of Father and Mother. Father looked tired. His evening bottle of rice wine was already half-empty. He looked uneasy and impatient. He must be anxious to get back to his new wife. He might fuss, but he wouldn't be a problem.

She had reported improved revenues at the casino each month since Prem had taken over as floor manager. She knew her father was pleased Prem was working for much less than Chit and there were no more unauthorized withdrawals from the cash box. She had told him she had something important she wanted to say. He must think it was about the casino.

Mother was still looking sourly at her husband. She should feel happy he was staying home tonight. Father had taken to sleeping with Rung at the house in town. It had been more than a year since her mother and father had spent the night together. The last time had led to a fierce argument that awakened her in the next room. She heard him shouting that Chaem was trying to bewitch him. Maybe Mother was finally beginning to understand he was never coming back and the pain was evident in her frown.

Mother Chaem had doted on Elder Brother Chit, often ignoring Ploi. Now Chit was gone and Father was going. Mother would cause a fuss, but she had a powerful weapon to win her over. Father was harder to figure out. Maybe he loved her enough to respect her wishes. But if he was in a bad mood he might try to stop her. Did he even care who she married?

She watched as Father took another big swallow of rice wine. Good, he was relaxing, but not too far gone with drink. Mother was glaring, first at Prem, then at Paen and then at Ploi. Was she angry or fearful? It didn't matter. There was no way back now. She ignored Mother's look and took Prem's hand. It was moist with perspiration.

"Mother and Father, as you know, Prem has done a wonderful job as floor manager at the casino. Income is up and expenses are down. He has worked smoothly with me and the other staff. More than that, he has cared for me and protected me. Prem loves me and has asked me to marry him. I have agreed. We would like your blessing."

"I knew it. You let that Chink into your bed," Chaem cried. "You don't know what you are doing. They say they love you, but they don't. He will use you for a while and then desert you. This one will reduce your status and bring you only suffering."

"Mother, that is not what will happen. I know exactly what I am doing. I love Prem. He loves me." She returned her mother's glare with her chin thrust forward. She pulled Prem closer to her.

"And I love Ploi," Prem said in a voice pitched high with tension.

"Prem and I can live here in the big house or we can live behind the casino. It's your choice," she said.

"Prem? I thought his name was Huong or something," Father said in puzzlement.

"His name is Prem now and we love each other. We will marry as soon as possible," she said.

"What do you mean, marry? Marry? You are still young. You could marry someone better than this. We are members of the royal family of Nakhon Srithammarat. The governor will be displeased," her father said. "Marry? He has no money. Look, I can find you someone much better. Someone with breeding, with status and wealth, with influence. Even a big shot like Sia Leng could be interested. I have seen how he looks at you. If you are going to marry a Chink, at least marry a rich one."

"We don't need your permission, but we would like to stay within the family. That is up to you. This is the man I want and we will be married," she said in a steady voice as she stared down her father and mother.

"Kamnan Paen, sir, I will dedicate myself to making your daughter happy and I will work hard at the casino for the family," Prem said.

"No, no, we can't accept this," Mother said. "I'm sorry, but you can't do this to me, to our family."

"Right. You will get over this. Just come home and we will find a proper husband for you," Father said.

"Like you come home?" she asked. "If you don't accept this marriage then you won't see me again and you can run the casino yourself."

Father looked uncertain. She had gotten her way with him before by standing her ground and she would not back down now. She knew the casino was the key. Father had given up dealing with the casino, asking only for a monthly cut of the profits. He no longer wanted to face Sia Leng and his constant demands for reports and profits. She knew he had promised his new wife a trip to Penang. He needed money and there were problems collecting the rents from the land along the river.

"No, I need you. The family needs you."

"Fine we will run the casino and make money for the family, but unless you accept Prem, you won't see me here again and you will never see your grandchild."

"Grandchild?" Mother said. "You are having a baby?"

Paen turned to his wife. "How could this happen? You are to blame for this. You failed to keep her under control."

Chaem reddened with anger. "Me? It is you who insisted she work at the casino. It was you who left her with all those men around."

"You failed to teach her any morals."

"No, it was you who taught her morals by example—the morals of sleeping with anyone you want."

"Mother, Father. Enough. We are leaving. We will come back only when you can be reasonable," Ploi said. "Until then don't expect to see us or our child."

Ploi and Prem started to leave, then turned around to *wai*.

"Wait, when is the baby due?" Mother asked.

"In six months, but you will never see it unless you accept this marriage," Ploi said, more harshly than she intended.

Mother collapsed to her knees in tears.

Father stared at her for a moment.

"No reason for me to stay around," he said as he opened the door. "Chaem, you have made a mess of this family. It's your fault," he shouted and slammed the heavy teak door behind him. A moment later the door reopened. Without saying a word Paen walked back in, grabbed his bottle of wine and stomped down the steps.

She watched as Father stumbled up the path. She would raise the family's status, not lower it. Prem would help her make the casino successful. They would be rich and respected, much more than Elder Brother Chit. They would have many children and Father would want to come home again.

7

SOMNEUK
In the Forest

The afternoon rain had left the forest cool and silent except for the slow drip-drip from the trees to the soft leaves of the forest floor. Even these small sounds threatened to pull Somneuk's mind away from his determination to concentrate on his breathing. In-out, innnn-ouuuut. Drip-drip-drip. The drops sliding down the big leaves of a young teak tree reminded him of the tears that meandered down the face of Tum's mother. He had felt helpless and guilty then and nothing had changed. He shouldn't think of that now. Back to the breathing. Maybe closing his eyes would help.

In-out, in-out. He concentrated on each breath. He tried to trace the breath entering his nostrils and sliding down his throat to his lungs. In-out, in-out. This method, *anapanasati,* was not as easy as Phra Tissa said. Maybe he should try meditating on a shape or a concept. Maybe walking meditation would be better—but not in a wet forest.

Damn, he had lost his concentration again. The harder he tried, it seemed, the faster his mind would slip away from his breathing to something his teacher said, to the sounds of the forest, to an itch in his crotch, to wondering how his mother and sisters were doing with the warehouse business. The last time he had visited, they seemed to be doing well. The warehouse had never looked so neat. There was a bustle of activity with merchants bargaining on storage rates and coolies wheeling merchandise in and out. He felt glad he wasn't needed, but also miffed he wasn't needed. It was all for the best. He was free to pursue his own life wherever it led.

Damn, damn, damn. In-out, in-out, in-out. A feeling of peace started to expand within his chest with each breath. He must be getting it right. Maybe he could do this, maybe he even had a talent for meditation.

Damn. Shit. Lost concentration again. He would never get this right. And he shouldn't curse, even to himself. He wasn't a rough sailor anymore. He was... he didn't know what he was, but he wasn't that sailor yelling at a crew to get to work or haggling over the price of shipping a ton of rice.

He opened his eyes and looked out over the clearing in the forest. A tangle of trees, vines and bushes struggled up the hillside in front of him. They were all fighting to get a bit of sun. The pale, cloud-filtered light of late afternoon picked out a hundred different shades of green. White mist rose from the soaked forest and mingled with the clouds drifting down from the big mountain west of the town. In the distance the mournful call of a gibbon sounded through the trees—"*pua, pua, pua.*" It does sound like "husband, husband, husband." He smiled to recall the legend in which the gibbon was Morah, an adulterous wife condemned by the god Indra to live as a gibbon and wander the forest forever calling for her husband without ever finding him. That punishment had always seemed a little harsh to him, but the distant sound did have a tone of unrequited longing.

Off to his left, the high-pitched whine of locusts started up like the sound of one of those electric motors he had seen in Bangkok. A bird trilled a quick series of notes and got an immediate answer from the other side of the clearing. He let his mind drift with the different sounds. He marveled at each of them in turn—the complex songs of the birds, the deep, rubbery sound of the frogs celebrating the rain, the damp rustle of the leaves in the fitful breeze. He listened to each as they rose and fell, thinking of the stories each sound had to tell.

A little later – he didn't know how long – his reverie was interrupted by the sound of a large body pushing clumsily through the underbrush behind him. Even in the forest, he couldn't be free of interruptions. Phra Panya, sweating in the humidity, came puffing out into the clearing. Clad in a bright saffron robe that kept slipping off one shoulder, he struggled with a large bag.

"Som, look what I have found. Some flowers of Chab pepper, roots of the wild betel leaf bush and some Plumbago root. Three of the six herbs listed by the hermits in the literature," the monk announced.

He smiled, glad to hear his teacher and friend use his new name. No more Chao. Now he was Somneuk or Som. No more a Chinese merchant and sailor, he was Somneuk, a Thai studying herbal medicine and meditation. No more a son with duties to his father, he was his own person. Maybe it was selfish to feel good about this, but he had spent most of his life trying to be that other person. It hadn't worked out very well. He had ruined his father's business, wrecked a ship and killed an innocent boy.

"What are they used for?"

"The betel root is good for muscular aches, the Plumbago helps with diseases arising from the bile and the Chab pepper reduces the symptoms of all kinds of incurable diseases."

"How do you know?"

"You are always asking that, but it's in the literature—the tale of the six hermits who tested the herbs on themselves," Phra Panya said. "So, it's proven."

"Have you tested them yourself?"

"I have prescribed the betel root a couple of times and the patients said they felt better."

"Muscular aches tend to get better with rest and time, so how do you know the herbs helped?"

"The patients all felt it helped them. And that woman with the growth under her arm—she said the Chab pepper reduced the pain."

"That's good, but it's only one person. Let's gather as much of these herbs as possible. Back in the temple we can do more testing—like they do with medicines in Europe."

"That's a lot of work," Panya said. "We should just help whoever we can."

"What is that long vine there?"

"That's another kind of wild pepper vine. It provides relief from problems of mucus."

"Well, at least if it doesn't work as medicine, we will have lots of pepper for our stir-fry," he said and stood to help his friend carry the big bag of herbs. "We'll need to make sure we label everything. Let me get my notebook."

Two days later, he was sitting in the compound of Wat Tawan Tok bent over that notebook and listening to Phra Tissa, the temple's healer.

"Som, you are a good student. The best I have ever had. Your records of what cures what are helping refine our treatments," Phra Tissa said, sitting back on the long root of a *somphung* tree. "I appreciate this, but you need to think about the future. If you want to do this as a layman, then you have to charge people, like a doctor, and you have to find your own place of business. You already know enough to set up your own clinic. Maybe just down the road from here. You can't stay in the temple forever as a layman. The abbot is already asking me how much longer you expect to stay."

Was Tissa telling him he had to leave the monastery?

"But there is so much more work to do. We have already documented that some of the traditional Chinese herbs work only when the patients believe in them. We need to do more research, test with more patients, refine the dosages, and find ways to increase the concentration. We need to be certain whether the herbs work and how to use them."

"Uncertainty is part of life," the elderly monk said.

"Maybe we can eliminate some of the uncertainty," Som said. "We know we can't rely on the old Chinese or Khmer texts. We must follow the Buddha's teaching in the Kalama Sutra, examine the effects carefully, look at all the variables and experience the results for ourselves. As you have taught me, the Buddha says we cannot rely on the authority of the old teachings without testing them for ourselves."

"That is difficult and you rarely find out enough to reach a conclusion," Tissa said. "So, most of us ignore the Kalama Sutra. Phra Panya gets good results because he is so full of faith. He gets the patients to believe they will get well. Often they do."

"We shouldn't promise cures unless we are sure they work."

"Our medicines work better when the patients believe. So, we need to encourage belief."

"I don't know," he said. "I am already responsible for one death; I don't want to cause any more by giving the wrong medicine or the wrong dosage. Even if we decide the medicines are safe, we need to be sure they work and we can't be sure without a lot more study. I would not feel right charging people for unproven medicines."

"Then you need time to test willing patients and a way to live without income. I don't think you can survive without the support of the *Sangha*," Phra Tissa said. "You should think about ordaining."

8

SAIFAN
In the Mosque

Saifan walked barefoot into one of the side rooms of the Krue Se Mosque. He had often come here for Koran study, but today was different. Normally Imam Wae Muso would teach from the front of the room, sometimes writing in Arabic on the chalkboard. Today, the Imam sat to one side. The chalkboard was in the corner. Standing near the doorway was an elegantly dressed stranger, who examined each of the villagers as they entered the room.

Salim, an assistant to the Imam, sat down and turned to Saifan.

"That guy comes from the *Istana*. I have seen him with the raja. He's a real big shot."

When the last of the Krue Se people had entered, the stranger strode to the front of the room.

"I have called you here today because of your loyalty to your raja, your culture and your religion," the man began. "All of these are threatened by the aggression of the infidel Siamese, who grow more arrogant each day."

A murmur rippled through the three dozen villagers in the room. Although the raja's *Istana* was only a half-day's walk away, the Krue Se villagers rarely concerned themselves with the affairs of the capital. They visited the elegant *Istana* only for resolution of disputes, annual fairs or the shadow puppet performances sponsored by the raja. Some of the villagers had met the old raja and there had been genuine grief at his passing, but his son had never come to Krue Se.

"The Siamese high commissioner, who arrived five years ago, has stolen the rights of the raja, which are truly the rights of the Pattani people. He has tried to convert good Muslims to worship their shiny Buddha images. He wants us to bow down to their king in Bangkok as if he were a god when we know there is only one God. Their soldiers and officials bully us, saying they are helping us to develop. They force us to use their language."

This time the murmur was louder and many of the villagers nodded their heads. They had all had problems with the government officials who insisted they submit written requests in Thai. Few of the villagers could read or write Thai at all, much less the formal language the bureaucrats demanded.

This problem, however, had turned out to be an opportunity for Saifan. He had started writing letters and filling out forms for his friends as a favor, but many insisted on paying him with some eggs or fish. Strangers were now coming to his door and offering to pay in coins for Thai language help. The income had been a welcome addition to the meager profits from the goat meat stall.

"They disrespect our women," the man said, re-adjusting his brilliant satin turban. "You all know about the insulting behavior of the Siamese soldiers and police. They pulled the head coverings off innocent women right in front of the *Istana*. They loudly offered money for sex. We cannot allow such insults. We must protect the virtue and honor of our women."

"Worst of all, led by the so-called commissioner, they insult and undermine our religion. The commissioner himself brought a dog to the mosque, allowing this dirty creature to walk into the prayer hall reserved for the devout. This man has a Buddha image in his office so anyone going to see him must bow before it and worship the portrait of the Siamese king, who is not our king."

"Our king, our raja, is determined to put an end to these insults, but he will need your help. We will need all of you to help us throw back the invading Thais."

"What can we do against their soldiers with their guns and cannon?" the Krue Se village headman asked. "We are farmers and fishermen, not soldiers."

"Yes, but you are also men, men of honor who must protect their women, their religion and their way of life," the raja's man said. He lowered his voice to a harsh whisper that had the villagers straining to hear. "We are already buying arms from a German dealer in Singapore. With our greater numbers we can drive out the Siamese soldiers."

Saifan recalled his father's stories of past defeats by the Thai king.

"But sir, our forefathers have fought many times," Saifan spoke up. "Each time the Thais always came back in greater numbers," Saifan said. "My own great grandfather was wounded and imprisoned in an uprising that was quashed in a few weeks. Why will this time be different?"

The elegant stranger looked displeased for a moment, then smiled.

"That is an excellent question and something the raja has considered most carefully. He will not move rashly, but will gather new allies. The other rajas, so often divided by petty disputes, are joining together under the leadership of Raja Abdul Kadir. The rulers of Saiburi, Kelantan, Trengganu, Rengae and others are beginning to see they must work together. Even the English are concerned about the abuses by the Siamese. Their governor in Singapore is on our side. The cowardly Siamese will not dare stand up to the *farangs*. If the British falter, then we can turn to the French. They have already humiliated the Thai king with a few warships sailing right up to his palace, crushing Siamese defenses along the river. How much easier it will be for them to aid us in Pattani."

He thought of the Siamese troops and ships he had seen in Pakpanang and Nakhon. Could it be so easy? He thought of his brother unjustly convicted by the Siamese courts, tortured in a Siamese prison and somehow murdered by the Siamese jailers. His face reddened at the memory of his humiliation at the Pakpanang jail and his anger rose. If it were possible to defeat the Siamese, then he was willing to fight. For Abdul.

9

DAM
In the Police Station

Dam stood at attention and saluted the police chief. Although thinner and a head shorter, the chief seemed to look down on him as he paced around him. An infantry captain transferred from the regular army, Captain Serm had the upright posture of a military man and the dangerous air of someone who had seen combat.

"You look like a policeman. You have your uniform nicely pressed. Your sword is shiny. Your belt is polished. You seem to know how to salute," the chief said slowly and softly. "Are you really a sergeant in His Majesty's Royal Police?"

"Yes, sir."

"Then why don't you act like one," the chief shouted, rising on his toes to push his face up to Dam's chin.

"Why am I getting reports that you are beating people and acting like a bandit, a member of an illegal *Angyi*? I know you became a local policeman before the national police force was established. Do I have to remind you those days are past? Do I have to remind you the Pakpanang police became part of the national force more than a year ago? Do I have to remind you this station has been under my command since then and I have made clear the standards of conduct?"

"No, sir," Dam said in a voice that cracked embarrassingly.

"Truly? From these reports, it appears I do. We are servants of His Majesty who, you should not forget, has appointed a Danish officer to lead the national police force. We must be civilized. Ten days ago, Colonel Schau asked me to look into complaints from three Pakpanang merchants. They swear you beat them, in one case smashing three fingers so they were permanently crippled. The complainants said you work for a local money-lender."

"Sir, those reports are lies. Boss, sir."

"Shut your mouth," Serm said and smacked Dam on the side of the head. "Do you think I am stupid? Do you think I would speak to you without checking those reports myself? I found out you are fortunate only three reports of misconduct have been made. Most of your other victims appear too frightened to complain."

The chief continued to circle him with a furious stare.

"In less than five years here you have risen from the youngest and lowest man in the station to a sergeant in charge of a squad. You did good work against those pirates in the bay. You showed bravery in battle. You were wounded. You led the police to round up those drunken sailors. Five of you arrested 20 sailors armed with knives and clubs. You somehow get men to follow you into dangerous situations and you seem useful in a fight. Most of our men serve their two-year commitment and then leave, but you've stayed on. So, although I am not sure you can change, I am not going to give up on you."

"Thank you, sir."

"Shut your mouth and listen."

"You will stop working for this Chinese gangster. You will apologize to the three merchants who complained and everyone else you abused. I will check on this, so don't forget anyone. Henceforth you will follow the laws of the Royal Siamese government and my rules for this police station to the letter. You will thank me for reducing your rank to private. If you do this, I will let you stay on here."

It was unfair. Other policemen took payoffs. Other policemen beat suspects. Why was he singled out? He looked at the angry face of the captain. There was no mercy there. Nothing he could say would change the captain's decision. He had to remain a policeman. It was all he had. He swallowed and, without looking up, said "Thank you, boss."

"I will be watching you. Do not make me feel like a fool. Now get out," he said.

He saluted stiffly and left the office, his face still stinging from the chief's slap. He felt tiny and powerless. Back to being a private. All those years wasted. All the dangers endured. Bad things happened to him one after another. His mother died just when she was free. Useless doctors. Debtors too cheap to pay their debts, too cowardly to stand up to him, but sneaky enough to inform on him. No gratitude from Jate who still called him a stupid buffalo. Why did he keep working for Jate? He didn't need him anymore. The captain was right. He would cut loose from Jate and his gang and earn the admiration of the chief. He had to change his luck. He had to change his life. As he walked back to his table in the common room of the station, he saw two officers smirking at him. They must have heard the chief's dressing down. A surge of anger swept through him. Why did the chief have to humiliate him like this?

Tomorrow, he would be ousted from the officers' room and his sergeant's stripes would be taken away. He would no longer be allowed to wear the heavy sword that slapped so nicely against his thigh in his dress uniform. He would be back to carrying a heavy Mannlicher carbine like the other raw recruits instead of the Mauser C96 handgun he had just bought. As a private, he would have to follow the orders of someone newer than him, someone who had never faced the guns and knives of bandits. Worse, he would have to apologize to his victims, even those who were in the wrong for not paying their debts. It was unfair.

He could expect no sympathy from Jate. That squatty Chink would be furious at his demotion. Jate wouldn't care that doing his dirty work had been the cause. Someday Jate too would regret making him hurt people. The captain, Jate, that fucking *farang* colonel in Bangkok, they were all abusing him. Just like his father did. Just like the plantation owner abused his mother. Someday they would regret this.

He would change. He would even change his name. Dam brought bad luck. He would be smart and look after himself. He would refuse to be used. Without a family to help him, without money, without connections, he had only the police force and his ability in a fight. So, he would use those. Step by step he would regain position and power. He had friends in the force. He had his *takrut*. He pulled the necklace of tin tubes from under his shirt and rolled them in his fingers. This had power. He would see the abbot again. He needed that *yantra*—the one that could help him win the favor of others.

He had been too focused on protection in battle. Bravery was not enough. Killing bandits was not enough. He had been defeated by reports, sniveling complaints and bureaucrats sitting on their asses. He would find a way to rise despite all the paper policemen. The people he saved from crooks and bandits, the ship owners who got their property back from the pirates he caught, the victims of the crimes he punished—all these would give him honor. They would be his way forward. He would never be humiliated again.

10

PAKDEE
In the Istana

Pakdee scratched at his new beard and tugged on his white crocheted *taqiyah* so it fit his skull more tightly. He looped a string of prayer beads over his wrist and tried to appear calm. He felt like a *Likay* actor in costume and longed for a mirror to check his appearance. He practiced what he hoped was a look of scholarly earnestness. He sat on a low bench outside the raja's meeting hall. Beside him was Salim Hussein, the raja's secretary, holding a sheaf of documents. The secretary shuffled the papers, then shuffled them again. He's as nervous as I am about playing this role.

It had taken an hour of negotiation, inducements and threats before Salim had accepted a small sack of gold coins for his role in the plan. Their relationship was a wary one. Salim had sold him bits of information about Abdul Kadir's activities before, but now he had been paid more to do more.

Tension between the Malay rulers and the royal Siamese government had worsened in the past month. The commissioner asked him to do more to forestall any unrest. He had persuaded three British merchants to warn Swettenham that supporting the complaints of the Malay rulers could lead to violence harmful to British business interests in Siam. The key had been convincing Duff that concessions for new mines in Thai territory would come far more easily if he spoke to Swettenham.

Duff reported the governor had not been entirely convinced, but would limit his efforts to writing to the king asking him to slow the moves to wrest authority from the rulers. On getting the British governor's letter, however, King Chulalongkorn, had resisted the pressure. He gave full backing to ending all the Malay rulers' remaining taxation and judicial powers.

From Duff and his spies in the *Istana*, Pakdee had learned that the raja, frustrated by the failure of his appeal to the British, was ready to go beyond complaints. Raja Abdul Kadir had begun planning an armed uprising in hopes some European power would come to his aid. The Germans were looking for a foothold in the region. Abdul Kadir might also have been hoping for some kind of support from the French colonial government in Saigon, even without approval from the government in Paris. Phraya Sukhumnaiwinit told Pakdee he didn't think the Europeans would take the risk, but ordered him to find a way to get more direct influence in the raja's *Istana*. Salim—offered a substantial bribe and threatened with disclosure of past sales of information—had agreed to introduce Pakdee as a Malay scholar with excellent Thai language skills. The commissioner wanted him to take over translation of documents to and from the Thai government. That would put him in a key position. Would the raja agree?

The heavy carved teak doors opened and an *Istana* servant beckoned as a line of villagers backed their way out of the chamber. He was about to enter when he thought he recognized one of the villagers. Was it Saifan? It looked like him, but taller and heavier. There was a fringe of beard around his face. He watched as the young man spoke to an older man in the group. The face of the younger man had an expression of devotion, an expression he had sometimes seen on his younger brother. It must be Saifan. He put his head down and turned away as the villagers passed him. He watched them leave through the main door. Saifan had grown in the five years since he had last seen him. He would be what—20 years old? Already a man. But what was his brother doing in the palace of the Pattani raja? Had he recognized Pakdee?

He turned to see Salim looking at him in puzzlement.

"What are those folks doing here?" he asked the secretary.

"His Highness is trying to reach out to his people. He wants support. That group was from Krue Se village."

His family must have moved to Pattani. Was it just Saifan or were his mother and father here too? They would be stunned to know he was alive.

I should contact them, go to see them, at least let them know I am alive. Mother would be so happy. But once Father found out I am working for the Siamese government, he would think I am a traitor to the Malays and to our family. Yes, Father would be furious. What would Saifan think? He was in the *Istana* so he must be a supporter of the raja. How would he explain the death notice? Or waiting five years to show up? He felt like running out the door to embrace his brother and tell him all that he had suffered. But that would be stupid. Going to his family would ruin everything he had accomplished since prison. It would destroy the new Pakdee and betray Sukhumnaiwinit, the man who had saved him from prison. My family abandoned me. I owe them nothing.

Salim was staring at him. "Come, we cannot make the raja wait. You must be convincing or we will both be in trouble."

He suppressed the emotions boiling within him and tried to focus on the role he had to play. He followed Salim into the raja's chamber to find the raja looking at them impatiently. They bowed deeply. The raja nodded and gestured for them to sit. He and the secretary lowered themselves to a thick Kashmiri rug. The ruler slouched back in a large armchair.

Abdul Kadir was just about his age, but he looked older. This was the man Father had named him for. His Western-style jacket was open to show a white shirt stretched tight over a large belly. Beneath his cleft chin was a double fold of skin. A luxuriant handlebar moustache and thick black eyebrows divided his squat face in thirds. A black *songkok* sat not quite straight on his head. Below the thick neck a little black bow tie bobbed as he spoke.

"So, is this the fellow you have been telling me about?" the raja asked in the slightly nasal tones of Pattani *Jawi*. "The one who has been doing the translations for us."

"Yes, Your Highness. This is *Haji* Wan Mohammed al Fatani. He is a student from the school of Shaykh Dawud al Fatani and expert in both *Jawi* and Thai."

"Why have I never heard of him before?"

"He is newly returned from studies in Mecca and Medina," the secretary said, repeating the story he and Pakdee had agreed on.

Abdul Kadir turned to Pakdee.

"Your Thai is good even though you have been away so long?"

"I love to read, Your Royal Highness, and I brought many Thai books with me. The books and poetry do not have the gravity and beauty of our language, but they are enjoyable. I have also kept up an extensive correspondence with my Thai friends in Nakhon Srithammarat."

"From Nakhon. Yes, I hear it in your accent."

"My great, great grandfather fought for the Raja of Pattani. He was deported to Nakhon as a prisoner of war, but my family has always wanted to return. I am fortunate to finally have the opportunity to be of service to Pattani."

Abdul Kadir nodded and smiled.

"So, your family has long been loyal to Pattani and have shared in our suffering and subjugation to the infidel Siamese. That is propitious."

"Indeed, Your Highness, but I am sure, with your leadership, Pattani will once again shrug off oppression and flourish."

"We must all work together to end domination from Bangkok," the raja said, raising his voice so others in the room could hear.

"The Thais have killed and scattered so many of our people over the centuries," he said. "They have cut up the great kingdom of Pattani into seven sultanates, but we are still one people. Soon we will reunite and regain our birthright."

Abdul Kadir turned back to Salim, "Now, what is it you want?"

The secretary spoke up to deliver the rest of the story he had memorized.

"Your Highness, *Haji* Wan has helped me in his free time with the translation of all the Thai documents I have shown you over the months, but we are falling behind. Honored Royal Highness, I would like to beg your indulgence to employ him full time and allow him to work in the *Istana*."

"How much?"

Pakdee suppressed an urge to say he would work for free. The raja would trust his motivations more if he asked for payment.

"Twenty baht per month will suffice, Your Highness. It is an honor to work in the *Istana*, Your Highness, but I have expenses I have to pay."

Abdul Kadir flicked the back of his hand. "Fine, it is done. But you must not only translate what we give you. You must be on the alert for information to help us understand the Siamese. Seek out documents, posters, telegrams, books—anything that explains why they are so determined to destroy me and how they plan to do it."

"Yes, Your Highness."

An aide crawled up to the raja, whispered something and gave him a small slip of paper.

Abdul Kadir gestured to his secretary to come closer. Salim squinted in concentration as he read the note. He leaned forward and whispered in the raja's ear.

"So, this note says something about a spy. *Haji* Wan, tell me what you think."

Salim bowed to the sultan, stepped back and handed the paper to Pakdee.

He read the note quickly, working hard to keep his face impassive.

"Your Highness, this note indeed warns of a spy in your court. It says 'Your Royal Highness beware a spy in the *Istana*. He is working for your enemies.' The handwriting and style suggest it comes from an educated Thai person. From the phrasing, he is likely a Bangkok Thai. It is signed 'a friend of the Pattani people,' but anyone can write that. It could be that indeed there is a spy, but more likely this is a Siamese attempt to sow suspicion in the *Istana* and distrust among your supporters. With your permission, I will keep this note for further study. But, Your Royal Highness, please be careful. The Thais are deceitful."

The raja grunted and leaned forward, speaking quietly.

"Salim, you must watch the staff carefully in case this warning is true, but I think the *haji* is right; this is a trick to cause confusion. My people all love me, especially those in the *Istana*. I doubt any of them would work for the Siamese, but watch everyone."

"Yes, Your Highness. I will make this my highest priority," Salim said and stepped back as the raja rose from his seat and addressed the two-dozen people in the room.

"The Thai have sought to dominate the traditional rulers of Pattani for four centuries," Abdul Kadir said loudly. "We have sent regular tribute to Bangkok, but that is not enough for them. In the last five years they have prevented my succession to the full honor of my father's throne; they have taken away my role in the courts and they have stolen the funds needed to serve my people and maintain the prestige of the raja of Pattani."

Abdul Kadir's voice rose and his face grew red as he launched into what Pakdee knew were his common complaints against the Siamese.

"The *monthon* commissioner seizes my power for himself. He insults Islam and allows our women to be humiliated by the crude oafs he calls policemen. This cannot be endured any longer. I will make them regret their transgressions against me. I already have ..."

The raja stopped.

"Uh, so, I have petitioned the king in Bangkok to consider the actions of his commissioner. All the Malay rulers are behind me on this. We are now waiting for a response, but we must be alert. *Haji* Wan, you have made a good start, please begin working full time and report to Salim daily."

"Yes, Your Royal Highness."

A slight nod indicated the audience was over. Pakdee rose, bowed and backed towards the door as Salim crawled forward to hand some documents to the raja.

He sighed in relief, but kept his face somber and focused on the floor. Once out of the *Istana* he found a seat under a tree and looked at the note. He read it again. He had had no choice but to translate it with slight omissions. The note read: "Your Royal Highness beware a spy newly arrived in the *Istana*. This fake *haji* is working for your enemies." It was signed "A friend of the Pattani people." If the raja had been able to read Thai... He slipped the note into his shoulder bag. Who could have sent it?

Now, he was in position in the *Istana* and ready to alert the commissioner of any moves by the raja. Most important, he would be able to engineer the next part of the plan he had presented to Phraya Sukhumnaiwinit. If he was betraying his family, his race and his religion, so be it.

11

SOM
Ordination

"Elder Brother Som, are you sure?" Prem asked Somneuk as he adjusted the filmy white robes on his shoulders.

"Of course, I am sure," he said a little louder than intended. "Anyway, it's too late now. The donations have been made. Mother is happy. There is a crowd ready to proceed to the temple. The abbot is waiting."

"Yeah, but no women, no entertainment, no money, only two meals a day, all that chanting," Prem said. "Better you than me."

"You as a monk—that I would like to see," Somneuk said, ruffling his brother's hair. "As mother says about us: 'Even on the same stalk of bamboo, the knots are unevenly spaced, so even brothers may be of different minds.' For you it would be hard to give up all those girls you chase, the games you play and the food you love. For me, none of those things are important," he said. "I have been living at Wat Wang Tawan Tok for weeks now and the routine of the monks has not been a problem."

"I don't chase women anymore," Prem objected. "I follow the five precepts—well, most of the time. But now you will have more than a hundred rules."

"About Father," Somneuk said. "Maybe he would not have gotten so angry if I hadn't left. I don't know. I must do what I can to make up for that. Mother seemed so happy when I told her I was thinking of ordaining."

"Yes, it is a good thing you are doing—for Mother and for Father. Making merit for his spirit and all that."

"I am glad Mother is happy, but you know that is not why I am doing it. It's for me. I just seem to fit in the monastery better than in normal life. I will have the peace and quiet I want, the time to study and the chance to learn more about medicine, maybe help some people."

"Yeah, it's all good, but don't forget you can leave any time."

"We'll see, but for now it feels right."

"Then we better get going."

The brothers climbed down the stairs of the friend's house they had used for the preparations. Mother looked at him with a proud smile and gestured to a wooden stool. He sat before her. She touched his hair softly, pulled up a lock and then snipped it off with a small silver scissors. Grandfather picked up the big-bladed straight razor in work-toughened hands and scraped the back of his skull, leaving a pale strip of scalp. Then Prem took his turn.

"Sit still, unless you want to lose an ear," he warned with a laugh as he shaved another strip down the middle and then handed the razor to a wizened monk who finished the job.

Somneuk could feel the cool of the morning breeze on his damp scalp. He closed his eyes as the monk gently shaved his eyebrows and brushed the hairs into a bowl made of lotus leaves.

A cheer went up when he came to the door. The crowd had been waiting for an hour, already starting the libations from a row of brown bottles on the veranda. Many carried gifts of saffron robes, candles and baskets of provisions for the monks. A five-piece band, seated in a small cart started up with the wailing of a pipe and high-pitched rasping of the two-string fiddle. The powerful voice of the fat female singer seated in the middle of the cart rose above the music. Two drummers, their long wooden drums slung around their necks, started pounding out a steady beat. The procession started up with two old women leading the way, bending their hands with surprising energy and grace, dipping in front of him and then twirling away. Prem handed him three lotus blossoms and a bundle of joss sticks and pushed him forward.

Behind them, his mother's cousins passed around gourds of arrack and bottles of rice whisky. He had seen much more of these relatives since Father's death. His three aunts and his grandmother had come by with food wrapped in banana leaves. The men had sat down to provide fatherly advice. They had made much of his new Thai name, shortening Somneuk to Som. Everyone on the Thai side of the family had supported his decision to ordain, but all assumed he would stay in the monastery only for the remainder of the rainy season. They told him his time as a monk would make him a mature man who could take his place in the world and in the family. They urged him to marry quickly, to buy land, rather than investing in a new ship. The only real wealth was land, good flat paddy fields, or hillside orchards. There would always be a market for food, they told him.

"Let me ordain first and then we'll see," he had told them.

As the procession wound through the town, more people joined in. Many of them he had never seen before. More liquor was passed around in the swelling procession. The dancing grew wilder, and the music sped up, propelling the crowd through the narrow lanes and over the moat around the town. When they reached the carved gates of Wat Wang Tawan Tok, the dancing slowed and the singer fell silent. He felt Prem's arm around his shoulders.

"Prince, your noble steed has arrived," he said and hoisted him onto his back with a grunt.

It was good to have a strong brother.

From his perch, he could see the procession following behind as they walked slowly around the prayer hall. After one full circuit, one of the Thai cousins stepped forward to take over the role of the horse. More wiry young men competed for the honor. He was relieved when, after three times around the hall, the procession stopped in front of the ordination hall. Mother and his sisters stood beside the entrance. They carried what he would need as a monk—saffron-colored robes, a large alms bowl, candles, a bathing cloth and a towel.

The abbot, Venerable Brahmavamso, waved him inside where more than a dozen monks and three lines of novices sat in front of an array of bronze Buddha images glimmering in the semi-darkness. The abbot took his place in the center of the first row as Som's relatives placed their donations in front of the monks. He knelt before the abbot and bowed three times. He took the three sets of robes his mother had given him and laid them on a mat in front of the Abbot Brahm.

"Honored Sir, I respectfully ask for your compassion to ordain me as a novice so I may one day be freed from the cycle of existence," he recited. The abbot placed the robes in his hands. Phra Panya and another monk escorted him into a side room where they helped replace his filmy white outfit with the windings of a monk's robes. The shoulder fold kept slipping and he had to tug it back into place as he knelt once more before the abbot.

"You were born on a Friday, so your monk name must begin with an S. Your new name is Somdhammo and your preceptor's name is Venerable Tissa," Phra Panya told him.

Another new name and another new life—this time as a novice

monk. No longer the Chinese sailor Chao, nor the guilty son Somneuk, but the Buddhist monk Somdhammo whose life would be simple, peaceful and under control. He was grateful to the abbot for agreeing to ordain him in the middle of the rainy season retreat. The abbot had decided his seriousness of purpose, his long stay at the monastery as a layman, his efforts at meditation, and his help with the temple's herbal medicines had qualified him for immediate entrance into the *Sangha,* the brotherhood of monks.

The abbot said: "May the *Sangha* hear me. The candidate, Somdhammo, under the Venerable Tissa, has been examined. If the *Sangha* is willing, may he be allowed to come forward."

He approached the line of monks, bowed three times and knelt with his hands pressed together. He chanted the Pali verses he had practiced for much of the previous week.

> *Sangham Bhante upsampadam yacami.*
> *Ullumpatu mam bhante Sangho anukampam upadaya.*
> *Dutiyampi Sangham bhante*

"Venerable Sir, I respectfully request the *Sangha* to ordain me." At a nod from Tissa, he chanted the Pali verses that meant: "I take refuge in the Buddha. I take refuge in the dharma. I take refuge in the *Sangha*."

Then Abbot Brahm spoke up. "Somdhammo is the acolyte of Venerable Tissa. He is free from the Eight Obstacles. He has his robes and bowl. He begs admission to the *Sangha*. Let those who are agreed keep silent. If anyone does not agree, let him speak up."

What if someone objects? What if someone says his carelessness had caused the death of a boy? What if someone says he disrespected his father? Abandoned his mother?

"The *Sangha* is silent," the abbot said. "Therefore, Somdhammo is admitted to the *Sangha*."

I am now a monk. Panic rose in his throat. What would this new life bring?

12

PAKDEE
Deception

Pakdee checked his reflection in the windows besides the entrance to the *Istana*. His beard was fuller now and there were unfamiliar worry lines on his forehead. He looked exhausted. But his knitted white prayer cap fit his head well and he moved the dark prayer beads through his fingers as he had practiced. His long white robes resembled those of a scholar from Mecca. He had become this new person for more than a month now, but he still wasn't completely comfortable. Just a few more days.

The large wooden doors to the *Istana* compound swung open with a rumble and a series of creaks. He watched a procession of Siamese government officials walk slowly through the outer gate and approach the steps to the reception hall. Raja Abdul Kadir emerged from the hall and stepped forward to welcome them just as he had done the day before. He smiled and greeted the Siamese vice minister of the interior, Phraya Sri Sahadheb. The smile faded as he acknowledged *Monthon* High Commissioner Phraya Sukhumnaiwinit.

Pakdee fell in line with the *Istana* staff following the Siamese officials into the hall. They bowed to the raja, now seated in a large chair next to the Siamese vice minister. The raja nodded to him. His heart pounded as he thought about what would happen next.

The first meeting between the vice minister and the raja had gone well. As expected, Abdul Kadir had complained he had been robbed of authority and revenue by the *monthon* commissioner who now controlled his administration. He demanded Pattani be administered like the Malay sultanates further south, with real authority in the hands of the traditional rulers. He wanted his financial powers and judicial authority restored. Malay, he insisted, was the language of his people and therefore should be the official language of the Pattani government. Phraya Sri Sahadheb had politely acknowledged the raja's complaints. He had been briefed by Sukhumnaiwinit who warned that the region was on the brink of rebellion against the Siamese throne. His task was to soothe the raja's injured feelings.

Following Abdul Kadir's example, most of the other Malay rulers had sent their own petitions to the king. Some had also joined in the Pattani raja's complaints to the British. Pakdee's informants had told him Abdul Kadir had bought weapons from a German arms dealer. The other rulers also sought arms for their followers. Representatives of the rajas and sultans were holding meetings in the mosques to rouse popular anger against the Siamese government. How could they avert an uprising that would surely lead to deaths on both sides?

King Chulalongkorn had responded to the written petition from Abdul Kadir by offering negotiations, along with a warning against violence and a ban on bringing arms into the Malay areas. The plan was to have Vice Minister Sri Sahadheb do what he could to soften the anger in Pattani and defuse or delay any conflict. He had watched in admiration the previous day as Sri Sahadheb smiled and nodded sympathetically as Abdul Kadir repeated his litany of grievances. The vice minister had offered to draft a letter to the king explaining the raja's position. His Majesty, he said, would likely be sympathetic to the raja's concerns as long as they were politely and properly explained in an official letter that recognized the sovereignty of the Siamese king. Abdul Kadir had grudgingly accepted the offer. As expected, the raja had insisted on a *Jawi* language translation of the letter before he would sign it. So, he would now have to play the role they had anticipated for weeks.

Late the night before he had gone to the guest house where the Siamese delegation was staying, entering through the servants' entrance to avoid the *Istana* guards at the front entrance. The commissioner gave Pakdee two documents. One was a copy of the Thai language letter to King Chulalongkorn that Sri Sahadheb had presented to Abdul Kadir. The other was a list of points he was supposed to omit or obscure in his translation.

"Keep the same number of sentences and the same layout," Sukhumnaiwinit said. "Your translation must appear complete, so a casual read will not reveal much difference from the Thai version."

"I think I can do that."

"The differences can be subtle, but the *Jawi* version must not show the acceptance of a lesser role that is clear in the Thai," the commissioner said.

"Yes, I can do that," Pakdee said, "but what if there is another warning about a spy?"

"I questioned everyone in the office. No one admitted to knowing anything about that letter," the commissioner said. "In any case, we have no choice now but to move ahead with the plan. It is the best way to regain control without loss of life."

He had returned to the *Istana* and worked until almost dawn completing the *Jawi* translation. It had to convince Abdul Kadir the letter asserted his rights and made his demands. Father and Saifan would see this as a betrayal, but he could not think of family now. If the plan failed, an armed rebellion would be hard to stop. So, he was saving lives, Malay lives. If it succeeded, his hopes of being someone, of being able to protect himself, of rising in the Siamese system could be fulfilled.

Standing to one side of the raja, he looked out over the assembled officials, the Malays with their black *songkoks* and white *taqiyah* prayer caps, the Thais in their white uniforms with colorful medals. All stood stiffly before the seated raja and vice minister, each trying to edge slightly forward. He inched back, happy to be out of sight behind two of the raja's burly guards. The velvet bag holding the *Jawi* and Thai letters felt hot against his chest. He could feel the rapid beating of his heart. There was a mumble of conversation and then the raja's secretary called in a loud voice: "*Haji* Wan Mohammed al Fatani."

This was the moment. He bowed to both dignitaries and then knelt to present the bag to the raja. Raja Abdul Kadir pulled out the two documents inside and focused on the *Jawi* language letter. Then he looked up and held out the *Jawi* letter.

"Haji Wan, read your translation aloud so all can hear it," he ordered.

His throat went dry and his tongue felt thick. He could see Phraya Sukhumnaiwinit nodding encouragement. The text looked blurred for a moment. Then it cleared and he began to read.

"Louder, please," the raja said.

He cleared his throat and started again. It seemed to take forever to finish. Finally, there was no more and he handed the paper back to the raja.

"This is a little blunt, not as elegant as I might write it, but, if that is the tone of the Thai letter, I like it. It is time to be clear about the problems that have been visited upon us by the actions of the commissioner. Is this a full and accurate translation?"

His heart raced, but he forced himself to reply calmly. "Yes, Your Royal Highness. This is full and accurate."

The raja smiled. "Then I will sign."

He took an ornate silver pen from an assistant and bent over the Thai language letter. High Commissioner Sukhumnaiwinit watched anxiously from the side of the vice minister and then caught his eye with the slightest of smiles.

"Thank you for your services," the raja said and nodded.

He bowed and retreated backwards. Looking back at the three high-ranking dignitaries, all looking pleased, he felt a sudden stab of guilt and one of his afternoon headaches coming on.

What will come of what I have done today?

13

SOMDHAMMO
A New Life

Phra Somdhammo grabbed at the robe slipping off his shoulders. He raised the end of the saffron-colored cloth high above his head with one hand and re-rolled it, tucking it in again. It had been more than a month since his ordination and he still had trouble keeping his robes from slipping.

The abbot started the chant, then the monks joined in. Their sonorous voices were soothing and the rhythmic chant was lulling Som into a half-sleep. He had been up late the night before studying a medical text he had found in the library at Wat Mahathat. It had been a relief to get out of the temple after the rainy season retreat and walk through the town. He had been a monk for less than half of the three-month retreat. How would he survive the full retreat next year?

He felt the quick thrust of an elbow in his side and saw Phra Panya glaring at him. He had forgotten to chant. He tried to pick up the verse. Memorizing the chants was his least favorite part of the monkhood. He liked the sound of it, but understood only bits of the Pali language of the chants, so they were mostly meaningless to him. Deciphering the Khmer language of the medical texts he had found stored in wooden chests at Wat Mahathat was more useful. The texts, some written on palm leaves, gave interesting suggestions on herbs helpful in dealing with different conditions. Starting points, at least, for experiments.

Life as a monk had been more difficult than he expected. Getting up an hour before dawn for prayers was one thing when you could skip it if you had a late night, but more difficult when it was required every day. As a layman he had enjoyed the time to study or meditate, but now that he was a monk, his free time had disappeared. The morning alms rounds through town took more than an hour. Sometimes his alms bowl would be filled in a few minutes, but the abbot insisted that the monks complete their route for the day.

"The people wait for us so they can show their devotion. We cannot disappoint them," he said.

He tried to practice his walking meditation during the alms rounds. He sought to focus his attention on the feeling of his bare feet touching the ground, one step after another, ignoring the morning crowd of people along the road. With his stomach grumbling, he sneaked looks at the food placed in his bowl. He was supposed to receive everything with calm acceptance, but he couldn't help noticing when he was given a special treat, like Chinese dumplings with bean paste. His mother and his sisters had prepared many of his favorite foods and traveled to Nakhon to place them in his bowl the first few days of his monkhood. Lately, however, they came only on special religious days. It was a long journey from Pakpanang and they were busy managing the warehouse. His thoughts now drifted to them more often. He missed the girls' chatter, their shy questions about life and the giggling that seemed to have no cause other than their youthful spirits. Recently their questions had been more practical: shipping costs, the value of different cargoes and the best way to store perishable goods. They were clever. They understood some things better than Father. Toh seemed to know how to deal with customers and Wan was meticulous about the record-keeping. They were learning the business so quickly.

Most of the women coming to the temple were older than Mother, with dark-red, betel-stained teeth and gray hair. They paid most attention to the older monks, asking for advice about their grandchildren, family quarrels or dealing with the death of a relative. He was too young to have any credibility as a counselor. Still he had to sit silently beside Phra Tissa as he listened to the women's problems. That was part of his duty as a disciple of the elderly preceptor. The problem was it took another two hours out of his day.

The abbot had assigned him to teach reading and writing to the temple boys. Today one of them had put a frog in the clay water jar. The boys had hooted and laughed when the frog jumped out as he was about to drink. Then one of the boys had whacked another with his writing slate and he had to separate their angry, squirming little bodies to prevent further injury. It was not teaching the class that bothered him or even the impish naughtiness of the boys, but the fact that it took more time out of his day.

Even worse was being assigned to go into town for one ritual or another such as blessing a new shop or performing a ceremony to remove bad luck from the site of an accident. In the temple, funeral rites occupied many evenings and marriage blessings took many mornings.

He was surprised at the amount of ritual activity. Father had thought religion was a waste of time, so his mother had gone to the temple on her own or with one of her sisters. Once he started making long voyages on The Wind Uncle, his only religious activities had been Chinese rites to appease the various sea and weather gods. The only purpose he could see in any of those rites was to reassure the fearful. How could chanting the dharma in Pali help a young couple deal with married life when they couldn't understand a single word of Pali? Some of the supposedly Buddhist rites seemed to have little to do with the Buddha's teaching. He was trying his best to read through the Buddhist texts in the temple library, but there didn't seem to be any mention of these rites, or monasteries, or even Buddha images. None of these things, now seen as essential elements of the religion, existed in the time of the Buddha. When he asked the senior monks what the Buddha had said about sacred white cords and lustral water, they had no answer and grew annoyed if he asked again.

All these duties meant there was little time for what he wanted to do most—to practice meditation and learn more about medicine. He helped Phra Panya dispense herbs to the sick in the late afternoons. The portly monk was popular for his generosity with the medicine and his good humor. His stories, jokes and comments seemed to cheer up even the most seriously ill. Panya, however, was more eager to dispense the medicines than to see if they worked. He often forgot to record what medicine had been given to which villager. Any sign of recovery was welcomed as due solely to his treatment.

Each patient had a page in the medical ledger he had started. Panya had agreed to write down symptoms, treatments and results with specific amounts and dates, but he often forgot. Sometimes he got so caught up in chatting with the patient that he failed to record anything at all. Som tried to fill in the missing information, but often Panya couldn't remember.

"It doesn't matter. They are recovering," he liked to say. "Recovery is all that counts."

Phra Tissa also seemed uncomfortable with Som's medical work. His preceptor had unshakeable faith in the treatments described in the old palm-leaf texts and wanted no variation or experimentation.

Whenever he told the old monk a traditional treatment wasn't helping, Tissa would just smile and say, "That is what is written."

He tried to use the early afternoon, when most of the monks took a nap, to grind herbs and try different mixtures. Some of these experiments came from the old Khmer writings; others came from Chinese books on herbal medicine. Often, he would crouch over these books in the light of a candle long into the night. He tried to reconcile the Khmer and Chinese understandings of disease, but there were so many differences. The conflicts were even greater with what he had learned from Western medical texts. His experiments further complicated his record-keeping and often left it uncertain what worked and what didn't. It had only been a month, so maybe things would become clearer—if only he could find more time.

His meditation practice also was proving difficult. Not only was there little time in the day left for meditation, but Phra Tissa was unable to guide him through the problems he had in keeping focused. Too often his mind was like that frog jumping out of the water jar and skittering out the door. Thoughts would stray from the object of his meditation to a patient's problems, to worries about his mother, to concerns about Prem, or to wondering what good would come from all this time devoted to meditation. Memories of the storm and the lifeless body of Tum often intruded. Sometimes the image of Father's slack face and panicky eyes would rise before him. Pulling his mind back to his breathing or his steps was difficult. Phra Tissa's own meditation practice was mostly an opportunity for a nap in the lotus position. Like the abbot, Tissa wanted him to concentrate on learning the chants rather than meditation.

With a start, he realized he had fallen behind the chant. He was on a different verse than the rest of the monks. Then the chanting stopped while he continued on alone for a moment. The monks put down their fans and clambered to their feet. As he started to rise, he found the abbot glaring at him.

14

PAKDEE
Disappearance

Pakdee looked into the small mirror he had pulled from his shoulder bag and an unfamiliar face looked back. His beard and mustache were gone. His long hair was gone. His pale skull gleamed in the light streaming through a porthole. Three days after assuring the raja of the accuracy of his translation, he had learned Abdul Kadir planned to send copies of the Thai letter and the Malay version to another translator. The raja now had doubts about his translation after hearing the confusing news of Sahadheb's discussions with Swettenham in Singapore. The British governor had expressed surprise Abdul Kadir had accepted Siam's new measures for governing Pattani. A new translation would soon reveal his deception. So, he had abandoned his belongings and hurried to the port. This had been the plan all along. It was just happening faster than expected.

"Haji Wan must vanish," Phraya Sukhumnaiwinit had ordered. "No one, not even our own staff must be able to connect him with you or me."

He wrapped a cotton *phakaoma* around his waist, pulled the front up between his legs and tucked it in behind his back. Looking like a worker who had just completed his time in the monkhood, he descended the gangplank. He was about to drop the bag into the sea when he stopped and opened it. He pulled out the note that had almost doomed him and tucked it into his waist. The bag went into the water with a quiet splash.

He walked down the dock as a group of *Istana* guards rushed towards the steam ship. Would they recognize him? He lowered his head and the guards passed without a glance.

Raja Abdul Kadir will be furious once he understands how he had been deceived. With the departure of Haji Wan, his wrath would fall on Salim. That couldn't be helped. At least the man had been well-paid.

He still had to get away from Pattani. There should be a boat willing to take him up the coast. At the end of the pier, he climbed down to the sand and walked along the long curve of Pattani Bay.

Dozens of brightly-painted boats were pulled up on the shore and a half-dozen more were anchored in the shallow bay. Finally, he saw one with a couple of crewmen getting ready to sail. He waded out to the boat and stopped to admire the intricate paintings on its sides. There were green-feather wings, big curves of blue fish scales and what looked like eruptions of blue and gold spray all interwoven. As the stern swung towards him, two large painted eyes stared back at him. It would be good to have them checking for pursuers as he sailed north and away from Pattani and all its anxieties. He showed the sailors a few coins and the deal was quickly agreed. He clambered aboard and the two crewmen unfurled the sail. It filled with the breeze flowing across the bay. He would soon be safe. Settling back against a sack of rice, he relaxed for the first time in weeks.

Two days of slow sailing brought him back through the inlet to Songkhla Lake and the *monthon* office. He slipped in through a back door and changed into his office clothes. He told the monkhood story to anyone who remarked at his shaven head. He had gone home to ordain and make merit for his parents who had passed away from a fever. The other officials were sympathetic about his loss, but later teased him about deserting them during the hard work of the vice minister's visit and the negotiations with the raja.

15

DAM
A Buffalo No More

Dam saw the man out of the corner of his eye. It looked like trouble.

He was patrolling the docks on the southeastern side of the river, a regular assignment since his demotion. The docks were lit only by the half-moon in a clear night sky. He could hear the lap of river waves against the pilings and the muffled sound of shops closing up for the night. He reached under his shirt to touch the necklace of tin tubes. Footsteps sounded on the weathered wood to his left. More footsteps behind him. They were not making any effort to be quiet. If only he still had his pistol.

He was relieved to see Nit's jowly face in the moonlight. Two more of Jate's men approached from behind a warehouse. He was still uneasy, but he raised his hands in a *wai*. Jate must be upset about something.

He had followed Captain Serm's orders to stop working for the Chinese businessman, but he hadn't said anything to his old boss. He might be betraying the man who had given him direction, had dominated his life for so long, but he felt relieved he no longer had to endure Jate's insults. Jate should understand and leave him alone.

"Dam, we haven't seen you for a long time," Nit said. "Where have you been?"

"I have been busy with police work. I no longer have my own unit, so I can't get away. And I have changed my name to Sakda. You should call me Sakda."

"Sakda—what does that mean?"

"Man of power and influence. One who wins out over others."

Nit burst out laughing. "Well, Private Sakda, I guess if you get demoted and lose power and position, you should at least have power in your name."

"Changing my name is just the first step. *Luang Paw* Klai told me it is only, what did he call it, a symbol. My new name is a symbol of how I am changing my life."

"Well, Dam, that might be a good thing for you, but the Boss is unhappy that you have forgotten him. He wants to see you."

"I am on patrol. I will try to find time later."

"Now. He wants to see you now and we have to make sure you come."

Dam looked at the three men ranging around him. Two had knives tucked in their waists and one held a heavy cudgel. Maybe he could take them. Maybe not. "Well, if we can make it quick," he said.

"The house is nearby. You know where it is," Nit said. "We will come along in case losing your name has caused you to lose your memory. Don't make this into a problem."

"No problem," he said, offering a smile he didn't feel.

With Jate's men on each side and one behind him, they climbed up the back stairway and entered the room where he had picked up the unconscious body of that *khaek* boy. Jate sat at a wooden table, a pair of candles lighting his face.

"Dam, I am glad you have come to see me after all this time," Jate said in a friendly voice. "I was sorry to hear that you have had problems."

"Yes, I am no longer a sergeant—just a private again. And I have a new name. I am now Sakda."

"To me you are still Dam and you will have to work your way back to sergeant again. A private isn't so useful to me."

"Sakda. Call me Sakda."

"I'll call you whatever the fuck I want and you will come whenever the fuck I call you. You have to prove to me my stupid mountain buffalo can be useful again."

A flash of anger seared him for a moment. No, he had to stay calm. He had changed. He would not be stupid.

"It is because I did your dirty work that I am no longer a sergeant. The police chief knows about you and the debt collections. He had names and details. There were complaints all the way to the royal court. I can't continue to serve you and remain a policeman."

Jate glowered and shook his head.

"That scrawny puppet of the *farangs* doesn't know as much as he thinks he does. You let him walk all over you, so now we are forced to make some changes. You will no longer have the pleasure or the payments for collecting debts. I can find others for that. However, I will need information from time to time—warnings of any police action that will affect my businesses. I want to know if there are any more complaints about me. If there are any signs my shipments have attracted the attention of customs officials or the police. You can do this without getting into trouble if you don't act stupidly."

That word stupid again. People thought he was stupid because he was big and clumsy, because he spoke with the rough southern accent of the hills, because he couldn't recite poetry or all that other shit that men do to appear to be something they are not. Jate had always treated him like a child, giving him detailed instructions for even the simplest task. He wasn't stupid. The only thing stupid thing he had done was continuing to work for Jate after joining the police.

"Yes, Boss. I can supply information."

"Then we agree. I want you to meet with Nit from time to time to let us know what is happening with the police. You won't have to risk the anger of that skinny captain by meeting with me."

"Of course. As long as we are careful, I can be helpful—but because there is risk and work involved, I will need payment each time I meet with Nit."

"You ungrateful lizard," Jate spat out. "Who gave you food and money when you had none? Who helped you buy your mother out of slavery?"

Jate had never given him anything—it was always payment for services. This was not the time to rouse Jate's temper.

"Boss, you are right, of course, but that is all past. I am in a position to help and I truly want to help you. This is just business. You taught me this. I take risk. You benefit, so you pay."

"I'll see first whether what you do is worth anything. Then, I'll think about payment. Now get out of here."

He climbed down the back stairs. This was the last time. He would not risk losing his position in the police for a man who had always used him like a club to batter someone with. He would avoid meeting Nit whenever possible. He would provide information that was late or worthless—just enough to avoid Jate's anger. Play the game, but from now on look out only for his own interests. Jate just didn't know it yet.

16

PAKDEE
Opening a Wound

SONGKHLA, FEBRUARY 14, 1902

Pakdee gathered the files for the morning briefing and handed them to his assistant. He looked around his office. It was large, second only to the commissioner's. At the commissioner's instructions, the office had been decorated with carved teak furniture, a silver tea set and an altar with candles and Buddha images. A recent portrait of King Chulalongkorn looked over his shoulder.

Three of his staff were working in the adjoining office. He had gotten them transferred from Somsak's clerk staff. One was banging away on a typewriter—the same one he had once used himself. Two others were Malay staff he promoted to serve as intermediaries to the *Istana* staff he had contacted as *Haji* Wan. They had each been well-bribed to send him information on the raja's plans and activities. Another set of informants helped him understand the feelings in the villages of Pattani and in the royal palaces of Saiburi and Rangae. The young man he had recruited from Krue Se was especially important. High Commissioner Sukhumnaiwinit now depended on Pakdee for much of his information on resistance to the reform of local administration. As personal private secretary to the commissioner, he was the key advisor and conduit to the leader of the *monthon*.

He took a last look in the mirror, secured the top button on his high-collared white jacket and headed towards the high commissioner's office. They had to think through the next steps against Abdul Kadir. The raja had reacted with rage and dismay when he learned the letter he signed agreed to the king's appointment of a secretary for the Pattani administration and the government secretary's signature was required for any decree. Now that secretary was waiting in Songkhla for a ship to take him to Pattani.

"Close the door behind you," Phraya Sukhumnaiwinit ordered as he took the files from his assistant.

So, this would be just the two of them.

"How do you think the raja will receive the secretary?" the commissioner asked.

"There will be indignant protests to the king and maybe to the British," Pakdee said, "but we are in a strong legal position because the raja signed that letter. Now it will look like he is trying to go back on his word. Fortunately, my *Jawi* language version has somehow disappeared from the *Istana's* files."

"That was well done," Sukhumnaiwinit said, "but I am not worried about our legal position. The raja still has those German weapons hidden somewhere, and he has called on the British officials in the Straits Settlements to seize all of our Malay states. The Pattani raja is seen as the leader of the Malays by the other rulers. This could easily erupt into another revolt."

"My informants tell me that Abdul Kadir has called on his supporters in the countryside to come to the *Istana* a week from today. I think he is planning something."

"Would he try to use his palace guards to arrest the secretary?"

"It is a possibility."

"He must know that would bring down the wrath of the Royal Siamese Government."

"Maybe he feels he has nothing left to lose."

"Then he is mistaken."

Phraya Sukhumnaiwinit stroked his mustache and looked up at the large portrait of King Chulalongkorn on the wall.

"Violent unrest in the south would upset His Majesty so soon after all his problems with the French and those uprisings in the northeast," he said. "We need to act decisively. There is an old proverb that applies here: 'When grasping, grasp firmly; when squeezing, squeeze to death; when aiming, aim straight at the heart.' We need to send troops and a warship with the new secretary. We will call it an honor guard. It will be an overwhelming force the *Istana* guards will not dare oppose. Instead of the raja arresting the secretary, we will arrest the raja. We will squeeze his defiance to death."

"What about his supporters who will be meeting at the *Istana*?"

"If we act quickly, before any weapons are distributed, we can crush them without problem. The meeting of local leaders actually works well for us. We can arrest them at the *Istana* and hold them, so there will be no uprising in the countryside. What do you think?"

"It is a drastic plan, a bold plan," he said. "It should solve the immediate problem of the raja, but it will inflame feelings against the government. The Malays will feel dishonored. If they lose their raja, it will be hard to bring them willingly into the new Siam."

"They won't lose their raja; we will just find someone else to appoint, maybe the old uncle. So, the people will have their raja, but a raja without power or weapons. Once Abdul Kadir is arrested and moved far away, the other rulers will fall into line."

"I am worried that will open a wound in the Malay people."

"Better a wound than losing the whole limb," Phraya Sukhumnaiwinit said. "You saw the reports on His Majesty's talks with the British governor in Singapore. Swettenham had the audacity to tell His Majesty Pattani and the other *khaek* states had become a danger to Siam and the king should 'get rid of them,' presumably by handing them over to him. This is what the imperialist party in London wants and they get support from Swettenham. The man even warned that the Malays would rise in rebellion against us and drive us from the peninsula."

"But the king stood up to him and refused to consider losing any more territory," Pakdee said.

"Yes, but he had to agree to the appointment of British advisers to our Malay states."

"That might not be so bad. We've had British advisers before and they ended up working well with us. It is the local rulers we have to worry about and Abdul Kadir is the most dangerous. If he rebels, the other sultans might follow."

"So then, you agree. Arrest the raja?"

"It will cure the immediate pain, but it will be a wound that will never heal. If we do this, we need to treat him respectfully."

"I will issue the orders to the military commander and the secretary. Alert your network to report any action from the raja."

He bowed and backed out of the office. He needed to send instructions to the network and brief the navy. But before anything, he had to do something about Krue Se.

17

SAIFAN
Confusion

Saifan hurried to the mosque, his worn leather sandals raising puffs of dust in the path. He washed at the entrance and hurried into the prayer room, though he was not going for prayers. As he entered, he saw the same villagers who had met at the mosque a week earlier. That official from the *Istana* had told them the raja was calling on them to show their support for their true ruler and their opposition to the secretary arriving from Bangkok to interfere with the raja's rule.

He had explained the raja wanted the villagers from Krue Se and all the villagers around Pattani town to come to the *Istana* to show their support. Imam To' Guru Wae Muso and all the leaders of Krue Se had agreed. But then, only a day before the planned march, a letter had arrived saying the march had been postponed and the villagers should plan to come the following week.

Now the Imam was reading another letter and shaking his head.

"Is there a new date for the march?" Saifan asked as he sat in front of his teacher. "I heard some of the other villages have already gone."

The Imam ignored him as he frowned at the letter in his hand.

"Listen everyone. I have gotten a note from the assistant to the Imam of Raja Chabang Tiga Mosque in town. It is confusing, but this is what he wrote:

> 'We are undone. The Imam is taken. Three days ago, soldiers came with the ship. They seized all of us waiting at the *Istana*, herded us to the prison. For two days we had nothing but rice gruel and water. We had to tell them our names and where we lived, what we did, before they would release us. Some are still in the prison where there is hardly room to move. We saw the *Istana* guards, their hands tied behind them, lying face down on the ground. The townspeople say the raja, the Imam and senior *Istana*

officials were taken by closed coach to the ship and pushed aboard. The ship is gone. Siamese soldiers with long guns are everywhere and many Siamese officials have moved into the *Istana*. They are showing what they say is a letter of abdication, but it is in Siamese, so it must be fake. They say the uncle of the raja has taken his place, but no one has seen him. There was word today from Saiburi saying three more rajas have been removed and there are soldiers in all seven Malay cities. The *sharia* courts are closed and the officials ordered to go home. From now on the only laws will be those approved by the Siamese king. All court documents must be in the Siamese language. They are destroying our language and our lives. All this is beyond endurance."

The group of villagers sat silently for a moment. Then several spoke at once. Wae Muso tried to quiet them, but the shouts from the normally soft-spoken villagers grew louder.

"We cannot allow this."

"They are destroying us."

"Our father is taken."

"Defend the religion."

"What can we do?"

"We must fight back."

"What do you know about killing or fighting?"

"Maybe some foreigners will help."

"The foreigners in the south are as bad as those in Bangkok."

"They have all the guns."

"We have our *kris* and our courage."

"But they have all the guns and the ships and the soldiers."

The Imam waited until the shouts died down to an angry murmur.

"Please be calm. Yelling does nothing," he said. "We must act in accordance with our beliefs. The Prophet has written: 'If you fear treachery on the part of a people, break off with them. God does not like the treacherous.' We must resist the Siamese treachery by pulling away. Ignore their laws. Refuse to go to their meetings. Withhold tax payments and let God punish them."

The old religious scholar looked uncertain. Wae Muso was 60 years old and had focused his life on studying the Koran. This was too much for him. He needed help to show some backbone.

Saifan stood up and faced the room of angry villagers.

"The Imam is wise," he said, "but it is written in the Holy Koran that 'Oppression is more serious than murder.' And this is oppression." He heard several shouts of agreement behind him and pressed on.

"There are many passages in the Koran calling on us to fight the unbelievers and end oppression. The book of Al-Baqara, verses 190-191 says 'fight in the cause of God those who fight you, but do not commit aggression; God does not love the aggressors. And kill them wherever you overtake them, and expel them from where they had expelled you.' Surely it is not aggression to defend ourselves from the Siamese oppressors and expel them from Pattani."

The Imam looked anguished, Saifan thought. Maybe his words were too strong. There had been troubles at the death of the last raja, but that disturbance had passed without touching Krue Se. The Imam must be hoping the village again could remain undisturbed. But the arrest of the raja was too much to take. The Krue Se villagers had been fortunate not to have been arrested at the *Istana* with the other supporters. That mysterious letter had stopped them from going. Maybe he would have died in prison like his brother. Was that letter a trick of the Siamese to reduce the show of support for the raja? Why only Krue Se?

Growing up in Pakpanang with no Malay ruler, no official *Jawi* language, no *sharia* court, and only a small prayer hall instead of a full mosque, he had felt his life had been without weight, without a center, that he floated on the edges of life like the flotsam in the river. In Pattani, all that had changed. The grandeur and ceremony at the *Istana* had given him a sense that being Malay and Muslim meant something bigger than family or village. There was a history and an importance to their lives and a long tradition reaching back centuries. There was pride in having a ruler who respected the traditional ways and enforced both Malay *adat* and *sharia* law. And those traditions protected Krue Se from a confusing outer world dominated by unbelievers. There was a feeling of community in Krue Se. There might be disputes over land or space in the market, but everyone in the village worshipped together at the mosque. They all spoke *Jawi,* and they depended on one another in a storm or a flood. When he worked in the market or came to prayers people called him 'brother'. There were no money lenders charging outrageous interest. There were no Chinese merchants buying low and selling high. They rarely saw any Siamese officials with their strange rules and frequent demands for payment. It was a good life, a peaceful life. And now it was being threatened.

18

PLOI
After Birth

Ploi looked up at Prem with a tired smile. She held their first child in her arms. A warm feeling of contentment seeped from the baby into her body. The birth had come after four hours of labor. It seemed much longer. Her mother and the midwife had stayed with her, encouraging her throughout. She heard Prem stomping back and forth on the wooden platform outside the door. Every few minutes he would lean in and ask whether it was over yet.

"If you are going to keep bothering us, get in here and make yourself useful," she finally yelled at him. The midwife told him to sit behind her so he could support her back and she could grab his thighs when the contractions came.

When the baby at last slid out into the hands of the midwife, Prem kissed her neck. He gently lowered her head to the pillow.

"We have a son—a new member of the family," he said.

"Give him to me," she commanded.

The midwife pulled two cotton cords from her bag and tied off the umbilical cord before cutting it. The baby relaxed into her arms and she lay back with a sigh. Prem looked horrified by the blood on the baby's face and bits of white tangled in his dark, damp hair.

"Is it alright?"

"It is fine and healthy," the midwife said as she wiped the baby with a damp cloth.

Ploi took the baby's hand. She counted the fingers and then the toes. "He has all ten fingers and ten toes," she said, looking up at Prem with a weary smile.

He beamed at his new child before noticing the midwife gathering the bloody placenta into an earthen jar. She pushed the jar into his hands.

"It is the father's job to bury it," she said.

Prem looked around uncertainly until Mother pushed him towards the door.

Ploi looked down at the baby and then up at her mother.

"Do you think he looks like Father?" she asked.

"I hope not," Mother said. "He looks like most babies, yellow skin wrinkled like an over-ripe mango. But he will look better in a few days."

"Send word to Father so I can show him his new grandson," she said.

Father would be proud of her and happy to have a grandson. Her older half-sister, Un, had two girls, but they were in Bangkok with Un's mother and never visited the south. Elder Brother Chit had two or three children with different women, but no longer lived with any of them. The last word from Chit was that he had broken up with his rich Phuket woman and was headed to Penang on a new business venture. He came to her to borrow money for an investment he promised would pay back double within a year. She would never see any of that money again, but it was worth it to have Chit further away. She and this new baby would be all important to Father.

Elder Sister Cheuy was still at home, but she was devoted to their mother and helped run the household. She had shown no interest in any of the men who had shown up eager to marry the *kamnan's* daughter. No, she had given Father the only grandson he could actually hold in his arms. So, where was he?

Father seemed to have resigned himself to her marriage to Prem.

"Now she is your responsibility," she had heard her father tell Prem three months earlier. "You will have to take care of her and take control of her. It's not my job anymore," he said.

Good, he accepts the marriage, she had thought. But he still looks at me like I am a child.

"I can take care of myself," she said. "Who do you think has been sending you money every month? Without that money, where do you think you would be? Without my 'loans' where would Chit be?"

Father had spent little time at the house in the final months of Ploi's pregnancy. He claimed he didn't want to attract the attention of the spirits known to haunt pregnant women. It was just an excuse to spend more time with his third wife.

She watched as the midwife took the baby and sprinkled it with white and yellow powder before returning it to her. His skin was so soft and his fingers were so tiny and perfect. She put his little hand to her lips. His eyes looked up unfocused and then slowly closed behind their long delicate lashes. She felt his chest rise and fall against her as he breathed. So tired. Slowly, contentedly, she relaxed into sleep.

When she woke, she felt the baby at her side. His eyes were closed but he was making tiny sucking noises. His delicate lips sucked in and then pushed out. He must be hungry. She pushed aside the cloth over her shoulder and offered him a nipple. Without opening his eyes, he latched on to the breast. A strange thrill leapt from her breast down to her toes. He reached up both hands to hold onto the breast. His grip was strong. She brushed back the fine hair on his forehead and marveled at the perfection of his eyebrows. He was beautiful.

There was a rustle. She looked up to see Prem leaning back against the wall, watching her. He had a dreamy smile on his face. He should be smiling. She had gone through all this trouble to give him a son. To give them a son.

"What shall we call him?" she whispered. "No Chinese names."

"I talked to the abbot at Wat Tai. He says the stars indicate the boy will be a great speaker and since he was born on Saturday, the name Praphot would be good."

"Praphot," Ploi said as the baby wriggled against her, "sounds dignified and important. I like it."

"My son, Praphot," Prem said as he watch the baby struggle to find a breast."

"But he squirms like a tadpole," Ploi laughed, "so his nickname will be Awt."

She shifted to offer him a breast. She relaxed back onto the mat with a sigh as the baby began to suck.

Even without looking, she could feel Prem's contented gaze.

The mood was broken by a scraping sound as Cheuy and the midwife dragged a large clay stove across the floor to her sleeping mat. What were they doing? Two servants came in with armfuls of firewood and her elder sister started to make a fire. Mother hovered behind them with the mid-wife, telling Cheuy to move the stove closer to Ploi.

"What are you doing?" she asked. "Just leave us alone."

"We are preparing the fire to help you heal after the birth. Now you must wrap yourself and move close to the fire," Mother said. "You will need to do this for nine days. I did this after you were born. And your aunt roasted by the fire after your cousin's birth for 29 days."

"Why? It is the middle of the hot season. We need to cool down, not heat up."

"It will protect you and the baby from ghosts and disease. Everybody knows that. I have explained this to you before, but you must have been thinking of something else," the midwife said as she placed a tray with five pairs of flowers, five candles and five baht beside the fire. "This is a powerful rite that my mother taught me."

Ploi propped herself up on one elbow, careful not to disturb the baby. Smoke from the fire was swirling around the room.

"Is this necessary?"

"Absolutely."

The midwife pulled a small silver knife from her bag.

"What are you doing?" Prem asked.

The midwife ignored him and gave the knife to Ploi. "Keep this under your pillow. It is your magical weapon to fight off the supernatural dangers to your child. You must keep this knife with you and stay close to the fire."

"For nine days? No, it's too hot. Nine days, no, I need to get up. I need to care for the baby. I need to check the casino accounts. Our payment to Sia Leng is due today," she said.

The fire rose in the stove, casting a red light on the baby's face. He pulled away from the breast and cried.

"This can't be good for the baby. It's too hot and too smoky," Prem said as he came and sat beside Ploi.

Finally, someone was speaking up for her. She was too tired.

"These are women's matters," Mother said. "We know what is best. It is what we always do. The smoke will improve Ploi's complexion."

"My mother never did this," Prem said.

"She was in a Chinese household. She lost her traditions."

"My brother and I turned out fine. My mother is still healthy," Prem said, leaning over and wiping the sweat from Ploi's forehead with a corner of his *phakaoma*.

"Men have nothing to say about this," the midwife said. "These are women's matters best left to women to decide."

"Nine days. Why nine days?" Ploi asked.

"That is the most auspicious number. It will lead to progress and good health," Mother said. "Some women roast by the fire for even longer, especially for the first child. It is for your own good."

"It must always be an odd number," the midwife said. "If an even number your health will suffer."

Ploi looked at Prem and shook her head.

"Well, one is an odd number," she said. "I will put up with this for one day, but that is all."

"Yes, this ends tomorrow," Prem said, stroking his wife's sweat-dampened hair.

Mother and the mid-wife exchanged horrified looks. So what? They couldn't tell her what to do with her own baby.

"One day only," she said.

"Daughter, you never listen to me," Mother whined.

"It is my body and my baby and we will do this roasting thing for just one day," she said and stared at her mother until she looked away.

"Then I will need to perform the fire-leaving ceremony," the midwife said, "but I warn you, nothing good will come of abandoning tradition and putting the mother and baby at risk. Don't blame me if something goes wrong. There are many dangers awaiting both mother and child. You are offending the spirits."

19

SOM
Medications

The old woman spit a stream of red betel nut juice onto the sandy dirt of the temple compound.

"It's my belly. Hurts somethin' awful. I have the running stomach now for two days," she moaned to Phra Panya and Phra Som who were seated on a low bamboo platform under the shade of a large Bodhi tree. A dozen people gathered round—all seeking treatment.

"It is the hot season, so an excess of heat is causing various problems," Phra Panya told her. "The elements of water, earth and wind can be problems, but this time of year, it must be fire."

"Yes, I feel like I'm roasting like a pig in the coals."

"Do you have fever?" Phra Som asked. If the patient had been male, he would have felt his throat or his wrist, but a monk could not touch a woman.

"Maybe. I feel hot beyond belief."

"Phra Som, please prepare a decoction of sugar cane leaves. That will reduce the fire and re-balance the elements," Phra Panya said.

He nodded. For once he agreed with the older monk's prescription, though he doubted the idea of the four elements. The more he read about medicine, the more confused he became. The Thai and Khmer texts said all ailments could be explained by the four elements getting out of balance. The type of illness was also determined by the age of the patient and the time of day. Cures depended on eating or drinking something to bring the elements back into balance. Chinese medicine books talked about qi, the energy holding together mind, body and heart. The Chinese texts, however, listed hundreds of treatments different from the Khmer palm-leaf books. The Western books he had found were even more different, focusing on structures in the body and little animals too small to be seen. It was hard to believe. It might not be possible to decide what caused disease, but he could at least record which treatments seemed to work and which didn't.

He took some leaves from one of the bundles behind him and pounded them in a large stone mortar. Checking that Phra Panya was busy chatting with the next patient, he added some salt, sugar cane juice and palm sugar to the mortar as he mashed the leaves. His records showed this mixture provided a quicker recovery from diarrhea than sugar cane leaves alone. He poured the mixture into a long bottle, stoppered it with a plug of wood, and handed it to Phra Panya who insisted he always be the one to hand the medicines to their patients.

"Here, this will have you feeling better in two days," he told her with a confident grin.

"Mix it one part to five parts of boiled water and drink two cups after each meal," Phra Som added.

"You will be as young and lively as ever," Phra Panya told her. "But don't get too frisky or you'll wear out your old man and we'll be treating him next."

The old lady cackled with delight and *waied* the two monks, clutching the bottle to her chest.

A young girl pushed forward supporting a pale woman in an embroidered cotton *phasin* with a bandage wrapped around her head.

"What have you done to your head, my child? Did you fall?" Phra Panya asked.

"Nothing like that. It is inside my head that hurts. It feels like an elephant is stepping on it," the woman said. "I have trouble seeing. It is like I am looking through cheap window glass."

"Did you throw up?" Phra Som asked.

"Yes, once," she said.

"Has this happened before?"

"Yes, several times, but this was the worst. The pain is terrible."

Phra Panya reached into the basket behind him and pulled out two cups carved from a cow's horn. "The best treatment is the application of the heated cup, child. That will reduce the pain completely within two hours," he said.

Phra Som sighed and pulled out his notebook.

"Headaches like this usually go away on their own within a few hours. We've had three cases like that in the past two months."

Phra Panya glared at his assistant.

"So, do nothing when she is suffering?"

"No, there is a treatment that has proven immediately effective,"

Phra Som said without looking at Phra Panya. "I have made some sticking plasters soaked in opium paste. These will ease the pain and help you sleep. When you wake up, the headache will likely be gone. The evidence for this is clear."

He placed the plasters on the mat as the young girl began unwinding the bandage around the woman's head. She then put the plasters on both temples and both women *waied* the young monk.

"The plasters alone will not suffice," Phra Panya said, pushing in front of Som. "You should light nine candles and nine joss sticks to the old image of the seated Buddha and make a donation to the temple. After your donation, spend some time in quiet contemplation of a Buddha image. This will heal the injury to your spirit, which has generated suffering in your inner self. Then your rapid recovery will be assured."

Stupid, but he better not say anything. He had already clashed with Panya on his frequent suggestions that their patients make donations. The older monk insisted that making merit through a donation would improve the patient's karma and helped cultivate a generosity of spirit that aided healing. Panya just wanted to look good to the abbot who was constantly encouraging donations. Bringing money into the temple was one reason the abbot supported the medical practice that crowded the temple compound with villagers and disturbed the monks' routine. They needed those donations to buy the herbs and treatments they could not find in the forest—like the opium he had used for the headache plasters—and the funds were needed to make repairs to the prayer hall and keep the kitchens supplied with charcoal. Still, it didn't seem right to tell people donations would help cure them when there was no evidence this was true.

"We are getting close to meal time. Phra Som shall take all the minor problems. All of you with more serious illnesses come to this side," Phra Panya directed.

So, he was qualified only for minor problems? He turned to the remaining villagers and started asking about symptoms. He used a concoction of forest leaves to treat eyesores, washed cuts with vinegar, and handed out more bottles of the sugar cane leaf decoction for diarrhea before the bell began its steady ringing for the second and final meal of the day.

As he was putting away his materials, Phra Panya approached.

"I know you are clever, but you are junior to me. Don't differ with my advice again or your time giving out medicines will be over. I would be forced to report your lack of discipline and respect to the abbot."

"I was just trying to…"

"No excuses," Panya interrupted. "I am your teacher and you must respect your teacher. You have much to learn about illness, about people and especially about humility."

Som looked at his friend in surprise and confusion.

"But our records…"

"Your records are not the problem. If your records indicate a different treatment, you can tell me later—not in front of the patients and the temple boys."

"I apologize. I meant no offense."

"No more contradicting me. Do you understand?"

"Yes, honored sir. I understand." Som bowed and *waied*.

"Good. Then we won't have to speak of this again. Let us go eat, we are already late."

The older monk hurried towards the main prayer hall. A feeling of disappointment spread through Som like blood seeping through a bandage. The temple compound that had seemed rich with the green of the trees and the orange of the roof tiles in the golden light of the early morning only a few hours ago was now washed out in the white glare of the midday sun.

20

PLOI
Wife and Mother

Ploi lay back on the big sleeping mat as the gray light crept across the polished wood of the floor. She felt content and yet something was nagging at her.

Prem slept beside her, his *phakaoma* riding low on his hips. She looked at the line of short, curly hairs that peeked above the cloth and smiled as she thought where they led. Over the past three months, she had often initiated their love-making. She knew that delighted him. She no longer reached the same peak of pleasure she had before Awt was born, but it felt good. She could still rouse Prem to heights of excitement.

Now that her breasts were swollen with milk for the baby, Prem paid them more attention than before. They spent more time nuzzling and touching. If her back ached from carrying the baby, Prem would start by rubbing her back with coconut oil. Then his attention would turn to her feet. She loved it that he did not see her feet as low or unclean. He massaged the oil into them with his powerful fingers. Then he would progress to her calves and thighs. This was part of his effort to arouse her, get her ready to make love, so she pretended indifference. He liked to kiss her upper thighs, getting closer to her sex, until she could not stop his kisses from sending a shudder through her body. Then he would smile with satisfaction and turn his attention to her hands, kissing the palms and working his way up her arms to what she knew was his real goal—the large taut breasts that had doubled in size since the baby. Last night she could bear it no longer and had reached for his manhood, pulling him to her.

She looked to the corner where Awt slept in a cloth cradle as peacefully as his father. He was like his father in his greed for her breasts. She was glad she was able to meet both their needs. Six months old now, Awt crawled around the house at amazing speeds. There weren't many places to hide in the plain rooms of the big house, but he seemed to find them. Last week they had searched for him for 20 panicky minutes before finding him asleep under a rice winnowing basket. Since then, the serving girl was relieved of her other tasks and assigned to watch him all the time. She enjoyed watching the girl play peek-a-boo with Awt and crawl around the veranda with him, but she felt no compulsion to join them. It was nice to have the time to herself after six months of focusing only on the recovery of her body and the child it had produced.

Giving the child to the girl's care also meant she was no longer the sole target of Mother's constant admonitions and advice. Her surveillance sprang from love, but it was annoying. She didn't need someone criticizing every move she made with her child. Mother was still worried she had ended the "roasting" by the fire too soon. If the baby threw up or had a loose stool or tumbled from the steps, she would mutter it was due to insufficient roasting. Mother used the baby's bath time each day to inspect every inch of him to see if anything was amiss. Now that the servant girl was handling the baths, she could see her mother's inspections as amusing, even endearing. Fortunately, Mother's objections to her marriage were now forgotten. Even Cheuy had become entranced with the baby. She loved singing to Awt as he fought against the need to sleep. Somehow her toneless singing pacified the child. The baby had become the center of the household.

If only Father had shown such interest. He spent more and more of his time with other disgruntled followers of the governor, many of whom had lost their official positions. They spent their evenings drinking, playing cards and muttering complaints against the high commissioner in Songkhla.

Father had visited a few days after the birth and had approved her choice of Phrapot as the name for the infant. He spent a few minutes looking at the baby before saying it had Prem's narrow face, rather than his own square jaw and broad forehead.

When Mother came in with some mashed banana for the baby, Father turned away. Later, she heard a loud argument about Mother's spending. Father had stomped off without saying goodbye. Since then, Mother had asked for her household expenses from the casino receipts so she wouldn't have to go to Paen for money. Then came the news that Rung, Father's third wife, was expecting. She found Mother in bitter tears. Now Father visited only when he knew Mother would be away at the market or visiting relatives.

"You will soon have another brother or sister," he told Ploi.

"Half-sister."

"She can be a playmate for little Awt."

"So, you will be bringing your new baby here?"

"No, probably not. Your mother would make a fuss. Not worth it."

"Then our family will be further divided—Elder Sister and big mother in Bangkok, Elder Brother and his children in Penang or Phuket or somewhere. Even here we live in the same town but separate houses."

It was unfortunate, but she had become used to the divisions in the family. Better than all the shouting when they were together. There was something else that wasn't right. She looked over at the bundle of notebooks against the far wall. With more free time, she had started receiving daily reports from the casino. In the past week she had gone over the details in the accounts ledgers and had written the monthly report to Sia Leng. There were none of the serious problems she had feared. Prem and the staff managed the gambling as steadily as before. However, there had been a slight drop-off in revenues. If this continued, it would not be good for the family. Maybe the decline was due to the rains and fears of another big flood. Maybe more of their rich customers were going to the big casinos in Bangkok now that steamer fares had come down. Maybe the entertainment they offered had become stale. Some customers had come just to hear her sing. Her personal touch had been missing for the past eight months.

"Prem, wake up," she said and prodded the sleeping form beside her.

"Good morning, sweet one," he mumbled.

"There is something I have to do," she said and nuzzled his neck.

"Again? Good, I seem to be ready—like every morning."

"No, not that. Well, that too, but later this afternoon I need to go back to the Jaikla. I have been away too long."

21

TUN WAY
Remembrance

Tun Way stared at the dark clouds beyond the river. The setting sun tinted red the edges of the massive monsoon clouds that shimmered in the reflections on the river. When Su Sah sat beside him on the veranda, such sunsets were beautiful. Now, they looked ominous. Why this feeling of foreboding? What more could hurt him? There was a cold void in his chest where once he had felt the warmth of joy. She was gone.

Head down, he leaned against the wooden railing of the veranda. The sun peeked out from under the clouds and sent spears of light across the river, but Tun Way ignored them. He saw only the pale face of his wife as she breathed her last breath. He reached for the glass of brandy balanced on the railing and finished it off.

"Sir, the child won't go to sleep," said a voice behind him.

He turned around. The girl he had hired to care for the baby was standing timidly at the door. She bowed and said softly, "She is asking for her grandmother."

The little girl, named Ngwe Lay by Su Sah's parents, had become more active and demanding in the past few weeks.

"How old is she now?" he asked.

"Close to three years," the girl said. Each day dragged slowly by, yet the years passed without anything to mark them. He had been startled a year after that terrible day when Su Sah's parents had arrived, smiling and carrying sweets and presents. He had flared with anger, asking what they were celebrating. Su Sah's mother explained they had come to mark the little girl's birthday.

Would it always be like this? Her birthday serving only to bring back memories of Su's death. For her second birthday, he sent the child to spend the week with her grandparents, saying he had urgent work in Rangoon. Nearly three years now? The pain was still fresh. Wasn't it supposed to heal with time? Su Sah's mother and father had offered to care for the child, but he refused. Would giving her up have helped lessen the memories. The child was a painful reminder of her mother, but she was all she had left of his wife. He really should do more with the child, but she seemed shy around him while she chatted merrily with her nanny.

"Three years old. Shouldn't she be able to go to bed by herself by now?"

"Usually I tell her a story and that puts her to sleep, but tonight it's not working. She says she wants her grandmother to read her a story."

"Well, her grandmother is not here, so you will have to do."

"Perhaps you could tell her a story or recite a poem," the girl suggested timidly.

All those times he recited a Mon tale or a poem to Su Sah—now no more. How could he tell those same tales to a child who couldn't understand much of what he said anyway? When he tried to talk to her, she just looked at him with big eyes—eyes that reminded him of Su Sah.

"Tonight is not a good time," he said and poured another glass of brandy. He flicked his hand to dismiss the girl.

He leaned back on the rail. It would be hours before he could sleep.

22

PAKDEE
Moving Up

SONGKHLA, OCTOBER 5, 1903

"Mr. Pakdee, sir. The ship from Bangkok has arrived. The high commissioner has asked for you," the office boy said from the doorway.

In the 20 months since the arrest of the raja, much had changed in the offices of *Monthon* Nakhon Srithammarat. More officials, police and soldiers had arrived from Bangkok. Some 30 officials reported to Pakdee now. He oversaw the drafting of local regulations and their translation into *Jawi*. He administered Songkhla port and business relations with the British throughout the *monthon*.

His personal staff had taken over the room used by the clerks. Somsak and his team were now crammed into a small room on the bottom floor. On Phraya Sukhumnaiwinit's advice, he had taken Somsak and the clerks out to dinner to thank them for their sacrifice. It had cost most of his salary for the month. Maybe it was worth it. Now Somsak gave him a deep *wai* whenever they met. Almost too deep.

He had continued to lead the reform of *monthon* courts. Prince Damrong's plan was to improve the courts so the foreigners would accept their authority. In the majority Malay areas, he had chosen village leaders and imams to interpret the laws on inheritance and marriage. He allowed them to settle minor disputes in line with *adat*, the local Malay traditions.

His own status in the office had risen. He had registered a family name—Charoen-nitthitham, meaning 'progress in just law' as suggested by Sukhumnaiwinit. The commissioner consulted with him more than any other official. It was rumored he had played some important role in the arrest of the Pattani raja, but no one could say exactly what. Other rumors hinted at high level connections in Bangkok. It was amusing to see the deference he received because of these rumors.

Sometimes he would finger the crystal around his neck when questioning his staff. This always seemed to make them nervous and more willing to admit to shortcomings. Sometimes, though, he detected flashes of disdain behind the shows of respect from those officials who had been at the *monthon* office before him.

His reputation had soared when his spies located the stash of German weapons purchased by the raja. He had ridden at the head of a procession of ten cartloads of weapons to the gate of the *monthon* office and presented the rifles, machine guns, hand grenades and boxes of ammunition to Commissioner Sukhumnaiwinit in a public ceremony. He had made his boss look good. Everything was working out well.

Sukhumnaiwinit continued to help him improve his written Thai, but trusted him to draft reports to Prince Damrong. The commissioner explained the subtle shades of meaning in the official Siamese vocabulary as well as ensuring he appreciated the complex levels of status and responsibility in the Siamese government service.

"Each person's title and even his name can change with a change in his official position. You must know what each title means. You must understand family connections, how each official came to his position, whom he has married, who has supported his rise, who are his enemies and what alliances he has formed. You must never oppose someone with a more powerful patron than your own. I have connections within the royal family, but I am not of royal blood. I too have enemies. Being far from the palace gives one greater freedom to work, but it makes one vulnerable to slander."

"Then I am in a far worse situation because I have no allies in the palace. I have no family. I'm entirely dependent on you."

"That is not completely true," the commissioner said. "I have made certain your role in our success in dealing with the raja and reforming the courts is clear to Prince Damrong. This is vital, but still not enough. One day I will return to Bangkok. I can support you from there, but who knows what position I'll have. I've taken a first step to help. Prince Damrong has approved a new position for you—Principal Assistant to the Monthon High Commissioner. We will have a ceremony announcing this tomorrow."

"That is most kind. I am forever in your debt."

"Yes, and one day that debt may need to be repaid, but you have more pressing problems now. Your new title will mean little without support. We need to establish your own circle of influence now, while we have the chance."

"Is that necessary? I have your support. That's all I care about."

"It's not enough. First, you must ensure all those appointed as judges know you were instrumental in their rise. Second, you must establish a line of income. Enduring power must be supported by funds. Wives can be helpful with that. You must have followers and you must have the money to support them when they have problems."

"What can I do? I have no family money, no estates. My official salary is not very high."

"I will raise your salary with your new title, but it won't be enough. You have information, contacts, legal influence and position. All those can be converted into money, but you must never do that at the expense of the Siamese people or His Majesty's government. If you move too quickly or encroach on someone else's income you will earn enemies who can bring you down. So, think carefully. I will say no more."

His head whirled as he thought of the possibilities and the problems. Maybe it was not a good idea to rise. It was more important to be safe. He thought of his climb up the stairs of Jate's house. Seeking too much had led to disaster. But Principal Assistant to the Commissioner—surely that title would protect him. He would be positioned for further promotion. If he could rise to deputy commissioner or even commissioner one day, no one could touch him.

"Thirdly," Sukhumnaiwinit broke into his thoughts, "we must take advantage of your legend."

"What legend?"

"Your rapid rise is stirring jealousy among the other officials. They don't want to believe you have risen above them because you are more capable. So, I have given them another reason to accept your rise—a story that explains your success in a way that does not shame them or tempt them to oppose you. You must appear invulnerable."

"How is that possible?"

Sukhumnaiwinit smiled, "I have always loved the old legends and I have a good imagination. I started the rumors in the market some time ago and they have spread."

"What rumors?"

"It's a great story, if I say so myself. A boy was born to a minor wife of Prince Damrong. When still a baby, the boy was examined by a renowned monk. The monk said the boy had great abilities and magical powers that would one day make him 'king of the south'. The monk placed a magic crystal around the boy's neck and said it would enable him to see into the heart of anyone he questioned. The monk's words caused great consternation among the other wives who all wanted their own children to rise high in royal service. They hired a couple to kidnap and kill the boy. The kidnappers, however, wanted a son, so they took him far away to the south. There he grew into a young man who entered the service of the *monthon* commissioner, rising rapidly to become his principal assistant."

"No one will believe that," Pakdee laughed.

"You would be surprised what people will believe," Sukhumnaiwinit said. "A few of your colleagues have seen the crystal. They think it confirms the story."

"Won't Prince Damrong be angry when he hears this?"

"I have already explained my plan to him and he thought it was quite amusing."

"What do I do if someone asks me directly if this story is true?"

"You must, of course, deny it, but deny it in a way that leaves room for doubt."

"It's a great story, but I still doubt anyone will believe this tale."

"Things will happen soon to support the story. First of all, there must be a marriage with someone close to Prince Damrong's family."

"Unfortunately, I have no family contacts. I know few women, much less anyone from Prince Damrong's palace. I will need your help."

"No, you won't," the commissioner said. "Prince Damrong, His Majesty King Chulalongkorn and, most importantly, the first Queen, all understand that a young official in an important position requires an appropriate spouse," he said with a smile at Pakdee's look of confusion. "The ship from Bangkok did not bring only documents and produce."

Sukhumnaiwinit clapped his hands and gestured to the office boy standing at the door. He pushed open the heavy door and a young woman walked in. She wore a French-style dress of green and yellow silk with a high-collared lacy blouse. Her hair was cut short in the palace style. Light glinted from the rings on her fingers and she carried a silver betel nut box that she handed to the office boy behind her. She turned to Phraya Sukhumnaiwinit, bowed and *waied* him in a curtsy as deep as the narrow dress would allow. She repeated the *wai* to Pakdee with a slighter bow and a demure smile.

"Honored sir, my name is Apinya and Her Majesty Queen Savang Vadhana has told me I am to serve as your wife."

23

TUN WAY
Determination

Tun Way closed his book in frustration. It was hard to concentrate on the old Mon language of the poems. These poems had once brought him delight. He read them to Su on evenings like this, with a pale moon rising from behind the hills and the last light of the sun reflecting from the water of the river. He had loved looking up from the page to see her smile in the last light of the day. It would be dark soon, but it would be difficult to sleep. Another glass or two would help.

He heard a faint clatter from the road and watched a buggy come around the curve into the drive. Who now? He had few visitors these days. That was just as well. He couldn't endure people for long with their silly chatter and their awkward efforts to ask how he was feeling. The buggy stopped in front of the house. In the gathering darkness he saw it was U Htun Htin, Shwe Hongsa and Aung Mon. The three friends walked gingerly up the muddy path.

"Tun Way, it looks like you have gotten a head-start on us," Aung Mon called as they reached the steps. "Aren't you going to invite us in for a drink?"

Tun Way looked at the bottle in his hand.

"I'll get some glasses."

When the three had settled on the mats in the main room and each had a glass of brandy, he looked at the three. "What brings you here this time?"

"It's the British. They have delayed permission for the school," Shwe Hongsa said. "It was supposed to be approved today, but they have been listening to the Burman officials in the municipal office who claim a Mon language school will cause divisions and unrest."

"They've approved schools for the other ethnic minorities—the Shans, the Karens, the Kachins. Why do they discriminate against the Mon?" Tun Way asked in sudden anger.

"The Burmans say that we are not really a separate ethnic group, but part of the Burman people," Htun Htin said.

"They just don't want us to protect our culture," he retorted.

"We do have a lot of customs in common," Htun Htin said.

"The Burmans copied from us," Tun Way continued. "Maybe they should consider themselves Mon since we brought them religion, learning and culture. It is only through war and excessive breeding they came to dominate. And now they get the foreigners to help."

"Well, it is not definite yet that the municipal office will reject us. It's just a delay, but it puts back the plan to start construction next month," Shwe Hongsa said. "The Mon Language and Culture Society and the school under it have to be registered at the municipality. Only then can the land can be transferred and construction started."

"If the land is still in your name," Tun Way said, "you don't need permission to build something on your own land—perhaps a big house with many rooms. If sometime later that big house is used for a school, so what. Let's go ahead and start."

"We could do that," Shwe Hongsa said, "but there are many other things that will require registration—hiring teachers, buying books, admitting students. We need to be properly registered to do all that."

"We are always so careful to follow the rules," Tun Way added, "even though these are not our rules. This is our city and we should be able to do what is right for our own people."

Aung Mon tossed back the remainder of his brandy and smacked the glass on the floor. "Right. Screw these Burman and British bastards. This is Mon land and we are Mons."

"Right, this is Mon land and we are Mons. Let's do it," Htun Htin echoed.

Tun Way smiled grimly. The darkness that had clouded his mind was clearing.

24

SOM
Inspection

The temple bell rang just as Phra Som was settling into his meditation. He looked outside his little wooden cell to see the other monks hurrying towards the prayer hall. This was not the time of day for prayers or meetings. Why was the abbot calling them? He sighed, uncrossed his legs and struggled to his feet. He followed the other monks into the hall. Next to the abbot was an unfamiliar monk and a small man in a white official's uniform.

"Today we are honored to welcome the Monthon *Sangha* Inspector, Phra Somdet Koson, and the Monthon High Commissioner Phraya Sukhumnaiwinit, to our humble monastery. As I explained to you last year, a new law – the Sangha Act of 1902 – now governs all Buddhist temples in Siam. This law unifies Buddhists in the proper practice of our religion. The *Sangha* inspector will stay with us for several days. We must show him how well we are following the *Sangha* Act."

"I am here to inspect the temples of *Monthon* Nakhon Srithammarat," Phra Somdet Koson said. "Previously I was assistant abbot of Wat Bowonniwet in Bangkok. I am also the personal representative of Phra Wachirayan, the abbot of Wat Bowonniwet. As you should already know, Prince Wachirayan has been entrusted by his half-brother, His Majesty the King, to improve the quality of Buddhist teaching in the land. I have noted the efforts of the Venerable Brahmavamso to implement the new rules in Wat Wang Tawan Tok and I am pleased to announce the Sangha authorities in Bangkok have accorded him the title of *Phra racha khana chan thep*. So, you may now address him as Phrathep Brahmavamso."

Som watched the abbot struggle to keep a smile from spreading across his face.

"This is one of 62 titles now used throughout the kingdom," the abbot said proudly. "These titles are awarded by the Supreme Council for achievement in passing the Pali examinations, promoting learning, encouraging merit making and adhering to the practices approved by the Council."

This explained some recent actions of the abbot. So, it was not just the abbot's own initiative to call for donations and push monks to focus on the Pali examinations, but a policy approved by the higher *Sangha* authorities.

"I would like to mention four points in the law," Phra Somdet Koson said. "Point number one: the approved Pali texts are the heart of our religion and must be used in our sermons to the people. Too many sermons focus on the superstitious tales of the *jatakas*. These tales cannot be found anywhere in the Buddha's own teaching. They are filled with myths of animals turning into humans and other magical events that distort our beliefs. This must end."

"Point number two: there is inappropriate interaction with women. These actions cannot continue."

"Point number three: monks are undertaking physical labor beneath the dignity of the *Sangha*. Monks should not be building structures, cutting trees or cooking meals. Monks should devote all their efforts to learning Pali, chanting, conducting approved rituals and studying the scriptures."

Who then would keep the temple buildings in good repair? Set on the edge of town, Wat Wang Tawan Tok had fewer lay supporters than other temples in Nakhon. The people would resent healthy young monks sitting idly while lay followers did all the work.

"Point number four: in some temples there is too much emphasis on meditation. Meditation has its place, but only when there is a proper understanding of the Buddha's teaching. Without that understanding, meditation can lead to magical thinking and false claims. Some monks say meditation gives them the power to fly or to see the future. The Buddha himself made no such claims."

There was now an audible buzz from among the monks and the abbot smacked his fan on the wooden platform three times.

"Please be silent. The honored high commissioner has something to say."

Phraya Sukhumnaiwinit stepped forward amid whispers from the monks. "Thank you for your attention," the commissioner said in precise central tones. "These changes have the full support of the entire state administration. I was a monk like you for 15 seasons and I understand the challenges of monastic life. These new rules are part of His Majesty's reforms to strengthen our nation. They will help bring all the towns of Siam under one religious system just as they are coming under one administrative system. We need your help to make Siam a modern, civilized nation. Are there any questions?"

There was a rustle of whispers like a wind sweeping through dry rice stalks, but no one stepped forward with a question.

"Good," the abbot said as he rose. "You may now return to your tasks." He led the commissioner to the gate where his carriage waited. Phra Tissa and Phra Panya escorted the inspector to the abbot's quarters. The other monks left the prayer hall, but gathered in small knots.

Phra Pat, one of the few monks serious about meditation, beckoned him, but Som shook him off and headed back to his cell alone. His head was swirling with the inspector's words. Would they affect his hopes of a peaceful life of meditation and medical service? The emphasis on the original teachings of the Buddha was a good thing. The myths in the sermons of the older monks clashed with the dharma. If the new rules would stop the magical practices of some monks – blessing amulets, "curing" illnesses with chants, predicting the future and claiming supernatural powers – that would be good.

He had barely reached his hut when three of the younger monks converged on him.

"Elder Brother Som. We want to hear your thoughts," said Phra Pat. "You have been to Bangkok—why is the Patriarch sending monks to inspect us? And why did the high commissioner come with him?"

"I think there are two parts to this," he said. "The first part is about the dharma. We must admit that much of what is said in our sermons is nowhere to be found in the Pali scriptures. The Patriarch is probably concerned that Buddhism in the countryside is drifting away from the teachings of the Buddha."

"Our chants are all in Pali taken from the scriptures. Isn't that enough?" asked Phra Awn, a young monk struggling to learn Pali.

"The lay people don't understand the chants," Pat said. "And, as we all know, many of our monks don't either."

The other monks laughed and Awn playfully pushed Pat back against the railing of the porch. "You couldn't mean me," he said.

"Even when monks understand the Pali scriptures, very little of it gets into their sermons," Som said.

"Because it's boring," Awn said. "Phra Panya's *Jataka* stories always get a crowd."

"Somehow we have to find ways to teach the dharma without putting everyone to sleep," Som said. "This is a challenge."

"Why did the high commissioner come if this is only about teaching the dharma?" asked Daeng, who had ordained four months earlier.

"That has puzzled me too," Som said. "The patriarch is close to his half-brother and we know the king wants to modernize and unify. Our Buddhist religion can bring people together, but not if every temple and every abbot is following different rules."

"I was surprised the *Sangha* inspector was not more supportive of meditation," Pat said. "That was how the Buddha achieved enlightenment."

He nodded. That had worried him too.

"The inspector is just one monk and there are hundreds of temples with many revered monks," Awn said. "There have been noises like this from Bangkok before, but in the end little changes."

The discussion continued on for some time, but Som's attention drifted away as the monks returned to the same questions again and again. If these changes really take hold, how would his life change? Did he want to persuade the villagers to make bigger donations? Did he want to spend even more of his time on Pali ceremonies? Should local temple practices be determined by faraway Bangkok?

With these new rules, did he still want to be a monk?

25

DAM
Dazzled

Dam was drifting into sleep when there was a loud banging on his door. What the fuck? Who could be bothering him this late at night? He had already worked a full day at the police station and he had done a full week of work at night. Since his mother's death, he had no one else in his life. If it was one of Jate's men asking for something, he could go screw himself. It was time for the boss to realize his 'black buffalo' no longer depended on him. It was now the other way around. The knocking grew louder.

"Dam, come on out," he heard. It didn't sound like any of Jate's men.

He pulled open the door. It was three of the policemen from the station. They were all officers about Dam's age.

"It's Sakda now," he said with a scowl.

"Yeah, that may be your official name, but we are used to Dam, and it fits you so well—no one is darker than you," said Jaet, the sergeant who was the oldest of the trio. "Let that be your nickname among friends."

"Alright, but in reports and in front of the captain, it should be Sakda," Dam said.

"Anyway, how about coming with us to have some fun tonight," Lek said. "We are heading to the Jaikla Casino. It's about time we got lucky and this may be our last chance."

"What do you mean?"

"An order has come down from Bangkok to close down all the casinos in Nakhon by the end of the year."

"I don't care. I never gamble. That is for fools."

"It's just for fun. You don't have to bet. The casino serves free drinks—especially for policemen. There's music. It'll be fun."

He looked at the young policemen who seemed eager for him to join them. They were now his only family, he supposed. He nodded and went back inside to pull on a shirt and trousers.

Twenty minutes later they were gliding across the dark river. A pair of paddlers in the narrow boat propelled it across the calm water. The clear sky at the start of the cool season allowed the moon and the stars to light the river. As they neared the shore, the oil lamps of the casino on the bank above the river outlined the large, tile-roofed building. A row of lamps led the way up the bank from the floating dock. When the boat arrived with a bump, the four clambered onto the dock.

"Time to supplement our pay," Jaet called to his friends. "I feel lucky tonight."

He smiled at this foolishness. He would never gamble away his money the way his father had. He didn't feel lucky; he never had. Any good luck that came his way had been followed by bad. After all his efforts to free his mother, she had died alone. Jate had pretended to care about him, but only used him. Now he had no one, needed no one. His hopes to rise in the police force had been damaged because of that unfair report against him. Sometimes violence was necessary. He just had to be smarter about it.

Back across the river, the police station was lit by one lamp dim in the distance. He would have to use the police to make a better life than his mother had ever had. No one would ever use him the way she had been used by her master. What was life anyway? Eat, shit, fuck, and at the end you die. It felt like a dark and empty future, but it was all he had.

He watched his friends clamber eagerly up the steps from the dock and he followed. As his eyes adjusted to the brighter lights at the casino door, the woman greeting the group came into focus. Her voluptuous figure shone in a gold-embroidered *phasin* and a swath of light blue silk that covered the swelling of her breasts. Bare shoulders were smooth and honey-colored. Large eyes seemed to look deep into his. Her smile seemed so warm and friendly. He opened his mouth to speak when he stumbled on the top step and nearly fell. He heard her giggle. What right did she have to laugh at him? He wanted to say something that would wipe the amused look off her face. But she smiled and extended a hand to help. It was warm and delicate.

Everything changed. He wanted to say something clever to impress her. Make her laugh with him, not at him. He wanted to draw close to her, but he struggled to find the words. With a final, friendly look, she had turned away, leading his friends into the casino. She swayed in the tight *phasin*, moving away from him before he could say anything.

The rest of the evening he sat cross-legged in a corner of the crowded room, sipping the rice wine offered by the casino. He watched as his friends got excited over their bets. They whooped with delight when they won and groaned when they lost. They're like children who can't control themselves.

Mostly, however, he watched the beautiful casino owner. He tried not to stare. She moved with such grace around the gambling mats, sharing a joke or promising a bettor he would win next time. Twice she caught him looking at her and smiled. It seemed to promise something, but he didn't know what. She was obviously intimate with the tall floor manager. He saw the way they looked at each other as they sang a love song duet. Why did no one look at him that way?

The pile of coins next to the cashier was also impressive. Bettors eagerly dumped their silver and gold in front of the cashier to be exchanged for handfuls of bright ceramic betting tokens. He tried to estimate the evening's take, but it was hard. Money quickly moved in and out of the iron cash box next to the cashier. It must be hundreds of *baht*. It would be nice to get some of that. Too bad the casino was closing. The betting went on into the early morning when his friends had finally lost all their money.

"Dam, time to go. We are finished. You'll have to pay for the boat back across the river."

They were fools to throw their money away, but they were the closest things to friends he had. Money was power and he wouldn't waste it on a few moments of fun. As they started to leave, he hesitated. He wanted to talk to the casino owner, who was busy checking a ledger. Just to talk to her would be fine, but if he were clever, there might be some way he could benefit from the casino, some way they could benefit together. He forced himself forward.

"Excuse me, madam. I am Police Sergeant Sakda. I want to thank you for an enjoyable evening," he said.

It was good to be able to tell people his rank again. He had gotten his sergeant stripes back just the week before, after two years of indignity as a lowly private. His willingness to take the late shifts and the dangerous assignments had paid off.

"Well, Police Sergeant Sakda, I noticed you did not join your friends in betting. That, you know, is what a casino is for."

"I think a casino is for making money and you have done that very well. Too bad the *Monthon* Commission wants the casinos to close."

"Yes, that is unfortunate, but nothing is official yet."

"Let me know if I can be of any help."

She looked at him and cocked her head to one side. Better to leave her with a question in her mind.

Dam drew himself up to his full height and snapped off a salute.

"I look forward to seeing you again," he said, pleased to have regained some control. He turned and strode off into the night.

26

PAKDEE
Palace Wife

Pakdee pushed aside the tray of *khao chae*. The cold soggy rice and the array of little dishes of vegetables with it were supposed to be elegant palace food. Once the hot season arrived, Apinya told him, all the upper-class families ate *khao chae*. It was unlike anything his mother had ever served. Her food was always hot and spicy, usually served with crispy flat bread. After less than a week of *khao chae*, he was sick of it. He was also tired of eating alone. Apinya said it was improper for her to eat with him, though she and the slave girl she brought from Bangkok would come in and out with additional dishes. If he invited her to sit with him and talk, she would apologize and say she had to attend to the food. She would spend hours creating tiny sweets from sugar and bean paste in the shapes of different fruits. Sometimes she would carve a papaya or a pineapple into elaborate designs that seemed too pretty to eat.

He longed for the meal times he'd had with his family in Pakpanang. Those had been noisy affairs filled with the aromas of his mother's cooking. His mother would make the *roti paratha* stuffed with spices and minced goat meat and toasted on a heavy iron grill. With a great flourish his father would make a metal pot full of orange-colored tea, sweet with palm sugar and rich with goat milk. He and Father would argue about ways to expand sales. Saifan and Father would discuss a passage in the Koran. He would tell Mother the latest gossip from the market. Now mealtimes were stiff and boring. Was this really the way Thai aristocrats liked to live?

Moving to a bungalow set back from the beach on the north side of the Songkhla inlet should have given him and his wife more of a family feeling than living at the *monthon* offices. Unfortunately, the bungalow was too far from the office to come home for the midday meal. Even when at home, he saw little of his wife. She was always busy getting dressed or bathing or making up her face. He was forbidden to watch any of these processes. Another important occupation was her work to set up a troupe to perform the traditional *Khon* masked dance-drama. In this she received encouragement from Phraya Sukhumnaiwinit, so he couldn't say anything against it.

"We need to bring proper Thai culture to the south," she said. "National unification, the queen told me before I came south, cannot be limited to political administration, but must extend to culture. The high commissioner agrees and has given me a small budget to put on performances here in Songkhla like those in the queen's palace."

This now consumed much of Apinya's time. She hired artisans to make the elaborate masks and costumes for the *Khon*. She worked with local musicians to learn the music and recruited the wives and daughters of other officials as performers. She expressed surprise that he had never seen a *Khon* performance. She saw it as another of his many cultural deficiencies.

She was quick to correct even the slightest of his mistakes in the use of the royal language. She never overlooked any hint of a southern accent in his speech, lamenting that he had spent too much time in the south. It helped him improve his use of the language, but it was irritating. If he dressed too casually for some event, she would send him back to change. Often, she helped him dress, paying particular attention to the crystal he wore around his neck. She seemed to appreciate him most when he was in his formal white uniform with the medals and braid of a royal official. She had encouraged him to grow back his mustache—"to look like His Majesty the King." He supposed he should appreciate her efforts. He knew she wanted to help his career, but she made him feel ignorant and clumsy.

Sukhumnaiwinit had explained away Pakdee's various cultural mistakes by hinting that, although high-born, he had been raised by lower-class foster parents and he had been placed in government service in the south at an age when other well-born young men entered the royal pages school in Bangkok. Despite this explanation, he could feel himself dropping in Apinya's esteem with each error in speech or comportment.

Now he sat by himself in silence, eating elaborate, but tasteless food. Married life had turned out that way too. It had begun with elaborate ceremonies officiated by Phraya Sukhumnaiwinit—first the betrothal only two days after Apinya's arrival and then the wedding a week later. Apinya had looked beautiful in an elegant silk costume studded with glass beads. Together, they made offerings to the monks at the big temple in town. Sukhumnaiwinit introduced them to the abbot with a look of great satisfaction. The night before he had schooled him in all that he had to do for the wedding.

"To become a proper Thai gentleman, you must know how to perform all the Buddhist ceremonies," he said before explaining each step in the marriage rites.

All this reminded him of his father's lectures on how to be a good Muslim. Above all, a believer in Islam had to remain a believer in Islam. "As for those who disbelieve after having believed, then plunge deeper into disbelief, their repentance will not be accepted; these are the lost," he remembered his father quoting from the Koran. But all that was in the past, part of a person different from the person he was now.

Even before his arrest, he had questioned much of his father's teachings. Beatings, conviction and prison taught him there was no Allah looking out for him. It was not that he believed in Buddhism either, but it seemed to allow more room for doubt. Just as he had learned to go through the motions of daily Islamic prayers, he had learned to go through the rituals of Buddhism without commitment. These rituals were simply tasks to be mastered.

He had emulated the commissioner in many Buddhist ceremonies— at the opening of a business, the dedication of a building or the funeral of an important person. He had become adept at the elaborate gestures and Pali phrases about the Triple Gems needed for the ceremonies. He learned how to make offerings to the monks, start a chant or "inspect the water" in the rites. The wedding was a similar set of rituals that meant little to him other than the chance to get ahead.

First there was the blessing of the monks and the chanting of passages from the *Tripitaka* in the early morning. Then, in the afternoon, the staff of the *monthon* administration and many of the leading citizens of Songkhla had gathered for a Brahmin ceremony linking him to Apinya with a white cord around their wrists and heads.

One by one the guests poured water from a large conch shell over their hands and gave their blessings. Sukhumnaiwinit made a gracious speech lauding him for his service to the *monthon* and thanking King Chulalongkorn for arranging a palace-trained bride for the rising star in *Monthon* Nakhon Srithammarat.

The number of people at the wedding surprised him. Maybe they came because of his capture of the raja's weapons. Maybe they came because of his duties managing the port and the courts, but he could call none of them his friend. Still the generous wedding gifts had eased his immediate financial worries. For the first time in his life he had savings to invest. Did it matter that most of those gifts were not made out of friendship but out of expectation of future favors?

Apinya also was without true friends at the wedding. Her family, she explained, was too involved with important affairs in Bangkok to make the long trip to Songkhla. Her father's duties in the finance ministry prevented him from attending. Her mother, his sixth wife, was a lady in waiting for Queen Savang Vadhana. The queen, Apinya said, needed her mother in Bangkok. She had three elder sisters and an array of half-brothers and half-sisters, but none of them could find the time to attend the wedding. The only person with her was a young maid named Toi.

After the wedding ceremony, the newlyweds had returned to his rooms in the *monthon* office. Apinya had looked so pale. Suddenly she burst into tears. He tried to comfort her, but she turned her back to him and cried herself to sleep.

The next day had been awkward. He woke up to find his wife staring out the window at the sea. She was already dressed and asked to be left alone. With nothing else to do, he walked down the hall to his office and spent the day dealing with correspondence. Returning to his room, he found Apinya waiting for him, dressed again in her wedding dress with her face carefully made up. She knelt before him and touched her forehead to the floor.

"Honored sir, I apologize for my inappropriate behavior last night," she said. "I have dishonored Her Royal Highness as well as my father."

"That is alright. I think we were both very nervous. Don't worry about it," he said.

"No, it is not alright. I failed in my duty, but it won't happen again. I am ready to consummate the marriage."

He had been surprised but pleased. She was beautiful. Her face was soft, with pleasingly plump cheeks. Her eyes, which he at first thought a little too small, now looked dramatic when outlined in dark kohl. He could see the swell of her breasts pushed up by the tight silk wrapping of her top. Desire rose within him as he looked down at her.

By the wedding day it had been many weeks since he had made a visit to the "ladies of the green lantern" in the Chinese section of Songkhla.

Before that, he had been a regular customer at one of the better brothels. He enjoyed the politeness of the madam, the good manners of the girls and their treatment of him as a person of importance.

There was a wonderful variety of women available. If he felt like a quiet, pale Chinese, there were three he could choose from—new arrivals from China imported to service the wealthier merchants in town. If he felt like one of the dark-skinned local women, like the pretty coconut vender he had admired so often from his window, there were two he liked for their earthy enthusiasm for the act. There was even a black-skinned woman from India whose large breasts seemed out of proportion to her slim body. Most of these women were somehow still slaves—some sold to the madam by their fathers, others born of service women and raised in the brothel. If he felt like talking, the madam was always ready with witty political comments or gossip from her other customers. Although he enjoyed his visits, there was none of the feeling of conquest and passion he had gotten from his lovers in Pakpanang. The women's professional competence and willingness to please was no substitute for the thrill of love. It was just business. Love with his wife should have provided passion.

That hope had gradually faded. The disappointment of their wedding night was hard to forget. Apinya joined him on the sleeping mat whenever he asked, but he always had to ask. She insisted on undressing in the dark without even a candle so he got only the dimmest glimpses of her body.

Their love-making had become routine. She usually lay unmoving beneath him and hurried to wash when they were finished. Did she think he was somehow unclean? She would turn away from the kisses he had learned to enjoy in the brothel. She would softly brush away his hand or turn her body away if he tried to touch her sex. If he kissed her breasts, she would make a soft noise of discouragement.

His eagerness in the first week had tapered off and his hope he could teach her to enjoy their nights together had faded. They now slept together only every third or fourth day. Sometimes a week or more would pass. It was not that she ever rejected him; just that she showed no enthusiasm, no desire. Perhaps that was normal for a high-born woman.

He just wanted to be wanted.

27

DAM
Shutdown

Dam sucked his stomach in and buttoned the last two buttons of his dress uniform. It was unusual to wear it for routine business, but it made a good impression. He checked to make sure his newly-regained sergeant's stripes were in place and smiled with satisfaction at the ribbons he had earned for his work against the Chinese secret societies and the pirate gangs of the Pakpanang estuary.

Under the watchful eye of the police captain, he had avoided working for Jate. With the wealthier citizens of Pakpanang he had been careful to be polite and correct. He gave in to the need to use his fists and feet only with the lowlifes and criminals. The restraint he had to show with so many made the feel of battering the guilty that much better. The fear he could see in a suspect's eyes—that always made him feel good. The ability to spark such fear meant that his cases often ended in a confession and the grudging approval of Captain Serm.

Dam smoothed the tight white cloth of the uniform. He had put on a bit more weight in the last two years, but he carried it well. Drawing himself up to his full height, he stepped off the boat onto the pier of the Jaikla Casino. He hoped the young woman would be there. He still remembered the glow around her and her slightly condescending smile. She would not feel so superior when she heard his order.

"Stay here," he told the two young privates with him as he rapped on the casino door. He was disappointed when that tall fellow answered the door.

"Where is the manager?"

"What is this about?"

"You may remember me from an earlier visit. Now I am here on official police business to talk to the manager of the Jaikla Casino."

The man, as tall, but not as thick as him, hesitated a moment as if he were going to shut the door. He could take him no problem, if it came to that.

"Official business," he repeated and stared unblinking into the man's eyes.

"Come this way," the man finally said and led the way through the large main room, past the teak-paneled high-stakes room and into a small office. There she was, sitting behind a small pile of ceramic markers and a long narrow ledger. Her thick hair was brushed back and her soft lips were pursed in concentration. She was wearing a frilly white blouse with narrow straps that revealed the smooth flesh of her shoulders and neck. Somehow, she looked both desirable and unapproachable, both competent and sensual.

"Ploi, dear, there is a policeman, a sergeant, here to see you on official business."

"I think I know what this is about. Prem, dear, I can handle this."

He pushed past the man who didn't seem to want to leave.

"It's alright," she said with a smile and the man stared coldly at him before leaving the room.

"Miss Ploi, I regret to inform you the government has ordered the closure of the Jaikla Casino in accordance with the Gambling Revenue Act of 1902. The provisions of this act provide for…"

"I know the provisions," Ploi interrupted. "I have been preparing for this order for some time. What I would like to ask is why now? Why here in Nakhon? There has been no action anywhere else in the country. Why Jaikla?"

What should he say? He had prepared a speech explaining the detailed provisions of the act, but was unsure how to answer her questions.

"The Gambling Revenue Act requires the closure of tax concession casinos at the discretion of the chief of police," he said.

"So, the police chief, who was gambling here earlier this month, as, if I am not mistaken, were you and several of your men, suddenly decided that it was time to close the Jaikla Casino?"

"It was legal then. Soon it will not be," he tried to explain.

"Why now?"

"I believe there was an order from the *monthon* high commissioner," he said. Why did he have to say anything? He should be in charge here.

"Ah, the monk."

"The high commissioner is not a monk."

"He was for many years and is still one at heart. So why now? To shut us down before Chinese New Year—our biggest day of the year. How much time can you give us?"

Her direct look was disturbing. He had planned to ask for a bribe to delay the shutdown since his boss had given him a month to close up all the casinos. Being so close to her in the small room he could sense the warmth of her breath. She smelled like coconut and flowers and something earthier. He had volunteered for this assignment because he had been unable to stop thinking of her. He had tried to tell himself this was stupid, that he had to abide by the Five Rules of his *yantra*— including the rule against coveting other men's wives. Despite this, he felt drawn to her. Sometimes just before he fell asleep, he could see her once more glowing in the lantern light that night in the casino. Her smile. The touch of her hand. So, when the notice came up in the action log, he made sure he was the first to volunteer.

The captain had given him a strange look, but then agreed. "You have to do this properly, no strong-arm stuff. Jaikla has a lot of connections."

He spent two late evenings going through the file on the gambling law, a file left untouched for more than a year. Now he searched for the right explanations.

"It's not just Jaikla, every casino in the *monthon* must close when the district police chiefs decide the time is right. I am sorry, but it is the law," he offered.

She didn't seem upset, but stood up and looked at him coolly.

"You know the Na Nakhon royal family enjoys outings here, the head of the Chinese merchants' association and the Nakhon self-help group all come here. Some of them may still have our tokens and they will lose their money if we close before they can redeem them. Even the monk commissioner must be practical. How much time?"

"A month," he blurted out. No chance now to bargain for a bribe, but he didn't care. What he really regretted was that so soon after meeting her, the closure of the casino meant he might never see her again.

"And after that?"

"After that the casino can no longer operate legally," he said.

"And, of course, we would not want to operate illegally."

"If you did, I would learn of it and I would have to arrest you."

"Then there is no choice, is there?" she asked.

"Not really."

"Then the Jaikla Casino will shut its doors," Ploi said. "But we will not be closing quietly. We will have a final month of gambling with special games, new singers, free food and liquor. We will make this the best month ever at the casino. Perhaps you would enjoy it."

"I don't gamble, but I might visit to see that all goes according to the law. If you have any questions, it's my duty to help. It can be quite confusing since some traditional gambling games are still allowed and others are allowed on special occasions, like *Songkran* or the Tenth Month Fair. Just ask for me and I will see what I can do to help."

He felt her eyes look into his for a long moment.

"Thank you. I am sure your advice will be useful. Please feel free to come to the casino in our final days. Even if you don't gamble, you are always welcome. Maybe we can find something to amuse you. Now we are finished here, aren't we?" she said as she sat back down at the desk.

She nodded and turned back to her ledger. She had dismissed him like she was his boss, but he didn't care. He would come to the casino as often as possible during its last month. There would be reasons to talk with her. He could advise on permits for games on the *Songkran* holiday. After that? As he walked to the door, he thought about what might lie ahead and felt a bubble of excitement rising within him.

28

SOM

A Proper Temple

NAKHON SRITHAMMARAT, APRIL 3, 1904

A shriek and a loud laugh interrupted Phra Som's morning meditation. He looked up with irritation and then a smile. *Songkran* was beginning early at Wat Wang Tawan Tok. He poked his head out of his hut and watched as a gaggle of young folks from the village splashed water on the robes of Taen, one of the novice monks. The girls and boys chasing him with pails of water were his friends, but neither friendship nor his new status protected him from the wet blessing of *Songkran*.

Taen abruptly turned and seized a pail from one of the women chasing him. He gave a delighted shout and upended it on her back. Two of Taen's fellow novices sprinted around the corner of the prayer hall with a large wooden bucket and tossed water over the young villagers. That ignited another chase as the villagers swerved to catch the novices. Shouts and laughter filled the compound that usually resonated only with the chanting of prayers.

The sounds of the competition between the village youth and the young monks and novices rose even louder as the villagers surrounded the outnumbered novices. A dozen villagers joined the fray with new supplies of water. The novices grinned and awaited the inundation they knew was coming. According to local tradition, the village youth would douse the novices, but not the older monks. They would then form a procession behind a village elder to bring gifts of flowers and incense to the temple, asking forgiveness. Both monks and lay people would parade down to the canal for boat races. The young monks of the temple had been practicing for weeks to avoid being beaten by the team of powerful young women who had won the race the previous year. Before the villagers could deliver their watery blessings, however, Abbot Brahm, appeared behind them with an angry shout.

"Stop right now. I will not tolerate this any longer."

Som was surprised because there had been similar scenes each of the three previous *Songkran* celebrations. Never before had Abbot

Brahm intervened. He looked at the two monks standing beside the abbot. He recognized one of them as Phra Somdet Koson, the Sangha inspector who had visited the temple the previous year.

The giggling subsided, and the youths looked at the three senior monks in surprise.

"I have established new rules and practices to bring our Wat Tawan Tok closer to the proper practice of Buddhism," Abbot Brahm said. "Please act with propriety and come to the prayer hall. In the village, you can celebrate as you like, but not in my temple."

The villagers looked disappointed. They began to drift away, still holding their buckets of water, as the temple bell tolled. The abbot led the monks towards the prayer hall. Som pulled his robe over his shoulder and descended the three wooden steps of his hut.

In the prayer hall, the monks settled down in half-lotus positions in front of the raised platform where the abbot and the two Bangkok monks were seated. Som sat with the 16 full-fledged monks of the temple. Behind him sat the nine novices. Along the sides the temple boys squirmed into position. Villagers began entering the hall, pulling at their wet clothes and looking around uncertainly.

"Phra Som, what is this about?" asked one of the elderly women who cooked for the monks.

"Auntie, there are monks here from Bangkok. They appear to have something to say to us."

Around him there was a buzz as villagers and monks whispered among themselves.

"Quiet please," the abbot said, smacking the staff of his fan against the wooden platform. "Quiet. Today we are honored by the visit of two important monks who come from the Supreme Council in Bangkok to view our temple. Let me now invite Phra Somdet Koson to speak. I expect all of you to pay attention."

Abbot Brahm nodded to Phra Somdet Koson who frowned at the villagers still straggling into the hall.

"I have come from His Holiness Prince Wachirayan, and from the Supreme Council of the Sangha. I am here to speak of the important reforms taking place throughout the land. From what I saw this morning, these reforms are as urgently needed here in Wat Wang Tawan Tok as they are in the backward temples of the northeast. However, I am confident, that under the leadership of Abbot Brahm, this temple will make rapid progress."

"First of all, the rule against contact between monks and females is necessary to maintain the holiness of the monkhood. This rule cannot be ignored, not even for *Songkran* and not even for novices. Monks should no longer compete in the longboat races."

There was a hiss of whispers among the villagers. Phra Somdet Koson frowned and then continued.

"Most important is improving the quality of sermons to reflect a correct understanding of the dharma. The birth stories of the Buddha will no longer be included."

Several of the monks turned to Phra Panya, who blushed at the attention. Phra Panya was popular among the lay people and many of the monks for his entertaining sermons that centered on the birth stories. Phra Panya not only had a powerful voice that reached the furthest corners of the prayer hall, but also had a knack for changing his voice for each of the characters in his tales—demons, animals, old men, hermits, kings and princesses.

Ignoring the stir in his audience, Phra Somdet Koson continued.

"It has also come to my attention that some sermons are delivered in the southern dialect and the correct Pali references are omitted. I listened to a sermon at Wat Mahathat last evening that was nearly incomprehensible. The abbot of Mahathat has agreed that henceforth all sermons will be delivered with correct pronunciation. Your abbot has agreed to do likewise. Monks who are uncertain of the correct pronunciation will be given instruction. I am told you have three monks, including the abbot, whose pronunciation is acceptable."

Som realized he was one of those. Most of the other monks had never visited Bangkok or studied the central dialect. It would not be easy to get his fellow monks to speak in the more subtle tones of Bangkok rather than the swinging tones of the south. Abbot Brahm was looking at him. He is going to make me responsible for this language training—yet another task that would take time away from medicine and meditation.

Abbot Brahm spoke up. "To give us an example of a proper sermon, I have asked Phra Somdet Koson to speak on the Brahmajāla Sutta."

Phra Somdet Koson nodded to the abbot and turned to his audience.

"The *suttas*, as all of you should know, are the sermons of the Lord Buddha and his leading disciples. They were memorized and repeated for many years before being written down more than two thousand years ago. Let me begin with the original Pali."

He drew a breath and began a long chant in Pali as villagers looked at each other in puzzlement. The novices looked around uncomfortably as the chant continued.

Som already had read the Sutta, the first of the Long Discourses of the Buddha. It discussed in great detail the ten precepts of devout Buddhists together with ways to put them into practice. It also elaborated on 62 incorrect beliefs that must be discarded to achieve peace of mind.

Phra Somdet Koson explained how incorrect beliefs prevented an understanding of the dharma. By the time he reached the second false belief, half a dozen villagers had quietly crawled to the entrance and disappeared into the bright sunshine beyond.

Two hours later, as the sermon droned to a conclusion, Som saw the only villager left was the gray-haired chairman of the temple committee who sat nodding with sleep in front of Phra Somdet Koson. Several temple boys were sprawled asleep along the walls and some of the elderly monks snoozed in the half-lotus position.

The sermon had been scholarly, but tedious. The dharma had to be more than just the words of the Buddha. It was an experience—one he was still struggling to attain. Dharma experience must come not from just the *suttas*, but from living a good life, helping others and practicing right concentration. There must be some way to help people understand and experience the dharma without putting them to sleep. But how?

29

PAKDEE
New Needs

"We must move to a bigger house," Apinya announced the moment Pakdee stepped onto the veranda of their rented bungalow. He took off his sandals and looked at his wife standing in the doorway, stiff with determination. It would not be easy to deflect her from her course, but as the husband he had to ensure their family decisions were careful and rational.

"We don't even use all the space we have here," he said, "and we have only been here a couple of months."

"We will soon have need for more space. The *Khon* troupe is coming together and needs a place to rehearse. A lot more practice is needed or they will embarrass me. The troupe will also need a place to store costumes and instruments."

"Can't that be done at the *monthon* headquarters?"

"With the staff expanding so quickly, you are already running out of room for office work, much less cultural work. And you know how important the high commissioner considers my cultural work."

"Yes, your work is important, but I don't think there is any suitable house available for us in Songkhla."

"Of course not. I have already looked. It is clear we must build our own mansion, one suitable for the principal assistant to the high commissioner of the *monthon*. I have already spoken with a builder and Phraya Sukhumnaiwinit has promised to allocate some land."

"You spoke with my boss without consulting me?"

"It was in the context of the work on *Khon* performances that he assigned to me."

"He is my superior. Anyway, it will cost a lot of money that I don't have."

"You need an income appropriate to your position. You are now the second most important person in *Monthon* Nakhon Srithammarat with many responsibilities. I too have responsibilities—for bringing culture to the *monthon*. We need income to fulfill those responsibilities."

"I am working on it, but these things take time."

"This is urgent. We need to have our mansion ready within seven months."

"Is there so much of a rush for the *Khon*?"

"Not entirely," Apinya said, her voice dropping to a whisper. "There is a personal reason we need more servants and more space."

"What now?" No matter how much Apinya got, she always wanted more. More clothes, more servants, more jewelry, more everything. She would just have to accept limitations.

"I am with child."

30

PREM
The Attraction of Risk

PAKPANANG, APRIL 4, 1904

The crowd had already pushed out the flimsy bamboo walls of the gambling hut twice since noon. Prem had to prop a line of boards against the outside of the wall. He tried to calm the excited bettors. There were too many people trying to lay their bets on the *Thua* mats in the makeshift betting hut. The big bettors were focused on *Po*, pushing to get closer to the mat. The betting had an undercurrent of urgency.

"Huat, where is the music? Why are you charging for drinks? Where is that big wheel thing you used to have?"

"It is Prem now, my name is Prem, not Huat," he explained for the third time. "Our permit for the *Songkran* festival covers only the traditional Thai and Chinese games and only for four days. So, no roulette. I apologize for the lack of drink and music, but with only four days to recover our expenses, the Jaikla family can't be as generous as we would like to be."

A cry of disappointment rose from the *Thua* mats as the final cowries were removed and there was no winner. Prem put his arm around a distraught bettor he knew owned a half dozen fishing boats.

"When I gambled, I often lost," he told the disappointed fisherman. "It's like fishing. Sometimes you lose your bait, but you can't let that stop you. Eventually you get lucky. But if the big fish are not biting, try for some small ones."

As usual, Ploi was trying to get the customers excited. A smile, a touch, a word of encouragement, a cheer for a winner. Somehow, she got all the male bettors trying to impress her with their daring. The cries of the bettors mixed with the clatter of cowries and betting counters. It was the music of money.

They had kept the casino building on the river operating as a nightclub and restaurant, but without gambling it wasn't profitable. They were forced to end the services of the singer and the five-man band. Ploi sang and sometimes he joined her for duets, but customers were getting tired of their act. Sia Leng still owned a portion of the nightclub, but without the gambling tax concession, he had lost interest. The Chinese businessman had closed all his other casinos in accordance with the law, though there were rumors he was financing cockfights out in the countryside.

By midnight, the crowds had diminished. Customers were drifting out to watch the shadow puppet performances starting on the field outside the temple gate. Those would go on until dawn. He chuckled as he caught a joke by the performer speaking in the crude language of the character *Ai Teng*. He smiled at Ploi who had leaned up against the wall of the betting hut. She gasped.

"The baby kicked," she said. "This is a feisty one."

It was good Ploi was pregnant again. More children—maybe a girl this time. The slowdown at the nightclub was not entirely unwelcome. It gave her more time to rest and gave him more time to be with her.

He took her arm and led her outside the hut. It felt good to have her lean on him. They sat on one of the stone benches outside the prayer hall. He grasped her shoulders and massaged the stiff muscles along her neck.

"A long day, eh?" he said. "You look tired."

"Oh, that's good. Don't stop. Yes, I had to sit down for the evening session."

"I'm pretty tired too—too many people gambling too hard. Two more days to go, so we should make enough money for a couple of months. *Songkran* is a life-saver."

Ploi swiveled on the bench so her feet rested against Prem's thighs.

"Looks like these feet are eager for a massage too," he said, pressing his thumbs down the middle of her soles."

"Mmmm. Somehow that makes my whole body feel better."

"That is our specialty here at Jaikla—making you forget your pain and suffering."

"Don't stop."

He liked the warm touch of her skin. He loved that she wanted him to touch her. Sometimes she seemed more devoted to the nightclub than to him. She was putting so much effort into it. Once the new baby came, she would have to slow down.

"We have to find a way to attract more people to the restaurant and the nightclub," she said. "Aside from days like today we are barely covering our expenses."

"Pakpanang is not Bangkok," he said. "Most people stay at home at night. Our main customers – the Chinese merchants, the royal officials and the few foreign businessmen – are getting bored. There are six other restaurants along the river and no one is making much money."

"I know all that. It is obvious the real money is in gambling. Sia Leng has gone back into it. Cockfighting and bullfighting—games for rural folk deep in the countryside where the police won't bother to go," she said. "Not our thing."

"We still have some capital. I think I could get a river boat for a good price. We could move produce from the hills down to the port more efficiently than those little canoes. Or I could plant our acreage on the western side of the road with fruit trees instead of rice. The water never seems to come at the right time for the rice fields there," he said. "Don't worry, there is always some way to make money."

"But it wouldn't be much. Our experience, our reputation, is for entertainment – nightclub, food, music, gambling – that is what people think of when they hear the name Jaikla," she said. "What if we opened the upstairs gambling room again, but only for those we trusted? We would have the only high-end gambling den in the province."

The weariness disappeared from her face and her words came faster.

"There would be no tax and we could work out a new deal with Sia Leng. It would be far more profitable. We would only serve the big bettors. Not only would that increase revenue, but it would reduce expenses. We always spent too much on space and staff catering to the little guys. This could work out well."

"How long do you think it would be before the police heard about it and arrested us," Prem said. "You remember how Sia Leng got the police to raid the gambling dens that were competing with us. Everyone who tried an underground casino was put out of business within months."

"Yes, but things are different now. There is no gambling tax farmer to spy on the illegals. There are no legal casinos to reward the police for the raids on the illegals. No rewards, no police action."

"You never know. Maybe a new police chief will want to impress his *farang* bosses in Bangkok. Maybe the *monthon* high commissioner will decide to enforce the gambling law. A fine could wipe out all the profits. We could even go to prison. I don't want the mother of my children in prison," he said. "Trust me. I can find some other way to earn a living."

"Never as much as a casino. The profits would be big. We would be important again."

She looked eager and excited. *Ayah*, she is determined to do this. She misses the bustle of the gambling den. She wants to be the center of attention again. My attention should be enough.

"Let's think about it carefully," he said.

"We still have the roulette wheel and the staff would be happy to go back to gambling and good tips again."

She would not give up. She never did. The last three years of running the casino had been exciting and rewarding for her. She enjoyed the power the casino profits had given her. She loved the grudging respect in the eyes of her father when she handed him his allowance each month. Too bad his appreciation didn't last very long. She loved the power it gave her over her brother Chit. Last year, he had come to her twice to beg for loans. His business venture in Penang was just about to reap big profits, he claimed. Ploi had given him most of the money he asked for, but only after he signed away all rights to the Jaikla Casino.

"Prem dear, you know nothing is as profitable as gambling," she said. "Nothing is as much fun. Think how much money we made just in our last two days. Everyone came—even the mayor. Each night we made three or four times our normal take. The casino was never so crowded. They loved the singing, our singing, but most of all they wanted a final win, a stroke of luck at the end. We still have our singing and our music at the nightclub, but the excitement is gone. Nobody wants to spend much for songs or food, no matter how good. They are only willing to spend their money for the thrill of winning more. Gambling on the special holidays is just not enough."

"It would be illegal and dangerous," he said. "The *monthon* commissioner sees gambling as a vice. Maybe he's right. There is something sinful about living on the addictions of others. Besides, it would be dangerous for us. We will soon have another child. We have to think of our children."

"You worry too much. The commissioner is all the way down in Songkhla and he is busy dealing with the *khaek* troublemakers. It is the local officials here that count. The district chief is Father's drinking buddy. Think of our best customers—the mayor, the wives of the district judge, the head of the Pakpanang Port Association, and even some of the royal family from Nakhon. What policeman would dare arrest these high-ranking people?"

Ploi's words tumbled out in a surge. He couldn't help but smile. This was an argument he was unlikely to win, but he shouldn't give up too easily. "Think of the risk. You know the king has banned all royal relatives and high officials from gambling even in the legal casinos. Would those important people risk their reputations, their positions and even their freedom just to gamble?"

"The risk is part of the attraction. The double risk of gambling and violating the law would pull in the rich and powerful whose lives are too easy. Gambling adds the thrill of danger to lives that are boring."

"Ploi, sweetheart—that is true not only of the gamblers."

"I don't want just to survive. Working hard, just scraping by. Stuck in the house with only the children and the servants for company. What about father and mother? I used to give them 40 percent of our profits from the casino. Now we barely break even and they are complaining there is not enough to live on."

"You don't have to take care of your father. Think about the risk."

"What if I could eliminate the risk?" Ploi asked in a soft tone. "What if I could ensure we would never be arrested?"

31

PAKDEE
Money for a Mansion

"I have found the solution," Apinya announced before Pakdee was halfway up the steps to the bungalow. He was tired after a difficult day in the office. He couldn't find a rickshaw and the long walk home through the hot and humid air of the town had been exhausting. He loosened the high collar of his uniform. It was soaked with sweat and chafed his neck. Why couldn't she at least let him sit down and drink some cool tea before launching into the speech he suspected she had spent most of the day preparing?

"The solution to what?" he asked.

"To finding the money for a proper place to live."

He suppressed a groan. Apinya had not let up in her insistence on a grand residence. As her pregnancy went forward, she seemed to gain not only weight but determination. She had engaged the builder who had built the residence for High Commissioner Phraya Sukhumnaiwinit, though she had made it clear that she wanted something larger than his elegant but rather small house. Many nights were spent shuffling through large sheets with drawings and floor plans.

"His family is in Bangkok. Ours will be here. We will have children and servants. We will entertain and stage *Khon* dramas. It must be big."

"We will talk of this after I bathe."

He had already explained that his official salary was small and he was still new to the position, so it was not an easy matter to generate revenue. But his role in port management did look promising. Every ship coming into the port had to have his approval to unload its cargo. There were still concerns about weapons being brought in for the raja's followers so all ships were supposed to be searched. After months of finding nothing dangerous, he had begun issuing exemptions to the search requirement to those shippers he trusted. These exemptions generated gifts that ranged from small blocks of goods to leather bags of silver coins left on his desk. He made it clear to the shippers that the exemptions were not certain. If he had information that weapons were being shipped in, even exempt ships would be searched and the punishment would be doubled. He was less concerned about the arrival of goods subject to tax. That was the responsibility of the harbor tax concessionaire, who had taken advantage of the security searches to make it harder to avoid tax. The harbor revenue was good, but he was a long way from being able to afford the mansion Apinya wanted.

He took his time with his evening bath. He pulled off his jacket and unwrapped his *phajonggraben*. He tied a *phakaoma* around his waist. He dipped the tin scoop into the big earthen jar in the water room and held his breath. He let the chilly water sluice down his chest. The cold was a delightful torment after the heat of the day. He poured a scoopful over his head and squeezed the water out of his moustache. He peeled off the wet *phakaoma* and rubbed himself with a dry one. He stepped into the long tube of his *phatung* and pulled it tight across his stomach. Apinya disapproved of the *phatung* he found so comfortable, but it would be better to argue about that than about the mansion. Maybe she's already gone to her sleeping mat. She had been sleeping more lately—saying it was good for the baby. Good for all of them, really.

As soon as he emerged onto the back veranda of the bungalow, he saw Apinya waiting. She looked pleased as she *waied* him and knelt at his feet.

"I have found a solution to the problem," she said. "You always say that our income will be increasing, that we don't have much now, but we will before too long. So, the obvious solution is to borrow the money we need now and pay it back when the income is flowing in."

"That is a good idea," he said with a smile. "Unfortunately, the banks and money lenders all want some surety, land or gold or something to take if we don't repay the loan. I have already checked."

"Your position can be your surety and I have already found a willing lender."

"You have? And what does this kind money lender want as collateral?"

"Nothing—well, only your signature on a contract to repay the loan."

"Truly? That sounds good. Who is this person?"

"He is a prominent Chinese merchant from Nakhon Srithammarat town who wants to start up businesses in Songkhla. The man is wealthy and understanding of our position. He came to the house with a half-dozen men. He is a bit rough-looking and crude but he understands our situation."

"You did all this without telling me."

"You were busy at the office and we need to move quickly. Anyway, my responsibility is to take care of our money and our status."

"Who is this crude, but understanding money-lender?"

"He is a Teochew, a Sae-Liu, so he has good connections with the merchant who has been bringing in the musical instruments for the *Khon*. He is well known in Nakhon. His name is something like Jay—no that is big sister." Her face brightened. "It's Jate. Jate Sae-Liu."

The blood rushed from his face and he was unable to speak as Apinya looked at him, puzzled.

"It's a fair arrangement. He asks only a small interest rate and can give us as long as we need to repay. It's perfect. We can have our mansion in time for the baby if we hurry."

He leaned back against the wall. He felt weak and unbalanced. Jate. It had been years since he heard that name said aloud, but he heard it in his head every day.

"It really is the best way out for us."

"No, I cannot do this," he said, surprised at the harsh determination in his voice.

"Why not, it is perfect."

"No, we will never do business with this Jate."

Apinya opened her mouth to protest and then went silent at the fierce look on her husband's face.

"I will find some other way," he said, turning his back on Apinya.

He stared out into the little garden. He could never deal with Jate. But all those expenses and debts! It was hopeless. The unpaid merchants would complain to the commissioner. Sukhumnaiwinit would be disappointed. The *monthon* staff would laugh at him. He could lose his position. Apinya would be humiliated. With a baby on the way, they would have no money. There was no way out. It was like the black iron gate of prison was swinging shut on him once again.

32

DAM
Police Protection

Dam paused at the back door of the Jaikla restaurant. The moonlight picked out the jumble of wooden buildings along the river and glinted off the dark surface of the water. He looked up at the path above the restaurant, then back towards the water. Across the river, the silhouette of a fishing boat glided along the far side. Satisfied no one was watching, he slipped through the door and moved carefully through a storeroom before emerging into the candlelight of the main dining room. He ignored the stares of the waiters cleaning the tables. He walked to the office where Ploi sat with the accounts.

"Good evening Miss Ploi," he said with what he hoped was a confident smile. "Have you eaten yet?"

"Good evening, Sergeant Sakda. To what do we owe the honor of your visit?"

"You can call me Dam. That is what my friends call me," he said, trying not to stare.

The light from two candles gave Ploi's face a warm glow. The cloth over one shoulder had slipped so he could see the side of one breast thrusting against the thin material. *She has become even more beautiful after the birth of her child.* Her face was softer, more rounded, but still marked by her large dark eyes and high cheekbones. Her thick hair, cut short in the traditional style, framed her face. She sat upright on the mat with her legs folded behind her in a posture that showed she was still supple. Her *phajonggraben* had ridden up over one knee and his eyes followed the smooth flesh of her leg up to her thigh pressed tight against the satin.

"Fine, then Sergeant Dam," she said with a smile, "why are you here? We made our payment only last week. Business is good, but that doesn't mean we can pay you more."

He had rehearsed his words on the boat ride across the river, but he took a moment to think what he should say.

"First, you need to be more careful. Word has reached the high commissioner of illegal gambling dens springing up since the closure of the legal casinos. He has issued orders for each district police station to set up special anti-gambling forces. The police are unhappy about this because the government won't pay a reward for closing underground casinos the way the gambling tax concessionaires used to. Most policemen think there is more money in recovering stolen goods or settling disputes. So, I was the only one to volunteer for the new Pakpanang anti-gambling force."

"That was a good move, but obvious," Ploi noted. "Don't expect a bigger payoff because of that. Your work will now be easier because you don't have to worry about other policemen conducting a raid."

"Well, I will have to come to your restaurant more often to check and I have to spread the payment to my men," he said.

"We will have dinner for you and your men whenever you come. And you are welcome to the second floor," she said.

The gambling room he had helped Ploi and Prem design had turned out well. Two doors blocked a narrow staircase. The first door was flimsy pine with a sign saying "supplies." He had recommended Ploi hire a heavy-set Sikh friend to guard the door. As a British dependent, the Sikh could not be arrested without the permission of the British consul in Songkhla. The second door was thick ironwood with a strong steel lock. A third door of cast iron with a sliding view slot stood at the top of the staircase. The room had a wall recess to hide the roulette wheel. The trays of betting tokens and the iron cash box could be hidden under the floor. There was a secret exit out the back. It should work well.

"Come up and see the gambling room in operation," she said.

Dam was proud of the design, but he had only seen it under construction. "No. I don't want to be seen by the gamblers. You never know who might be a spy ready to turn you in for a reward," he said. "The commissioner seems to be serious about gambling. This is personal for him—maybe from his time as a monk. Perhaps he wants to curry favor with the minister. Or, who knows, maybe he just wants to increase the pressure so he can get a bigger payoff. All I know is that the Pakpanang police have been ordered to do more."

"Would it help if I gave you tip-offs about other gambling dens?"

"That would be good," he said. "I can build my reputation by closing them down."

"I can't give you information on Sia Leng's operations—we are too close and I don't want attention focused on the former legal gambling operators. But there are others—people hosting card games in their homes, villages with weekly cockfights, and there is an underground lottery. I don't know who is behind it yet, but it competes with mine."

"That I already know," he grinned. "That's my second news. Jate is the one who launched the lottery. Its customers are mostly coolies in the tin mines and in the port."

"That doesn't compete with us," she said.

"Not yet, but he wants to win more customers in the big towns. Jate will do everything he can to make his lottery more popular than yours. It will be hard to stop him. Unlike a casino, a lottery operation is nowhere and everywhere. Like you, he uses secret codes and distributes tickets and prizes through a network of people who profit from the lottery."

"The market is big, but competition from Jate will force us to offer better prizes, so lower profits for both of us," she said.

"It's worse than that. I hear he is planning to open gambling dens in Sichon and Tungsong. If those go well, soon he will do something in Pakpanang. You should know he has the backing of one of the Chinese secret societies—the Teochew *Angyi* in Nakhon. The *Angyi* is powerful."

"Sia Leng might get us support from the Hokkien *Angyi*."

"I fear a strike at your operation. Jate's gang is bigger than ever."

"Just make sure your informants are alert," Ploi said. "I will talk to Sia Leng to see what he can do."

"There is another problem," he frowned. "Your father borrowed money from Jate and he is not making the agreed payments. You need to tell your father to pay off his debt. Jate is getting impatient."

He watched her smile vanish. She stared at the account ledger.

"He borrowed from Jate? Father's stupid fishing boat venture. Now, I will have to help him even more."

"Do it soon. On this, Jate will get the support of the Chinese business community as well as the *Angyi*. They don't like to see debts unpaid."

33

PAKDEE
The Raja's Return

By late morning the heat was already intense. The sun glared out of a clear sky and slanted off the azure water of Pattani Bay. Pakdee squinted between two *Istana* officials. He wanted to see the raja's face as he stepped ashore, but he knew it would be dangerous for him to get too close. He mustn't chance being recognized, even though he no longer looked like the Muslim scholar who had advised the raja two years earlier. He was dressed in the stained cotton sarong of a sugar cane juice vender. He pushed a battered cart with a pile of canes and a steel wringer to squeeze the juice from them.

He had discussed his trip with Phraya Sukhumnaiwinit and the new high commissioner for Pattani, Phraya Sakseni. Sakseni had been eager for Pakdee to come, but Sukhumnaiwinit had discouraged him.

"This is no longer our responsibility. Prince Damrong has split off five of the Muslim states into a separate Pattani *monthon*. Looking after them is the job of the new commissioner. I've had enough," he said.

His boss's words were disappointing. His successes in dealing with the problems in the traditional Malay areas had given him his opportunity to rise. He had made key contributions to the defeat of Abdul Kadir. Now his value was no longer clear. He had to concentrate on finding more income for his family. He was drawn to Pattani. Malay resentment could erupt again into violence.

Phraya Sakseni had arrived in Pattani a month earlier to head the *monthon*. He had brought officials with him and took on some members of the old *Istana* staff. He had the backing of the secretary to the raja, but there were dark rumors and secretive meetings that alarmed Sakseni. The new Pattani commissioner had come to depend on Pakdee for advice and information.

"I would truly appreciate it," Sakseni had appealed to Sukhumnaiwinit, "if you would let Pakdee come to Pattani and help with this—just temporarily."

The *monthon*'s biggest problem was now gliding towards the dock. Abdul Kadir Kamarudden, was aboard the weekly steamship from Bangkok. The former raja had been released from house arrest in the northern province of Pitsanulok and allowed to return to Pattani. Pakdee had recommended leniency, but now the release seemed premature.

He told his informants in the important mosques to be alert for signs of rebellion. He used his network to spread stories of Abdul Kadir living in luxurious confinement in the north. The *monthon* staff had been ordered to stay away from the port when Abdul Kadir arrived.

Despite these preparations, he was concerned at what he saw on the bright water of the bay. Nearly a hundred boats – fishing boats, sailing junks and a pair of steam yachts – were escorting Abdul Kadir's ship. More than 500 people crowded the dock. They seemed to have forgotten how foolish the raja had been in fomenting rebellion.

As a condition of his release two weeks earlier, Abdul Kadir had issued a statement renouncing any role in Pattani political affairs. Would this show of support lead the former raja to renege?

He watched carefully as two sailors leaped onto the dock and secured heavy lines to the massive iron mooring bollards. They pulled out the gangway and stepped back. A man in a black velvet fez peered at the throng. A murmur swept through them and swelled as Abdul Kadir, looking older and heavier in a black jacket, stepped onto the gangway and paused to look out over the crowd.

A cheer arose and soon changed into a steady chant.

"*Daulat Tuanku. Hidup* Pattani. *Daulat Tuanku. Hidup* Pattani."

Abdul Kadir raised his hand and nodded to the crowd. He looked at the police guard sent to escort him and shook his head. Without a word, he walked to the first of three waiting carriages. Everyone seemed disappointed, but Pakdee was encouraged. The man had looked weary and fearful. Was there a glint of defiance in his eyes? We will have to discourage any thoughts of a return to power.

He felt someone tugging on his *phatung*. It was a young boy begging for sugar cane juice. He smiled and spun the wheel of the wringer, catching a stream of the greenish-yellow juice in a thick tumbler. The boy gulped it down and held up the glass for more.

If the government could show the local people the benefits of being part of the Siamese nation, maybe it would all work out.

34

SOM
Forest Monk

Phra Som sat in his hut trying to meditate, but the noise outside made it more difficult than usual. He sighed and clambered to his feet. He looked out of the hut in surprise at the crowd jostling in front of the ordination hall. Phra Tissa sat in a lotus position at the entrance to the hall with dozens of people milling before him. Phra Panya bustled about, trying to get the villagers to form orderly lines.

Som adjusted his robes and walked towards the crowd.

"Quiet. Wait your turn," he heard Panya say in a stern tone. "Everyone will get a chance. Phra Tissa needs to concentrate to get the numbers right. If you interrupt his concentration you will be the one to blame for a losing number. Think how you would feel if you were interrupted during your important business on the sleeping mat."

The crowd laughed and an old lady with a wide gap between her front teeth called out, "What would you know about such business?"

"We monks also know how to—sleep," Panya shouted back with a wink. "Phra Tissa needs to concentrate so you can prosper, but don't forget to share your prosperity with the temple. The more merit you make, the luckier you get."

"Why not give us all the same number?" a young, heavyset woman asked. "That would save time and give us all an equal chance to win."

"Then you'll each win less," Panya said. "Besides, the numbers come from dreams and visions that are not always so clear. The esteemed seer must interpret these for each person and each lottery date."

The underground lottery has come to our temple, Som thought. The crowds begging the elderly Phra Tissa for winning numbers had grown each day since the underground lottery began three months ago. Phra Tissa had told people he dreamed of a three-headed dragon battling five ogres in a large circular arena. One of the villagers bet the number 350 and won a large prize. Since then, more of Phra Tissa's visions had led to winning numbers. The temple was taking the place of the gambling dens shut down by the government at the start of the year.

With the evening sermons now delivered in central Thai using approved material, attendance had dropped off. Phra Panya had been affected more than anyone. Once the most popular of the temple speakers, he struggled with the new style of sermon. Som and Abbot Brahm had provided notes on the *suttas* for him to use, but his delivery was no longer fast-paced and laced with jokes. He complained that even his most enthusiastic admirers looked bored. He asked to be excused from speaking.

So, when the interest in Phra Tissa's lottery predictions picked up, Panya put himself in charge of managing the crowds coming to get numbers. He would trumpet the success of past numbers, relate the predictions to magic in the birth tales of the Buddha and appeal for pledges of donations to the temple. The abbot, initially opposed to Phra Tissa's predictions, changed his mind after the first big lottery winner made a 100-baht cash donation. It was like the temple is the casino, getting the house cut.

The gambling and the pressure for donations was only one of the problems afflicting Wat Wang Tawan Tok. The abbot had been awarded the title of *Phra racha* of the *thep* level, but he wanted a higher title. He seemed convinced that donations and building improvements were the services most noticed by the senior monks in the capital.

This desire for titles was a kind of greed and attachment. Already unpopular with the abbot, Som knew that anything he said would be seen as a personal attack on the abbot. But silence felt like cowardly compliance with actions against the dharma.

A sharp crack and a crash silenced the villagers for a moment. A team of workmen was working on a new prayer hall. The abbot said it would be taller and grander than the old one. Som had tried to explain to the abbot that more money was needed for medicines and space for the sick people who came to the temple. Abbot Brahm, however, had dismissed his arguments, insisting "a beautiful new building will inspire greater faith in the teachings of the Buddha and earn greater merit for all of us. Look at Wat Mahathat—it is venerated because it is large and filled with hundreds of Buddha images."

It was foolish to try to compete with the largest and most revered temple in the south. Wat Mahathat had many more monks and many more followers. It also held relics of the Lord Buddha—something that

Wat Wang Tawan Tok could never match.

We should be offering something different, such as effective medical care, training in meditation and teachings that reflect the purest scriptures. The abbot, however, had simply ignored his suggestions. A group of younger monks had agreed with Som and encouraged him to press the argument with the abbot. That had only annoyed him and divided the monks into two camps. Supporters of the abbot, including most of the older monks, outnumbered the young monks behind Som. Phra Pat, one of those young monks, hurried towards Som.

"He's here, and he is going to give a sermon for monks in a few minutes in the prayer hall. Come quick. You need to meet him."

Som strode towards the prayer hall. There had been talk for weeks that Phra Sawat Purithatto, a renowned forest monk and meditation teacher, would visit Nakhon as part of his *thudong*, or wandering ascetic practice. As his eyes adjusted to the dimness of the hall, he saw several of the young monks gathered around a slim figure sitting on the floor. The monk's robes were dark and stained, unlike the bright orange of the temple monks. His skin was brown and weathered. His arms and shoulders looked powerful, but he sat with an ease that seemed to relax the curious young monks around him. It was hard to estimate his age. He looked up with a smile as Som found a place in the circle.

"Thank you for welcoming me," Sawat said in a deep voice tinged with the tones of the northeast. "I left my temple in Udon several weeks ago at the end of the rains retreat and decided I should *thudong* in the south, an area I had never seen before. I spend most of my time in the forest in meditation but, like my own teacher Phra Ajahn Sao Kantasilo, I also feel an obligation to teach the dharma during my wanderings. I try to explain what I understand of the teachings of the Buddha. Here in Nakhon Srithammarat, one of the oldest Buddhist sites in Siam and especially here in an historic temple before fellow monks, I am humbled. Perhaps it would be best if I just answered any questions you might have."

"Did you really walk all the way from Udon? Why not take the steamship?" a monk asked to laughter from the other monks.

"There is nothing wrong with taking a steamship or one of the new railway trains if all you care about is arriving at your destination. For *thudong* monks, however, it is not a geographical destination we seek, but the experience of the journey. I took a train ride once, and the countryside passed in a blur. I had the same companions for the whole trip and they slept most of the time, so what did I learn? Very little. Walking slowly through the forest I can stop to look at a caterpillar or pry open a seed pod. I can observe the dharma of nature—the trees, the animals, the rocks and the water. Most importantly I have the time to observe my inner self."

"Aren't you afraid of the beasts of the jungle like wild elephants and tigers?"

"Yes, I am sometimes afraid, but it is in dealing with fear that I strengthen my mind and spirit through *samadhi*—pure concentration in peace and stillness."

"How does that happen?"

"Normally our minds are disturbed by fleeting thoughts that are gone before we can fully understand them," he said. "Our thoughts tend to go to extremes. One moment the mind soars high into the sky; at another it plunges deep into the earth; then it darts back up into the air. Who on earth can overtake such a mind? You need a strong will to control it. I suspect you have all dealt with this problem in your own meditation practice."

The monk had perfectly described Som's own meditation problems.

"Experience in a dark forest or a charnel ground sometimes brings a crisis of fear that provides the occasion for you to gain control. Let me tell you about one such crisis."

Phra Sawat dropped his voice and leaned slightly forward. The circle of monks edged closer.

"I had practiced my teacher's meditation methods for two years and felt I was becoming quite capable. My teacher told me, however, that my practice was not yet deep and strong. He told me: 'If you are afraid of the wild beasts of the forest, you must seek them out and become their friend.' So, when I heard villagers say that tigers from the hill had just killed a buffalo, I decided to try to get close."

"Walking up the hill I heard an unusual sound in the thick brush above the path. A tiger poked its head out of a bush and looked straight at me. It was huge. I felt like someone had poured cold water down my back. At the same time, sweat beaded on my brow. The blood drained from my face. For a moment all thought of meditation and dharma fled from my mind. I wanted only to run away. Yet I knew if I started running, I would be killed. I regretted I had not come with a companion. That way, of course, I would only have to outrun him rather than the tiger."

The monks laughed and then hushed to hear more of the tale.

"The tiger growled and leaped into the path before me. My breathing was fast and my heart pounded, but I slowly sat down into a full lotus position right there in the path. I tried to meditate, but my mind wouldn't focus. I was terrified of the tiger. I was afraid I would shit my robes. They were already soaked with sweat. The tiger roared again. I was shaking as if I had a jungle fever. Only then did I realize my mind refused to focus out of sheer fright. I straightened my back and cajoled my mind to face death if it came. I concentrated on my breathing, slowing down and feeling its light touch as air entered my nostrils and was pulled down to my lungs. Then the mind became calm. I heard the tiger's growl and noted it simply as a sound. Like the wind brushing the trees, it was just another noise. My spirit rose high into the air. I could look down and see myself sitting calmly on the path. I watched from far above, totally detached as the tiger sniffed and circled around me. When my spirit returned to my body, I felt no fear. I could look into the tiger's eyes. I could smell his pungent odor. I could almost feel his breath on my neck, but I was serene."

"What did the tiger do?"

"It killed and ate me, of course," Sawat said with a grin.

The monks laughed. "No really, what did the tiger do?"

"Truly, I don't know. From concentration on my breathing my mind found a peaceful understanding and I was able to see my attachments. One by one I sought to separate from them—from desire for food, affection for fellow monks, love of my mother and finally my attachment to life. Death would come. It mattered little when. My fear of the tiger seemed foolish. It might have been an hour or perhaps two, but when awareness of my surroundings returned, the tiger was gone."

Som edged forward. "Is it possible to achieve this level of concentration – to leave your body and fly above the world – by studying the Buddha's teaching and practicing the various methods of meditation here in the temple? Without facing tigers?"

Sawat smiled at him. "Perhaps. There appear to be many paths to enlightenment. Achieving a deep understanding of the dharma from the scriptures may be one, but for me, study and practice were not enough. I could never achieve the depth of concentration that would allow me to overcome the distractions of my own attachments until that meeting with the tiger. A monk must be a warrior battling the unwholesome forces within. A warrior needs skill, courage, experience and knowledge, but the ultimate learning comes from his own fear. A warrior can truly test himself only in the field of battle. If fear is defeated, the mind will be suffused with courage and peace."

"And you can really fly?" one of the young monks asked.

"Flight is the ultimate non-attachment taught by the Buddha."

The circle of monks was silent as they thought about Phra Sawat's words. The silence was broken by one of the temple boys peering in from the doorway. "The abbot needs three more monks for funeral prayers. Who is coming?"

There was no movement for a moment, then the monks rose to their feet and *waied* the forest monk before following the temple boy.

Som remained behind. He looked around at the ornate decorations of the prayer hall, the paintings on the walls, the lines of shiny bronze Buddha images and the glistening teak floor. It all seemed unnecessary. He wanted what the slim figure sitting before him had found. He made a sudden decision.

"Phra Sawat, when you return to the forest, would you accept this unworthy monk as your student?"

35

PAKDEE
Business Arrangement

Pakdee looked through the sheaf of bills on his desk once again. He added up the figures and groaned. Apinya had piled up debts to builders and suppliers at an alarming rate. Massive teak pillars from northern Thailand, a whole team of wood carvers, the best window glass from Singapore. His income had risen, but expenses climbed even faster. There was no money to pay for all of that. He would lose everything. Maybe he could just disappear. But there was a baby coming. He couldn't leave.

He had reached agreements with shippers and importers on regular payments for quick access to the port. British and Chinese mine companies had paid well for tin concessions. The office of high commissioner's principal secretary was profitable, but it would take time to earn enough to cover the costs of the mansion. He might also have to share some of the money with his staff and maybe even Somsak, who had been promoted to internal inspector. Money was just too tight right now. He had appealed to Apinya to economize. She always agreed, but then went ahead and spent more money. She insisted they have a house and a manner of living "suitable to our high rank."

The house was the largest expense, but the others such as clothes, servants and the *Khon* troupe were also high. She didn't understand why he had rejected her proposal to borrow money from Jate and he couldn't explain it to her.

Jate was responsible for his humiliation, his years in prison and the loss of his family. Next time, it would be the other way. He thought of Jate in a court room listening to one of Pakdee's judges pronounce sentence on him—10 years in prison—no, life in prison—no, execution. He smiled at the thought, someday, somehow…

That would never happen if he could not solve his debt problems. He was the one who could end up in prison. He had tried to explain the problem to Phraya Sukhumnaiwinit, but his mentor had simply said he did not want to get involved in the private affairs of his subordinates. Despite the commissioner's project to turn him into a proper Siamese gentleman, he would be dimissed if he became an embarrassment to the government. The commissioner had made it clear there would be no special favors. So, he had to make sure his creditors did not complain to his boss. It was essential to find some way to pay them, or at least offer a plan to pay them.

A knock on the door and his assistant peered in. "A Chinese merchant to see you, sir, Sia Leng. He says he has an appointment."

He gestured for the man to come in. Seeing these Chinese businessmen was tedious, but often useful. When Sia Leng had asked for a meeting, he had checked on him. A former gambling tax farmer, the man had found ways to replace the income from the gambling. He now imported mining machinery and was said to have a good deal of cash.

"Come in, come in," he said as the heavyset man stepped through the doors and raised his hands in a respectful *wai*.

"Honored sir, it is kind of you to meet with a humble businessman like myself," he said.

Pakdee noted the heavy gold chains around his neck, two rings with large rubies and his well-cut Western clothes.

The greeting led to the inconsequential chat and the drinking of tea required to start such meetings. Sia Leng praised government efforts to control the Malay rulers, build new roads, improve the docks and dredge the entrance to the harbor. The man managed to imply all this was due to Pakdee's great abilities. This Sia Leng obviously knew flattery never hurt with government officials. But what did he want?

The man noted the economic impacts of the casino shutdowns.

"This has caused losses both to the government and to those who operated the gambling dens," he said with a sad expression.

"Your role as gambling tax farmer for the *monthon* is known and appreciated," Pakdee said. "But that is finished now."

He had expected a complaint on the casino closures, but there was little he could do. Shutting the gambling dens was a royal policy Phraya Sukhumnaiwinit had implemented with particular enthusiasm. The commissioner insisted there was a connection between the casinos and the crime, poverty and opium addiction that afflicted many of the towns of the *monthon*.

"It is unfortunate for you our national policy and our national honor have required the closure of the gambling concessions. I am powerless to change national policy," Pakdee said. "Eventually, gambling will be outlawed in all areas, even in Bangkok. *Monthon* Nakhon Srithammarat was simply the first to see this change."

"That is understood and accepted," Sia Leng said to his surprise. "I would not presume to ask for a change in policy. However, I am sure you realize implementing this policy will be a great challenge. Thai people, from the lowliest fisherman to the wealthiest aristocrat, love to gamble. They have enjoyed this pastime for centuries. Cockfights, bullfights, cricket fights, even fights with fish—all for betting. The people love all the different card games and the cowrie games like *Thua* and *Po*. Even poor slaves bet their meager cash on their favorite numbers in one lottery or another. Shutting down the legal gambling dens does not shut down the desire to gamble. In fact, it continues more than ever, but now the government gets no revenue from it."

"That is so," Pakdee agreed, "but we have little choice but to do our best to implement the government's policy."

"Perhaps I can be of service. As the former gambling tax concessionaire, I have information useful in the control of illegal gambling. If I help you locate these gambling operations, the owners and the customers can be fined. These fines will allow the government to replace at least some of its lost gambling tax revenue."

"That would indeed be of benefit. I have orders to coordinate with the district officers and the police to enforce the gambling laws. If you would bring such information to me, I would be grateful."

"I would be happy to do that, honored sir. However, once the police start acting, my sources of information will dry up, unless I am trusted by the gambling operators."

"And you would keep that trust by…?"

"To be trusted, I must be one of them. I must run gambling dens myself. This would, of course, be only to maintain my ability to report to you on illegal gambling."

"I see, but letting you operate gambling dens would undermine the objective of the policy—to eliminate gambling."

"True, but completely eliminating gambling, sadly, is an impossible goal," Sia Leng said with an exaggerated sigh. "I would help you achieve a more realistic and useful goal—controlling and gaining revenue from a vice that can never be completely eliminated."

"This would not be viewed well by the civilized nations that have criticized us for gambling," Pakdee objected, repeating something the commissioner often said. "You must understand that what we do on gambling and opium is part of a bigger plan. We need to gain the respect of the *farang* nations to maintain our independence."

"Who would tell them of our little arrangement?" Leng asked, raising his thin eyebrows. "The government could still proclaim gambling is illegal and would win sympathy for its efforts. The information I could provide would give you a steady stream of arrests to impress the *farangs* and a stream of fines to provide income for the royal government."

Pakdee leaned back and looked at the man opposite him.

"And you, of course, would get the income from your gambling operations without interference from the police."

"Oh, no, no. My operations would have to be raided as well. If not, the others would no longer trust me. Just not so often and not without some advance notice."

"Still you would be fined and lose money."

Sia Leng smiled. "I am willing to pay. Such fines would just be part of the costs of doing business, like paying for tokens, staff, *Thua* mats or cowries."

"So, you would profit, the government would gain income from the fines and the *farangs* would be impressed by the raids and arrests."

"It would be a business arrangement in which all parties would benefit," Leng said with a smile stretching across his broad face.

"I understand your thinking, but Phraya Sukhumnaiwinit would never agree. You recall how he handled the case of Chin Sung Huat—rejected a $1,000 donation and sentenced him to six months in prison."

"Yes, everyone was impressed when the commissioner said even a $10,000 donation would not reduce the sentence by a single day," Leng said "The commissioner gained much face and the ordinary folks now feel free to speak up to the commissioner about problems caused by even the most powerful people. That is why I have come to you. The word is that you better understand the practical needs of business, especially when it hurts no one. In this case, not only is no one injured, but we generate income for the government, employment and enjoyment for the people and a steady stream of police raids to show the *farangs*."

"But all this would create work, risk and responsibility for me."

"And that work should not go unrewarded," Leng said. "Funds could be made available to compensate you for that work."

"I hope you are not suggesting I take regular bribes," Pakdee said trying to look appropriately stern.

Sia Leng's mouth dropped open.

"Such payments would be illegal, of course, and hard to disguise," Pakdee said. "I prefer to operate as above board as possible."

"Then what?"

"I understand you are cash rich at the moment and have already begun to lend out some of that cash. You are recognized as a money lender."

"Yes," Leng said cautiously.

"At the moment, I have had some unexpected expenses and would be willing to accept a loan from you. I would propose to repay the loan in amounts you would enter in your accounts each month, even if, say, sometimes the payment was not quite in full or not quite on time."

"Of course, I can be most flexible on loan repayments," Leng beamed. "Then we have an agreement. It will be an honor to be of service to the high commissioner's assistant. Just let me know how much you need."

Once the big Chinese had backed out of the room Pakdee sat back and took a deep breath. Apinya could finish the mansion. He would have the funds for all the dinners he was expected to host for subordinates. The pressure would be off.

What would this new arrangement mean in the years to come? For the first time since leaving prison he was acting against the wishes of Phraya Sukhumnaiwinit. The commissioner had always insisted that gambling and opium dens had to be closed down. But the *monthon* required money to build the roads, canals, ports and railroads needed to unify the region. The gambling fines would help with that. So, really, he was acting in the best interests of his mentor and the country. But it was yet another secret he had to guard.

36

PLOI
Business Disputes

Ploi counted a stack of gold coins and slipped them into one small leather bag. She put another stack into a second bag and placed the rest into the heavy iron box in front of her. The last few months had been even more lucrative than expected. She had been right about their customers. Making gambling illegal had only whetted their appetites for risk and reward. The upstairs room at the restaurant was busy every night. There were fewer customers than at the old casino, but they bet more. The gaming also boosted income from the restaurant. Some men would bring their wives and children for a meal and then disappear upstairs while the family ate at the restaurant. Hungry from gambling they would order food sent up. The hoist system she had devised was working well. It sent food from the kitchen in a large box raised by pulleys along a track set in the wall to the gambling room.

She looked up as Prem opened the door. He kissed her neck and smiled at her.

"Not now," she said. "I am working on the accounts."

"It looks to me like you are finished. Such hard work should be rewarded," he said. "I finished the repairs to that broken window. I think we should reward each other." He massaged the muscle of her calf and began to work his hands upward, but Ploi pushed them down.

"My feet, please. The toes too."

Prem hesitated and then complied, pressing both thumbs into the soles of her foot. She knew he loved to touch her, but disliked taking orders. She also knew that touching often led to much more. Today, there just wasn't time.

"Sergeant Dam is due here any moment and I have to deliver Father's payment after that," she said. "So just a foot massage." He would be disappointed and perhaps even annoyed. Prem didn't like being told what he could and couldn't do, even if it was obvious. But he usually gave in if she insisted.

"I am the man of the house. That means what I say goes," he often complained. She would try to soothe him by saying, "Of course, dear, but you wouldn't want to pressure me when I am not ready. No fun for either of us."

That was always a telling argument, but if he needed further persuasion, she would add, "You don't want to be like your father." That ended any discussion. Prem blamed his father's domineering ways for his brother's departure and his mother's unhappiness.

Today Prem appeared content to massage her feet and calves, moving his hands occasionally higher to see if he could arouse her for something more. She liked the feel of his powerful hands on her and she had to suppress the tingling racing up the insides of her thighs. It would be nice, but there was no time.

Disappointed by her apparent disinterest, Prem returned to stroking the bottom of her foot with one hand and reached over to heft one of the leather bags on the table with the other.

"This feels like a lot. Your father does nothing to help the casino. Why does he get so much?"

"It's really his casino."

Prem shouldn't question her decisions on money. He didn't understand how important it was to make sure Father was pleased with her work.

"It has been our ideas, our money, our work and our risk that have earned this money," Prem said. "It's okay to give him something, but not so much. We need to build up our reserve in case of problems."

"It's the family business, and he is still the leader of the family, even though he has moved away. In your family business was there any question about your father getting the proceeds?"

"That was different. It was his ship, bought with his sweat. He was the manager. He had the customer contacts, and made the big decisions. He should have listened to us more, but he did the work. That gave him the right. Your father does nothing for the casino. He has his own business affairs, and he doesn't share any of the proceeds."

"There are few proceeds right now – the debt he owes for the fishing boats – he has to make those payments. He has lost his position as *kamnan* and that has disrupted income from his land rentals. Some tenants have complained to the *monthon* government and his old connections in the Nakhon royal family seem helpless to do anything."

"He will have to control his expenditures just like we did when the casino was first shut down," Prem said, stopping his massage.

"He already has. Some of his men have deserted him because he reduced their pay and the others are unhappy. All that makes it even harder to collect his rents."

"That's not our problem."

"It's a family problem." She looked up at Prem. "Father is still the head of the family and we have to respect him."

"Maybe you should ask your mother about that."

Why did he have to bring up the problems between her father and mother? She had to deal every day with Mother's complaints and she was tired of it.

A knock on the door. Sergeant Dam poked his head into the room.

"May I come in?"

"Not now," Prem said.

"Oh, it's alright," she said.

It was a welcome interruption to an argument that wasn't going to be resolved. She saw annoyance flash across Prem's face, but she smiled and moved to the door. "Come on in."

The burly policeman sidestepped Prem and saluted her. She nudged Prem towards the door.

"Prem dear, we can talk later. Let me take care of this first."

She knew Prem and Dam were uncomfortable with each other. Prem had warned her Dam had a bad reputation and she should avoid becoming too dependent on him. But the man had done well so far. Dam was enthusiastic about his role as protector of the gambling den. He or one of his men dined almost every night at the restaurant, providing extra security and demonstrating that the operation was tolerated if not exactly legal. His presence was a warning to gamblers to avoid causing problems. If there was an altercation, the police were just downstairs. So far, the transition from legal to illegal operation had gone smoothly.

Prem frowned at Dam before shutting the door behind him.

"Miss Ploi, I hope you are well."

"Yes, and the gambling is going well too," she said, standing up and holding out a small bag of coins.

Dam stared at her for a moment and smiled.

"Good. I can see why you have so many customers."

"The important thing is to be sure their gambling is not interrupted," she said.

"I wanted to let you know that police in Songkhla and Trang have begun to make raids on underground gambling dens," Dam said as he settled his bulk on the mat in front of Ploi.

"Our monkish *monthon* commissioner, I suppose."

"Maybe, but the Songkhla police tell me the information for the raids is coming from the commissioner's assistant."

"Just make sure we know about anything happening in Pakpanang."

"Of course. Nothing so far, but there will be a raid tomorrow in Tungsong. It is just a card game in someone's house, but there will be fines for anyone who gets caught. We also got word from the *monthon* office to prepare action against a bullfight in Sichon district."

"It seems strange the information is coming from Songkhla rather than Nakhon."

"The police in Nakhon knew about the gambling, but didn't think it was worth arresting anyone. It's just villagers testing their bulls."

"So, the *monthon* office is serious. We'll have to be careful."

"You needn't worry about the police. I'll know about any action in Pakpanang, but there is something you do need to worry about. Jate is really pissed off, excuse me, really angry at your father. He has missed his last two payments."

"I sent Father the money to make those payments."

"All I know is what Jate's men tell me," Dam said. "They think Paen is vulnerable now that he is no longer *kamnan*. Jate knows about your casino reopening and your lottery. He is jealous of your profits. You heard about the robbery in Chien Yai last week. It was a *Fantan* game, and the robbers were Jate's men. It was done, not just to get the money, but to put a gambling competitor out of business."

"We can add extra security in the restaurant, but it won't be easy for anyone to get into the gambling room."

"I can have dinner at the restaurant more often."

"You are always welcome, but perhaps you could do one other thing." Ploi looked up at the policemen who towered a head above her with a chest even broader than her husband's. It was not just his size, but his manner and his dark face that were intimidating.

"You know Jate. Can you get a meeting with him?"

"We are no longer close."

"Would you explain to him our casino is providing the money to pay my father's debt? Tell him it is not in his best interests to cut off these funds and it would be dangerous to take action against anyone as prominent as Kamnan Paen."

"Your father is not *kamnan* anymore and Jate is not getting his money."

"Well, tell him I will press my father to make the payments."

"I am not sure a meeting is a good idea. Jate is difficult."

"Please do what you can."

"Just get your father to pay his debts."

37

SOM
Thudong

Phra Som sat on the steps of his hut. Spread out on the ground before him were his belongings. Everything had been given by family or friends, but it seemed like a lot for someone who had renounced material possessions. There were six candles and a small kerosene lamp, four sets of saffron robes, five bathing cloths, two straight razors, a shaving bowl and brush, three cakes of soap, two sleeping mats, a mosquito net, a tea pot and three tea cups, two alms bowls with cloth carriers, his father's pocket watch, two cotton sheets, a satin cover, two blankets, two shoulder bags, three large towels and a packet of handkerchiefs he had never opened.

How did there get to be so much? The biggest problem was his books – more than 30 volumes – and a pile of medical magazines and copies of Thai language editions of the *Bangkok Daily Mail* and the *Siam Observer* newspapers. Added to that were a dozen cardboard-bound notebooks filled with medical notes. He had been a monk for four rainy season retreats and things had just accumulated.

"Are you going to *thudong* with a horse cart?" a voice rang out. Phra Sawat strode across the compound. He had a yellow cloth bag and an alms bowl on one shoulder and two large umbrellas on the other.

"Phra Sawat, good morning," Som said. "Thank you for coming back after the end of the rains retreat."

"Did all of this stuff come out of that little hut?"

"I don't know what I should take," Som said.

Sawat surveyed the belongings and pulled out the alms bowl, one set of robes, one towel, a shoulder bag and a small metal teapot.

"With this," he said, placing one of the large saffron-colored umbrellas on the little pile, "you have everything you need."

"An umbrella?"

"It is like an umbrella, but it's actually an essential piece of *thudong* equipment called a *klot*."

Sawat opened it. Hanging from the broad, umbrella-like top was a curtain of thin cloth. Sawat ducked under it and disappeared.

"This is your *thudong* home—it will protect you from the sun, the rain and the cold. It will keep insects off you when you sleep at night. It will be your private space for meditation. Without a *klot, thudong* is impossible."

Sawat leaned out of the *klot,* closed it with a snap and hoisted it onto his shoulder.

"The rest you can throw away or give away."

Som looked at the eight monks who had gathered around them.

"My books—Phra Pat, can you look after them for me? I will be back before too long. As for the rest of this stuff, everyone take what you want."

Shyly at first, the monks started picking up his belongings. Then they moved more quickly. There was a tussle over the kerosene lamp and an argument over the razors, but within moments, everything had disappeared into the arms of the monks.

Phra Sawat laughed. "See, it isn't so hard when you have friends to help."

Som looked around at the monks, some of whom looked abashed at their sudden greed. They were indeed friends. Pat had helped him make his medicines and had become adept at treating infected wounds. Daeng and Awn had been serious about meditation. They had sat with him for many hours, sharing their progress and disappointments. Several had joined in his dharma study group or his central Thai class and most had supported his complaints about the abbot.

"Thank you all," he said with a grin. "Not just for helping me unburden myself from these attachments, but for being my friends. I know it has not always been easy."

He thought of his arguments with Phra Tissa and Phra Panya over medical treatments and his objections to Abbot Brahm's obsession with buildings and donations. He had gotten the abbot's permission to leave only the night before. The abbot had seemed torn between disappointment at losing an effective medicine maker and relief at getting rid of an irritant.

He looked around the temple that had been his refuge for so long. He smiled at his friends and then looked at the monk who would be his teacher and companion. Sawat picked up his *klot* and handed the other one to Som. He followed Sawat through the temple gate as the other monks called out encouragement. He saw the abbot watch from the prayer hall entrance for a moment and then disappear into the building.

They turned onto the narrow path leading towards the forested mountains west of town. Within minutes they were in the welcome shade of the large trees lining the path. For the first two miles they could see the flat green expanse of paddy fields beyond the trees. As they walked farther along the path, the rice fields gave way to orchards—rambutan, mangoes, papaya and bananas. As the path grew steeper, they found themselves surrounded by dark symmetrical rows of rubber trees. The trees leaned out over the path as if they wanted to protect the travelers from the harsh sun. Or were they just greedy for the sunlight?

They walked in silence until the last of the rubber plantations was left behind. The path narrowed and thorny bushes reached out to clutch at their robes. A high canopy of teak, ebony, durian and ironwood trees made it seem like dusk.

"Now the *thudong* begins," Phra Som said. "I will be your guide, but the forest will be your teacher. Listen to it, feel it around us. Be aware of the rustle of the leaves in the wind, the droning of the cicadas. Appreciate the musical discussions of the birds. Note and dismiss the sounds of animals. Above all, be aware of what is happening within your mind as you walk."

"You mean my thoughts?"

"Not just your thoughts. Start with the sensation of each foot as it touches the ground, of each muscle as it stretches and contracts. Note how your chest rises and pulls in the air to breathe, how that air tickles your nostrils and caresses your throat before it enters your lungs."

"That's a lot to think about," Som said.

"Not all at once. Choose one thing at a time and focus on that, but if you become aware of something else, don't be upset. Accept it, consider it, discard it and then return to your focus."

"I thought we would sit to meditate," Som said.

"We will, but meditation does not occur only while we sit and say 'now I am meditating', it is something we can do all the time."

"Where will this lead? What is the objective?"

Phra Sawat smiled, "Let's just walk and learn."

38

SAIFAN
Mosque Scholar

Saifan peered through the entrance to the small side room of the Krue Se Mosque. Seated cross-legged in neat rows on their mats were eight young boys. Each pair of boys sat behind a copy of the Koran held open in a hinged wooden stand. He stroked the fringe of beard on his chin. The beard made him look older, more like a true Islamic scholar. Today was a first test. Imam Wae Muso had summoned him to his small house behind the mosque and told him he was ill and would appreciate it if he would take over instruction of the village boys for a few days.

"We are just beginning Book 23, *Al-Mu'minum*," the Imam had said. "Nothing difficult there. Just make sure their pronunciation is more or less correct and they have a basic understanding of the meaning."

No, there should be nothing difficult, but would he be able to convey the thrill of the words of God recorded by the Prophet Muhammad. How could he explain the joy of submitting to those words? His first Koran lesson had been on the dirt floor of the temporary prayer house in Pakpanang with only three other boys. The teacher, he knew now, had mangled the Arabic pronunciation, and the lesson had confused him. Later lessons by better teachers and especially his studies over the last nine years in Pattani had revealed the beauty of the language and the profundity of the teaching.

"Boys, some of you know me already, but for the rest of you, I am Saifan, a student of Imam To' Guru Wae Muso, who has asked me to take his place in instructing you for the next few days. I understand you are just starting *Al-Mu'minum*. Who can tell me what that means?"

The boys, dressed in similar long white shirts, round prayer hats and striped sarongs, looked around at each other. Then a tall boy in the front row raised his hand. The Imam had said this 10-year-old, Sulong, was the best student in the class. Unlike the village boys from Krue Se, Sulong came from a wealthy and religious family in Pattani town.

"Al-Mu'minum means the Believers, honored teacher," Sulong said.

"That is correct. This tells us what we must do as true believers according to the teachings of the prophet. It explains what we must believe and how we must act to be worthy members of the community of Islam. These are things you should already know, but now you must be able to read them in the beautiful language of the Holy Koran and understand the deeper meaning of the verses so you can apply them to your daily lives."

He looked out at the eight innocent young faces before him with their dark brown eyes looking up at him with respect. It felt good to be a teacher.

"Now listen carefully and read after me."

He had to repeat each verse several times before the high-pitched voices of the boys got close to the correct pronunciation. It took nearly two hours to get through the first 11 verses.

"Your recitation still needs more work, but enough for now. Who can tell me what these verses mean?"

The boys looked sleepily at each other and tried to avoid Saifan's gaze. There was a long silence.

"It is important to understand the meaning of the verses. Let me translate:

'In the name of Allah, the Beneficent, the Merciful.

Successful indeed are the believers,

Who are humble in their prayers,

And who shun what is vain,

And who act for the sake of purity,

And who restrain their sexual passions,

And those who are keepers of their trusts and their covenant,

And those who keep a guard on their prayers.

These are the heirs who inherit Paradise. Therein they will abide.'"

The boys had perked up at the mention of sexual passion, but what would nine and ten-year-olds make of that?

"The most important things to understand is that as Muslims we must believe in God as almighty and all-knowing and in Muhammad as his prophet," he told the boys. "As believers we are offered the possibility of living in Paradise forever, but only if we are good Muslims. What does it mean to be a good Muslim?"

Sulong waved his hand and said eagerly, "Pray five times a day."

"Yes, but not just to pray—to pray properly, never asking for selfish gifts, always remaining humble, asking only to be of service to God. And what does it mean to keep your covenant?"

"It means tell the truth," Sulong said.

"Correct. Keeping covenant means you must not make up untrue stories," he explained. "You must not lie, not even to protect yourself. Liars are forbidden to enter Paradise."

The boy frowned. "What if the Siamese police come looking for your uncle? Teacher—this really happened. My father told the police his brother was away in Narathiwat when he was hiding next door. Will my father be denied Paradise? That doesn't seem fair."

"You bring up an important point. Our most important covenant is between us and God. Since God is all knowing, it is fruitless to lie to him. The next most important covenant is within the community of Islam. If you try to deceive your fellow Muslims, you weaken the community, so do not lie to fellow Muslims, especially to your parents and your teachers. This is important. Lying to the Siamese police, however, is not a sin because there is no covenant of trust between that infidel government and our community. The Siamese are unbelievers who lie to us, imprison our raja, insult our women, and kill our brothers, so your father has committed no sin. Indeed, he has protected the community of believers. All must be understood in terms of the struggle between belief and unbelief, especially in these difficult times when the Malay people are suffering from oppression."

He saw the boys were excited by this, but he was afraid that excitement would divert attention from the study of the Koran.

"That is enough for today, but tonight at home sit quietly and think how you can be a better believer. We will continue this tomorrow."

Each of the boys came forward, grasped Saifan's hand and pressed their foreheads to it in a gesture of thanks. He had really helped the boys understand the verses. Tomorrow he would teach the verses on life, death and resurrection. It was good to be their teacher, but it will also be good to get home. He thought about Arwa with a smile. He had gotten married only three months earlier, and he still hungered for the touch of his pretty wife. She was only six or seven years older than his students. She was lively and fun. He would have to teach her to read, but for now he read to her from the Koran or from the book of Malay poetry he had bought in Pattani town. She, in turn, would tell him the Malay folk tales her parents had taught her.

He gathered up the extra copies of the Koran and put them away in cabinets along the wall. Arwa would be waiting for him. Like her name, she was soft and light to his touch. This is why Abdul was so interested in women. There was great pleasure in the embrace of his new wife, but it was more than that. She would have his dinner waiting. Then they would chat about the day. He would tell her about the success of his class. She would tell him the gossip from the market or the difficulty in finding fresh fish. He would enjoy the sight of her slim body, the scent of her, the feel of her.

As he hurriedly left the small room, a fellow member of the Mosque committee gestured to him.

"Come, we have received a letter from Raja Abdul Kadir," he said. "He calls on us to join him in a struggle against the Siamese."

No, no, he needed to get home. They didn't need him to be there. He would slip out the back door.

"The Imam wants all the men of the community to come," the man said. The Imam, looking pale from his illness, came through the portal followed by a half dozen men. Two more came through the rear door.

Saifan swallowed his annoyance.

"I'm coming."

39

TUN WAY
Ashes

Tun Way looked at the three friends gathered around him on the veranda. They looked more content than he had seen in a long time. The reason was further up the river. He could see the rectangle of the school building, his school building, with moonlight glinting off the freshly painted boards of the two-story wooden structure. It was such a relief to see the building finally nearing completion. It was a dream become real.

A strong breeze curled through the group. U Htun Htin closed the top button of his jacket under his long, thin neck. Wisps of gray hair were showing at his temples. Next to him Aung Mon sipped at the tea cup of whisky Tun Way made sure to have on hand when his portly friend visited. He too showed signs of age in the tracery of red veins on his large, flat nose. His double chin wobbled in the light of a pair of oil lamps. The long, slim figure of Shwe Hongsa had fared better in the three years they had been working on the Mon Language and Culture Society. He too looked up the river at the school site. His bony knees poked at his checked *longyi* as he leaned against the porch railing. That *longyi* looks like it was made of material manufactured in Madras. They had all vowed to wear only locally woven cloth, but that was long ago, the pledge mostly forgotten. Better not to say anything right away because Shwe Hongsa had volunteered to help teach in the school. He would have to find a suitable time to remind his friend that only Mon cloth would be allowed once classes started.

"My friends, I am pleased to call this meeting of the board of the Mon Language and Culture Society to order," he said. "Thank you for coming at this late hour. With determination and dedication, you have overcome all the difficulties that have faced us. Soon we will have our own building for the school, a Mon library and adequate space for cultural events. Despite the lawsuit filed by the government teachers, despite the problems with the building contractor and despite the shortfall in funding, we shall dedicate the new building next month and open classes two months after that."

The group clapped and Htun Htin rose to his feet.

"Many worked on this, but progress was due to the leadership of Nai Tun Way and the many sacrifices he has made," Htun Htin said. "I propose we name the school building the Nai Tun Way building."

There were nods of agreement, but that wasn't what he wanted.

"Thank you for the kind words," he said, trying to sound grateful, "but I have told you before the school should not be named for me. If, somehow, we attract a large donor, we could name the school for him. However, if you would be so kind as to indulge me, I would like to propose the girl's section of the school be named the Su Sah School for Girls in memory of a woman who led the way for female achievement in Bago," he said, surprised at the choking feeling that rose in his throat.

He swallowed hard. "Learning is the way forward for our girls as well as for our boys. As soon as she is old enough, my own daughter will study at the school."

He closed his eyes and saw Su Sah's face before him. She was smiling at a sign saying 'Su Sah School for Girls' in Mon. This was how he could keep her memory alive without so much pain. Everyone would remember her as the kind and effective nurse who studied medicine and respected Mon culture.

Then little Ngwe Lay could go to school. She was a quiet girl, strongly attached to her nanny. She would run to her room if guests approached the house. She had no playmates. She loved stories, but had been slow in learning to read. She preferred having her nanny read to her. Worse, she had not learned how to add or subtract. School would be difficult for her, but it might just be the cure for her fears and shyness. He had been right to keep her away from the Burmese school in town. Soon she could begin her education in a Mon school.

"That's good," Shwe Hongsa said. "Your example will help recruit the children of other leading Mon families. So far, we have only a few who have agreed to pay for a place at the school. Our people all say they want their children to learn proper Mon, but they send them to government schools that teach only in the Burmese and English languages. Even the monks who teach in Mon are finding it difficult to keep their students. Without Burmese and English, the parents say, it is difficult to go on to higher education or find a city job."

"But once the school is in operation," Tun Way said, "feelings will change. They will see good teachers giving students a strong sense of Mon history and culture as well as competence in mathematics and science. When I was in Rangoon, I could proudly tell the Burmans their beloved Shwedagon was built by Mon monarchs centuries before there were any Burmans here. Such knowledge gave me confidence I could outperform the Burmans in my classes. It is up to us to revive our history, to breathe new life into our music and our literature. We will use the cultural events at the school—music and poetry—to encourage pride in Mon culture and market the school to parents."

"The problem is," Aung Mon spoke up, "that most of those who come to the music performances or dance-dramas that you and I have arranged are not the parents, but the grandparents. The younger parents and their children seem to prefer that new cinema place. Half of our audience is asleep by the end of our performances."

"We have been forced to hold those events in a tin-roofed shed," Tun Way said. "When it rains, you can hardly hear the music. The new school will have an auditorium with a proper stage and comfortable seats, even better than the cinema. Things will change. We may even charge admission."

"That will be helpful," Aung Mon said. "Our performers might play for free once or twice, but not more than that."

"That brings us to the most important item on the agenda tonight—finance. You have all seen the accounts. We spent the last of the money we borrowed to finish the school building. We need another major donor."

"Times are hard," Htun Htin. "The economy."

Their incomes, like those of many other landowners, had dropped due to the bargaining power of the Chinese rice mill owners. There were just too many farmers producing too much rice. More and more peasants were abandoning the lands of the traditional landlords and clearing patches of scrub land for themselves. The network of small rivers and canals lacing the Bago Region not only gave small holders access to water for the fields but also brought small ships to pick up their crops.

Their silence was broken by a timid knocking. Aya, a plump matron in a purple *longyi* stood at the doorway. Little Ngwe Lay stood behind her, clutching the cloth of the ankle length garment.

"Miss Ngwe Lay had an afternoon nap, so she is going to sleep quite late tonight," Aya said. "She should say good night to her father since he has no time to tell her a bedtime story."

"We are in a meeting."

"It will take only a moment," the matron said, pushing the little girl forward.

"Honored father... honored guests. It is time for me... to say good night," the girl said softly, then turned and fled back into the house.

The three friends chuckled.

"She is a cute one," Aung Mon said. "Like her mother."

Htun Htin elbowed Aung Mon in his well-padded ribs. His friends had learned to avoid mentioning Su Sah in front of him. He should be getting over his loss by now, but it was difficult. Ngwe Lay did indeed look like Su Sah. It was painful.

He stared at the doorway as Aya bowed and retreated after her charge. One of Su Sah's unmarried cousins, a forty-something woman had been sent by Su Sah's mother. She had taken over the running of the household and the care of the baby. He knew he should be grateful, but the woman persisted in telling him what to do. Read to the girl, take her out for a trip, find friends for her. She didn't seem to understand he was too busy for all that. Probably he should do more with the child, but why did she think she had the right to pressure him? Each time she brought the girl to say good night, had her sing a song for him or urged him to tell her a story, her looks of disappointment seemed like accusations. She was telling him he was a bad father. Maybe he was.

"I have talked to everyone I know about donations for the Society. There is nothing more I can do," Htun Htin said as he turned his attention back to the meeting.

"Maybe we can apply for a government subsidy," Shwe Hongsa suggested.

"The government school teachers, all Burmans, will protest again, just like they tried to stop the construction of the school," Htun Htin said. "They see us as a threat to their domination of language and culture in the schools. They have the local government on their..."

Shouts from the road along the river wrenched their attention away. A young man, his *longyi* pulled up in both hands to free his legs, was running towards the house.

"Fire. Fire at the school."

By the time the runner reached the gate, the four men had risen and started down the path to meet him.

"What is going on?" Tun Way asked, as he recognized one of the painters he had hired to work on the school building.

"Come quickly. There is a fire. It happened so fast."

The four clambered into a small boat to cross the river. By the time they were halfway across, the fire was lighting up the night sky. When they reached the school gate, they could see the dark figures of the workmen in front of the building, flames already shooting out the long rows of windows on the second floor.

The workmen rushed back and forth to the school pond with small buckets of water that had little effect on the fire. The four friends grabbed the empty paint tins and rushed to the pond. They ran back and forth with the water, but the flames grew higher. When the horse-drawn fire pump arrived from town 20 minutes later, the tile roof had already collapsed, bringing down the second floor in a flurry of sparks and smoke. The big teak pillars were blackened. The only parts they had managed to save were the front porch and the flag pole. The town firefighters worked the big pump sending a stream of water onto the glowing embers. Finally, the fire died out, as much from the lack of fuel as from the water.

Tun Way sat on the ground, exhausted by the unaccustomed physical effort and drained by the loss of his school.

The foreman of the work crew bowed to him.

"Sir, we did everything we could. We don't know what happened."

"Did you see anyone? Hear anything?"

"We heard some horses on the road, but that's not unusual. We were all in our sleeping shack. Some of us were already asleep. We have been working long hours to finish it."

"So, anyone could have set the fire while you were inside and rode away before you knew anything."

"Maybe, but it also could have been a cheroot tossed away still burning or a spark from a cooking fire. There were fumes from the paint."

"But someone could have set the fire deliberately."

"I suppose. But it might have been an accident."

"No, this was deliberate—to stop us from having a Mon school," Tun Way said, the bitter taste of smoke in his mouth. "To suppress the Mon people."

He looked at the smoldering ashes of the school. He could still feel the heat of the fire on his face and the growing heat of anger in his chest.

40

SOM
Jungle Guru

"Som, you've been an excellent student and you have made great progress," Phra Sawat said as they sat together in the cool prayer hall of Wat Pa Tong, several days walk north of Bangkok.

"Because you've been an excellent teacher," Som said.

He had traveled with Phra Sawat on *thudong* for more than a year. They had talked with the learned monks at Wat Boworniwet in the busy capital for the three months of the rains retreat, walked along the high banks of the Mekong River and stopped at humble temples all across the northeast before heading back south a month ago. But most of their time had been spent walking together through the vast forests, talking about the dharma, meditation and the means to end the suffering that had afflicted him since the wreck of *The Wind Uncle*.

"That's the problem," Sawat said.

"What do you mean?"

"There are some things you can only learn on your own. When we heard the roar of a tiger for the first time, you were afraid, but then I helped you overcome your fear. When we arrived at a village and the people seemed hostile, you looked to me for courage. When you have problems trying to meditate, you ask me for help."

"You were always so confident, it helped me remain calm," he said.

"Can't you be calm on your own?"

What was Sawat getting at? Was it that magical stuff again? In recent months, Phra Sawat's teaching had emphasized astounding accounts of his own meditation experiences. Surrounded by younger monks, novices and temple boys he told of flying high above the forest or traveling to distant lands. Once he had described these experiences as feelings arising from intensive meditation, but lately he seemed to say they had actually taken place.

"Your mindfulness has been a model for me, even though I have not achieved your special abilities. What is wrong with trying to follow your path?"

"You need to find your own. You need to be able to calm yourself when your only resource is the dharma and your own consciousness."

"Can't you teach me?"

Sawat smiled. "See, you are looking to me again."

It felt like Sawat was rejecting him. After all their time together Sawat had become something more than a mentor, more than a brother. The thought of separation made his head ache.

"What should I do? Why can't we do it together?"

"The villagers say that a pair of tigers killed a buffalo calf last night. They found drag marks and a blood trail going up the rocks of a stream just a short distance from here. One of the novices can show you."

"You want us to seek out the tigers?"

"Not us. You. Seek out your worst fear, whatever it is, so you can defeat it with your own strength."

What was his worst fear? That he would harm others, like little Tum? Or Father? That his life was meaningless? That he would die without accomplishing anything? Or just that he would die?

Someday his body would be like the crumpled body of Tum. Or paralyzed like Father. Would looking for tigers help with any of that?

The next morning, he carried his *klot* up the hillside, using a rocky path washed bare of vegetation by the rainy season downpours. But now the dry season had reduced the stream to a trickle down the broad, sloping rock face. A few pools of water in the rocks squirmed with tadpoles and green slime. At one spot he had to pull himself up the rock using the long roots of a tree. If he fell, would anyone find his body? It felt strange to be walking in the forest by himself, without the muscled legs of Sawat leading the way.

The dense scrub of vines, stickers and small trees made either side of the path nearly impenetrable. Further up the hill the foliage arched over the stream bed, turning the path into a narrow green tunnel.

Would tigers use this path? Or would they make their own? Then he saw a line of crushed bushes leading away from the rock face. This must be the path they use. He would stop here.

I don't actually have to face a tiger. I just have to face my fear of the tiger. It would be like facing the storm aboard *The Wind Uncle*, when he had risen above his fear and felt himself looking down from a great height. He wanted that feeling of non-attachment again.

He cleared a small area by the side of the path hardly visible in the fading light. He spread his bathing cloth and opened the *klot*. He thought of Sawat's teaching: "If fear is defeated, the mind will be overwhelmed by courage and enjoy profound inner peace. If fear is the victor, the monk will be suffocated."

He sat on a flat section of rock and began his meditation. It did not go well. He wasn't finding the normal peace. He could not help listening for the sound of a tiger. After an hour he took a string of meditation beads out of his shoulder bag. A Burmese monk had given him the beads as an aid in mantra meditation. They were made of polished sandal wood. One of the beads was larger than the others and shaped like a bell. That was the "*guru*" bead, the monk had told him.

"Hold the beads in your right hand, draped between your middle and index fingers. Starting at the *guru* bead, use your thumb to count each smaller bead, pulling it toward you as you recite your mantra. Do this 108 times, traveling around the string, until you once again reach the guru bead."

He took seven deep breaths to clear his mind and then began saying aloud "Buddho… Buddho… Buddho"—the mantra the northeastern monks had taught him. He inhaled at 'Bud' and exhaled at 'dho.' After each chant he moved his fingers down the string. Like members of a family, each of the hand-carved beads was slightly different, separate and individual, yet similar and connected by the string.

He tried focusing on the tip of his nose, but there were too many things to think about—the breathing, the mantra, the beads and the sounds of the jungle. His mind drifted to the little islands that poked out of the waters of the Mekong, to the blue-coated French soldiers who lounged at river ports, to the Khmer ruins that looked down on the vast plains to the east, to the… Focus. His mind was like one of those monkeys that collect coconuts. Despite being tethered by a rope held by its master, the monkey would dash about in different directions and had to be pulled to the right tree.

After the first round of 108 beads, he reversed direction and began again. Weary from the climb up the mountain, he fell asleep before dawn. He was awakened by the far-off sound of tigers roaring. They seemed too far away to be dangerous and his meditation drifted again into slumber.

The next day he ate part of the rice and vegetables in his alms bowl.

Leave the frogs—maybe the scent will attract a tiger.

The day passed slowly. He imagined a tiger coming down the path and leaping on him. Could I remain calm and mindful if that happens?

That night he again tried to prepare himself for death in the jaws of a tiger, but this night he didn't hear even a distant roar. Where had the tigers gone? The next day, after finishing the last of his rice and fried frogs, he decided to spend one more night in the forest and then return to the monastery and temple at the foot of the mountain. Perhaps he had done enough to face his fear and achieve the peace Sawat had described.

He fell asleep soon after dark. Then he was awake again. There was a crashing sound. His whole body buzzed with energy. He peered out of the *klot*. Tigers?

The sounds of breaking trees were like gusts of wind rippling a sail. The tall bushes along the waterway swayed like waves in an angry sea. Then, in the dim moonlight, he saw a large dark shape emerge from the foliage, then another and another. A line of five elephants climbed up the rock waterway, pushing the bushes aside. They were heading towards him. The lead elephant was a large male, with tusks at least six feet long. It raised its trunk and let out a loud trumpeting sound that made him shiver.

Fear paralyzed his body. He was right in the path the elephants seemed certain to take. The big male lurched upward from the rocky stream bed and onto the narrow path. It stopped six paces from his *klot*. It trumpeted again, thrashed the bush with his tusks and stomped on the ground.

The ground trembled beneath him. His own limbs shook from fear. He felt like his heart had stopped. Sweat dripped down his forehead. Thoughts raced through his head. He should climb a tree or light a candle—elephants would fear fire, wouldn't they? Crawl away from the path.

Phra Sawat would be disappointed. I am a meditation monk devoted to *thudong* practice with all its dangers. I am a human being and a monk of the Lord Buddha. The elephant is only an animal, and it's not afraid of me. If I am afraid of it, then I am lower than an animal.

Regain mindfulness, control my thoughts. What did it mean to die? Perhaps death meant nothing, or perhaps it was a return to wherever we were before birth. The Buddha had not feared death.

He focused on his breath and the beating of his heart gradually slowed. How did he look to the elephant—an unnatural clump of skin and orange cloth in the darkness?

His mind became calmer. He felt cool as the sweat evaporated in the night air. The big elephant also calmed. It was no longer pawing the ground. It gave a soft grunt and looked straight at him. The giant animal must be concerned for his females and the small one.

He watched as the elephant moved forward again, slowly taking the last few steps before reaching him. Almost daintily, the huge beast stepped around him and off the path, crushing the bushes next to the *klot*. It stopped and sniffed the air with its trunk upraised over his head. Its gray flanks looked like the Nakhon city wall, dusty and wrinkled. It grunted again and stared at him as the other elephants climbed up to the path, stepping past the spot where Som sat. When the juvenile passed, it took a jaunty swipe at the *klot* and knocked it over. The big male trumpeted and then followed the others up the path. The crashing sounds of the elephants faded in the night.

He was alone again. Joy swelled within him.

41

PAKDEE
Royal Visit

Pakdee re-tucked the end of his *phajonggraben* for the fourth time. He smoothed his mustache. If only he had a mirror. His white jacket had no speck of dirt. His silver buttons glinted in the morning sun. He looked at the boat tied up at the pier. It was a 34-foot dugout that drew less than two feet of water. The boat's small steam engine was fully stoked, the boiler hissing and muttering. A yellow awning shaded much of the boat. A Persian rug and an array of silk pillows had been laid out on a small platform near the bow. It was hardly fit for the king, but it was the best he could find to cruise the shallows at low tide.

Pakdee thought back to the last time His Majesty had come to Nakhon. He had failed miserably to impress the king. Despite his tongue-tied incoherence, the king had approved his written appeal and reversed his conviction. Would the king remember the prisoner who had stuttered into silence before him? Did the king know of his service to the high commissioner?

There was a clatter of hooves on the laterite road to the waterfront and the honor guard at the pier straightened their lines. He consulted his pocket watch. It was 9:00 am. The king was exactly on time. The villagers on both sides of the path cheered as King Chulalongkorn, the fifth king of the *Chakri* dynasty, absolute ruler for nearly 40 years, waved and walked towards the pier.

The king was dressed in a white shirt and tan trousers. His head was protected by a solar topee like the British wear. This was the man who had changed his life. This was the head of the government he served. This was the leader working to modernize the nation. He felt the urge to pay the traditional form of respect—lying face down before him, touching his head to the ground. But the king had banned this display of servitude, however heartfelt it might be. Instead he bowed deeply as the king approached. When he looked up, he saw the king looking at him with a quizzical expression on his face.

"Phraya Sukhum says we have met before and you do look familiar, but I can't recall where. I have read your reports, but there is something else. He has challenged me to remember you, so don't tell me. I will think of it by the time the day is over."

Surprised to be addressed so directly, he cursed his boss for playing this game. He hesitated for a moment as his flustered brain searched for the words in the royal language he had practiced for weeks, determined not to repeat his failure four years earlier. It was confusing because the king spoke the common language, but Pakdee's reply was supposed to be in the royal language with all its complicated Khmer words.

He was starting to panic once again when the words came. "The dust under the feet of Your Majesty honors me with your attention. I am unworthy."

"You are the principal assistant to the high commissioner, are you not?"

"Yes, dust under the feet of your honored Majesty."

"Both Prince Damrong and Phraya Sukhum have given me good reports of your work in quelling the Pattani raja's rebellion without loss of life. They tell me you have made useful recommendations on adapting our national legal system so it does not cause unrest among my Malay people."

"Dust under the feet of Your Majesty, I fear they give me too much credit."

The king's voice suddenly turned gruff. "You accuse your superiors of reporting falsely to me?"

"No, Your Majesty, no, no," he croaked. "I just did my best to obey their commands."

The king chuckled. "No matter—you don't have to be so modest and so formal. We are going to spend several hours together on this little boat and I would appreciate it if you would speak frankly and simply. If you speak the royal language, it will be an ordeal for both of us. There is much I would like to learn about this area and Phraya Sukhum tells me you are a native of Pakpanang."

"That is correct, dust under the feet of Your Majesty.... I mean yes, honored sir."

A white-coated navy aide from the royal ship helped the king step into the boat and he gestured for him to sit below the king next to the platform. More navy men, two royal aides and the Pakpanang district officer sat in the back of the boat. The long, narrow dugout pulled away from the pier and cut through the glassy surface of the bay. Tall monsoon clouds piled up on the horizon like fluffy kapok in the market. The sun was strong and he was thankful for the canvas awning shading most of the boat.

"I understand we are taking this boat because of the shallows," the king said as he watched the dark green of the coastal mangroves stream past.

"Yes, honored sir. The bay here has been silting up for centuries. In fact, at one time, long ago, Nakhon town, called Ligor by the *farangs*, was on the coast, but silt from the rivers and sand brought in by the currents created new land between the town and the sea. Because the bay is now so shallow, most sea transport to the province has shifted to Pakpanang. There too, silting is becoming a problem. The people of the town, supported by the district officer, would like permission to dredge the bar so large ships can enter the river in the dry season. Once past the bar, the river is deep enough for large steam ships to sail upriver for a considerable distance."

The king leaned back on the cushions and watched the low green shoreline broken by the occasional fishing boat or fisherman's hut. Two white spires poked out above the trees. The gilt and orange of a temple building glimmered through the leaves. Along the shore, clusters of fishing boats painted red, blue and yellow lined up on the sand. They heard the distant barking of dogs and the shouts of children as they glided by.

The king kept him busy with questions about the sights they passed until the boat reached the mouth of the Pakpanang River. The brownish water of the silt-laden river flowed into the blue-green water of the sea. Clumps of mangrove trees poked out of the water, tiny islets of green in the vast, flat expanse of water. Occasionally a white egret, startled by the boat, would launch into the air, complaining shrilly at the intrusion.

The helmsman turned the boat to starboard, and it slowed as it fought the river current. As the boat churned upriver, houses appeared on the banks. Most were thatched huts but, as they drew closer to Pakpanang town, more large wooden buildings and the occasional one of concrete appeared. Both sides of the river were lined with wooden piers and floating docks moored to tall tree trunks driven into the dark river mud. At a command from the district officer, the boat moved closer to the right bank and then across the river to the other shore to let the king see the latest buildings—warehouses, factories, rice mills, and some imposing private homes.

"The river is as broad as the Chao Phraya," the king noted. "I count 31 Chinese and Malay ships. It is good to see large ships can come this far upriver," he said, writing in a leather-bound notebook.

Pakdee had spent hours studying the reports from the Pakpanang district staff for this trip. He had spent most of his life in Pakpanang, but there was much he had never known. The government reports made the town seem bigger and more complicated than he remembered.

"Once past the entrance to the river, it is at least six meters deep for eight miles upriver. In the rainy season at high tide, it is much deeper," he told the king. "Ships as large as HMS Pali and HMS Sukreep should have no problem coming up the river. In the rainy season, smaller steamships can go far into the interior with some waterways reaching all the way south to Songkhla Lake."

As he spoke, dozens of small boats paddled out from both banks of the river, with boatmen, their heads wrapped in red *phakaomas*, *waiing* to the king.

"I am surprised to see so many people and so many buildings," the king said. "How many people live here?"

"The population, honored sir, is now more than 46,000. It is the largest town in Nakhon Srithammarat province, aside from the capital. If you compare Pakpanang town with Songkhla, the annual tax income of Pakpanang is only 20,000 *baht* less than all of Songkhla province. There is no port town on the east coast of the southern Peninsula busier than Pakpanang. It is also becoming a center for education as well as commerce. This year, as a result of Your Majesty's support for education, there are four schools in the district with nearly 100 students."

He looked at the houses, docks and wats along the bank. Pakpanang was growing fast. Then his eye caught the stairway going up the back of one of the buildings. That must be Jate's shop—the place where he had made the stupid decision to follow his lust instead of good sense. It was more than nine years ago, but the old feelings of humiliation and pain of that night swept through him with terrible power.

The king looked at him.

"You look like you've seen a ghost," he said kindly.

"Yes, sir. Something like that."

The king turned and waved to the small boats edging nearer to the royal boat. A boat paddled by nine women dressed in elaborate costumes glided past. Pakdee thought he recognized some of the dancers from his wife's *Khon* troupe. Three large fishing boats came up behind them on the freshening breeze. A half-dozen sun-darkened crewmen clung halfway up the mast of one of the boats trying to get a better view of the king.

The king's boat then swerved to starboard as a tall smokestack came into view. The district officer spoke up.

"Your Majesty, we are now approaching the Koh Hak Gnee rice mill. This is the first steam-driven rice mill in the south. The Hak Gnee family is greatly honored you agreed to preside over the opening ceremony."

The rice mill ceremony took more than an hour, with speeches by the patriarch of the Hak Gnee family, the district officer and the king. All predicted great success for the rice mill and for rice exports from Pakpanang. At the conclusion, the king re-boarded the boat and ordered the boatman to head further upriver.

As the boat moved further into the interior, the number of houses diminished. They saw newly planted rice fields beyond the banks, glowing bright green in the noon sun. At a branch in the river, the Hak Gnee patriarch, who had insisted on joining the boat trip, pointed to the brown stream pouring through the fields.

"This branch of river runs down to *Tambon* Tung Pung Krai—most productive rice area of the whole *monthon*. If planted full, harvest greater than Klong Rangsit," he said with the halting accent of a Chinese immigrant.

The king looked appreciative and the elderly Chinese was emboldened.

"Your Majesty, if area planted, we build ten more steam rice mills. Big market in Singapore and *khaek* states. Need more labor. Good to allow Chinese people to own farmland."

The king nodded noncommittally.

The Chinese merchant was going too far to propose a change in the long-held policy of preserving certain occupations, especially rice-farming, for native Thais. He should keep his mouth shut, but the king seemed interested.

"Your Majesty, labor is not the immediate problem, it's the cost of transport," the district officer intervened. "If we could get large ships over the shallows at the mouth of the river during the dry season when most of the rice is harvested, the export costs would be lower."

The king looked interested and Pakdee stepped in as agreed the night before.

"I believe the Hak Gnee family might have something to offer on this," he said, nudging the old man.

The rice miller cleared his throat and said "Your Majesty, we honored to start fund for annual dredging of river mouth. We give 80,000 baht."

"That is an impressive amount," the king said. "Will there be an adequate return on such an investment?"

"We believe," he said, "…if also get permission to cut big trees in mountains up river. We float them down to sawmill we build near rice mill. We put finished boards on ships in Pakpanang send Bangkok and around region—even China has shortage of lumber."

The district officer looked unhappy at this new request.

"It is getting late," he said. "We are scheduled to have dinner at my house before Your Majesty has to return to your ship."

The dugout turned around in a graceful arc and headed northeast towards the mouth of the river. The rest of the journey was quiet as the king observed the countryside and the boats coming out to greet him.

At the district officer's new house, built of varnished teak on a rise above the river, a group of local dignitaries—officials, Chinese businessmen and even two British mine operators—waited along with crewmen from the royal ship and a long line of policemen. Leading the welcoming group was High Commissioner Phraya Sukhumnaiwinit. They all bowed as the king disembarked.

The king sat before an elaborate array of dishes spread on a mat before him. A pretty woman in a silk *phajonggraben* and a lacy white top, placed rice on the king's plate.

"Your Majesty, these are dishes of the south—fish stomach curry, orange curry, roasted lobster, fish in pandanus leaves, chicken curry and *sataw* in oyster oil. Some of these may not be to Your Majesty's taste. So, we have also prepared a Chinese-style hot and sour soup."

"That will do nicely," the king said, reaching for the small soup bowl. "Delicious. I will be sure to mention this in my trip report."

Phraya Sukhumnaiwinit smiled. "This is all from the best restaurant in Pakpanang, which is owned and operated by this woman. Uh, what is your name?"

"Ploi, sir. Your Majesty, our restaurant is just across the river, but we can prepare food for delivery to your ship for your journey home."

"Perhaps you would be kind enough to send me the recipe," he said. "I like to do a little cooking myself."

"Of course, Your Majesty," she said.

The king nodded and turned his attention to the soup.

Pakdee watched as the woman bowed and *waied* gracefully. Most of the men at the table also were watching her. It's not because they were hungry for the rice she was serving. There were other women helping with the meal, but all the male eyes had been captured by the restaurant owner. He too smiled at her as she bent to spoon rice onto his plate. The smooth golden skin of her shoulders drew his eyes to the top of her breasts. Her body seemed to promise soft delights. Then he noticed a tall man at the back of the room watching him intently. No. No more chasing other men's women. The big man, who looked too muscular to be working in a restaurant, was pushing the restaurant staff to serve the other guests. Anyway, he had a wife of his own to play with. He sighed and tried some of the Chinese soup the king seemed to be enjoying.

"Since the Chinese are such a prominent part of the Pakpanang population," the king said, "it is entirely appropriate for me to enjoy this type of soup. It's rather spicier than I am served in the palace."

This was his cue. "Your Majesty," Pakdee said, "may I introduce one of the leaders of the Chinese community, not just in Pakpanang, but throughout the *monthon*."

He gestured to Sia Leng, sitting several places down the line of dignitaries. The heavy-set Chinese crawled on his knees up the line, careful to keep his head lower than the district officer and the commissioner.

"Sia Leng, once a leading tax farmer for Your Majesty's government, is now in many businesses—shipping, machinery, trade and transport. He has kindly paid for our meal today."

The king nodded. "I heard earlier today we might profit from a change in our policy towards the Chinese—allow them to farm and take advantage of unused land. What do you think?"

"Your Majesty, I believe the current policy is a good one," Sia Leng said. "Yes, allowing the Chinese to farm might boost productivity, but there would be resentment among Thais. They think of the land as their most important asset. There is a danger that Hokkien and Hainanese would come in great numbers, but few would stay. Once they have some money, they go back home to be big men in their villages. We Teochew, however, are different. We stay, start businesses and gradually become Thai. That tall young man at the back, Prem, owner of the restaurant with Miss Ploi, is a good example. His family runs a warehouse business. Unlike me, he speaks Thai as fluently as any native. He shows that Your Majesty's policy toward the Chinese is working fine as it is. Accept those who want to make this their homeland and let us do the businesses the Thais don't like."

The king looked thoughtful. "I have just visited Pattani. The people there don't seem so eager to be part of Siam."

"Your Majesty understands the heart of the problem," Phraya Sukhumnaiwinit said. "The *khaek* will be more difficult to integrate into our nation. They cling stubbornly to their *adat* and their religion. Pakdee has been very helpful to me in understanding how the local people think and feel."

"The honored high commissioner is correct, Your Majesty," Pakdee spoke up. "Unlike the Chinese, the Malay have been here for centuries and have lived by their own rules, with their own religion and their own language. It is not surprising they resist. We must do what we can to make the changes in political system more palatable."

"Yes, of course," the king said. "But we don't have much time. The French are scheming to take our traditional lands on the north and the east. The British are more subtle, but they too advance on our tributary states. Between them, Siam might be nibbled away to nothing. We must demonstrate we are a modern nation, capable of effective rule."

Pakdee glanced around the crowded room. "We have made progress," he said so that all could hear. "There is increasing acceptance of the courts and the new laws."

The king looked somber for a moment, then his eyes lighted up and he looked at Pakdee with a knowing smile.

"It took me long enough to remember, but I believe you are a good example of progress through effort and education."

The king turned to Sukhumnaiwinit, looking pleased. "You have accomplished a great deal with this man, but not enough to fool me. I'll collect my bet, thank you, before I return to Bangkok."

The discussion continued until mid-afternoon. The king looked weary. Pakdee knew the king had been afflicted with some kind of kidney disease for several years. The king was often tired, but he refused to let the illness curtail his travels or his work. Sukhumnaiwinit stood up and bowed to the king. He thanked all the guests for coming. He said the king had important business to discuss with Nakhon officials.

Sukhumnaiwinit ushered the king into the district officer's study, motioning Pakdee, the deputy governor, the chief of police and the district officer to join them as planned. The king sat in a large chair behind a teak table. Sukhumnaiwinit knelt before him.

"Your Majesty, I would like to report on events concerning the Muslim Malay that we could not mention with so many others present. Pakdee has remained in close touch with his informants throughout the region and has prepared a report for you."

"Your Majesty," Pakdee said and cleared his throat. "I regret to inform you there are still groups dedicated to restoring the Pattani raja, despite his conviction and his pledge to refrain from politics. Your Majesty's mercy in allowing Abdul Kadir to return home was wise, but it has not changed his determination to regain power. While he appears to be following the conditions of his release, he is working secretly to foment rebellion. My informants tell me there is a steady stream of visitors to the raja. They come from all parts of the south and return with messages from the raja—sometimes verbal, sometimes in unsigned letters. These are presented at mosques and spark anti-government discussions. They include scurrilous rumors that cast the royal government in a bad light. Unfortunately, there is just enough truth to those rumors to make them believable. No matter what we do, the people see dark motives. The honored high commissioner helped set up government schools to allow local people get the education they need, but many people hesitate to let their children attend for fear they will lose their religion. Bringing in more police to end cattle theft and robbery is believed to be a plot to suppress local people. Anything done to support Buddhism is considered an effort to undermine Islam. I fear there will be violence."

The king nodded wearily.

"None of this is unknown to me. We tried to use the approach the British have employed successfully throughout their empire—advising and supervising local rulers to prevent them from uniting—but we were not successful. We treated these areas as our own, but it was not true, for both the Lao and the Malay consider that their provinces belong to them. We said we were going to trust them, but we didn't."

"Your Majesty," Sukhumnaiwinit said, looking alarmed at the king's description of past policy. "That may be true, but we couldn't risk the Malay rulers colluding with the British against us."

"So, we had to send commissioners and secretaries to supervise them," the king said. "We had to either manipulate the local rulers as puppets, or, if that was not possible, to spy on them and undermine them with their own people. I believe you and Pakdee were most successful in this regard."

"We had little choice, Your Majesty. We faced the risk of losing all of the *khaek* areas," Sukhumnaiwinit said.

"I approved all of your actions at the time," the king said. "But we have come to learn that an administration so full of deviousness cannot bring mutual trust and peace of mind."

There was a long silence in the room. Pakdee was startled to hear the king express deep doubts that reflected his own.

"Your Majesty, what else could we have done?" Sukhumnaiwinit asked.

"I am sorry we have not found a better solution to these problems," the king said. "But we are now on a path to integrating the Malay provinces into our nation and making it a modern state. If we fail, we will fall to the imperialist powers. So, we cannot fail. We must bring the negotiations with the British to a successful conclusion. We must integrate at least Pattani into our nation, but with an understanding of local feelings. So please continue your work. Prince Damrong and I do not want honeyed reports that sweeten bitter realities."

"Yes, Your Majesty," Sukhumnaiwinit and Pakdee said together.

Sukhumnaiwinit presented the king with detailed reports from Pakdee's network. The king glanced through the reports, asking brief questions. When he finished, he looked both grim and tired. One of the navy officers suggested the royal boat would lose the favorable tide if they did not leave soon. Sukhumnaiwinit led the king out of the house towards the river where the ship's boat was moored. Putting on his plumed hat, Phraya Sukhumnaiwinit joined the king in the boat, taking Pakdee's place as planned.

Two dozen Nakhon and Pakpanang policemen lined the path down to the pier. Pakdee followed the royal party with a sense of great relief.

All had gone well, but he was still shaken by the depth of the king's concerns about the south. He watched as the boat swung into the current and headed towards the far end of the bay where the king's ship lay at anchor. Another steamboat to take him and the other *monthon* officials back to Songkhla pulled up to the dock. The group piled aboard, chattering about the success of the royal visit. He turned for a last look at Pakpanang and his eye was caught by the stare of a beefy policeman looking across the dock.

It was him. The one who had beaten him into silence. The same broad, dark face he saw when he awoke in a sweat in the middle of the night. The big-knuckled hands extending from the white uniform were the hands that had blackened his eyes and broken his ribs.

The boat pulled away from shore and the big white figure stood still in the evening sun. He felt the stab of another headache, but could not tear his gaze away until the figure was nothing but a white smudge on the distant shore.

42

DAM
Black Tiger

Dam threw open the door and kicked a half-empty pot of rice across the floor. It was unfair. He was being screwed over once again. He tore off his uniform jacket and threw himself onto the sleeping mat on the floor of his little house. The room was littered with discarded clothing and dirty dishes. Noi wasn't coming back. He had to find someone to clean the house and wash his clothes. Just because he had slapped her a bit. That was over a week ago. She had burnt the rice again, filling the house with an acrid smell. That was the least of his problems. He thought back to his meeting with the police chief.

"Sergeant Sakda, you have been effective. The work against that gang of thieves raiding warehouses was well done, especially getting the leader to confess," the captain had told him. "You appear to be following my orders to stay away from that Chink gangster. Because of this, I recommended that you be promoted to lieutenant and given command of all the rural units."

About time, he had thought. He had worked hard and taken risks to get this promotion, but he saw that the captain looked unhappy.

"Sir. Thank you, sir."

"Unfortunately, however, my recommendation was overruled at the *monthon* office."

"Why? Who?"

"I don't know. Maybe the *monthon* police commander. However, I think it goes beyond that. You have an enemy. The high commissioner may not understand your tough methods are sometimes the only way to get results. The commander said there are notes in your file at the *monthon* headquarter saying you beat *khaek* prisoners, take money from Chinese businessmen and pay little attention to the law. You have to admit these reports are not completely without foundation."

"But I have changed," he complained. "It's unfair. No one has done more to suppress crime in the district. You can't do that by being polite.

No one has stopped as many criminals as me."

"Yes, though a lot of them end up dead."

"Only if they resist arrest. Anyway, it's the only way to be sure they don't return to crime."

"Yes, well, so many deaths upset the aristocrats in the *monthon* office. You need to be more careful. Complaints may still be reaching the high commissioner and his staff. Every negative report is believed while positive results are ignored. There is nothing I can do."

"So, who is the new lieutenant?"

"Sergeant Suchat."

"That weakling. How am I supposed to take orders from him?"

"I will not put him in charge of your unit—commercial crime is more his thing. You will still be responsible for violent crime, gambling suppression and theft. But watch how Suchat operates. He is careful with suspects. Gets proper evidence. Keeps up with changes in the law. He is polite to other officials. He writes excellent reports. He mixes with the officials in Songkhla—even goes to those dance-drama things."

"That's not me." Dam spat on the floor. "That's not what a real policeman does."

"The job of a policeman is more than just stopping criminals. You are an officer in the royal service. You represent His Majesty's government and your own future depends on how you operate within that government. You have the support of your men, but you need relationships with the superiors in Songkhla and even Bangkok to advance. You should cultivate friendships with the judges, the prosecutors and the district officers so someone will defend you if you are attacked. Right now, it is just me and there is only so much I can do."

"I don't know how to do all that ass-licking stuff."

"Then you will be a sergeant forever."

He bunched up a dirty *phatung* as a pillow and stared up at the ceiling. Large spider webs clung to two of the corners. He watched the futile struggles of a fly caught in one as the spider slowly climbed towards it. Which one was he? The spider or the fly? He felt trapped by all those laws and regulations. Even worse were the social niceties, polite words, and gestures officials used to show their status.

Make friends with the polite little government officials who would shit themselves if they faced a pirate? Make alliances with the double-talking officials from Bangkok? I don't think so. I am the Black Tiger. The people out in the villages appreciate what I do. They want me to break up the gangs. The farmers want to get their missing buffaloes back. The ship owners want their cargoes back from the pirates. The people know I get results and don't care how I do it. The prosecutors like my ability to get confessions even if the judges don't like the complaints that criminals make once they are in the safety of the courtroom.

No, he wouldn't change. He couldn't. The *monthon* office would just have to see his value. Maybe if he could identify that enemy....

He looked at the mess in the room. He would have to find a new woman. Noi should have understood his moods. That day had been wasted in writing reports. Even after years in the police force, he still struggled with the spelling and the phrasing. Then that new kid had laughed at his opening sentence. He had barely controlled the hand that wanted to swat his snotty face. Then he got home to the stench of burned rice. Noi should have apologized. Instead she talked back. So, he slapped her. Not even hard. She rushed out and never returned. No big loss. She was getting too demanding anyway. He would have to resort to the teahouse behind the market. At least the girls there never asked for jewelry or clothes. They were weary and plain. There was no excitement, no challenge, and no beauty. Not like Ploi.

She had those large eyes and that challenging smile. There always seemed to be some deeper meaning to everything she said and everything she left unsaid. He thought of how beautiful she looked, even after two children. She lit up the restaurant like a flame. He often lingered long after his meal so he could have a word when she came down from the gambling room.

She had been good for his income too. The monthly payments meant he could afford to buy a better gun, better whisky and put real silver buttons on his uniform. He had been careful to spread most of the money to his men, tightening his grip on their loyalty. Along with the rewards for returning stolen goods and providing extra protection to some of the wealthy ship owners, the casino money had made his men the best paid squad in the whole *monthon*. The big shots might not like him, but his men did. They were the ones who counted in a fight.

And a fight was looming with Jate. In only a year, Jate had expanded his gambling business across Nakhon. Starting with cockfights, bullfights and a three-digit lottery, he had started to open gambling dens in Thung Song, Sichon and Nakhon towns. He had been surprised at how much the *monthon* authorities knew about Jate's activities. Finally, they had orders to crack down. The priority was to cripple Jate's businesses.

He had already led several raids. Sometimes he sent out word to one of Jate's men so the damage was not too great, but lately orders for raids were coming in at the last moment. This month he had seized large amounts of money and arrested the men running the gambling. It was good to see Jate suffer. His problems with the law were compounded by competition with the Jaikla Casino. Ploi's casino, operating right on the river bank, was never raided. He told Ploi that was due to his protection, but there had never been an order to raid Jaikla. It was strange the *monthon* headquarters seemed to be unaware of the Jaikla Casino when they had such accurate information about Jate.

All would be perfect, if it weren't for Ploi's stupid father. He still hadn't cleared his debt with Jate. He had tried to persuade Jate to give Paen more time to repay, but his onetime boss had dismissed him like he was still an ignorant slave boy from the hills.

"So, now you are the errand boy for the *kamnan* who is not a *kamnan* anymore," Jate had said with a sneer.

Surrounded by four of the henchmen who had once worked with Dam, he had laughed off his suggestion to give Paen a few more months to pay the overdue installment on the loan. He knew it was hopeless, but Ploi had asked him to talk to the guy, so he did.

"You, better than anyone, should know what we do to those who don't pay their debts," Jate had told him. "Go tell your new boss to pay up."

He had felt like smashing the man, but he knew he couldn't win against the four men with Jate, men he had seen in action with their long, curved knives. Two maybe, but not four. He had controlled his anger and walked out. The raids on Jate's operations had been pay back enough.

After his warning, Paen had made payments for a few months, but the moron had missed his last two payments. Jate wouldn't stand for this shit much longer.

If it came to a real battle, where would he stand? Jate still had the *Angyi* behind him and Paen still had contacts in the Nakhon royal family. Chinks against Thais. Why not just let them fight it out among themselves? If it weren't for Ploi....

43

PAKDEE
Farewell

Pakdee reviewed the list of tasks Commissioner Phraya Sukhumnaiwinit had given him for the visit of Prince Damrong. He had found a suitable motor vehicle for the prince and the commissioner to inspect the new road being built through the mountains to Trang. Helping a prince inspect the roads was a big change from laboring on those roads as a convict. He had come a long way.

With the successful defeat of the sultans and the imposition of central government rule in the south, Phraya Sukhumnaiwinit's tenth year as commissioner was going smoothly. Some of that success had been due to his own efforts. Raja Abdul Kadir had been removed from power. Work on reform of the courts was going well. His reports based on informants throughout the south had given Phraya Sukhumnaiwinit and Prince Damrong evidence to defend their softer approach in the south. Tax revenues were finally rising despite the closures of gambling and opium dens. Fines and property seizures from gambling raids were adding to *monthon* income. The latest visit of His Majesty King Chulalongkorn had gone well.

The royal visit had enabled him to identify the policeman who had beat him years ago. Sergeant Sakda. Now, let the bastard feel what it is like to be unjustly abused. As long as he was in government, the oaf would never get promoted and would never know why. At first, he had been tempted to confront the man and let him know who was now in control, but that would threaten his own status. No, it was safer to keep that a secret. There was a pleasure in thinking how puzzled the policeman would be to be always left behind while others advanced, to be plagued by negative reports passed on to each of his commanders. Someday he would find a way to hurt Jate, the real cause of his suffering. Now that he had power, there was a lot he could do.

His own family situation had also improved. The loan from Sia Leng had enabled him to clear his debts and complete construction of the mansion. Revenue from the mining concessionaires and shippers was more than keeping pace with his expenditures. Apinya had given birth to their first child, a daughter they called Riem. She was a cranky baby, often crying and demanding to be held, but he didn't mind. He had his own family now. His own house and a daughter. When he got home late, he would often peek into Apinya's room just to watch his wife and daughter sleeping peacefully.

Apinya was happily busy with decorating the house and organizing the *Khon* drama troupe. Its first performance had been a great success, attended by Phraya Sukhumnaiwinit and his wife, along with the leading figures in Songkhla society. A second performance in Nakhon had attracted the governor and other members of the old Nakhon royal family. Apinya was still a reluctant sleeping partner, saying it was too soon after Riem's birth. But that was nearly two years ago. She said she had to save her energy to care for their daughter even though the two nannies did most of the work. She seemed to feel that having borne one child, her reproductive duties were done. In a way that had worked out for the best. Earlier this year, Apinya had brought a pretty young woman to him after dinner.

"Her name is Duangjan," his wife said. "She is as lovely as the full moon, is she not?"

He had to admit the girl was nice-looking, with a round face, plump cheeks, large eyes and a shy smile. She had clear pale skin and the figure beneath her loose white blouse looked inviting.

"My mother sent her from Bangkok where she has learned proper manners, music and domestic skills. If you like her, she will join our household."

"She looks fine," he had said, "But do you really need another maid? You already have two slave girls plus the nannies, the gardener and the cook."

Apinya looked at him with a strange smile. "No, no, she is not for me. She is for you. A man of your status should have more than one wife. The Songkhla governor already has four and his needs are not as strong as yours. More important, you need more connections in the capital. Her uncle is an official in the commerce ministry. She has been working with my mother in the palace. You can't reject her. She and her family would suffer a terrible loss of face. You have been slow to act on this, so I had to help you. Look at her. She will be fun for you. I will, of course, be the major wife and in charge of any others."

Duangjan had proved a shy, but willing bedmate, removing the temptations of the green lantern girls. She was someone he could tease and laugh with. He suspected she reported faithfully to Apinya, but he didn't mind. With one wife for official functions and status and another wife for fun, his home life was now enjoyable. Within days he noticed that other officials appeared to approve of the new wife. Even Somsak was finally paying him proper respect. He must be pleased about his promotion to head the administration section. He had taken on the exaggerated politeness of the aristocrats who visited from Bangkok. The man must spend a fortune on uniforms and all those dinner parties he hosted for senior officials. How did he find the money?

His thoughts were interrupted by the sound of footsteps on the floor above him in the house the Nakhon governor had provided for the prince's visit. Prince Damrong and Phraya Sukhum must be up and ready to travel. He hurried up the stairs and into the sitting room. He bowed and *waied* deeply. Prince Damrong, reading at a large teak desk, ignored him. Phraya Sukhum gestured to him to come in.

"Are the vehicles ready?" Sukhumnaiwinit asked. "Has everyone along the route been instructed to give His Royal Highness a proper reception? Where is the governor and the honor guard?"

He was about to answer when the prince spoke up.

"That can wait, Sukhum. I have just received a telegram from His Majesty. I agree with his decision, but here, read it for yourself."

The prince handed the telegram to Phraya Sukhumnaiwinit. The commissioner sat down on the long settee and read the telegram. It looked short, but Sukhumnaiwinit sat silently for several minutes.

Finally, the prince said, "Good friend, this is a major honor. You will serve in a very important position as Minister of Public Works. Your ability has already been demonstrated by the roads and canals you have constructed in *Monthon* Nakhon Srithammarat. You will be raised in rank. You will be a member of the king's cabinet and you can be nearer to your family and friends in Bangkok. You and I may no longer be working together directly, but we will be living close to one another. We can do things far more enjoyable than defeating the plots of unhappy sultans. So, you agree?"

"This is the wish of His Majesty the King, so of course I will comply even though I am unworthy."

"Excellent, though I'll have a devil of a time finding a decent replacement for you," he said and then turned from the commissioner to his deputy.

"Pakdee, you will make this transition easier. I expect you to support the new commissioner with the same devotion and intelligence you have served Phraya Sukhumnaiwinit."

"A new commissioner?" he said. His heart seemed to stop. He was not only losing his friend and mentor; he was not even being considered as a possible replacement.

"Yes, of course, there will be a new commissioner, an experienced man, I'm sure, coming in from the ministry. Now, take down this message and send it as a telegram to the royal palace in Bangkok:

'I fully support Your Majesty's decision and I have already ordered Phraya Sukhumnaiwinit to hurry back to Bangkok. Stop.'"

He wrote down the brief message, added the formal honorifics at the beginning and end and hastened out the door. His head whirled. His boss, friend and mentor was leaving him behind. He would have no one to protect and advise him. He would have to adjust to a new commissioner. Who would it be? How would they work together?

The life that had seemed so stable a few moments ago was now filled with uncertainty.

44

SOM
Death of a Monk

Light filtered through the forest canopy, speckling the dark back of Phra Sawat as he climbed a narrow path. They had rolled down their robes to the waist as they walked through the midday heat of the dry season. Som watched the movement of the muscles under the skin of Sawat's back as he walked. This was where he was meant to be, following his teacher in the deep forest.

He looked over the edge of the path that dropped off to the water gurgling around rocks below. At least they would have fresh water to drink tonight and the soothing sounds of the water to help them sleep. From a tree beside the stream, a blue-backed kingfisher uttered its loud alarm at the intruders. A small lizard rustled the dead leaves beside the path. Far in the distance a gruff cough sounded like a jungle cat, maybe a leopard.

He turned his awareness to his feet. Heel, then toes on the rough stones of the path. The thick callous of his feet allowed no pain, but he could feel the contours of each stone he stepped on. First one foot, then the other. His mind slipped into reverie. He thought about the years since leaving the safe, but irritating confines of Wat Wang Tawan Tok. He felt grateful to the wiry figure in front of him who had led him through deep jungles and the confusing customs and language of the Lao and the Khmer. Sawat had shared lessons with him, but also stepped back so he could find lessons on his own. He had helped give meaning to the encounter with the elephants. He had helped him improve his meditation practice. He could now control and sustain concentration. His focus on breathing or walking was simply an entry to a state of mind that allowed him to consider questions of dharma. Despite all that, he felt uneasy about Phra Sawat's claims of supernatural power—claims he made in talks to others, but rarely to him.

For their second rains retreat together they had stayed in Phra Sawat's home monastery in Udorn where his mentor was welcomed like a long-lost son. With the giggling assistance of the northeastern temple boys, he learned to speak a few words in the Lao dialect used throughout the northeast. At Phra Sawat's bidding, he taught the temple's local healer how to make and administer some of the herbal medicines he had found most effective.

At the end of the rains, they had headed south again, this time with three novices from the Udorn temple. Sawat urged Som to serve as their mentor so Sawat could focus on his own meditation practice. Sawat was changing. He no longer engaged in discussions of the dharma and often declined to eat anything for a whole day. Sometimes in the evening he would ask the novices about their dreams. He encouraged them to seek an understanding of their own karma through signs found in their dreams.

Why was Sawat becoming so interested in dreams, magical signs and mystical experience? His stories of visions and flying guaranteed an interested audience, but when Som questioned his mentor about his claims, he refused to discuss them. None of this was helpful in understanding the Buddha's teachings. In his own discussions he tried to relate what he had learned from the *suttas* to his experience in the forests. He sought to explain some of the conundrums of the Buddha's teaching. How can one be mindful and yet be empty of desire? How can one want to make merit without wanting the benefit of merit? How can one respect and preserve life and yet welcome death? How can one seek enlightenment and yet eliminate all desires, including the desire for enlightenment?

Discussions with the young monks were interesting. He felt like a teacher while still Sawat's student. It was too bad the three novices decided to stay in Ratchaburi to study with a learned abbot there.

A short stop at Wat Wang Tawan Tok had proved disappointing. Several of his friends had left the monkhood. The abbot had been cold and formal when he paid his respects. He was still registered at the temple, but the abbot didn't seem to want his return. Phra Tissa had passed away and Phra Panya had taken over as the seer who could predict lottery numbers. He had been surprised at Panya's warm greeting. After two nights of telling Panya of the new herbal medicines he had found, the plump monk confessed that the lottery number business was not going well.

"I'm just not giving them many winning numbers. They may not realize it but my numbers are no better than chance," he said. "The old ladies who can't calculate the odds still come to me, but the people able to make the donations have drifted away. I would like to revive the medical treatments we dropped when the lottery numbers were going well. Why don't you come back and we can work together again?"

"Phra Panya, that is kind, but we used to have lots of arguments and you refused to keep careful records," he said.

"But I have forgotten most of the recipes and what worked and what didn't, so I need your help."

"There is still more I want to experience in the forest, but perhaps one day," he said.

From Nakhon, the two monks headed west, walking along the spine of limestone mountains and forest in the center of the peninsula. Now their path wound high above a small stream. The only sounds were the whisper of water in the stream and the songs of birds that flitted and dived over the bubbling water.

"Look there," Sawat pointed to a dark spot in the limestone hillside above them. "A cave. This is the cave I have been seeing in my dreams. It is calling to me. The cave has something to teach me."

The way up was overgrown, but the faint trail showed someone had come this way before. The cave entrance, partly shrouded by green vines, was much larger than it had appeared from below. Long limestone daggers hung from the cave roof. Overturned at the side of the cave entrance was something that looked like a cracked alms bowl.

"Monks have used this cave before," he said.

Sawat hurried to the entrance and peered deeper into the cave. He turned around in excitement.

"Yes, and one ended his life here. This must be why the cave was calling me. This is why we are here," Sawat said.

Once his eyes adjusted to the dim light of the cave, he saw a tangle of dirty yellow cloth. A leg bone protruded from the cloth and a white rib cage lay half buried in the dirt of the cave floor.

"A tiger, perhaps a cobra, or maybe disease, but this was the last place of mindfulness for this monk," Sawat said. "It reminds us that one day we will all be like this—whitened bones in a scrap of cloth."

"If it was a tiger, maybe we shouldn't stay here," Som said.

"Whatever it was, it happened more than a year ago. We have heard the coughing and growling of tigers many times in our travels, but they've never bothered us. Let's ask this man's spirit to allow us to share his cave. That spirit may come to us in our meditation or in our dreams. By reliving his death, we may come to understand what lies beyond this life."

Som felt uneasy about spending the night with the bones of a fellow monk. He doubted his dreams had anything to teach them, but he collected the bones scattered around the cave and piled them together with the skull on top. He placed the alms bowl next to them and spread the torn robe over the bones.

"We should return to the village we passed this morning and report the death," he told Sawat. "Maybe the villagers knew him. In any case, I will ask them to make merit for his spirit."

"That's fine, but tonight he will be our teacher," Sawat said. "One of the benefits of our practice is to prepare us for death, to understand death. There will be visions—signs of our karma. We have been given this opportunity to meditate on death. We shouldn't reject it."

They filled their bottles from the stream and found room in the cave to open their *klots*. Som sat in the half-lotus position and began his meditation facing the pile of bones. Sawat did the same on the other side of the cave.

The fading light of evening filtered through the loose-woven cloth of the *klot*. It seemed like his view was cut into hundreds of tiny squares. Was this the last view of the monk whose bones rested an arm's length away? Did he even see the teeth of the tiger or hear the approach of the python before death? Would it be better to see death coming or to have it strike while sleeping? What would it be like to know for certain the end of life was moments away? He focused on this moment—the last breath his body would ever take. It was terrifying. How could reality continue without him? He laughed at himself. This was the height of arrogance and selfishness.

He thought back to the storm at sea. Death had been imminent. He knew then that the world was indifferent to his life or death. The huge waves of the storm could smother him or not—it made no difference. How had he forgotten this lesson? He had buried it in his mind for eight years, but now it unfolded before him like the view from a mountaintop. Reality was indifferent, nature didn't care—why should he?

Self—it was his attachment to self that made him fear death. He longed for the non-attachment that allowed him to soar far above his body. As he meditated, he sought to imagine himself drifting up and away from his body, into nothingness.

Could the world exist without this so very important person – Chaoxiang, Somneuk, Somdhammo, Som – whatever he called himself? It was difficult to imagine a world without him when every single perception of the world had come through his eyes, his ears, his mind. Could the world go on without him? His family would adjust. He had already been apart from them for so long, it would not be a problem. He had no wife, no son or daughter to carry his existence into the future. Phra Sawat might miss him, but he would soon attract other disciples. His medicines could still help others even when made by other hands.

The world would go on as usual without him. So why should he be concerned? He hoped the monk who died in the cave had come to this understanding before death, that he had not suffered from fear, panic or pain, that he had met death with calmness. He wondered if he could do this for himself as the darkness of death approached. Even the exhilaration of departing from his body was itself an attachment. Perhaps he was wrong to seek it. Maybe Sawat and his claims of flying, of seeing the future were wrong too. What then should he seek? Was non-attachment, emptying his soul of need, was that a worthy goal? He thought of his father struggling for breath, his face slack, his eyes staring sightlessly. He could hear again the sound of his sisters weeping and his mother groaning.

This would come for him too. Was he selfish to concentrate on his own feelings, his own understanding? He could do more. He should do more—not so the world would miss him, but so his life would make a difference, so that others would benefit, so his life would still send at least a small ripple through the world after he was gone. Seeking an end to his own suffering, seeking his own peace—that was not enough.

45

PREM
Married Life

Prem rolled sleepily onto his back. The thin satin sheet had slipped to his waist and he could feel the cool morning breeze on his bare chest. Was it time to get up? His left hand bumped against a small body. Must be Awt. He withdrew his hand, fearful of waking the active five-year-old. Once he was awake, the little boy would be full of questions and demands, insisting Prem play with him or carve him a toy or take him fishing. He started becoming so demanding at two years old when his sister Phraphai was born. He had only just gotten over his jealousy of the little girl when a second son, Praphan, nicknamed An, came along a year ago. He turned to his right and peeped over Ploi's shoulder. An was sleeping on his mother's arm. Just beyond him slept little Phai, now almost three and already annoying her big brother by trying to follow him everywhere he went.

He smiled at the thought of his children playing together as he had played with Som and their sisters, inventing games and little plays in which they each played a part. Awt, however, didn't want to have much to do with his sister or his little brother. He preferred to run around with a gang of boys from the town nearly a kilometer away.

He sat up and looked around the room. Set to one side of the main room, it was bare except for the woven sleeping mats, a few Chinese-style wooden pillows and clothes hung on nails along the walls. He looked at Ploi. The satin sheet had fallen away, baring the smooth tan skin of her back. There was a bit more flesh covering her ribs than six years ago when they had first slept together, but she was more beautiful than ever. Her long neck tempted a kiss, but he contented himself with a slow sniff that drew in the aroma of her body and the coconut oil she used on her thick, short-cropped black hair. Her breasts trembled slightly with each slow breath and he felt his morning erection pushing against the cloth of his *phakaoma*. He leaned over and kissed Ploi's neck, savoring the slight saltiness of her taste on his tongue. She leaned back into him, pressing the warm skin of her back into his chest. He reached over her arm and drew her closer, nestling one hand beneath her left breast. He watched as a single drop of milk slid down the soft curve of her breast. Soon An would be up and demanding his first feed. Maybe there was time before he and the other children woke up—if they were quiet and careful. He moved his hand down over the slight curve of her stomach to the dark curls below. She moaned quietly and pushed back against his erection. Her eyes flicked open, and she smiled sleepily. Prem pressed his hand lower, but Ploi took his wrist in her hand and pulled it away.

"Not now, Father."

"Why not, Mother?" He grinned at the terms they had begun to use after their second child was born. No longer 'lover' or 'sweetheart,' but 'father' and 'mother.' He supposed this was a good thing. They were now more than lovers; they had a family together.

"You'll wake the children and I have work to do. The monthly report to Sia Leng is due and I've only just started it."

He sighed and fell back. With each child, their love-making had diminished a bit more. They had to find a time when the children were either asleep or out to play. But if the children took something away, they added much more. He loved watching them, feeding them, playing with them and now, with Awt, teaching them. If only Ploi wasn't so busy with the casino.

Managing an illegal gambling den had become more complicated and stressful than before, but Ploi had insisted on handling it all herself. There were secret meetings with that ugly policeman, special reports written in code for Sia Leng, and runners dispatched to tell their big customers of gambling dates or to pay off the lottery winners. There were no more duets with Ploi. She wanted him to manage the restaurant that provided a legal front for the upstairs gambling room. The casino took most of Ploi's time from evening until well into the night and she had to make monthly trips to Songkhla.

He felt neglected some times, but the children were taking up more of his time, especially now that Awt had begun to learn his letters. He had already taught him the first 40 letters of the alphabet, skipping the archaic ones that were hardly used anymore. Awt quickly grasped the complicated rules of spelling, but he was easily bored. The longest he would sit still was an hour or two. Then he would run for the door.

Recently, little Phai had been to joining their lessons, sitting silently behind her brother, studying the letters he wrote on the slate blackboard. He wasn't sure whether she understood what he was teaching. It was difficult to get her to talk, but her large eyes always looked interested.

He gave Ploi's neck another sniff as she moved back towards the baby who eagerly clutched one breast in his chubby little fists. On his other side Awt was kicking aside his covers and struggling to his knees. He rubbed the sleep out of his eyes and looked up at him.

"Can we take the boat out today? Lek caught a big fish yesterday. I need to catch a bigger one."

He tousled his son's hair. "Well, you know the fish don't always cooperate, especially the big ones."

"But I want it, so I can show Lek."

"We can try, but first I have to help your mother and then we have to work on your letters."

Awt frowned. "But the fish bite early in the morning."

"We will check the tide, but I am busy this morning. The evening would be better if the tide is going out. And we have to get some bait first."

"Then I am going to play with my friends."

"Alright, but no fishing until you do your letters."

"Sure, Pa, sure," Awt said as he pulled the tail of his *phakaoma* through his legs and tucked it into his waist at the back. He pushed open the door and scrambled out, heading for the cook room at the rear of the house where Ploi's mother already had a pot of rice gruel bubbling on the charcoal stove. Little Phai was struggling after him, her plump legs tangled in her *phatung*.

"Wait. Awt, wait for me," she called as she disappeared through the door. "Wait for me."

Prem looked back at Ploi. She sat on the mat with An sucking lustily at her breast.

"He's like one of those sucker fish that stick to sharks. Maybe we should rename him '*Pla doot*.'"

"Or maybe the 'the big leech,'" Ploi laughed as she watched her son feed. "I think he is old enough now to start eating mashed bananas. That way I can make the trip to Songkhla. If I leave early in the morning, he can have banana and goat's milk during the day and I can get back to feed him at night."

"Why don't I make the trip for you for a few months?"

"Our agreement was that I would report to Sia Leng. He doesn't want anyone else—not even Father. Anyway, you don't know what is happening with the casino; you spend all your time in the restaurant trying out new recipes or buying supplies in the market. It's not a problem. Sia Leng says he is content with my written reports until I am free to travel. I could even take the baby with me now that the monsoon season is over. The steamer makes a faster and more comfortable trip than the sloop."

"I could go with you."

"We need someone to oversee the restaurant and the nanny."

He watched from the window as the nanny, a skinny 14-year-old girl, chased after Awt who was running up the path to the road waving a skewer of chicken livers from the kitchen. He knew he was needed at home and at the restaurant, but still felt miffed at being excluded from the casino business, the family's main money earner. He had to admit the casino had gone smoothly despite the government's ban. That policeman seemed to be keeping his well-compensated promise to protect the casino, but there were still risks. Several other casinos had been raided in the past few months. They got off with fines, but the courts could always decide on a prison sentence. What would he do if Ploi were arrested? What if he were arrested too? What would happen to the family then?

46

PLOI
Trouble

Ploi's eyes flicked open. She must have dozed off. It was late, and it was dark. The candle on her table had burned out. She should have been on her way home long before this. What was that sound? Tim? He should be waiting to escort her home. Prem had left earlier to help put the children to sleep. They would fuss if he was not there to tell them a story. Was that a groan?

It was well past midnight, but the air was still heavy and warm. The windows were closed and shuttered for the night. There was a crash from the restaurant below. The first door. It was made of thin pine. Someone was breaking in. Where was Tim? There was a thud that made the wooden building tremble. Then another and another. Someone was chopping through the heavy second door. They might get through that, but then they would have to deal with the iron door at the top of the stairs.

It would take a long time to get into the gambling room. If they did, she would take the hidden exit out the back. She peered out the rear windows. Dark shapes were pulling at the disguised door to the exit below. It was built to open only from the inside. Then she heard the sound of chopping from the back. The wood of the exit was splintering. If they came up that way, she would be trapped.

All the casino proceeds for the week were in the safe hidden in the floor of the office. Would they find it? She pulled aside the mat hiding the safe. She gathered the wads of twenty-baht banknotes in a bag and then added six sacks of gold and silver coins. With some effort, she hoisted the bag over her shoulder. It was too heavy, so she left the bags of small coins behind. She closed the safe and covered it with the mat.

Her heart was pounding even faster than the chopping sounds from below. Could she get out the window and onto the roof? No. She looked out into the main gambling room. There was nowhere to hide. The roulette wheel had been folded back into the wall. The

Thua and *Po* mats were rolled up against the wall. She heard muffled voices along with the sounds of breaking wood. Someone must hear them. Where were Dam and his police guards? What would the thieves do to her if they found her?

She pulled back into the office and closed the door. What about the food box? She bent over the food delivery system and pulled on the ropes hoisting the big box to the second floor. She could hear footsteps on the ladder to the hidden exit. That came out behind a large teak cabinet. It would take two men to move it. She knelt on the floor and crawled backwards into the food box, closing the doors. It was completely black. She had to fold her knees into her chest and bend her head. Holding onto the rope she lowered the box so the top was at floor level. Her arms strained with her weight. From above they would think it was an empty closet and from below all they would see was the bottom of the box.

She heard the sounds of the teak cabinet being pushed back and bare feet rushing into the gambling room. There was a sharp smack of wood against wood. The door – they were already in the office – only a few feet away. She could hear the food cabinet doors pulled open. Did they see the rope?

There was a moment of silence, then a whisper and the doors slammed shut. A moment later she heard the clank of metal against metal. The wooden floor groaned. They must be trying to pry the safe out of the floor.

Her fingers were numb from holding the rope. It slipped and a foot of rope slid through her hand and the box lurched downward. Did they hear? How much longer could she hold the rope? She twisted it around her wrist and flexed her painful fingers, now wet with sweat—or was it blood? She heard the rasp of heavy iron being dragged across the floor. They had the safe out. There was a clang as the iron door was opened from the inside and more footfalls on the wooden floor. There were grunts and a crash on the stairway.

The rope moved again pulling her arms up to the top of the box and dropping it another six inches with a short squeal as the box rubbed against the frame of the hoist system. She held her breath. Had they heard it?

There was another crash and then a series of thumps from the stairway. There was a muffled snort and a whinny from the path outside the restaurant. They must have a cart. They were going to get away and there was nothing she could do. At least she had taken out the gold and the banknotes. She smiled when she thought of their disappointment at the meager value of the coins. The pain in her wrist was getting worse. She tried to shift to the other hand, but her fingers, numb and wet, let the rope slip. She tried to grab it again, but it whipped outside the box. It slid down with a screech and crashed to the floor of the kitchen. Ploi's head and shoulders fell out of the box onto the cool tile floor of the kitchen. There was a shout and a curse from the front entrance. They must have heard. They were coming for her.

She crawled out of the box, dragging the heavy bag behind her. The kitchen was dark, but there was nowhere to hide. They had her now. She stood up and waited for the door to burst open.

There was more shouting from the front. Then a crash—a gunshot? Then another. A clatter of hooves against the hard dirt of the road. Another gunshot, farther away. Then silence. She waited in the dark. She heard voices—Father? Prem?

She cautiously opened the kitchen door.

"Ploi, are you there? Ploi."

It was Prem. She slipped through the door and Prem rushed up to her, crushing her in his arms.

"Are you hurt? Did they hurt you?"

"No, they never found me, but my hands are cut," she said.

Prem took her hands gently and held them up to the lantern sitting on one of the restaurant tables. The fingers were cramped and curled. Patches of skin had been torn loose and oozed blood.

"We need to get you to a doctor."

He put his arm around her shoulder and led her outside where Father and two of his men were crouched over a body. Hunched beside them was Tim, dark blood seeping from his hair down his jawline.

"Tim, are you injured? What did they do?" she cried.

"It's not too bad—just a headache. Never saw them coming. I'm sorry I couldn't stop them. Once they got into the restaurant, they forgot about me and I ran for help."

"Too late to stop them," Father said in disgust. "They got away with a horse cart. Ploi, what did they take?"

"It was the safe, I think."

"And all our money…

"No, it was just the small coins. Here are the gold, silver and banknotes." Ploi pointed to the bag on the floor behind her. Father tore open the first leather bag and started counting.

"Fifty coins each, 800 baht in notes," Ploi said. "Don't worry, it's all there."

"That's not so bad then, but I will still track down and kill the bastards," her father said, holding up his heavy revolver. "At least I got one of them. We have to find out who he was working for."

They all turned to the body. Tim took a rag and wiped the blood and dust from the dead man's face. He was just a boy.

Tim looked up with fear in his eyes.

"Boss, this means trouble," he said. "This guy. It's Jate's eldest son."

47

PAKDEE
Drama

Pakdee heard the entwined wails of two horns and the thump of a drum as he climbed the stairway to his house. Must be the final rehearsal before the show. Apinya's *Khon* drama group was scheduled to put on a performance for the beginning of *Songkran* the next day. He knew the *Khon* performances had boosted his status with the new high commissioner, Phraya Chonlaburanurak, but he was tired of all the people in his house and all the noise.

The door swung open and he stepped back in surprise. Big eyes stared at him from a green face with white tusks protruding out of an open red mouth. One of the ogres from the *Khon* slipped past him in a rush. He pushed through the door to the central platform of the house.

On one side sat the 10-member orchestra with two string violins, drums, half circles of brass gongs, a bamboo xylophone and a pair of small horns. On the other side a man and a woman in elaborate costumes danced gracefully in time with the ching of tiny cymbals. It was Duangjan. She had recovered rapidly from the birth of Nui, his first son, two months earlier. He enjoyed watching the subtle movements of her body, now even more voluptuous. He loved the graceful gestures of her hands, so flexible that her fingers curved back almost to her wrist. She must be Sita dancing for Rama.

He had gradually become familiar with the story depicted by the dancers as they rehearsed at his house. Apinya had explained, rather impatiently, the details of the long tale of the *Ramakien* depicted in the *Khon* drama. She thought it strange he didn't already know the story. He explained he had grown up in the south where most of the drama performances were the *Manora* or the tale of *Phra Aphaimani*, but he knew his wife was puzzled and disdainful of his ignorance.

"In the palace, we all had to learn to dance the different roles of the *Khon*," Apinya had told him. "No males were allowed, so the women had to take the male parts—even the ogres. I most often danced the part of Phra Lak, but I know all the roles."

For this production, however, Apinya's troupe would have both men and women in the cast—just like the latest public performances sponsored by the king in Bangkok. She had even gotten painters to create a scenery backdrop—the new trend in the capital. Apinya had thrown herself into the production with an intensity that surprised him. She was delighted when she won approval from High Commissioner Phraya Chonlaburanurak to perform on a stage in front of the *monthon* headquarters. The commissioner, like his predecessor, saw *Khon* as one way to bring the culture of the capital to the provinces of the south.

At first, he had enjoyed the color, bustle and sounds the troupe brought to his house, but today, he wanted only to rest after a busy and frustrating day. Apinya had tried to get him to perform in the production, but he declined. She had recruited other officials. Somsak proved particularly adept, taking the role of Rama. In comparison, he would only embarrass himself. On stage for all to see, even the satin costumes and heavy makeup might not disguise the Muslim goat-meat seller from Pakpanang. It was better to be seen as a patron of the *Khon* rather than as a clumsy performer.

He much preferred the simple fun of the shadow puppet performances he had grown up with in Pakpanang. Just a white screen and puppets cut out of stiff buffalo leather. The narrator took on all the parts, making funny comments about the story as it unfolded. There were jokes about local dignitaries or cutting comments about political affairs. There were stories of noble heroes and nasty villains, but there was also lots of buffoonery from the clowns along with dirty jokes and comments masked by double meanings. Whenever there was a shadow puppet performance in the courtyard in front of his building, he would come back to his office at night, pleading urgent work. Then he could sit on the balcony and watch the shadow puppets for an hour or two.

Nevertheless, he knew he had to keep up his role as a government official who appreciated royal culture. He had read through the poetry written by the kings of the current dynasty. He had become adept at the formal written language needed for government reports and he felt more comfortable using the royal language in his meetings with members of the royal family. He had to admit that Apinya had been helpful. She had slipped into the role of advising him on aristocratic traditions, though he suspected her upbringing in the palace had its limitations. Chatting with Duangjan had helped him perfect his central Thai accent, but speaking with women so much had caused some embarrassment. A couple of times he had used phrases spoken only by females, sending his fellow officials into spasms of giggling.

Still, Apinya's sponsorship of the *Khon* troupe, her elegant appearance, her musical evenings and the proper language he had learned from her had enabled him to win the acceptance of most officials in the office. His palace-raised wives and rumors of his mysterious family origin had led the central Thais to accept him as one of their own, while his fluency in the southern dialect and *Jawi* had won support from local officials. For nearly four months before the new commissioner's arrival, he had served as acting commissioner. His administration of the *monthon* had gone smoothly and he had accomplished a lot, but that ended with the new commissioner's arrival. At least he had earned a higher official title. He was grateful to Prince Damrong for naming him deputy high commissioner in charge of the courts, police, contracts with foreign businesses, and Muslim affairs. The additional authority was welcome, but he missed the wide-ranging discussions of political and cultural affairs he had enjoyed with Sukhumnaiwinit. At least he had been rewarded with a promotion, even though it wasn't the one he wanted. Surely now, he was in position to succeed his boss.

That must be the reason for that anonymous letter. Fortunately, he had found it in the pile of correspondence for the commissioner. It had been in a plain envelope. Since he often screened the commissioner's correspondence, he opened the envelope. It was a single sheet of paper with only two sentences: "High Commissioner, please keep a careful eye on your deputy. He is not what he seems to be and his loyalties are not what they should be. – A True Thai"

Who could this True Thai be? Why was he trying to poison the commissioner against him? He had queried the clerk who collected the mail but he insisted he hadn't noticed that envelope. It must be someone with access to the office. Who?

That question had bothered him throughout the day, but there was nothing he could do about it. It seemed out of place. Just when everything was going well, this was like a fishbone in his throat. Maybe Apinya would have some ideas—if she could spare some time from her *Khon* troupe. But maybe she would blame him for making an enemy.

Although Apinya no longer shared his sleeping mat, they had

reached a working partnership that met other needs. He provided the money and the official status she desired. She managed the household budget, their savings, her cultural activities and the minor wives.

The newest wife, Ying Yue, was the pale third daughter of a Chinese mine operator. The girl had been presented to him to cement an agreement on a tin mine in the northern mountains of the *monthon*. It didn't hurt that the girl's pearl white skin was a pleasing contrast to his darker-skinned wives. Apinya had approved the choice as a way to build alliances with the wealthy Chinese in Songkhla. Before that she had pushed forward Saengdao, the daughter of a middle-ranking military officer stationed in Nakhon, saying he needed connections in the army. The officer, who had five daughters, was grateful to be relieved of one. So now he had four wives—the same number allowed by the Koran. Father would be jealous. Despite his frequent threats to take additional wives, Father had never dared to upset Mother and anyway he could never afford any more mouths to feed.

The new wives were working out well. Duangjan was pregnant again. Ying and Saengdao were wonderfully different. Ying was submissive and attentive to his every need. Saengdao was aggressive and demanding, urging him to do things he had only done with Green Lantern girls. Apinya ran a strict household with each of the wives taking responsibility for particular tasks and all working to ensure he was satisfied. When there were conflicts and squabbles, Apinya settled them with decisive finality.

More wives meant more 'milk money' payments to their fathers, but income had increased as his power in the *monthon* administration became established. The financial difficulties of a few years ago had eased despite the expenses for the new wives, the *Khon* troupe and Apinya's clothes. Money flowed in from port fees and from the Chinese and British businesses competing for mining concessions and other favors. It was understood by shippers, importers and miners that modest payments to a special account along with the usual gifts would ensure their business went smoothly. These connections had not only been lucrative, but had also given him the contacts among the shadier shippers. Those contacts enabled him to tip off police to seize a shipment of arms to Pattani and several large packets of opium headed to the tin mines. Those seizures had won him favorable comment in reports to the king and in the Bangkok press. After a year and a half in office, Phraya Chonlaburanurak had come to depend on him.

Yes, all was going well.

Apinya had not even noticed his arrival. Just as well. He was tired of her non-stop chatter about which dancers were doing well and which were not. She insisted on perfection and anything less meant a scolding and detailed complaints. Some dancers were lazy. The lead singers kept forgetting the lyrics. The musicians wanted more money and the local craftsmen couldn't make the papier mâché masks properly. On and on. She didn't seem to notice when his attention drifted away. Her complaints seemed meant to release her anxieties rather than to find a solution. Why should he bother to listen?

There were many more serious problems in the *monthon* than the clumsy dancing of the Sita actress. He faced challenges implementing reforms ordered by the ministry. He had to outwork and outthink the other staff. When the current commissioner moved on, he would be in line to become commissioner, a well-deserved reward for his work and the risks he had taken to consolidate government control in the south.

His old boss, now with a new title and name—Chaophraya Yommarat—was well-positioned as a cabinet minister to help him. Prince Damrong, the most powerful person in the kingdom after the king, knew him well. Even the king, although they had met only a few times, seemed to appreciate his abilities and his work.

He settled down on a mat and leaned back against the teak wall of the house. There was too much work to do to spend his time worrying about an anonymous letter. He had spent the day with 32 judges from district courts throughout the *monthon*. He had to ensure they understood the new Revised Criminal Code. The law had been written and rewritten for six years with advice from foreign advisers—French, Japanese, Belgian and even a lawyer from Ceylon. Under the new law the police had a reduced role in prosecutions. It was now illegal to whip prisoners. The accused were entitled to legal counsel. It was a good law. Too bad it had arrived far too late to have helped him.

Some of the older judges refused to understand the new procedures. He had already slated those for retirement. The problem was to find people to replace them. The commissioner hadn't shown much interest in the courts since he took office more than a year ago. He was more interested in state ceremonies and economic development, especially building roads. He delegated the legal work to him. He found it interesting, but it was less exciting than political affairs.

The continuing political problem was the resistance of the people in the Malay provinces to the king's reforms. His informants reported that Abdul Kadir had not given up hopes of returning to power. The former raja did little in public, but he and his sons were stirring up dissatisfaction. They had appealed to the British colonial authorities in Singapore for support.

The British had acquiesced to the arrest and replacement of Abdul Kadir four years ago. Since then, negotiations had been underway to clarify Siam's relations with its Malay territories and the Malay areas under British protection. Once an official treaty was in place, administration of the south would be much easier.

He watched as the monkey general Hanuman and his army gathered on one side of the central platform with the opposing army of ogres on the other. He liked Hanuman and the antics of his monkey soldiers. He grinned at Hanuman's boastful declarations and the angry retorts from the ogre king *Totsakan*. Then the armies danced towards each other. The performers twirled their wooden weapons and strutted back and forth on the polished floor. Soon the battle would be joined. Would it be the same for the Malays in the south? Were the complaints and threats of the old raja just theater? Or would they lead to a real battle? Once the fighting began, it would be hard to stop and the deaths would not be the colorful fakery of the *Khon*.

48

SAIFAN
Pondok

Saifan cleared his throat and rapped his walking stick on the rough brick floor of the mosque. He looked at the 22 boys sitting cross-legged in front of him. This was the culmination of a long effort—the first day of teaching in his own school, a *pondok* with three new thatched huts just outside the mosque wall. One hut provided a classroom for use when the mosque was busy. Cooking and eating took place in another. Books and papers were stored in the mosque. Five of the boys were boarding in one of the huts. The other boys came from Krue Se village. Their families were paying two baht each for their lessons.

He looked at the schedule on the chalkboard nailed to the wall. Top of the list was the Koran and explanations of its meaning, then the prophetic tradition of Islam, Islamic jurisprudence, Islamic ethics, Islamic history, Arabic, *Jawi* and Thai. Most other *pondok* schools in Pattani were unable or unwilling to teach Thai, but language was an important weapon in the struggle against the infidel Siamese government.

"If we cannot understand them, how can we defeat them?" he said when asked why he taught Thai. Most parents, however, wanted their sons to learn Thai for more practical reasons—doing business in the city now dominated by Thais. It was the reason he was able to attract students, but it wasn't why he started the school.

"Today we continue our study of the Holy Koran," he said. "I will first recite a verse. You will not understand the meaning of this verse because it is in the Arabic language of the Prophet Mohammed as conveyed to him directly from Allah. You should open your ears to the beauty of the sounds. I will then explain the meaning. An educated Muslim must know both how to recite the verses and how to understand their meaning. So, listen with your whole being. Remember my explanations. Think how to apply them in your lives. Our religion is not something trapped in books or empty rituals. It must be lived."

He took a deep breath and recited the first verse of the Koran, memorized long ago. He had learned to project his voice and to let the tones of the Arabic words rise and fall in an austere melody. He was pleased to see his students stop their fidgeting as the sounds washed over them.

"Now I will translate into *Jawi*, so you may understand the solemn meaning of the verse."

"In the name of Allah, the Gracious, the Merciful.
All praise belongs to Allah, Lord of all the worlds,
The Gracious, the Merciful,
Master of the Day of Judgment.
Thee alone do we worship and Thee alone do we implore for help.
Guide us in the right path —
The path of those on whom Thou hast bestowed Thy blessings,
Those who have not incurred Thy displeasure,
And those who have not gone astray."

He paused a moment and surveyed his students. They seemed to be listening, though the chubby one in the back already looked sleepy.

"The beginning of this verse is the standard beginning for all chapters in the Holy Koran," he said. "It identifies mercy as one key attribute of Allah and his dominion over the world as the other. Therefore, all praise is due to Allah. We need not look to any other source for help— not to political power, not to wealth, not even to family. In the end, it is only Allah who can save us from eternal suffering. However, we must do our part by striving to follow the right path. Then, when we come to the day of our death – the Day of Judgment – we will not be afraid because we have not strayed from the path."

He stopped and took a breath. He seemed to have their attention.

"That is why you are here today, to learn the right path and to seek the guidance of Allah through his prophet Mohammed and the Holy Koran. Now repeat the verse after me."

He recited the first line, and the boys tried to imitate the unfamiliar sounds. Then they repeated each of the lines in turn. He corrected their pronunciation and made them repeat the verse again and again. For more than an hour he led the recitation until he was satisfied. He then queried them on the meaning of the verse, explaining that the words gracious and merciful came from the same Arabic root word, that mercy must be shown to all in the world, even the unbelievers. It is only by the grace of Allah that all the things men need in the world are provided to them—food, clothing, community and companionship. It is only by the mercy of Allah that believers are rewarded with eternal life.

As the sunlight coming through the doorway crept across the floor, the boys were tiring. He had to be careful not to let his enthusiasm push them beyond what they could absorb. Some boys were eager to learn, but most were there at their family's insistence. Unfortunately, there didn't seem to be any with the keen intellect of his old student Sulong. That boy had been a challenge, but an interesting one. He was always questioning how the teachings of the Koran could be applied to life now in Pattani.

Saifan had spoken to Sulong's father about the boy's talent and energy. As a result, his father had sent Sulong to Mecca for further study. The boy was doing well, judging from the letters he had received describing the wonders of the holy city and the wisdom of his teachers.

He looked at the students bent over their Korans.

"It is now question time," he said. "You may ask questions on any point of the day's lessons or any concern you may have."

The boys looked at each other. There had been no question time in the classes with the Imam, so this was the first time for them. Most were not allowed to question elders at home either.

"Honored teacher, there is a man in my village who has dreams and predicts the future. He says he is inspired by Allah. Is that possible?"

"It is hard to say anything is impossible if it is the will of Allah, but the Koran, the word of Allah, tells us that claims to predict the future can be tricks of Satan. The Koran says: 'O you who believe! Intoxicants, gambling, idolatry and divinations are abominations of Satan's doing. Avoid them, so you may prosper.'"

"This one line shows us how much of Siamese society is abomination. That society is made evil by its rice wine, gambling dens, bronze images everywhere and its childish faith in soothsayers and fortune-telling monks. Don't be tempted or deceived by this corruption. The Koran is clear: all that is the work of Satan to lead you away from the righteous path of Islam. We will learn much more of this path in the days ahead. Today let us focus on the first verse. Are there any questions?"

He could see the boys were struggling to come up with questions. Finally, one of the older boys, one he had taught in his previous classes at the mosque, spoke up in a voice that was just starting to deepen.

"Honored teacher, today's verse says Allah is the master of Judgment Day. Is that only for Muslims? Does Judgment Day come for the unbelievers as well? It doesn't seem fair that only Muslims must follow the path while others can drink, eat and enjoy themselves."

"Allah is all-powerful and the judge of all mankind, so yes, the infidels, whether Buddhist or Christian, must face his judgment. If they sin, if they resist the teaching of Allah, they face eternal suffering. Following the path of Islam is not easy, but it leads to an eternal paradise that is not available to others. Do not look on the sins of the flesh as privileges, but as the prelude to suffering."

"But the unbelievers seem to prosper and to dominate us," the boy said, his brow clenched with uncertainty. "My father says we suffer under their rule. Last week a policeman killed a fisherman, claiming he was a smuggler. Do we have to wait for Judgment Day to see him punished?"

"Judgment Day is certain, and the punishment is terrible," he explained, "but the Koran allows us to seek justice before that. There is a verse on this that shows we have a duty to punish such crimes, but in just proportion. Listen and remember:"

"O you who believe! Retaliation for the murdered is ordained upon you."

As he quoted the verse, he thought of Abdul. He had failed to retaliate for his brother's murder. Someday, somehow there would be something he could do.

49

PLOI
Revenge

Ploi woke with a start. The room was dark with only a faint hint of light through the windows. Something was wrong.

She looked at the three children on her left. Each seemed to be sleeping peacefully. She reached out with her right hand and found the warm flesh of Prem's back. She listened for his breath. There it was, steady and quiet. She could barely see. She heard footfalls on the path outside. Who could be coming this late at night? There was a pounding on the door. She gave Prem a sharp nudge.

"Wake up. Someone is at the door."

"What?"

"Someone is at the door."

"The girl will get it."

"No. You go."

Prem groaned and stood up, retying his *phakaoma* around his waist. She stood up with him and pushed him ahead. The pounding at the door came again.

"Ploi, open up. Open the door. It's me."

It was Daeng's voice, but he sounded strange, his voice higher than usual.

She pulled Prem with her as she hurried to the door. Prem drew back the iron deadbolts and threw the door open. Daeng looked up at them with a face distorted.

"They stabbed him. They stabbed him right at his own door and left him in his blood."

"Who stabbed who?" Prem asked.

But she already knew. It was Father. They had feared this ever since the night of the robbery when they found the body of Jate's son. For weeks, there had been threats and plots. Father's men had fought off one attack two weeks after the robbery. Then last month another attempt had failed when Sergeant Dam had gotten word of a planned ambush on the road to Nakhon. She had ordered extra precautions, but Father was more afraid of looking fearful than he was of Jate.

"Prem, get dressed. We have to go now. Jate has attacked Father, hasn't he?"

Daeng nodded and tried to speak, but no sound came out.

She ran down the steps and onto the path to Father's house. Daeng, Tim and three other men hurried to keep up with them.

They were all breathing heavily when she turned to Daeng.

"What happened? You and the other men were ordered to be on guard. How did you let this happen?"

"He went out drinking with friends. They were supposed to get him home safely," Daeng said between breaths, "but they must have left him at the gate to the house. We didn't know he was back until we heard the shouts. By the time we got to him, he was bleeding so much. Nothing we could do."

"How bad is he?" Prem asked Daeng who was struggling to keep up.

"Bad," he panted.

"But still alive?" she asked.

"He looked up at me. Said 'get them'. Saw no one. They must already have run—maybe into the forest. So, I came. To get help. Others trying to find them."

She ran steadily, but the dread growing inside her seemed like a weight pulling her down.

Rung knelt on the path near the front gate, bent over a body. A cluster of men crouched behind her. Blood was smeared on one cheek. Her blouse was dark with something that glinted wetly. She rocked back and forth, making a faint keening sound like a wounded animal.

Ploi pushed Rung back and took Father's head in her hands. His eyes stared up in the faint light of the lantern one of the men held over them. He did not look peaceful in death. His chin sank back into his neck and his betelnut-stained teeth jutted out. A jagged red wound slanted from one ear across his neck to his collar bone. Blood from wounds in his stomach and chest still seeped down his side.

He was gone.

Nothing made sense. She had tried so hard to gain his approval, to win a nod or a smile, to make him proud. She had given him grandchildren. She had secured the family wealth. Now it all meant nothing.

Jate had done this. Robbed her of her father. Taken away a world that made sense and left chaos behind. Helpless anger swelled within her. She felt like she would burst. He would have to suffer too. He would pay.

She felt Prem's hands on her shoulders. He said something into her ear. It made no sense. She shrugged him away and sat staring into the darkness. She heard nothing; she saw nothing.

Then, the burly form of Dam crouched on the other side of Father's body. She looked at his face. It was dark with the same rage swelling within her. Her eyes questioned that rage and his eyes gave her the answer she demanded. Jate would pay.

50

SOM
In the Charnel Grounds

Phra Som gagged and pulled his robe across his nose and mouth. The smell of rotted flesh and damp ash filled his throat. He looked back at Phra Sawat in alarm.

"It's like anything else," Sawat said. "You get used to it over time. That is why we are here — to know death, to smell it, taste it, and, in our minds, experience it."

Som looked around the field only a few paces from a path heading west to the Burmese border and a few hundred paces from the monastery where he and Phra Sawat were spending the rainy season retreat.

"Come walk with me," Sawat said. He opened the small gate in the rough stone wall of the charnel grounds. Som followed, feeling like he was being pulled along against his will. Piles of ashes and bones stippled the field. In some piles of ashes he could see the blackened flesh of a torso only partly burned. In one corner there was a large pile of rags and bones. The breeze shifted and the smell struck like a club. He could see skulls, rib cages, leg bones and blackened flesh amid the rags. This was where the monks from the nearby temple dumped cremated remains along with the bodies of those who had no one to pay the expenses of cremation.

"One day you and I will smell like this," Sawat said. "Whether burned or rotten, our flesh, this flesh we love so much, will fall away from the bones, will be devoured by insects until nothing remains but a bleached skeleton like this one here," he said, pointing to a set of bones missing only the skull.

"Birth, sickness and death—these are all normal and unavoidable. All we can do is achieve a state of mind undisturbed by these things."

Sawat cleared a space in front of the skeleton and set up his *klot*. He sat down and lifted his feet onto his thighs.

"This man, or perhaps woman, will be my teacher tonight. Look around and choose your own teacher."

Som looked over the field, backing away from the big pile in the corner. As he turned away, he caught a glimpse of a skull in the weeds. The dark holes of the eye sockets stared up at him. A wisp of dried skin and a few strands of hair clung to the top of the skull. It seemed to be waiting for him to say something.

"I suppose you could be my teacher," he said, brushing away the ashes in front of the skull and setting up his *klot* beside it. His heart pounded as he felt the empty eye sockets look through him. Fear was stupid. He was a *thudong* monk. He had faced the real dangers of the forest. He had meditated amid the roars of tigers and the trumpeting of elephants. Why should he fear a bit of old bone?

It was those ghost stories his father enjoyed telling the children before the annual Hungry Ghosts Festival. Father would command Mother to prepare a lavish meal before leading the family to the shrine dedicated to their ancestors. They would place the food at the shrine and burn paper money, calling on the spirits of the dead to bring good luck to the family business.

Father always took special delight in frightening his children that night. Hungry ghosts, he told them, were the spirits of people who led greedy lives or died violent deaths. Sometimes they would become 'rigid body ghosts' who could only move by hopping. Thump, thump, thump, Father would imitate the sound of hopping ghosts by smacking the floor boards of the house.

Som found himself straining to hear whether there were any thumping sounds in the field, but all he heard was the sounds of crickets and the rustling of leaves in the wind. He felt foolish. I am no longer a child. There is nothing to fear. He looked straight into the eye sockets of his teacher. What kind of life had this person led? Was it one of greed and disappointment or of good deeds and mindfulness? Had he died peacefully or in torment?

The fading sunlight glinted dark yellow from the skull. Shadows from the piles of remains stretched longer across the field. The evening breeze wafted over the half-burned remains and he gagged again on the smell. Foul-mouth ghosts?

Father's stories described at least a dozen different types of ghosts. The foul-mouth ghosts, he told the children, were sinners who became ghosts with vile-smelling breath—disgusting even to themselves.

Unable to sweeten or escape their own breath, they wandered the earth tormented by the stench of their own foul deeds. He wrinkled his nose to shut off the smell. What was that other kind of ghost? Needle-mouth ghosts? Greedy in life, these unfulfilled spirits had mouths no bigger than needles, so no matter how much food or drink was available, they could never satisfy their hunger or thirst. Maybe Father had become such a ghost. He had worked so hard, sacrificed so much, been so tough on his family, yet never seemed satisfied. Perhaps that was the lesson this skull had to teach him. Death will end the chance for fulfillment, so find fulfillment in a life without greed.

He closed his eyes and the image of the skull before him gained flesh and shifted into the face of Tum. Death had come to the boy before he had had more than a brief taste of life. That was his fault. He had failed to care for the boy. Tum's face looked back at him for a moment and smiled. Was he forgiven? The image of Tum faded and he opened his eyes. The field was lit by the moon as it rose over the tree line. He looked again at the skull before him. The pattern of white bone and dark shadow stayed with him. He slowed his breathing and focused on the skull.

Like this person, I'm destined to die, to think no more, to feel no more, to lie exposed to the sun and the rain. Where is death? Death is within me, the inevitable companion of life. And if it is within me, I cannot escape it.

He could feel the tension in his chest start to ease. If I run away, I will still die. If I stay here, I will still die. So, there is nothing to fear and no reason to run. He began to feel the familiar peace of meditation. He hardly noticed that a soft rain began to fall.

Hours later, he awoke with a start and a feeling of panic in his throat. Thump, thump, thump. Rigid body ghosts!

The sound was coming from the path beyond the field. A head appeared in the gray mist of dawn and floated along the path. It was followed by another head, then another. Thump, thump, thump. All the calmness of the previous evening's meditation vanished in an instant. It was a line of ghosts. Coming for him.

His heart pounded and he could feel cold sweat sliding down his neck. He must face fear. Breathe in, breathe out. Whatever is going to happen, let it happen. He found his heart beat slowing and his fear subsiding. Focus on what you really fear. Death.

As the morning light grew brighter, he was puzzled. The heads did not float on air, but appeared above the stone wall. He stood and walked to the gate. A column of young men carrying heavy bags and rifles trudged past in the mud of the path. The dawn light picked out the dull gleam of the steel gun barrels. Maybe this was something he really should fear, but fear had left him. He stood silently as several of the men *waied* to him. A heavily laden cart passed by. One wheel was uneven and made a thumping sound as it passed. He grinned at himself. What had seemed so frightening a few moments ago, now seemed funny.

The last man in the column stopped and *waied*. He was tall and dignified, with streaks of gray in his hair. Dressed in the Mon fashion, he carried an over-stuffed bag on one shoulder.

"Bless us, father, for we are in peril," said the man in halting Thai as he paused in front of him.

"You have my blessing, but I am not sure it means much," Som replied. "I hope you are in peril for good reason. May you find a way to escape unharmed."

"We save our nation," the man said as he *waied* once more and walked down the path after the thumping cart.

Som watched until the ragged column disappeared around a curve in the path, heading towards the border marked by three white *chedis*. They were moving on to their fates whatever they might be, just as he would move on to his own fate.

What did he want that fate to be? He thought of the Buddha's words... '*Paccattaṁ veditabbo viññuhi*—the wise will know for themselves.' No more fear—of ghosts, of death. His fate must not be shaped by fear or greed. Then by what?

51

TUN WAY
Guns

Tun Way looked back at the misty figure of the monk who had appeared by the side of the path. It would have been better if no one had seen his men with their guns. He cursed himself for letting his youthful companions take a few of the long Snider-Enfields out of the cart. They said they might meet with Burmese soldiers at the border and had to be ready. They just wanted to play soldier. If they did encounter a border patrol, they would have little chance. His boys had practiced loading and aiming the guns, but they had never fired them. They would be no match for British-trained troops. He had agreed to their pleading only to keep them happy and to lighten the load on the rickety cart.

Still, the eagerness of his young recruits was a good sign. For too long the Mons had been passive. They gave in to the Burmans and then to the British. Too many took jobs working for the Indian or Chinese businessmen in town. Too many were forgetting their Mon heritage, forgetting even the Mon language. Too few supported his Mon school, a school still in ashes.

The burning of the school should have ignited Mon patriotism. There should have been a surge of donations to rebuild the school. But no one stepped up. The leading Mons had nothing but excuses.

"It's a sign that this is not meant to be."

"You failed to protect the school."

"There is no more money. We already donated all we could and got nothing for it."

"Show us you can protect the school. Then we would feel better about donating for it."

All just excuses, but they had forced him to Siam to find weapons. He had to show the Bago Mons they could defend a Mon school. The only way to do that was to have weapons and men willing to use them. The Burmans would not dare to attack their school then. Weapons would give the Mons pride and self-confidence.

It had been a long journey—first far to the south of Siam. With the gold from the sale of two plots of land tucked in a sack under his shirt, he had slipped across the border at Ranong. After weeks of futile contacts with dealers in Nakhon Srithammarat and Songkhla, he was tempted to give up, but he could not go back to Bago empty-handed. Then, late one afternoon, a policeman had appeared at his inn in Songkhla, saying he was summoned into the *monthon* office.

The policeman escorted him to the long headquarters building with its swooping tile roof. Taken past two snarling stone lions, he climbed up the curving red tile staircase to the second floor. He walked along the veranda that extended the length of the building and gazed out on a busy courtyard with two low buildings that stretched like arms out from the main building.

A young clerk had led him down to one end of the veranda, past a crowd outside what appeared to be a large meeting room. The clerk pulled open the red-painted doors to a smaller room. Inside, a young man in a high-collared white uniform directed him to take a seat. The man was strikingly handsome, with close-cropped black hair, smooth tan skin and a neat mustache. He introduced himself as Deputy High Commissioner Pakdee.

Tun Way had started to introduce himself but Pakdee quickly interrupted.

"I know who you are and I know what you have been doing. I just want to know why. What precisely do you plan to do with these weapons you are seeking?"

The man was intimidating. He read detailed information about Tun Way's activities from a sheaf of papers on his table. He knew everyone Tun Way had contacted for weapons, even those at the mining camp. He had dates, amounts and types of weapons. If the Siamese wanted to arrest him, there was nothing he could do.

"Let's not waste time," the deputy commissioner said. "I know what guns you want and I know you've failed to buy anything. Such weapons may not exist right now, but if your reasons for seeking them are acceptable, there may be a way. Tell me the truth."

He drew a breath and then, in a mixture of simple Thai and English, he plunged into the story of the loss of Mon culture, the domination by the Burmans and the British, the effort to establish the Mon Language and Culture Society, the burning of the school and the fears of the

Mon community in Bago. The official listened and nodded in apparent sympathy. He helped with words when Tun Way struggled to find the right term. When he finished, he looked up at the deputy commissioner.

"So, these arms are just to defend a school and a cultural society inside Burma," Pakdee said, tapping a pen on the desk.

"Yes, sir."

"Are you really prepared to kill for this school?"

A question he had asked himself many times. It might not come to that, but if it did? He thought of how the Mon people had suffered—the loss of dignity, power, language and traditions. Could he kill for that?

"If we are attacked, we have to defend ourselves."

"You could trust the British police for that."

"No, the police defend the group in power and the system that keeps them there. The Mon people mean nothing to them."

"This little defense force gives you an alternative."

"Yes, sir."

"And if I requested information on the British in Bago, would you be willing to pass that information to me?"

Once he had the weapons back in Mon territory, he could not be compelled to do anything.

"Yes, I would do that."

"Then, I believe we have a common interest in understanding British actions on our western border. It so happens I have weapons. I have been ordered to dispose of safely. Perhaps you could help me."

The two agreed on a price that left him enough to purchase ammunition and find transport back to Burma. Three days later he was taken to see a load of rifles—some Enfield short rifles, musketoons. Indian Service rifles and a dozen Snider–Enfield infantry rifles. These were impressive, with their long barrels and lever-action breech blocks. They were used by the colonial troops in Burma, so the Mons would be armed at least as well as the Indian, Shan and Karen troopers in the British colonial force.

Mons in Songkhla told him there were cartridges for sale by Karen groups west of Bangkok, so he had hired a cart and oxen to transport everything back north. The heavy crates of rifles filled the cart. The last of his gold went to buy three dozen boxes of cartridges from the Karen. He sent word to his friends in Bago to send him the volunteers he had recruited to escort the weapons back to Burma.

Already away from home for three months, he wondered whether his daughter had missed him. Did she even care he was gone? He knew they were not close, but her nanny was doing a good job and she reminded him too much of Su Sah. He must do more with her once he got back home.

The ragged column trudged past the three white concrete conical *chedis* that gave this border point its name. It was still early so there was no one on the path. A simple bamboo pole blocked the path next to a thatched hut with a sign announcing the border of British Burma. There was no one on duty, so Tun Way raised the pole and waved his group through. The boys with guns had skirted through the forest south of the path. They were to meet up with them again two miles down the road.

Tun Way grimaced at the thumping noise of the cart. The cart was already past the border when a bleary-eyed official in a loose shirt and a tea-stained *longyi* pushed open the door and peered at the cart with a frown.

"Where are you going? I am the official here. Where are your papers?" he demanded.

Tun Way showed him the forged papers describing him as a merchant of agricultural equipment.

"Just bringing some plowshares and water pumps back to Palaw," he said.

"Let me see."

Tun Way threw back the tarpaulin to show a half-dozen iron plowshares lying atop boxes labeled "Holden & Brooke mechanical water pump assembly."

"How do I know what is in the boxes?" the official asked sleepily.

"We would be happy to show you, but you would have to help me move these heavy plowshares and then open the crates. I don't have a crowbar to open them, so it might be hard. I could buy a crowbar in the village or from you," Tun Way said and took a few of his remaining coins out to count them. The official reached for the coins, but Tun Way covered them with his hands.

"Why don't we save both of us the trouble?"

The official nodded and Tun Way let him pick up the coins. He motioned the cart driver forward and the two oxen leaned into their harnesses. The thump, thump sound of the cart wheels now seemed like the drumbeat of a march to a better future.

52

PREM
Buy Out

Prem watched as the long line of dignitaries climbed up the steps of the cremation platform. All the big shots were there. The governor had presided with a graceful speech praising his nephew. The *Monthon* high commissioner had led the offerings to the monks. One of Prince Damrong's younger cousins represented the royal family and the Interior Ministry. The police chief with his men in their white uniforms—they were all there, but, like him, they had failed to protect Ploi's father and none of them had found his killer.

He watched Ploi approach the police chief. Even though he was too far away to hear, he knew she was pressing him to take faster action against Jate. She had already met with the governor and the commissioner. She had pushed Sia Leng to see what he could do. Now that the cremation would soon be over, maybe she could find some peace. If only her brother Chit had not shown up.

After missing the bathing ceremony and seven nights of prayers Chit arrived the night before the cremation, smiling and greeting relatives like he was the family patriarch. He had insisted on playing a role in the cremation ceremony and Ploi's mother, Chaem, had let him, hoping perhaps that he would accord her honors at least equal to the other wives. Dressed in an elegant silk shirt and *phajonggraben*, Chit had bowed to the coffin of his father. Even as smoke started to rise from the tall temple chimney, he stood chatting with the governor.

In separate groups standing in the temple compound were Paen's three wives, each surrounded by a small group of friends and offspring. Ploi stood with her mother, staring at the smoke. He hurried to join her, pulling Awt, Phai and An with him. Even Awt had been well-behaved at the funeral, but the hours of chanted prayers had left the children anxious to get home and get out of their uncomfortable clothes. It had been a difficult day for them all.

Following the funeral, everyone went to the big house for food.

There seemed to be little mourning for Paen as the guests dug into the big trays of chicken in curry sauce, spicy seafood soup, chicken in coconut sauce, whole roast ducks, sour orange curry, and rice noodles with three kinds of sauce. Chaem busied herself overseeing the food and the guests. Paen's first wife had departed with her daughter in a flourish of fringed parasols soon after the ceremony saying she had to catch the steamer back to Bangkok. Most of the important officials were gone before sunset, but that didn't stop the party.

Awt raced around the house with his friends, shouting and laughing now that the enforced solemnity of the funeral ceremony was behind them. Phai had tried to keep up with them, but the boys had little use for a girl. Finally, she gave up and sat down beside little An. She gently waved a fish woven out of bamboo strips over his head. Maybe that would put him to sleep.

Paen's hard-drinking friends, family servants, former slaves, farmers who had rented land from Paen and a large assortment of relatives took eager advantage of the food and drink offered. Dozens of bottles of rice wine were emptied before the funeral feast began to subside.

He had tried his best to comfort Ploi, but his account of how he had dealt with his father's death didn't seem to help. Like Ploi he had not been on the best of terms with Father at the end. There was a lot he never got the chance to say to him. She brushed off his suggestion she talk with Som. She just stayed in her room staring out over the mountains to the west.

Chaem needed his help with the food and a few drunken guests. By the time the remaining food was parceled out, the mess cleaned up, and rickshaws called for those guests unable to walk, he was exhausted. He checked the children sleeping next to Ploi. He slipped onto the sleeping mat beside her and drifted into sleep.

There was a noise. It was the bedroom door closing. He looked around. Ploi was gone. He heard voices outside. He put on a clean *phatung* and a shirt and went into the central area of the house. He saw three angry faces in the yellow light of the lantern. It was Ploi, Chit and Chaem.

"Those are the only choices you get," Ploi was saying. "I take out all I have invested and you can have what is left—just the shell of the building, no equipment and no cash. Or you can go back to Phuket, stay away and I will send you a percentage of the profits."

"I am the son. I am the eldest. I should inherit. If you are nice to me, I will let you continue to work at the casino," Chit said.

"You signed away your rights to it to get a loan. Even Mother doesn't want you back. She knows the business wouldn't last a year with you in charge."

"Bullshit. I worked at the casino long before you started sticking your nose in. I can make it profitable," he said looking at his mother.

Ploi's mother looked tearful and uncertain.

"Son, I love you and will come to visit you, but Ploi is right," Chaem said. "You are no good for the business. Your own ventures don't seem so good. You have deserted three wives now. You take no responsibility for your children. You are too much like your father."

"Mother, how can you side with her against me. Father was right to leave you for someone more loving," Chit shouted. "You are all against me. It's not right. I am the son."

Drawn by Chit's angry shouts, Awn, Tim, Daeng and two other casino workers hurried up the steps to the house.

"Is there a problem?" Tim asked.

"Yes there is. I am the eldest son. I am the rightful owner of the casino and all my father's businesses. This bitch is trying to steal them from me. Explain to her you will only work for the rightful heir."

The men looked confused for a moment. Then Tim *waied* Chit.

"We are so sorry, Chit," Tim said softly. He looked at his fellow workers, then said more confidently, "We have worked for you and we have worked for Miss Ploi. We would prefer to work for her."

"When the storm hit, Ploi led us to safety," Daeng said. "When I lost the cash box, she defended me. I will stay with Ploi."

"This is crap. You are all against me," Chit shouted, his face red and contorted.

"Listen carefully," Ploi said coldly. "You have signed loan notes for thousands of baht and you have repaid none of the money you owe me and others. So, you can try to take the casino, if you want, but I will file suit to force you to repay the loans. The police and the courts will enforce your agreement to give up the casino and to pay back what you owe. Sia Leng will demand payment for his share because he will never agree to work with you."

"So what? I don't need that fat Chink."

"Maybe, but do you want him and the Teochew *Angyi* as enemies?"

Ploi asked. "You just heard the staff say they will not work for you."

"I will find new staff to replace these lazy, ungrateful bastards."

"And you really think you know how to run a casino when every business you start ends in failure?"

Prem watched as Chit spluttered. Ploi pushed closer.

"I will take all of the staff and all of the customers to start a competing casino. The *Angyi* will ban their mine workers and coolies from your casino. My police protection will cover only my new operation. Expect a police raid in your first month."

"You want your own brother to be arrested?" he said. "What has made you so cruel?"

"You."

"I could never survive with all of you against me."

"That is your problem. And this is your choice, take the casino and all its problems, work day and night like I have—and Prem and your mother and the staff—or go back to doing whatever you do in Phuket or Penang and get a bit of the profits monthly without lifting a finger."

"How much?"

"Five percent," she said.

"But that is our income, our children's inheritance," Prem spoke up for the first time. "He doesn't deserve a single baht."

"It will be worth it just to get rid of him," Ploi said.

Chit's face reflected the conflict between anger and greed.

"Half," he said.

"You must already be asleep and dreaming," Ploi said. "You get five percent for doing nothing, or become the owner of what will soon be a bankrupt business with Sia Leng chasing you for payment and a good chance of going to prison. You have seen my large friend, Sargeant Dam. He is in charge of casino raids. He would enjoy questioning you."

"What about one big payment? I don't trust you to keep making profits. Even if you do, you would find a way to cheat me."

"Why?" Ploi said, "Because that is what you would do? Fine, one large payment—the cash we have on hand right now. Nothing more."

Chit whined, begged, promised and threatened for more than an hour. Ploi was unmoved. Chaem supported her daughter and begged Chit to take his sister's deal. Finally, Prem had enough.

"There is nothing more you can say," he said, looming over the slighter Chit. "We will all go to sleep now. Tomorrow you will get on your horse and ride back through the mountains to Phuket."

"Not until I get my payment."

"If you sign the agreement, you will get it, but then I will never see you again," Ploi said coldly. "If you don't sign, you get nothing. And if you show up here again, you may not survive the attentions of the police or our friends in the *Angyi*."

Prem looked at his wife. She seemed to grow tall in the lantern light even as Chit shrank in front of her. He could never imagine cutting off his own brother like that. She wouldn't really get someone to kill her own brother. But Chit was a worthless brother and a threat to their family. Ploi was doing the right thing. She was strong. He looked at her face, hard and beautiful in the flickering light, and felt a little shiver.

53

SOM
Religious Magic

After three weeks of wandering in the deep forest north of the Three Pagoda Pass, Sawat and Som had come to a fork in the path.

"Now we turn east. We have been too long away from the Mekong, too long away from the heart of the country," Sawat said as he strode on the path to the left.

"A moment," Som heard himself say. For the past four years he had followed Sawat wherever he led, but now he was torn. He felt incomplete without his mentor. But it was strange to need someone's approval so much. Their recent disagreements over Sawat's mystical claims had hurt.

"We are not too far from Bangkok and Wat Boworn," Som said. There are some books waiting for me and I have some questions for the monks at Wat Po."

"Useless. Why bother with useless book knowledge when you can peer into the reality of the world through meditation. That will give you power, not concoctions of herbs."

"People are sick. They need medicine," he tried to explain. "This is something I can do to help, but I need to learn more."

"You have much to learn, but not about leaves and herbs. You can learn with me. You said you once flew over the ocean in a storm."

"I felt like I rose into the air and looked down at myself to see how small and insignificant I was. It was a feeling at a moment when I thought I would die. It wasn't real."

"The feeling was reality, but you haven't been able to repeat it. I can. I can fly whenever I want and I can teach you to fly. I have been leading you to this point since we started *thudong*," Sawat said.

"I have been with you for four years and I have never seen you fly."

Sawat smiled. "You simply didn't have the eyes to see. You have not reached that stage, but I can help you achieve this. Just like the Buddha flew to Lanka to drive away demons, I can fly anywhere I like."

"Those are tales from the Lankan chronicles, not part of our scriptures. Anyway, you are not the Buddha."

"How can you be sure?"

He struggled to find words. Did Sawat really believe he had achieved enlightenment? In his talks in the temples it had seemed like a way to attract attention, to show the value of *thudong*, to entertain the younger monks. But now, it was just him.

"Meditation has given me abilities beyond anything normal people know," Sawat continued. "I can cure disease with my hands. You can have these powers one day. Just follow me."

He stared at his teacher, who resumed walking, taking the path to the north. This was the error the Buddha warned against, the error of self-glorification. What were the words in the Kevatta Sutta? The Buddha said the miracle of psychic powers is of little importance. The real miracle is the miracle of instruction, helping people learn how to deal with their own suffering. He should remind Sawat of the Buddha's rule against showing off supernatural powers. But Sawat was already far down the path.

He started to follow, then stopped. He watched as Sawat grew small in the distance. He turned and took the other path.

54

DAM
Nakleng

Sergeant Dam and two of his men stopped at the front door to Jate's shophouse. An iron gate stretched across the front of the shop. Fishing nets, buoys, spars, fish traps and sail cloth were on display. Two of Jate's men sat on the floor leaning against the counter. One was Uncle Nit. The other he didn't recognize. Must be new. The new man pulled the gate back a few inches.

"I am here to speak with your boss," Dam said. "Uncle Nit, tell Boss Jate that Senior Police Sergeant Sakda is here to talk to him."

He had always gotten along with Nit. The older man seemed to feel sorry for the mocking abuse Jate and his men had dumped on him. It was mockery he had only half understood at first. The memory of the names they called him – mountain buffalo or black buffalo – still made his face flush. But Nit had been different. He never mocked his ragged clothes or his slowness to understand what the boss wanted. He didn't join in the laughter when Jate taunted him.

"Good morning Dam," Nit said. "It's good to see you after so long. What is this about?"

"Routine police business."

"The boss is not too happy with you, so it might be better not to bother him. You should stay away. He was never good for you."

"Captain's orders. I am working on an investigation. It's important."

Nit frowned, but turned and trudged up the stairs. Dam gestured to the new man to open the gate, but he shook his head.

"Let us in, that is a police order," Dam said.

The man looked uncertain for a moment, then closed the gate, locking it with a click.

"The boss says only trusted customers come in," he said.

Dam felt his temper rising. This stupid motherfucker disrespected him in front of his men. There would be payback someday. Now he had to stay in control. He forced himself to stop pacing. This was typical of

Boss Jate. The bastard thought of himself as the top *nakleng* in Nakhon. How many times had he waited for Jate? How many times had his payment been delayed? He hadn't understood who it at the time, but now he saw it was a tactic to show who was the boss, to show Dam he didn't matter. He could be thanked or given a kick. It was all up to Jate.

No more. He was a *nakleng* too. Even better, he was a police *nakleng*. He was on the side of the law. His *takruts* and his *yantra* tattoos protected him. He had proved himself in battle with bandits and pirates. He had killed. His men respected him. He was a sergeant, in charge of his own unit. He was following the captain's orders to investigate a murder. He was fulfilling a promise to Ploi. He would find the evidence against Jate and put him at the mercy of the courts, of the police, of Dam himself.

That thought calmed him. He would look into Jate's eyes and say 'you are under arrest'. How satisfying it would be to report the arrest to Ploi, to testify against him in court and to see Jate kneel before the blade of the executioner.

Once he might have feared Jate, but not anymore. Once he had respected the stocky Chinese for his wealth and power. Once he had depended on him for money to buy food for his mother. Once he had done bad things for the man, hurt defenseless people. No more taking on Jate's bad karma.

He touched the string of tin *takruts* around his neck. Now, it was he who was in the position of power. It was he, the Black Tiger, who was known throughout Nakhon for bold actions against bandits—seven killed by his own hands and nearly a hundred arrested. It was Jate who would be next for Dam to throw into Pakpanang jail. Jate was certainly guilty. All he needed was the evidence.

The chief had ordered a thorough investigation. Not only the governor, but the high commissioner had made investigation of Paen's killing a high priority. He was one of many policemen working on it. Captain Serm said the commissioner saw the murder as a setback to his efforts to show that Nakhon was a civilized place. The governor's interest was more personal. Paen was a relative. For once, the governor and the commissioner were in agreement: Paen's murderer must be brought to justice. Sergeant Dam would be the one to do it.

The problem was evidence. The commissioner demanded evidence acceptable in court. After nearly five months, the investigation had produced little. The murderers had escaped. There were no witnesses. Police had received a tip from a member of a rival gang that three of Jate's men had suddenly gotten a lot of money, buying foreign liquor and two girls each at the brothel on the Sichon road. A fisherman at Jate's store in Nakhon when his son's body was brought in told police Jate had threatened to kill Paen. But after both informants were found with their throats slit, the usual sources in the Nakhon underworld went quiet. The head of the Chinese secret society had not only denied any knowledge, but had put out the word that anyone talking to the police would suffer. Worse, there were witnesses who claimed Jate had been sleeping at a temple in Nakhon at the time of the murder. He could crack those witnesses if given a chance, but the police chief and the commissioner would still need more to authorize an arrest.

He saw again Ploi's tear-stained face after the murder. Over the weeks, her tears had dried into a stiff mask. She offered a large reward for finding the killers and gave him a sack of gold coins to locate witnesses, to uncover evidence, to get Jate. Every time he saw her, she asked about the case. Each time they talked, she would conclude with the same sentence: "I don't care what you do, just get him."

He knew he had to do something. He had promised her justice, but the official investigation was stalling. This might be his last chance.

Finally, Nit reappeared. "The boss says he will see you, but only you."

He looked over his shoulder at his men behind him. "You can wait here. I am just going to ask some questions."

Nit gestured to the revolver strapped to his waist. "The gun," he said. "Or you don't get in. Sorry, Boss's orders."

He suppressed another flash of anger. Then he smiled. Jate must fear him. He pulled the revolver from its holster.

"No problem."

He felt his heart start to race as he followed Nit up the stairs. It felt like one of his operations against a gang of thieves. No, it was more difficult. Somehow, he had to get Jate to give him some bit of evidence that would help the investigation. Maybe he would boast about getting his revenge as he had often done in the past.

When they reached the top of the stairs, Nit knocked on the door. At a muffled word from within, he opened it and led him into the room. Jate leaned back against a large triangular cushion. The grip of a pistol protruded from under the cushion. A half-full bottle of Chinese liquor and a heavy glass tumbler sat on a table next to him. Jate looked like he had aged since Dam had last seen him. His scalp shone through his thinning hair in the light that raked through the window on the river side of the room. There were dark crescents below his cold eyes. His belly now sagged over the top of his *phakaoma*.

Why had he feared this man? Why had he done his dirty work?

Jate looked up at him with a grin that did not extend to his eyes.

"What can I do for you, Mr. honorable policeman, sir?" he said. "Lieutenant Dam, is it? Oh no, you didn't get that promotion, did you? Too bad."

He felt his face flush.

"I have been promoted again to senior sergeant and I am investigating the murder of Kamnan Paen. I have questions for you."

"Ah yes, I heard about that. So sad, but a man like that, a man who thinks he is so important, a man who overcharges for land rent, a man with an illegal casino, a man who doesn't pay his debts, such a man must have many enemies."

"Murder is murder and the murderer will be found and punished."

"Undoubtedly. All of us who cherish law and order look forward to that day. I am, of course, happy to help in any way I can. As you know, I have spoken with police detectives three times already, but to be questioned by the renowned Sergeant Dam is a special honor."

"In private," Dam said.

Jate looked at the burly man waiting at the door. "Nit, you can leave me and this very important policeman to discuss this case. I have nothing to fear from him."

Dam swallowed his anger once again as Nit closed the door behind him and clumped down the stairs.

"Now we are alone and you can tell me the truth," Dam said. "We have evidence three of your men have become suddenly wealthy. They were paid a bonus for killing Paen, weren't they?"

"Your questions are as clumsy as you are, fitting for a stupid buffalo," Jate said. "As you know, I am a generous man and I may have rewarded them for loyal service," he said. "But that has nothing to do with murder."

"We know that Paen owed you money and was often late in making his payments."

"Yes, that is true, but if I killed all those who were late in paying, my money-lending business would soon disappear. Are you so stupid to think I would kill off my own customers? A little persuasion, yes, but killing, no."

"Then there is the matter of your son. He was found dead at the scene of a robbery at the Jaikla Restaurant."

"The Jaikla Casino, you mean," Jate said as he rose to his feet, his face darkening. "A vicious murder. Why aren't you investigating that murder and their illegal casino operation instead of bothering a bereaved father like me? It seems you police care more about an old man who fails to pay his debts than my young son—a boy who hardly had a chance to live. Why do you ignore him and disrespect me? Dam, I was like a father to you."

"I have a witness who heard you threaten to cut out Paen's heart."

"Do you? I heard that this so-called witness suffered an unfortunate accident. So, it seems he may not make it to court," Jate said as he turned and looked out the window at the busy river below.

"Where were you on the night of June 30?"

"Let me think," Jate said slowly. "Where was I? Oh, yes, I took part in a donation ceremony and prayers at Wat Suan Khan,"

Jate turned to grin into Dam's face.

Why was he smiling? He must be lying, mocking me.

"What time did you leave the temple?"

"I have answered all these questions before. Apparently, the police chief didn't bother to tell you. If I remember correctly, I did not leave until the next morning and then went straight to my store in the city. Never came anywhere near Pakpanang. Maen, Nit and Sem can confirm this," he said.

"They are all your flunkies. The police and the courts will give little weight to their made-up stories."

"Dam, Dam, Dam, you do not seem to be neutral in your questions. Could it be you have been twisted by the favors of Paen's pretty little daughter?" he laughed. "Too bad she is married to someone else. Anyway, there were others who will testify I was still at Wat Suan Khan when the so sad murder took place."

"What others? More of your men lying to police will not help you."

"Oh, there were definitely others who will be believed, even by you. Now, who were they?" Jate said, tapping his head.

"I remember now," he said. "Phra Ajahn Klai, that nice young abbot at the temple. He will testify for me. You probably don't know that this young monk is so revered for telling the truth, he is known as the 'Golden Mouth Monk'. So, talk to Phra Klai, and you will learn that I had nothing to do with this terrible, terrible crime."

Could it be true? With a respected monk to vouch for him, the police would never arrest Jate. He must not have taken part in the murder himself. As a real *nakleng*, Jate should have killed Paen with his own hands. Maybe the coward had put his own safety above personal revenge. Everyone would believe the monk. There was none of the evidence the legal stickler of a commissioner would insist on having. Fucking Jate would get away with this murder as he had so many others. Ploi would be furious. His promise to get justice for her father would come to nothing. She would see him as a failure.

Jate took a step forward and thrust his head up close to Dam's chin.

"So, you have had your little amusement and now it is time to crawl back to the police station with nothing," he said, switching to the harsh, dominating tone that brought back memories of past humiliation.

Jate poked him in the chest and pushed him towards the door.

"You know the saying, 'free men are above associating with slaves'— and despite your fancy uniform with its silver buttons, that's all you are—an ignorant slave boy. So, don't come back here again. You won't be allowed in. Just go back to licking the ass of your captain," he said, pushing his finger into the soft flesh of Dam's neck.

"Just go back to sniffing hopelessly at the daughter's cunt. Just go back to being the stupid mountain buffalo you've always been."

Dam grabbed the finger poking his throat and bent it backwards until it cracked. Jate screamed in pain and grabbed the bottle of liquor. He saw it swinging towards his head, but he got a forearm up. The bottle shattered, sending a surge of pain up his arm. A shard of glass stuck into his cheek. Anger flooded through him. He looked at Jate's face and saw fear as well as pain in his eyes.

Holding the broken bottleneck in front of him, Jate backed away. His tone changed.

"Dam, control yourself, son. Think of all I have done for you. I've been a father to you."

Dam pulled the piece of glass from his cheek and wiped the blood from his face. He lashed out with a front kick that sent Jate spinning back onto the sleeping platform. As he moved forward, Jate reached under the cushion and pulled out the pistol. The barrel looked huge.

"You've attacked me in my own house. I have the injuries to prove it. Since you are so big, I had no choice but to protect myself," Jate said with a high-pitched giggle. "Naturally I was devastated to have killed my old friend, my adopted son, but I had no choice."

Dam watched in horror as Jate aimed the heavy old pistol at his chest where the tattoo of Five Devas peeked through his open collar. He couldn't move. He saw the man's finger tighten on the trigger. There was a click, and another and two more. He had a chance. He lunged forward, knocked the gun aside with his left hand and smashed a fist into Jate's left ear. He followed with two more blows to the face.

"I hated my father," he said, leaning down to Jate's battered face. "And I hate you."

He held Jate's head down with both hands and drove his knee up into it. He could feel the crunch of broken teeth. Another kick snapped Jate's head back. His body went limp and dropped onto the wooden platform. He straddled Jate's body and pounded his face. Jate's eyes rolled up into his head and blood streamed from his nose.

Dam paused, breathing heavily. Jate's head lolled back and lay still.

What had he done? He had no evidence against Jate for the murder. He would be sacked from the police for beating a prominent citizen. Nit might have a gun. What would he do when he saw Jate's battered face? He couldn't stop now. He couldn't let Jate go unpunished. He couldn't disappoint Ploi.

He ripped open the door to the balcony outside the room, pulling the limp body of his former boss through it. He looked down at the dock area below and saw what he was looking for. A desperate energy surged through him. He picked up Jate's body and hurled it down. The body landed with a crunch on one of the big anchors stored next to the house. One anchor blade pierced Jate's back. Dam stared at the blood flowing bright red onto the checked pattern of the *phakaoma*. The body twitched and then lay still.

There was a pounding on the door to the room behind Dam.

"Is everything alright?" It was Nit.

"Uncle Nit. Come quick. There has been a terrible accident."

55

PREM
Best Served Cold

Prem heaved a sack of catfish onto the worn wooden tabletop in the restaurant kitchen. The fish, fresh from the market, were still squirming.

"Catfish red curry is on the menu tonight," he announced to the cook who was washing a large pot of rice. Chaem looked up from the big wooden chopping block she was using to slice leaves from the kaffir lime tree in their yard.

"Are they fresh?" she asked.

"They are still lively enough to wriggle out of the frying pan if you don't chop them up first," he said with a grin.

Chaem laughed and went back to her task. Paen's death had been a shock for her, but it had also helped heal the long-festering wound of his leaving her for a younger woman. Just a few months ago, she had been sour most of the time. Only her grandchildren and her work in the restaurant had distracted her from her anger at Paen. She had not understood why the rest of the family was not more upset at him. Her father had even suggested she should accept the new woman into her house. That would have been a reasonable solution to most wives of important men, but not for Chaem.

Every time he and Ploi went to visit her father Chaem would tromp around the house in frustration. Then she would interrogate her daughter about her father. Chaem had continued to consult with a variety of soothsayers and monks to ask them whether Paen would grow bored with his new wife and return to her. She also spent money in secretive dealings with strange women selling talismans and spells. After Paen's funeral, however, she had seemed calmer, yet livelier. She came to work at the restaurant with real interest and had added several new dishes to the menu.

He looked around the cluttered kitchen. What should they prepare today? Each day's menu had to reflect the three different types of customers they attracted—southern Thais, Chinese and central Thais.

He used recipes from his mother to fill out the Chinese menu. Chaem had taken over the southern Thai part of the menu with its fish stomach curry, stir-fried *sataw* with shrimp, sour orange curry with bamboo shoots, deep-fried fish with tumeric, and soft-shelled crab in a coconut cream curry sauce heavy with cumin and saffron.

Today she was making another southern specialty—fragrant rice salad with sweet-sour pomelo, grated coconut, dry shredded shrimp, sliced kaffir lime leaves, lemongrass and turmeric leaves served with powdered chili and sweetened fish sauce. This was a dish served cold, but with spices to heat up the tongue. He looked at the piles of ingredients filling an array of bowls in front of Chaem.

"Don't make too much. I hear the 'walking stomach' sickness has broken out in the port again. Sick people don't go out to eat and even those who are well may be afraid to eat at a restaurant."

"Our customers know we wash all our vegetables in vinegar and everything is well cooked," Chaem said.

"But the rice salad is served cold. That could be a problem, so don't make too much."

Chaem shrugged and stopped her chopping. She wore a bright new *phasin* and moved with energy and authority, ordering the helpers to gut the fish and peel the bamboo shoots piled on the table. She looked younger than before and still attractive. Paen had been a fool to leave her.

Was this how Ploi would look in 20 years? It wouldn't be so bad growing old together. He would have to guard against developing a belly like his father. Already he was a bit heavy. Being around food all day and tasting the various dishes had added an inch of fat to his waist. Maybe it's good. Makes me look more substantial—not a lean and hungry sailor anymore. No more work on the ship to keep his stomach hard. I can live with that—no more backaches from all the pumping we had to do to keep *The Wind Uncle* afloat. He looked at his hands—no longer hard and cracked from hauling on the salt-crusted ship's lines. That was good too. Life was easy now.

Still there were times he missed life on the sea. There was an excitement to running before a strong monsoon wind that the restaurant couldn't match. The demands of the restaurant and the children meant he had little time to see old shipmates. They came to the house from time to time to invite him to go out fishing or drinking, but often Ploi had some urgent task around the house that stopped him from joining them. Whenever he did go out, Ploi would be noticeably cold when he got home, turning her back on the sleeping mat, not even accepting the offer of a foot massage. In any case, he didn't have the same energy as he once had. In the first year of marriage, he and Ploi had enjoyed each other every night and sometimes during the day. She seemed to take as much delight in the act as he did. She was always exciting. Teasing him when she undressed. Touching him in new ways, slowing, then speeding up her movements so she could achieve release when he did. Those were nice memories.

"What are you smiling at?" Chaem asked. "If you have a joke, share it with us."

"Just feeling good," he said and then frowned.

Things had changed. Now, Ploi would hold him off when he stroked her breasts. She said she didn't want any more children yet. But children brought so much happiness and making them was so much fun.

On was already six years old and Prem was trying to get him to take his schooling more seriously. If only he were like Phai and An who did their lessons dutifully. Maybe he should send On to the Pakpanang Boys School.

Ploi had lost most of the weight she had gained when she was pregnant with An, but still bemoaned the weight that remained and the stretch marks that showed faintly on her honey-colored skin. What was she worried about? The additional weight had made her softer and more beautiful than ever. He loved the soft feel of her arms and the curve of her stomach. Now she insisted on satisfying him with her mouth or her hands, so he felt vaguely unfulfilled. Part of the joy of making love was to see the look on Ploi's face as she came to orgasm.

Why was she so reluctant to have another child? A big family was what everyone wanted, wasn't it? Both Chaem and his own mother had delighted in each new grandchild and urged them to have more. The last two children had come rather easily, but he knew Ploi begrudged the time away from the casino required by each pregnancy. She hated becoming large and clumsy. Customers looked at her differently when her stomach pushed out the waist of her *phasin*, and she didn't like it.

Her father's death and her triumph over Chit should have meant Ploi no longer had anything to prove. Still she spent more time than ever at the casino, meeting with Sia Leng, or working to expand their underground lottery business. When she came to him to discuss the business, it was to complain about the quality of the food, the speed of the restaurant service or the cost of ingredients. Today, even though it was still early, she had retreated to her office upstairs to consult with the staff about the introduction of a new game. He hated being left out, but this might not be the time to barge into her office uninvited. He would only hear more complaints about the restaurant service.

Now she was spending more time with the police, demanding they do more to find the killer. Her last visit to the police station had degenerated into an argument with the captain. Prem told her to let them do their jobs, but that triggered an outburst against him.

She was meeting more often with Sergeant Dam. He seemed to show up at the casino every day or two. She said the meetings were to report on the investigation into her father's murder. Prem offered to join her, but Ploi refused.

"What do you know about criminal investigations?" she asked. "Sergeant Dam is working on this investigation himself. He has promised they will find the evidence to get Jate."

What if Jate was not the murderer? Paen had other enemies, but he knew mentioning this would only make her angry. She had no doubt Jate had been behind the murder and she was determined to get revenge. He knew she had talked to a man known as a killer for hire. Somehow, he had to get her to give up this obsession with revenge.

"If a dog bites you, don't bite it back," he quoted an old saying to her. That had triggered an outburst of rage for which she had later apologized, but that was the last time he mentioned her father's murder. Maybe it was good that big lizard of a policeman was working on the case. At least it was legal and wouldn't put Ploi at risk. If Jate's family and friends thought she was behind something happening to Jate, they would seek revenge and the cycle of violence would never end. Their own children would be at risk. He just did not like Ploi and Dam spending so much time alone together. He had seen the look in Dam's eyes every time he came to see Ploi. The oaf must think he is in love with her.

That was nothing new. Many of the casino customers were at least half in love with his wife. Their eyes followed her around the casino. They rushed to chat with her. They eagerly complimented her when she showed up in a new outfit. They applauded her songs. And she flushed with pleasure at the attention.

Until recently, he had been confident she would never respond with anything more than thanks. She had always made it clear, with a look, a smile or a touch that he was not just her husband, but her love. Since her father's murder, however, she seemed to blame him for not doing more to find the murderer. He felt like he disappointed her.

What more could he do? He had approved the reward they offered for information. He had talked to the police chief and his friends in the two Chinese secret societies. But she placed her hopes on that ugly policemen. Dam was different somehow from the casino customers. There was something obsessive about his feelings. He was always at the casino. Maybe Dam provided the family business with protection, but he didn't like it.

He was bringing a heavy sack of rice into the kitchen when he heard the front door open and a heavy tread on the stairs to the second floor. It must be that damn policeman again. The fucker felt free to go straight upstairs without even announcing himself. He dropped the sack and hurried out to the main room. He heard the clank of the iron door at the top of the stairs and the slap of feet on the wooden floor above. There was a long moment of silence and then a shriek.

He rushed up the stairs, threw open the door at the top and hurried into Ploi's office. He was stunned to see Ploi with her arms around Dam. Ploi turned to him with a triumphant smile.

"The bastard is dead, crushed."

"Who is dead? What is going on?" he asked.

Ploi pushed Dam away and ran across the room to hug him.

"Jate—he has paid for his murder. Father can rest in peace."

"What have you done? What has he done?" he asked.

Dam drew himself up, straightened his jacket and smiled in triumph.

"There was an accident during an official interrogation and a person of interest to our investigation died of his injuries," he said.

"We pursued him until he cracked," Ploi cried. "The idiot attacked Sergeant Dam last night. There was a struggle, and the devil fell to his death. It was the bad karma he earned by killing Father."

"I have already reported this as an accidental death," Dam said. "The suspect became agitated at my official interrogation. He ran out onto the balcony, slipped and fell to the ground."

"He died in agony, with an anchor sticking through his stomach," Ploi said. Prem stared at Ploi. A strange smile twisted her face. "We got him!" she shouted.

56

DAM
Hearing

Dam pulled at the high collar of his dress uniform. The heat of the day was still seeping out of the wooden walls of the district office. Sweat kept running into his eyes. Normally Captain Serm made him feel anxious, but today it was good to have him here. It must mean something. Most of the policemen from the station sat in rows behind him. He avoided looking at the group seated to his left. That was where Jate's family sat in a buzz of angry whispers. He recognized Jate's teenaged son, his first wife and his third wife. The second wife, he knew, had disappeared years before—not long after that quick rape trial.

The district officer sat at a table at the front of the room, flanked by two secretaries. Why did he even have to go through this? He had killed criminals before and all he had to do was get his fellow policemen to agree on a story and report to the chief. That was it. He always got a cheer from the bad guy's victims. They called him a hero.

Now, the *monthon* office had ordered an inquiry. They were trying to make him feel guilty. Fuck that. It was because Jate was wealthy and his family wanted revenge. The captain had told him the *monthon* office was satisfied with the outcome until Dam's role was reported. Then the deputy commissioner ordered the police chief and the district officer to investigate.

He reached under his shirt to feel the delicate tin tubes containing his *takruts*. Their power had stopped Jate's gun from firing. The magic signs of the *yantras* had not only protected him from the gun, but guided Jate's body onto the anchor. It was amazing.

When told of the hearing, he returned to the temple for an additional *yantra*. Ajahn Klai designed it to protect him from accusations.

"You need the *yantra* of four spires," the abbot had told him. "This symbol will influence the feelings of others and protect the bearer."

When he returned to the police station, the captain called him in.

"I don't want to know what happened," he said. "I want to know how you will explain it. This could reflect badly on all of us."

He told his story to the captain, who kept interrupting to correct his grammar or to suggest a change. Then they spent hours rehearsing. Now he would have to perform.

The district officer announced the start of the inquiry into the death of Jate Sae-Liu. Reading from the official report, he said Jate's death was due to a fall onto an iron bar that led to massive internal injuries and bleeding. He called the first witnesses.

The two policemen who had accompanied Dam told the hearing that they had found the body below the steps to the house. No, Dam was not near the body, they said.

He looked to his left to see how Nit was reacting to the testimony. He seemed impassive. What was he thinking? Would their deal hold? If not, he was screwed.

Captain Serm stood to report that Sargeant Sakda had been assigned to the team investigating the murder of Kamnan Paen. Jate had been on the list of those to be questioned.

"Sergeant Sakda's presence at Mr. Jate's shop, therefore, was entirely consistent with his duties in this regard," he said.

"Yes, completely. He was there at my orders," the captain said.

The district officer nodded and Serm returned to his seat.

"Sergeant Sakda, you were the only witness to the fall that led to the fatal injuries. Is that correct?"

"Yes, sir."

"Please tell us what happened."

"Thank you, sir. As my colleagues have explained, we visited Mr. Jate's shop as part of a murder investigation on orders of our honored captain. Mr. Jate said he wanted to speak to me without others present. He told Mr. Nit to leave the room. Mr. Jate appeared to have been drinking before my arrival and he continued to drink from a bottle of whisky while I was present. The remnants of the bottle, sir, are in evidence. I asked him routine questions about his whereabouts on the night of the murder and his relationship with Kamnan Paen. During the process of this questioning, Mr. Jate became agitated. He struck me with the whisky bottle, causing injury to my right forearm. Realizing he had committed a felony by striking an officer of the law, Mr. Jate threw open the door and ran to the outside stairway. He must have been drunk. He appeared to trip on the door sill. His face smashed into the railing and his body flipped over the railing to the ground below. I called out to Mr. Nit to tell him there had been an accident. Mr. Nit ran down the stairs to the body below. He was soon joined by my two police colleagues. I believe they did everything they could to help him, but were unsuccessful."

"Were you angry that Mr. Jate had struck you?"

"No, sir. I was surprised and puzzled. As Captain Serm has testified, I have known Mr. Jate for many years. He employed me when I was still a boy. He was kind to me and helped me join the police. I always thought of him as a father figure since my own father left us long ago."

"Did you strike the deceased?

"No, sir."

"Did you push or throw him over the railing?

"No, sir."

"Why would the deceased attack you?"

"I have asked this of myself many times. Perhaps my questions as an impartial police officer upset him. He may have expected me, as an old friend, to be softer in my questioning, but I had to do my duty. Maybe he felt unhappy about something. I understand his eldest son died recently, but I have to say I don't think he would have gotten so upset if he had not been drinking."

"Did the deceased's responses to your questions indicate his guilt in the matter of the Paen murder?

"No, sir. As a representative of the law, I considered Mr. Jate innocent until proven guilty. I found no evidence against him. In fact, he gave evidence of his presence at a temple in Nakhon far from the murder scene."

"So, if you did not consider him guilty, there would be no reason for you to take any action against him, no reason for you to attempt to arrest him?" Captain Serm spoke up.

"That is correct sir."

"I therefore recommend that this hearing come to the conclusion that the police were not responsible for this unfortunate, accidental death," the captain said.

There was a burst of angry murmuring from Dam's left. The district officer raised his hand.

"One moment," he said. "The *monthon* office has asked us to be most thorough in this matter. I would like to hear from one other witness at the scene. Mr. Sontaya… Mr. Sontaya."

"Yes, sir," Nit spoke up.

"You are known as Nit, correct. And you have worked as an employee of Mr. Jate for 12 years."

"Yes, sir."

"Did you see Sergeant Sakda injure Mr. Jate in any way?

"You mean Sergeant Dam, right? Then no, sir," he said, sparking furious hisses from the family.

"Did Sergeant Sakda, that is, Sergeant Dam, appear angry when you saw him on the second story landing?"

"No, sir."

"Do you believe the sergeant pushed or threw the deceased from the stairway?"

"I did not see that, sir."

"You have known Sergeant Dam for several years. He has quite a reputation as a tough policeman. Do you believe he was capable of harming Mr. Jate?"

"District Officer, sir. I have always known Dam as a quiet and obedient young man. He admired Boss Jate. I don't believe he was capable of harming him."

There was another angry outburst from Jate's family and he saw the son run out of the room, his heavy footsteps making the wooden floor tremble.

Dam exhaled. Nit had resisted the family pressure. Their deal held. He had pledged his support for Nit to take over the gang instead of Jate's son. Nit had already won support from the older men in the gang. The promise of backing from the police had strengthened his hold on the gang members reluctant to follow the orders of a boy.

He kept his eyes looking straight ahead as Nit made his way back to his seat. He watched as Captain Serm and the district officer conferred quietly. Behind him, the other policemen were smiling. He knew he wasn't the most popular officer in the station, but at least the other policemen admired him for his toughness. None of them wanted to see a fellow policeman disciplined for doing his job.

"It is the finding of this inquiry that the death of Mr. Jate was due to an accidental fall. The police department and the officers involved acted in accordance with proper procedure," the district officer said. "No disciplinary action or criminal charges are warranted. The details of this finding shall be reported to the high commissioner."

There was a cry from Jate's wife and shouts from the family, but the district officer ignored the uproar.

"We extend our condolences to the bereaved and hereby conclude this hearing."

There was a cheer from the police who surged around Dam to clap him on the back. He touched the string of thin tin tubes around his neck. They had saved him once again.

57

SOM
Homecoming

The small boat moved smoothly with the flow of the river pulling it towards the sea. Som felt rising excitement. He tried to calm those feelings as the trees of the forest thinned, and more buildings appeared along the banks of the river. The sun was behind him now, glinting off the sweaty shoulders of his two paddlers. They were hastening their pace, trying to reach Pakpanang before dark.

He stared at a large building with a tall smoke stack on the northern bank of the river. That had not been there the last time he had come this way. But that was almost four years ago. There were more buildings now—rice mills, a saw mill, three shipyards, large houses with tile roofs, not thatch, and an imposing white government building. A variety of boats crisscrossed the river, from small dugouts to Chinese junks as big as *The Wind Uncle*. His boat glided past two large steel steamships anchored in the middle of the river.

He was back home. He would see his brother. How were his mother and his sisters? He had written to them whenever he could. The last letter from Prem said he already had two children. His sisters had written they were busy with the warehouse business. The older one, Toh, had married a Chinese medicine shopkeeper and had a baby son, but that was two years ago. Wan was still unmarried, devoting herself to Mother and the business. They had sold the old house and moved into rooms above the warehouse to save money. Prem wrote that he and Ploi had opened a restaurant. He could hardly imagine his big, outdoor-loving brother serving food. But he had sounded proud of the business—said he even had the honor of serving the king. Prem described his son and daughter with obvious love.

He had missed so much.

Prem had written that the restaurant was a bit downstream from the police station. He spotted the peaked roof of the station.

"Move closer to the shore," he told the paddlers. He looked at a large building, but that was a warehouse. Next to it was a cluster of thatched-roofed houses. Then he saw what must be the restaurant. The two-story building was lighted with a row of lanterns as the sunset sent long shadows across the floating dock below it.

"There, land at that dock," he said. The boat swung around with the current as one of the paddlers leaped onto the dock and held the bow of the little boat. Som scrambled onto the dock, stood and adjusted his robes. What if his visit came at a bad time? He took three deep breaths and then climbed the wooden steps up the bank.

At the door he hesitated again. Perhaps he should find a place in one of the monasteries along the river for the night and return in the morning. A large man in a white shirt and *phajonggraben* with a cloth over his shoulder saw him through the open door and looked at him in puzzlement.

"Honored sir. How may I be of assistance?"

Som felt a smile growing on his face and tears starting to fill his eyes.

"Prem?"

"Chao? Is that you? I mean Somneuk, uh, uh Phra Somdhammo. Som!"

He nodded and suddenly found himself crushed against the big chest of his younger brother.

"Yes, it is me."

Prem jumped back and made a deep *wai*.

"I can't believe it. It has been so long."

"Yes, too long. I'm sorry, but I have thought of you, mother and the girls so often.

"So much has changed. You have to meet my wife and children," Prem said.

"Yes, a boy and a girl—I got your letters."

"Now two boys and a girl," Prem said with a smile. "You have to see them. But first—Ploi! Ploi!" he shouted. "Come see who is here. Ploi, come down. See who is here."

Prem's grin widened even more. There were soft steps on the stairway from the second floor. A beautiful woman in a lacy white top opened the door and came out with a look of annoyance on her face. She changed to a more respectful expression and *waied* to the monk.

"Honored sir," she said, her hands clasped in front of her face.

"Ploi—this is my brother, Phra Somdhammo. I read you his letters. He is back home. He has traveled all over – even to the Khmer land and the Mekong River – and now he is back home."

"There is much to talk about," Som said, "but now I have to find a place for the night. Then I want to see Mother and Toh and Wan."

"Wat Nantharam is only a short walk away. You can stay there. I know the abbot. Then tomorrow we will take you across the river to the warehouse. Toh's shop is nearby. But this is a difficult time. There is sickness in town. People are staying home. Look at the restaurant—almost empty. Some say it was the crew of a Dutch ship, others say it came from that big steamship from Calcutta. People are sick and some are dying. Toh and her husband are working long hours. There is a big demand for medicines, but nothing seems to help much. Wan has been ill and mother is caring for her."

"What do the doctors say?"

Prem's face was grim.

"They say it is cholera and more will die. Wan is young and strong, but she is very ill."

There were herbs in his bag that had proved useful with diarrhea in Bangkok earlier in the year. The main problem was giving the patients enough water and salt. He would start with Wan and then set up a place to isolate the other patients, train people to give them the herbs, give them a thin, salty soup and dispose of the waste.

"I think I can help."

The grateful look in his brother's eyes told him he had made the right choice. This was more valuable than any of Sawat's magic. He could help people, help his own family. Finally, he was where he was meant to be.

58
PAKDEE
Gain

Pakdee flicked open the telegram from Bangkok. It was the news he had expected for months. Good thing he had long ago arranged for all official telegrams to go through him. This was information he wanted to present himself to high commissioner. The commissioner would want to discuss the implications for *Monthon* Nakhon Srithammarat. He opened the big cabinet behind him and withdrew a thick sheaf of papers tied with a ribbon. He leafed through them, thinking back to his discussions with Sukhumnaiwinit and Prince Damrong. A few quick notes for the commissioner. He retied the file.

One other matter. He took an envelope from his desk and reread the message from his informant in Krue Se. Abdul Kadir was stirring up anger in Pattani once more.

After the appointment of the Pattani high commissioner, Pakdee had turned over most of his network to the office there, but he made sure the man in Krue Se still reported directly to him. It might be nothing more than talk, but it was disturbing. He would have to increase the payments to his man. He might have to do more than just report. He sat back to think.

The treaty was a triumph. Finally, everything was going his way. Jate had died an ugly death and it came at the hands of his other tormentor— that big policemen. It was unfortunate the man had been cleared by the inquiry. How sweet it would have been if he had been held responsible for the death. At least he had been made to squirm for a few weeks and he would have a permanent black mark on his record. Overall, a victory.

Yes, all was going well. His mission for Prince Damrong in Kelantan had been tricky, but Duff had taken the bait and reported to the British that the Siamese planned to build the railway south with German engineers. Duff was obviously angling for a role in building the railroad, so he used his influence to lobby for the treaty. That turned out to be the last push needed to get British concessions.

As he walked down the hall, nodding to the officials he passed, he smiled at the thought that only he in all of southern Siam knew of the agreement changing the region forever. As he arrived at the commissioner's office, he looked at the carved teak portal and the sign proclaiming the office of the high commissioner. Someday, this would be his. The man at the desk in front of the commissioner's office scrambled to his feet, *waied* to him and opened the heavy teak doors. Phraya Chonlaburanurak glanced up from the document he was working on, looking grateful for the interruption.

"Pakdee, I am glad you are here. I would appreciate your help with this dispute over concession income. The British adviser in Kelantan, quite rightly, is following up on our demands for more revenue from the concessions awarded to Duff. It's no surprise the man is protesting, complaining and delaying. He seems to think his friends in Singapore and London will back him up once more."

"High Commissioner, as you know, we support the adviser, who has turned out to be more sympathetic to the Kelantanese people than to British businessmen already fat with profits. His Royal Highness was wise to appoint a Britisher like Graham there. Prince Damrong will insist we back him up. You recall that he was ready to resign if London gave in to pressures to let concessionaires like Duff get away with paying less than agreed."

"Yes, yes. But can you find a way to let Duff know we stand behind the adviser?"

"Already done sir. That trip to Kota Bahru I took for His Royal Highness—I had the chance to see Duff and let him know he will have to pay up. He wasn't happy, but he may have gotten the impression his company will get contracts for the railroad."

"But we already have those German engineers."

"That is changing."

He held up an envelope with the telegram.

"The treaty?"

"Yes, sir, His Majesty signed the Anglo-Siamese treaty in Bangkok yesterday. We have given up a lot—Kedah, Kelantan, Perlis and Terengganu, but we have gotten important compensation in return—full control over Pattani, Yala, Satun and Narathiwat. No more special legal status for the British. Without a treaty we might have lost all the Malay states with no compensation. What's more, the British have agreed to finance the railroad south, provided we use British engineers."

He placed the telegram on the commissioner's desk.

"A line has now been drawn—what is ours is clearly ours and what is theirs is clearly theirs. We will no longer be drawn into the legal and debt problems of the sultanates or the intrigues of their rulers."

He waited as the commissioner read the long telegram, referring occasionally to the file he had placed alongside it.

This was a hard-won triumph for King Chulalongkorn, Prince Damrong and Phraya Sukhumnaiwinit, but also for himself. They had taken serious risks in arresting the raja. It could have exploded in rebellion. He had played a role in the maneuvers orchestrated by the prince, even the last-minute threat of using the Germans for the railway. Now it looked like success. Prince Damrong and the king's American adviser Edward Strobel had worked out a compromise with the British and cleared away internal Siamese opposition. Strobel had been strong in rejecting British attempts to claim Pattani. It had been the last thing the American had done before succumbing to a long illness.

Was this what he thought about as he lay on his deathbed, far from home? Did he see the treaty as the greatest accomplishment of his life? Or, as life ebbed away, were his last thoughts of loved ones back in America? Death, even after a life of accomplishments, even after a long, painful illness, cannot be welcome.

How would he think about his work when his time was at an end? He had served the king well. He had helped build a more modern nation, a Siamese nation. But hadn't he also betrayed the Malays—his own people? What would Father or Saifan think, if they ever found out? But they had betrayed him first. Left him alone in prison. He had to become a new person, a Siamese official, with a different name, with a different language, with a different life.

"So, this is good?" the commissioner asked, looking up from the documents.

"Sir?"

"The treaty, will it make things better now?"

"We have gained a lot, perhaps too much. Making Pattani part of Siam will challenge our sensitivity, our generosity and our wisdom. We must be wise enough to let go of what we have lost and patient enough to consolidate all we have gained."

Part Three : Family

1

PREM
Illness

The first pink of dawn warmed the sky as Prem helped Ploi and Chaem prepare a bowl of rice, fried fish wrapped in banana leaves and a pot of curry. Two of the casino workers paddled them downriver to Wat Nantharam. The morning light was still silvery as a line of saffron-clad monks walked slowly out of the temple gate. Som was the last in line.

Chaem scooped rice into the black lacquer bowls of the monks as each paused before her. Ploi put a spoonful of red curry into each bowl and Prem gave each a fish. Finally Som stood before him. His brother was finally back. It felt good to place the fish in his bowl. But, according to the rules, he should say nothing to him.

Prem returned to the temple an hour later, when he calculated the monks would have finished their morning meal. He found Som waiting for him at the temple gate.

"Mother will be so happy to see you. And the girls too."

"I was away too long," Som said.

"It seems like a lifetime," Prem said, hoping he didn't sound like he was criticizing his brother. "You can't imagine how often they ask whether I have gotten a letter from you. I know you wrote whenever you could, but we never had enough. We loved hearing of your adventures. But there were so many months when there was no news.

"I was on *thudong*. We traveled in the forest, rarely staying anywhere for too long. Often we only had a cave or our *klots* to sleep in. During the rains retreats it was better, but it was difficult to send mail from some of those *wats* in the far north. I am sorry it was not enough."

"Don't worry about it. It is just so wonderful to have you back. Come, I have arranged a boat."

Prem felt his heart swell with conflicting emotions. He struggled to separate them. There was love and anger. There was respect and doubt. Why had Som stayed away so long? All those times he needed his brother and he wasn't there. Didn't he feel some responsibility for the family? He had changed. His face was thinner yet he looked stronger, settled, more mature.

As they walked towards the river, he matched Som's steady pace but a half-step behind. Even his body had changed. The soles of his feet were thick with callouses and his legs were wiry with muscle. He was thinner. His back was dark and speckled with what must be old insect bites. He didn't seem to hurry, but it was hard to keep up.

At the temple dock they boarded a small boat. The paddlers made a few quick strokes and the boat swung into the current.

"There are more buildings now," Som said. "What is that tall pillar?"

"That is the smokestack of the steam rice mill," Prem said. "A lot has happened here while you were away. The town is growing. We even had a visit from His Majesty the King."

"Yes, you wrote."

"Pakpanang is now one of the busiest ports on the whole coast," he said. "The family has been busy too. You must come see our children. They are dying to meet you. I read your letters to them over and over. They want to hear more about the elephant. They want to hear about the Mekong River. You have done so much and I have just stayed here. Dammit, you left me behind and stayed away so long."

Som turned around and half-smiled. "And you were ready to leave your beautiful Ploi and your exciting work in the casino? Prepared for the life of a *thudong* monk? That is a different younger brother than I remember."

It was true, he had never even thought about leaving; he just missed his brother.

"How long has it been, five years?"

"Only a bit more than four, but it seemed longer to me too. How is mother? And the girls?"

"Mother expanded the warehouse. Younger Sister Toh is married. Younger Sister Wan does all the bookkeeping and correspondence. They are making more money than Father ever did. Business is good."

When they landed at the warehouse dock, it was deserted. The main entrance was closed by an iron gate. He led Som to a side door that opened into the big storage room with long rows of goods covered with canvas. All the hours they had spent in this place, working for Father, all the arguments between Som and the old man. It still seemed strange to be in the warehouse without the sound of Father shouting orders, quoting Chinese proverbs and telling tales of his adventures at sea. Whatever Father's failings, he had always looked out for what he thought were the best interests of the family. Did Som understand that? The final year had been the worst—the shipwreck, Som leaving, Father dying. Had Som found whatever he was looking for? Why was he back?

He led his brother around the warehouse. There were no sounds other than the echoes of their footsteps. They skirted a large stack of wooden crates and came to the staircase.

"Mother, look who I have brought to see you," he called as they mounted the stairs. At the top, he looked around at a large room with desks, chairs and piles of documents.

"Mother, it's me," he shouted.

There was no answer, so he pushed through another door with Som behind him. Mother was bent over a form on a raised sleeping platform. She looked thin and there were strands of gray and white mixed into the dark of her short-cropped hair.

"Oh, Prem, I am so glad you've come," she said. "Wan has gotten much worse. I'm so worried. Your sister went to get more medicine, but she has not…" She halted as Som rushed forward and knelt in front of her, touching his head to the floor at her feet.

"Mother. I am back," Som said with a note of pleading in his voice. "I regret I was away from you for so long. Please forgive me."

"Chao? Is it you?" Mother sobbed. "It has been so long."

"I'm sorry. I am so sorry," he said. "But I am home now."

Mother turned her gaze to her youngest daughter who smiled weakly up at them.

"Wan, see who has come to see you," she said.

"You came back," she whispered.

"Wan. I am here, here to help," he said. He turned to Mother. "Is it cholera?"

"Yes, Toh thinks so. She started getting sick three days ago but today it got much worse," she gestured to a pail and a pile of brown-stained cloths. "It is like she has been squeezed dry. Toh has given her medicine, but nothing seems to work."

Som hesitated for a moment and then felt for the pulse in her neck. He must be counting her heartbeats. He looked worried.

"If it is cholera, I have something that has been helpful in the past."

Som turned to him. "Prem, go to the market and get some drinking coconuts, some salt and palm sugar. Mother, boil some water and set it aside to cool in two pots. We will use the warm water in one to wash our hands with soap."

Som took a yellow cloth bag from his shoulder and began pulling out small packets of herbs. Some were wrapped in banana leaves; others were in leather bags. He opened one of the bags and sniffed at the contents.

"I call this mixture *Krisanaklan*. It has shavings of agar wood and extract of clove along with a few other herbs and some salt and sugar cane juice. When the cholera hit Bangkok port, it saved many people. It slows or even stops the diarrhea so the body has a chance to recover."

"So, she will get better?" Prem asked.

"I think so," Som said. "Prem, why are you still here? Go now. She needs fluids."

He got to his feet and hurried out the door. The market was nearby, but it took a long time before he found someone selling coconuts. He ran back into the room carrying a half-dozen coconuts tied together by a twist of coconut fiber.

Wan appeared to be sleeping. Som and Mother were sitting on the floor beside her. Som was reading from a notebook.

"In Bangkok, 21 people took this medicine for six days and 19 survived," he read.

"So, two didn't?" Mother asked as she pushed a pot of steaming water towards him.

"Well, I noted that another 38 cases were treated differently—with Chinese medicine or nothing at all and only 12 survived," he whispered. "So, this is her best chance," he said. Som measured out two spoons of the power into the pot and stirred.

"Give her a cup full every few hours," he said. "And as much coconut water as she can drink. Prem, open a coconut for her."

He used a heavy knife to lop off the top of one coconut and then opened it in four quick strokes. He poured the cloudy coconut water into a thick glass. Som nodded to him. Oh, right. As a monk, Som should not touch a woman.

He held up his sister's head and put the glass to her lips.

"Drink this," he said.

"You need the liquid and the sweetness," Som said. "Then we'll give you the medicine." Wan took a few sips of the coconut water and then some more until the glass was empty.

He looked behind him at the sound of footsteps on the staircase. Younger sister Toh entered and went to her knees.

"I have some medicine for her—elk's horn," Toh said. "It is what my husband recommends."

"Is that what you have been giving her?" Som asked.

"Who are..." Toh looked at Som for the first time. "Elder Brother Chao?"

"Yes, Toh. It's me."

"It has been so long."

"I know, but now I am back. Have you already tried the elk's horn?"

"Yes, that is what the books say," she said.

"But it hasn't worked, so it is time for something new," Som said.

"I have this *farang* medicine," Toh said, holding up a bottle with foreign writing on it. "Just came into the shop. Holloways Pills—cures fever, nausea, chest pain and dizziness."

"Useless," Som said. "Already tested it."

Som poured a glassful of the medicine into a tea cup and blew on it. When it was cool, Toh put it to her sister's lips. She gagged at the taste, but at Som's urging, she finished the glass and lay back on the wooden pillow.

"Wan, how are you feeling?"

"Weak, my stomach hurts," she said.

"Your body may be weak," Som said, "but your mind can be strong. You can meditate lying down," he said. "Close your eyes and concentrate on your breath until your mind is clear. If you still have pain, concentrate on the pain. Examine the pain. How does it rise and fall? Where is it coming from? Don't fear it or try to run from it. If you understand your pain, you will realize it is no different from any other experience. Accept it. It is just something happening in your mind."

Wan closed her eyes. Her breathing slowed.

"Now, we must let her rest," Som said.

He could hear care and confidence in his brother's voice. He had always been the logical one, but now there was a strength and assurance he hadn't seen before. That assurance is soothing Wan and calming Mother.

"Toh, can you help your mother care for Wan? Try to get her to drink as much coconut water as possible. Then every four hours give her one glass of the medicine. I will add some boiled cucumber leaves to make it more effective. Cook some rice with too much water, then pour off the water for her to drink after the coconut water. Once she feels stronger, make a paste of boiled onion to eat with rice water. Mother and sister, can you do that?"

In a few minutes, Som had become the man of the family, a doctor, a monk and a source of confidence. It was a relief, Prem thought, but he should do something too.

"What can I do?" he asked Som.

"You must make sure Wan gets everything she needs," Som said. "You need to care for Mother. Make sure she doesn't get too tired and fall ill herself.

"I will stay with them as long as I can," Toh said. "But I am also needed at the medicine shop. There are many in the town with the same illness and they are desperate for medicine. My husband Tan makes several different medicines that sell rather well."

"Are people are getting better?" Som asked.

"Some are, but many are not."

"Can you take me to your shop while Wan sleeps. This is why I came back. I will mix more medicine. I believe I can help."

2

SAIFAN
Holy War

Saifan sat on the cool tile floor of the mosque and crossed his legs. Imam To' Guru Wae Muso had sent word a special preacher would talk to them tonight after the evening prayers. He looked around the room and recognized several of his friends and neighbors. Two of his older students sat at the back of the group. It was good his students were taking his Koran teaching to heart, to care about the *ummat*, to protect their community. Next to him sat Hamidy, his best friend from the market. He sold vegetables from a stall next to Saifan and his father. Only two years older, Hamidy too had grown up outside of Pattani, on the shores of the Songkhla Lake. Neither was fully accepted by the Krue Se villagers, but unlike Saifan, Hamidy didn't seem to care.

The Imam stood at the doorway, shifting his weight from one foot to the other, looking at the men seated in the room. Many were bent over leaflets handed out by a stranger at the mosque entrance. Saifan looked down at his copy. Printed in *Jawi* on rough paper, the large letters at the top said "Satan Deceived the Leaders." He looked for the name of the author, but could find nothing.

The pamphlet listed nine tactics the Siamese state was using to subvert Islam and weaken Malay society. There was a buzz around the room as people read the pamphlet. Saifan went down the list.

"1. The Siamese *kaffirs* demand we obey people outside of Islam." This is true. More and more officials were coming from other provinces to work in Pattani, though none had yet appeared in Krue Se village.

"2. Officials appointed by the Siamese government impregnated Muslim women in several areas: The offspring become outcastes. They do this to destroy the Malay family line." That is far-fetched. There were so many Muslims in the south and, as far as he knew, very few Muslim women married non-Muslims.

"3. The Siamese government is destroying the culture of Malay Muslims." This charge was often made in the heated debates after the arrest of Raja Abdul Kadir and the changes in the leadership of most of the Malay provinces. They may try, but they can succeed only if we let them.

"4. The Siamese government perverts the translation of the Koran." The government was sponsoring a translation of the Koran into both Thai and Malay. He didn't know of anyone who had seen these translations yet. The answer was for Malays to learn the true meaning of the Koran through classes like his.

"5. The Siamese government is about to issue a law to persecute religious leaders who won't obey their commands." He hadn't heard this, but it might be true. The Thais seemed to be tightening control over the people in other ways, so why not in religion?

"6. The Siamese government is luring Pattani Malay Muslims into worship of money." People in the village did seem more commerce-minded, but people had to make a living. Some Malays had always been too eager to make money. No pressure from the Siamese was needed. Still, there was a lot less attention to money and profit-making in Pattani than in Pakpanang. But maybe Pattani was heading in that direction.

Before he could read the remaining points, there was a flurry of activity at the door. Two men wearing elaborately wound turbans of embroidered silk marched in, surveyed the waiting group of villagers and then stood on either side of the door, puffing out their chests, each with one hand on the kris tucked into their waistbands. A small man in long robes and a large, brilliant blue headdress walked to the front of the room, the Imam trailing behind him. The man had long hair that swept in smooth waves over his shoulders. He smiled and nodded at the seated men. At the front of the room he extended both hands and touched his right hand to his heart.

"*As-Salam-u-Alaikum wa-rahmatullahi wa-barakatuh,*" he said in a soft, musical voice. Everyone in the room looked up at him straining to hear. The Imam moved beside the man and introduced him as an important scholar and holy man. His name was To'Tae and he was renowned for deep insights into the heart of Islam, his long periods of abstinence and his mystical experience of God. He was also a close confidante and spiritual advisor of Raja Abdul Kadir.

"It is said that because of his closeness to God, he has performed miracles," the Imam said.

Saifan looked at the Imam. There was something about his expression that suggested he didn't believe in the supposed miracles.

"This holy man has carried a letter from the raja, asking us to support his preaching. The letter says our customs, our *adat*, our traditional rulers and our religion are under dire threat. So, please listen what To'Tae has to say."

The elegantly dressed figure stepped in front of the imam and looked out over the assembled men. For a moment he looked straight at Saifan.

"In the name of Allah, I thank you for coming here tonight. Like all of you, I would prefer to be doing something else tonight. My prayers and rituals take much energy. I have a *pondok* that demands my time and my wives complain that I do not give them enough...attention," he said in a soft voice with a smile.

There was a smattering of laughter from the audience.

"But I find I can no longer live the life I want to live with my students, with my community, with my books and yes, with my wives. Why not?"

He paused and again surveyed the crowd, seeming to fix each of the listeners in his gaze.

"Because we are under attack. Our Malay language is being replaced by silly sing-song Thai."

His voice rose in volume and pitch. "Our rajas and sultans have been ousted and their places taken by impostors who suck up to their masters in Bangkok. Our *adat*, the Malay wisdom of centuries, has been replaced by new laws strange even to the Thais. Our women are attacked in their villages and lured into the harems of powerful unbelievers. Our men are insulted, beaten, imprisoned and killed by policemen who can't even understand the language of their appeals for justice. The Siamese intruders come to rule us, but can't be bothered to learn the language of Pattani. They humiliate us by demanding taxes to pay for our own oppression. Our beloved centuries-old Pattani sultanate has been broken up into seven small pieces. The ignorant masters in Bangkok are not embarrassed even to tell us how we should translate the Holy Koran," he ended in a shout.

The villagers stared at the man who seemed to loom over them.

"You can read all this," he said in a voice suddenly quiet, "in the pamphlets you were given earlier. I will not waste your time or insult your intelligence by telling you things you already know."

Saifan looked around the room. Everyone had fixed their attention on To'Tae. The room was silent.

"No, I did not come here to recite the crimes of the Siamese government and their minions. I came here to tell you it is time to do something about it. Our duty as Muslims, our duty as Malays, our duty as human beings is clearly laid out in the Holy Koran. Verse five of Book Nine says: 'Kill the polytheists wherever you find them. And capture them, and besiege them, and lie in wait for them at every ambush.'"

"So that is what we must do. First, we must stop cooperating in our own humiliation. We must refuse to pay the extortionate taxes demanded by far-away masters, taxes that pay for the officials who discriminate against us, the police who abuse us and the guns that kill us. That is an important first step, but it is not enough."

"We must do more," someone shouted from the back of the room.

"Yes, we must do more," To'Tae said. "We must become Islamic warriors of Pattani and fight the infidel Siamese. We must attack them in their offices, in their courts, in their so-called schools. We must ambush them along the roads so they will fear to leave their cities polluted with sin. We must make them feel the pain of their aggression. We must punish their crimes as commanded by Allah."

There was a buzz around the room. Saifan felt his heart beat faster. Finally, he would get justice for the murder of his brother. This is how he could prove himself to be a true Malay Muslim. He was surprised some people seemed to disagree. Next to him, Hamidy was shaking his head and frowning.

The imam spoke up.

"We in Pattani know first-hand the abuses of the Siamese, but Islam is a religion of peace. Do not forget that in Book 7 Verse 33 the prophet says: 'You shall not kill any person—for Allah has made life sacred.'"

"That is true, kind imam, but you fail to recite the last part of that verse. What is it?"

The imam looked chastened, hesitated as all looked at him, and then mumbled, "It concludes — 'except in the course of justice. If one is killed unjustly, then we give his heir authority to enforce justice.' But you must be an heir to seek such revenge. Allah opposes aggression without justice."

"Do we not have justice on our side?" To'Tae demanded. "We are not the aggressors. We are defending ourselves from Siamese aggression.

We are all Muslims of Pattani, so we are all heirs to the raja who was sent in chains to a northern prison. We are all heirs to the fisherman killed by policemen. We are all heirs of the woman raped by a Siamese official. So, as heirs, we are all enjoined to seek justice. That justice, the Koran tells us, can only come from killing the oppressors."

A tall man he didn't recognize stood up.

"These injustices are made possible by the removal of our traditional leaders," he said. "You all know that the raja was unjustly imprisoned, but many other officials of the raja's government have been pensioned off or simply dismissed. I was a *Qadi* judge in charge of the raja's Islamic justice system in the capital. Two months ago, I was 'retired', dismissed without cause. Two of my Malay colleagues in the civil service were offered positions in Sukhothai—far away from their homes. When they declined to leave their homeland, they were fired. We can no longer govern our own communities. The positions of police, district officers, judges, health officials are now in the hands of the Siamese infidels."

There were shouts of agreement and To'Tae nodded. "You all know this to be true. But an important question is why? Why are they doing this? Why are they so eager to have their people in key positions? You know they don't like to live here. They think Pattani is 'uncivilized.' They call us *khaek* as if we, not they, are the ones who came here from afar. Transfer to Pattani is seen as punishment for the Siamese. So, why?"

To'Tae paused and looked around the room.

"I fear it is to prepare the way for a full assault on our way of life, our traditions, our language and our religion by people who know nothing of our lives. It is part of the government plan to make us into imitation Thais, who speak Thai, worship their king, celebrate their bizarre holidays, kneel before their idols and become slaves to their vices of alcohol, opium and sex. Once they have all the positions of power in their hands, it will be easy to punish anyone who wants to live as a faithful Muslim, as a true Malay."

That was what had happened to Abdul, Saifan thought. He thrilled to the feelings throbbing within him. Ever since he learned of his brother's death in prison, he had been angry and confused. Abdul's only transgression was daring to be friendly to the woman of one of those powerful infidels. For this he was unjustly punished. For this he was murdered. Father had moved the family to Pattani to escape that injustice, but the evil had followed them. He felt a surge of energy and found himself standing.

"To'Tae is right," he said. "We must stand up against oppression. My own brother was a victim of a so-called justice system perverted by money and bias against Muslims. He paid with his life. The word of Allah calls on us to resist, even kill, those who persecute us. Book 2 Verse 191 says: 'You may kill those who wage war against you, and you may evict them whence they evicted you. Oppression is worse than murder.'" He felt Hamidy's hand on his arm, pulling him to sit down.

"Excellent, excellent!" To'Tae cried, pointing to him. "This man understands. We are simply responding to oppression. If we are good Muslims, we must follow the word of Allah and seek justice. We do not want to invade the Siamese areas; we do not aggress against them. It is they who are the aggressors. The word of Allah is that we must kill these aggressors and evict them from our beloved land."

The imam shot an angry look at Saifan. "I still say it is wrong to kill and it is dangerous to talk like this when the Siamese are so much more powerful," the imam said. "You will only bring violence and suffering to Krue Se. We should not be talking about this in my mosque."

To'Tae shook his head. "You forget that those killed by warriors of Islam die by the will of God. So, there is no sin attached to their deaths. There is no other conclusion—we must kill the oppressors. Once they have seen enough of their people killed, the oppressors will crawl back north and leave us alone."

The imam turned to the crowd, now rumbling with anger, and held up a hand. "Remember how you were all ready to rush to the *Istana* to defend the raja, but when you got there, you saw the soldiers with their long guns, that big warship with its cannons and the rows of police with clubs. And what did you do? Nothing. To fight the Siamese state with all its weapons is to die uselessly, to leave your wives without husbands, your children without fathers and achieve nothing."

"It is natural to fear death," To'Tae said in a softer tone, "but we must look to the Koran for guidance. In Book 3, Verse 157, it is written: 'If you are killed in the cause of Allah—forgiveness and mercy from Allah are better than anything.' Some of you may be ready to become martyrs and to be welcomed into Paradise, but for those who are not, I have created talismans of great power. These symbols of our just God will deflect any bullet fired at you by an infidel. When you fight for Islam, you are never in any real danger."

"But there is no hope of victory," an older man said. "We have fought the Siamese for centuries, one battle after another. We always lose and we always suffer for it."

"That is because our leaders, like your timid imam, have failed the people," To'Tae said. "This time I will lead you into battle with guidance from Allah. As the Koran says, 'When the disbelievers plotted against you, to imprison you or kill you or expel you, they planned this. But Allah also plans, and He is the best of all planners.'"

There was a confusion of voices as several men shouted at once. To'Tae held up his hands until the room quieted. "This time, I promise you we will be clever. We will sow confusion by burning their district offices and attacking their police stations in many parts of Pattani. We will have guns. We will be protected from bullets by the holy talismans."

Saifan sat thinking, as the arguments went on with To'Tae providing more verses from the Koran to deflect any objections to his call to battle. The imam left the room shaking his head. Hamidy leaned over and whispered into Saifan's ear.

"We must be careful. We have families and we have responsibilities. The Siamese will fight back and they have all the power," he said.

Saifan could not accept that, just giving up.

"Our highest responsibility is to our community and our religion," he told Hamidy. "We have to do something."

A chorus of voices rose. "We are ready to fight. We will follow."

"And I will lead you to victory," To'Tae shouted. "Allah Akbar!"

The villagers shot to their feet, echoing his cry, shaking the room. "Allah Akbar! Allah Akbar!"

Saifan found himself on his feet shouting along with the others. At last there would be retribution. At last there would be justice.

"When do we fight? Where do we attack?" one villager asked.

"That is not to be discussed tonight," To'Tae said in a calm voice. "The first thing to do is to stop paying tax. Then we will take bolder steps. All I want you to do now is prepare. Find weapons if you can. Learn how to use them. The call to holy war will come. Just be ready."

3

SOM
Chasm

When Som returned to Wat Wang Tawan Tok a month earlier, he found many of the monks eager to see him, even those he didn't know. His first night back a dozen monks and several novices gathered around him in the ordination hall. The monks and the temple boys were eager to hear of his travels, especially his encounter with the wild elephants. Most seemed to enjoy the tale for its excitement rather than its lesson about mindfulness. Only three asked about the meditation techniques Phra Sawat had taught him, but that gave him the chance to explain.

He focused on the teachings of his first few years with Sawat. He still didn't know what to think about Sawat's claims to be able to leave his body and fly above the forest. His strange predictions of future war with terrible machines raining death on the Thai people seemed far-fetched, but it was Sawat's insistence he could cure disease by touching the head of the afflicted that had led him to part ways with his old friend. When some of his patients in the north told him they would prefer the spiritual healing offered by Sawat to Som's foul-tasting herbs, he began to realize that staying with Sawat was a problem. If he didn't oppose Sawat's spiritual healing, he would be responsible for continued illness, even death. If his treatments failed, he could be responsible, but not if he let his patients go without treatment. Still, the memory of Sawat's form fading into the distance was painful.

The return to Wat Wang Tawan Tok had never felt like a true destination and the cold welcome from the abbot had reinforced that feeling. Still, the reception from some of the younger monks encouraged him. They seemed to appreciate his detailed descriptions of his meditation methods—the use of isolation, the benefits of alternating breathing meditation with walking meditation and concept meditation. Above all, they appreciated his willingness to talk about his failures, obstacles and difficulties in meditation. The talk went on late into the night until a temple boy came in to say the abbot didn't want them to waste any more kerosene for the lamps. He went to his sleeping mat feeling good about the young monks.

The next day, his old friend, Phra Pat had returned his medical books with a smile.

"I am afraid we gave away your other things long ago, but no one wanted the books, so I kept them. I've read some of them, but they were confusing."

"Pat, I get confused too. Sickness and health are more complicated than any of the texts can explain."

"What was most helpful in treating the sick," Pat said, "were your notes about which treatments worked for which ailments. The problem was Phra Panya didn't keep up the records. Sometimes we would use your treatments, but sometimes Panya would say your medicine didn't have the right taste—not sweet enough or astringent enough for a particular disease. So he would use a treatment that he had heard of from somewhere. Some patients recovered quickly, some didn't, but we never recorded it."

"It's not your fault," he reassured Pat. "It is difficult to be sure what works. Sometimes people just recover on their own. That was often the case when we were in the forest with no medicine available. Sometimes just giving people something to take, even if it was just tea, would lift their spirits and help them recover. If I could stay in one place, I could follow up on treatment success. That is one reason I decided to return."

"But are you sure you want to come back to Wat Wang Tawan Tok?"

"Why not?"

"You were unhappy here before. That was why you left, wasn't it? The new rules are even tighter now. The sermons to the lay people are boring. Even Phra Panya has given up. The abbot listens only to the Sangha Council in Bangkok and his big donors in the market. No one teaches meditation, and few practice it."

His second meeting with the abbot, Abbot Brahm, had been awkward. The abbot had asked nothing about Som's meditation practice or his *thudong* experience. He asked, instead, whether he had finally memorized the chants for funerals. He told him that his rainy seasons stays in temples in Bangkok and the northeast had given him different versions of the chants. When he told Abbot Brahm of his stay at Wat Boworniwet, the abbot asked whether he had met the supreme patriarch. He told him the patriarch, Prince Wachirayan, had several times discussed meditation and dharma with Phra Sawat and him. He thought the abbot looked unhappy with that, but seemed relieved when he told him he had not communicated with the supreme patriarch since leaving Bangkok two years ago.

"I have received the great honor of an invitation from the supreme patriarch to attend Mahamakut University," Abbot Brahm announced. "Undoubtedly because of my success here."

Som smiled because he had attended some of the first classes at the Buddhist university set up by Prince Wachirayan and he knew the purpose was not to reward performance but to upgrade older monks seen as weak in their understanding of the canon. The classes used texts written by the patriarch explaining basic Buddhist ethics in simple Thai.

"Many of our older monks in the countryside have misunderstandings about these things," the patriarch had told Sawat and Som one afternoon at Wat Boworniwet. "We need to create a common understanding to unite monks throughout the land. There should not be a northern Buddhism, or a southern Buddhism—there should be only one Buddhism—at least in Siam. Just as His Majesty is re-organizing and unifying the administration of the state, we must re-organize the administration of the religion."

The university would be a good experience for the abbot, but he might have difficulty with the classes in Pali that went far deeper into the language than the usual chants. But that was not his problem.

"Congratulations. I am sure your university studies will be rewarding," he said.

The abbot had then said he wanted Som to work under Phra Panya to expand the medical treatment services. Donations from people seeking treatment had fallen off in recent years, he said, and needed to be increased. Under the new rules, Som was registered at Wat Wang Tawan Tok under Abbot Brahm and therefore was supposed to follow the abbot's orders. The only alternative was to seek registration at another monastery under another abbot.

"You must have noticed the new buildings and the improvements to the ordination hall," Abbot Brahm said. "I have made Wat Wang Tawan Tok one of the most important *wats* in Nakhon. The Sangha Council has been most generous in its praise."

Four new *chedis* had risen in the courtyard, the ordination hall had a new coat of whitewash and the prayer hall was now decorated with multicolor bits of glass, making it sparkle like a huge jewel. "But we must not be satisfied with past success. I have plans for a new prayer hall and much larger Buddha image. Already," Abbot Brahm said, "two rice millers, the Nakhon royal family and a Chinese mine owner have promised part of the money we need for the construction. But more is needed."

The abbot unrolled a large paper with plans for the new building and spread it on the floor. He pointed to the key features, including an upswept roof and a set of gold-plated stands to hold the tiers of Buddha images in the prayer hall. Som had found his mind drifting away from the drone of the abbot's voice as he explained the need for a grand hall that could compete with Wat Mahathat for attention. By the time the bell rang for the second meal, he had made his decision. That night he told his friends he would move to another monastery.

"You have been to temples all over Siam," Phra Pat said. You've studied medicine and have had more success treating people than anyone here. You've learned meditation with several masters. You should establish your own monastery, temple and meditation center. You will not be satisfied with anything else. Since you know members of the Sangha Council in Bangkok, you should be able to get approval for a new temple. Under the rules, you would just have to show enough support for buildings and maintenance of at least four monks. Then you will be the abbot. If you do that, I'll go with you."

"That may be difficult, especially if Abbot Brahm is opposed."

Phra Pat laughed. "Oh, I think he'll be happy to see you leave. Remember how annoyed he was with all your questions before—and that was when you were a new monk. Now you have experience and a reputation that will make it difficult for him to control the monks who follow you. You saw how they reacted to your *thudong* tales. Just make a few suggestions to Abbot Brahm with your usual irritating logic and he'll be happy to see you leave."

"But I don't want to be an abbot—responsible for all the necessities of a temple and monastery."

"You may not have a choice. You can't keep traveling forever. And if you want to register at another temple, where will you go? The temples in Nakhon are all traditional—performing ceremonies and taking in young men for a few months of the Buddha's teaching. I don't think there are any that concentrate on teaching meditation."

That was true. What if there could be a monastery that recreated the experience of meditating in the forest? A practice that offered some of the benefits of *thudong* and, at the same time, offered the benefits of a village temple—teaching the dharma, educating young men, helping monks with their meditation practice and treating the sick. If there were a temple that did that, then his practice would not have to stop for the rains retreat. Would local people support such a place? One that didn't offer marriage or funeral ceremonies? One that didn't send out monks to toss holy water, open new buildings or bless fishing boats?

He recalled an old monk in a temple near the Mekong telling him about a dream. In his vision he saw the land split wide open. On one side was a lush forest, on the other was a beautiful temple with orange and green tiles glinting in the sunshine. He saw people trying to reach across the chasm. There was no bridge and the crack was too wide to leap over. The old monk said he was puzzled at the meaning of the vision. Phra Sawat suggested the dream showed the split between the practice of *thudong* and the official Buddhist traditions, a chasm too wide to cross. Maybe his purpose in life was to build a bridge.

4

TUN WAY
Disappointments

Nai Tun Way leaned back in his rattan chair and drained his glass of brandy as he watched the sun set over the river. Little Ngwe Lay was playing by herself at one end of the veranda while Aya prepared dinner in the cook shed behind the house. The last sunlight picked out the skeleton of the ruined school building. It had been a year and a half since the school had burned down and there had been little progress in rebuilding it. He had spent his own money to clean up the site, but the rest of his funds had gone to buy the weapons needed to defend the school. The wealthy Mons in Bago had not understood the benefit of those weapons. The timid fools—they thought it would encourage more violence against them and make them vulnerable to the British-led police. They were sheep.

"We must be patient," the biggest Mon businessman had told him. "British law will constrain the Burmans. If we stay within the law, we can prosper."

"Maybe you can prosper," he had replied, "but only because you suck up to the British in Rangoon and make business deals with the Chinese here. We need the Mon Language and Culture Society to bring the Mons together."

That appeal had not gone over well.

Even his friends were giving up. Shwe Hongsa wanted to support Mon studies at the proposed Burma Research Society in Rangoon. Why should Mons depend on foreigners to preserve their own culture? How humiliating is that? Too many Mons thought like Shwe Hongsa. They just took the easy way, going along with the colonial government, doing business with the Chinese, borrowing money from the Indians—all to get a little richer and avoid trouble. They didn't want to hear his appeals for donations or his scorn when they declined.

His friends visited less often now. U Htun Htin had sold some of his land along the river to the government to build a new pier and warehouses. As part of the deal he got a 20-percent share in the completed facility. Htun Htin had warned him the British considered him a radical.

"Tun Way, be careful. They have a file on you. They are watching," he had whispered at their last meeting more than five months ago.

Aung Mon had a new young wife and was working hard to keep her happy. He had stopped drinking. He looked slimmer and healthier than he had in years. But he rarely came to visit. Whenever he was invited, he would say he was taking the wife shopping in Rangoon, or heading up to a hill station to avoid the heat.

Shwe Hongsa was an even bigger disappointment. They had started to gather traditional Mon tales and poetry to be published as a series of hard cover books. But the publisher had backed out and the documents were gathering dust in his study. Worse, Shwe Hongsa had taken a job at the government school, teaching history. Their last meeting had ended in an argument.

He poured another glass of brandy and turned to his daughter. Each year she looked more and more like Su Sah. She had the same delicate nose, but in a rounder face. Her dark hair was long and tied back the way Su had often arranged her hair. The honey color of her skin was the same. It stabbed his heart to look at her. She was a quiet girl who seemed content to play with her toys or read her books by herself. She must be bright because she could already read both Burmese and Mon. Aya had insisted on teaching her Burmese over Tun Way's objection. He didn't like it, but he knew the housekeeper was right. If the girl was ever to go to school, she would need Burmese. He had been forced to let the two house servants and the gardener go. So now Aya had to cook and clean the house as well as care for the little girl. Ngwe Lay had taken to trailing Aya around the house as she worked. There were no other children nearby for her to play with since the gardener and his family had moved away. Yes, she should start school soon. But how could he proclaim the need for a Mon school when he sent his daughter to a Burmese school. It could wait another year.

When he and his troop of teenaged fighters had reached Bago, he realized there was no immediate need for the rifles. There was no school to protect yet and there was no safe place to keep the weapons. If found by the police, it would mean jail. Just knowing the weapons were available was enough. He had taken one rifle out and stored it in three layers of oiled cloth buried in the space beneath his house. The rest went up into the mountains with the boys who took turns manning the little campsite they called their guerrilla base. The boys enjoyed practicing their military tactics in the forested hills. They begged for permission to fire the rifles, but that would use up their small store of ammunition. On his last visit he had allowed three shots each to practice.

Even at the campsite, he felt alone. The boys were of a different generation and it was hard to talk to them. He didn't understand their jokes or their chatter in a slang that incorporated too many Burmese words. Sometimes he found them chatting in Burmese only to go silent as he approached. All his problems were so much worse without Su Sah. Her death had left a deep ache that never seemed to go away. But the image of her in his mind was growing less clear—like seeing her through the morning mist of Mt. Kyaiktiyo.

Then she appeared in front of him.

"Please, Papa, play with me." It was Ngwe Lay, looking up at him.

Like Su, her eyes were large and dark brown under perfect curves of eyebrows. He stared at her for a moment.

"What do you want to play?"

"Dolls," she said, holding up a yellow-haired doll. Why did the doll look like those strange, pale British women so many Burmese marveled at, with their ghostly skin and their bizarre hair?

"Where did you get that doll?"

"Aya gave me."

"You should have dolls that look like Mon women," he said.

"We play?"

"No not tonight," Tun Way said. He turned away from the little girl, finished off the glass of brandy and poured another. He sat staring into the gathering darkness.

5

SOM
A New Path

Som sat with Mother, Prem, Ploi and Toh on the veranda of the restaurant, watching a large steamship head up the river against the ebbing tide. Wan's recovery was going well, but she had stayed home to rest. He would check on her later. He loved having the family around him, but they didn't understand what he wanted to do. He wasn't explaining it well.

"It comes from what I learned from *thudong* and from my visits to so many temples. I want to do something different. No big buildings, no golden Buddha images, no chanting and rituals. I want to give the monks something like the experience of the first followers of the Buddha. I want to focus on the original teachings in plain, understandable language. Like the Buddha, the monks at this monastery will practice meditation of all types, but nothing to extremes. We will mentor each other. No boss. No hierarchy. No interference from Bangkok. The mission will be to reduce suffering, and to provide the peace, the teaching and the space for monks to meditate."

"But it can't just serve the monks," Prem spoke up. "It would be like running a restaurant solely for the cooks and owners. You have to think of the customers."

"Don't forget even the simplest meditation center will need land, building materials and construction labor," Ploi said. "The monks will need food and robes, candles—a lot of little things. For all that you need money. How will you attract donations?"

"Even if it is in the forest, a temple has to mean something to the people nearby," Mother said.

"That's right," Prem said. "And if it means something to them, they will support the costs."

"You have to be practical," Ploi said. "No money, no mission,"

They were right. He had to think this through.

"I suppose we will have to accept donations. I didn't like Abbot

Brahm's focus on getting more and more donations, but you are right; some donations are necessary."

"What will you give the donors in return?" Prem asked.

"Monks repay the people by teaching the dharma," Mother said, "by accepting young men as novices, by educating the young, by soothing their worries with prayers and by providing wise guidance to solve their problems. The buildings provide a sense of beauty and awe that takes people away from the drabness of their ordinary lives. A monastery is a refuge for the old. It cares for orphans. Ceremonies and chanting add solemnity to important events in life—marriage, death, even opening a new building. The images of the Buddha give people symbols of the dharma that they can see and touch. They help people feel there is a spiritual power protecting them against the uncertainties of life. That is the way it is for all the temples I have known."

"That is true, Mother, but trying to do all those things means that the temple does none of them well," he said, impressed by his mother's thoughtfulness. He had noticed how much more self-confident and talkative she had become in his absence—or perhaps it was the absence of Father that made the difference.

"Is it wrong to have a sanctuary that concentrates on meditation above all else?"

"Will that be enough to get the support you need?" Prem asked. "Ploi and I can make some donations, but you will need support from local people wherever you build the temple."

"The answer is obvious," Toh spoke up. "You must provide medical care for the community. You already have a reputation from treating people during the cholera epidemic. Your *Krisanaklan* herbs are the best-selling medicine in our shop. You love finding new treatments, tracking their effects, perfecting them. Do that in your new temple and you will never lack support from the people."

"But that will lead us back to Abbot Brahm's plan to demand donations in exchange for treatment. I can't do that," he said.

"You don't need to demand anything," Toh said. "If people recover from illness, they will show their gratitude. You don't have to say a word. More important, if you find new medicines, then we will make them and sell them in our shop to those who can't travel to your temple. That way your medicines can help more people and support the everyday needs of the monks." They were right. He could create a new kind of temple for medicine and meditation. The next day, he began looking for a site with the family comments in mind. It had to be in a forest, but it could not be too far from the people to come for treatment. It shouldn't be too close to another temple. It couldn't be on good land for farming, or someday there would be a struggle over land rights. Most importantly, it had to be welcomed by the local villagers.

He spent several days explaining his needs to the officials at the district office and getting their approval. He sent a letter to the Sangha Council. Then he sailed up and down the Pakpanang River. But there was no idle land along the river. Much of the forest that had once shaded its banks had been cleared to plant rice. Pakpanang town was spreading along both banks and there were new roads reaching back to villages chopped out of the forest.

Then one morning, Prem walked into the temple compound followed by a lean, dark man. He looked familiar.

"Som, Phra Som," Prem called. "I have brought someone to see you and perhaps offer a solution for the new temple."

He looked up from his spot under a large tree at one end of the compound and squinted through the morning sun at the two men approaching him.

"Is that Nuey, our old crewman?" he said with a smile as he stood. The man *waied* and knelt before him.

"Yes, honored sir. Since the wreck of *The Wind Uncle* I have been working as a fisherman. I have a wife and two children now and we live in the village on Talumpuk Cape."

"I've told him about your plans for a new temple," Prem said. "He says there is a forest behind the village. The soil there is too sandy and sometimes floods with sea water, so no rice can be grown there. The village of mostly fishermen and boat builders is growing fast."

"Now more than 400 people live there, but there is no temple and no monks to receive our donations," Nuey said. "We have to sail back up the river to go to a temple in town on holy days. The older people are especially unhappy."

The next day the three took a boat down the river and across the shallow bay to Talumpuk village. Yai, the village headman, was delighted with the idea of establishing a temple nearby. He led Som, Prem and Nuey to a clearing in the forest about 15 minutes walk south of the village.

Som walked slowly around the clearing. The soil was sandy and shaded by some large trees. Some wild banana plants, the broad leaves partly shredded by the wind promised a bit of food. An old coconut grove lined one side of the clearing and a pair of giant Mimosa Rain Trees guarded the other side. A large Banyan Tree offered a pleasant place to meditate. There was some thorny bush that would have to be cleared away, but it shouldn't be too difficult. Fallen trees strewn nearby could be used for building materials. He spotted a broad green tangle of *Fah Thalai Jon* plants at the high water mark. He could use them to make medicines for sore throat.

"What about drinking water?" he asked.

"We'll have to dig to be sure," Yai said, "but elsewhere on the cape you can reach fresh water at about six meters. If that doesn't work, you'll have to store rainwater for drinking."

Peering east through the undergrowth Som could see the shining water of Pakpanang Bay. Behind him, the gentle waves of the gulf whispered against the sand. The clearing looked to be less than two meters above the water level.

"What happens in a storm?" he asked.

"The middle of the cape is usually high enough to escape the waves," Yai said, "but every few years a big storm hits at high tide. Then you might get your feet wet. All the houses in the village are built on pillars the height of a man. You better do the same."

Som felt the sea breeze against his back. It would be cool here as long as they had some shade. The wind seemed to lift him up and tell him this was the place. Back at the village, the elders said they would support the temple if the monks would come to the village for morning food donations. Yai said the village had 20 craftsmen who built boats. They would donate their labor for the buildings, he promised.

On the boat trip back up the river, Prem and Nuey chatted about their days on *The Wind Uncle*. Som sat quietly watching the sea breeze fill the sail and pull them smoothly along. Fate was pulling him along to something now becoming clear. He could become a healer, a meditator and a guide for others. This is what I can do, what I am meant to do.

6

PLOI
Outside the Heart

Ploi heard voices from the restaurant on the floor below her office. Prem had already gone out with some of his old buddies and she had stayed to finish up her report to Sia Leng. It sounded like their burly Sikh guard and... Dam? He was late. For months, Dam had stopped coming to the casino to avoid suspicion they had conspired to kill Jate. She had prepared a small sack of gold coins to reward him, but he had never come to pick it up. The thought of Dam hurling that Chink filth onto an anchor was still satisfying.

Heavy footsteps on the stairway. Dam? It should be safe to meet now, this late at night. He pushed open the door and peered in with a timid smile that looked odd on such a big man.

"Come in, come in. It has been a long time, but you were smart to stay away."

"Yes, far too long."

"I have a reward for you," she said and walked over to the floor safe, pulling back the planks that covered it. She found the leather sack and held it up to him. "A small reward."

"Not needed."

"I have to reward you some way." She looked up and smiled. He was really large and powerful, but he looked uncertain. She knew what he wanted and perhaps she wanted it too. She moved closer and stood on tiptoes to sniff his chest. She could feel the excitement stirring within him. She took his hand and pulled him closer. She reached up and stroked his face. She shouldn't do this. But she had to reward him. He obviously wanted her and had for a long time. The way he had looked at her when she accidentally touched him or bent down so he could see her breasts. It had been fun to tease him, but now she couldn't forget what he had done for her. He gave her revenge when no one else could.

The thought of his large body was exciting. But she wasn't doing it just for that. This would tie him to her more surely than gold. She moved his hand to her breast. Looking down she could see the effects even through the heavy twill of his uniform trousers. His other hand reached behind her and pulled her against him. Then he dropped both hands to his sides.

"I can't," he said and pulled back.

"What? You don't want to?"

"No, no, I have wanted you ever since I first saw you so long ago. I dream of you at night. When it is boring in the station, I close my eyes and think of you. But I can't do this."

"But why?"

"My powers. My *yantra*. I lose my protection if I lay with another man's wife. It is all that saved me from Jate's pistol, all that protected me in the inquiry. It is protection I must have to continue my work."

"So, your little bits of tin are more important than me," she said. She moved back close to him and looked up into his face. She took his hand and again pressed it against one breast.

"Feel my heart. It is beating for you tonight. If you reject me, it will never beat for you again."

Dam groaned and bent his head to the curve of her neck to inhale the smell of her. One hand slipped under her blouse and stroked her breast. The nipple hardened. He pulled her against him. His manhood pressed into her stomach. She felt a rush of warmth between her legs. Her heart beat faster. Life was exciting again.

7

SOM
Doubts and Promises

The breeze coming off the sea felt cool against his sweaty back as Som stepped back to survey the work so far. The last of the four huts was finished, except for the roofing. They were rough and clumsy. The strips of split bamboo woven together for each wall showed cracks where the weave had not been tight enough. They stood on rickety wooden pilings like aged, arthritic legs. The door on the second hut did not quite close and sagged off its leather hinges. Sad-looking, but at least the huts would provide shelter in the coming rainy season. Dwarfed by the tall pines around them, the huts blended into the forest.

He grinned encouragement at Prem who was straining to pull a large rock into the small circle planned for sermons. Three of the monks were working on the roofing of the third hut, hoisting thick thatch onto the bamboo poles and lashing it into place. Like him, they had pulled their robes down to their waists to cool off. Their bodies were speckled with sunlight filtering through the trees.

With all the construction work there had been no time or energy for meditation. That had been the key reason Phra Pat and the other young monks had left Wat Wang Tawan Tok to join him at his little meditation center. He had thought more would come. Phra Panya had sounded enthusiastic, but at the last moment changed his mind.

"I have many followers at Wat Wang Tawan Tok who don't want me to leave," he explained.

That left him with the bare minimum of four needed to apply for Sangha permission for a new temple. At least the four were hard workers.

Abbot Brahm had laughed at his plans, but gave him permission to leave. "You'll find out it is not so simple to run a temple," he said. "It is a lot easier to criticize than actually get things done."

Maybe the abbot was right and he had been foolhardy. They needed to get the shelters finished, but he also needed to make time for meditation. There was still no place for the medical work. There was just too much to do. How could he manage a temple? How could he lead other monks? How could he respond to the needs of the villagers?

A large jumble of lumber, window frames, doors and roofing tiles was piled on the sandy soil of the clearing. This was all that existed of the planned medical buildings. Two ship owners—old friends of the family, Toh's husband, and the family of one of the young monks had donated the materials. Prem and Ploi had paid for 30 sacks of cement. The building would have a diagnostic room, a medicine preparation area, two treatment rooms and a large shaded veranda for patients waiting for treatment. Like the monk's huts, the medical building would be raised at least five feet off the ground. But erecting such a large building was beyond the capability of his unskilled monks. Where were the workers who volunteered to build it? They were supposed to be at the site that morning, but the sun was already high overhead and no one had appeared.

Until now, everything had been going so well. Toh's shop was providing initial raw materials for medicines. More would come from his searches through the forest covering much of the cape that curled half-way around Pakpanang Bay. He would still have to make a trip into the mountain forests for materials, especially the agar wood needed for medicines to deal with diarrhea. Where would he find leaves of the sweet wormwood plant for a tea he had read about in the Chinese *Handbook of Prescriptions for Emergencies*?

He needed new supplies of cinchona bark for malaria. Even though it was still the dry season, Talumpuk Cape was afflicted by swarms of mosquitos. His stomach rumbled. Only a half pot of rice was left after the morning meal. The village had vowed to provide food for the monks. Most importantly, the headman had promised carpenters, boat builders, who could erect the main building. But no one had come.

He looked at the lumber and mortar transported to the site by an old friend of Father's. Even with Prem helping when he could spare time from the restaurant, the monks would never be able to build the medicine hall before the rains. The new temple would be in trouble even before it started. Without buildings, the Sangha Council would not give official approval.

"Let's take a break and finish the food we have before noon," he told the monks. After eating the last of the rice and dried fish they had brought with them from town, the monks rested in the shade of the pines.

He pulled his feet over his thighs and focused on his breath. He tried to feel the air flowing in and out of his nose and down into his lungs. In and out. How could they finish the building? Maybe he should start offering medication right away. But once the rains began there would be no place to do this.

He was too distracted to meditate. This, he thought is the problem with a temple—too many worries. Maybe the whole idea was flawed. Maybe he should go on *thudong* again. What about all the people who had donated? He eyed the pile of wood, bricks and cement and his heart sank.

Then he heard a murmur of voices. He looked towards the narrow path from the village. A dozen men, chatting loudly, with bags on their shoulders and tools in their hands, were coming up the path. A half dozen children ran ahead and burst into the clearing. Som could feel a smile of relief and welcome spread across his face.

8

PLOI
Deception

Ploi pulled the heavy silk wrap away from her chest as the little boat fought against the current to cross the river. She had pulled it too tight in her haste. She needed to get home soon or Prem would have questions. She had paid for the steamboat from Nakhon instead of the cheaper sailboat to give her some time in the little house behind the police station. It was her reward for all her hard work. An afternoon of excitement and danger. She tugged at the silk again. Her breasts were still warm and her nipples still sore. These were not the only parts of her that were sore. She smiled and shook her head at the memory of the past two hours.

As usual, Dam had been playfully rough with her. As usual, she had teased him. He was getting soft and old, she told him. She would have to find a more vigorous lover. She loved the fire her teasing could ignite and the heat he exploded inside her. That fire was much like their first time, now nearly six months ago.

The opportunities to meet him during the periods it was safe for her to have sex were rare, but even more exciting for that. Dam was powerful and rough, but he made no demands. He seemed to enjoy her taking control, pushing him back on the mat and riding him. She liked looking down on his face dark with concentration and desire and then see him lose control as he climaxed. The ability to tease and entice this large man stirred something deep within her. This was power. The precautions to keep their secret occupied much of her thought. She had to fool everyone and she was doing it. There was a strange pleasure in the planning and anticipation of their trysts.

Their love-making had an urgency and a power that had been missing in her nights with Prem. He was still tender, but their fun together on the sleeping mat had to be snatched between the time the children fell asleep and they themselves fell into slumber, exhausted by work at the restaurant and the casino. Prem always sought to be in command and it irritated her. Besides she was not ready for another child. The three were already too much. She tried to keep track of her monthly bleeding and to time the love-making for the days the midwife said would be safest. Other nights she had to satisfy Prem with her mouth or her hands.

Despite all the new buildings and the new people attracted by the town's rapid growth, Pakpanang was still a small town. There were eyes watching all the time. People didn't have enough to do, so they minded everyone else's business. The last time she had spent an hour with Dam had been a near disaster. Prem asked her why it had taken her so long to get home from the boat pier. One of the market ladies bringing fish to the restaurant had told him she had gotten off the boat an hour earlier and would be home soon. Taken by surprise, she had to make up a story about going to the temple to light a candle in thanks for a successful journey.

Prem had looked puzzled.

"But you have never done that before. Why now? Are you nervous about the sea voyage? Maybe I should go with you next time. Don't forget I am an experienced sailor."

Today she had prepared a tale of wandering through the market to find material for a new dress. She clutched the bolt of silk that would back up her story. Truly, it would be better if she didn't go to Dam anymore. She was crazy to risk her family for a man she didn't love, not really. But he made her feel emotions she never felt with Prem. Excitement, yes, but more than that. Dam made her feel like she was the only thing that mattered in the world. He was a powerful force, focused only on her. With him, she always felt in control.

Prem still loved her, she was sure, but now she had to share his love with the children. He spent more time with Awt and Phai than he did with her. He had taught them not only to read and write, but also to do arithmetic, using problems from the restaurant. Even with her, Prem talked only about the restaurant or the children. He didn't seem to notice that she was restless. He had become boring. It wasn't his talk about the children that bored her, but that he said little that she couldn't see for herself. She wanted the best for the children and she could see how good he was with them. She was glad he had trained Awt to take orders from customers. Phai liked to sit at the entrance and greet each of the customers as they entered, bowing and *waiing* to each. Repeat customers she greeted by name, endearing her to all.

Someday Awt, An and Phai would help her run it. No, it was better if at least one of her sons went into the police. Dam couldn't protect the casino forever. A policeman in the family would be perfect. The children would have to understand the casino might be illegal, but it was hurting no one.

The customers came because they wanted to, because they enjoyed it, because it brought some excitement into lives dulled by work in the mines, by the meaningless procedures of government offices, by waiting for customers in the market, by the boredom of working on a ship. Gambling, along with the music and the comradeship of shared risk, added something to their lives—or else they wouldn't come. Her children would have to see the casino was good for community. Once they were old enough, she would bring them upstairs to hear the laughter of the winners and see the excited looks of the gamblers as the final cowries were removed from the bowl.

But they might not see things her way. Prem had begun taking them once or twice a week to the new temple and meditation center at Talumpuk. What they learned there might not be good for the casino—all that monk stuff had little to do with the real world.

"They need moral education too," Prem had explained, ignoring her protests that the children were too young to understand Som's complicated explanations of the dharma. At least Som was not the usual monk preaching the rote memorization of rules.

It was just a waste of their time—like Mother had wasted her time by dragging her to the temple to sit painfully still as an old monk droned on and on. At least Som was more amusing. The one time she had accompanied them had not been too boring. He had kept even Awt entranced with his tale of an encounter with an elephant. But when he started to explain the meaning of the tale, Awt got bored. Little Phai, though, seemed to understand and tried to meditate herself. She folded her little feet behind her and closed her eyes, imitating her uncle.

Awt, however, dashed off towards the beach as soon as the stories ended and the meditation began. He liked to spend time with the fishermen who pulled their boats up on the beach near the temple. Prem was patient with his son's persistent questions on tides, wind and fishing spots. The little boy enjoyed helping the fishermen weave their fish traps from bamboo.

"He likes to do things, not to meditate," Prem told her. "He is already begging to go out with the men at night to catch squid."

"That is never going to happen," she had responded. She could still feel the warm, strong pull of the water on her legs during the storm. Sometimes she would dream of it. The river was a dark monster, clutching at her with soft, but powerful fingers, trying to drag her out to sea, pulling her down. She struggled to climb the slippery bank. Just when she was escaping the current, Elder Brother Chit appeared before her and pushed her back into the river. The water closed over her; she couldn't breathe. She would awake gasping for breath.

No, Awt and all her children must stay safe on land. They would help her run and expand the family business. That was now the meaning of life, something she had lost in the weeks after Father's death. A dark emptiness had swept over her. She had had no interest in Prem, the casino, or even her children. There had been no gaming in the upstairs room for four months. It was only after Paen's funeral, Jate's death and Dam's hearing that she had begun to feel like entertaining the gamblers again.

There had been some anxious moments when Dam came to her one night to report that Jate's teen-age son Ong was trying to get Nit and the men to make another raid on the Jaikla Casino, insisting he should take over leadership of the gang from his father.

"Dam, there is a saying: 'When cutting down rattans don't leave the sprouts; when killing the father, don't spare the offspring.' I will not live my life in fear."

That fear had faded a few weeks later with Dam's report the boy had nearly died in a boating incident. Dam had suppressed a grin as he explained that Ong had been knocked from a boat coming into the dock at night. His old friend Nit, the only one with him, had pushed the boy down and held him under water. When he let him up for air, he asked "Who will lead the gang?" It took a few dunkings before the boy spluttered "Uncle Nit."

"Ong isn't very bright, but eventually he got the idea. Let Nit run things or die," Dam said. "The next week, the boy persuaded his mother to send him to school in Penang."

"So we don't need to worry about him?"

"Not as long as Nit is there."

After that, the future of Jaikla gambling was clear. All her work was for the children. They gave meaning to the money clattering into the receipt box. Whenever she counted the monthly take, she put aside the usual portion for casino operations, a portion for the household expenses, an allowance for Prem, the agreed percentage for Sia Leng and payment for Dam. But now, before calculating any of the other payments, she took out a couple of gold coins for the strongbox she had hidden in the back wall of the house. Once those coins would have been for Father. Now they were for the children.

She was startled out of her thoughts when the boat bumped on the pier below the restaurant. She looked up the steps. Prem was waiting at the top. He must have seen her as the boat crossed the river. Would he question her again? Didn't matter. She would give him the story and he would have to be satisfied. Good thing he was so eager to please her.

"Ploi, my love, why are you so late?" Prem called to her as he came down the steps to greet her. "I heard the Songkhla boat came in hours ago."

"I took some time to go to the cloth market, but it was hard to find something I liked." She held up the bolt of cloth. "But see, I found some silk for a new dress. I'll try it out on you first."

"You want me to wear your dress?" he asked with a grin.

"No, silly. I'll wear it for you to see, before anyone else."

"Why did it take you two hours to find a bit of silk? I missed you," he said, reaching down to help her up the stairs. His hands were warm and she saw him look down at the silk top that had slipped a bit. Maybe she had loosened her top too much. No, it was a good distraction.

"I can show you how the dress looks when I wear it," she said with a smile. "And then I can show you how I look when I take it off," she whispered into his ear.

He looked at her in surprise and smiled. He quickened the pace up the steps. It was good she could still get him excited. Most days she just didn't feel the urgency he still seemed to feel.

It made things worse on those days when he tried to act like the boss and grabbed at her.

"Come, we have an hour before the casino opens. See me upstairs," she said.

9

PREM
Family Time

A shrill scream sounded from the central platform, followed by a stream of angry complaints. Prem looked up and sighed. Awt and Phai were at it again. He knew his daughter worshipped her elder brother, but was often outraged when he contrived some mischief against her. If he ignored her, she would plead for his attention. She was happier with his pranks than his absence.

He re-tied his *phakaoma* as he rose and went to the door. He was already sweating from the humidity that made the first weeks of the rainy season so unpleasant. He looked up at the dark clouds beyond the rice fields behind the house. The rain would soon cool things off.

"What is it now, Phai?"

"He stole my book and tore out some pages to make paper animals," she said, pointing at her brother. "He is a thief. A destroyer of books."

Awt laughed. "Books are not for girls, anyway. I just made good use of the paper that was wasted on her," he said.

"Awt, you know that is not true. Girls can learn. Look at your mother—she can read and write and handle all the calculations for our business. Now you apologize to your sister. If you play nicely together, I will let you have some of those big durians."

Now tall for his eight years, Awt hesitated for a moment. His scorn for his sister's complaints was competing with his desire for the rich durians brought in that morning from the market.

"Well, for durians, I suppose I apologize for making that silly book into something useful."

"Awt," he warned.

"Alright, Father, I apologize to my silly little sister... sorry, to my so intelligent, educated, wonderful sister for tearing out a few pages from her important book," he said with a grin and a deep exaggerated *wai*.

"I'll go get the durians."

Awt dashed across the platform towards the kitchen.

The boy was getting harder and harder to control. He often went missing most of the day, running with his gang of friends from the village. They hunted for frogs in the forest or cast their nets for shrimp in the river. Awt's constant pleading had led him to buy a little boat for the boy. That had upset Ploi who thought it was too dangerous for him to be out on the river by himself. He had argued that the boy was a strong swimmer and a good paddler.

"Besides," he had said. "If we don't get him a decent boat, he will just go out with his friends on their old, leaky one. It will also give us something to take away when he misbehaves."

That was a telling argument for Ploi, who was often frustrated in her efforts to discipline her eldest son. Lately, when she smacked his backside for some infraction of her rules, he only laughed and ran off. Some days he did not return home until late at night.

Awt was a bad influence on Phai. She often tagged along after him even though Awt and his friends ignored her. Sometimes she would bribe them with sweets from the restaurant to be allowed to join their adventures. Normally she was quiet and studious—already better at her sums than her brother. She completed all her written work, surprising Prem with her ability to make clever rhymes about the family, the monks walking down the beach at Talumpuk or the animals that came into the family compound to nibble at the garden. She had a calmness about her that was impressive in one so young.

It was only Awt who could rouse her to noisy protest or long, detailed complaints about his latest outrage. Her little brother An was even quieter. At five, he had his mother's slim body, but not her bold spirit. He liked to follow his brother and sister, imitating whatever they did. An had begun coming to the teaching sessions he held each morning before he left for the restaurant. Like his brother and sister, he would take out a slate and chalk, scribbling on it in an effort to imitate his older siblings. He would have to start paying more attention to An now. He seemed a little lost since the birth of the latest child. An was used to being the baby of the family, getting lots of attention from his mother, his grandmother and his aunt. But now that attention was diverted to little Praphon, or On, born a month ago.

There had been a miscarriage that had sent Ploi into deep despondency. After that, Ploi had been much more reluctant in their love-making. She had insisted they take measures to avoid another pregnancy. He had resigned himself to the idea that An would be their last child, so it was a pleasant surprise when Ploi announced she was pregnant again. He had been puzzled at first. Perhaps he had failed to withdraw in time or they had mistimed the few times he had completed the act inside her. It didn't matter. It was wonderful to have another son, but he felt sorry for Phai who so wanted a little sister. The pregnancy had also meant a return to normal love-making.

"Well, I can't be more pregnant than I already am," Ploi had said. She became more attentive to Prem's needs and quick to praise his virility.

"Even when we try not to make a baby, we still get one," she told him. He had never understood why she didn't want more children, but he was grateful she had changed her mind.

He watched his children troop out of the kitchen. Awt carrying two of the spiny brownish-green durians. Behind him, Phai and An each carried one of the smelly fruits.

"Let me get a knife so I can open them for you," he said. "We'll have a durian feast. We'll see who can eat the most."

"I can," Awt announced, "because I am the biggest."

Prem ducked back into the sleeping room. Ploi lay on the mat, half asleep as On snuffled at her breast. He was dark for a child who had yet to be exposed to the sun. His brown face and curly hair contrasted with the smooth skin of his mother's breast. He was a large baby—bigger than the others—and active, demanding to be fed several times each night. Both of them were tired, especially since he had to take over from Ploi at the casino. That demanded late nights. When he returned home tired and ready for the sleeping mat, he faced Ploi's detailed questions about the casino. How many customers? Who were they? How much was bet? Any big winners? What was the profit? She was relentless, even though they were both exhausted. She worried that income was down during her absence. Despite his objections, she had announced she would return to the casino next week. He would arrange for the baby's cradle to be set up in a corner of the dining room so she could come down and feed him.

He drew his knife from its wooden sheath and re-emerged onto the central platform where the three children sat cross-legged in front of the pile of durian.

"Alright, whoever has finished their sums for today gets the first one," he said as he cut into the tough rind of the durian. He chuckled at Awt's scowl and pried out a large yellow segment of durian. It felt heavy and soft in his fingers as he handed it to Phai, who smiled triumphantly at her brother.

"I'm next," Awt said.

"But you haven't finished your sums," Prem said.

"I have done some of them and An hasn't done any."

"He doesn't have any to do. He is too little."

"Doesn't matter. I'm next. Right An?"

An nodded.

He shrugged and handed the next piece of fruit to his oldest son while An waited patiently.

How could they all be so different and all come from the same parents?

The sweet, earthy smell of durian hung in the humid air. He looked up as Ploi carried the sleeping On out onto the platform. She sat down with her children. She was so beautiful. Her eyes were large and soft in the pale morning light sifting through the clouds. The light cloth thrown over her shoulders hid only one of her breasts swollen with milk.

"Any left for me?" she asked.

He fumbled with another durian, hardly feeling the spines pressing into his hands.

"Of course. Anything for the love of my life and the mother of my children," he said with a broad smile. He thumped the durian to see if it was ripe. Twirling his big knife with a flourish, he cut it open and handed her a fat segment tapered on each end. She smiled at him and bit into it. The baby on her lap sought her breast and settled with a sigh to feed.

He leaned back against the wooden walls of the house. He watched as his wife and children enjoyed the creamy fruit. Phai nibbled delicately. An struggled to fit a big section into his mouth. Little specks of yellow spotted Awt's cheeks as he looked up for more. Ploi smiled down at the baby who was sucking at her breast while lifting one chubby foot into the air.

Was there anything better than this?

10

DAM
Bravery

Dam peered through the predawn mist sifting down the mountain. No one was stirring in the cluster of buildings below. He could see the dark shapes of at least a dozen water buffalo in a corral. Seven or eight thatched huts clustered along a rocky stream below a large teak house on thick wooden pillars. That must be the house of *Sua* Thuam—Tiger Thuam, the big *nakleng* of the mountains west of Nakhon. The orders were to arrest Thuam and bring back stolen cattle and money.

It wouldn't be easy. First, he and his men would have to climb down the hillside thick with tangles of vines and stickers. Then they would have to smash through the heavy door at the top of the ladder leading to the house. By then Thuam would be alerted and there might be a fight. They had to move fast and get into the house while the bad guys were still sleepy and confused.

How did I get assigned to this action so far from Pakpanang? In the briefing the night before, the captain told him Thuam had long been a problem for the authorities in Nakhon. He was renowned as a cattle thief and *nakleng*, but the district officer had found it difficult to take action against him. Thuam had the respect of the local villagers because he kept order in the surrounding seven or eight villages. Three years earlier Thuam and his men slaughtered a band of brigands from Trang who had dared to rob one of his villages. Thuam had personally led the attack, killing the head bandit with a slash of his short sword. Since then he became known as Tiger Thuam, becoming more and more arrogant in his defiance of the police.

He might be brutal, but he wasn't stupid. The clever fucker shared his wealth, giving poor villagers some of the buffaloes stolen from the lowlands below. If the victim of one of his cattle raids came to him and paid the proper respect, along with a fee, Thuam would help find the "lost" cattle and return them. This activity would probably have been tolerated, but Thuam had branched out into more dangerous crimes—raiding cockfights, small gambling dens and bullfights to steal the betting money. Two weeks earlier, he had attacked a den in Sichon and killed three men who tried to stop him. The den was one of Nit's gambling operations and two of the men killed were from Nit's gang. The other was a local official.

When word of the murders reached the *monthon* headquarters in Songkhla, the deputy commissioner ordered tough action. The Nakhon police, however, had been reluctant to move. Tiger Thuam was reputed to have amulets making him invulnerable to bullets. The police kept finding excuses to delay taking action, insisting more men and arms were needed for an operation so far from the city.

Nit, furious at the death of his men, had appealed to Dam to do something, promising support from his gang. Dam had been reluctant, but then the provincial police commander decided that only a policeman with a tough reputation could stand up to the big *nakleng*. Sergeant Dam, he said, was the man.

Trapped by my own reputation—the man who killed Boss Jate. The guy who came through fights without losing a man. The Black Tiger. He was screwed. Since he had started sleeping with Ploi, he felt he was losing his magical protection. He consulted Ajaan Klai. The old monk was unsympathetic.

"You moron. I told you, you must live a good life to ensure the power of your magical protections. That means never sleeping with a married woman. You should give her up," Klai said.

He had tried, but he had to see Ploi almost every day at the restaurant or the casino. He tried to send one of his men to collect the payments, but Ploi refused to deal with anyone but him. Each time he saw her, he felt his face flush and his body tingle. He resolved to turn her away if she came to his house, but after long weeks between visits his resolve melted before her mischievous smile.

He tried to avoid dangerous duty, but his reputation as a fighter worked against him. Whenever the Pakpanang police chief had a tough job, he assigned it to Dam. On one assignment, against an opium den guarded by toughs, he had nearly vomited with fear. He had stood paralyzed as one of the toughs ran at him swinging a long, curved *khaek* sword. Fortunately, two shots from his men left the thug bleeding at his feet. His men thought he had stood his ground unafraid.

When he went back to Ajaan Klai, the old man told him the help of the Lord Buddha was needed to overcome Dam's sins and to protect him from harm. He said Dam had to make a large donation to cast a new bronze Buddha image and smaller images to act as talismans against injury. One of the new images was strung around his neck along with the thin tin tubes containing his *yantra*. He had also distributed the heavy little amulets to each of his men. Would they be powerful enough to overcome his sins?

With the first glimmers of sunrise over the trees, he swallowed hard. He had no choice. He signaled to his men and started the climb down towards the house. One group of men moved off to the right to set up an ambush between the big house and the huts along the stream. He could hear the whisper of the waterfall near the huts and low grunting of the buffalo. When they reached the steps up to the house, he waved the men carrying a battering ram forward. He looked up. The steep ladder meant that it was going to be difficult to swing the ram with any power. Maybe they should shoot at the door and call on Thuam to surrender. Was there another way up? If they didn't get in fast, it would be bad.

Then he heard the slap of bare feet on the floorboards above his head. There was a rattle and scrape of metal as the steel deadbolts were drawn back and the door swung open. This was it. He put the amulet in his mouth and drew his heavy Mannlicher pistol. He checked the six-shot magazine, took a deep breath and then swung onto the ladder, dashing up to the door as a bare-chested man in a rumpled *phakhaoma* stared at him in confusion. Dam smashed the butt of his gun into the man's chin and pushed his body back onto the main platform of the house. His men rumbled up the ladder behind him. He waved them to the rooms to the left and right and then moved forward with a group of men to the main room ahead of them. A man came out of one of the rooms rubbing his eyes. He shouted in surprise before one of his men chopped him with a rifle butt. There were more shouts from the room ahead. He ran to the door, but a volley of shots from the windows sent his men scrambling for cover.

Suddenly he was alone and he couldn't move. Panic tasted sour in the back of his throat. All Thuam and his men had to do was open the door and he would be dead. He pressed up against the wood of the door, trying to gather the courage to do something. The shutters on the windows on either side of the door creaked opened. Bullets whizzed past him and he hugged the door even closer. The sound of bullets was squeezing him into the door like he used to squeeze the water from raw rubber. He could see the dark snout of a pistol poking out of one window and waited for it to turn on him.

Why don't they just shoot me? Maybe they can't see me in the recess of the door. The gunman at the window must be focused on the shots coming from his men. The gunfire drew screams and curses from inside. His *yantra*, his tattoos and his amulet were protecting him, so far. He flinched as his men's bullets smashed into the walls, splintering the wood only a yard from his head. Oh, shit, his own men might shoot him by mistake.

After five minutes of gunfire, the shots from inside slowed and stopped. Maybe those inside were dead or out of ammunition. Good. Maybe they would surrender now. He leaned back against the door and held up his hand to get his men to cease fire.

"Thuam," he shouted. "You are under arrest for robbery and murder. No more of your people need to die. Come out and give yourself up," he shouted.

"I am Tiger Thuam," a voice called from inside the room. "You stupid motherfuckers can never arrest me. I will kill you all."

Dam motioned his men forward to crouch beside the windows. He was about to shout again when the door was yanked open from the inside. He stumbled into the body of a man who swung a big knife at his head. The steel sliced through his ear and clanged in a glancing blow against his skull. He drove forward and knocked the man over, landing heavily on top of him. A wave of dizziness swept over him and the man squirmed free. He pulled back and picked up the knife from the floor.

His chest and arms were covered in tattoos. Several strings of amulets swung from his neck. It was Tiger Thuam.

"Surrender," he said.

"No way," Thuam said as he started forward, lifting the knife above his shoulder.

Dam lifted his pistol and pulled the trigger. Nothing happened. What was wrong? Where were his men? Dam frantically checked the safety. The gun was not fully cocked.

"You can't kill me, no one can," the man laughed and took a step closer to Dam.

He thumbed down the cocking lever and brought the pistol up again as Thuam started to thrust the knife downward toward his face.

The blast snapped the gun back. The man stared at the small red hole in his stomach. The knife clattered to the floor. The man fell to his knees and then onto his side.

He had survived. His magic was stronger than Tiger Thuam's. He felt dizzy with relief. It was wonderful to be alive. He looked around the room as three of his men cautiously entered. Beyond Thuam's body, he could see a woman and a small child lying in pools of blood spreading slowly across the floor. His heart, soaring a moment ago, fell like a rock dropped off a cliff. Not a child.

11

NGWE LAY
Loneliness

Ngwe Lay missed the yellow-haired doll. She was so pretty. When she held her up in the sun, her hair shimmered and sparkled. What happened to her? Aya promised a new doll, but that was so long ago and she was still waiting. Now Aya was sick. She made funny sounds when she breathed, like dry coconut fronds in the wind.

For the first week of the illness, it had been fun to play nurse. She brought Aya a dish of rice gruel each morning. One of the farmer's wives came each day to do the cooking, empty the bedpan and wash clothes. She was no fun. Wouldn't play with her and hurried home.

So, she was the real nurse—like her mother. Grandma had come several times to teach her what she had to do for Aya. Already she knew how to make tea mixed with the milk the Indian vendor delivered each morning. She knew how to reheat the day's curry and rice and to stir-fry the morning glory from the garden. She brought a pot of the milk tea to Aya twice each day, in late morning and then again in the evening.

Normally the evening was the time Aya would read her stories or listen while she read from the Mon poetry Papa gave her. Boring. Why didn't Grandma come to live with them? Oh, because Granddad is sick too. There was no one to talk to. Aya fell asleep soon after drinking the tea. She would just have to get better soon. Sickness was boring.

Then Grandma got sick too. Now, they wouldn't even let her come to visit. The last time she came Grandma said she didn't want Ngwe Lay to catch the fever. She looked so sad and tired.

Papa would be home soon. But he had been away so long and she felt alone in the big house. She missed the sounds of her father's feet on the boards of the house, of the rocking of his chair when he had his evening drink. He didn't say much, but at least he was there.

This time he had been away too long. Why didn't he come back? Or write? All the other times he had left he had returned within a few weeks. On the longer trips he had sent letters she could read aloud to Aya. The letters told her of the difficult journeys through the mountains and the sights along the way. The Siamese cities sounded nice. Someday she would go to Siam. She would go with Papa and he would talk to her instead of writing.

If they traveled together, it wouldn't be like at home where nothing much happened. There would be lots to talk about. If they traveled together, Papa couldn't close the door to the study.

She looked around her on the veranda. She still had three other dolls, but they were old and not so pretty. Maybe Papa would bring her a new one when he came back. A bit of movement across the river caught her eye. It was a line of boys walking home from school. They skipped and pranced like the monkeys that sometimes came down from the hill into their garden. She could hear the sounds of their shouts, but couldn't make out the words.

Someday she would go to school, too. She was already nine years old. That was old enough. Lots of boys younger than her were going to school. Her father had promised her, but said she should wait until the Mon school was ready. She looked across the river where the dark pillars of the burned down school building peeked through a gauze of green vines. Papa said she was learning just as much at home, but she wanted to be with other children. Maybe this year Papa would come back with the money to rebuild the school. Money was the problem. Whenever the men came for the meetings, she could hear them talk about money for the school.

She watched as the boys chased each other up the path to the village. Why weren't there any girls going to school? Her mother had gone to school. She looked back into the main room where a row of pictures lined the big wooden chest against the back wall. Mother carrying books. Mother getting a sheet of paper from a foreign-looking man in funny-looking clothes. Mother with other women in their nurses' uniforms in front of the big hospital. Mother and Papa at their wedding.

She wanted to know more about those pictures, but Papa was always so gruff when she asked. At best she would get a few words from him. Aya said Mother had been an educated woman, a nurse who, everyone said, might have become Burma's first female doctor. Ngwe Lay loved it when one of the nurses, especially the fat one, Ma H'La Yin, would tell her stories about her mother—how she had stood up to an old doctor, how she had chosen Papa instead of a British doctor, how she had cured a disease or saved a child.

Someday she would go to school to be like her mother.

No one would tell her exactly how her mother died, but she suspected she was to blame. Nobody told her, but she figured it out all by herself. Mother died the same year she was born—the same month even. Had bringing her into the world been too hard for her? She heard the nurse say having a baby was a painful and dangerous business. Other women had survived it—why not her mother? Was there something about Ngwe Lay that had been too difficult for her? The way her father looked away from her when she asked about her mother made her feel she had done something wrong. Somehow, she would have to make it up to Papa. He had been away so long. Maybe he didn't want to come home. He always looked so sad and angry. He took away her doll. Maybe he didn't want her either.

Ngwe Lay wanted to curl up next to Aya and have her stroke her hair and tell her she was a good girl. But Aya was sick. Her breathing was noisy again. She should do something, but she didn't know what.

Now she just wished Aya would get better and Papa would get home. And bring her a new doll.

12

DAM
Dominance

Dam looked out the window again, squinting into the setting sun. He looked up and down the busy street below. He saw coolies sweating under bags of rice, Chinese merchants chatting loudly, venders selling steamed buns from large baskets, a pair of Thai women in *phajonggraben* giggling at a man in a police uniform, but no Ploi.

They had sailed down the coast on the same ship, but she had forbidden him to talk to her. She looked so lovely with the breeze rippling her dress on the deck and pulling it tight against her so he could see the long curves of her legs. He ached to talk to her, touch her arm. But the one time they passed each other along the rail, she looked through him as if he wasn't there.

He had followed her instructions just the way she said. He had stayed on the ship and watched her climb into a rickshaw at the dock, waited for 10 minutes, then walked to the address she had given him in the Chinese Kao Hong district, Nang Ngam road. A good name— "beautiful woman" road. But there were too many people. Too many Chinese. Too much noise. The town felt squeezed between the sea on one side and the lake on the other. He had gotten lost twice, but he wasn't supposed to talk to anyone.

Finally, he had found it. It was a large two-story house with a roof of Chinese clay tiles. The bottom floor was plastered brick with a second story of wood. He had walked through a narrow lane to the rear of the house and entered through the unlocked door. He made sure no one saw him.

He had climbed up the narrow stairway to the bedroom and waited and waited. It had already been hours. It would soon be dark. She had told him she would be busy going over the accounts with her Chinese business partner, that fat Chink, Sia Leng. Then there was supposed to be a meeting with the deputy high commissioner, what was his name? How could two meetings take so long? It wasn't right that he had to wait. He had already waited so long to be alone with her. She was always too busy or it was the wrong time of the month. Or fucking Prem was around. Damn it. He was the Black Tiger, feared by even the toughest *nakleng*. Her business depended on his protection. He was the man, so she should do whatever he wanted whenever he wanted it. He would throw her down and fuck her hard until she cried out. She would beg for mercy, scream with pleasure. Today, he would dominate. Tell her how to pleasure him. She would do whatever he wanted.

The sound of the front door scraping open. The lilt of a woman's voice. Her voice! Finally. He stood up, straightened his shirt and opened the door. He stopped himself from rushing down the stairs. Shouldn't seem too eager. Anyway, she had said to wait in the bedroom. He heard the rattle of rickshaw wheels, the creak of the door and then the soft sound of her feet on the stairway.

Her face shone like a candle in the gloom of the house.

"Good. You found it," she said as she reached the top of the stairs. "I hope it wasn't too much trouble."

"It was a long hot walk in this crowded town, but it's worth it to see you," he said, feeling the heat building inside him. "It has been nearly a month. We have so few chances in Pakpanang, but now we have time to be together the rest of the day and all night. Time together."

"Not so much, actually," she said. "There is a *Khon* performance and dinner tonight hosted by the deputy high commissioner. I really must go."

"Can't you skip the dinner? I have taken my last days of leave and traveled all the way here just for you."

He hated the whining sound of his voice, but maybe she would change her mind. Wasn't he more important than some stupid official?

"It's business," she said. "I've already accepted. We have an hour."

"Damn it. I have been waiting for you for many hours."

"I can leave now, if you want."

What had he done wrong? She treated him like shit. Her business was always more important. Or her family or her clueless husband. He should just tell her to go. Show that he didn't care that much, didn't need her. He should, but...

"No, stay with me, please."

"Then take off your clothes," she said, pushing him back on the bed. "We should make the most of the time we have."

He fumbled with the buttons on his shirt and pulled off his trousers, leaving them puddled around his ankles. He felt limp and small. What was wrong? He looked down. Nothing was happening. His dreams of what he would do to her weren't like this. She looked at him with a raised eyebrow. Embarrassing. But then she smiled and began unbuttoning the front of her dress. She slowly swayed from side to side. She was so beautiful.

He stared as her long fingers undid a button, paused, then undid another button, widening the opening in her dress. He couldn't move. The skin of her stomach was so smooth. The soft material fell to each side exposing the sides of her breasts. It caught on her nipples. Why wasn't he responding? He looked down. Shit. She cocked her head to one side.

"What happened to my big black tiger?" she said as she traced the tattoo on his chest. "Maybe you need some more encouragement."

She shrugged her shoulders and the dress dropped to her waist. She caressed her breasts, pressed them together, rubbed her thumbs over her nipples. He sat up and reached for her. She slapped his hand away.

"Patience. You are not ready for me yet."

She slowly swiveled her hips and the dress slipped to her feet. He leaned forward but she pushed him hard with both hands and he fell back onto the bed.

"You are weak today. I can push you around like a little boy and that's what you look like down there—a little boy."

She knelt on the bed, straddling him. She reached down with one hand and stroked him.

"Still not ready," she laughed. "I might as well go to that dinner now."

She started to get up. Why did she humiliate him like this? He could feel the heat building within him. He grabbed her wrists and pulled her onto his chest. He wanted to hurt her the way she was hurting him.

"Hmm, the hands are strong and the chest is hard, but it's not your chest or hands I want."

He threw her to one side and twisted on top of her. He pinned her wrists against the satin-covered mattress. The pulse in her neck throbbed inches from his lips. Her eyes stared up into his. She was smiling at him. Mocking? He glared back at her. What the hell?

"Oh, the big man is angry now, but the little man is still asleep."

She tried to sit up, but he slammed her back down.

He could feel her exhale beneath him. He nipped at her neck. He bent his head and found a breast. He sucked on it like a hungry baby. He could feel himself growing hard, finally. She reached down and pulled his cock between them. He could feel the soft curls covering her sex. He tried to shift to enter her, but she twisted to one side.

"No. Not this way. I want you underneath me."

"But..."

"Now, on your back."

He turned and lay back. He could feel her hands and then the wet touch of her tongue swirling around him. Then she straddled him again, positioned him with warm hands. She slowly sank down and enveloped him.

She leaned back with a smile on her face. She looked like someone holding the winning lottery ticket.

13

SAIFAN
Uprising

Saifan turned to look at the Yaha district police station. The cement and wood building sat on the other side of the canal, now filled by the final storms of the rainy season. A small wooden bridge crossed the canal. The plan was to cross the bridge with a half-dozen cattle surrounding the cart carrying the weapons To'Tae had distributed the night before. That would allow them to take positions in the rubber grove on two sides of the police station. Then they would start shooting.

He had never fired the heavy rifle. They just pushed it into his hands when he joined the others at the house of the former headman of the little town. He had watched in the dim light of a kerosene lamp as a former member of the Raja's guard, a man he knew only as Ghazi, demonstrated how to load and fire each of the guns. It looked simple. Pull up the bolt, then slide it back to open a slot for the heavy little cartridge. But then it got confusing. There were several types and each one worked a little differently. There were a dozen old British Indian army rifles, a pile of shotguns, several musketoons, two different kinds of German rifles and three Enfields. Saifan was proud he was selected to get one of the newer German rifles. But the bullets were smaller.

"Wouldn't a bigger bullet be better?" he asked.

Ghazi just laughed. "Load the right cartridge for your weapon, aim it carefully and it will work fine. Just don't put the wrong one in the chamber. It could jam or blow up in your face."

Saifan felt the cartridges in the bag pulling on his shoulder. He was sure he had taken only the right kind. He should double check, but there was no time. They were already crossing the canal.

The decision to attack was exciting, but after waiting for so many months, everything was happening too fast. No time to practice with their weapons. No time to understand battle tactics. The plan of attack was sketched on a map drawn on a piece of brown wrapping paper. He didn't understand why they were attacking Yaha, well to the south of

Pattani city. He tried to ask, but To'Tae told him to just do his job.

"I have received divine inspiration for this attack. Allah is the only planner we need," To'Tae told the group the night before.

"Tomorrow we attack here," he said. "It is south of Pattani, where they won't expect it. This attack will certainly succeed. I have seen it—a vision of the district office on fire and the Siamese policemen dropping their guns and surrendering. After a night of prayer and fasting, the vision came to me—our people capturing the police station, seizing stacks of weapons for bigger and bigger attacks. We will achieve a victory that will be cheered throughout the sultanate."

The Sufi sheikh, his turban glinting in the dim light, gestured to his assistant who moved around the room, handing each man a small bronze talisman with a golden cord. There was a quiet murmur as the men slipped the cords over their heads.

"Do not fear. Your faith in Allah and this sign of his protection will deflect all bullets and prevent harm to you in any form," To'Tae said. "No infidel bullet can touch you."

Saifan tried to keep from showing his doubts. These bits of bronze wouldn't stop bullets, but he could see the Sufi sheikh's words had lifted the spirits of the men anxious about the coming battle. A true Muslim should not need such mystical beliefs, only belief in God. The main thing was to strike back at the Siamese. The rallies against paying taxes had received good support, but they were just talk. Now there would be real action. Looking at the group of untrained men and their motley weapons, he wasn't so sure about taking up arms. To'Tae told the group this was the time to strike because the Siamese king was ill, weakening the spirit of the police.

"Our actions tomorrow will punish the oppressor. Allah's far greater punishment will soon follow. The infidel king will learn the wrath of Allah is terrible. It is inevitable. So too are the rewards in paradise for those who stand up against the infidels attacking Islam."

Saifan pushed aside his doubts. A strange excitement welled up within him. His legs shook with energy. At least the long years of submitting to abuse were over. The insults of Siamese laws and rules, the unfair struggle to compete with the privileged Thais and Chinese in the market, his humiliation at the police station in Pakpanang, the death of Abdul—all these would be avenged.

It had been difficult to sleep, lying on the floor of the house, bothered by strange men turning and snoring on either side of him. Would he fail in the battle? Would he be brave once the shooting started?

He didn't see To'Tae anywhere. Why wasn't he leading them? Where was that Qadi judge? The plan was for the group of more than 50 men to surround the police station soon after dawn. There should be only a handful of police there. They were supposed to shoot at the police station. While the police were distracted, a small group would set fire to the district office. Then all would shoot their weapons at the station until the policemen surrendered. They would tie them up, seize all their guns and post a proclamation with a list of demands on the station door. He had been selected to write up the demands in both Thai and *Jawi* and to carry the thick paper in his shoulder bag along with the extra ammunition.

At a signal from Ghazi, the group crossed the bridge, keeping the placid cattle between them and the station. Hamidy walked by his side. He had been surprised and pleased his friend had arrived at the last minute to join them. They had argued many times about the need for action against the Siamese.

"You should think of your family. Your first responsibility is to them. Your father is old. Your son is young. You are their main support. Don't risk it," Hamidy argued.

He had tried to explain it was for his family that he was ready to risk his life. "My father does not want to live under the thumb of the infidels. I don't want my son to be a slave to them and I must avenge the death of my brother. No, it is because of my family I must do this."

Hamidy had seemed unhappy with the answer, but when Saifan had awakened this morning, Hamidy had been waiting at the doorway, ready to go with him. It felt good to have a friend with him. Now there was no turning back for either of them.

After walking past the path to the police station, one group split off and headed down the road to the district office. Saifan's group filtered into the rubber grove behind the rough wooden fence around the station. Ghazi motioned to them to lie down and crawl up to the fence. There was no one outside the station. It had a first story of concrete with small barred windows. The second story was made of clapboards topped by a sloping roof.

According to Ghazi there would be less than a dozen policemen there. This shouldn't be too difficult. But crawling through the undergrowth with the heavy rifle and the bag of bullets was not so easy. The scrub bushes between the lines of rubber trees pulled at his clothes. He felt sweat dripping down his neck even though the morning was still cool. He had still not reached the fence when he heard the first crack of a shot. Had they been seen? No, it was someone shooting too soon. Another shot followed and then a few more in a ragged volley that sounded more like Chinese New Year fire crackers than a disciplined attack.

There was a flurry of movement in the police station and the black barrel of a rifle poked out of one of the barred windows. It looked like it was pointed straight at him. More gun barrels appeared from behind the piles of lumber in the police station yard. How did they get there so soon? There were more shots coming from the police station. He heard the buzz of what must have been a bullet ripping through the undergrowth next to him. A hand pushed his face down into the muddy ground and he felt Hamidy's body beside him.

"Keep your head down," Hamidy yelled.

There were more shots and a shout from Ghazi—"God is Great"— and echoing shouts from the other attackers. He spat the mud from his mouth and shouted with them. Then he remembered he was supposed to be shooting his rifle. He leaned on one elbow and pushed the bolt forward until it clicked. He tried to line up the sight with the barred window. He pulled the trigger and felt the gun slam into his shoulder. He saw a puff of cement dust two arms lengths from the window. Pulled too hard. He was supposed to pull it slowly. He fumbled for another cartridge and then pulled back the bolt and a shell casing popped up, almost hitting him in the face. Beside him, Hamidy looked like he was trying to burrow into the ground, his rifle held out in front of him as a pathetically small barrier against the gunfire.

Another bullet ripped through the bush next to him and he could not help pushing his face back into the wet ground. More gunshots crackled through the trees. He looked up and saw a haze of smoke hovering over the piles of logs near the station. There must be a lot of guns there. He slipped another bullet into the rifle chamber and pushed the bolt closed. Another bullet buzzed past his head. Could they see him? Beside him Hamidy was pulling a branch down in front of them—to hide them from the policemen? But it made it hard to sight his own rifle. He pushed the branch down trying to focus on the logs.

Behind the police station he could see a group of men hurrying across the canal and kneeling behind a line of heavy clay water jars next to the station. More shots were coming from them. Where should he shoot? He could see a policeman fumbling with his weapon beside one of the water jars. He aimed his weapon again, this time trying to pull the trigger more slowly. He braced for the kick of the heavy wooden stock. He saw the policeman stand up to run. Without thinking his finger tightened on the trigger and the rifle kicked against his shoulder. The policeman slipped to the ground. Was he dead? Had he killed someone? A ragged cheer rose from the line of attackers.

Splinters flew from the wooden walls of the second floor. There were more cries of "God is Great". But their shots didn't seem to be having any effect on the police. More and more gunfire was cutting into the rubber trees. There was a scream of pain to Saifan's left and he saw one of his group stand up with blood running down his face. Then he was snatched backward and thrown to the ground. Was he hit again? The fire from the police was growing. Off to his right there was a groan and then another scream of pain. Some of that fire was coming from the bridge they had crossed only a short while ago. How did the police get over there? With bullets coming from two directions it was hard to know where to hide. There was another scream along the line of attackers to his left where they were most exposed to fire from the bridge. He loaded and fired again, but couldn't tell where his bullet went. He saw several of the attackers on his left crawling backward and turning to face the fire from the bridge. Ghazi was shouting something in the Pattani dialect that Saifan couldn't quite understand.

"Outflanked… retreat," he thought he heard. He felt Hamidy pulling at his loose shirt. Were they supposed to move? Hamidy was crawling backward and to the right, heading deeper into the trees. Behind them there was the sound of horses and more gunfire. Were there soldiers coming up the road? A bullet smacked into the rubber tree next to Saifan's head and his eyes stung. He couldn't see anything. He touched his cheek and felt a thick liquid. He must be bleeding. He was shot, but his fingers could not find a wound.

"I'm hit. I can't see."

Hamidy pulled at him again and they crawled away from the fence. He still couldn't see. He felt the liquid slide into the corner of his mouth. It had an earthy bitter taste. It wasn't blood. He almost laughed in relief. It was rubber sap. One of those little coconut shell cups of latex must have been hit by a bullet and splattered into his eyes. He picked a sliver of coconut shell from his forehead.

"It's not a bullet wound," he shouted in relief. He stood up to wipe his eyes with his shirt sleeve. "I can see."

Something slammed into his shoulder and spun him around. He lay on the ground stunned. It was like that time when he was only six years old and the big billy goat butted him, knocking him to the ground and leaving him gasping for breath. Mother had run out to him and held him in her arms until he could breathe again. He longed for her soothing voice telling him he would soon feel better.

Instead it was Hamidy's raspy voice yelling at him to keep moving. He felt his friend pulling on his good arm and he turned to crawl behind him. He felt a searing pain in his left arm. He felt a sudden desperate need to run and energy flooded through him. He ran in a crouch through the trees, trying to stay close to Hamidy. They scrambled through one row of trees after another. He tripped and rolled into a soggy depression filled with weeds. He lay panting for a moment. Hamidy pulled him to his feet. He started to head back towards the bridge.

"No, not that way," Hamidy hissed and pulled him in the opposite direction. The two ran, hunched over, along a little stream for what seemed like miles. He clutched his aching arm. It still burned, but there was surprisingly little blood. The sounds of gunfire faded behind them. He was exhausted and out of breath. Where was his rifle? He must have dropped it. Hamidy didn't have his weapon either. How would he explain this to Ghazi or To'Tae? Where were the others? He could no longer hear gunshots or shouts. The only sound he could hear was the high-pitched drone of cicadas.

"The attack has failed," Hamidy said. "We must get away."

"What about the others? Shouldn't we try to find them?"

"Who knows where they are. There was no planning for retreat. Leave your ammunition and that stupid proclamation behind. If the police catch you with it, they will kill you."

"We can't do that. What will To'Tae say?"

"Do you want to die for To'Tae? Where was he today anyway?"

"Then we must bury the papers and the bullets somewhere we can come back for them later."

Hamidy sighed. "Then do it quickly."

They walked on for at least two more miles, coming to the end of the rubber trees and a dirt road. They headed east on the road until they came to another road that Hamidy said led towards Krue Se to the north. A pile of rocks covered with vines could be seen through the trees to one side. Hamidy rolled over three of the rocks and scraped out a shallow trench in the soft black earth. Using one hand Saifan put the two bags of ammunition in the hole and placed the proclamation on top of them. Hamidy rolled the rocks back over it.

"We can remember this place – the rocks by the crossroad – and come back for this later."

"Yeah sure, but we must get to the coast."

They walked all day. The burning in his shoulder had turned into a deep ache. Hamidy rolled up the sleeve of his shirt and wiped the dirt out of the wound.

"It's not so bad. The bullet went straight through, I think."

He tore a piece of cloth from his own shirt and bound the wound tightly and then pulled the shirtsleeve down over it. They met several others along the road and nodded in an attempt at a friendly greeting. For a few baht they were allowed to clamber onto a bullock cart of paddy trundling east. When they heard the roar of a motor coming up the road, they peered over the sides of the cart as two truckloads of soldiers passed them heading west. It was long after dark before they crossed a dirt road onto the beach. It was deserted, but several fishing boats were moored offshore and five more were lined up on the beach.

The soft sand felt good. He had to sleep. What had happened to the attack? It was all confused. He could still see the body of the policeman he shot lying motionless on the ground. Did he die? Who was that man? Did he have a family? Saifan could be a murderer. A violator of the Holy Koran's command against killing. But he was fighting against the oppressor. His arm ached. He might have died too. If others were captured, they might name him. He would go to prison like his brother. Or would they just kill him? The police would treat him as a killer and a traitor. What would happen to his family in Krue Se?

"Saifan, wake up."

He opened his eyes to the gray of dawn. The sun was just starting to brighten the sky over the sea. Hamidy stood next to a young man.

"We have a boat. We must leave now."

14

PAKDEE
Reign's End

The *monthon* office felt dark and cool. A rainstorm at the end of the wet season had left puddles of water in the courtyard. Water still dripped from the roof. The heavy clouds made the late morning feel like early dusk. Pakdee looked at the documents on his desk, but didn't have the energy to deal with them. Everything had changed. Nothing made sense anymore. The king was dead. The Fifth Reign was over.

The news had come the previous day. He had known the king had health problems, but how could he die so soon? Only 54 years old. Too young. The last time he had seen him, the king was still energetic and dedicated. It was hard to believe. He picked up the telegram that had arrived only five days earlier.

"His Majesty has improved in all respects," it said. Next to it was the telegram that had arrived three days later carrying the news the king had died and 30-year-old Crown Prince Vajiravudh had succeeded to the throne. What would happen now?

It was only two years ago he had joined the royal entourage on a visit to three of the Malay states. King Chulalongkorn met with British and Malay officials, advancing the negotiations for the long-delayed treaty. The king had been pleasant, reasonable and well-informed. He had charmed the British with his modesty and his fluent English. Some days he had seemed tired, but he always kept to his schedule, staying up late to write notes in his diary or draft long, fact-filled letters to his children. His Majesty had seemed to draw energy from the painstaking progress made in reducing the threat from the British. Now he was gone. What would happen to Siam?

The transformation the king had led was still incomplete, but it was far more secure now than when the king had come to the throne so long ago. Prince Damrong would ensure the reform process continued, but would he have the support of the new king?

Would Pakdee himself be able to win support from the crown prince, the new king? What would happen to him? King Chulalongkorn had nullified his conviction, had appointed him to his high position and had treated him fairly. He would always remember their discussions during their travels together. The king had been friendly and open to his ideas. Together with Phraya Sukhumnaiwinit and Prince Damrong, the king had given him guidance and protection.

Sukhumnaiwinit, now named Chaophraya Yommarat, was a member of the cabinet in charge of construction and the capital. He had often talked about his days in England. The crown prince had been one of his pupils. It was the crown prince who had given Sukhumnaiwinit his first title as royal preceptor. Sukhum had proudly showed him the gold tablet signifying his rank.

His old mentor must still be close to the new king. That would be good for him. He would protect him. There would be chances for advancement. There would be changes in the government. The current commissioner, never comfortable in the south, would seek to return to the capital. The new king would have to appoint a replacement. Who could be better than the deputy commissioner? He had already been acting commissioner. He had served long and faithfully. He had the trust of the minister. Yes, he would finally be *monthon* commissioner, at the top of all the layers of officials that stretched from Songkhla to Pattani in the south, to Surat Thani in the north and Phuket in the west. No longer would anyone question his family background or giggle at his misuse of a royal word. He would be in power. He would be safe.

He shuffled through the pile of documents before him. More details on the attack at Yaha. No mention of Saifan among the dead or captured. Maybe Hamidy had convinced him to stay home or maybe he had escaped. The action would be proclaimed as a victory for the government, but really it was a sign of failure. Despite all his efforts, the Malays still saw the government as invaders. The king had understood the problem. Without him, there would be calls for a crackdown on all dissent—more police, more soldiers and harsher punishment. Resentment would get worse. What could the new king do?

He felt like the damp air of the morning was spreading within him, leaving him cold and numb. He rose and lifted the brass-topped walking stick leaning against his desk. It had been a gift from the king after his final trip to Europe. The metal felt cold to his touch as he walked along the veranda. He looked into the offices he passed. The officials and clerks were huddled in small groups, some of them silent, some of them whispering. He heard sobs coming from the office that handled the logistics of royal visits. Somsak was draping the portraits of the king in black crepe.

Walking along the lake front, he saw the dock sides were quiet. The waterfront normally bustled with coolies wheeling barrows of goods, market ladies calling out the prices of cloth and shoppers demanding discounts. This day, however, the market stalls were empty and only a few people walked the streets, their heads down.

When he reached home, he saw that the door, normally open to catch the sea breeze, was shut. No smoke rose from the cooking area behind the house. He climbed the steps to the main platform and pushed open the door. His third wife rose and *waied*. The make up on her pale cheeks was smeared. Black streaks from the kohl around her eyes ran down the side of her nose. Without speaking she led him to the main room where the other wives and the children sat in a circle around Apinya. She was already dressed in the black *phasin* she wore to funerals. Behind her, also in mourning attire were his other wives, Duangjan, Siriporn and Ying Yue.

"What are we going to do?" Apinya asked. "He is gone. We must mourn with the queens and consorts. We must take the next ship to Bangkok. The commissioner is going. Somsak is going."

"I would like to, but I have responsibilities here," Pakdee said. "The high commissioner leaves for the capital on the steamer tomorrow. While he is gone, I must act in his place."

"Then I must go. I should be there to help," Apinya said.

"Shouldn't you wait to be invited?"

"No. Now is the time. I must be there with Her Royal Highness. I will take Duangjan with me. Siriporn will stay here to take care of you and Ying is still recovering from childbirth."

"Fine. If you really feel the need to go, then fine."

"It is important to be in the palace. Important for us to be seen as loyal. I must also try to understand what the new reign will bring. The first days are important. I need to meet people in the Crown Prince's, I mean His Majesty's palace. You should come when you can."

"My duty is here. Prince Damrong will understand that I must, above all, do my duty."

"Don't you understand? Everything will change. I thought there would be more time, but now the process has begun. Everyone will re-align. New groups will seek connections to the new king. There will be promotions and demotions. Even all the way down here, we will feel the impact. We must find patrons in the new alignment."

"You shouldn't worry. The government needs me. Prince Damrong and Chaophraya Yommarat will protect me," he said with more confidence than he felt. "They know what I have done all these years. When High Commissioner Charoen moves on, I will certainly be appointed to replace him. It is just a matter of time."

"You are naïve. You have been passed over twice already. That is because you are not one of the elite. You try to imitate us, but something is off. And they know it. All the people of power have long strings of relationships, years of favors and courtesies that reach up to the king. Do you think the prince and the minister can protect you when they may not even save their own positions? Aside from those two, you have no friends in the new royal palace. You have no relatives to protect you. Your paddle is too short to reach the water."

He was taken aback by his wife's alarm and bluntness. She had always pretended to believe the stories of his mysterious birth and the legend of the crystal he wore around his neck. She had coached him, not always patiently, on the intricacies of polite Siamese behavior. She had ensured he was properly dressed. She had corrected his mispronunciations, and she had seemed satisfied with his accomplishments. Now she was saying he had fooled no one.

He had gone to Bangkok for four of the annual meetings of the *monthon* commissioners and he had met with many of the officials in the Interior Ministry, but he had never felt comfortable with them. Aside from Prince Damrong, he had no ties in the large and complicated royal family. The brothers and half-brothers of the king, the cousins and nephews all seemed to find him unimportant. As Apinya often pointed out, he did not move easily in the royal circles. His manners were not quite right. There was still a hint of a southern accent in his speech. He did not write poetry or stage plays like the new king. He had never been trained as a royal page. He had never served in the military. His English was serviceable, but stilted, unlike the fluent speech of all the princes and aristocrats who had been educated in Europe. He felt more at home in a *phatung* than in the top hat and trousers now fashionable in the capital.

Despite that, they must see all he had done to serve the king. He had helped defeat the Pattani raja. He had helped Prince Damrong set up the Islamic Family Court system. This move had undercut Malay complaints about the defeat of the raja. He had set up the network of informants that kept the high commissioners in all three southern *monthons* aware of the feelings of the Malay people. Less than a month ago, his warning had helped defeat that foolish attack on a police station. Already, the leader of the uprising was under arrest, along with most of the villagers deceived into joining the attack.

What if Apinya was right? What would happen to him? What would happen to Saifan, with no one to protect him? No, it wasn't possible. Just a woman's fearful imagining. Prince Damrong was the king's uncle and a powerful leader in the cabinet. He was the Minister of the Interior and acknowledged leader of national reform. Pakdee's old mentor was the king's former tutor and a popular cabinet minister. Surely the new king would listen to him. These two would be enough to protect him. They understood that he did not need to be a palace aristocrat to serve the king faithfully and effectively. No, he had nothing to fear.

"You go ahead to Bangkok," he told his wife. "It will all work out. Before too long, you will be the wife of the high commissioner of *Monthon* Nakhon Srithammarat."

15

SOM
Sermon

Phra Som looked out over the villagers gathered in the forest clearing. The monks had arranged seating on large stones and coconut tree logs raised up off the sandy soil. Off to one side was the long medical building now nearly complete. Several of the older women sat in the shade of the building's sloping tile roof. There were more people than usual for the weekly sermon. Several of the women and some of the men had tears on their cheeks. The sermon this day would be especially difficult, but especially important.

He had resisted the village headman's request for regular sermons. He explained he wanted to provide the monks in his meditation center with an experience similar to that of a forest monk. He said the main activities would be meditation and medicine. He welcomed the villagers to come to him with medical problems or for guidance on their own meditation practice, but the village headman had been adamant.

"We are simple people," he said. "We know how to pry mussels from the rocks, lure bass into our traps and bring squid to our nets, but most of us cannot read. We don't meditate—we are too busy making a living. We don't understand the dharma, but we want to. We need instruction. We need the help of the Buddha to face the difficulties of life."

How could he refuse? He thought back to his first sermon. What a disaster. He had tried to explain the *Kalama Sutta* as the basis of the search for personal truth. He quoted the sutta.

"Don't believe something because you have heard it repeatedly,
Nor because it is a tradition,
Nor because it is in a scripture,
Nor because of your own bias,
Nor because one who seems to have great ability says it is so,
Nor because it is taught by a monk.

Believe it is true only when you yourself know it to be true, on the basis of personal experience, evidence and reason, with a mind free of hostility and ill will, a mind that is undefiled and pure."

It took several repetitions and lots of questions before the villagers began to understand the *sutta*. There was a long discussion of bias. Finally, the villagers ran out of questions, but many of them looked troubled. Then, a teenaged boy stood up.

"So, you are saying we should not believe our parents?"

"You must think carefully and decide for yourself what to believe," Phra Som said. There was a murmur in the crowd.

"Then, we shouldn't believe the village headman?"

"Well, the headman often has good reasons and wise advice, but you must try to understand the reasons and wisdom for yourself." The murmurs grew louder and Yai, the headman, glared at Phra Som.

"Then, we shouldn't believe His Majesty the King?" the boy persisted.

The voices from the assembled villagers grew angry. "You will destroy our land," one man shouted. "What kind of Buddhism is this?"

He looked at his fellow monks for support but they looked confused.

The teenager still standing, spoke up again, raising his voice to be heard above the clamor. "But then you also said that we shouldn't believe something just because it is taught by a monk. So, we don't need to believe anything you have just taught us."

"Yes, that is so. There is no need to believe me just because I am a monk. You must consider, study and think for yourselves," he had said with some relief.

His answer quieted the crowd and Phra Pat spoke up.

"Phra Som has given us much to think about. Please join us in the chant to bless new things." Phra Pat launched into a familiar rhythmic Pali chant. The villagers joined in. The chant calmed everyone. After the chant, the villagers left the clearing and he felt relieved.

Each week since then he had tried to choose less difficult topics for his sermons. This week it was clear what he had to do. The news of the king's death, filtering to Talumpuk village only the day before, lay heavy on the congregation. Many of the villagers had taken their boats up the Pakpanang River to see the king pass by only five years earlier. It had been the highlight of their lives. The headman still told of the day he had eaten dinner with the king at the district officer's house. The visit of the king had changed the way many felt about their own lives. For the first time, they felt part of something much larger than their village, bigger even than the old kingdom of Nakhon.

Interest in national affairs had increased. Often now, villagers brought newspapers from Bangkok for the monks to read to them. Phra Pat had started a bulletin board with such articles nailed to a coconut tree at the entrance to the village. He and the other monks had started teaching the youngsters to read. His little temple was becoming important to the village.

More and more people came up the path. The logs were filled and several villagers had spread mats to sit on. They want reassurance, solace. They should understand that life arises through causes, conditions and effects and there is no truly existing self. No, too complicated. Not the time for another confusing debate on Buddhist doctrine. He drew a calming breath and looked out at the waiting villagers. "I am glad to have you all here together at this time of sadness. We can help each other deal with this latest sorrow and we can learn from the teachings of the Lord Buddha," he said, aware that all the eyes in the crowd were now focused on him.

"The Buddha taught that the First Noble Truth is that suffering must come with life. Old age, sickness and death are unavoidable. That does not mean such suffering must lead to sadness and despair. Yes, life is suffering, but it is what we do with life despite that suffering that is important. The Buddha said: 'As aging and death are rolling in on me, what else should be done but to live by the dharma, to live righteously, and to do wholesome and meritorious deeds?'"

He heard muffled sobs from the villagers and continued.

"This, I believe, is exactly what His Majesty the King has done. He lived righteously. He performed many meritorious deeds that brought happiness to his people, that protected us from foreign invaders, that allowed us to earn our livings in peace, that established order in our lives."

There were murmurs of assent from the villagers. Several wiped tears from their eyes.

"His Majesty left us too soon," an elderly woman said.

"That may be true, but we never know when our time will come. That is as true of kings as it is of fishermen on a stormy sea," he said. "There is a verse in the *Tripitaka* that says:

'Even the beautiful chariots of kings wear out,

Our bodies also undergo decay.

But the dharma of the good does not decay.'"

Would this comfort them? He had to focus them, on the future, on living their lives the right way.

"You can see the Buddha is calling on us, even in our much smaller lives, to strive to do meritorious deeds. We should help one another, be kind to one another, encourage our young people, and comfort our old people. Yes, life is suffering and everything is impermanent, but we can rise above that through awareness, understanding and compassion. The good we do does not decay; it does not die. So, let us honor the king and lighten our suffering by remembering all the things he has done and, most important, by following his example."

The four monks began the funeral chant. The villagers joined in and the sonorous sounds drifted through the trees.

Two hours later, he was discussing the sermon with Pat when Headman Yai hurried up the path to his hut.

"We have a man who is very ill. Can you help him?"

"Who is it? What is wrong with him?"

"It's some Malay man who came ashore from a fishing boat. He has a high fever. There is something wrong with his arm. His friend says they are wandering scholars of the Koran. Do you want to help?"

"Of course. I must gather my medicines. Then we'll see what we can do."

16

SAIFAN
Recovery

Row after row of trees staggered past him like drunken soldiers. Something terrible was chasing him. He had to run, but his legs were paralyzed. There were booming sounds. Coming nearer and nearer. A giant bee dove at his head. He ducked and tried to cover his head but he was terrified to find he had a black snake in his hands. He threw it away and tried to run from the sounds. More bees flew past him. He ran again and stumbled on something soft. He fell to his knees and looked into the face of a man. But where the mouth should be was a large, red hole rimmed with broken teeth and dried blood.

Saifan awoke with a start. He was drenched with sweat, but he felt cold. His eyes were dry and his head ached. Where was he? Sunlight filtered through the walls of split bamboo. It was a tiny room. He could almost touch the other wall. A single window was shuttered with more slats of bamboo. A prison? He could hear the sounds of birds and then the sound of a bell. He shook his head. The last thing he remembered was Hamidy crouching over him, feeling his forehead. He tried to sit up, but fell back onto a small kapok pillow. He felt the ache in his shoulder. His hand met a thick bandage. He sat up. He could see two bowls filled with foul-looking liquids and a stack of white cloths.

The door opened and a boy in an orange robe peered in.

"Where am I?"

The boy quickly shut the door without a word.

He looked down and saw his chest was bare but a long, black and white cotton *phatung* was tied around his waist. He was trying to gather the energy to stand up when the door opened again.

A tall Thai monk in a saffron robe came into the little room.

"I am so glad to see you awake. We were very worried," the man said in the southern dialect. "How are you feeling?"

"Where am I? Who are you?"

"Good, you are alert. You are in Wat Talumpuk. I am Phra Som. I have been treating you. I am pleased to see the medicine is working."

The monk reached out and felt Saifan's forehead. He drew back and leaned against the rough bamboo wall.

"No fever," the monk said, and then grasped Saifan's wrist. He tried to pull away, but the monk's grip was surprisingly powerful.

"Be calm," he said. "Your heart is beating regularly. However, you are still weak. I'll bring you some rice gruel, vegetables and fish."

"I shouldn't be here," he said.

The monk bent over one of the bowls and slowly began adding a powder from a small leather sack, stirring the mixture. It had been a long time since he was this close to a Buddhist monk. He had no eyebrows. Of course, they shave them. The face was leathery but unlined. The expression seemed kind, a half-smile on his lips as he mixed whatever was in that bowl.

"Don't you want to know who I am and how I was, uh, injured?"

"It is of no importance. I know you were shot and the wound became infected. But you are recovering. Drink this."

The monk smiled and held out the small bowl.

He sniffed at the bowl. It smelled like the forest after rain, but when he put it to his lips, there was a sharp bitter taste.

"I know it doesn't taste good," the monk said, "but it will suppress any fever and help the wound heal."

He finished off the bitter liquid. The monk nodded and left.

A moment later, Hamidy burst in.

"You are awake!" he cried. "I thought you would die. How would I explain that to your wife? But don't worry. I sent her a letter saying that our return was delayed because your teaching of the Koran was so well appreciated."

"You lied to her?"

"Get used to it," Hamidy said. "No one can know what happened to us or how we ended up here, so far from Pattani. Just remember you are a wandering teacher of the word of Allah."

In the days that followed, Phra Som came to the hut three times a day with medicine and sent two of the temple boys with food. He found his appetite growing. At first, he could hardly choke down the rice gruel with bits of fish and green onions, but by the second day he hungered for something more solid. The boys brought him some stir-fried prawns with morning glory, later a soup of chicken, onions and tomatoes, grinning at his appetite. The food made him feel stronger. He opened the door and looked out. He was surprised there was no stupa or any of the gaudy red, green and yellow buildings he had seen in every other Buddhist temple.

Phra Som was sitting on a mat in the shade of a large pine. Next to him were three other monks. Two of the temple boys who had brought him food were sitting behind them. In front were four or five men dressed in the simple clothes of fishermen and one man in a rich red *phatung*. Next to him was a small girl. All sat quietly without speaking. Their eyes looked closed. Phra Som looked at peace, with a joyous glint in his eyes—the way the imam often looked after evening prayers.

Meditating. He knew Buddhist monks were supposed to meditate, but he had never seen it before. Prayers. I haven't prayed for days. He looked for the sun, filtering through the trees. Evening was approaching so that must be the direction of Mecca. He took the bowl of water left for him in the hut and washed his hands. He walked slowly to the long, building across from his hut. It looked empty, but when he opened the first door, he saw an old woman sleeping on a mat. Next to her was a man with a bloody bandage around his head. He closed the door. The next room was empty.

He knelt down and began to pray.

17

SOM
Marriage

Som hesitated before responding to Prem. He was hardly the one to deal with such problems, but he had to try.

"As they say, the female heart is as unstable as water rolling on a lotus leaf," he said gently. "Tip the leaf your way and perhaps she will roll back to you."

"And you know this from your vast experience with women?" Prem said with a sour laugh.

"Maybe not with women, but with people."

"And how do I tip this lotus leaf?"

"You have been married, for what? Ten years? You should know by now. What does she like? What wins her attention? What makes her feel good about herself?"

"Once I knew, but now I am not sure anymore. She has changed. I just want to change her back," he said.

"Maybe it is not Ploi you need to change, but Prem. It is hard to change yourself, but a lot harder to change someone else, even harder to change them the way you want. Ask yourself: what can you do to be happy with the way she is now?"

"I don't know. She is obsessed with the casino. She works there late into the night, even after the restaurant closes. Sometimes I stay and wait for her, but sometimes it takes her too long and I have to go home alone. I don't know what it is exactly, but I feel like she doesn't want me anymore. We still make love, but not so often. She shuts me out of things. She travels to Songkhla for meetings. She visits the lottery sales people, but it is never convenient for me to travel with her. When I question an expense, like for those new silver-edged cowrie shells, she gets angry. When I ask her to do something, like come with me to visit you, she finds an excuse. Sometimes she just ignores me like I haven't said a word."

"Maybe she doesn't like coming to the temple."

"But she should respect my wishes. I am the husband. I should decide. Father always decided. Whatever he said was the rule, even if it was unreasonable."

Som laughed. "Are you saying you want to be like Father?"

"No, I guess not, but I wish Ploi were a little more like Mother."

"Mother now operates her own business and makes all her own decisions."

"What I mean is that I want her to do things together with me. When we started living together, well, we were together all the time. It was just the two of us in the back room of the casino. We ate together. We slept together. We worked together, and we loved together. We used to go over the accounts together, but now she doesn't want to show them to me. She says I should trust her. We used to go everywhere together, but now she takes trips by herself. A proper woman shouldn't travel alone. She goes missing for hours and I don't know where. We used to entertain the customers together, but now she wants me to stay downstairs. The betting is illegal, she says, so the bettors don't want too many witnesses. That doesn't make sense. I used to love to sing with her. To watch her as she cheered the winners or consoled the losers. Just watching her was a joy."

"Now, perhaps it is time to find other joys."

"What joys? There are the children, of course, but that is not so easy. Awt is always getting into trouble. With the restaurant I don't have much time to spend with him and he has gotten bored with serving the customers. So he disappears for the whole day. He comes home cut and dirty from fights or playing, I don't know. I have trouble getting him to study his lessons. He is cruel to Phai too. I don't know why he teases her so much, but I often find her in tears from something he has done. She just submits to him. I know he is the Elder Brother, but she should be more like her mother and stand up to him. The baby is starting to run about and causes all kinds of alarm when we can't find him. These are joys, I guess, but they come with even more worries. Ploi just doesn't seem to be with me the way she was before."

Som didn't know what to say. He knew something of the dharma and meditation. He knew something of the monks he had traveled with. These problems between husband and wife were unfamiliar.

It was not just his brother's problems, but those of the villagers who came to consult him. Runaway sons, crippling debts, family feuds, abusive husbands—the villagers brought it all to him. Most difficult were the conflicts between lovers or family members. What did he know of the relations between a man and a woman, between a father and a son? Maybe he would never know. The path of a monk, the practice of meditation, they seemed to lead away from family, certainly away from women.

He looked at the monks sweeping the veranda of the medical building. Maybe they would become his family. Maybe the patients, two of them now resting in the shade of the veranda, would give him enough to care for. He looked at his brother. He had to help him.

He had spent much of his life rebelling against his father's rigid authority. Perhaps that was why he had become a monk. But why was Prem's son rebelling? Prem was anything but stiff or demanding. The boy just had an energy and impulsiveness he didn't understand. The times the boy had come to the meditation center, he could barely sit still for prayers before he was running down to the beach or climbing one of the big trees. Maybe the boy would calm down as he grew older.

Ploi was even more of a mystery than most women. Didn't all women with young children grow more focused on home and family? Mother had been like that. All her energy had been devoted to protecting her children from Father's harshness. It was only when they were safely grown and Father was gone that she had plunged into the warehouse business. According to Prem, Ploi had gone the other way, becoming more focused on the business even as she had more children. Maybe it was the death of her father.

At Prem's urgent pleading, he had gone to their house before the funeral to try to help Ploi deal with her father's death. He had been taken aback by the depth of bitterness welling out of Ploi. He had tried to explain to her what he had learned about death—that it came to everyone, that death was natural.

"What is natural about a knife slicing through your neck?" Ploi had asked. He had no answer, and he knew his words had done little to lessen the darkness engulfing her.

"You are right. I don't know much about women," he told his brother. "But I have learned from the teachings of the Buddha. Above all else, it is this one thing—suffering comes from attachment. If you are too attached to Ploi, her every word that does not nourish your attachment will cause you suffering. You must accept that she is a separate person.

You cannot control her movements, her words. You cannot use her to feel good. You must allow some space between you."

"Then she will drift away. I'll lose her."

"Do you imagine that you have her now?"

"I did once. We had each other."

"That was an illusion. The illusion is over. You must see things as they are. She is not yours. You are not hers. Enjoy her. Value her. Appreciate her. But she is not your possession. She is a person with her own spirit and her own ever-changing journey in life. You cannot stop her from changing. You cannot become attached to a past version of your life together and insist it is the only way life should be. That way lies suffering. Both of you will change, but you cannot control how the other person changes."

Prem shook his head and looked down. "I love her," he mumbled.

He sighed. Maybe the words he thought so wise were not helping.

"Prem. Let us think of something else for a while. Sit comfortably. Draw a deep breath. Look at the trees, then close your eyes. Feel the air come into your nostrils, pull it down into your lungs."

"I know what you are trying to do," Prem said. "It won't help."

"Just concentrate on your breath for a moment. In and out. If thoughts enter, examine them and discard them to focus on your breath. Breathe in; breathe out."

He watched as Prem shook his head sadly. Then he drew a deep breath and settled into a half-lotus position. Som placed his brother's hands, palms upturned on his knees. The sound of birds fluted through the damp air of the forest. He sat on the mat next to his brother and watched as Prem's breathing slowed and his eyes closed. He took a long, slow breath himself.

"Breathe in; breathe out. Breathe in, breathe out."

18

TUN WAY
Mon Resistance

Nai Tun Way trudged up the tiled steps to the second floor of the *monthon* office. He was weary. Much of the long journey from Bago had been on foot. He didn't want the British to know he was traveling across the border, so he walked at night. When stopped by the authorities at the border he identified himself as a trader in agricultural machinery. He had spent a week at the Mon camp in the forest. That had been even more exhausting than the journey up the mountain.

The movement was not going well. There was one spat after another among the boys. They had gotten bored with life in the jungle. They missed the bustle of Bago and their friends, flirting with the girls in the market, and their mothers' cooking. They argued over the simplest camp tasks and the limited food. They demanded he solve their disputes. But no matter what he said, someone was always unhappy. More important, he was unsure of the next step. The boys must feel his uncertainty. Some of the group wanted to take more action, but he couldn't decide what to do. Their efforts in the past five years had been pathetic.

Their attempt to burn down the police station at Toungoo had failed when a brief shower had doused the flames. But it had aroused the police and his boys had barely escaped. They printed and distributed leaflets calling for Mon rights, but they hadn't excited much interest, except in the Police Special Branch.

The chatter in the markets was all about silly Burmese pamphlets prophesying the ascent of an avenging Burman king to replace the British. People knew the slogan "Burma for the Burmans," but knew nothing about the hopes of the Mons. Worst of all they had failed to rebuild the Mon school while new schools teaching in English and Burmese were starting up every month.

They had to do something more spectacular, something to attract attention and inspire hope in the Mon people. Some of the boys had wanted to attack the British. They were the foreign overlords who ruled in ignorant supremacy over all the people of Burma. They were bringing in hundreds of thousands of Indians who already outnumbered the indigenous people in Rangoon. An attack on the British would gain support from the Burmans, the boys said. After all, the Burmans were Buddhists too and there were many more of them than the few arrogant British. Maybe it would be wise to join with the Burmans first, then seek autonomy within an independent nation.

But he had seen the power of the British in Calcutta: the disciplined, well-equipped troops, British and Indian. Worse, joining forces with the Burmans would ensure the Mon would be exploited forever. The British, in some ways, were better overlords than the Burmans. At least there was room for Mon language and culture.

So, it had to be a Burman target—one that would send the message of Mon resistance. The disaster at Toungoo showed them they needed a well-planned escape route. They needed help from the Thais.

At the top of the stairway a young man dressed in a plain cotton *phajonggraben* and a white, round-collared shirt was waiting for him. It was the same office assistant who had taken his written request for a meeting with the deputy high commissioner two days before.

"Is the meeting approved?" Tun Way asked even before reaching the top step

"Yes, His Excellency, Deputy High Commissioner Pakdee is prepared to meet you. Please come with me."

He nodded and followed the man along the long veranda. He felt in his bag for his coded notes. This was his payment for Siamese support. They detailed British military movements along the eastern border from the Three Pagoda Pass all the way south to Kawthaung across the inlet from the sleepy Thai port town of Ranong. He and three of his soldiers had traveled the southern portion of the long border with Siam, looking for their first attack target. They also searched for information the Thais wanted. That border was still ill-defined, and the Siamese worried the British would push eastwards, nibbling away at Siamese territory. He had to make sure the Siamese remained concerned.

The man ahead of him pushed open a heavy door, and they entered the same office he had visited two years earlier. It was cool and seemed dark after the brilliance of the morning sunshine. Sitting behind a large desk was the deputy commissioner, looking as elegant as ever. He wore a high-collared white jacket with bright brass buttons. His neatly trimmed mustache appeared lightly waxed and his hair was combed straight back, glistening with pomade.

"Nai Tun Way, I am glad to see you again. I was not sure I would. It has been a long time since you promised to keep me informed, yet I've received only two reports from you."

"My apologies, Your Excellency, but the Police Special Branch are watchful. I did not want to risk a report falling into their hands. So, I have come to report to you in person."

"Very well. What have you got?"

He pulled the notes from his bag and flipped past the first two pages, which were Mon poetry. Then he found the paragraphs meant to look like notes on Mon mythology, but recorded his observations in his own code. Armored cars were ogres, police units were bands of monkeys, British officers were demi-gods, and locations were disguised as places in Mon literature.

"The British are re-equipping many border posts with armored cars and new rifles brought in from India. We learned at least 10 crates of rifles were delivered to the Kawthaung encampment two months ago. They are recruiting more local men into their forces, creating four new army companies for border duty and reinforcing six police stations between Sinbyudaing and Kawthaung. British officers remain in charge of all company-sized units whether police or army. Here are the places where they are camped."

He paused to let Pakdee jot down some notes. Then he detailed the new police posts and the road-building that was making it easier to move men and machinery closer to the border. Under questioning from the deputy commissioner, however, he had to admit the police were needed against bandits and the roads could be intended to facilitate shipments of agricultural products to market.

"Transportation links and military and police forces near the border, however, could be a threat to Siam," he said, "especially since most of the border runs through heavily forested hills. The British teak companies are pushing into those hills for timber—much as they do in the north. With the British, it is business that leads to conquest."

He paused and looked at Pakdee. He seemed to nod in agreement, so he pressed on.

"Once they have harvested all the teak in Burma, they will start pushing for concessions in your territory, or just start felling trees. Siam is vulnerable. Already you hold just a narrow strip at the neck of the peninsula. If the British take that strip, then the Siamese kingdom will be split in two. Nakhon Srithammarat *monthon* and all of the south will be separated from the capital. They will move in the name of commerce, but the impact will be political."

"So, you can read the minds of the British?" Pakdee asked.

"I know their character and I know what they have done in the past," Tun Way explained. "Their wars against the Burman king were all about commerce. The king foolishly resisted, and he's now in exile. This gives the Mon an opportunity."

"How so?"

"Even though the British allow the Burmans into their civil service and military, they don't trust them. They counter the possibility of Burman revolt by strengthening the ethnic groups that have long struggled against the Burmans—the Shan, the Kachin, the Karen, the Karenni…"

"And the Mon?"

"Not yet. The British have fallen for the Burman lie that the Mon and Burman cultures are the same and our people are one. It is that lie I am trying to expose."

"With your association? The one that has not actually done anything?"

"Yes, the association is struggling, but it can grow quickly if we can re-ignite pride in being Mon. Language and culture are only part of the struggle. There must be a military side to it. We must demonstrate the Mon are not content to be the little brothers of the Burmans."

"How will you do that?"

"Our group of patriots is eager to strike the first blow. It will be against a police station carefully chosen near the border."

"Tun Way, the situation has changed. The British are no longer such a threat. They are abiding by our treaty and they are focused on the problems in Europe. His Majesty the King has excellent relations with the British. Now is not the time to cause problems."

"My men are brave and eager. I cannot hold them back much longer. What I need from you is assurance we can escape across the border if necessary, so no evidence falls into Burman or British hands."

"If you choose to come into our country, I cannot stop you, but if you start an armed conflict with the British, I cannot help you."

"Then why did you sell us the guns?"

"That was a different time and you said they were for self-defense," Pakdee said, his tone now cold. "An attack on a police station is not self-defense."

Tun Way closed his eyes in frustration. He could see again the smoke rising from the school, feel the heat of the flames against his face. He recalled the laughter of the Bago education administrator scoffing at the idea of Mon language school.

"So you won't help us?" he asked.

"I am helping you," Pakdee said. "Your little activities have already put you in danger and the British police are rather efficient."

"But we have taken risks for these reports for you."

"Now is not the time to take any more. Be careful."

"But the reports."

"Don't worry about them," Pakdee said. "We don't need them anymore."

19

PAKDEE
Chulalongkorn Day

Pakdee looked at the big clock newly installed on his office wall. He had an hour before the ceremony was to begin. Enough time to look at some of the correspondence on his desk. He loosened the top button of his tunic. He had already read through the proclamation of the day to honor the late King Chulalongkorn. Two years had passed since his death. Moving through that time had felt like trudging through river mud at low tide. He was still deputy to the *monthon* commissioner, but his relationship with the new commissioner was strained. Somsak, his old fellow clerk had been promoted to second deputy and his influence was increasing. Maybe that was a good thing. Somsak, trying to live up to his big-shot brother in Bangkok, had desperately wanted the promotion. Now he should be satisfied. With all they had been through together, Somsak would be an ally. He had a way of talking with the commissioner that Pakdee had never mastered—a clever compliment, a tone of admiration or the use of a royal pronoun. Maybe he had been spoiled by his unusual relationship with Phraya Sukhumnaiwinit.

Somsak could help explain the realities of the south to the commissioner, who didn't seem interested in the customs, language or culture of the region. Several times he had allowed his impatience with the commissioner to surface when he said something stupid. Sukhumnaiwinit had warned him about this long ago. What had he said?

"The boss is always right, especially when the boss is wrong."

"Your boss will always believe that your first duty is to protect the boss, just as his first duty will be to protect his boss. In return he will provide loyal subordinates with protection and rewards."

He missed his old mentor, now far away in the capital. He missed Sukhum's quick intelligence and his wide reading. He missed his ability to look at himself with a kind of amused detachment.

At the crucial moment, however, Sukhum and Prince Damrong had failed him. When he should have been the logical replacement for the outgoing commissioner, he was overlooked. The new king had chosen one of his half-brothers, Prince Yukhitamphon Krom Luang Lopburi Ramet, as the new *monthon* commissioner, with additional powers as viceroy of the south. At the office, of course, he had to pretend to be delighted and honored with the appointment. When he complained to Apinya, she had laughed at him.

"How could you compete with Prince Lopburi Ramet? His Royal Highness is a true aristocrat, a member of the royal family. He is a half-brother of the king. They studied in England together. His wife, Princess Chalermkhetra Mangala, is also a member of the royal family. What's more, he is a graduate of that famous *farang* university Cambrit—in political science and administration. He is perfect for the position."

"He is so young—what 23? He can't even grow a mustache. He looks like a little boy," Pakdee grumbled. "He has no practical experience. Yet he is not only *monthon* commissioner, but regent for the whole south."

"Be careful what you say. He is a half-brother of the king. Who are you? Far below him. Just be grateful you continue to work as deputy commissioner. Make sure you serve His Royal Highness well. That is the only way our family will survive."

She was right, but he still felt frustrated. The new commissioner was polite, but distant. He did not seem to have the same drive to understand the people of the south that Phraya Sukhumnaiwinit had shown. He could not speak the southern dialect and he brushed aside Pakdee's offer to teach him a few *Jawi* words. The prince had embarrassed him by making gentle fun of his English pronunciation.

Fortunately, the prince and his wife had shown interest in Apinya's *Khon* troupe, attending all the performances. It gave him the chance to chat informally with the prince. He was no longer sure where he stood. Sometimes Prince Lopburi Ramet asked sharp questions about his reports. At other times, the prince didn't even meet him for days at a time. His policy recommendations were politely considered, but often ignored. The prince seemed to listen to Somsak more than anyone else. Luckily, Somsak had been willing to help when he asked him to convey important information to the commissioner.

Pakdee felt he still had the confidence of Prince Damrong Rajanubhab, his boss's boss. The prince saw his reports, he knew, but only after they were reviewed and edited by the commissioner. Once a year he met the minister at the *monthon* commissioners' meeting in

Bangkok. Last year, however, Prince Damrong had seemed distracted and uncertain. There was an uneasiness about the whole government. So much had changed so quickly. The death of the king had removed the most important symbol of continuity for government officials, for everyone really. There were rumors of discord in the cabinet meetings and a number of the king's uncles had been moved to new positions. Some had left government entirely, usually citing health reasons.

King Vajiravudh had certainly been working hard, not only creating new offices and organizations, but issuing proclamations and government statements along with an amazing number of essays, plays and poems. All this effort must be an attempt to complete the transformation of Siam into a civilized, modern nation, respected by the *farang* powers. Fortunately, the imperialist pressure had eased. The big powers were now busy with their quarrels in Europe. Britain had adhered to the treaty of 1909 – the last great accomplishment of the late king – and there had been progress getting rid of extraterritoriality.

All this only made the the former Malay rulers more desperate. The old Pattani raja was still stirring the pot and young men paid with their lives. Luckily, Saifan survived the first uprising and had stayed away from similar violence a year later. Both uprisings had been put down by the army and the police, but not before more people were killed.

He had argued for pardons for the villagers captured, saying they had been deceived by those two Sufi charlatans with their magic amulets and promises of paradise. The government, however, had ignored his advice, fearing leniency would encourage more insurrections. His agent had managed to destroy the bits of evidence pointing to Saifan's guilt, but many other foolish boys were still in prison.

He reread the coded note informing him Saifan was back teaching the Koran in Krue Se. Maybe now he would accept the inevitable and live quietly as a citizen of Siam. Live a peaceful, happy life. It would not be easy for his stubborn little brother. The rhetoric from the capital must be infuriating to him, proclaiming that to be part of Siam you had to share the same blood and religion and be personally loyal to the king. He picked up a copy of one of the king's speeches that had arrived by post the week before: "When we know that something gives us dignity, we do our best to preserve and cherish it. Since the king gives dignity to the nation, he also gives dignity to every member of the nation. It is therefore the duty of all the members of the nation to do their best to preserve their king. Those who harm the king must be regarded as those who harm the nation, who destroy the dignity of the country and who break the peace and happiness of the community. They must be regarded as the enemy of all the people."

Yes, there was a need for loyalty, but why did the king's call for loyalty have to be repeated so frequently? Was it effective? Only a few months earlier, the government had arrested and tried a number of army officers for plotting against the king. It was the emotional reaction of foolish young men who had felt insulted by the king's establishment of the Wild Tiger Corps as a military organization outside of the army. The officers had misunderstood the king. He wasn't trying to dishonor the army, but rather to spread military spirit through the civil service with marching, weapons training, and camping. The rebels would pay for their foolishness with time in prison, just as he had paid for his own foolishness. Maybe they too would learn something from it.

There was a knock at the door and the commissioner's young secretary came in and *waied*.

"Pakdee, sir. Officials are gathering outside. You should be in place before His Royal Highness the High Commissioner comes out," he said.

Why wasn't the secretary wearing his civil service uniform? He had on khaki-colored shorts with knee socks. He wore a military-style shirt with a broad leather belt around his waist with another crossing his chest diagonally. A row of brightly colored medals was pinned to his chest and four large chevrons covered one sleeve.

"That is quite a uniform," Pakdee said.

The secretary beamed. "Yes, sir, I have been promoted to sergeant major in the Wild Tigers. I am in Deputy Commissioner Somsak's company. We camp out together in the forest. We learn teamwork and tactics, so we can fight if there is an invasion. It is very exciting, and the training has built discipline and unity among the clerks of the office. I think it would be greatly appreciated, sir, if you would join."

He felt a flash of annoyance at the secretary presuming to tell him what to do. "I am considering it, but right now I am too busy with a variety of tasks to take off for days of camping and exercises. I will join as soon as I have some time."

"As you know, His Royal Highness believes joining the Wild Tiger Corps is an important way to show our loyalty to His Majesty the King. He says His Majesty has a special interest in Nakhon Srithammarat and might even join the next big camp outing in the *monthon*."

"That would be a great honor," he said as the secretary *waied* and backed out of the room.

Maybe joining the Wild Tigers would be a good move. In the two years since the new king came to the throne, he had not had any opportunity to speak with him. The high commissioner rarely mentioned him in his reports. The commissioner himself had never said he should join the Wild Tigers. Why was it so important? His work in defeating the Pattani raja should be enough to prove his courage and his loyalty, but few people knew what he had done. He had to get closer to the king and this might be the only way. He would put it on his list of tasks for the year ahead. It would be a busy year. The railroad was coming to Nakhon, more tin mines were opening up, Chinese migrants were flooding in, trade was growing, more work was needed to suppress bandits and he still had to keep track of Malay discontent and the plots of the former raja. The work of implementing a fair judicial system was far from complete. There was no time to dress up in fancy uniforms and run around in the forest.

Would the Wild Tiger Corps solve the loyalty problem? People were now more likely to see flaws in the top leaders. It was a conundrum he had discussed with Phraya Sukhumnaiwinit. The king needed loyalty to ensure smooth running of the government, but if he elevated people simply on the basis of loyalty, incompetent officials would threaten smooth administration. That had been true under King Chulalongkorn, but the king had been fortunate in having so many brothers who were both competent and loyal. The new king did not appear so fortunate or so trusting of his powerful uncles.

The high commissioner's speech was unlikely to touch on the real issues worrying Prince Damrong. Officials were often urged to find ways to increase government revenues, but too much was spent on the king's extravagant personal projects. The country needed an influx of Chinese labor for expanding mines, rice mills and industry, but the government was deeply suspicious of Chinese loyalties.

The fluctuating policies on gambling were a particular headache. His agreement with Sia Leng had worked out well, but the pressure to stamp out illegal gambling was rising. He had won praise for raiding gambling dens, lotteries and card games, but the new commissioner had questioned why there was still so much gambling despite the raids.

How much did the government really care about stopping gambling? There were still legal casinos operating around Bangkok. Gambling was still allowed on special holidays and some royal organizations had started holding lotteries to raise money for special projects.

He had been able to finish paying for Apinya's mansion, but then his wife had insisted on two more expansions—one for each of the last two wives after they had given birth. It was probably best to put an end to that. Five wives were enough. He had hardly slept with the newest one. She seemed so frail, but she enjoyed reading so they had much to chat about on the nights she was assigned to his sleeping mat. Yes, five wives were enough, especially now.

He descended the staircase to the courtyard of the *monthon* office. Arrayed in front of the flag pole were the governors and district officers from all over the *monthon*. Most had more than one wife, but things were changing. A ministry circular last month urged government officials to avoid the distractions and expenses of many wives, although members of the royal family were apparently exempt. He could see the sense of this, but it was annoying. He had taken more wives to be part of aristocratic society only to be told his wives were a distraction. Apinya hadn't said anything about this change, but she tried to keep up with the trends in the capital. On her last visit to Bangkok she had been dismayed by the changes in the palace. Only two years ago the women's area of the palace had been a vast complex of buildings, theaters and houses with its own system of law and security—all run by women. Now, she told him, the inner palace was nearly deserted. Many of her friends had been forced out of the safe world of the palace to find housing and husbands on the outside.

Even though Apinya ruled the mansion with a sharp tongue and the occasional slash of the long rattan rod she carried, more and more disagreements were bubbling up to him. In the office, there were rules and incentives to ensure order and efficiency. At home everything was personal. Who got new cloth for a *phasin*, who got a better role in the *Khon*, whose child was given a top-knot ceremony, who came to his sleeping mat at night—everything was contested.

For two nights in a row, dealing with arguments among his wives had sent him to bed alone with an aching head. He had once again been waking up from nightmares of being locked in a cell. Sometimes he would see the tear-stained face of Malee, the girl he thought would join him in a new life so long ago. Once he dreamed of finding her body bruised and still on the stairs to Jate's house. In his most frequent dream he was being questioned by a judge and found he had no tongue; trying to gesture he found he had no arms.

Of all the issues his wives squabbled about, the only one he cared about was the sleeping arrangement. It was nice his wives competed to please him, but sometimes it was just a nuisance, especially when he was tired from work. Like everything else in the mansion, Apinya took charge of the appointments for his sleeping partner, explaining it was necessary to give each of his wives similar opportunities or household jealousies would worsen. Apinya, however, no longer made sleeping appointments for herself. She explained her 'sacrifice' prevented ill feeling and provided him with more energetic partners.

He laughed at himself. When he was young, he had to plot, please and flatter his way into a woman's favors and he had paid a terrible price for one miscalculation. Now, it was all on offer, with a choice of women. Yet there were some nights he just wanted to sleep. When he was young, he had no power and no regular sexual pleasure. Now he had power and more sex partners than he needed, but it only made life more complicated.

There was a quiet murmur in the crowd. He looked up and saw the high commissioner, His Royal Highness Prince Lopburi Ramet, moving to the platform at the top of the twin stairways. Somsak bowed to the prince and handed him his speech. He began with a Buddhist invocation and then an eloquent description of the great work being done by the king.

In the four years since Sukhum had moved on to the cabinet in Bangkok, Pakdee had often served as acting high commissioner. Now his role was simply to support the prince. Every needed measure had to be carefully explained to the commissioner. Even after the most thorough explanation, there would be delay after delay. No matter what decision the commissioner made, everyone had to greet it with the reverence due great wisdom. It was just as much a show as the *Khon* dramas of heroes, monkey soldiers and ogres.

Now, as the high commissioner appeared to be coming to the end of his speech, his role would be to applaud, praise and support. He was just another prancing soldier in the monkey army.

20

PLOI
Family Names

Ploi slammed the paper down on the desk in front of the clerk.

"What does this mean?" she demanded. There was surprise and fear in the eyes of the clerk. Good. He could be intimidated. She felt the others in the provincial office turn to look at her. What did she care? She would reverse this injustice.

"Well, uh, honored Madam, it means your application for the surname of 'na Nakhon' has not been approved," the clerk said.

"Why not?"

"I am sorry, but I am just a clerk," he said.

"Then call your supervisor. This injustice must be corrected."

The clerk hesitated, then rose and walked to a large desk at the back of the room. An older man behind the desk gathered some papers and followed him to Ploi and Prem.

"I understand you have questioned the decision made on a request for an official surname," he said.

"I submitted my application two weeks ago, but it has not been approved. Obviously," she said, "an error has been made."

The man bent over the papers. "No, I am afraid this decision is official," the man said. "See, it has been initialed by the governor."

"And why was that decision made?"

"There have been many similar rejections of applications for the 'na Nakhon' surname. I have a circular from the governor's office that explains this." The man went through his papers, pulled one out, nervously cleared his throat and read slowly: "In accordance with the Law on Surnames promulgated on March 22, 1913, His Majesty the King has determined that no surnames with the particle 'na' may be approved without royal consent and shall be given only to those whose ancestors were members of the official ruling class with long established residence in the locality. With respect to surnames in Nakhon Srithammarat province, the governor has determined that the 'na Nakhon' surname should be restricted to the immediate family of the late ruler."

"But the former king was my father's father's great uncle," Ploi said.

"Then your father can appeal," he said, "but several applications like this have been rejected. His Majesty thinks royal surnames shall be granted only to the offspring of major queens, not those of the concubines. So, tell your father that he must appeal on the basis of descent from a major queen."

"My father is dead," Ploi said.

"Then an appeal will be very difficult. I am most sorry."

The official handed her the paper. It was insulting, but there was nothing she could do. She crushed the application in her fist.

"Ploi dear, it would have been good to honor your father, but don't be upset. There are many other names we can choose," Prem said.

"Like what?"

"I would like to suggest Samutapanich, in honor of my family's business in the sea trade and shipping. My mother has chosen this surname. This way we would all have the same last name. I think that was the king's intention—to link families together with the same name, like in the Western countries."

"Your mother and sister may run a warehouse, but there is no ship anymore," she said as they sat outside the office. "We need a surname that will advance our business and our main business is the casino."

"But that is illegal. Our legal business is the restaurant."

"It may be technically illegal, but that is what we are known for and that is how we earn most of our income," she said.

"Do we really want to tie our family name to a business that could be shut down by the police at any time?"

"I have decided. Let the governor's family have their little 'na Nakhon' royal surname. Our family will be known for confidence and daring."

"Why can't you listen to me for once?" Prem pleaded.

"Your family will still have your father's Chinese family name. Among the Chinese, you will always be Sae-Tang, so what do you care about a Thai surname? Let me have the Thai name."

Prem was silent. She took his hand and sniffed at his palm. "Please."

Prem exhaled. "If it will make you happy."

"Good," Ploi said as she filled in a new form with the name in bold letters. "From now on we are the Jaikla family."

21

NGWE LAY
Visitors

Bago, October 2, 1913

"Miss Ngwe Lay, put your dolls away," Auntie Ma said. "We have visitors."

She looked up from the dolls standing around the little bed she had made from scraps of wood. "But I cannot stop now. The doctors are still discussing the case of this poor woman," she said, stroking the hair of the doll. "She is quite ill. It is a very complicated case."

"Now," Ma said with a look that meant there was to be no argument. She heard the faint clip-clop sound of hooves on the road by the river. It was a man on horseback and a couple of men walking behind.

Could it be Father? She squinted into the brilliant sunshine of the late afternoon. It was hard to see with all the dancing sparkles of light from the river. Father had been away so long. No, it didn't look like him.

"Who are those men?" she asked.

"I don't know," Ma said with a frown. "First put your toys away and go to the back room until I call you. Tell Aya to come to the veranda."

She placed her dolls in their satin bag. As she stood up, she noted she was already a half a head taller than Ma. Where Ma was broad and sturdy, she was slim, but strong. She could chop right through the pork bones for soup.

Aya had never fully recovered from her long illness. So when something needed to be done around the house, Aya showed her how to do it, and she did the real work. She had learned to pound the chilies and tumeric for curry and to cook the rice so it wasn't too dry or too wet. Ma went to work early each morning and worked all day at the hospital in town. By the time she got back it was usually dark. Then the three of them would work together to prepare the meal and clean the house. Tonight, it would be river prawns in a red chili sauce.

Life had been so sad after Grandpa and Grandma died. She had felt so lost at the funeral when the monks had told her to toss the bamboo flowers onto the box holding her Grandpa. It had only been three months earlier that Grandma had died of the big fever that made so many people sick. Grandpa got better from the fever, but then he died anyway. No one could tell her why.

"Sometimes people just don't want to live anymore," Ma had explained. "Your grandfather lost his daughter and then his wife, the person he had lived with so long. I think maybe he was just too sad to keep on struggling."

"What about me? Didn't he want to live for me?"

"I am sure he did, but maybe not enough," Ma said.

It was good that Ma told her things honestly. There were no secrets with Ma. Not like with Father who never seemed to want to tell her anything. After the funeral, Ma said she would come to live with Aya and Ngwe Lay until Father came home. She said it should only be a month or so, but that was many months ago. Maybe Ma would stay even after her father came home. She liked living with Ma. She could answer the questions that Aya couldn't. She explained about sickness and food and books. She helped her understand the big words in Father's letters. She even taught her about all the confusing things about her own body. Someday she would be a nurse like Ma.

Best of all, Ma told her about Mother. She liked the stories where Mother saved the life of a woman by devising a treatment better than anything the doctors could do. Or when she succeeded in delivering a baby stuck in the wrong position. She liked hearing that Mother stood up to the stuffy old doctors. She especially enjoyed hearing the story of how Mother had rejected an arrogant British doctor to choose Father. Why didn't he ever tell her any of this?

She put her dolls on the shelf in the back room and listened at the door. She was getting too old for dolls anyway. She would soon have her ear-piercing ceremony. That would mean she was grown up. Aya had already made her a dress. It was so beautiful. And there were earrings of gold with little rubies. She would look like a grown-up lady. They were just waiting for father to come home.

She could hear a man's loud voice and then Ma's voice, equally loud, answering back. She heard Father's name. She heard something about letters in a demanding tone. Then there was the sound of heavy feet on the floor boards of the house. Suddenly the door opened.

"So this is the daughter," a man in a blue jacket said in Burmese. "Good afternoon, young miss, I am Lieutenant Tin Oo. What is your name?"

"There is no point talking to the child," Ma said. "She knows nothing."
Ngwe Lay felt insulted.

"Good afternoon, sir. My name is Ngwe Lay and I am twelve years old. I can speak Burmese and I know a lot of things."

"I am sure you do, Miss Ngwe Lay," the man said with a smile. He waved his hand and one of the men pulled Ma out of the room. He turned back to her with a nice smile.

"Would it be alright if I came into your room and sat down on the mat here so we can have a chat?" he asked.

"Yes, I think so. My father is the owner of this house, so I suppose I can give you permission."

"Thank you. I am so sorry we did not get the chance to meet your father today. Where is he now?"

"He is far away on important business," she said. "He is gathering money to build a wonderful school for the Mon people."

"That is very good. But do you know where he is?"

"I am not sure, but it takes a long time to get there. You must walk over mountains, go through forests and cross rivers. It is far away, so it is difficult for him to get home."

"Did he ever mention a group of men hiding in the forest?"

"Well, he has some students he takes on hikes in the mountains, but they aren't hiding."

"Did he ever say where they take these hikes?"

"Somewhere in the east, I think. Father is very busy."

The man looked disappointed.

"What about guns? Have you ever seen your father with a gun?"

Ngwe Le felt like her heart stopped. One night she had seen father cleaning a long gun and then wrapping it in a thick cloth. When Father saw her he looked upset, but then told her this was their secret and she must never tell anyone about the gun."

"No, no, no. Never," she said. "Father never had a long gun."

The man nodded like something she said had pleased him.

"No matter. When do you think your father will be getting home? We heard he might be back already."

"Did you? Then it must be very soon," she said, relieved he didn't ask any more questions about guns. "He wrote to me in his letters. I will soon have my ear-piercing ceremony."

"You must be a very smart girl to read his letters."

"I can read quite well, but sometimes Auntie Ma has to help me."

"Can you really read your father's letters? Show me."

She felt a little sorry for the man who didn't seem to realize that she was quite grown up and well-educated and could read Father's letters very well. At least that was what Auntie Ma said.

She jumped up and ran to the box inlaid with carved slivers of oyster shell where they kept her father's letters. She pulled them out with a flourish.

"See. He writes to me quite often and uses all the grown-up words," she said. She took the top letter and began to read. She was careful to say each word clearly, but after a few sentences the man looked blank.

"You don't understand Mon," she laughed. "You really should. The Mon language has the greatest poetry and most wonderful tales."

"I am sure you are right. Let me look."

She handed the bundle of letters to the man and watched as he flipped through them.

"I need to have someone translate these for me, so I will have to borrow them for a few days," he said, handing them to one of the men who stood behind him.

"No, no, that is not proper!" she gasped in alarm as the man put Father's letters into a leather satchel. "These are my personal property and I don't think I can let you take them away."

"I promise I will bring them back to you in a day or two."

She couldn't see Aya or Ma anywhere. The man stood up and gave her a short salute. "Aya and your auntie will be coming with us to the police station to help us with our inquiries. They will be allowed to return to you tonight. Don't worry about them."

She watched as the men left, taking Ma and Aya with them.

She waited and waited. It was strange to be in the house all alone. The man said they would be back, but by supper time, there was no sign of Aya or Auntie Ma. She ate the curried prawns by herself, but there was a lot left over. After washing the dishes and storing the prawns in a heavy ceramic bowl, she sat on the veranda waiting for them to return.

The moon rose high over the hills. It was so quiet, she could hear the frogs along the river, and the crickets and the sound of the wind in the mango trees. Some dark clouds drifted across the moon, so she lit another lamp and went back inside to read her lesson for the day. She must have fallen asleep over the book when she heard footsteps on the veranda. At last they were back. She looked out of the window, but couldn't see much. The moon must have set. Then she heard the door open and someone stepped softly into the room. The yellow light of the kerosene lamp picked out a man's form. She drew back against the wall. Then, with a surge of delight she saw Father's face against the dark sky outside.

"Father, Father!" she shouted and ran skittering across the floor.

"Shush. Shush. Quiet."

"Father, you're home," she said, throwing her arms around him.

"Ngwe Lay, is that you? You are so tall?" he said as he awkwardly tried to return her hug and then pry her arms from around his waist.

"Enough. Enough. We'll talk later. Now there is no time to waste. Gather your things—one bag only. We must leave tonight."

22

SOM
Medicine

Som stood on the bow of the sailboat as it nosed into the dock. He stepped quickly onto the weathered wood, his calloused feet barely feeling the rough texture as he strode towards the back door of his sister's medicine shop. He puzzled over the note delivered the day before. It said: "Come tomorrow to the shop for an important meeting. Bring a sample of the dysentery medicine *Krisanaklan Tralilane* and a list of ingredients." Was someone in the family sick?

He and his monks, now ten altogether, had been busy for more than two months gathering, grinding and mixing the herbs for the *Krisanaklan*. The demand was sparked by another outbreak of dysentery afflicting thousands in Pakpanang and nearby. His records showed the medicine had proved better than other treatments in helping people survive the illness. Recovering patients were spreading the word that the monk from Wat Talumpuk was a great healer.

It was good his herbal concoction had been helpful, but now he and the other monks had little time for meditation or discussion of the dharma. There had been an influx of people seeking treatment. The monks had to spend time helping the carpenters from the village build additions to the medical building. It could now hold up to 30 people.

In the past week even that number had been exceeded. The room was crowded with patients on sleeping mats. More mats had been placed on the broad porch. Most of his time was taken up in meeting patients, asking about their symptoms and deciding on the dosage. He kept notes on each patient, describing the symptoms, the treatments and the outcomes. He tried different mixtures of the main ingredients to see which combination worked best. Although he hated to lose the opportunity to see the outcomes of the treatments, he had started giving jars of the medicine to take away. He asked them to report back to him in a week, but he knew from experience that once they recovered, most would decide it wasn't worth their time to return.

He had also been supplying his sister's shop. At first sales had been slow compared to other traditional treatments for dysentery, but demand had picked up and Toh had appealed for new supplies.

Toh was waiting for him at the door and ushered him inside. It took a moment for his eyes to adjust to the dark interior of the shop after the glare of the sun on the river. Sitting at a table were Toh's husband Tan and three men in army uniforms. He inhaled the complex aromas of the medicines stored in row after row of glass jars behind a wooden counter. He thought he could detect the smell of ginger, Chab pepper, ginseng, plumbago root and camphor.

The military men stood up and *waied* him.

"Venerable Teacher, thank you for coming to see us," said the shortest of the three men. "We need your help with a serious problem. As in many of the towns of the south, our military camps have been afflicted with dysentery. At times, more than half of our men are too weak to leave their barracks. This puts the entire nation at risk. Our camp doctor in Nakhon, Captain Somwang here, treated the sick with a medicine bought from this shop."

"Our shop has a wide variety of treatments available that we would be happy to provide to the army," Toh's husband said.

The military man wearing spectacles spoke up.

"I am the doctor for the camp in Nakhon. I have tried most of the traditional remedies and the results have not been very good. Unfortunately, Western medicines are in short supply, expensive and even those are not especially effective."

"Therefore, we are interested in your *Krisanaklan*," the doctor said. "I have given our soldiers six different treatments and kept records. Those receiving the *Krisanaklan* medicine recovered far quicker than those receiving any other treatment. I purchased all the medicine available in Nakhon and conducted further treatments. Again, the outcomes were good, and I have reported this in some detail to our commander. I was ordered to find a steady supply of the medicine, but when we spoke to the shop owners, they told us you are the sole supplier. When we spoke yesterday, you said that your supplies come from Phra Somdhammo."

The doctor turned to him. "Venerable Teacher, we would like you to supply us. The army, will, of course, compensate you for expenses and make a generous donation to your temple."

Som sat silent for a moment, feeling pulled in different directions by the doctor's words. "I am pleased to hear that others, including a trained doctor, have found my medicine useful, but we are already making as much of the medicine as we can. How could we possibly manufacture enough medicine for the army?"

"My husband and I could arrange production," Toh spoke up. "We can find space and workers to make more than in the forest temple."

Toh was a shrewd businesswoman and had already hinted that she and Tan were interested in making several of the medicines he had found effective. Was that a good idea? He wanted to keep close control over the selection and preparation of herbs—and he wanted to get information on outcomes so he could improve his formulas.

"We can promise to make donations to the temple that will enable you to build a beautiful prayer hall or cast large Buddha images," Tan said eagerly. "There is big money in this."

"We don't need big money," Som said.

His sister gave him a pleading look.

"I don't want our temple to turn into a business, but I do want to help more people. I realize that means producing more medicine, but I want to keep the price low."

"The army can help with this," the doctor said. "We can offer a procurement contract to control the price and ensure a high volume."

"And quality," Som said. "I will have to train the workers, inspect the process and check the production."

Tan and Toh nodded eagerly.

"I can provide reports on treatment outcomes," the doctor said.

"Excellent," the senior officer said. "I will draft the contracts."

"We will arrange the workers and, the production space," Tan said. "We can also produce your other medicines."

Everyone around the table turned and looked at him. They were right to want to make more medicine to help more people. But he could see the desire in their eyes. They wanted to be important and make money. Even his sister. Was it bad to make money by doing something good? But they were not responsible for keeping his temple a place for peaceful meditation. He would have to spend more time on the medicines. There would be calls for more buildings—a prayer hall, a stupa, a big Buddha image. He had seen it happen at Wat Wang Tawan Tok. What would all this do to the monks? What would it do to him?

23

NGWE LAY
Refugees

Ngwe Lay bent her knees and ducked her shoulder under the pole. With a grunt, she straightened up, lifting the pails of water and stepping away from the well. Behind her a line of women waited for water. It was not far to their hut, but it was uphill and the water was heavy. As she walked, she smiled and exchanged greetings with the people she knew as she wound her way through the huts of the refugee camp.

"*Mongora 'au*, Miss Ngwe Lay," one of Father's men said.

"*Mongora 'au*, Nai Kyi Win," she replied. Here everyone spoke at least a little Mon, but she also heard chatter in Burmese and Thai. Some families had been here for generations, but usually people moved out once they could get enough money to buy land or a shop.

She slowed her pace to walk on boards placed along the path still ankle-deep in mud. Because of Father, their hut was one of the bigger ones, but he was often gone. Whenever he was away, she would stay with her friends. She missed Aya and Auntie Ma, but there were girls her age in the camp. That was fun. Her best friends were Zin Min, and Yin Non Son. They loved to chat and she loved to listen. She had never had girlfriends before.

It was almost a year since she and Father walked out of the forest to this camp. Burma was just on the other side of the mountains, but it had taken more than a week to walk here. Now it was home.

She poured both pails of water into a big jar. That was for cooking and washing. For drinking they used another jar that captured the rain still falling almost every day. She heard her father inside the hut. It was good he was back, but she never quite knew what to say to him. Sometimes he was distracted and said nothing for hours. Sometimes he tried to tell her what to do. Other times he was like a teacher, correcting her Mon or lecturing about some long-ago event in Mon history.

"Father, the jars are full. I am going to school now."

Father came out of the hut, blinking in the sunlight. He wore his usual jacket and *longyi*, looking grouchy. He couldn't seem to see the good side of their new life. He missed the old house and he was always complaining about the lack of privacy. Here there was just a two-room hut. No polished floors, no paneled walls, no river, no veranda, no library, no place to just sit and think quietly, he grumbled on and on.

The camp was crowded and noisy, but there was a little market, celebrations of holidays and evenings with music or dance-dramas. Best of all, there was a school. Every day she got to go into the dirt-floored school with 30 others. She studied with the older ones, even some grown-ups, who already knew how to read and write in Mon and Burmese. It was fun. Now she had to hurry. Where was her box of pencils?

Father watched her as she found them next to her bed.

"When you are at school, go see Head Teacher Nai San Tin," he told her. Tell him I am willing to teach a course on Mon history. I'll be stuck here for several weeks and might as well teach at the school."

"Yes, Papa, but you know the school is pretty busy with the courses we already have."

"Surely they can spare a few hours a week for our own history and language. Young people need to understand where they come from."

"But we are in Siam now."

"Mon history is not just about Burma. Mons have been coming to this country for centuries. Many important people in Siam are Mons. Even in the royal family."

"Really?"

"Yes, the first king of this Chakri dynasty was the son of a Mon aristocrat who came to Ayuthaya. He was a great warrior and helped push the Burmans out of Siam. He was the great, great, great grandfather of the current king. He…"

"Papa, I have to go. I'll be late."

"Don't forget to ask about my Mon history course."

"Yes, Papa," she said as she grabbed her books off the rickety table and whirled out the door.

Class was starting when she reached the wooden school room, already full of students. Her usual seat on a bench in the last row was taken. She liked sitting at the back so she could watch everyone and no one could watch her. But now she had to walk to the first row, right in front of the teacher, who gave her a slight frown as she sat. Everyone must be looking at her. She bent over her book and tried to follow the teacher.

This morning, it was Thai language again. Thai wasn't too difficult. The letters were funny looking, but, in some ways, it was like Burmese. The hard part was saying the ends of the words. Their Thai teacher was always fussing with them about that. She was better at it than most, better even than Zin Min who had been in Thailand a lot longer. But all the girls were better than the lazy boys.

"Now, let's read the poem I assigned to you yesterday," the teacher said. "Who is ready to read?"

She shuffled through her papers and found the poem. It was by someone named Sri Prad. Only one of the students raised a hand.

"Yin Yin Nwe—this is a surprise," the teacher said. "Go ahead. Let us hear it."

It was that boy who was always teasing her. He wasn't very good at Thai, so now she could laugh at him. He was tall. Zin Min said he was handsome. Kind of dark, but his eyes were bright. Why was he looking at her and grinning? He started reading slowly:

"Shall I leave you with the sky? No!

Indra would sweep you high above.

Shall I leave you with the earth? No.

Earth's lord would you seduce.

Shall I leave you with the water? No!

The sea dragon would take you for his own.

It is only fit to leave you with yourself until I return."

He turned, smiled and bowed to her. The class erupted in laughter and she could feel the blood rush to her cheeks. Why was he doing this to her? She looked down and studied her papers.

"Well Yin Yin, that was better than your usual, but you will have to learn to face the front of the room, even if there is someone of special interest on the side," she said to more laughter from the class.

The lesson seemed to last forever. When it was finally over, she rushed home before anyone could tease her some more. Why were boys so annoying? He didn't really think she was so pretty the gods would seduce her. Did he? What if he did?

24

PLOI
Lucky New Year

Ploi smiled as she looked around the packed gambling rooms of the Jaikla Casino. More than a dozen bettors knelt on the big *Thua* mat, all staring at the bowl of cowrie shells placed in the center. She loved the sound of the rapid-fire clacks of the gamblers smacking down their ceramic betting tokens on the four corners of the mat. Behind the *Thua* mats an even larger group watched as Tim dropped the metal ball into the spinning roulette wheel.

"Red, red, red," one gambler shouted. Another called out "even number, please."

There were groans and cries of triumph as the ball settled into the slot for black 12. The Sichon district officer looked distraught as the croupier raked in his stack of tokens. She had to do something.

"Honored District Officer, sir," she said as she gave him a deep *wai* she knew would show off her bare shoulders. "It is an honor to have you back with us."

"Ploi, it is good to see you, but your wheel is abusing me."

"I will have to punish it then for such disobedience. No more oil for a week until it squeals like a beaten dog," she said with a smile. "But if I recall correctly, that same wheel was far too kind to you only last month. Luck is like the weather. Sometimes it is good, sometimes bad, but you still have to live your life."

"You bring sunshine with you, so please stay with me to help warm up your impudent wheel," he said.

She stroked his arm and smiled up at him.

"Your arm feels warm. Perhaps the weather is improving already," she said. "But before you get too hot and take all our money, let me treat you to some of this *farang* whisky – Scotch – brought all the way from across the ocean."

She handed the officer a glass of whisky with water and ice and lightly touched his arm.

"My next song will be dedicated to you," she said, motioning to the small band that shifted into the languid rhythms of a love song popular in the capital. The drummer played at a slower rhythm and horns softly wailed.

She felt the emotion of the song rise within her, swelling with the sad tones of lost love and loneliness. Around the room, the gamblers paused. Good. She could still attract attention even after four children. She let her voice soften to a whisper and then gain volume with the painful lyrics telling of the lover's death. She sang and walked slowly between the gambling mats, focusing on each of the customers in turn.

It's important to make everyone feel like I am singing just for them. The lantern light glittered off the silk of her new *phasin* and the gold chain that dipped into the valley between her breasts. When the song ended, there was a moment of silence. Then applause that swelled. They still liked her. Now, a graceful *wai* to complete the show.

Prem was leading the clapping, as he should. But why was he not downstairs overseeing the restaurant? Deliveries of food orders in the gambling room had been slow, so he should be doing something to speed up the service.

She pulled him aside into the small room that served as her office.

"I hope you have put some extra people in the kitchen. Some of our gamblers have been waiting 20 minutes for their orders."

"We didn't expect to have so many people, but we are catching up."

"We have a full house. Isn't it wonderful?"

"Maybe not. To get this many people, you had to send out pamphlets. I'm worried the casino is attracting too much attention," he said.

"Those pamphlets just said, 'Come to have fun at Jaikla,' and our new sign says 'Jaikla Restaurant.' We promised a special menu of delights on the eve of the New Year. We must take advantage of the king changing the calendar to add the *farang* New Year. As you can see, our people like to celebrate the New Year just like they do in Shanghai or London. So now we have two new year celebrations every year."

"I know what is on the sign, but everyone still thinks of Jaikla as the casino. The newspapers say the king thinks gambling dens encourage crime and cater only to the Chinese."

"Look around," she said. "There are just as many Thais as Chinese. Anyway, the Chinese we attract are the merchants and the businessmen, not the scrawny coolies that go to other dens. Some of those places are dark and dirty with half the clients lost in opium dreams. Our Chinese clients are people of influence and, if you have influence, you are immune to arrest. So be nice and polite to them."

"I am polite enough. But nice manners and pretty smiles won't protect us. Two of Sia Leng's casinos have been raided in the past three months and some bettors were arrested. The local authorities want to show the king they are tough on gambling. The king wants to show that Siam is a civilized nation."

"Yes, but even His Majesty holds lotteries to raise funds for special projects, like buying weapons for the army, or ships for the navy."

"Those lotteries are all legal and approved at the highest level. Our casino is not. All I'm saying is to be discreet."

"Don't worry," she said. "Those raids were all arranged with Sia Leng beforehand, like the capture of our lottery proceeds last year, to make money for the local government and to show the authorities are tough on gambling. Besides, we have the leader of the anti-gambling task force on our payroll. Lieutenant Dam will ensure we are protected."

"I just think we should be careful."

"Thank you for your concern. Now please go down and speed up the food service."

Prem looked like he wanted to say something more, but then turned and headed back towards the stairway.

25

TUN WAY
Too Soon?

Tun Way made a deep *wai* in the Thai style as Deputy Commissioner Pakdee stepped down from the motorcar. He had been trying for a year to get Pakdee to visit the Mon camp in Chumphon. Set in a clearing on a path down from the hills that formed the border between British Burma and Siam, the camp now had nearly 500 residents. Further to the east was the main road carrying traffic north to the capital. It had been recently widened for the smoke-belching trucks that have replaced the horse carriages and elephant caravans of the past. And only a few miles away construction crews were completing the railroad that would make travel between Bangkok and *Monthon* Nakhon Srithammarat even faster by land than by sea. Inspection of road and railroad construction was one of Pakdee's duties, so he finally agreed to make an inspection tour with a side trip to the Mon camp.

Tun Way felt indebted to Pakdee for getting official permission for him and his men to be in Siam. Pakdee had deflected British Special Branch inquiries about Tun Way and had found housing for him and his daughter in the Mon camp. In return, he had continued to give Pakdee information on British activities along the border. His men made frequent forays across the border all the way from Ranong to the Three Pagoda Pass. That had not been without risk. It was the capture of one of his men that brought the Burmese police to his home. He had barely escaped with Ngwe Lay and a few possessions. His camp inside Burma, in the hills east of Bago, had to be abandoned. For the past two years he and some of his men had been stuck in this little camp at the edge of the forest.

Now, he needed Pakdee's support for his new plan. He should have worked harder to improve his Thai, but he could speak enough to make himself understood. He put on a smile as he escorted the deputy commissioner through the camp. As always, the Thai was neatly groomed, his mustache trimmed and his thick black hair glistened. He wore a white, high-collared jacket with silver buttons and carried an impressive, brass-headed walking stick.

"Welcome to our celebration of *Thingyan*—our traditional New Year, like your *Songkran* celebration, honored Deputy Commissioner," he said. "I have been your guest so many times, I am grateful to serve as your host for once, however poorly."

"There are some matters we need to discuss, but I also look forward to spending the New Year celebrations with you," Pakdee said. "I want to see how the Mons celebrate."

"Our celebration is similar to yours. We feel at home in Siam—too much so."

"Why is that?"

"Our Mon people have been coming to Siam for the past four centuries to flee oppression by the Burmese. Once in Siam, Mons become comfortable and never return to fight. That is why our camp is near the border—not in areas long settled by Mon people further north. I try for years to get them interested in struggle inside Burma."

"Perhaps fighting is not the solution," Pakdee said. "Can't you protect your heritage some other way?"

"I tried to make the Mon Culture and Language Society, but they burned our school down. Our teachers co-opted to teach in racist Burmese language schools and our businessmen bribed with contracts from British and Chinese. Many Mons held in debt slavery by the blood-sucking Indian money lenders."

"Nai Tun Way, you have my sympathies. I appreciate the information you have provided, but you don't seem to be making progress."

"We will change that. I will organize new activities. My men here are anxious to return. We will wage cultural war of self-protection with pamphlets attacking colonial government, calling for Mon language schools, and rejecting use of Burmese. We just need assurance we can come back into Siam if necessary."

"Yes, yes, but your misadventure five years ago did not go over well. Prince Damrong was most unhappy."

"I apologize for the error, but we were unlucky. At least no weapons were captured by British. Since then we make more than dozen incursions without loss of weapons."

"Yes, that is true, but several of your supporters have been arrested."

"If dare nothing, achieve nothing. Increasing activities will provide better information. I must take personal charge inside Burma."

"Hmmm, that is part of what we need to discuss," Pakdee said. "I must inform you my government no longer feels the need for your information. We have an embassy in Rangoon. Our merchants travel freely around the country. Most important, we believe the British are no longer tempted to expand their colonies at our expense. So we will no longer sponsor your information-gathering trips."

This was bad news, Tun Way thought, but not unexpected. For the past six years the British-Siamese agreement on the Malay states to the south had been working well, even though the Malays in Siam were restless. The new British governor of the Straits colonies had denied support for the Malay uprisings.

"Our relations with the British are good," Pakdee said. "Both the British and the French are bogged down in that terrible war that has already expanded to Turkey, China and Suez. His Majesty is paying close attention. He has friendly connections with the British and the Russian royal families. He was trained by the British and held an officer's commission in the British army. His Majesty follows his old British regiment with particular attention. So, you must do nothing to threaten our relations with the British."

"I don't ask for much. Just access to border and for border officials to look the other way from time to time."

"I will have to think about this," Pakdee said. "It could put me at risk."

"Let us first give you proper welcome," Tun Way said, waving to the group of women waiting beside the camp office. "Happy *Thingyan*."

Three girls in yellow and green silk sarongs *waied* gracefully. They held bouquets of wildflowers. Ngwe Lay was one. She looked lovely. Too much like Su. He looked away as she raised a bronze bowl of water filled with white jasmine flowers. The flowers suffused the hot afternoon air with a sweet fragrance—the same fragrance he remembered from their wedding.

He turned back to see Ngwe Lay shyly pouring water on Pakdee's hands, murmuring a blessing in Mon. The deputy commissioner looked pleased with the greeting, smiling at the three women. Ngwe Lay looked up at him, smiled and then giggled as she turned away.

What was she doing? Pakdee had a reputation for his interest in pretty women and he had thought having women from the camp greet him would be a way to gain his sympathy. It was a surprise when the camp committee recommended Ngwe Lay be one of them.

She is too young for this. But she was taller than any of the women in the camp. As he looked at her now, he could see why Pakdee was interested. Although slender, the silk top wrapped around her breasts was well filled. Her body was that of a grown woman. It was too soon. Too many things were happening too soon.

Only two nights earlier, Ngwe Lay took part in the courting game of *sabaa* played in the camp as part of the *Thingyan* celebration. He had watched from the back of the room as two groups of young men and women sat facing each other on long benches. Each of the youngsters held a circular wooden disk, the *sabaa*.

He had watched *sabaa* with Su more than sixteen years earlier. That had been his first chance to show her he was interested in marriage. She had pretended it was all just in fun, but it had been an important step in his courtship. It showed her he was serious and they came from the same tradition, unlike that big-nosed British doctor.

It was strange to watch the boys rolling their *sabaas* at those of the girls. There were shouts and jokes that elicited giggles and some repartee from the girls. It all seemed rowdier than he remembered. We were more refined in the old days. Why was Ngwe Lay getting so much male attention? She was fifteen years old—old enough perhaps for marriage according to Mon custom, but still so young. It would be a relief to have her safely married, but none of the men in the camp were suitable. Most were poorly educated. Some would return with him to Burma. None had much money or land.

But what would happen to her while he was away, perhaps for a long time? When she was little, Ngwe Lay was safe at home with Aya and Ma. It was no longer so simple.

He had dragged her to a foreign country. Who would look after her here? What would happen to her when he returned to Burma? The lewd double meaning of some of the boys' jokes appalled him. She was too innocent to protect herself. He had failed as a father. It could get worse once he was away. But he could not back out of the plan to work in Burma. The Mon people depended on him.

He watched as Pakdee chatted with the girls who led him into the meeting hall and served him Mon delicacies of pumpkin soup, fish curry and tea leaf salad, along with a deep red sweetened tea of hibiscus flowers. The deputy commissioner seemed particularly attentive to Ngwe Lay, who was explaining how to make Mon-style green curry with fish. Ngwe Lay's cooking skills had surprised Tun Way during the past year in the camp. She had learned from Aya all that time he was stuck in Siam or hiding in the hills above Bago.

Somehow, she had become a woman without him noticing. Clearly, however, the young men in the camp had noticed. One boy after another had sent their *sabaas* rolling towards Ngwe Lay's. The one to claim hers with a direct strike was a dark-skinned boy, Yin Yin, one of his own men. The arrogant whelp fancied himself adept with women, often boasting of his conquests over their campfires in the forest. Why would Ngwe Lay smile at that rascal? The boy was a good talker, but when there was work to be done, he was hard to find. His father had been a farmer known for his prodigious consumption of rice wine and his limited production of rice. He had already told Yin Yin he wasn't wanted for the next incursion and the arrogant fool had walked away in anger. No, this boy was not suitable at all. He would have to find a way to keep them apart. But how? If he was going to be spending more time in Burma, she would be unprotected, not just from Yin Yin but from all the other boys staying behind in the camp.

The next day, he was surprised when Pakdee offered to give him a ride in his noisy automobile, but less surprised when he suggested that Ngwe Lay come along. He looked at the strange-looking vehicle making grumbling noises on the road beside the camp. It didn't look safe.

"This is a Morgan Runabout Deluxe. It can average almost 40 miles an hour—if the roads are smooth enough," Pakdee said proudly.

"It sounds like an angry bull. Dangerous?" he asked.

"Absolutely not. We drove all the way from Songkhla in only two days, picking up petrol at government stations in Thung Song and Ban Dorn along the way. With careful driving there is no danger whatsoever."

Pakdee ushered Ngwe Lay into the rear seat alongside him, leaving Tun Way to sit beside the driver. He gripped the metal post holding up the canvas roof of the vehicle as it accelerated to an astonishing speed. The car took them down the dirt road to the main road.

"Now we can really go fast," Pakdee called from behind him. He could hear Ngwe Lay laughing with excitement.

It seemed like hours before they returned to the camp, covered in red dust. His daughter didn't seem to mind. At dinner that night Ngwe

Lay sat next to Pakdee and explained each of the Mon dishes. Pakdee seemed delighted with the dinner and the Mon music afterwards. This was the time to push his request for border access.

"We need your support. The Mon people need your support," he said after a detailed explanation of his plans.

"That is not so easy," Pakdee said. "This is not the time to annoy the British. Besides, if you go back into Burma, who will look after your lovely daughter?"

He is going to refuse to help. He looked at Pakdee smiling at Ngwe Lay and had a sudden thought. It might solve all his problems.

"My daughter. Yes, that is a problem, but if I went back into Burma, I would be concerned about her. Would you be willing to take her into your household?"

Pakdee looked surprised, but pleased.

"As what?"

"I don't know. As ward? As servant? Maid for your wife?"

"We don't need any more servants and you undervalue her," Pakdee said. "She is a beautiful, intelligent and charming young woman. In only a few days we have become quite friendly."

"The responsibilities of a father are great," Pakdee said. "What would you say if I asked for her as a wife I would protect and treasure?"

26

PLOI
Raid

Ploi scrutinized the three women who entered the restaurant. They wore colorful *phasins* and thick gold chains. The heavyset lady leading the group was the wife of a rubber merchant and a frequent customer. She *waied* to the women and nodded to the guard at the wooden door to the staircase. He opened the door, and the women went up to the second-floor gambling room. It looked like it would be a good night for the casino. The upstairs casino had been closed so Jaikla could open its usual *Songkran* gambling hut near Wat Nantharam. It had been a relief to operate legally once again to celebrate the traditional New Year.

The holiday take had been good this year. The war spreading everywhere had created rising demand for rice, rubber, tin and fish from Nakhon. As long as the actual fighting stayed away, war was good for business. And what was good for business was good for the casino. With help from Sia Leng and Dam, she had reached an agreement with Jate's old gang, now run by Nit. She agreed not to open a casino in Nakhon town and Nit agreed not to interfere with her operations in Pakpanang. Sia Leng would control gambling in Songkhla, Pattalung and Trang. Nit would expand his casino in Nakhon and run the bullfights and cockfights without competition. They agreed to alternate the underground lotteries, with Sia Leng holding his lottery on the third and fourth weeks of each month. Ploi took the second and Nit the more profitable first week when Chinese mine workers got their pay.

The lottery made money, but wasn't much fun. It was the casino she enjoyed, and she had made it the best in the south. Jaikla attracted gamblers from as far away as Pattani, Songkhla and Chaiya. The steamship lines along the coast meant it was only a few hours for the wealthy to get to Pakpanang. She had arranged a small flotilla of boats to bring customers from the steamship pier to the casino.

A group of men chatting loudly in Teochew and Cantonese pushed through the restaurant door. These big gamblers were rice merchants from Pattani, where the government was making it difficult for casinos to operate. They would tell their wives they came to Pakpanang to discuss rice prices with the big mills, but they would also enjoy a few hours at the casino and conclude the night with the women at one of the green lantern establishments across the river from Jaikla.

"Welcome to Jaikla," she said with a smile and a *wai* to the men. Prem greeted them in Teochew, describing the southern Chinese delicacies on offer from the kitchen. Prem was useful in dealing with the Chinks. She could charm them and attract them, but she never understood these burly men with their narrow eyes. Many were more comfortable in Chinese than Thai. There were always bursts of loud laughter at some joke that Prem told—a joke she could not understand and he would never explain. It was probably coarse and sexual. Why did men feel they had to be careful about what they said to women when they were so careless and rough about what they did to then? It didn't matter. As long as they brought their bundles of paper banknotes to spend on the games, food and drink, that was enough.

"It will be a good night," Prem called to her with a smile. "Maybe we should start our duets again. We haven't sung together for weeks."

"We should practice first," she said. "I brought in a singer from Hong Kong. I probably won't sing tonight."

Prem's face fell. He should understand they had demanding customers who came from far away. It wasn't like their first years together anymore. They had to meet a higher standard now. She climbed up the stairs, pleased to hear the distinctive clack of betting tokens being raked in from the *Thua* mats. She *waied* to each group of gamblers, greeting many of them by name. She walked to the group around the roulette wheel. "You gentlemen are working hard. You must be thirsty," she said with a laugh.

"Bring some drinks for the roulette players," she called to one of the two girls carrying trays.

She *waied* in response to their thanks and continued through to the big room she had added for the Chinese games, *Fantan, Po Pan* and *Po Kam*. There was a gasp from the *Po Pan* mat as the dealer removed the outer box and revealed the top face of the *Po Pan* cube.

"White wins!" the dealer cried to a mix of cheers and groans.

"You big winners should treat your friends to some of the delicious *dim sum* we have on tonight's menu."

She left the Chinese gamblers to their orders and discussion of the price of rice on the Singapore market.

She knelt down next to Tim who sat on a mat next to a large basket of betting tokens with the heavy strong box behind him.

"Twelve hundred baht so far."

She nodded in satisfaction. All was going well.

"Miss Ploi, someone to see you," the door guard called out.

She walked back through the betting mats, chatting with the gamblers as she went. At the top of the staircase, she saw the guard holding a boy by the arm. The guard gave her a folded paper.

"He says this is an urgent message. Only for you."

She unfolded the paper. In heavy letters it said: "Raid tonight. Not my unit. Go now."

"Who gave you this?" she asked the boy.

"A big man. Police," he said.

She gave him a small coin, and he scurried back down the stairs. She took a deep breath and strode to the center of the room.

"Dear friends," she said loudly. "I am sorry to announce that we are closing early tonight."

"But I am winning," one man siad.

"I just ordered food," complained another.

"There is no time. We may have a visit from the police. Please go down to the restaurant and have something to eat—all meals are free."

A few of the gamblers headed down the stairs while others crowded around Tim to exchange their betting tokens. She ordered the dealers to collect the cowries and cards. The croupier at the roulette wheel was folding it into its recess in the wall. Counting the tokens was taking too long. She crouched down and started helping Tim. The last of the gamblers were still waiting for their money when she heard heavy footsteps on the stairway and banging on the iron door to the betting room.

"No time. Keep your tokens. Go now," she told them. Two of the dealers pushed back the false wall concealing the rear exit. The gamblers rushed through the narrow door and clambered down the dark stairway. Loud sounds of metal against metal came from the entrance. They must be trying to smash the lock.

"Take the strongbox," she told Tim.

Ploi turned to the musicians. "Start playing. Something loud with drums," she told them. The music would hide the sounds of the gamblers fleeing out the back. Once Tim and the last of the gamblers had disappeared through the door, the dealers moved the wall back.

There was a loud crack, and the door swung open. A half dozen policemen she didn't recognize rushed into the room. A tall man in a round-collared shirt and rough *phajonggraben* seemed to be in charge even though he was not wearing a police uniform. He waved a large gun and looked around in puzzlement.

"Where are the gamblers?" he demanded.

"There are no gamblers. This is a restaurant," Ploi said. The man ignored her as the policeman overturned the mats. Two of the policemen kicked in the door to her office. The idiots didn't notice it wasn't even locked.

"Find the gambling equipment," the tall man ordered.

"What are you doing?" Ploi demanded.

"You are Ploi Jaikla?" he asked.

"Yes, and you are intruding in my restaurant."

One of the policemen put the big betting token chest on the floor before them. He used an iron crowbar to pry open the lid. Brightly colored ceramic betting tokens spilled out.

"Your gambling den, you mean."

"This is just a place for music and singing," she said.

"You can now do your singing in court," he said. "You and everyone here are under arrest for running an illegal gambling casino."

27

NGWE LAY
Mon Wife

The automobile eased to a halt in front of the tall wooden gate. Pakdee's driver sounded the horn. After a moment, the big gate swung open.

"This, my dear, is home. I know you will like it here," Pakdee said.

She looked up at the sprawling mansion on thick pillars of teak. She could see at least six roofs of orange tile glistening in the sun. A broad staircase led first to a small pavilion with its own tile roof and then up to the gated entrance to a broad wooden platform connecting the buildings. It was even larger than her house in Bago.

In the shady space under the house she could see three women lounging on a wooden platform raised off the beaten earth of the floor. A half-dozen children were playing some kind of game with big, shiny seeds. They all looked up as the car slowed to a halt.

Pakdee leaped out of the car as the children rushed to greet him. He laughed as the children clung to his legs.

"Children. *Wai* properly and greet your father politely," a heavy-set woman in a silk *phasin* said from the top of the staircase. She came down the stairs, careful to avoid stepping on the hem of the *phasin*.

"Father, welcome home," she said as she made a polite *wai* to Pakdee who returned the greeting.

"Girls, what are you waiting for? Come greet your husband." Four women came out from under the house and one scurried down from the platform above.

Husband? Pakdee had said he already had five wives, but somehow Ngwe Lay had thought they would all be old. These were young women—quite pretty, even the plump one. He had assured her they would all welcome her as they were tired of bearing children.

She saw the plump one staring at her.

"Who is this you have brought with you?" she asked.

"Ah, Apinya, dear wife, this is Miss Ngwe Lay," Pakdee said. "Her father is a friend who has asked me to care for her. Ngwe Lay, please pay your respects to my wife Apinya. You can call her Mae Yai. That means big mother."

She climbed down from the car, adjusted her *longyi* and made a respectful *wai*. She looked up and saw the woman frowning at her.

"Well, I suppose we could use another hand in the kitchen," Apinya said. "What is her name?"

"Ngwe Lay," Pakdee said.

"What a strange name," Apinya said. "Who can pronounce that? We'll call her Lay. How long must we keep her?"

"She is not a servant. She was given to me as a consort."

"No, no. We discussed this. Times have changed. You already have too many wives. His Majesty the King has said too many wives brings waste and inefficiency. It is not civilized. She will have to go back."

Would he really do that? She would be ruined. She couldn't go back. She didn't want to go back. He had promised.

Pakdee looked unhappy, then determined.

"We can discuss this later, but it is already done. Now find a place for her and her things," he said pointing to the driver who was carrying two cloth bags of Ngwe Lay's belongings.

Did that mean she was safe? That he wanted her to stay?

"There are no more rooms. She can sleep with the housemaids. She is just a girl herself."

Ngwe Lay looked around at the wives and children, now in a half-circle behind Apinya. They didn't look friendly.

"Then she will sleep in my room," Pakdee said, pulling her towards the staircase. Apinya's frown was duplicated on the faces of the other wives arrayed behind her. Pakdee led her up the wooden steps. At the pavilion, they washed their feet in a carved wooden trough. Then they stepped through the gate at the top.

"Don't worry. Apinya will get over it," Pakdee whispered as he looked back at the wives staring up at them. "She is only upset because I didn't consult with her first. She always seemed happy for me to have more wives, so she will get used to this. They all will."

He opened a door, and they entered a long room with a high ceiling. At one end was a desk and chair next to a cabinet topped with packets of paper. At the other end was a platform covered with a thick mat. Satin sheets were folded on top.

"You can rest here while I talk to Apinya, uh, Mae Yai. Then we will bathe and eat. Don't worry. It will all be fine."

She didn't know what to say, so she said nothing. Pakdee stepped over the raised portal and closed the door behind him. Ngwe Lay lay back on the mat. The wood of the platform was still warm, but the patch of sunlight coming through the narrow, barred window had moved across the floor as evening approached.

Why didn't Mae Yai like her? She would take good care of Pakdee. She blushed as she thought of their nights together during their three-week journey from Chumpon.

The first night had been frightening and painful, but Pakdee had been patient and kind. If only Aya or Auntie Ma had explained to her what she was supposed to do. Zin Min had tried to explain what should happen after the quick wedding ceremony at the camp. But she hadn't got it quite right. It had been awkward and embarrassing, but after the first night, there was no more pain. After two or three times, it actually felt good. It was like playing with their bodies like she had played with her dolls. Now she had a man's body to play with. Pakdee was much older, but he was still slim and his stomach was flat. She was amazed and a little proud that she could make his organ swell and stiffen. She enjoyed seeing the eagerness on his face when she unwrapped her breast covering and untied her *longyi* and let it slip down her legs.

It was good there was no separate room for her. She liked sleeping with Pakdee, watching his chest rise and fall, hearing the soft whisper of his breath through the bristles of his mustache. She didn't know it was important to a Thai man, but Zin Min had told her that a man's male spirit, his *hpon*, resided on his right side, so she must always sleep on the left. She liked him holding her and sniffing at her neck in the morning. Each night they would chat after sex. She would ask questions about his work, his family, what he liked and disliked. Unlike Father, he answered whatever questions she asked. He never said she was too young to understand. He was interested in her life and truly sorry that she had lost her mother without ever knowing her. He told her he had lost his mother and father too.

Their journey from the refugee camp took them along the coast south from Chumpon to a meeting in Chaiya with the *monthon* commissioner there. Then they drove to the port town of Ban Dorn where they feasted on sweet-tasting sea crabs at the mouth of the broad Tapi River. The road wound through the mountains south of Ban

Dorn. In some places it was steep but fun racing down the slope with the breeze whipping her hair behind her.

Several times during the journey Pakdee stopped to inspect work on the railway line. Hundreds of sweating Chinese and Thai laborers carried the heavy boards they placed between the steel rails. Occasionally they heard explosions that Pakdee explained were needed to level the rocky limestone terrain. Each night they stayed at a guest house at a district or provincial office. Often Pakdee had to leave her to attend meetings, but he seemed to enjoy answering her questions about what he had seen and done. He hadn't, however, said much about his major wife, Apinya. The woman seemed so fierce. Why didn't she want her in the household? What could she do? Why had Father abandoned her in this strange place?

28

PREM
Suspicion

Prem awoke to the cackle of two roosters competing to end his sleep. The pale light was climbing the far wall. He felt for Ploi's body beside him. It was one of the joys of the morning to feel the soft warmth of her body beside him, to nuzzle her neck and feel his need grow within him, even if it didn't lead to anything more. But his hand felt only the slick material of the satin sheet crumpled on the sleeping mat. She must have risen early. He looked around. The children were asleep in a row, each child a little larger than the one before—all except for Awt, who now insisted on sleeping in a separate room with two of the boys who worked at the restaurant.

On the mat closest to him slept five-year-old On, his dark skin and big head contrasting with the lighter complexions and delicate features of An and Phai, his quiet ones. On was so different. He was more like Awt, full of demands and aggressive energy. How could the same parents produce such different children?

How old was Phai now? Not yet 12 and already as tall as her mother. She had dark eyes that missed nothing. Phai was the scholar among his children. She had already read all the books in the house and learned everything he could remember from his own schooling. She could write more Chinese characters with far more skill than he could and just as well as Awt, who had studied with a private Chinese tutor. It was like she was the daughter of Phra Som. She enjoyed their regular trips to Wat Talumpuk where she begged Som to teach her more. She often returned from the temple with books Som had lent her. But what could she do next? The Pakpanang School had been in operation for more than a decade, but didn't accept girls. There were schools for girls in Bangkok, but she was too young to study there on her own. It wouldn't be too many years before he and Ploi would have to find a husband for her.

Little An, only a year younger than Phai, was short and slight. He wasn't much bigger than On, even though he was five years older. An was the easy one. He was always happy to help when there were tasks to be done, unlike Awt and On, who had the same marvelous ability to sense approaching work and to disappear—often together.

Both Phai and An had finally gotten over Awt's reluctance to do anything with them. They had taken to walking or reading together. His oldest son seemed to care only for his gang of friends. They would disappear on boats in the bay, into the forest or along the docks for most of the day. Strangely, Awt, who ignored Phai and An, delighted in teaching his youngest brother how to bait a hook, weave fishing nets, paddle a boat and catch frogs at night by lantern light.

The children were changing so quickly it was hard to know what they would become next. The three youngest now spent much of their time with him at the restaurant. Phai and An had proved helpful, taking orders, greeting customers and even learning to cook some of the Chinese specialties he enjoyed making. It was the one part of his Chinese heritage that Ploi encouraged. It brought in customers. When his mother came to the restaurant, the four of them would work in the kitchen—making hot and sour soup or steaming *pao* filled with bits of red pork. On avoided the kitchen except to grab something to eat. He was more interested in the activities in the gambling room, often sneaking in to watch the action. Now that there was no more gambling he often disappeared with Awt and his gang of friends.

Prem rose from the mat, careful not to disturb On and headed out to the central platform. There he saw Ploi, bent over a large sheet of paper. He could see the complex lines of the design drawn on the paper.

"Still working on that?"

"Of course. This is our future. We won't even have to build the boat ourselves. I can buy one of those big rice barges and convert it. It may not look like it, but there is a huge amount of space in those things."

Ploi smiled up at him and pointed to the drawing.

"See, we can put a cook room at the back. We can have two floors below the deck and one more floor above it. I have designed a separate room for the Chinese games and another for the roulette wheel and the cards. There will be even more space than at the Jaikla Casino."

"Ploi dear, haven't we suffered enough from gambling? We spent five nights in that miserable jail. We were humiliated in court and forced to pay a fine of more than 1,000 baht. Enough. Let's just live quietly and make the restaurant successful."

"You can manage the restaurant if you want. Once we move the gaming to the boat, you can expand upstairs into the old gambling room. The restaurant is your business, the casino is mine. It has paid for this house, for our food and for all the money we've saved. Without it there would be no money for Mother. Just because we had one minor setback, we can't give up on it. Besides, by putting the gambling rooms on a boat, we will be far safer. Lieutenant Dam says none of the police, not even that detective unit that raided the casino, has authority over what takes place on the sea."

"If Dam is so smart, how come we got raided? Why didn't he protect us the way he was paid to?"

"I've told you three times already. The police came from Nakhon, not Pakpanang. Yet Dam was still able to warn us so we didn't lose the gambling funds. Even more important, all our customers escaped. Without Dam, it would have been much worse."

"Why do you always defend that big clumsy oaf?"

"Can't you use more polite language," Ploi said coldly. "The children hear you and they'll start speaking the same crude way. Awt already does. He spits like an old Chink coolie. Where does he get that from?"

"I would teach him better behavior if he would stay around long enough. Maybe he gets it from the honorable policeman."

"Without Dam, we would have been out of business long ago. The fine we paid is just a cost of doing business. You know we can afford it. And the court decided against any more punishment for us because there was so little evidence. It was Dam who got rid of most of it. He even got the betting tokens to disappear from the police station. If we could have gotten the roulette wheel away, there wouldn't have been any evidence at all."

"If he had done his job properly, there wouldn't have been a raid. Anyway, if the gambling is out at sea and the police have no duty to stop gambling on ships, then we won't have to pay the guy anymore."

"No, you don't understand," Ploi said. "After all his success in suppressing gangsters like Jate and Tiger Thuam, Dam is now the most famous policeman in the *monthon*. He has the respect of both police and *nakleng* throughout Nakhon. I still get useful information from him. He makes sure that Nit and the *Angyi* leave us alone. His reputation protects us. No, we could not survive without Dam."

"We? I can survive just fine without him," he said.

A strange expression flitted across his wife's face. Why was she so attached to Dam? All those private meetings. All those trips to Songkhla she had to take on her own. All the money she paid to Dam. The light in Dam's eyes whenever he came to the casino office.

He felt his heart shrink inside him. She turned back to her plans for the boat. She leaned on one arm over the paper and drew with small, careful movements with the other. Her expression was calm as she worked. Under the dark crescents of her eyebrows, her large eyes were focused on the paper. Her full lips were pursed in concentration and her smooth skin was pale in the morning light. Her long, graceful legs stretched the fabric of her *phasin*. Her blouse had slipped from one shoulder and he could see the firm swelling of one breast.

Of course Dam desired her. Anyone would, but she would never betray him. They had been too long together, had gone through too much for anything to part them. He pushed the thought from his mind.

29

NGWE LAY
Minor Wife

Ngwe Lay looked at the four bare wooden walls of the room. Pakdee had left for work and she was alone again. Father had often left her with just Aya for company. She had hoped living with Pakdee would be different. Father had told her she would be part of a big, happy family, that the other wives would be like sisters.

She could hear chatter outside the window that opened onto the central platform, but she couldn't quite make out the words. Three of the wives were sitting on a mat. It looked like they were sewing clothes. Maybe she could help. Mae Yai came out and peered over the shoulders of the three sewers.

Ngwe Lay put on a loose white blouse and opened the door. All four women looked at her and she hesitated. She made a deep *wai,* which the older woman did not return.

"Maybe I can help?" she said.

Apinya looked at her with a slight frown. "We are making costumes for the *Khon.* Do you know how to sew?"

"I can try. I can learn, sir" she said, realizing as soon as she said it that something was wrong.

The younger women giggled. The older one sniffed. "Do I look like a man? Say— 'I would like to try to learn, madam,'" she said.

"Yes, madam, I would like try to learn. Madam."

"We have a performance in two weeks. No one has the time to teach you. You would only make a mess of the fabric and waste our time. Go back to your sleeping mat—that seems to be the only place where you have any skill."

"She must do really good work on her back. Father hasn't taken anyone else to his room in weeks," Siriporn grumbled. "But he'll get bored. I know how to get him excited—even after three children."

"Yes, I am sure you are right. She can't sing or dance and she speaks strangely," said plump Duangjan.

"Like a retarded child," Apinya said. "Don't worry. I'll restore the regular schedule soon. Now, you," she said, turning to Ngwe Lay, "go back to your room and stop interrupting our work."

Her cheeks burned. How could they talk about her like that right to her face? She bowed and backed away. She threw herself down on the mat and tried to stop the tears seeping out of her eyes. It would be hours before Pakdee returned. She would rub his back and touch him as he instructed. She was learning what pleased him and what didn't, but there was nothing for her to do until he returned.

She looked at the only two books she had brought with her. She had read the Mon folk tales twice already. Why hadn't she asked Father for more? Now he was gone and she couldn't even send a letter to him. He was with his group of men somewhere in Burma. He hadn't even told her how long it would be before he returned.

A bitter, acid taste seeped into the back of her mouth. Her head felt strange and her stomach hurt like that time she had eaten a crab curry that had been left out too long. But she had eaten little except for rice gruel and morning glory stems. Could that make her sick?

Maybe she could ask Pakdee for some Thai books. She needed to improve her Thai. She didn't want the other wives to laugh at her. She wanted to understand the stories of the *Khon* drama group.

From watching the rehearsals over the past few nights, she could see the stories were like the Mon stories of Rama. The dance, with the colorful costumes and music, was like the Burmese *Yama Zatdaw* performance that Auntie Ma had taken her to see in Bago. She missed Bago. It would be so nice to be sitting on the veranda looking out over the sleepy river that wound down from the hills in front of the house. She missed doing the housework with Aya, listening to Ma's stories of events in the hospital. She missed Aya. She missed Auntie Ma. When would Father return? Would they ever go back home? But now she was married. She would never see her home again.

The tears she had held back now poured forth, sliding down her face onto the mat.

30
PREM
Fatherhood

Prem sat hunched over the ledger book. Restaurant income was down again and he would soon have to take another one of his gold chains to the pawn shop to pay for supplies. He had hoped the restaurant could use the empty gaming room upstairs to attract more customers. Instead, without the casino, customers had drifted away. Most nights the upstairs tables were empty. He had just paid the final month's salary to the last two cooks and let them go. Now it was just he and Chaem doing the cooking. Fortunately, Phai was happy to help as a waitress.

Unfortunately, Ploi showed no interest in the restaurant and would not allow any of their savings to be spent on it. She was always at the shipyard where her rice barge was being fitted out. That was taking all of their savings. Why was it so expensive? Ploi insisted on polished teak paneling and heavy brass fittings. She bought Persian rugs, a whole new set of gambling tokens, a new roulette wheel, and elegant lamps and dozens of cushions. Then there were the bronze statues Ploi commissioned of Lakshmi, the Hindu Goddess of Good Fortune and Kung-Te-Tien, the Chinese goddess of luck. Thousands of baht, for what? He had tried to get her to be more careful, but she refused to listen. The last time he tried, it turned into an argument.

"Your customers come to gamble, not to admire the good luck goddesses or the beautiful doorknobs," he had told her. "They won't bet more because the cowrie shells are new. You are wasting our money and we have very little left."

"We will make it all back with the casino boat," she said.

"I just wish you would listen to me at least a little. I am the man of the family and I should have the final say."

"Yes, of course, you are the man and can lead on most things, but we agreed long ago the casino was mine and the restaurant was yours. All the money for the boat came from casino earnings."

"I don't remember any agreement exactly. It's just the way it has worked out because you have no interest in the restaurant and ignore my ideas about the casino. The restaurant never made much profit because we priced the food to attract gamblers."

"Don't worry," she said, patting his arm. "Once the boat is in operation, I'll order lots of food from the restaurant at a good price and the restaurant will be profitable again."

"It's just that you never listen to me and you always put the casino before our family."

"It is because of the casino our family has a big house, has clothes to wear and food to eat. I put the family first. That is why the casino has to be successful. You used to understand that. Now you object to everything I do."

"I'm just not happy with everything you are doing. I have the right to say something, don't I?"

"Why are you so unhappy? You don't really believe the casino will fail. There is a big and growing demand for gambling. With the shutdown of the legal casinos all over the country, the big gamblers, the Chinese businessmen, the Thai aristocrats, the government officials, they will all come to the Jaikla floating casino."

"You put the family at risk. We were lucky to get only a fine after the raid. You could have gone to prison."

"No way. I was careful to make arrangements with Sia Leng and his man in the *monthon* commission. With the boat we will start the gambling only when we are far from land. There is not much risk."

"You have become too dependent on that oaf of a policeman. He has evidence he can use against us anytime he chooses. I don't like it."

"You worry too much. Sergeant Dam is under control."

"How can you control a police *nakleng* who boasts of being the 'Black Tiger?' You should stay away from him. Find another policeman to provide protection."

"What do you have against him? If he is a *nakleng,* that is to our advantage. Dam is perfect for the job. He hates his boss; he dislikes all the rules coming down from Bangkok; his men follow him without question; and he is in charge of anti-gambling activity in Pakpanang. Who could be better?"

"He is too full of himself. He thinks he is invulnerable. We will regret ever working with him. What's more, he is a bad influence on Awt and On. Why is he spending so much time with my sons?"

"I know what is best for the casino and Dam is best."

"But not for our family."

"My casino and my family—they prosper together."

Prem gritted his teeth and looked up as Awt stuck his head in the restaurant door.

"Going fishing. On and I are going to show Uncle Dam how to catch the big ones."

Prem felt a flash of anger. Why were his sons going fishing with that guy who didn't know an oar from a fishing pole?

"I'll take you fishing," he said. "You don't need Dam."

"Aren't you busy with the restaurant?"

"No problem. There won't be many customers today. Your Grandma can handle it. I'll come with you."

"Can we all fit? You and Uncle Dam are both pretty heavy?"

"Don't worry. I know how to handle a boat and the weather should be calm today."

Awt shrugged and dashed off, shouting "On—Dad is coming too."

31

PAKDEE
Resignation

Pakdee nodded in reply to the *wai* from the secretary manning the desk outside the high commissioner's office.

"What does he want?" he asked.

"I don't know, but it's something big in the overnight telegram. He's quite excited."

"Why didn't it come to me first?"

"It was marked private for the high commissioner."

Pakdee smoothed his mustache and straightened the folds of his *phajonggraben*. He pushed open the heavy doors to the big office and bowed.

"Good morning, Your Royal Highness, sir."

Prince Lopburi Ramet responded with a quick and careless *wai*.

"This morning I received a personal telegram from the minister with important news affecting us all. I will announce it to the staff in a few moments. His Royal Highness Prince Damrong Rajanubhab has resigned. We will have a new minister and I expect more changes will follow that might affect me personally. There are important posts in Bangkok that need to be filled."

It was stunning news, but not a complete surprise. One by one King Chulalongkorn's half-brothers, who were uncles of King Vajiravudh, had been moved to less important positions or pushed into retirement. There had been rumors of arguments between the king and Prince Damrong, his most powerful minister. Some said it was due to the king's dissatisfaction with the British treaty; some said it was disagreement over funding for a new battle cruiser. Apinya said the gossip from the palace indicated the conflict was something about Prince Damrong's daughter. Still, it was a shock. For all the years Pakdee had been in government, Prince Damrong had been the Minister of Interior and the most powerful person in the land beside the king.

"Did the telegram give a reason?"

"Ill health."

"Oh, of course."

"Uncle Choei will be the new minister."

"Chaophraya Surasri? How will that affect us?"

"Don't worry yourself about such things. You just do your duty."

Pakdee nodded. "Are there any instructions from the new minister?"

"Not yet. He will be careful to consult with the king before doing anything. He is not as adventurous as Prince Damrong... and he is already rather old," Prince Lopburi said, almost to himself.

"Your Royal Highness, is there anything else?"

"I will speak to the staff later this morning, but I want you to draft a notice to post. Explain that the change was made solely to allow Prince Damrong to care for his health. His Majesty the King's policies will continue to be implemented smoothly and effectively throughout the south."

"Yes, Your Highness, sir." He bowed and backed out of the room.

He walked wearily back to his office. His only high-level supporter in the ministry was gone. Chaophraya Yommarat was still in the cabinet, but in a different ministry with no regular contact with Pakdee. With Prince Damrong out, he was alone, unprotected.

As he arrived at the office, his secretary handed him a letter. He sat at his desk and tore it open. It was from Prince Damrong, a personal note written in the prince's own elegant handwriting. The prince wrote he had worked for the royal government for many years and felt tired. He thanked Pakdee for his efforts and devotion, listing many of their accomplishments—dealing with the Pattani sultan, establishing the Malay family courts, helping quell the two Malay uprisings, inspecting the nearly completed railway and shutting down the gambling and opium dens. He appreciated the prince mentioning his work. Then the paragraph at the end caught his eye.

"Many changes have occurred in the Sixth Reign, as is to be expected. Do not neglect to respond appropriately to those changes. We must all obey and support the king. Soon there will be a new minister. My old friend Pan Sukhum has praised your ability to adapt. That ability will be more important than ever. No position is secure forever. Make yourself essential to Prince Lopburi Ramet. Study the writing of His Majesty the King. He needs the support of people like you. Adapt. I am doing that myself. Finally, I will have time for writing and history. Truly, the only constant is change."

32

PREM
Hero

Prem watched the red disk of the sun slip behind the dark mountains of Nakhon. The sea breeze dropped and the little boat rocked gently in the outgoing tide.

"Let's go back now," Dam said for the third time. The big policeman had been uneasy throughout the afternoon on the boat. He said he had grown up in the mountains and didn't know how to swim. He had nearly fallen overboard earlier when a fish had hit his line. He dropped the line to clutch the sides of the boat. Awt had laughed and grabbed the line, pulling in a good-sized bass.

"One more fish," On pleaded. "Awt has five and I have only four. I need to get one more."

"What do you think Sergeant, sorry, Lieutenant Dam?" Prem said. "Can you stay out a little longer for On? The boys will understand if you have to go back before they are ready."

He had watched Dam throughout the day. The big man needed On's help baiting his hook and seemed fearful once they were out in the broad bay, far from land. He tried to cover up his nervousness by praising Awt's expertise with the paddle and shouting in triumph every time one of the boys caught a fish.

"Alright, if On wants to, we can try for one more fish," Dam said. "Why don't we start paddling back as we fish?"

The man had no right to be close to his sons or to his wife. Life would be so much better if he were not around. He could feel annoyance tightening like a rope around his chest.

Awt and On baited their hooks and let them drift seaward on the ebb tide. The baits disappeared slowly in the dark water. A few stars peeked through the clouds. To landward, the red tint on the clouds was fading. To seaward, the line between the sea and the sky was dissolving as the darkness deepened. It felt like they were floating in a vast emptiness with no boundaries. The boat rocked as Dam stood up and moved clumsily to the stern.

"Don't stand up, you big buffalo! You'll tip us over," Prem yelled.

"Fuck you—just want to light a lamp. It's too dark," Dam retorted.

"Sit down and sit still."

Dam sat down with a bump and fumbled with a kerosene lamp. He balanced the lamp on his knee and pulled up the glass. He turned up the wick and struck a match. It didn't catch. He threw the match arcing into the black water where it hissed and died. He struck another match as On gave a shout and tugged hard on his line to set the hook.

"I got a fish! A big one."

"I'll help you," Dam said.

On brought the thrashing fish close to the boat. Dam lurched upward to grab the line, knocking the lamp into the water. He reached for it, but that tipped the boat to one side just as Awt scrambled forward to help his little brother. Water poured over the side. Prem tried to steady the boat with his paddle, but Dam overreacted to the tipping and leaped to the other side. Suddenly they were all in the water.

He stroked to the surface and looked for his sons. Awt was already clinging to the bottom of the overturned boat. Where was On? Prem heard a splash and a gasp as his youngest son's head broke the surface. He pulled him to the boat.

"Just hold on to the boat. Stay calm. Don't do anything else yet."

"No problem," Awt said. "We've turned the boat over lots of times. We can right it easy, just like you showed us."

He felt a surge of pride that his son's voice held no panic. Even little On didn't seem upset. He just lay on the boat, his arms draped over the stern, as he looked around in the faint starlight.

"Where's Uncle Dam?" On asked.

He didn't see the man anywhere. Then he felt a swirl in the water beneath him and felt a hand gripping his shin. Dam was down there. The hand on his leg pulled him down and he swallowed a mouthful of water. He kicked down and the grip slipped down to his ankle.

"We have to find Uncle Dam. He can't swim," Awt shouted.

One more kick would do it. The hand on his ankle seemed to be weakening. One more kick. He looked at his two sons, their eyes wide with concern.

He took a deep breath, let go of the boat and plunged his head into the water. Bending at the waist, he reached down and grabbed Dam by the wrist just as his hand was sliding off.

He straightened up and kicked for the surface, pulling the heavy body after him. Two strokes brought him to the boat. He heaved Dam up onto the boat bottom now just a few inches above the water. Dam's eyes fluttered, and he coughed up water. Awt grabbed him under the arms from the other side of the boat and helped Prem pull him further up onto the rough planks.

"Dad, you saved him!" On shouted in relief.

Was that what he had done? Why?

33

NGWE LAY
A Proper Thai Wife

Ngwe Lay heard the door open and pulled herself out of her half sleep. Was Pakdee back already?

But it was the servant girl Jiap peeking around the door.

"Lay, Mae Yai wants to see you," she said. "Now."

What could this be about? Mae Yai Apinya never spoke to her, except to order her to help in the kitchen or do chores around the house. She adjusted the top of her *phasin*, giving it another roll to keep it secure. She wiped her face with a damp cloth and retied her long hair. Don't want to give Mae Yai anything to scold her about.

When she emerged onto the central platform, Mae Yai was seated on a stool, with the other wives, Duangjan, Siriporn and Ying Yue, on the floor around her. She looked like a queen in an elaborate dress with puffy sleeves and a necklace of gold and gems. Her legs were encased in a heavy silk garment. They told her it was called a *phajongraben*, something to wear if she wanted to be a proper Thai woman.

Must bow deeply and *wai* the Thai way—just get this over with as soon as possible.

"Lay, you have been with us for two months and you still have no idea how to be a proper wife. You chatter when you should be quiet. You sleep late. Your stitches are like the wandering of a blind cow. Only Father's kindness prevents us from concluding your performance on the sleeping mat must be just as bad."

She heard giggles from the other wives and felt herself blushing. If only she could go back to Bago.

"You are not up to the standards expected of a wife of the deputy high commissioner of the *monthon*. I chose each of the other wives to be sure they were worthy, but you sneaked in without my approval."

"I did not sneak. Honored Pakdee chose me."

"There you go again. Men have no idea how to choose a proper wife. They end up with someone who can't do anything—someone like you."

"I try but nobody helps."

"So, you blame me for your failings. That is the problem. No humility. No manners," Mae Yai said with a scowl. "I suppose there is nothing else to do but try to train you. I don't know how long Father will keep you around, but I can't tolerate any more of this. Listen carefully."

"I listen."

Apinya shook her head and sighed. "Start by speaking properly. Say it this way: 'I am listening, Mae Yai, honored madam... Go on, say it.'"

"I am listening, Mae Yai, honored madam."

Duangjan handed Apinya a sheaf of paper.

"It's too bad you are so ignorant you cannot read this for yourself. I will have to recite it for you."

"I can read," she said, but Mae Yai ignored her. She took a pair of glasses out of a lacquer box and adjusted them on her nose.

"This is from the poem *Gridsana Teaches Her Younger Sister*." She began to read in a lilting voice:

"Do not be like those bad women

Who are not grateful to their husbands,

Who are not ashamed to yell back,

Who are inconsiderate, who think only

Bad things of their husband. ...

The sewing, the repair of clothes

Are all the work of a good wife.

Without being reminded, the sewing should

Be done at once. Do not chit chat

Too much with your friends...

The cooking must be done on time.

You must obey your husband;

Do not procrastinate or talk back

Or fight with him physically or verbally.

Do not nag...

You must get up before your husband

And go to bed after him.

Perform your duties as you are told."

Apinya put down the paper and looked at her. "Do you understand? This is just a small part of what is expected of a proper Thai wife—something you may never be."

"I try. Mae Yai, honored madam."

34

PREM
Acceptance

Prem paced back and forth in front of Som's hut, trampling a path in the sand still damp from an afternoon shower. He looked back at the medical building where he could see Som kneeling beside a patient on the long open porch. He would have to wait for his brother to finish the treatments. They couldn't speak there.

He had to calm himself. He looked at the trees surrounding the clearing. The temple, monastery and meditation center had expanded over the past two years. Money from Som's medicines had paid for a large hall used for books, paintings and statues about the Buddha's teachings. Som called it the Dharma Theatre. Donations from grateful patients had given Som enough money to enlarge and improve the medical building—more patient rooms, two treatment rooms and a covered area in back for medicine production.

The first expansion was made for patients during the dysentery epidemic and the second to increase medicine production to meet the needs of the army and Toh's shop. Now, patients came in with a wide variety of ailments. Both buildings were far more substantial than the little huts where the monks lived. There was still no prayer hall—the biggest building in most other temples. Som stubbornly refused all appeals to be like other temples. The number of huts, however, had expanded to some two dozen—not only for monks, but for townspeople who wanted to listen to Som's sermons and learn to meditate. Talumpuk village too had grown. There was now a new row of houses for fishermen cashing in on demand for dried fish that had doubled since the outbreak of the war.

If only his restaurant could have grown like this.

He replayed the events on the river two days earlier. He had almost committed murder. He could still feel the impact as he kicked down on Dam's hand on his leg. He could still see the look of concern on On's face when Dam didn't surface. He could still hear the shout of praise from his son—"You saved him."

Som walked slowly across the sand swept clear of debris each morning. He looked peaceful and happy. Why couldn't he feel such peace himself?

"I need to talk to you," Prem said, raising his hands in a respectful *wai*. "Can we go inside?"

"There is a nice breeze out here. Let's just sit on the steps and chat."

"It would be better to go inside," he said.

Som's smile faded.

"Come in here," Som said, opening the door to an empty patient room. "What is it?"

"I think Ploi has been unfaithful," he said in a whisper.

"Are you sure? Pakpanang is a small town in love with gossip. I haven't heard anything."

"No one would tell you. You are a monk and not known for idle chatter. But one of the market ladies says she saw Ploi walking towards the police station after coming back from Songkhla. Why?"

"Doesn't she have an arrangement with the police to protect the casino?"

"Yes, that may be the problem. She is always meeting with this man Dam. I can see in his eyes he wants her."

"But that doesn't mean she wants him."

"I don't know, but these day she does whatever she wants. She follows her impulses. She might have an impulse for someone different."

"I suppose that is possible," Som said. "One of her impulses was to sleep with you, remember. You used to say you loved her impulses. Don't you have impulses? You used to visit the green lantern houses whenever we got to a port."

"But not since I married Ploi."

"Really? I saw Nuey last week. He said you and some of the old crew went out drinking in Nakhon. You spent the night at that new hotel and women were sent up to the rooms."

He felt the blood rush to his face. He would smack Nuey for this.

"That motherfuck... sorry. Nuey shouldn't have said anything. We had too much to drink. Ploi was away in Songkhla buying something for the boat. It had been a long time. She is always too busy, too tired or too far away. It didn't mean anything. Yes, it was an impulse—just an impulse, a man thing. A woman, a wife especially, should be different."

"You know the village women come to me with their problems and I am not sure they are so different from the men. They just control it better. Your lapses and impulses should help you understand her, forgive her—if indeed she has done anything to forgive. One market lady's comment is not much to go on."

"There is something else. On—he is darker than me, broader than the other children. He looks a little like that damn policeman."

"Kids change as they grow up," Som said. "I shouldn't have to tell you that. You are much broader and heavier than me. Maybe On is dark because he is out in the sun so much. Maybe he takes after grandfather. He was pretty dark."

"It's just that I can't get this thought out of my head. What if On is not my son?"

"On is not your son just because you provided the seed for him. You love him, raise him, teach him, protect him. It is those things that make you his father.

"But how can I live with the suspicion my wife has betrayed me? It gnaws at me like a rat trapped in my chest."

"Do you love On? Do you still love Ploi? If you do, you must think only of what you can do to show that love. What Ploi has done or not done is her concern. If you are attached to a certain type of conduct from her, you can never be at peace because you cannot ensure that her conduct will please you."

"But I'm the husband. She should please me, shouldn't she?"

"Prem, you must admit that sometimes you do things you regret later. If you cannot control your own conduct, how can you control hers?"

"But she is the wife and I am the husband. I should control her."

"Like Father controlled Mother?"

He thought of the times he had seen his mother crying after Father berated her. Sometimes there were bruises on her face. He couldn't imagine Ploi weeping like that. Even if he hit her, she wouldn't submit.

"I would have to hide the kitchen knives," he said with a glum grin.

"And what about On? You are not his father because of one night on the sleeping mat. You taught him to read and write, to fish and paddle a boat. You can teach him how to be a man, or you can reject him and let someone else be his father. Your choice."

"Elder Brother Som, sometimes I get so angry. The other night I almost killed Dam," he said.

Slowly he told the story of the boat capsizing and his attempt to drown Dam. As he told the story, he felt like it had been a dream.

"I almost became a murderer, yet my sons think I am a hero. Even the moron Dam is grateful. He doesn't seem to remember the kick— just that I dove down and pulled him out of the water. He doesn't know I wanted him dead. I always thought I was a good person, but now I know I am evil."

"I never thought I would be saying this to you," Som said as he grasped his brother's shoulder, "but perhaps you are too hard on yourself. We cannot always control what we want, but we must try to control what we do. In the end, you did the right thing even though you wanted something else."

"Thank you for saying that, but I feel guilty for trying to drown him and angry at myself for failing to do it."

"Let's assume all your dark suspicions are true. What then? Would you be strong enough to forgive her? If not, what can you do? Abandon your family?"

He didn't want On growing up with Dam as an 'uncle,' but it would be worse if he left and Dam became the father. Just seeing them together hurt. How could he reject little On? How could he leave his other children?

"No, I need him. I need her. I need all of them."

"Then your need is your suffering. Of all the suffering there is in this world, this is not so bad. Can you live with your doubt?"

He slowly nodded, but could he?

35

DAM
National Police

Dam yawned as he watched the members of the Pakpanang police force gather in front of the station. Another boring speech was coming, but there was no way to get out of it. What were those district patrolmen doing here? Not really police, they were useless in a fight. Then he noticed a dozen men striding up from the dock. They were dressed in a motley assortment of clothes from trousers to *phajonggraben*. Two of them looked familiar. They had been in court for the casino case. They were the fuckin' plain-clothes detectives who raided Ploi's casino. Those lizards had embarrassed him and humiliated Ploi. What were they doing here?

There was a stir among the policemen when the police chief, Captain Nitiya, came out of his office and stood at the top of the station steps. Unlike Captain Serm, Nitiya had been sympathetic to Dam's methods because he got results. Nitiya had already told him he would recommend Dam as his replacement whenever he was transferred.

He nodded respectfully to the captain, but the man didn't seem to see him. Next to the police chief was a pale young man in a brilliant white uniform and knee-high riding boots. He looked about 18 years old. There was a colorful array of medals on his chest. He couldn't have earned all those. Too young and mild-looking.

"I have called you all together to provide you with important information affecting all of us," Captain Nitiya said. "As some of you may have read in the newspapers, His Majesty the King, in his great wisdom and his concern for the well-being of the Siamese people, has recognized the importance of police work and the difficulties we all face in protecting the people. To enable us to work with greater efficiency and effectiveness His Majesty has merged the provincial gendarmerie, the criminal investigation detectives and the district patrol units under the Ministry of the Interior. He has appointed Lieutenant General Kramrob as the first director general of the new national police force.

The general has authorized a single hierarchy of ranks with a basic division between commissioned and non-commissioned officers."

What did all this mean for him? He was already an officer, a lieutenant, in line to be the next captain of the Pakpanang police. What was a 'commissioned officer,' anyway?

"As part of this reorganization, I have been promoted to Police Major and transferred to Chiang Mai where I will oversee all the police in the province," the captain continued.

Finally, he would get his promotion, long overdue, to be chief in Pakpanang, run things the way they should be run. But what was the captain saying?

"...excellent choice. So now let me introduce my replacement as commander of all units of the newly combined Pakpanang District Police. He is Police Captain Mom Luang Pravej Deeprasertkul."

The captain's office assistant began clapping and after a pause, the rest of the policemen joined in. Captain Nitiya held up his hand to signal an end to the applause.

"Captain Pravej studied law at the royal pages' school and served with distinction as an attaché in the Siamese embassies in Britain and France. He graduated with honors from Police Cadet Academy and most recently taught law at the academy. I expect all of you to respect his knowledge and to assist him in making Pakpanang and, indeed, all of Nakhon Srithammarat, a safer and more orderly place to live. Captain Pravej would now like to address you."

This pale little fucker was stealing his job as police chief. How could he do that? No field experience. Unlike Captain Serm and Captain Nitiya, no military experience. He looked like he would faint at the first sight of a pirate with a sword or a tattooed *nakleng* with a pistol.

"Gentlemen of the new national police force. I bring greetings from the royal palace and from my uncle, Lieutenant General Kramrob. I have studied the reports from Pakpanang for the past year and understand we face many challenges. Of particular importance is adjusting our methods to the legal requirements of the Penal Code, which has been in place for more than seven years now, but has yet to be fully implemented. Equally important is the Code of Criminal Procedure, which requires each of you to carry a report book to note the details of your actions. As policemen we are the guarantors of order in society, so in our own behavior we must show proper order in accordance with the law."

Proper order? Report book? What about the damned Chinese secret societies? What about the brigands who don't think twice about slitting your throat? What about the *nakleng* who rob and kill while the district officers look the other way? What about the rag-head Muslims attacking police stations? How will this pretty little fellow communicate with the villagers who speak only the southern dialect or *Jawi*? He lost track of what the new captain was saying.

"… commissioned officers. Both have completed their training at the Police Cadet Academy. Please welcome the new deputy chiefs. They were my students so I know their quality. But I also look forward to selecting the best of you for the Academy so you too can become commissioned officers. Until then, however, those who have not been through the academy will be considered non-commissioned officers. The top rank will be sergeant. I will be observing each of you very carefully. Captain Nitiya has told me you are all experienced and competent. I look forward to working with you."

More was said, but Dam stopped listening. It sounded like he was going to be demoted again. He stared in fury at Captain Nitiya who looked steadily at the new captain until his speech finally concluded. He then disappeared into the office.

The other policemen stood in small groups buzzing with talk. He looked back at the new chief gazing over the assembled policemen. He doesn't really expect us to abide by all the rules in those silly books, did he? How was he going to keep the pirates from raiding into Pakpanang Bay if they didn't fear the police? What was he going to say to the villagers who lost their cattle or their belongings to the *naklengs* in the countryside? How was he going to keep order in the towns without deals with the *Angyi* and the other Chink gangsters? How would he get confessions? This guy was going to be worse than the judges in letting bad guys go free. What about his arrangement with Nit's gang? Could he still protect Ploi? He had already failed her once.

The men in his unit gathered around him.

"You should go to that Academy," one of the men suggested.

"Because I am so good with books and lectures?"

"If that's what you have to do to win promotion, then do it. It's what we will all have to do. That's what the new captain said."

"You think that pale little law professor is going to promote the Black Tiger?"

"He may not like your methods, but all the bosses like convictions. They like the money we seize and the fines we generate. They like it when we share the donations from grateful crime victims or from negotiating settlements."

"Yeah, they like the money, but how can we get the results that earn money when our hands are tied by report books, laws and rules?"

"We are now part of the National Police Force. We'll find a way."

He listened as his men suggested tactics to evade the rules, but all he could think of was that this was yet another personal setback. He must have failed to renew the power of his *yantra* for influence. Or maybe its power was used up saving him from drowning. Was it punishment for sleeping with Ploi? He would have to go back to the abbot. In any case, he would have to be careful to stay legal—at least until they understood this new lawyer-policeman better.

He left his men still talking and trudged along the river bank. A fisherman with a throw-net draped over his shoulder peered over the bright water of the river. The man hurled the net with a sweep of his arm and a flick of his wrist. The net swirled into a large circle before dropping into the water with a splash. The fisherman waited for the chain around the edge of the net to sink to the bottom, then slowly pulled the net to the bank. A large fish thrashed in the net.

That is me. Trapped in a mesh of rules and laws. I should get out before the net closes. I should get far away from Pakpanang and the police. I can do something different.

"Uncle Dam, Uncle Dam. Look here. Look at me."

The shouts came from two boys in a boat piled with debris. The tall boy at the back held the boat steady while the little one stood on the bow, posing on one foot and spreading his arms like a cormorant drying its wings. Ploi's sons, Awt and On. What mischief were they up to today? He had gotten the older one out of scrapes a couple of times already—stealing fish traps or fighting with other boys. Now the little one was becoming an accomplice. The last time he saw them on a boat was that night two months ago. Their faces looked so worried as he lay coughing and exhausted on the bottom of the boat. They cared for him. No one else did. Maybe their mother, but it was hard to be sure.

"Where are you two rascals going today?" he asked as the boat glided to the dock and On leaped ashore.

"We are hunting for floating treasure," Awt said. "After last night's storm, there are lots of things floating around. Look, we have two fish trap buoys, a big coil of rope and an oar."

"You sure those were floating free and not snatched off someone's dock?"

"Of course not," Awt said as he tied the boat to the dock. "We collect only stuff that has no owner."

He grunted in surprise. On slammed into his thigh and hugged him.

"Uncle Dam, come with us. We are going out on the bay. Come with us, please."

He smiled at the tiny hands of the boy who barely came up to his waist. He enjoyed spending time with the boys. He remembered Ploi telling him, "You should take special care of On."

Why? She had smiled, but refused to say more.

He looked at the boy and thought once again—yes, the boy must be his. His skin was dark and his face was broad, unlike that Chink of a husband. It must be true. He had a son.

"I don't think I am ready for another boat trip just yet. I have swallowed enough river water for this year. Tomorrow, I have a day off. I'll take you up into the mountains and I'll show you how to shoot a gun."

"A gun, really? Wow—but father and mother won't agree."

"You don't have to tell them. Say we are going to hunt for durian."

He was guilty of sleeping with another man's wife. A man who had saved his life. What kind of gratitude was he showing by continuing to see her? No wonder he almost drowned. No surprise to be demoted again. It was his own bad karma. But he had tried stopping himself from seeing her before and he couldn't. He was as addicted to her as his father had been to his gambling—selling his own wife and son for one more chance. What if Prem found out? But the man had saved his life. The fool must not suspect anything. He wanted to be with the boys. On was his only child. He had to stay close.

36

NGWE LAY
Pregnant

Ngwe Lay struggled out of her dream upset and confused. Aya was calling her to come help her gather some morning glory stems for lunch. She could see the sun glinting off the river and hear the creak of an ox-cart trundling along the dirt road in front of the house. She could see the silhouette of her father on the porch, but she couldn't see his face. He was just a shadow. Why didn't he smile at her?

A dream, just a dream, but it made her feel empty. Father had never come to visit her in Songkhla. He sent only one letter, saying he was returning to Burma with his band. Just another sign he didn't care about her. He abandoned her with these strange people who didn't want her. It was bearable only because Pakdee said he loved her.

She looked at the angle of the sunlight streaming through the single window in the room. It must be late. She should get up, but she felt so tired. She couldn't go back to sleep, but she didn't want to get up. She turned onto her back and the satin sheets rubbed across her breasts sending a little thrill of pain through them. She touched one breast. The area around the nipple had grown darker and larger in the past two months. And the breasts themselves had grown full and heavy. What was happening to her? The other wives had stopped teasing her for being small; now they teased her for being big.

"What magic! She has transformed little mangoes into big papayas," Siriporn had laughed.

Then Mae Yai had taken her aside, prodding her in sensitive places and putting a cord around her waist. She asked about her meals and the sick feelings she sometimes had.

"Humph, you feel tired, sometimes feel like you are going to throw up. It can only mean one thing," she said with a strange expression.

"What is wrong with me?"

"Nothing. You are pregnant."

She was going to have a baby. No, she was too young. She couldn't be a mother. Mae Yai must be wrong. What would Pakdee think?

Dazed, she allowed Mae Yai to lead her down to the space under the house where the other wives were sewing.

"This one is pregnant. Take care of her. She's ignorant, so it is up to us to make sure she does nothing to endanger the baby," she said.

"Father is giving us another child," Siriporn cried. "We should be grateful."

After that, the wives still teased her, but with a kinder tone than before. As her stomach swelled, the other wives became more sympathetic. She needed them. Aya and Auntie Ma had never spoken to her about pregnancy or childbirth, but she knew her mother had died in childbirth, or soon after. Could she die too? Just being pregnant made her feel different, but, except for the nausea, not so bad. She didn't know what would come next, but the wives offered her advice and sympathy. Sometimes they brought her special foods good for the baby, but they said that meant she had to stop taking meals with Pakdee.

"Pregnancy requires warmth, so you must eat foods that maintain the heat," Mae Yai said. The other wives brought her ginger tea, young coconut meat, salty foods, tamarind and warm liquids. It was nice to have someone other than Pakdee being nice to her. They insisted she eat soups made with a slippery green vine that felt strange in her throat.

"It will make the baby slide right out," Siriporn said, cuddling her youngest to her breast. "I have had three, no problem. Soon you will have one of these."

Mae Yai was as insistent on the foods she must avoid—pickled foods, spicy curries, shellfish and eggplant. These 'banned foods' could make birth difficult or cause problems for the baby. Coffee and tea were also forbidden as they would diminish the intelligence of the child.

Some of the instructions seemed silly—like avoiding eating a whole banana to prevent obstructions in the womb, but the attention was nice. It was like she was allowed entry into a secret society—the society of mothers, with its shared rituals. It was a society that excluded Pakdee. Once it was determined she was already four months pregnant, Mae Yai decreed she must move out of Pakdee's room.

"She needs more rest and quiet. She doesn't need you bothering her at night," Mae Yai had told Pakdee. "It's not safe for the baby."

It was disappointing that Pakdee submitted so meekly to Mae Yai's command, but there was no questioning the power she wielded in the household. Each morning all the wives were expected to greet her with a *wai*. Mae Yai then issued her instructions for the day.

The servants cleared out a small room where the *Khon* troupe's instruments and costumes had been stored. That was now her room. She missed her nights with Pakdee. Sometimes she could feel a heat and tension rising in her that made her long for his touch. There were moments when she was desperate for him to enter her. She tried to attract him with a look, a touch, but Pakdee feared doing anything that might affect the baby.

"Duangjan has lost two babies to miscarriages and Apinya one," Pakdee explained. "Ying Yue gave birth to a baby who died soon after, so we must be careful to do nothing to hurt your child. You must follow the instructions of Mae Yai. She is the expert on this, trained in the palace school for midwives."

Pakdee still came to chat with her, but he avoided touching her.

The wives encouraged her to go for walks around the mansion.

"You need to be active or the birth will be difficult, but don't lift anything heavy," Siriporn told her.

She was always happy to get out of her little room. She especially enjoyed playing with the children. Mae Yai gave her the task of providing the spirit house with fresh food, drink and fruit each morning.

"Keep the spirits happy and they will protect the baby," Mae Yai said.

It was good to have tasks to do and to have something to chat about with the other wives, but today, she just felt like lying back on the mat and returning to her dream of home.

The flimsy door was flung open and Mae Yai strode in.

"It is time to get up, bathe and eat. I've arranged for your first pregnancy massage. Hurry up now. The woman will be here soon."

"Mas-sage—what is that?"

"It will help the pregnancy. The woman will rub coconut oil into your skin and massage away your aches and pains. More importantly, she will determine if the baby is in the correct position. If not, she knows how to push on it until it is correct."

"Just a few more minutes," she pleaded.

"We pay this woman for her time. You have to be ready when she comes," Mae Yai insisted. "Now."

It had become difficult to move this heavy new body, but she clambered to her feet as quickly as she could. She must not annoy Mae Yai.

37

PAKDEE
Royal Changes

Pakdee unbuttoned the top two brass buttons of his heavy white dress uniform. Red dirt speckled one sleeve and sweat stained the collar. It had been a long day. He had risen early to accompany King Vajiravudh from the high commissioner's official mansion to the hills west of Songkhla Lake. The king traveled in a long column of automobiles with police, *monthon* officials and railway engineers. The king sat chatting with Prince Lopburi Ramet throughout the trip. After a quick look at the rails already laid, the king and the prince had left for a nearby Wild Tigers encampment. He had asked Prince Lopburi whether he could go along.

"But you haven't joined the Wild Tigers," the prince said.

"I am planning to, Your Royal Highness, but the office has been so busy…"

"No matter. Deputy Commissioner Somsak is coming with us. I need you to escort members of the king's retinue back to Songkhla. Make sure to care for them properly according to their status."

That task had taken hours because some of the king's staff had been unhappy with their accommodations. He had to call in favors with wealthy merchants to find them more elegant housing. Then others complained about the spiciness of southern food. He had to go back to the restaurant and order a blander version of their menu. It was growing dark when he finally returned to the *monthon* office.

Babysitting. That's all it was. And a missed opportunity. Nearly five years into the reign of the new king, he had yet to speak to him. He had tried to follow Apinya's advice to make friends in the king's palace, but all seemed in flux there. He didn't even know who to approach, and he had felt uncomfortable asking for help from Prince Lopburi. The young prince had rejected his recommendation of leniency for rural Muslim religious leaders arrested for criticizing the king in their sermons. He tried to explain that severe punishment would only arouse more rebellious feelings, but arguing with the prince had achieved nothing.

He had to be more disciplined—think first about his relationship with the prince.

Apinya had offered assistance, but that had come to nothing. She found her relatives more concerned about saving their own positions than helping her husband. They all had been moved out of the royal palace to look after the various wives of King Chulalongkorn in their new homes. The inner palace that once thronged with the king's more than 70 children, his many wives and consorts, and all their servants, was now nearly empty. Apinya told him her own mother and one of her sisters had left the Grand Palace with Queen Sukhumla to live in her son's much smaller palace. Long settled relationships and alliances were changing. The man at the center of all this was right here in Songkhla, but Prince Lopburi had kept Pakdee away from the king, busy with a variety of mundane tasks. Throughout the visit all movements were carefully scripted, with no opportunity for him to have a word with the king. Unlike Phraya Sukhumnaiwinit, who arranged for Pakdee to be a primary escort during royal visits, Prince Lopburi took that role himself. During travels, the prince always occupied the seat next to the king, and the two seemed to have a great rapport. It was natural. They were half-brothers, born only two years apart, raised in the same palace. They were educated together in England. Often, they laughed over some private joke.

After a five-day visit, the king was due to leave Songkhla the following day, so it could be many months before there would be another chance. Perhaps at the annual *monthon* commissioners meeting in Bangkok. He would have to plan his approach to the king more carefully.

Footsteps on the veranda outside his office. Who could that be at this hour? It sounded like quite a group, but when the door opened only Prince Lopburi entered. Normally, the prince summoned Pakdee to the commissioner's office, but even those occasions had become rare in the past year. The prince closed the door behind him.

He stood up quickly and bowed. "Your Royal Highness."

"Pakdee, you look rather disheveled. We must keep up appearances, you know."

"Yes, Your Royal Highness," he said as he struggled to re-button his jacket.

"However, I am glad to find you here. I have spoken to the king about you."

"That is very kind of you sir."

"I informed His Majesty of your long experience here, especially your ability to understand the *khaek* and your work with the courts. His Majesty asked many questions."

"What questions?"

"About your sympathies for the *khaek*, about those weapons you disposed of, among other things."

"But sir, everything I have done has been with your approval or the approval of your predecessors."

"I do not expect to debate these issues. I simply wanted you to know that there are concerns at the highest level. You have not been successful in winning the loyalty of your subordinates and you have few friends among the senior staff. To be a senior official you must have loyal subordinates and a network of friends."

"Honored sir, I don't know what to say."

"Don't say anything. Just improve your work."

"Your Royal Highness, I..."

"And get that jacket cleaned before the farewell ceremony tomorrow," the prince said as he opened the door to leave. "Sloppiness by any one of us reflects poorly on all of us."

38

PLOI
Launch

Ploi watched from the deck of the boat as the first guests made their way down the wooden steps from the restaurant. She was dressed in a pale yellow *phasin* with a silk top that bared one shoulder. A broad strip of embroidered green silk covered the other shoulder and swept from one breast to her side. It showed elegance and high class. She touched the gold necklace, recently reclaimed from the pawn shop. If tonight was successful, the necklace would never go back.

Another group of people, mostly women who were old customers, gathered at the top of the steps where Mother was checking names against approved reservations. This was going to work. It had to. She smiled at Prem beside her. He had resisted her plans to restart the casino, but he finally agreed that the boat was the safest way to do it. In the early days he had grumbled about the costs and the risks, but recently he had been calmer. Maybe it was good he was spending more time at his brother's temple in the woods of Talumpuk.

She had gone with him twice, but it had been a boring waste of time. There was nothing there but trees and mosquitoes—and interminable discussions of the dharma. How could such boredom take his mind off his worries? But somehow he was usually calmer after a visit. He had finally ceased his incessant grumbles about the risks of working with Dam. He probably feels closer to the man after saving him from drowning. He has no idea who he saved. Life is strange.

She looked back through the door of the main room of the casino where Dam sat cross-legged in the shadows on the edge of the *Thua* mat. He too had seemed calmer lately, less insistent on her visiting him. It was up to her, he had agreed, and that was what she wanted. Nothing, not even the excitement of her encounters with Dam, could be allowed to interfere with the launch of the new floating casino. Nights with Prem had become less tense and more frequent. She didn't want any more children, so they had to take care, but Prem was more willing than ever to do what she wanted. She smiled to herself. *Now I understand Father a bit better. Different lovers fulfill different needs.*

She broadened her smile and sank into a respectful *wai* as the first customers crossed the dock to the boat.

"Welcome to the Jaikla riverboat dinner cruise," she said. Prem *waied* still more customers and gestured to a serving girl with a tray of drinks.

"Please take a glass and find a comfortable place to sit," he told three men, Chinese mine owners down from the hills in northern Nakhon.

"When do the games begin?" asked a broad-faced man wearing a heavy gold chain.

"We'll explain the arrangements for entertainment once we are out on the water," Ploi said. "I am sure you gentlemen are all adept at the various ways of striking it rich. We wish you good luck."

The three laughed and reached for the whisky on offer as Ploi turned her attention to five heavy-set women stepping carefully onto the dock. Four of the five were matrons over forty years old, with chubby arms protruding from the puffed sleeves of their blouses. Their brightly colored *phajonggraben* stuck out on the sides, making their broad hips look even broader.

"*Mae* Ploi, we are so happy to see you again—it has been far too long since the *Songkran* festival," said the smallest and oldest of the group. She was the wife of the *kamnan* of Sichon and a distant cousin of the governor. Her arrival meant word of the casino boat, spread discreetly mouth to mouth, had reached the elite in Nakhon.

"Madam Lamai, I am so glad you could come on our little cruise."

"We will be serving a special menu of Thai and Chinese food that I'm sure you will enjoy," Prem added as he *waied*.

"My friends are especially interested in seafood—shellfish mostly," Lamai said with a twinkle to her voice.

"Yes, we want to see lots of cowries," one of the friends giggled.

"I am sure you will find plenty on this trip," Ploi said. "If your taste is for cowries, find your places around the big mat in the far corner."

"We will bring the food to you."

She glanced back up the river. The sun had almost disappeared behind the mountains. The sunset lit the clouds with an orange light like the paper lanterns sent floating skyward at *Loy Krathong* festivals. Those sky lanterns lifted into the air by the heat of a candle were supposed to bring merit and good fortune, so perhaps this sunset lighting the clouds would bring fortune to the Jaikla family.

A buzz of voices pulled her attention back to the dock. It trembled with footsteps and the staircase above it was crowded with people—Chinese merchants talking loudly about rice prices, aristocratic ladies with serving girls carrying their betelnut cases, an elderly man with a large white mustache, a plump young man in an elegant *phajonggraben*, a group of giggly teen-age girls, a man she recognized as the district officer of Tung Song, two fishing boat captains and the owner of the big steam-driven rice mill with two of his wives behind him.

It was going to be a profitable evening.

Nearly eight hours later, specks of starlight glinted off the river as the boat, pulled by a breeze filling the big sail, glided back up the river. The staff had already put the roulette wheel into its compartment below the deck and were starting to roll up the gambling mats. The guests, tired from the games, were chatting quietly. Some chortled at their good fortune. Others boasted how much they had lost and how little they cared. The serving girls offered a final round of drinks. It was always good to leave them feeling they got more than they paid for. When she did the accounts, she was sure it would be one of their most profitable nights ever. Was it because of the long time between opportunities to gamble? Or the novelty of gambling out in the bay, far from the cares and rules of the land?

Two days from now they had scheduled another excursion that would just be a dinner cruise with no gambling. Prem had insisted this was necessary to show their dinner cruise business was legitimate. Only trusted customers would be allowed on the gambling cruises. All others would be shuffled to the dinner cruises.

It was a good idea to reduce the risk, but why has Prem finally become supportive? He must have come to accept that the gambling operation was the best way to make money for the family. She should thank him, but she didn't see him in the main room. She stepped out onto the deck. There he was at the big wooden tiller, steering the ship. She was surprised to see the big form of Dam standing next to him. She had never seen the two of them together like this before.

The two men in her life made a strange pair. Prem was fun-loving but gentle. His manners might be rough, but he always sought to please others. He was good with people—loved gossiping and telling jokes.

Everyone liked Prem. He loved to play, with her, with the children. He enjoyed singing with her and they had gotten great applause for their duet tonight. That had been a good idea. Inviting him to sing with her should make him feel better about the casino—and it made her feel good to trade musical double meanings with him. Like the old days. Songs, games, company, food and children would keep him happy— and sex, of course. She would reward him on the sleeping mat tonight.

Dam was so different. Often angry at some slight, he could go hours without saying a word. A couple of times she had seen him lash out at others with a ferocity that was frightening. But he listened placidly to her own chatter about the casino or the children or her family without the joking comments Prem would have made. He never argued with her. Unlike Prem he never pointed out her inconsistencies. Occasionally he would talk about a police operation, not to boast about his daring as he did with the men who asked about the exploits of the Black Tiger. When he talked with her, he spoke about his mother or his fears he would fail his men in a moment of danger. Each time he had risked his life, he told her one night, there was a moment when he couldn't seem to move, a moment when he feared his men would see him as a coward.

Sometimes he would explain the details of a new tattoo or a new *yantra*, but mostly he just listened to her without a word. He liked it when she talked about her sons. She wasn't sure Dam was On's father, but she was sure it was useful for him to believe it. She needed him— for the casino, for protection, but also for the thrill it gave her that this moody and violent man cared about nothing in life as much as her.

Both men meant a great deal to her. Those love songs about loving only one person in the world were unrealistic. Father had loved three women, each in a different way. She loved two men—maybe someday there would be another. What would Father have thought of that? He had never seen any of his women as having the same needs he did. He would have been puzzled and upset. She had often puzzled and upset him, but he would have been impressed with her success tonight, with all she had done to strengthen the family. Now she had to keep it all going—the casino, Prem, Dam, her mother, the children—the family.

39
SAIFAN
Imam

Saifan paced nervously on the rough bricks of the mosque hallway. Shadows of the late afternoon were creeping across the floor. It would soon be time for evening prayers. It seemed strange that Imam To' Guru Wae Muso would not be there to lead the prayers. His funeral the day before had brought mourners from Pattani town, Yala, Narathiwat and even Kelantan.

Now there was no imam to lead the evening prayers. Perhaps the mosque committee would make their decision by then. He could hear nothing from the meeting room behind the heavy wooden door. It had already been two hours.

"Don't worry," Hamidy said with a smile. "The committee will make the correct decision."

"Some of them, I think, still see me as an outsider."

"It's your grating Pakpanang accent working against you, but I think they can see beyond that. They know you joined in the uprising to restore the raja. They know you risked your life, that you suffered a wound and nearly died."

"But to be the imam is to be a teacher and a leader, not a soldier."

"Which is a good thing, because you were a lousy soldier," Hamidy grinned.

"True. I am better explaining the Koran and leading prayers than aiming a rifle."

"You will be a good imam, even if you still don't quite speak real Pattani *Jawi*. The old imam didn't agree with the uprisings, but despite that, he took you back as a teacher of the Holy Koran. Despite that, he supported your *pondok*."

"We had our differences—about teaching, about the Koran, about To'Tae and fighting the government. But despite all those differences, he always treated me with respect. His death is a great loss."

"He was very old," Hamidy said. "He had a full life, and he is now in

Paradise. He had many children. Experience gave him wisdom."

"He was right. It was foolish to attack the Siamese when we were so ill-prepared."

"Not only were we foolish, but we failed to learn from sad experience," Hamidy said. "The failure of To'Tae's attacks was not enough. Our people were deceived again by false promises and followed that other Sufi, *Haji* Bula, to fight the Siamese. The outcome was the same. We could not stand up to the guns of the government."

"But we had to do something for the raja," Saifan said.

"And where is the raja now?" Hamidy asked bitterly. "He left us to go live in Kelantan after the government rejected his request for a pension. Maybe the raja believed he could win back his palace and his position. I doubt he believed the Sufi prophecies of victory. If he had, he would have come out to lead us himself."

"He is the rightful ruler, isn't he? But perhaps you are right. If he believed, he would have been with us at the police station. Actually, I always doubted To'Tae's claims to see the future or provide magical protection. I just wanted the Siamese to suffer a bit of what we have suffered, what my brother suffered. I should have listened to you."

"Despite the Sufi prophecies, our people rot in a Siamese prison and five of our men rot in their graves," Hamidy said. "Their wives are without their husbands. Their children are without their fathers."

"I was almost one of them," Saifan said. "If it hadn't been for you, I would be in the sandy soil of that beach village."

"That monk in Talumpuk. He was the one who saved you."

"It was Allah who saved me," he said. "Now I must try to do his will. As imam or as a simple teacher, I must obey the will of Allah."

With these words, he felt calmer. It didn't matter if he were chosen imam or not. Whatever happened was the will of God and he had to submit to that. But if he were imam, he could better serve the community of believers. There were many ways he could strengthen the mosque, attract more followers. Most important was to provide understanding of the Koran and what it meant to be a good Muslim.

There were also the challenges of dealing with the Siamese government. Unlike others in Krue Se, he had lived with the Buddhists and their strange practices and with the Chinese and their money grubbing. He had felt the power of their guns. He could caution against the emotions so easily aroused. It was not that he hated the government any less. Seeing men die, seeing others locked away for years had planted hatred deep in his heart. He just needed to make sure that the simple people of Krue Se did not become the victims of Siamese power or fake holy men. He needed to protect the Krue Se community the way Hamidy had tried to protect him from his own eagerness to prove loyalty to the raja.

The door opened and the five members of the mosque committee came out and greeted him. "Brother Saifan, we have carefully considered the opinions of many in Krue Se for this important decision," the eldest of the committee said. "These are difficult times for our community, for our mosque, for our religion. We need someone with knowledge, wisdom and bravery. It is a heavy decision, but we are united in deciding to invite To' Guru Mustapha to be the imam. We hope you will continue to teach in the mosque, but we feel at this time the people of Krue Se need a man of Pattani, someone who grew up here, an older man, to lead the mosque."

A dozen questions spun through his head. After all the work he had done for Krue Se, after fighting for the Malay community, why had they rejected him? Mustapha was older, but his understanding of the Koran was simplistic. His Arabic pronunciation grated on the ears. His lessons were limited to monotone readings from the commentaries and repetition of the verses of the Koran. His students routinely slept through his lessons. He spoke little Thai and understood nothing of the Siamese government. How could he lead Krue Se when the government was intruding ever deeper into the lives of the villagers?

"I thank you for considering me," Saifan felt he had to say. "I will be honored to serve under the new imam, to support the mosque and to educate our youth."

"That is for Imam Mustapha to decide and he would like some time to consider. He has asked you to suspend your classes for a few weeks while he decides how to organize mosque activities."

No classes? Why would Mustapha do that? Why had the committee decided against him? He had known some of these men for nearly 20 years and yet they didn't yet see him as a neighbor. He thought of his time in Talumpuk Village. The villagers had been kind and the abbot of the little temple had saved his life. The man had nursed him with his own hands. He stayed by him through his fevers without fear of contamination. Those Buddhists had accepted him, yet his own people had not, at least not completely.

The monk had saved his life even though he was Malay. He had never thanked him.

He saw Hamidy waiting for him in the corridor.

"Brother Hamidy," he said, "it looks like I will have some free time now."

"They didn't choose you?" he said.

"I was not worthy. So now I have the time to make a trip I should have made long ago."

40

DAM
Investigation

Dam rebuttoned his uniform and tried to smooth out some of the wrinkles. The oh-so-elegant Captain Pravej always seemed to notice such trivial faults. What did the captain, the skinny lizard blocking his promotion, have to complain about now? A smudged report? A word misspelled in his notebook? Some complaint he was not speaking politely enough to the criminals he questioned? Or would this be the day he was demoted back to sergeant because he didn't qualify for officer's school?

But maybe it was another job. He was bored and frustrated. It had been months since the last action. Work was little more than routine patrols and training his men. And paperwork. Every year there was more and more of it. And no promotion. He enjoyed the gambling cruises with Ploi, but those were frustrating too. To be so near her and yet unable to touch her. Prem was always around. The guy had saved his life, but he had the woman he wanted. Worse, she no longer managed to get away to visit his little house behind the police station. All her time was devoted to the Jaikla gambling boat. She didn't want him anymore. It would be good to lead a police operation again, to feel the excitement in his blood, the crunch of his fist on some bastard's face.

He pulled open the door to the captain's office and snapped off his best salute.

"Lieutenant Sakda, I have received an unusual letter from a senior official in the *monthon* office. Apparently the commissioner would like us to undertake a particularly sensitive investigation. "

"I am ready to help, sir. Who are we going after? Smugglers? Thieves?" Dam asked, pleased at the prospect of getting out of the station.

"Let me read you part of the letter addressed to me," the captain said, unfolding a piece of paper. "Captain, under your command you have an experienced officer, one Lieutenant Sakda, who has led many successful operations—the elimination of Tiger Thuam and his gang, the suppression of pirates in Pakpanang Bay and several successful raids on illegal gambling operations."

Dam tried to suppress a look of surprise at this unexpected praise.

"You may inform him that despite this success, he has not qualified for higher rank because he has has a powerful and persistent enemy in the Songkhla headquarters. This person has repeatedly recommended against his promotion and inserted negative information into his official file."

"I knew it. I have been sabotaged, but why would someone do that?"

"Let me finish," Captain Pravej said. "This official is now under investigation. You are to head the Nakhon part of the investigation. I am supposed to turn over this investigation file to you."

He pushed a bulging brown cardboard file across the desk to Dam.

"I am not sure I like the idea involving you in an investigation in which you have some personal interest, but those are my orders."

"Yes, sir."

"The details in this file are confidential, but I am supposed to tell you that you are authorized to pursue the investigation wherever it may lead," Captain Pravej said. "My instructions are to provide you with whatever support you need."

"I'll use my own men," Dam said. "They know how to keep their mouths shut."

"You are supposed to begin by looking into the harboring of a *khaek* rebel at a Buddhist temple near Talumpuk Cape," the captain said, referring to the letter. "Who brought this rebel, most likely wounded in an attack on a police station, to the temple? Who paid for his treatment? Who arranged his passage back to Pattani? Read the file. Interrogate those involved. Headquarters wants weekly reports. Work quickly."

41

PAKDEE
Accused

Pakdee stood before Prince Lopburi's desk, looking at the portrait of King Vajiravudh. The painting of King Chulalongkorn had been moved to the other wall and that of Prince Damrong had been destined for the storeroom until he had it placed in his own office. So much for the permanence of even the most powerful men.

The prince was reading from a sheaf of papers on his desk and scowling.

"First Deputy High Commissioner Pakdee, I regret to inform you that troubling questions have been raised about some of your actions. I have therefore had no choice but to initiate an investigation."

"An investigation? Questions? What questions? I have always served honestly and faithfully."

"Yes, yes. I am sure the investigation will prove you innocent, but the integrity and loyalty of the civil service is of great importance to His Majesty the King. I would be remiss in my duty if I did not look into these questions," Prince Lopburi said.

Pakdee's mind raced. Had someone reported the loans from Sia Leng? The lack of action against Leng's casinos? Or the payments from the shippers? The gifts from the tin mine operators? Who would do that? He shared some of that income with others in the office. If those payments stopped, everyone would suffer.

"Honored sir, I believe I can clear any suspicions, but I need to know what they are and who is raising them?"

"Who? That is not important, but you will be informed in due course if the investigations show those suspicions to have any basis."

There was a cold look in the commissioner's eyes.

"I suggest you review your files and make sure all is in good order. Receipts and payment documents are particularly important."

"Your Royal Highness, I assure you all is in order."

But it wasn't. How could he account for the loans and the special payments made over the years? How could he explain his mansion, the big household staff, the lavish *Khon* performances?

"I hope so," the prince said with a grim look. "Because I must relieve you of your duties until these matters are satisfactorily explained. Please brief Deputy Commissioner Somsak. He will take over your duties temporarily. I have scheduled a hearing in 30 days."

42

PREM
Race to the Cape

"Put up the second sail," Prem shouted to Awt who was crouching on the bow of the narrow little boat.

Awt scrambled to the bow and raised the jib they rarely used. The boat surged forward in the stiffening breeze. Good boy. They might still make it to Talumpuk Cape in time. Dam had an hour head start, but fortunately he had chosen to go the long way around by horseback.

"You must get to Wat Talumpuk before Dam," Ploi had told him. "You must convince your brother to say nothing."

He was still puzzled by the urgency of it all. He had been working in the kitchen when Ploi and Sia Leng appeared at the kitchen doorway.

"Prem, dear, we need your help," Ploi had told him. "Lieutenant Dam is going to Talumpuk on an investigation that could imperil the man who protects us at the *Monthon* Commission Office. If our friend in Songkhla is implicated, it could threaten our business."

"Why don't you just tell him to stop?" Prem asked. "You always say you can control the man."

"I tried, but he wouldn't listen. There is something personal about this. He said he can finally remove the obstacle to his career. He rushed out before I could explain how important this was. He said he had to go to Talumpuk. Something about your brother's temple and some *khaek* with a gunshot wound. He plans to question Phra Som and there are things he must not learn. This is dangerous not only for us, but for your brother."

There was a grim satisfaction in Dam turning out to be the problem he had always predicted. Finally, Ploi needed her husband to preserve the family business. She must now realize that this was his rightful role—protecting the family. He had to beat Dam to the temple. But even if he got to Som in time, could he persuade him to go along? They had to sail faster.

"Well done son. Now lean back so I can tighten sail," he said.

Awt's eyes shone with the excitement of the race down the river. The boat heeled over with a gust of wind. He threw his slim body backward to level the boat. The boy was now almost as tall as he was. It was good to be doing this together. Awt was always on the lookout for some adventure. For once it was with his father, not his gang of friends or the damn policeman. The wind was brisk, but the current – slack when they left Pakpanang – was turning against them. That would slow them down. He angled the boat to starboard. If he cut behind a string of small islands, the tide would have less power. Already bay water was starting to cover the dark mud of a tiny islet. In another hour nothing but a scraggly tree would be above water. By that time, they would have to reach Talumpuk, or Dam would be there before them.

Finally, he could see the low, dark line of trees on the cape. Grey clouds loomed behind them. He smiled at Awt and the boy grinned in triumph. He pushed the tiller over and the boat glided into the beach. He could see the tiled roof of the medical building through the trees. When they reached the temple area, Som was sitting on the porch of the building examining the arm of a man in a white Muslim prayer cap.

"Elder brother Som," he said with a hurried *wai*, "we need to talk privately, urgently."

"A moment and I'll be finished," Phra Som said and turned back to his patient, ignoring Prem's impatient fidgeting.

"The wound has healed well. There is no need to thank me or make a donation. I am just glad to see you again. I appreciated our discussions. Perhaps Islam and Buddhism are not as different as people think. Your prayers and our meditation have similar benefits. Please wait while I speak to my brother. We'll talk some more if you have time."

"Is that the man you treated for a gunshot wound?" he asked as the man walked back into the medical building.

"Yes, but he has completely recovered," Som said. "How did you know?"

"You must get rid of him immediately. The police are coming. If they find him, they will arrest him and maybe you too. And there is more to it. The police are gathering evidence against a friend of ours in Songkhla. They must not learn about the wound."

"But I have to tell the truth," Som said, with a puzzled look. "What is this about?"

"I don't understand what the police are investigating, but Ploi says it would hurt our family if they find out you treated a wounded man. It's even worse if he is caught here. Why did you let him return?"

"He wanted to thank us for our help," Som said.

"That could get him arrested, maybe executed. You can say you treated a different man six years ago. Or say you don't remember, but don't say anything about the bullet wound."

"I need to know more about this. I..."

The muffled sound of hooves came from the sandy temple entrance. The brothers watched as Dam and two other policemen rode into the meditation area and dismounted.

"Prem, I didn't expect to find you here," Dam said, rude as always. The man had been better lately, but the guy had no manners. Ploi complained about his own manners, but Dam was worse. It was good to have beaten him to the temple. He would enjoy telling Ploi about how he had warned Som just in time. But that *khaek*, where was he?

"Just visiting with my brother. I have to get back to town. Farewell elder brother," he said before *waiing* and turning away.

"Honored Abbot," Dam said. "I would appreciate your assistance with an official investigation."

"Of course. Come with me into the Dharma Theater. I'll show you the latest additions to our collection. It will be a good place to sit and talk quietly. We'll open some coconuts for you and your men who must be thirsty after your ride."

Som nodded towards the medical building and Prem took the hint as his brother led the policemen away. Prem opened three doors before he found two Malay men.

"Quickly, you must come with me right now. The police are here looking for you," he said pushing the two men out the rear door. They ran to the beach and launched the boat, now overloaded with the four of them. Once the sail filled and the boat was well off shore, he looked back. One of the policemen was standing on the beach staring at them as they sailed away.

43

NGWE LAY
Finding Father

Ngwe Lay sat in the cool shade on the central platform of the big house. Columns of mist rose from the garden after an evening shower. The baby had fallen asleep after feeding, but Ngwe Lay wanted to keep holding her against her breast. She brushed the fine strands of hair back from the baby's little face.

"Hla Kun Way, Hla Kun Way," she whispered, the syllables tripping off her tongue like poetry. "Hla, my beautiful child, my beautiful daughter."

The words reassured her this was real. The long pregnancy, all the things she had to do to please Mae Yai, the terrifying, painful hours of labor—it was all a half-forgotten dream. This little face was real. With delicate eyebrows, a perfect little nose and long eyelashes, she was beautiful. The tugging of her tiny mouth on her breast was real. The hand with its little fingernails clutching her finger was real. Just watching her breathe was the most wonderful thing in the world.

Footsteps on the stairway. Pakdee and Mae Yai pushed open the door and hurried onto the platform. They were heading to her. They might wake the baby. She put a finger to her mouth.

"Shhh—she just went to sleep," she whispered with a smile.

"Put her on the mat. We need to talk," Mae Yai said.

She didn't like being separated from the baby, but did as she was told.

Pakdee should be happy to see the baby, but he looked so serious.

"I am sorry, Lay, but this is important. I need your help. I need to find your father," Pakdee said once they moved away from the sleeping baby. "Is he at the refugee village?"

"I don't think so. I wrote him about the baby. The village headman wrote back to say he's somewhere in Burma. He promised to send my letter with the next one going to his camp."

"I have a problem at the office only he can help with. He must get back here in less than a month or bad things might happen to me. I might have to go away."

"If Father is sent away, there will be no money," Mae Yai said. "Who will feed you and your baby? Where will you live? You better do something to get your father back here. Now."

Ngwe Lay felt shaky. It was like one of the earthquakes that sometimes shook Bago. What could happen to Pakdee? Why was Father involved?

"I will write again," she said. "What do I say?"

"It is about the weapons I sold him. I will write the letter. You just write a cover note. Tell him this is important, very important for me, for the family and for you."

She nodded, but she could feel the fear rising in her chest. They didn't understand how difficult it was to get Father to do anything. How hard it was even to find him. All those weeks when she needed him and he was away. All those times she begged him to stay and he went anyway. This was bad. Bad things would happen and it would be her fault because Father would never come.

44

PLOI
Linked

Ploi sat at her desk and watched Sia Leng pacing back and forth, his heavy footsteps sounding like the long drum in a *kathin* procession. Prem sat on a mat making a stack of mah jong tiles. He piled them up until they tipped over, then started piling them again. She looked back down at the list. It was important to be thorough. She had written everything they knew about the investigation, the threats they faced and possible actions to take.

"Sia Leng, what is our risk from the payments you made?" she asked

"If this investigation finds out about them," Leng said, "we could have a big problem. They were loans, but we got careless about documenting his repayments. Some of that money was from Jaikla. If we are questioned, we'll just have to apologize for bad record-keeping, but insist that Pakdee has always repaid the loans. It will look bad, but it's nothing criminal."

"But it could trigger an investigation into our gambling interests," Ploi said. "Dam could also come under suspicion—just when the boat casino is doing so well. What about the raids on our competitors?"

"If they add everything up," Leng said as he paused his pacing, "it will be obvious that others have been raided far more often than us and fined more than us."

"And in Nakhon, it was always Dam leading those raids," Ploi said. "We should have had him lead raids against some of our operations—your dens in Trang and Phuket or my lottery."

"If Dam's investigation implicates Pakdee and us, it would raise questions about Dam's own performance against gambling," Prem said, "but the moron doesn't see the danger he's in."

Trust Prem to say something negative about Dam. He didn't understand that Dam was emotional and cared so much about his job in the police. He didn't care about anything else. Maybe me, maybe On. But I haven't paid much attention to him lately. A mistake. She should have kept him motivated, but she was too busy with the casino boat. There were too many sharp-eyed gossips in Pakpanang alert for scandal. And, really, she was getting tired of him. The thrill was gone.

"I will talk to him again," she said. "He is pushing the investigation because he thinks getting rid of Pakdee will remove the obstacle to his promotion. I need to get him to see he could get caught up in a scandal that will hurt all of us."

"Why would Pakdee stop Dam's promotions?" Leng asked.

"Who knows? I need to talk to Pakdee. Whatever it is, he needs to promise Dam he will stop it so we can all survive," she said, ticking off one of the lines on her list.

"It's not just the gambling," Leng said. "It's something about those *khaek* rebels Prem's brother helped. If your family is connected to the *khaek* rebellion, your business will come under greater scrutiny. You will lose influence and connections. Phra Som could even be charged with a crime—harboring the enemy, sedition or something like that. What did he say when Dam questioned him?"

"I warned him not to say anything," Prem said, "but I didn't get the chance to explain why. The last I saw of him, he was talking to Dam. I had to get away with the *khaek*. There was nothing more I could do."

"If only you could have gotten there sooner," Ploi said.

"I sailed as fast as I could. We were lucky to get there before Dam."

"You needed to convince your brother. You know him. He can be difficult."

"He just wants to have all the information, examine things from all angles before coming to his own conclusion," Prem said.

"That makes him difficult," she said. "Worse, he thinks he has to tell the truth even if it causes damage."

"I told him Dam's investigation could lead to the arrest of the *khaek* and might hurt our family," Prem said. "If he sees the danger to others, he'll do the right thing. You can talk to Phra Som yourself. I got a note saying he will come upriver in a day or two. Anyway, I got those *khaeks* away from Dam. That was lucky. You didn't even know they were there. If Dam had found them, it would have been bad."

"Where are they now?" Leng asked.

"We put them in one of the huts near the big house," Ploi said. "They should be safe there until we can get them on a ship back to Pattani. Without them, the only evidence Dam will have is whatever

Som told him. But if we are to save Pakdee, we need to figure out what started all of this."

"My contacts in the *monthon* office say it has been building for some time," Leng said with a sigh. "Pakdee doesn't get along with his boss. He just doesn't know how to treat a prince. He is too aggressive, not respectful enough. He has also failed to win the support of the staff. One of them has been feeding damaging information to the high commissioner. It was the *khaek* stuff that got the high commissioner's attention, but once started, it could spread like rot in a basket of rice."

"Why would Pakdee risk everything by helping the *khaek*? It doesn't make sense," she said. If everyone's motivation was clear, then she could figure out what to do. Right now, nothing was clear.

"Must be money," Leng said. "That raja still has money and he uses it to stir up unrest."

"You're just guessing," Ploi said. "We need to know. I don't suppose there is much we can do about the high commissioner, but maybe we can do something with the person undermining Pakdee—pay him off, or threaten him, but we need to stop this thing before it gets worse."

"I don't know who it is. I need to get back to Songkhla," Leng said. "There is nothing more I can do here."

"I'll go with you," Ploi said.

That would give her the chance to meet with Pakdee, she thought, maybe talk to the *monthon* staff. She could invite them all for a dinner cruise. Bring the boat down the coast to Songkhla Lake. Offer a free introductory meal for *monthon* officials. Maybe even get the prince to come.

"I should go too," Prem said.

"No, we need you to stay here to speak with your brother. He may be required to come to Songkhla. In any case, you must get the *khaek* away from here as soon as possible. I'll take the casino boat to Songkhla."

"What? Why?" Prem asked.

"It will be a chance to talk to officials, listen to gossip and offer favors," she said. "We can't just sit here and hope for…"

A pounding on the door interrupted her. Prem started to rise when the door swung open and Daeng stumbled into the room with Saifan close behind.

"They got him," Daeng said.

"Who got who?" Prem asked.

"Brother Hamidy went for a walk early this morning and didn't return," Saifan said.

"The noodle vendor on the main road told me the police arrested a Malay man and took him away," Daeng said. "I went to the police station and Dam told me he was a rebel being sent to Songkhla for interrogation. So we came here."

"We must save him," Saifan said.

The idiot doesn't deserve to be saved, Ploi thought, but they had no choice. The *khaek* was the beginning of a string that connected them all. It could lead to Phra Som, to Pakdee, and then to Dam, Sia Leng, Jaikla and her family. They were all at risk.

"Yes, of course, we'll do what we can for him. We leave for Songkhla immediately," Ploi said. "But, Saifan, you cannot come with us. Go back to Pattani."

45

PAKDEE
Defense

Pakdee rifled once more through the files. He could only find receipts of his "loan" repayments for the first three years of his arrangement with Sia Leng. There was nothing after that. How would he explain the additions to the house, the costumes for the *Khon* group, his donations at funerals? Would they really look into all that? Everyone at the office, except maybe the high commissioner, had something to hide. Why would they single him out?

The guns—that was a great success, getting those away from the raja. But how could he explain selling them. There should be a receipt from that Mon fellow somewhere. It wasn't exactly policy to arm the Mons, but at least it wasn't the Malays.

The payments to Hamidy were another problem. There was no paperwork to show that he was paid as a spy for the government. He had his report warning of the To' Tae uprising. He could explain that the information had come from Hamidy. That should get the man out of jail. He should be given a medal for all the lives he saved and for his service to the government. Someone was confusing the prince, turning white into black. He could explain Hamidy's role, but what about the help for Saifan—paying for his passage back to Paṭṭani and making a donation to that temple? Hamidy should be smart enough to know what to say and what not to say. But would the abbot be discreet? His defense would depend on it. If the monk talked too much, he could lose everything—his position, his house and his family. He could go back to prison.

There was a knock at the door. It was Somsak.

"Deputy High Commssioner Pakdee, please forgive the intrusion, but I am concerned about the unfair charges against you. Is there anything I can do to help?"

"Somsak, it is so thoughtful for you to ask," he said.

"Of course, we are all in this together," said Somsak with a serious look. "When the record of any senior official is questioned, it damages the reputation of all of us."

Somsak's support was a great relief. The man was popular among the staff, taking them to lunch almost every day and sponsoring *Songkran* excursions and *kathin* trips—all stuff that he could have done if he wasn't so busy with real work. Somsak had never accomplished anything much. He wrote nice reports, praised the commissioner and annoyed no one. Maybe he could help him with the commissioner.

"So, we all have to work together on this," Somsak continued. "Let me know what I can do."

"Thank you. We have been together here a long time. When I first came, I served as a clerk under you."

"And we have both risen, me not quite as high as you," Somsak said with a smile.

"So, you know me. You can tell the prince how hard I've worked, how much I have done for Siam—capturing the guns, providing information on the rebels, organizing the port, all that."

"I am sure the prince is aware of all you have done, but I would be happy to speak up in your defense."

"Actually, Somsak, my friend, there is one more thing," he said. "I fear someone on the staff is passing harmful information, distorted information to His Royal Highness. Any idea who that could be?"

"No, not at all. Everyone respects you. Rising from the clerk's room to become deputy commissioner—that is quite an achievement."

He looked at Somsak. The man was always polite and complimentary, lavish with his praise.

"Well, if you hear anything, I would appreciate you telling me. We need to get rid of these suspicions as soon as possible for the benefit of all of us."

"Don't worry," Somsak said, "by the end of the month I'm sure this will all be cleared up."

46

SAIFAN
Responsibility

"It is my fault," Saifan said. "I shouldn't have brought him with me. But he wanted to come. I should have stopped him from leaving the house."

He looked at Phra Som, who sat across from him in the shade underneath Ploi's big house. Despite all the turmoil, the Buddhist priest looked calm.

"Your intentions were good. No one could have foreseen this, this investigation," Phra Som said. "You cannot blame yourself for what you did not know."

The monk was trying to calm him, but his emotions still boiled. Hamidy had been a good friend. He had never wanted to join the rebellion. He went along just to protect him. Now he was in prison. How could he be calm? It was unjust.

"I will do what I can," Phra Som said. "I will go to Songkhla for the hearing. Too many people saw you and Hamidy come to the temple. Many people saw you were gravely ill, but perhaps they won't ask for the details of your wound."

"You would lie for me?"

"I haven't decided. Truth is important, but so are people's lives. A bullet wound would connect you with the police station attack. Hamidy would be convicted. You would be hunted. This Pakdee person would be dismissed. Somehow that would hurt my brother's family. Lying affects my own karma. The Buddha was clear that lying is wrong. Perhaps I should trust the courts to find justice."

"Even if you help, Hamidy will still be under arrest. Is there other evidence against him? Is there nothing we can do? Can we trust the police to let him go?"

"I hope so. I don't want to see anyone suffer," Som said.

"We teach that good motivations and a pure heart must lead to good outcomes, don't we?" Saifan said. "That is what our religions say, but in my experience, it isn't always true. Especially with the police."

"The good outcome is within us—the peace of mind that comes with acting honorably for the benefit of others."

"The arrest of Hamidy is an evil action, so I need to do something, even if it is inadequate."

"Take care you don't make things worse," Som said.

He had to think. What if he gave himself up? Wouldn't that worsen the case against Hamidy? Who would care for his wife and child? Should he just return home and do nothing? What was it the Koran said?

"We can never be sure of the outcome of our actions," he told Som. "The Prophet has said 'Only Allah can determine what will happen to us. He is our Master: let believers put their trust in Him.'"

That was it. He had to do something. Whether or not he succeeded was up to God. Hamidy had saved his life at least twice. He owed him.

"But you must use your intelligence to do something effective," Phra Som said. "They are not after Hamidy or you. Prem says you are simply the bait used to catch a bigger fish—the man who helped you, the deputy commissioner."

This had confused him. Prem and Som had told him that this man, Pakdee, had given money to Hamidy to pay for their escape boat, their passage back to Pattani and even made a donation to Phra Som's temple. Why would he do that?

Now Hamidy and even Phra Som—people who had done so much for him—were caught up in his mess. Som might be accused. Hamidy was under arrest. He had failed Abdul; he couldn't fail Hamidy. There must be something he could do. Send him food and money. Testify, take all the blame.

"I must go to Songkhla. I have to help."

47

PAKDEE
Hearing

Officials, clerks and police crowded the veranda as Pakdee left his office, but he felt completely alone. All eyes turned to him as he walked to the big meeting room trying to look confident. Two guards swung back the heavy doors carved with Chinese designs. Dragons curled down the door frames, a reminder the *monthon* office building had once been the mansion of the Chinese governor. The old governor was gone, but at least he had a pension and an honorable retirement.

Several senior staff members sat at the long teak table that extended half the width of the room. At the center, a large ornate chair stood empty. That must be for the high commissioner. More junior staff and some people he didn't recognize sat in chairs behind the table. Who were those people? The pretty woman he remembered as a business owner from Pakpanang. She sat next to Sia Leng. Was the big Chinese there to testify about his failure to repay some of his loans. No, he would never incriminate himself. Sitting apart from the others was a Buddhist monk. Why was he here?

Somsak entered with two clerks carrying armfuls of file folders and took the seat next to the big chair. Somsak had promised to help him. He should say something about his role in dealing with the raja. Somsak might not know the full story, but he had been in the *monthon* government during the struggle against the raja. He had witnessed his delivery of the raja's weapons. He could talk about all his hard work on the courts and his supervision of the harbor. Fortunately, he had shared some of the money from the unofficial harbor fees with the clerks, so that would make him an ally, wouldn't it?

Where should he sit? All the seats near the prince's chair were taken. Opposite the prince? No, that would look like a confrontation. He picked a chair slightly to one side and placed his own files on the table. He had piles of receipts, financial reports and copies of all the reports High Commissioner Phraya Sukhumnaiwinit had sent to the ministry praising his work.

There was a murmur of voices from the doorway. All those at the table stood up as the high commissioner walked in followed by his secretary.

As usual, His Royal Highness Prince Lopburi Ramet was dressed in a high-necked white uniform covered with colorful medals. A yellow silk sash ran from his right shoulder to his waist. His close-cropped hair was neatly groomed. Unlike most of the officials around him, he was clean-shaven. He looked around the room with eyes that took in everything and found nothing worthy of interest.

"Gentlemen, this is an official inquiry to deal with questions arising over the actions of our esteemed Deputy High Commissioner Pakdee Charoen-nitthitham. We owe it to His Majesty the King to ensure his officials are free from any suspicion. This is particularly important for the government here in the south where we must keep the respect of all the various groups in the population. This is not a trial, but an official hearing to remove any suspicions that might adhere to our senior official. Deputy Commissioner Somsak, please begin."

Good, Somsak knew of most of his effective work for the government. Officials had to stick together.

"Your Royal Highness, senior officials, witnesses and concerned citizens," Somsak began in an expressionless voice, "it is my sad duty to enumerate the suspicions concerning my honorable colleague, Deputy High Commissioner Pakdee."

Why was he starting off with the suspicions? He should create a good impression by talking about all the good things he had done for the *monthon*. He looked at the officials around the table. They avoided his eyes.

"The first question concerns his origins. Deputy Commissioner Pakdee began work at the *monthon* office 15 years ago. We know nothing about his family, his education or his prior work. All we know is that he was brought in from Nakhon Srithammarat by the then high commissioner, now Chaophraya Yommarat. He was promoted unusually rapidly while other officials were ignored. There is no record of any check into his background. Why was he so fluent in *Jawi*? How did he come to understand the details of the Islamic religion? At my request, all of the district offices looked for records of a male named Pakdee of his age. All have replied that they have no record of him. No birth certificate, no housing registration, no education record, no court record, nothing. We don't even know when or where he was born. That, of course, is not evidence of guilt, but it does raise questions we must seek to answer."

Irrelevant questions. He had worked hard for 15 years and no one had cared about such things. Why now? There was a tone of malice in Somsak's voice. What was he doing?

"In his many reports to the ministry, which I have here, he has consistently argued in favor of the *khaek*," Somsak continued. "He convinced the government to allow local courts to be established and to use *khaek* traditions to decide family issues. After the attack led by the charlatan To'Tae, Pakdee recommended that those captured should be educated on the benefits of citizenship in Siam and released to their families after less than a year, hardly a punishment commensurate with the crime of rebellion against His Majesty the King. This recommendation was therefore rejected by the ministry. We are left with these questions: Why did he side with the rebels? Where do his real loyalties lie? Is he the true Thai he pretends to be?"

What? He had simply done his duty as requested by the high commissioner to reduce the conflict with the Malays and help them become part of the Siamese nation.

"Your Royal Highness, I can explain," Pakdee interrupted.

"Deputy Commissioner Pakdee, please be polite enough to let Deputy Commissioner Somsak finish. You will have your chance to speak," Prince Lopburi said.

Somsak cleared his throat, nodded at the High Commissioner and continued.

"In his personal life Pakdee appears to follow the example of the Muslim sultans rather than the fine example of His Majesty the King. He has many wives in a grand house that is even larger than the high commissioner's Khao Noi Palace. Unlike every other senior official, he has refused to join His Majesty's Wild Tiger Corp. None of this is a crime, but it raises more questions."

"I didn't refuse, I..."

The Prince glared at him and he stopped himself. He must stay in control. Follow the rules. Somsak said it—none of this was a crime. Somsak looked at the high commissioner and took a deep breath.

"Those questions become more important when we examine his work record. He spent a great deal of time in Pattani. In 1905, the personnel log shows he was listed as on assignment in Pattani for six months. Yet there is nothing in the Pattani office log to show he worked there. How could an office clerk disappear for so long in the *khaek* states most opposed to our government? I have two witnesses who say he was seen in the *Istana* of Raja Abdul Kadir. Was he conspiring with the raja? Supporting him? Our financial records show payments made to unnamed persons in Pattani, payments authorized, as you can see here, by Pakdee. All this came at a time when the raja was mustering support for a rebellion."

It was that rebellion he was working to defeat. He had to explain his role disguised as the scholar who deceived the raja. But that would embarrass the government. It would call into question the arrest of the raja and much of the work that had gone into the treaty with the British. It would undermine Prince Damrong.

"Pakdee, is this true?" Prince Lopburi asked.

"Your Royal Highness, it is true I was in Pattani, but I was on an assignment for High Commissioner Phraya Sukhumnaiwinit."

"Is there any record of that assignment?"

"No, Your Highness, but you can ask the former high commissioner."

"Even more suspicious are these notes we found hidden deep in Pakdee's personal files," Somsak hurried on, holding up two scraps of paper.

"As you can see, these are written in a secret code," Somsak said as he placed them in front of Prince Lopburi.

"Each is a record of payment, with the notations KS and MbH along with a date. One is shortly before the rebel attack on a police station in Pattani and the other is two months afterwards. I believe that KS refers to Krue Se, the home village of several of those guilty of joining in the attack.

"Your Royal Highness, those notes were from one of my informants. It was his warning that allowed us to defeat the attack," Pakdee said.

"How do we know what the notes say?" Somsak asked. "Is there anyone else who can decipher this code? It doesn't appear to be a government code."

"It is a private code," Pakdee said. "I can translate it for you."

"But how can we know you are decoding it honestly? That is not all," Somsak continued, pushing several more papers in front of the commissioner who frowned as he read them.

"The highlight of Pakdee's career," Somsak resumed, "was the capture of weapons purchased by the raja to support an insurrection against His Majesty the King. Many of us recall the ceremony when he turned those weapons over to the government right here at this office. How was he able to find those guns when many others failed? Did he turn over all of them? Was this the raja's way of promoting his chief spy to even higher office? What happened to those guns after that? I have found they are no longer in our storeroom. There is nothing in the storeroom records but a brief note saying some were distributed to the police and the rest were sold. To whom? Why was the amount of money paid into the treasury so small? Only two years after those weapons disappeared from our storeroom, *khaek* rebels used similar guns to attack a police station. Were those the weapons missing from the storeroom?"

This was all preposterous. They were different weapons. Those must have come from a separate cache hidden by the raja. He had reported that to the commissioner. Why doesn't Somsak cite that report? He stood up to protest, but the commissioner gave him an angry stare and waved him to sit down before he could say a word.

"Fortunately, that attack failed and many of the rebels were killed, wounded or arrested," Somsak continued. "What was the deputy commissioner's reaction to that uprising against His Majesty? Did he demand punishment? Did he work to eliminate this threat? I have here a report signed by Mr. Pakdee describing his visit to the prison where the rebels were held. Was he there to interrogate them? No, according to his own report, he wanted to ensure they were properly treated. Why was he so sympathetic to those *khaek* criminals?"

The high commissioner frowned, his boyish face looked dark. His lips were pressed into a grim line. He couldn't possibly be falling for this one-sided inuendo, could he?

"Even more suspicious," Somsak continued, "is the story of two rebels who escaped to Pakpanang. One of them was shot and seriously wounded. He was treated by a monk at Wat Talumpuk. After recovering from his wounds, this rebel and his companion bought passage on a steamer returning to Pattani. Who gave them the money for this?"

Somsak was acting like his prosecutor. If only Tun Way could testify about the weapons. Where was he?

"How is Pakdee connected to these rebels?" Somsak continued, his voice becoming louder and faster. "The notes I showed you earlier, are for payments 'to HbH' and this one says 'to HbH, steamer.'"

Prince Lopburi bent over the ledger Somsak had placed in front of him.

"And those notes were written by…?"

"By the deputy high commissioner, Your Royal Highness," Somsak said.

"Who is HbH?"

"That is what we shall find out very soon, honored sir. We will not only hear from the policeman who led the investigation into these rebels, but from one of those *khaek* rebels recently arrested in Pakpanang."

Turning to the guards at the door, Somsak ordered "Bring in the prisoner."

Pakdee felt his stomach sink as a burly policeman pulled Hamidy, his hands manacled in front of him, through the door. That policeman—it was the monster Dam. Why was he here? This couldn't be happening again. Dam pushed Hamidy down into a seat at the end of the table and sat beside him. Had the man been beaten like he was so many years before? His face looked unmarked, but Dam knew how to inflict pain without leaving a mark. Why would the man stay loyal? He should have paid him more.

"Lieutenant Sakda of the Pakpanang police station was assigned to investigate this story of *khaek* rebels and he has arrested a suspect for questioning in this case. We will soon hear his report. It will answer some of the questions raised about Pakdee," Somsak said. "I am afraid his testimony will be most disturbing."

No longer was he called the honorable deputy high commissioner, not even Mr. Pakdee. It was obvious now that Somsak was the enemy. He watched as Somsak pushed a note to the prince, who nodded.

It was hard to breathe. Somsak had stabbed him in the back. The prince had turned against him. Dam would testify against him. That would convict him once again. He would be dismissed from royal service. He would be charged in court. He would lose everything. He would go back to prison. He would lose his family. His life was over.

48

PLOI
Shadows from the Past

Ploi watched from the back of the room as Dam took his seat. What was he thinking? His face showed no sign of the emotions that had burst out when they spoke the week before. She had tried every argument she could think of. She explained they were all on the same side as the deputy commissioner. Both Dam and Pakdee were helping to protect Jaikla Casino and Jaikla was crucial to the well-being of her family. Most important of all, she told him, the removal of Pakdee would hurt everything she had worked so hard to build. The casino, the lottery, the restaurant, the cooperation with Sia Leng and with Nit's gang— everything that provided income and predictability. If Pakdee was dismissed, the casino would close and Dam would lose his monthly payments. Without Pakdee there might be further investigation of police failure to stop gambling. Dam's own position was at risk. She reminded him of all she had given him, not just money, but her trust and her love. Her body. A son. In return his only job was to protect her.

Dam had lashed back with surprising fury.

"This is the slimy little lizard who has frustrated me for years. I tried so hard to do my job, risked my life to win promotion. Over and over I was about to be promoted and this fucker sabotaged me, humiliated me—for no reason. I should have been captain long ago. Did you know he was stopping me? Did you work with him anyway?"

"No, of course not. Sia Leng was the one who met with him and even he didn't know."

"What about that time in Songkhla when you had to rush away from me to go to some party with him. Did the two of you laugh at me?"

"Of course not. It was just business—a business that has paid you well."

"That's all you think about—business and what I can do for your business. I am tired of being used. I don't want your fucking money. I want to get rid of the stinking carcass blocking me. Don't worry. Once

I am chief of Pakpanang police, I can protect you better than ever, if I still want to."

"Do you think government officials will reward you for destroying a government official? They will wonder whether you will destroy them next. You will be seen as a threat. You could be the next to be investigated."

"I am not against any other officials. I can show them it is just this one I am after."

"Think about it. Why would this man, a senior official in Songkhla, undermine your career? There must be a reason. Who have you hurt over the years?"

"I did nothing against the lizard," Dam spluttered. "Yeah, maybe I hurt some people. Most deserved it. I am sorry about some of the people I hurt, but against this one I did nothing. I haven't ever met the bastard. That is why I want to get him; he sabotaged me for no reason, maybe just because I'm not an aristocrat, just because a former slave like me is so far beneath him."

"Are you sure you didn't arrest or kill a relative of his? Did you hurt some financial interest of his? Did he borrow money from Jate? You did some bad things for Jate. Think back. People don't act for no reason. Are you truly innocent of actions that have given you this bad karma?"

At this question, Dam's angry muttering gave way to silence.

In the days that followed, she had sent Dam notes with all the information she could find about Pakdee—the date he started work in Songkhla, his appearance, his reputation as a *Jawi* speaker who understood the people of the South, his work on the railroad, his supervision of the tin mine contracts and the shipping through the ports. She had to make him see the other side, see Pakdee as a person. But she heard nothing back from Dam.

Was he still angry with her? She had not been with him for months. There just wasn't time.

Now Dam was staring at Pakdee with a puzzled scowl. What was he thinking? Pakdee looked pale. He shrank back in his seat. He must know Dam was going to get him. Then Dam's eyes opened in surprise. He stared at Pakdee for a moment and put his head in his hands.

That pompous official began talking again.

"Lieutenant Sakda, you went to Wat Talumpuk to investigate the two *khaek* rebels harbored there. What did you find out?"

Dam turned to look at her and nodded before turning to face the high commissioner.

"Your Royal Highness the High Commissioner, I and two associates went to Wat Talumpuk to conduct an investigation as ordered, all proper and official. We spoke to the headman, to several of the villagers and to Phra Somdhammo, the abbot who is here today and who will corroborate my findings."

"Yes, and what were those findings?"

"As your excellency has noted, there were indeed two *khaek* men who sought shelter at the temple. One of them was seriously ill. Phra Somdhammo, well-known for his expertise in healing, attended to the man for five weeks, after which he recovered sufficiently to leave."

"And what was the nature of this serious illness?"

"As I am not a medical person," Dam said, "I would prefer to allow the abbot to answer that question."

"Surely you don't need to be a medical expert to say it was a bullet wound."

"I found no evidence of a bullet wound, but it would be better to allow the honorable abbot to provide medical information."

Had Dam changed his mind? Ploi wondered.

"You investigated this did you not?" the official asked, sounding surprised. "Answer the question."

"The honored Phra Somdhammo is the best person to answer this, sir."

"It is alright," Prince Lopburi said. "We will let the abbot speak. His testimony about a medical condition will have more weight anyway."

Dam must have decided to help, but what would Som say? The man was infuriatingly honest. Prem was supposed to explain to him what was at stake, but she was still unsure.

Phra Som turned to the prince.

"Your Royal Highness, Lieutenant Sakda is correct. Two men, preachers of Islam, did indeed arrive at Wat Talumpuk a few weeks after the end of the rainy season retreat six years ago," he said.

"That would be shortly after the police station attack led by To'Tae," Somsak said. "The police report at the time said several blood trails were found leading away from the battle showing at least three of the attackers had been wounded. Two of those were later arrested, but one was never found. I believe this was the man who escaped to Talumpuk

Cape. What was the condition of this man?"

"One of the men had a high fever and an infected wound in his arm."

"A bullet wound?" Somsak asked with a triumphant smile.

"No bullet was found. The man's friend said it was from falling on a nail in a sailboat during rough weather," Som said.

"Surely, you can tell the difference between a bullet wound and a nail wound," Somsak said sharply.

"The wound had not been treated and it was severely infected," Phra Som said. "I concentrated on saving the man's life. Fortunately, he survived."

"Was it a bullet wound or not?" Somsak asked, his voice rising in pitch.

"No, I don't think so."

"Lieutenant Sakda, you interviewed others at Talumpuk," Somsak said, taking two steps toward the policeman. "Your written report said you were told it was a bullet wound."

"Yes, that was what the village headman told me when I first interviewed him," Dam said, looking first at Pakdee and then back up at Ploi. "But I now consider that an uninformed opinion. The headman did not examine the wound, and he has no medical training. Perhaps he thought the bullet made this a more exciting tale."

"But your report was clear."

"My humble apologies for that, but now I have had more time to think about the evidence I collected and to consider the honorable abbot's statement that there was no bullet wound."

Ploi felt hopeful. Somehow both Dam and Som had decided to help. They might be able to save Pakdee. Jaikla might survive.

"Isn't it true that soon after treating this man for his mysterious wound, you received a generous donation from Deputy High Commissioner Pakdee in gratitude for saving the life of this rebel?"

Som smiled. "His donation was used to buy medical supplies for our treatment of people coming to us for help. Whether this was in gratitude for something, I have no idea. The Buddha teaches we should do good for the sake of doing good. The two men had departed some time before the donation was received and they received no benefit from it. As Buddhist monks we accept such donations both for the good they do for the sick people of Nakhon and for the benefit to the karma of those who make donations."

"These witnesses have been most unhelpful," Somsak said. "Your Royal Highness, we must now turn to the prisoner."

"They have answered your questions," the commissioner said. "Our purpose here is to find the truth. Please keep that in mind as you continue."

"Yes, of course, Your Royal Highness," Somsak said and turned to Dam.

"Lieutenant Sakda, you arrested this man in Pakpanang after spotting him sneaking away from Wat Talumpuk with another *khaek*, is that not correct? These two must have been the rebels treated at the temple, isn't that so?"

"Not quite, sir," Dam said. "I arrested this man because you gave me his name and description. It seems unlikely he was the same person at the temple six years ago. We arrested him in the Pakpanang market and there was no other man with him."

An official entered the side door to the room, moved silently to the side of the prince and went down on his knees extending what looked like an envelope. The prince opened it and began to read.

"Most unhelpful," Somsak muttered, looking unhappily at the commissioner, before turning to Hamidy.

"Your name is Hamidy bin Hasan," he said in a loud official-sounding voice. "Your initials are HbH, correct? Obviously, you are the same HbH shown in our records as receiving money from the deputy commissioner?"

"Yes, those are my initials, but I received nothing from any official. These could be the initials of many others—Halim, Hardee, Haatar, Hakim, Habib, Hajib, Hashi, Haddad, Ha..."

"Enough, enough," the commissioner said. "If initials are all you have, there is no reason to question this man. Let us recess for a short time and then reconvene." He turned back to the letter with a puzzled frown.

"Yes, Your Highness, we are just looking for the truth as best we can. We will soon deal with the most serious question yet," Somsak said loudly over the scraping of chairs as people started to leave the room.

Dam and Som had come through, Ploi thought. Because of her? But what was this most serious question? Were they all still at risk?

49

TUN WAY
Grandfather

Tun Way directed the horse cart driver to the front of the grand teak house he remembered from years before. A pair of women lounged in the shade under the house.

"I am here to see daughter Miss Ngwe Lay," he said.

The women looked uncertainly at each other.

"She is not here," the older woman said.

"What happened to her? Is she alright?" Tun Way asked. Her note said she had a baby. It was too soon. Had she gotten sick? Did he arrive too late once again?

"I need to see her now," he insisted.

"She is not here," the woman repeated.

"Well, where is she?"

The two women exchanged looks. The older one glared at him. She looked suspicious.

"Where is she? My daughter?"

"At the *monthon* office," the woman finally said.

He knew where that was—not far away. Why was she there? For medical treatment? A problem with the baby?

Tun Way ran back to the cart and jumped aboard.

"Go now, quickly," he ordered, pointing down the side street towards the lake.

When he arrived at the office, he ran up the big steps and turned towards a small crowd, mostly women, sitting on mats on the veranda. Where was she? Weary from his travel, his eyesight blurred. It was Su Sah staring at him in surprise. No, it was Ngwe Lay, but she looked older, heavier, content. Like her mother. She held an infant. His granddaughter?

"Father?" Ngwe Lay said in Mon. "You came."

"Of course I came. I hurried back as soon as I got your letter," he smiled. "Let me see the baby."

Ngwe Lay pulled back the cotton cloth so her father could see the child.

"She is beautiful," he said.

"Her name is Hla Kun Way," she said proudly.

"Hla—beautiful. Then part of my name," Tun Way said with a smile. "Strange, but nice. I am sorry I wasn't here to help you with the name, and everything else."

"That's alright. You are here now."

"I'll find some palm leaves and write the birth note for the child. That makes it official."

"Enough of this," said a heavy-set woman in a yellow puffed-sleeve blouse. "You are that Mon man and you are needed inside right away."

"Who are you? Why?"

"No time for questions. Get inside. Pakdee needs you," the woman said as she pushed him through the big doors.

50

PAKDEE
Crystal Clear

Pakdee tried to listen as Somsak droned through a justification for arresting Hamidy. The prince no longer looked interested. He seemed focused on the piece of paper that had been given to him. It had been a great relief when Hamidy and Dam were allowed to leave. With a word or two Dam could have condemned him, but he didn't. Why? He could have said something about the bullet wound. He could have had evidence against Hamidy. What was that traitor Somsak saying now?

"…most serious. Our ultimate purpose as officials of the His Majesty the King is to maintain the loyalty of our people and ensure order and tranquility. Anyone providing weapons to the *khaek* rebels is destroying that purpose. Indeed, it would be treason. Therefore, Your Royal Highness, any possibility an official has provided weapons to the enemies of His Majesty the King must be thoroughly examined."

"Yes, yes, please get on with it," the prince said, looking once again at the letter in his hands.

"As I showed before, the weapons Pakdee seized to such great acclaim were locked in the storeroom behind the office. But they are no longer there. The log book lists the weapons as including five musketoons, 48 Enfield long rifles, a dozen short Enfield rifles and 24 almost new Snider–Enfield Infantry rifles. The Enfield long rifles and half of the Snider-Enfields were distributed to *monthon* police in May 1910, but the others disappeared with only a note saying they had been sold. It is no coincidence that after the attack by the rebels under To'Tae, the Raja Abdul Kadir's religious advisor, the weapons captured included two musketoons, two short Enfields and one Snider-Enfield—a modern weapon very hard for the rebels to acquire, unless … unless they got it from our storeroom."

The prince frowned and looked at him.

"Deputy Commissioner Pakdee," he said. "Those weapons were under your control. Can you explain how they might have reached the rebels?"

"As Deputy Commissioner Somsak has said, most of the weapons were distributed to our police and some were sold," Pakdee said, holding up a ledger. "See the entry is here and there is another entry showing that the funds earned, paid in gold at a fair price, were placed in the *monthon* treasury."

"Yes, we know they were sold," Somsak almost shouted, "but sold to whom if not those *khaek* rebels? This is treason. I recommend that Your Royal Highness turn our evidence of this treason over to the courts."

"Somsak," the commissioner said in a stern voice. "You have asked a question. Let him answer. Pakdee, please explain."

"The sale of the weapons was part of an arrangement to support a Mon group that was providing intelligence and defense on our border with British Burma," he said.

"An interesting story," Somsak interrupted. "Did you have any instructions to do that from the high commissioner? From the ministry?"

"Not exactly, but we all saw the British as a threat," he said. He should have gotten approval. He should have done the paperwork, but would Prince Damrong have approved? Probably not.

"And did this mysterious group actually do any border defense?" Somsak asked. "Where is the mysterious purchaser? How were the weapons used on the border—or did they somehow get from the border into the hands of those *khaek* rebels trying to kill our policemen?"

"Your Royal Highness," Pakdee said, "it is sometimes necessary to take actions for the national defense that are not fully documented. I used my own judgement at the time."

"That is not proper procedure," the prince said. "It raises suspicions. More importantly, do you have any way to prove it?"

"Your Royal Highness, I, uh, I…"

There was a commotion of voices at the doorway and he saw Apinya pushing her way past the guard and pulling a dusty, disheveled man behind her.

"Here he is," she said as she stopped and made a deep *wai* to the prince. "Your Royal Highness, here is the man who bought the guns."

"This is not proper," Somsak said. "My apologies, Mrs. Apinya, but you should not be here. This is an official hearing."

"Come here," the prince ordered. "Madam Apinya, if you have information for me, you should have filed it earlier."

"He just arrived," she said. "Your Royal Highness, in your gracious kindness and interest in the truth, I believe you will want to hear him."

"Alright, then," he said with a nod as Apinya *waied* and backed away.

"Come closer," the prince said, turning to Tun Way. "Who are you then?"

"I am Nai Tun Way of Bago, Chairman of the Mon Language and Culture Society. Our school was attacked and fired. We needed weapons to protect the Mon community. Mr. Pakdee sold us the weapons needed. In return, we gave reports on British troops and police along border with Siam. I bought the weapons, took them to Burma. All are still there."

Pakdee felt like the tight band that had been squeezing his chest for weeks had finally loosened. Tun Way had come.

"We have no idea who this man really is," Somsak protested.

"Deputy Pakdee," the prince said. "Is this true? Did you sell the captured weapons to this man?"

"Yes, Your Royal Highness, that is correct. You can check to see that the note acknowledging payment is in his handwriting."

"Was this sale authorized?" he asked.

"Not officially, Your Highness. My responsibility was to ensure the security of the *monthon*. The threat to that security came not only from the Malay rulers, but from the British who were supporting the sultans and who had already taken control of the Burmese kingdom. I decided I should act without bothering the high commissioner."

"That was not a good decision," the prince said.

"See, his actions were not authorized," Somsak said. "Who knows who he was really selling weapons to, who he was really supporting?"

Somsak looked to the prince with a plea in his eyes.

"Your Royal Highness, there are just too many questions about the loyalty of this mysterious *Jawi* speaker who always seems to side with the *khaek*. He pretends to be a Thai of high birth, but his manners, his accent and his actions show otherwise."

"But you have proved nothing," Pakdee said. "You just want my position as first deputy. This is all about your own ambitions."

"That is enough," the prince said. "Both of you. There are indeed a lot of questions. I am not sure they have yet been resolved. However, I received an unusual letter earlier today from the Honorable Chaophraya Yommarat. He wrote that he did not want to interfere with my authority to evaluate my staff, but he said Pakdee had served him well for many years. He also suggested that if there are questions about Pakdee's background I should examine a crystal. Do you know what he was talking about?"

Pakdee felt for the crystal under his high-collared uniform. He had slipped it over his head as he did each morning without thinking about it. What was that story again?

"Yes, Your Royal Highness, uh, I have had this for a very long time," he said as he unbuttoned his collar and walked around to the prince's side of the table. "Here it is."

The prince took the pendant in his fingers and examined it carefully. He seemed to pay special attention to the elaborate silver setting for the crystal.

"How did you get this?" he asked.

He started to say it was a present from the former high commissioner, then he remembered.

"Well, I am not sure. I have had it as long as I can remember. I was told it was given to me by my father, a father I never really knew, as I was raised by stepparents."

"Do you know what this design means?" the prince asked as he turned over the silver setting.

"No, I am sorry, Your Highness, I do not know."

"I see," the prince said and picked up a frayed piece of paper.

"Chaophraya Yommarat also sent this note and asked me if I recognized the handwriting. It says: 'Your Royal Highness, beware a spy in the *Istana*. He is working for your enemies.' I don't know what this is about, but, Deputy High Commissioner Somsak, this does look like your handwriting. Can you explain?

Somsak's face was drained of color. He put one hand down on the table for a moment, then pushed himself erect.

"I have no recollection of this, Your Royal Highness. It must have been many years ago. It certainly has nothing to do with this case."

"Hmm. Why then did Chaophraya Yommarat send it to me? Think on this and perhaps your memory will improve. We will talk of it later," the prince said. "Do you have any further evidence or questions to submit to this hearing?"

"No, but we must beware of this man," Somsak said in a hoarse voice. "He is not one of us."

High Commissioner Prince Lopburi cleared his throat and turned towards the officials seated around the table.

"Are there any questions or comments on what we have heard today?" he asked.

The room was silent.

"Good. I do not believe we have heard any incriminating answers to the questions raised about our deputy high commissioner," he said. "No evidence has been presented showing the deputy commissioner sold weapons to Malay rebels or assisted the medical treatment and escape of two rebels. Questions about Mr. Pakdee's personal background may be the stuff of office gossip, but they do not appear relevant. Therefore, there is no reason for further action and this hearing into the conduct of Deputy High Commissioner Pakdee Charoen-nitthitham is hereby closed."

51

DAM
Ties

Dam watched as the doors opened and officials left the meeting room in a buzz of hushed chatter.

"So, nothing came of it all," he heard one say.

"What a waste of time," said another.

"What do you mean? It was worth it just to see the big shots get embarrassed. All the shouting and red faces. Better than *Likay*."

The crowd flowed down the wide veranda towards the stairs to the lower offices. There was Captain Pravej. He *waied* and the captain stopped.

"What should I do with this one?" Dam asked, nodding to Hamidy, whose hands were still in irons.

"There is no arrest warrant. He was held for questioning and now the questioning is over, so let him go."

"Yes sir," Dam said as the captain hurried to catch up with the *monthon* police commander.

The *khaek* smiled up at him.

"It looks like we were on the same side after all."

Dam shrugged and unlocked the man's hands. He headed towards the stairway. Dam followed and almost ran into Pakdee.

Pakdee stared at him for a moment and then raised his hands in a *wai*. He was older and heavier, but he had the same trim mustache and thick hair. It was him alright. How did a *khaek* criminal get to be deputy high commissioner?

"I am not sure why you did it," Pakdee said, "but this woman, Madam Ploi, told me your evidence could have hurt me, so thank you."

"Just gave the factual evidence from my investigation, sir. Just being professional."

"I appreciate that and uh, I would like to assure you I will also be factual and professional… from now on," the deputy commissioner said.

"So, from now on," he couldn't help saying, "no more screwing me."

"Yes, from now on. What is past is past," the deputy commissioner said.

Dam watched as more people gathered around him. In addition to Ploi and Sia Leng, there were a half-dozen officials, a dusty-looking Mon man with a young woman carrying a baby along with several women.

The *khaek* fellow touched his heart and then Pakdee's hand.

"Honored sir," Hamidy said in *Jawi*. "I am sorry I couldn't explain what you were doing. I would not have been able to return home."

"Hamidy, you did the right thing," Pakdee said. "I would like you to continue your mission if you are willing. Find Saifan. Protect him."

What was that about? Dam wondered. So, there was another *khaek*. More secrets.

"Yes, sir. I will take my leave now."

"First, let me say something," Pakdee said facing all of them. "I want to thank all of you for your help. Tun Way for coming all the way back from the hills of Burma. Sia Leng and Ploi for finding documents and witnesses to help me defeat this attack. Hamidy for his loyalty. Lieutenant Sakda for his professional investigation. Phra Som for his care for others. My wives for their support. My former boss for his timely letter. I give humble thanks for all that was done to save me and my family."

"We all had our reasons," Ploi said, "And this effort has tied us closer together. We share secrets and we share interests. We must continue to help each other."

"With this behind me and with Somsak's motives now in question," Pakdee said with a relieved smile, "I should be more influential as deputy high commissioner and I should still be the most likely successor once His Royal Highness Prince Lopburi decides to take higher office in the capital. With all the changes going on there I do not believe it will be too much longer. Then I will be in an even better position to show my gratitude to all of you."

Sounded good, Dam thought, as long as he got to be Pakpanang police chief and as long as the deputy commissioner didn't start ordering raids on the Jaikla Casino. Ploi was right, it was worth keeping his mouth shut. Maybe now she would understand his value. Maybe she would be grateful. In any case, he should finally be free of Jate's bad karma.

What about the rest of them? Would they help each other as Ploi wanted? Somehow, they were tied together. But wasn't it just for what they each got out of it? Were those the kind of ties that would last?

52

SAIFAN
Traitor Brother

Saifan stood with Prem in the shade of the overhanging roof of a side building attached to the *monthon* offices. He was glad Prem had insisted on coming with him. The big Thai had stopped him from charging into the hearing room.

"We don't want you getting arrested too," Prem said. "That would be more trouble for all of us and would do nothing for your friend."

He had arranged for them to carry big baskets of cloth and dress as cloth sellers. That had taken far too much time. The ship bringing them south from Pakpanang had been delayed by light winds and they had trudged into the courtyard of the *monthon* office just in time to see Hamidy pulled into the meeting room by that policeman.

It seemed like hours before they emerged again and stood on the veranda to one side of the big doors. They just stood there.

"At least he is not being taken back to the jail," Prem said.

"But he is still manacled. What are they going to do to him?"

"I don't think there is any real evidence against him."

"They don't need evidence against Malays. They just assume we are guilty."

"Are you?" Prem asked.

Even this one. He doesn't know anything, but he assumes we are guilty. No need to answer.

Then the doors opened and officials walked out in their ornate uniforms with all their medals sparkling. One of the policemen spoke to the one holding Hamidy. He saluted and did something to the manacles. Hamidy's hands were free.

"See, I told you it would work out," Prem said. "Stay back. Don't let anyone see you. Let's just wait until all the police are gone."

But then Hamidy and the policeman went back into the room.

Long minutes later they emerged again. Phra Som came out. Good. Nothing was going to happen to the man who had saved his life. Prem's wife was there, some women, a big Chinese and then a slim man in the uniform of a senior official. He put his arm around Hamidy. There was something about the man.

"Who is that? The official with Pak Hamidy?"

"That is who this is all about—Deputy High Commissioner Pakdee. It looks like he has survived the hearing."

"He is the one who helped me? The one who sent money to Hamidy, who paid for our ship home. That doesn't make any sense."

"Well, that is what Ploi says. It must be true," Prem said. "The fellow is supposed to be from Pakpanang, like you. Maybe he is an old friend. Maybe that is why he helped. Do you recognize him?"

"No, I don't think so, no, no." He peered again at the man.

It couldn't be. He was dead. It was official. Would an official notice lie? They lie about everything. Abdul's face floated before him, grinning as he took off with that Thai girl twenty years ago. Abdul would be about this age. He had to get closer. He rose and started towards the double staircase.

"Wait a minute," Prem said, grabbing his shoulder. "It's not safe."

He faltered in confusion. The man stood chatting with the others. He took a baby from the arms of one of the women. He was thicker through the middle, but not by much.

Then he grinned at the women clustered around him. It was Abdul's mischievous smile. It was him. How did he get out of prison? How did he get here? In a high position? It made no sense. Why didn't he contact the family? How could he let them think he was dead? What about Mother? All the tears she had shed. All the nights unable to sleep. The light that had gone out of her. The life that had gone out of them all. How could he have done this to them? To him? How could he be working for the Siamese oppressors? He was a traitor to his own people. But he was alive. He had to bring him to Mother. He had to hold his hand again. In that uniform?

"They are coming this way," Prem said. "It should be safe for you to meet him now. My wife can introduce you."

His head spun as he pulled away from Prem's hand. He looked back at the group chatting and walking down the broad steps of the office.

"Tell Hamidy to meet me at the dock," he said over his shoulder as he hurried away. "I can't stay here any longer."

53

PAKDEE
Family Protection

Pakdee stood before the high commissioner's desk. He tried not to shift his weight from side to side. Be still. Look confident. Prince Lopburi still had not looked up from the documents he was reading when he entered.

"Your Royal Highness, you summoned me sir," he said as softly and respectfully as he could. He had not spoken with the prince in the week since the hearing. The commissioner must not be entirely pleased with the outcome. He was forced to take disciplinary action against one of his senior staff and he still seemed to have doubts about another.

"Ah yes, Pakdee. I wanted to let you know that I have informed the Minister and His Majesty of the outcome of the hearing. I have communicated with His Majesty the King about you and about Somsak."

"That is very kind of you sir."

"His Majesty agreed that a senior administrative post is not quite appropriate for a man with your strengths and weaknesses. The accusations against you are not easily forgotten and your sale of weapons without authorization was a serious misjudgement."

"But I was cleared. Somsak distorted the facts. Now he is under suspicion for writing that note."

"You were not authorized to sell those weapons. Recently I have learned the man who bought them is the father of one of your wives. Chaophraya Yommarat has declined to explain the details of your assignment in Pattani, but he did indicate that the note someone sent was an attempt to undermine his plan for the raja. He said that part of history is better forgotten. Let me be frank. It is only your mysterious connection with Prince Damrong that has saved you."

"My connection?"

"No matter. As the prince is no longer in government, I discussed this with His Majesty the King and he agrees we cannot have senior officials under suspicion. There are enough attacks on His Majesty already. You have seen the scurrilous cartoons in the Bangkok newspapers. We must be above suspicion and both you and Somsak are not."

"So, I will never advance beyond being deputy. I can never rise any higher?"

"I am afraid it is more than that," the prince said. "This conflict between two deputies who distrust and dislike each other reflects poorly on me. You will both be moved to other positions. Somsak will be transferred to Bangkok, an inactive position, while it is determined whether he wrote that note. I am bringing in two of my former students at the Royal Pages School to assist me as part of a reorganization of the *monthon* office."

He must show no emotion. Where would he be sent? Moving from Songkhla would be a disaster for the family.

"I would like to ask you to help them get acquainted with the local issues here, with the staff and with the various officials out in the countryside."

"Of course sir. I would be happy to help. So, I am staying here. The south is what I know and where I can be the most useful."

"That seems to be the case, but in what capacity? I have not yet decided. You will be moved to the temporary post of advisor to the regent for the south while you help the new deputies get integrated. You will also continue your work on implementation of legal reforms, especially with the Muslim family courts. Since I oversee all of the south, this means your area of operation will widen quite a bit. In a way, this could be considered a promotion. At the same time, His Majesty has agreed that I should seek a suitable long-term position for a man of your heritage."

"Your Royal Highness, I..."

"There will be no further discussion of this," the prince said as he rose from his desk. "My automobile is waiting."

He watched silently as the prince walked towards the door. The commissioner was shunting him off to an advisor's position with no power. Instead of being promoted, he was being tossed aside. He felt the blood rush to his face. This was unfair. He had to do something. But Prince Damrong was retired. Chaophraya Yommarat was in another ministry. He had no protectors. He had to say something.

"Your Royal Highness, I don't think..."

"Start moving your personal things to the basement office. Please make sure to leave all the official files," the prince said.

As the door closed behind the commissioner, he felt like the door was closing on his life. Everything he had done – surviving prison, studying the law, transforming himself, abandoning his family, spying against the raja, memorizing all those royal titles, refining his accent, learning the royal language – all that was for nothing?

An hour later he wearily climbed the steps to his house. He hoped everyone would be asleep. He didn't want to see anyone tonight, especially Apinya. She would be full of questions and caustic comments. Tomorrow would be soon enough to tell her the bad news. She would be furious and she would blame him. She might go back to Bangkok. Maybe that would be good. There was no way he could support so many wives and children. Without his position, those doing business with the *monthon* would no longer be so generous with their 'gifts' and loans. Even Sia Leng, despite their long connections, would undoubtedly pay less. Once it was clear he had lost power, the people who had saved him at the hearing would drift away. All that good talk about being connected, about working together would fade once they realized he couldn't help them anymore.

He could lose everything. The children—how could he support them? Some were already going to the new school in town and there were fees. It wouldn't be long before the others needed schooling and clothes. Eight of them. I should have spent more time with the children. Now they might be gone.

Apinya was his biggest expense. Despite improvements in his income over the years, she always demanded more money for extensions to the mansion, for the drama troupe, for new clothing, for entertainment and for the growing number of children. He had given up trying to keep track of these expenses. He just turned over all of his income to Apinya and then asked her for whatever was necessary for his own modest needs. What would she say now that his income was certain to fall, and fall by a lot? She would be dismayed by his loss of status. Did he want to go through this? What for?

He opened the heavy wooden door at the top of the stairs. A nearly full moon lit the central platform, casting deep shadows. He stopped in mid-stride.

There, standing in the center, was Apinya. Behind her, sitting on mats, were all of his wives. Even Ngwe Lay was there, the baby sleeping in her lap. Siriporn was nursing little Nok and Ying Yue cradled three-year-old Uan on her lap. They all looked so beautiful in the moonlight. Apinya rose and *waied* while the wives seated behind her *waied* in unison.

"Welcome home Father. We have been waiting. How bad is it?

"What do you mean?"

"There is a rumor you have been dismissed," Apinya said.

"Pretty good rumor. I only just found out myself."

"I told you many times you needed to find support in the palace."

"Yes, but you never tell me how to get it."

"No matter. How bad is it?"

He sighed. "I will still have a position, but it is temporary. Even then I will be just an advisor, so I will lose authority. Lack of authority means lack of income," he looked at Apinya. What he had to say next would make her angry.

"We will have to cut back on expenses. No more expensive clothes. No more gold jewelry. No more *Khon* troupe. No expansion of the house to build a room for Lay and her child. The mansion is already too big. I'm sorry, but there was nothing I could do."

"It won't be as bad as you think," Apinya said.

He stared at her. What was she saying? It was going to be very bad, but she looked unworried, almost cheerful.

"I have been planning for this since the king ascended to heaven," she said with what sounded like pride. "There are some things I haven't bothered you with. I didn't use all the money you brought in for daily expenses. I learned from what happened in the Bangkok palace."

"What do you mean?"

"I bought 500 *rai* of good farmland north of the lake and two rows of shophouses in the market. We are already getting rent from these properties. I have also lent out money to a group of market ladies to allow them to buy their produce in the morning. They pay me with interest each evening. The money is good, and the capital I have available for loans is now substantial."

Was that true? Did they really have this income? Why didn't he know this?

"Mae Yai, I…"

"And you are wrong about the *Khon* troupe. It is not an expense. It's an asset. We already have all the costumes and instruments we need, so not much more expense there. For the past two years we have been putting on extra shows and charging admission. All the minor dancers are students paying to learn. It is not much, but it means the troupe can more than pay its own way. We will survive—at least until you get a new position."

"Why… why didn't you tell me?"

"You were busy, and …" she hesitated. "And I wanted you to work harder to save your relationship with the prince."

A strange feeling rose in his throat as he looked at the smiling faces of his wives. They had all been in on this. They were his true protection, not his official position.

"In any case, we have some security," Apinya said. "We will have to be careful, but we will survive. We will be fine."

"You will have more time with us," Ying Yue said, pushing Uan forward. The little boy put his hands together in a *wai*. Three of the older child *waied* as well and, at Apinya's urging, came forward to hug his knees.

"Perhaps you will have more time and energy for your children," Siriporn said as she came forward with Nok squirming in her arms.

"And for your wives," Duangjan said with a laugh that started all the women giggling.

Ngwe Lay was in front of him. She held a tiny bundle. The newest baby. He bent over the tiny face. He had been too distraught over the hearing to pay her any attention. Her eyes opened and she gazed up at him. Her long lashes and the faint dusting of eyebrows looked dark in the half light. The delicate line of her lips curled. She was smiling. His new daughter was smiling at him. It was hard to breathe for a moment.

"We need to decide on a name," he said.

"Her name is Hla Kun Way."

"What does it mean?"

"Hla means beautiful," she said.

"Then we will name her Mayuree in Thai. The meaning is the same," said Apinya.

Pakdee hardly noticed the interruption.

He looked at Lay's face, glowing in the moonlight, then at the women arrayed behind her in a line, like beads on a string. Each wife held their children, his children. This was his family. It was complicated and often annoying. The connections among them might sometimes fray, but being a family held them together. Apinya might be the real leader, but he was important to them all. He looked at all the faces turned to him in the faint light.

This was what he had to live for.

Acknowledgements

This tale was sparked by stories Yuangrat and her sisters told about their ancestors and growing up in the south. Once Yuangrat and I started writing, however, our imaginations led us far away from the original accounts. Although this is a work of fiction, we have tried to be true to events in the south in the critical period around the turn of the century. With the exception of those listed in the section "Historical Personages and their Roles in the Story," all of the characters in the novel are fictional.

Our story is, in some ways, an appreciation of and a reaction to M.R. Kukrit Pramoj's famous novel, *Si Phaendin* (Four Reigns). It covers much of the same period in Thai history, but from the point of view of characters in the southern provinces.

We would like to thank Narong Nunthong, whose master's thesis "Kanpattirup Kanpokrong *Monthon* Nakhon Srithammarat Nai Samai Phraya Sukhumnaiwinit Pen Khaluang Thesapiban" (Administrative Reform of *Monthon* Nakhon Srithammarat in in the Era of Phraya Sukhumnaiwinit as *Monthon* High Commssioner) provided detail on the administration of the region. We are particularly grateful that Khun Narong met with us in Nakhon to answer our questions. Interviews with two other historians from Rajabhat University Nakhon Srithammarat, Prof. Somphut Turajen and Prof. Chatchai Suprakan were helpful in understanding Nakhon at the end of the fifth reign. Prof. Somphut escorted us through the exhibits in the National Museum of Nakhon and Prof. Chatchai gave us another useful book, *100 Pi Rongrien Pakpanang* (100 Years of the Pakpanang School). The book provided detail on the first school in Pakpanang and life in the town at the time of our story, long before Paul taught at the school from 1972 to 1974.

We also relied extensively on Tej Bunnag's classic study *The Provincial Administration of Siam from 1892 to 1915: A Study of the Creation, the Growth, the Achievements and the Implications for Modern Siam, of the Ministry of Interior Under Prince Damrong Rajanubhab*.

We are grateful to David Lyman for giving us access to the library of the Tilleke & Gibbins law firm, which proved particularly useful to our understanding of the legal reforms under King Chulalongkorn, especially the role played by the firm's founder, William Alfred Goone Tilleke.

We gained much insight from the letters of King Chulalongkorn and the numerous writings of Prince Damrong Rajanubhab. For our descriptions of life in Bago we depended largely on *The World of Burmese Women* by Mi Mi Khiang, who was a friend of Yuangrat's at the University of Michigan many years ago. For our descriptions of gambling, we relied primarily on James Warren's *Gambling, the State and Society in Thailand, c. 1800-1945*.

The character of Dam is loosely based on the life of Nakhon policeman Phantharak Rajjadej, known for his exploits against southern criminals as well as his mastery of traditional magical amulets and tattoos. Yuangrat had the chance to meet Khun Phan before his death at the age of 103.

For other aspects of life in southern Siam we relied on a variety of scholars too numerous to mention. Any errors of fact or interpretation are, of course, the sole responsibility of the authors.

Glossary of Non-English Words

Adat – customary law derived from long Malay tradition.

Ajahn – professor or teacher, sometimes used for Buddhist monks known for their teaching.

Ayah – an exclamation of dismay often used by males of Chinese ancestry.

Chaophraya – a high royal title usually awarded to officials at the minister level.

Chuan zhu – Chinese for 'ship lord'. This is the person with responsibility for planning the route of the ship, overseeing its financial affairs, and buying and selling the cargo. However, the *chuan zhu* does not have responsibility for the sailing of the ship.

Daulat Tuanku – the Malay equivalent of 'long live the king'.

Dharma – the teachings of the Buddha.

Dong quai – the roots of this Chinese herb are boiled to make a blood tonic. *Dong quai* has also been used to treat headaches, nerve pain, high blood pressure and inflammation.

Durian – a sweet but strong-smelling tropical fruit. It comes in large, spiny casings, but the fruit inside has the consistency of a thick pudding. It grows wild on tall trees in the forest, but is also extensively grown in orchards.

Fantan – a Chinese card game.

Farang – Thai term for Caucasian foreigner, possibly borrowed from the Arabic 'ferengi'.

Guru – religious teacher, also used to refer to the largest bead in a string of meditation beads.

Hidup – Malay term calling for long life.

Hpon – Burmese word for the male spirit believed to elevate men to a higher spiritual level than women. It gives a man spiritual power earned through good deeds in past lives. It is used to explain and reinforce social hierarchy and male status.

Istana – palace of a Malay ruler.

Jataka – a tale of one of the Buddha's incarnations, whether in human or animal form. The future Buddha of the tale may appear as a king, an outcast, a god, an elephant. In whatever form, he exhibits some virtue that the tale thereby inculcates. Often, Jataka tales include an extensive cast of characters who interact and get into various kinds of trouble, whereupon the Buddha character intervenes to resolve all the problems and bring about a happy ending.

Jawi – an Arabic alphabet for writing Malay. It is sometimes used to refer to the Malay dialect in southern Siam.

Chedi – Buddhist monument, typically a round, solid edifice that rises to a point. It often contains a relic of the Buddha or ashes of an esteemed person.

Kaffir – an Arabic term for a person who rejects or disbelieves in God according to the teachings of the Islamic prophet Muhammad, and denies the dominion and authority of Allah.

Kaffir lime – a type of lime tree whose fragrant leaves are used to give flavor to a variety of southern Thai dishes.

Kamnan – official in charge of a sub-district. Often the most powerful person in a rural area.

Khaek – person from the Indian subcontinent or the Middle East. Literally, visitor. It was also applied to Malays even though they had lived in southern Thailand for hundreds of years. Some Malays felt the term was pejorative and resented its common use by Thais.

Khapraputthajao – Thai formal first-person pronoun used in addressing a member of the royal family.

Khao chae – a style of Thai cuisine usually served in the hot season. It literally means 'rice soaked in cool water'. The recipe was adapted from a Mon dish and then modified for the royal palace. It is considered a palace food. When ice was not then available in Thailand, the water was kept cool during hot season by putting it in an earthenware vessel in a shaded place.

Khon – pronounced with a long rising tone, Khon is the name for the Thai dance-drama based on the *Ramakien*, the tale of the long struggle between Rama and an army of ogres who kidnapped his wife Sita.

Klot – a large umbrella equipped with an insect screen and a wooden pole that can be pitched and set up like a small round tent to protect monks from dew and insects.

Kris – a long Malay knife or dagger, often with a wavy blade forged with alternating strips of differently colored iron, sometimes believed to have supernatural powers.

Likay – a popular drama form that included music, dialog and colorful costumes

Lingam – a term borrowed from Pali for the male sex organ.

Longyi – an ankle-length tubular cloth worn by Burmese men and women, rolled or folded at the waist to keep it in place, sometimes with the additional help of a belt.

Loy Krathong – a Siamese festival celebrated annually throughout the Kingdom of Thailand and in nearby countries. The name could be translated as 'to float a basket', and comes from the tradition of making *krathong*, or buoyant, decorated baskets, which are then floated on a river. Loy Krathong takes place on the evening of the full moon of the 12th month in the traditional Thai lunar calendar, thus the exact date of the festival changes every year. In the Western calendar this usually falls in the month of November.

Luang paw – common term of address for an older, highly respected Buddhist monk.

Mae – mother, but sometimes used as an affectionate term for a woman.

Mae yai – a term for the first or major wife.

Mahjong – a tile-based game which was developed in China in the Qing dynasty

Manora – a type of dance-drama originating in Southern Thailand. The basic features of the performance include a lengthy invocation, a dance by the main character, and a play or skit. The invocation is enacted by slow rhythmic movements of legs, arms and fingers. The dramatic repertoire of Manora performance is based on

Thai legends of Manora, derived from the Buddhist Jataka tales, many of which were absorbed into Malay society centuries ago.

Monthon – an administrative area introduced by King Chulalongkorn (Rama V) beginning in 1892 to provide better control of outlying provinces. A *monthon* was governed by a high commissioner who was charged with overseeing several provinces, each of which had a governor. The *monthon* system was abolished in 1932.

Mingalaba – a Burmese greeting.

Nai – an honorific used in formal Thai speech or in reference to a upper class male. Also, can mean boss. Could be translated as Mr. It has a similar meaning in the Mon language.

Nakleng – Thai term for a man of aggressive strength. Often seen as a leader and usually has a following of tough men. Nakleng can be negative, meaning a gangster or a criminal, but also has positive connotations of decisiveness, power and loyalty.

Pha – cloth.

Phajonggraben – a traditional Thai garment. It is a tube of cloth fastened around the waist. The bottom front of the garment is pulled through the legs and tucked into the waist at the back to create a garment that has legs. It is usually secured by a belt and is worn by both men and women.

Phakaoma – the versatile rectangular cloth that men sometimes wear around their waists, particularly when at home. It is an informal garment that is typically used as a bathing cloth. It can also be used as a sash, a satchel, a head-covering or a towel.

Phasin – a traditional Thai woman's skirt made from a single piece of cloth, often embroidered or woven with colorful designs.

Phatung – long, tube-like garment covering from the waist to the ankle, usually worn by women. However, Muslim men also wear a similar garment.

Phra – usually refers to a Buddhist monk. It is also used in the titles and honorifics for high-ranking Thai officials.

Phrathep – title for a senior Buddhist monk.

Pla doot – sucker fish.

Pondok – Islamic boarding school.

Po Pan – Thai gambling game.

Pua – common Thai word for husband.

Pwe – traditional Burmese performance, consisting of dancing, singing, and dramatization. Similar to the Thai Likay.

Qadi judge – the magistrate or judge of the Shari'a court, who also exercises extrajudicial functions, such as mediation, guardianship over orphans and minors, and supervision and auditing of public works.

Qinghao – a Chinese herb from the sweet wormwood tree. It yields an effective anti-malarial medicine known in the West as artemisinin.

Ramakien – Thailand's national epic derived from the Hindu epic *Ramayana*. There are at least three versions, one of which was prepared in 1797 under the supervision of (and partly written by) King Rama I. His son, Rama II, rewrote some parts of his father's version for *Khon* drama. The work has had an important influence on Thai literature, art and drama (both the *Khon* and *nang* dramas are derived from it).

Roti – Indian flat bread.

Roti paratha – an Indian-influenced flatbread dish in Malay areas of Southeast Asia. It is usually served with dal or other types of curry, but can also be cooked in a range of sweet or savory variations made with a variety of ingredients such as sardines, meat, egg, or cheese.

Sabaa – Mon courting game.

Sakdina – the traditional Thai system for ordering society with specific ranks for each person from king to slave with precise numerical rankings for each. The system required those of lower rank to honor, obey and serve those of higher rank, particularly the person designated as their lord. Conversely those of higher rank were to provide for the welfare of those lower-ranking people assigned to them. Punishments for various infractions were more severe for those of higher rank. The system was strengthened by magical rituals intended to assure the loyalty of all to their lord and ultimately to the king. Sakdina required all subjects of the king to provide free labor for royal projects for several months of the year. Chinese migrants were not covered by the system. Sakdina developed over hundreds of years from the 15th to the 19th century before it was officially dismantled at the start of the 20th century by King Chulalongkorn. Many of the conservative, hierarchical values and attitudes of the sakdina system,

however, have persisted into the 21st century in Thailand.

Salat – the obligatory Muslim prayers, performed five times each day. Performing these prayers is the second Pillar of Islam.

Samadhi – pure concentration in peace and stillness.

Sangha – the community of Buddhist monks.

Sataw – bitter beans with a pungent smell popular in southern Thai cuisine, eaten raw, stir-fried, roasted or boiled.

Saw-oo – a two-string Thai violin played with a bow between the two strings.

Shamshu – Chinese liquor brewed from rice.

Sia – a term used by Thais for wealthy Chinese men as a sign of respect for their wealth.

Somphung – a tropical tree that grows large and tall.

Songkok – a cap, usually black, worn by Muslim males in Southeast Asia. It is similar to the Turkish fez.

Songkran – the celebration of the traditional Thai New Year. Often called the water festival, the celebration includes the pouring of water over elders, family and friends along with wishes for health and happiness in the New Year. Coming at the height of the hot season it is an excuse for young people to toss water on one another.

Sua – a Thai term that literally means tiger, but is used for men reputed to be bold and dangerous.

Suttas – the discourses of the Buddha.

Takian – a dense tropical hardwood from the forests of Southeast Asia.

Takrut – a type of Thai tubular amulet made of a metal beaten thin. It is supposed to protect the wearer from various dangers. Magical phrases, called 'yantra', are written or engraved in the metal of the tube.

Tambon – sub-district. Several villages usually make up a sub-district or *tambon* and several *tambon* make up a district or *amphur*.

Teochew – a dialect spoken by the people of coastal Guangdong province in southeastern China. An old dialect, Teochew preserves many of the old pronunciations lost from other Chinese dialects.

Thingyan – the Burmese New Year Festival that usually occurs in the middle of April. It is a traditional festival celebrated over a period of four to five days, culminating in the lunar New Year. It is similar to the Songkran festival celebrated in Laos and Thailand.

Thua – a gambling game in which the operator briefly shows the bettors a bowl of cowrie shells. The bettors then place their bets on the number of shells that will be left after the operator removes the shells in groups of four. The possibilities are three, two, one and zero.

Thudong – the practice of Thai monks walking on long journeys through the forest during the dry season. During these journeys the monks are supposed to observe at least some of an additional 13 rules of ascetic practice. All so-called Forest Monks will observe at least one of the austerities. These austerities are meant to deepen the practice of meditation and assist in living a holy life. Their aim is to help the practitioner to develop detachment from material things, including the body.

Wai – the traditional Thai greeting and display of respect made by clasping the hands together with the fingertips pointing up. Usually accompanied by a bow of the head. The higher the hands and the deeper the bow show greater respect.

Wat – Buddhist temple or monastery, which may include prayer halls, meeting halls, ordination halls and the huts of the monks.

Wisakha – the most important day in the Buddhist year. It marks the birth, enlightenment and death of the Buddha. On this day, good Buddhists go to the temple early in the morning to make merit by donating to the monks. Then they return in the evening to take part in a candle-lit procession.

Yama Zatdaw – a Burmese dance-drama telling the story of Rama. The Burmese name for the story itself is *Yamayana*, while Zatdaw refers to the dance-drama presenting the story. Like the Thai *Ramakien*, the story is based on the Indian epic, *Ramayana*.

Yantra – sacred geometrical, animal and deity designs accompanied by Pali phrases that offer power, protection, fortune, charisma and other benefits for the bearer. The yantra is tattooed onto the body.

Yot Mongkut – a round yantra design for good fortune and protection in battle typically tattooed on the top of the head.

Historical Characters

King Chulalongkorn (September 20, 1853–October 23, 1910) was a revered Thai king whose modernizing reforms transformed life throughout the country. He faced challenges from the colonial ambitions of France and Britain. France used armed force and diplomatic pressure to seize territory that traditionally owed allegiance to the Thai king. Britain used political and economic pressure to gain power over the Malay sultanates previously considered part of the Thai kingdom. King Chulalongkorn responded to the colonial pressure by radically transforming his traditional nation. He replaced local rulers with centrally appointed administrators, revised the legal system and established a professional, full-time military and police force. He negotiated a treaty with Britain that clarified the status of the Malay sultanates in the far south of Siam.

Prince Damrong Rajanubhab (June 21, 1862–December 1, 1943) was a half-brother of King Chulalongkorn. His many roles in a long career of public service included commander of the armed forces, head of public health and minister of education. As minister of the interior for some 20 years, he was responsible for implementing the far-reaching administrative and legal reforms of King Chulalongkorn. After the death of the king, he had differences with his nephew, King Vajiravudh, and resigned as minister of the interior in 1915. He then devoted his energies to writing the history of Siam.

Raja Abdul Kadir (1877–1933) was the eldest son of Sultan Sulaiman Sharafudin, the last traditional ruler of Pattani. Under King Chulalongkorn he was transformed from a traditional Malay ruler into an official of the royal Siamese government with limited powers. He resented the policies of *Monthon* High Commissioner Phraya Sukhumnaiwinit and rebelled against the Siamese government. He was arrested and held under house arrest for two years until he pledged to stay out of Pattani political affairs. He did not keep this pledge, however, and fomented unrest in the south, including armed uprisings in 1910, 1911 and 1922. After the failure of the first two of these rebellions, he went into exile in Kelantan, a sultanate under British influence.

Phraya Sukhumnaiwinit (1862–1938) was born as Pan Sukhum and later given the royal titles of Phraya Sukhumnaiwinit and later Chaophraya Yommarat. He was a monk and then a schoolteacher appointed as tutor to several of King Chulalongkorn's sons. He accompanied them to England for further education. He was given a royal title by the prince who later became King Vajiravudh. On his return to Siam he was appointed as the first high commissioner of *Monthon* Nakhon Srithammarat. He was later appointed Minister of the Capital, then Minister of the Interior and Regent.

King Vajiravudh (January 1, 1880–November 26, 1925) was a British-educated prince who succeeded his father King Chualongkorn as king. He was a prolific writer who promoted Thai nationalism and loyalty to the monarchy. He established the Wild Tiger Corps and advocated monogamy.

Prince Lopburi Ramet, originally named Prince Yugala Dighambara (March 17, 1882–April 8, 1932) was a younger half-brother of King Vajiravudh. He was a British-educated political scientist and administrator who served as high commissioner for *Monthon* Nakhon Srithammarat and Viceroy of the South during the reign of his half-brother King Vajiravudh and later as the minister of the interior in the government of King Prajadhipok.

Robert W. Duff was a former British police officer in Malaya who became a powerful businessman operating in southern Siam and the Malay states. He founded the Duff Development Company and used his political connections for business advantage.

Phra Sirithammuni was a Buddhist monk appointed as supervisor of the first government school in Pakpanang that later became the Pakpanang Boys School.

Tiger Thuam was the most famous Thai bandit of the end of the 19th century. Initially a buffalo thief, Thuam gathered a large gang that terrorized a wide area. He was reputed to have magical powers. An article in the *Bangkok Times* reported that his magic was so strong "no bullet can pierce him nor knife cut him." Thuam defied police and murdered officials who resisted him before police finally succeeded in killing him.

Edward Henry Strobel (December 7, 1855–January 15, 1908) was an American diplomat and legal scholar. A former US assistant secretary of state and law professor, he moved to Bangkok in 1906 to become the American Adviser on Foreign Affairs to King Chulalongkorn. He died in Bangkok in 1908.

Born in southern Thailand, **Dr. Yuangrat Wedel** graduated from Thammasat University and earned a doctorate in political science from the University of Michigan. She has taught and researched Thai political philosophy at Thammasat University, Ramkhamhaeng University, and Singapore's Institute of Southeast Asian Studies. She taught Thai culture at Assumption University and researched Southeast Asian economic developments at Chulalongkorn University's Institute of Asia Studies. This academic experience was followed by more than a decade of work in rural, community and child development for UNICEF and Plan International, a non-profit organization. Dr. Yuangrat has family links to a reform strain of Buddhism and traditional herbal medicine. One grandfather was a senior royal official in the south and one grandmother was a Mon from Burma.

With a degree in English literature, **Paul Wedel** taught at the Pakpanang Boys School in Nakhon Srithammarat as a member of the US Peace Corps and later produced educational television programs for the Bangkok government. Returning to the United States in 1975, Paul won a scholarship from the Columbia School of Journalism. His master's thesis focused on political struggles in Thailand. After graduation, he won a traveling fellowship to write about the aftermath of the Indochina War. He then spent the next 14 years working in Asia as a journalist for United Press International. Paul later served for 19 years as executive director and ultimately president of the Kenan Institute Asia, a Thai non-profit organization. He also taught courses on Southeast Asia as an adjunct professor for the University of North Carolina at Chapel Hill. He has written a book on how to use news stories to learn English and contributed to a biography of King Bhumibol Adulyadej. He is on the board of directors of the Fulbright Foundation in Thailand.

Married in 1977, Yuangrat and Paul are avid ballroom dancers who split their time between Bangkok and a cottage in the forest of Nakhon Nayok. Often accompanied by their two daughters, they make trips to southern Thailand to visit relatives and do research for their writing. As co-authors they wrote *Radical Thought, Thai Mind: A History of Revolutionary Ideology in a Traditional Society*. They write a blog on the relation between Thai history and current events, which is posted on their website at https://www.yuangratandpaul. online. *Beads on a String* is their first novel.